CATALOG OF THE
AMERICAN MUSICAL

A Project of the
National Institute for Opera and Musical Theater
Major funding provided by the
National Endowment for the Arts
and
American Express Company

CATALOG OF THE
AMERICAN MUSICAL

Musicals of
Irving Berlin ● George & Ira Gershwin
Cole Porter ● Richard Rodgers & Lorenz Hart

by
Tommy Krasker
and
Robert Kimball

Catalog of the American Musical
by Tommy Krasker & Robert Kimball

© 1988 National Institute for Opera and Musical Theater
Printed in the United States of America

International Standard Book Number
0-9618575-0-1

Library of Congress Catalog Card Number
87-061421

Photo Credits:
Photo of Richard Rodgers & Lorenz Hart
courtesy of Rodgers and Hammerstein

Photo of George & Ira Gershwin
courtesy of the George and Ira Gershwin Collection
—Music Division, Library of Congress

Photos of Irving Berlin and Cole Porter
provided by Bettmann Archives

TABLE OF CONTENTS

FOREWORDS

Like most of my colleagues, I've devoted my life to the creation of new works. We all know that the great musicals of the past are central to the American cultural legacy, but, as people often do, we've waited until the last minute to conserve our heritage. With startling clarity, the *Catalog* shows how widely the performance materials for these works have been scattered. It is a first step to bringing them to life onstage once more, a step I'm very pleased that the Institute could be instrumental in taking.

Harold Prince
Chairman Emeritus
National Institute for Opera
and Musical Theater

The American musical is part of what "American culture" means. We at the Endowment are justly proud to be associated with its perpetuation. As is often the case, it was professionals working in the field—and particularly the conductor John Mauceri—who apprised the Endowment of the need to stem the steady disappearance of scores, books and lyrics of classic American musicals. In partnership with the private sector and the National Institute, we initiated this effort to locate and secure all performance materials still extant. We trust this catalog will serve the field and be a cornerstone for preserving a unique dimension of our cultural heritage.

Frank Hodsoll
Chairman
National Endowment for the Arts

While there is no business like show business, the entertainment industry enjoys no special immunity from the bureaucratic peril of misplaced records. This catalog project has been more than "research," being in fact a "search and rescue mission," without which we believe a major segment of our cultural heritage would soon have been lost. For us at American Express, therefore, it has been very gratifying to support the tireless work that has gone into its preparation.

Louis V. Gerstner
President
American Express Company

INTRODUCTION

The *Catalog of the American Musical* represents the first phase of a national effort to locate and rescue original performance materials of the American musical theatre. Hundreds of musicals—particularly those produced during the years that spanned the two world wars—have been woefully neglected and, in some cases, lost forever. By focusing on authentic performance materials, the *Catalog* seeks to preserve one of our country's most highly prized art forms and protect it from further erosion. This first volume surveys the seventy-five book musicals of Irving Berlin, George and Ira Gershwin, Cole Porter, and Richard Rodgers and Lorenz Hart, documenting the location and completeness of all original piano-vocal scores, lyrics and libretti, and orchestra scores and parts.

This project was initiated in 1983 by Frank Hodsoll, Chairman of the National Endowment for the Arts, and John Ludwig, Executive Director of the National Institute for Opera and Musical Theater, in response to discussions with leading authorities on the American musical. Contributing to the genesis of the *Catalog* were Theodore S. Chapin of the Rodgers and Hammerstein Office; Robert H. Montgomery, Jr., Trustee of the Cole Porter Musical and Literary Property Trusts; conductor John Mauceri; Michael Price of the Goodspeed Opera House; and Roger L. Stevens of the John F. Kennedy Center for the Performing Arts. Its future was secured by major funding from American Express Company and the National Endowment for the Arts, and by generous additional underwriting by Mrs. Ira Gershwin, Mr. James O. Cole, the Rodgers and Hammerstein Estates, Mr. and Mrs. Earle M. Craig, Jr., the Wallace Funds, Mr. Irwin Winkler, and others.

Our search for original materials has taken us to such repositories as the New York Public Library, the Library of Congress, Yale University Library, Tams-Witmark Music Library, the Cole Porter Musical and Literary Property Trusts, the Irving Berlin Music Corporation, the Shubert Archive, the Rodgers and Hammerstein Theatre Library, and the private collection of Ira Gershwin.

The most dramatic and visible of our efforts has been the inspection of thousands of scores and manuscripts—by Jerome Kern, the Gershwins, Cole Porter, Rodgers and Hart, and many others—rediscovered in 1982 at the Warner Brothers Music warehouse in Secaucus, N.J. This astonishing find, which included partiturs by Frank Saddler, Stephen O. Jones, Maurice B. DePackh, Robert Russell Bennett, Hans Spialek, and other leading orchestrators of the period, brought worldwide attention to the quest to preserve rapidly disappearing scores, lyrics, and books of classic American musicals. Of the manuscripts discovered in Secaucus, those by the Gershwins and Rodgers and Hart are now at the Library of Congress, while those by Cole Porter are at Yale University.

Our research has proven most rewarding in the discovery of material previously believed lost. Missing lyrics from Rodgers and Hart's *America's Sweetheart* turned up at Tams-Witmark Music Library;

full orchestra scores to Porter's *Gay Divorce* were found at the Shubert Archive; the script to George Gershwin and Brian Hooker's *Our Nell* was traced to the Library of Congress Annex in Landover, Maryland. Frequently, we found that the components of a show were widely scattered. For example, material from George Gershwin and B.G. DeSylva's *Sweet Little Devil* was dispersed among collections at the Library of Congress, Amherst College, and Tams-Witmark Music Library. After weeks of inventory, we had located all but one item: a lyric that we eventually found in the private collection of Ira Gershwin.

Work on the *Catalog* has coincided with a renewed public interest in authentic productions of vintage musicals. The 1983 Broadway revival of Rodgers and Hart's *On Your Toes*, with original script, score, and orchestrations, proved so successful that the vocal score was published and the show made available for rental. Similarly, the Goodspeed Opera House's well-received 1987 revival of the Gershwins' *Lady, Be Good!*, which restored the original libretto, prompted a refurbishment of the entire rental package. Concert versions of first-rate musical scores (with their original orchestrations)—including the Gershwins' *Girl Crazy*, conducted by John Mauceri with the Boston Pops and at the Edinburgh Festival in Scotland; a trio of Jerome Kern gems (*Oh, Boy!*, *Oh Lady! Lady!!*, and *Zip, Goes A Million*), presented by John McGlinn at Carnegie Hall; and a string of neglected works ranging from Victor Herbert's *Eileen* to Kurt Weill's *One Touch Of Venus*, produced by the New Amsterdam Theatre Company—have piqued interest in lesser-known musicals and affirmed the reputation of celebrated ones.

The *Catalog of the American Musical* is designed to promote such diversity and craftsmanship, to assist and encourage producers, conductors, and performers in seeking out less familiar, equally deserving works of the American musical theatre. The 1987 concert performances of the Gershwins' political satires *Of Thee I Sing* and *Let 'Em Eat Cake* at the Brooklyn Academy of Music (under the musical direction of Michael Tilson Thomas) exemplified two different approaches to restoring works from surviving material: For *Of Thee I Sing*, partiturs were created from the published vocal score and recently rediscovered parts; for *Let 'Em Eat Cake*, a piano-vocal score was reconstructed from the authors' manuscripts and newly orchestrated in the style and spirit of the original production. Both works will soon be made available for theatrical performance, and will join other recent rental editions such as Irving Berlin's *Miss Liberty*, Rodgers and Hart's *I'd Rather Be Right*, and Cole Porter's *Jubilee*—all restored from original materials. The information in the *Catalog of the American Musical* will, we hope, alert the public to the performance potential of these and many other shows, as well as serve as an aid to scholars in further research in the field. In a sense, the preservation of the American musical theatre is really just beginning. This book is a first step—but a critical one.

Tommy Krasker
Robert Kimball
April 1988

ACKNOWLEDGEMENTS

There are many to whom we wish to extend out deepest thanks for their assistance in the preparation of this catalog—above all the creators, their families, and their estates: To Irving Berlin and to Hilda Schneider of the Irving Berlin Music Corporation; to Mrs. Ira Gershwin, to Ronald L. Blanc, attorney to Ira Gershwin and his Estate, and to Mrs. Gershwin's assistant, Mark Trent Goldberg; to Robert H. Montgomery, Jr., Trustee of the Cole Porter Musical and Literary Property Trusts, to Florence Leeds, executive secretary of the Porter Trusts, and to Jim and Alice Cole; to Mrs. Dorothy Rodgers, to Theodore S. Chapin, Managing Director of the Rodgers and Hammerstein Office, to Nicole Friedman, his assistant, and to Joe Lewis, librarian of the Rodgers and Hammerstein Theatre Library; to Dorothy Hart, and to Philip Zimet and Frederic Ingraham of the Lorenz Hart Estate.

We express special gratitude to American Express Company—Louis V. Gerstner, President; Susan S. Bloom, Vice President, Cultural Affairs; and Anne L. Wickham, Manager, Cultural Affairs—and to the National Endowment for the Arts—Frank Hodsoll, Chairman, and Patrick J. Smith, director, Opera-Musical Theater Program.

To Henry Cohen, Frank Military, William Reilly, Flo Gallagher, and Ethan Neuburg at Warner Brothers Music; to Dee Topol and Jeanne Segal at American Express Company; to Don Rose, Michael Feinstein, Richard Lewine, Ceciley Youmans Collins, Robert Lissauer, and Alfred E. Simon for their help with the Secaucus inventory; to John McGlinn for his research and expertise; to Ray White, Elizabeth Auman, Wayne Shirley and the entire staff at the Music Division of the Library of Congress; to Louis Aborn and Dale Kugel at Tams-Witmark Music Library; to Richard Jackson, Dorothy Swerdlove, Richard Lynch, and their colleagues at the New York Public Library; to Richard Warren, Jr., at Yale University Library; to Maryann Chach and Reagan Fletcher at the Shubert Archive; to Miles Kreuger and The Institute of the American Musical; to the staff and Catalog Panel (Michael Price, chairman) of the National Institute for Opera and Musical Theater; and to Janet Brenner, Michael Cerveris, Vicki Clark, Kim Criswell, Louise Edeiken, Amber Edwards, Ann Farris, Rob Fisher, James Fuld, Jessica Helfand, Harry Miller, Larry Moore, Donald Oliver, Ron Raines, Dean Seabrook, and Ron Spivak.

We also acknowledge, with appreciation, the published works of Ken Bloom, Stanley Green, David Hummel, Edward Jablonski, Jack Raymond, Brian Rust, and Steven Suskin.

Contributing Research:
Nancy Cotton
Technical Consultant:
Jack Stephenson
Additional Music Research:
Evans Haile

HOW TO USE THIS BOOK

For each book musical by Irving Berlin, George and Ira Gershwin, Cole Porter, and Rodgers and Hart, the Catalog provides basic information about the show, followed by a detailed inventory of surviving performance materials for each musical number.[1] Our work is based on examination of original performance materials as well as such secondary sources as programs and reviews. While we have attempted to present the information in a manner immediately and intuitively clear, the quantity of data led us to use a number of abbreviations, a full table of which is provided in the Appendix.

Show Information

Title: The title of the show as it appeared during the original New York run.[2] Alternate titles are noted in the Comments section.

Music and Lyric Credits: Only the principal authors are listed here. Songwriters who made additional contributions to the original production—or collaborated with the principal authors on later versions—are listed with the General Information that follows.

General Information about the original production (where known), including:

- *Type of show:* "Musical comedy," "operetta," etc. These classifications are drawn from an examination of the original materials, and do not necessarily match the picturesque phrases first used to advertise a show.
- *Number of acts* in which the original production was presented.
- *Opening date* of the original New York production.
- *Length of the original New York run.*
- *The world premiere date,* followed by the *location of the world premiere.*
- *The librettist(s),* followed by source material (if any).
- Any *additional songwriter(s)* who contributed material to the original production, either during its tryout or its original New York run. In addition, any songwriter(s) who collaborated with the original composer or lyricist on a later version (e.g., London production, film version, revival) is listed here.
- *The producer(s)* of the original production.
- *The director(s)* of the original production. Credits such as "staged by" and "book directed by" are incorporated into this category.
- *The choreographer(s)* of the original production. Credits such as "ensembles by," "musical staging by" and "incidental dance numbers staged by" are incorporated into this category.
- *The musical director/conductor* of the original production.
- *The orchestrator(s)* of the original production.

Synopsis and Production Information: A plot synopsis—drawn from the original script and score, as well as period reviews, clippings and photographs—is provided for each production. Following the synopsis is a brief commentary on other production elements, including supporting characters, requirements of the ensemble, and unusual sets or costumes.

Orchestration: The original instrumentation, with all doublings noted.

Comments: Additional information intended to further illuminate the work (e.g., mention of an original cast member whose style has left an imprint on the material, a word about the show's initial or eventual reception, details of its pre-Broadway travails).

Location of Original Materials:

- *Script.* Location of any script that provides full dialogue and stage directions from the original production, followed by a statement summarizing the number of lyrics contained in that script (in terms ranging from "all lyrics" to "no lyrics"[3]). Early drafts of the libretto are listed at the end of the Original Materials section.
  If a script has been published, the name of the publisher and the year of publication are noted.

- *Piano-vocal score.* Location of any score that contains the songs performed in the show—arranged for piano, with a separate vocal line—in their original sequence. (In most cases, the piano-vocal score will contain not only the songs, but music for dances, underscoring, and scene changes as well.) If the songs performed in the original production have not been assembled, an instruction is given to "See individual listings" on the song pages that follow; there the reader can note the extent and location of surviving material and determine the possibility of compiling a piano-vocal score.
  If the piano-vocal score has been published, the name of the publisher and the year of publication are noted.

- *Partiturs.*[4] Location of full orchestra scores. A location given does not imply that partiturs for all numbers in the show may be found there, merely all partiturs known to survive. The number of partiturs that have surfaced is noted at the end of the Original Materials section.

- *Parts.* Location of original orchestra parts. As with the partitur listing, a location given does not imply that parts for all numbers in the show may be found there, merely all parts known to survive. The number of songs for which parts have surfaced is given below.

- *Notes.* Further information about original materials (e.g., the location of early drafts of the script, the number of surviving partiturs and parts[5]).

---

[1] The Catalog includes only produced works for which these gentlemen wrote at least half the score. The section devoted to George and Ira Gershwin also covers the musicals that George wrote with other collaborators. For a documentation of Gershwin's folk opera *Porgy and Bess,* the reader is referred to Quaintance Eaton's *Opera Production I.*

[2] Three of the musicals included in this catalog—*Primrose* (1924), *Nymph Errant* (1933), and *Lido Lady* (1926)—were written specifically for the London stage; any references here to "New York" (e.g., "New York run") should be understood to refer to London in the case of these shows.

[3] "All lyrics" means that the script contains all the lyrics believed to have been performed in the original production, not that it contains every lyric written for every number.

[4] The authors use the term "partitur" in place of "orchestra score" or "full score" for its conciseness and lack of ambiguity.

[5] If no mention is made to the contrary either here or above, the reader may assume that all partiturs and parts survive.

Rental Status: If a show is currently available for rental in its original form, then the name of the rental agent is given (e.g., "Tams-Witmark rents the original show"). If a variation on the original version is rented, then the rental agent is given, along with a description of how the rental version differs from the original production. If there is currently no rental package available, then the musical is labeled "Currently unavailable for rental." Addresses for all rental agents are provided in the Appendix.

Music Publisher: The name of the music company that currently holds publishing rights to the score. Addresses are in the Appendix.

Information: Who to contact for further information. Addresses are in the Appendix.

Song Information

Following each page of show information is an examination of all songs written or intended for that show anytime before its Broadway closing. Also included are any numbers composed later (for road companies, film versions, or revivals) by at least one of the show's principal songwriters.

Songs that appeared in the New York production are listed first (in their original sequence), followed by songs dropped before the Broadway opening and songs written for later productions. In general, numbers added to a show during its New York run have been included in the running order, while those deleted after the opening have been grouped along with other excised material.

Finales of acts have been included only when they contain material not listed elsewhere. For example, the Act II Finale of the Gershwins' *Lady, Be Good!* (1924), which contains new lyrics set to "Fascinating Rhythm," is included; however, the Act II Finale of their *Treasure Girl* (1928), which simply reprises a number introduced earlier, is omitted.

For each song, the following information is provided:

Title of Song: The title judged to be the most accurate is listed here; alternate titles (if any) are noted below. Where a title is merely descriptive (e.g., "Finale Act I," "Opening") and no alternate title exists, the first line of the song is also given.

Author(s) of Song: Where known, the authors are listed, the composer preceding the lyricist. In the case of instrumental music, a lyricist is credited alongside the composer if the piece contains arrangements of songs on which he collaborated. If the authorship of a number is in any way uncertain, the credit reads "Author(s): Unknown."

Orchestrator(s) of Song: Listed where known. The majority of shows in this catalog were scored by more than one orchestrator (even in cases where the original program may suggest otherwise). Therefore, an orchestrator is credited for a specific song only where there is proof of his work (i.e., if the partitur survives and the authorship is clear). Otherwise, the credit reads "Orchestrator: Unknown," and the reader may refer to the show information section for a complete list of orchestrators known to have contributed to the show.

Although some songs may never have been orchestrated (particularly ones dropped from a show early in its inception), all numbers are treated as if they were scored unless proof exists to the contrary.

Location of Materials: A full table of abbreviations used in this section is provided in the Appendix.

- *Composer's manuscript.*[6] The location of the composer's holograph is given; if it consists only of a verse or refrain, then the abbreviation "v" or "r" follows. The manuscript is generally arranged for piano or piano-and-voice; where this is not the case, the abbreviation "lead" (leadsheet), "sk" (sketch), or "frag" (fragment) follows. A null sign (-0-) indicates that no composer's manuscript was located.

- *Sheet music.* All sheet music at the Music Divisions of the Library of Congress and the New York Public Library was examined. Both locations have extensive collections; furthermore, songs sent to the Library of Congress for copyright registration are, in many cases, the only copies known to survive.

  Other major collections we investigated include those at the Irving Berlin Music Corporation and Yale University Library for the works of Irving Berlin, and those at the Cole Porter Musical and Literary Property Trusts ("Cole Porter Trusts") and Yale University Library for the works of Cole Porter.[7]

  If a song was published separately, the location of the sheet music is given; if it was published solely as part of a "piano selection" or in a song collection, it is designated "Not published separately," and further information is provided below. Songs never published are simply labeled "Unpublished." In some cases, the title of a number gives little clue to its identity (e.g., "Specialty," "Letter Dance"), and one cannot be certain what music was used; in these cases, a null sign (-0-) is given.

- *Most complete music.* Gives the location of any piano-vocal copy that contains all the music written for the song.[8] Where there is no known piano-vocal, the location is given for that manuscript judged to be most complete. A null sign (-0-) indicates that no musical material was located.

  The version with most complete music does not always contain lyrics to all verses and refrains. Nonetheless, it often contains a basic lyric that may be sufficient for some readers' purposes. Any musical listing that includes a lyric is tagged with a lower-case "l";[9] the reader then can refer to the *most complete lyric* listing that follows to see if that manuscript contains *all* lyrics.

  This category lists the location of the most complete music and the form in which it exists. For example, "LoC (pv-l)" indicates that the most complete version of the music is the piano-vocal with lyrics at the Library of Congress.

  If multiple versions of the most complete music exist, they are listed, separated by a semicolon (in the case of multiple locations) or a comma (in the case of multiple versions at the same location). Where two or more entries must be combined to

---

[6] There is no category for lyricist's manuscript because relatively few hand-written lyric holographs survive, and the authorship of a typed lyric sheet is often difficult to determine.

[7] Late in his life, Cole Porter bequeathed to Yale all music manuscripts in his possession; Irving Berlin sent copies of his own songs to Yale upon the founding of the Yale collection of the Literature of the American Musical Theatre in 1954.

[8] This category is concerned only with the song proper, and not with subsequent dance arrangements or orchestral variations.

[9] The only exceptions are sheet music and piano-vocal scores, which are assumed to have a lyric unless noted elsewhere.

form a complete version, they are joined by an ampersand (&). For example, a listing of "LoC (sm, pv-l)" indicates that the Library of Congress has sheet music and a piano-vocal with lyrics, both of which contain the most complete music. Taken a step further, a listing of "LoC (sm, pv-l); NYPL (sm)" indicates that the Library of Congress has sheet music and a piano-vocal with lyrics, and the New York Public Library has sheet music—all containing the most complete music. But a listing of "LoC (sm & pv-l)" indicates that both the sheet music and the piano-vocal at the Library of Congress must be examined to assemble a complete version.

- *Most complete lyric.* Gives the location of any manuscript that contains all the lyrics written for the song.[10] A null sign (-0-) indicates that no lyric was located.

This category follows essentially the same format as *most complete music.* For example, a listing of "NYPL (sm)" indicates

that the sheet music at the New York Public Library contains the most comprehensive version of the lyric.[11]

- *Original partitur.* Location of the original orchestra score. A null sign (-0-) indicates that no partitur was found. Where a partitur has been reconstructed from original parts listed below, the location of this partitur is given, along with the year of the reconstruction.

- *Original parts.* Location of the original orchestra parts. A null sign (-0-) indicates that no parts were found. Where parts have been extracted from an original partitur listed above, the location of these parts is given, along with the year of the restoration.

Notes. Any other vital information about a song, including alternate titles, historical footnotes, or publication data.

---

[10] In general, alternate lines and early drafts and sketches are kept separate and listed below.

[11] The only exception to this format comes with the use of the books *The Complete Lyrics of Cole Porter, The Complete Lyrics of Lorenz Hart,* and Ira Gershwin's *Lyrics on Several Occasions.* Each title is simply noted by its abbreviation, and the names and addresses of the publishers are provided in the Appendix.

IRVING BERLIN

IRVING BERLIN was born in Temun, Russia on May 11, 1888 and came to New York with his family at age five. He spent two years in the New York Public School System and received his earliest musical education from his father, a cantor. Berlin began his career as a song plugger for publisher Harry Von Tilzer and was working as a singing waiter in Chinatown in 1907 when he wrote his first song, "Marie From Sunny Italy." In 1909 he was hired as a staff lyricist by Ted Snyder Co.; four years later he became a partner in the firm. As a charter member of ASCAP in 1914, Berlin served on its first Board of Directors. After World War I, he established his own publishing firm and in 1921 built the Music Box Theatre with Sam Harris.

In the 55-year span between "Marie of Sunny Italy" and his last Broadway musical, MR. PRESIDENT (1962), Irving Berlin wrote over 800 songs, among them such memorable successes as "Alexander's Ragtime Band," "Everybody's Doin' It Now," "That Mysterious Rag," "Call Me Up Some Rainy Afternoon," "When I Lost You," "When the Midnight Choo Choo Leaves for Alabam'," "Snookey Ookums," "That International Rag," "I Want to Go Back to Michigan, Down on the Farm," "Play a Simple Melody," "The Girl on the Magazine Cover," "I Love a Piano," "Oh, How I Hate to Get Up in the Morning," "Mandy," "A Pretty Girl Is Like a Melody," "You'd Be Surprised," "All By Myself," "Everybody Step," "Say It With Music," "Pack Up Your Sins and Go to the Devil," "All Alone," "Lazy," "What'll I Do," "Always," "Remember," "Blue Skies," "Shaking the Blues Away," "The Song Is Ended," "How About Me," "Let Me Sing and I'm Happy," "Marie," "Puttin' on the Ritz," "Soft Lights and Sweet Music," "How Deep Is the Ocean," "Let's Have Another Cup Of Coffee," "Say It Isn't So," "Easter Parade," "Heat Wave," "Supper Time," "How's Chances," "Cheek to Cheek," "Isn't This a Lovely Day," "Top Hat, White Tie and Tails," "Let's Face the Music and Dance," "I've Got My Love to Keep Me Warm," "Change Partners," "God Bless America," "It's a Lovely Day Tomorrow," "Fools Fall in Love," "Be Careful, It's My Heart," "White Christmas" (Academy Award, 1942), "I Left My Heart at the Stage Door Canteen," "This Is the Army, Mr. Jones," "You Keep Coming Back Like a Song," "Anything You Can Do," "Doin' What Comes Natur'lly," "The Girl That I Marry," "I Got the Sun in the Morning," "There's No Business Like Show Business," "They Say It's Wonderful," "Better Luck Next Time," "A Couple of Swells," "A Fella With an Umbrella," "It Only Happens When I Dance With You," "Steppin Out With My Baby," "Let's Take an Old-Fashioned Walk," "The Best Thing for You," "It's a Lovely Day Today," "You're Just in Love," "Count Your Blessings Instead of Sheep," "Sisters," and "Don't Be Afraid of Romance."

Berlin had contributed random songs to over twenty musical shows when producer Charles B. Dillingham asked him to write the score for WATCH YOUR STEP (1914). Following that stylish and spirited success, Berlin wrote songs for such diverse Broadway musicals as STOP! LOOK! LISTEN! (1915), YIP, YIP, YAPHANK (1918), ZIEGFELD FOLLIES OF 1919, four successive editions of the Music Box Revue ('21-'22-'23-'24), THE COCOANUTS (1925), ZIEGFELD FOLLIES OF 1927, FACE THE MUSIC (1932), AS THOUSANDS CHEER (1933), LOUISIANA PURCHASE (1940), THIS IS THE ARMY (1942), ANNIE GET YOUR GUN (1946), MISS LIBERTY (1949), CALL ME MADAM (1950), and MR. PRESIDENT (1962). Berlin's Hollywood credits are equally impressive and includes scores for TOP HAT (1935), FOLLOW THE FLEET (1936), CAREFREE (1938), ALEXANDER'S RAGTIME BAND (1938), HOLIDAY INN (1942), BLUE SKIES (1946), EASTER PARADE (1948), and THERE'S NO BUSINESS LIKE SHOW BUSINESS (1953).

Bucknell University, Temple University, and Fordham University each conferred on Irving Berlin the degree of Doctor of Music. Harry S Truman awarded Berlin The Medal for Merit. From Dwight D. Eisenhower he received a gold Congressional Medal, and from Gerald Ford The Medal of Freedom.

WATCH YOUR STEP

Music	IRVING BERLIN
Lyrics	IRVING BERLIN

Musical comedy in three acts. Opened December 8, 1914 in New York and ran 175 performances (World premiere: November 25, 1914 in Syracuse, New York). Libretto by Harry B. Smith. Additional music and lyrics by E. Ray Goetz, Ted Snyder, De Witt C. Coolman. Produced by Charles Dillingham. Directed by R.H. Burnside.

Synopsis and Production Information

Old Jabez Pennyfeather dies and bequeaths his fortune to any man or woman in his family who has never been in love. Two relatives appear: a very proper and bashful Englishman, Joseph Lilyburn, and an innocent young maiden, Ernesta Hardacre, who is spurred on by her greedy father, Ebenezer. Pennyfeather's money-grubbing lawyers and married relatives plot to disqualify the pair by luring them into amorous entanglements. Eventually, Joseph and Ernesta fall in love with each other, but don't admit it until after they receive the inheritance.

The show requires a host of supporting characters (including the ebullient Miss Birdie O'Brien, of the Comedie Francaise, and the dashing matinee idol Algy Cuffs), as well as a full singing and dancing ensemble. Settings include the Palais de Fox-Trot, the Metropolitan Opera House, a Fifth Avenue Cabaret, and the interior of a Pullman sleeper.

Orchestration

Unknown

Comments

The original cast included Vernon Castle as Joseph and comic Frank Tinney as "a carriage caller at the opera, a Pullman porter, a coat room boy." Irene Castle was credited as playing herself, and indeed, one of Vernon's numbers had him stepping out of character and referring to his wife -- contradicting the very premise of the show. WATCH YOUR STEP was, in fact, as much revue as book musical: The critic for the New York Times noted, "Mr. Castle has a name of some sort attached to the character that he is supposed to play, but Tinney [keeps] calling him Vern," while his colleague in the Press observed, "The plot lasted through the first act, but never appeared again in recognizable shape." Even the librettist's credit read "Plot (if any) by Harry B. Smith."

Location of Original Materials

Script: Shubert Archive (no lyrics)
Piano-vocal score: Library of Congress, Yale University
  (Published: Irving Berlin Inc. 1914)
Partiturs: Missing
Parts: Missing

The Shubert Archive script is dated July 24, 1931, but it seems to represent the show as originally performed in New York (although, mysteriously, Birdie is named Iona in this version). The New York Public Library has two early drafts, both incomplete: One is missing the first act; the other lacks the last scene. Neither contains any lyrics.

Rental Status

Currently unavailable for rental

Music Publisher

Irving Berlin Music Corporation

Information

Irving Berlin Music Corporation

Overture

Berlin/Berlin
Orchestrator: Unknown

Location of - Composer's manuscript: -0-
- Sheet music: Not published separately
- Most complete music: LoC (pv score);
    Y (pv score)
- Most complete lyric: INST
- Original partitur: -0-
- Original parts: -0-

I'm a Dancing Teacher Now

Berlin/Berlin
Orchestrator: Unknown

Location of - Composer's manuscript: -0-
- Sheet music: Not published separately
- Most complete music: LoC (pv score);
    Y (pv score)
- Most complete lyric: LoC (pv score);
    Y (pv score)
- Original partitur: -0-
- Original parts: -0-

Listed in the New York programs as "The Dancing Teacher."

Office Hours

Berlin/Berlin
Orchestrator: Unknown

Location of - Composer's manuscript: -0-
- Sheet music: Not published separately
- Most complete music: LoC (pv score);
    Y (pv score)
- Most complete lyric: LoC (pv score);
    Y (pv score)
- Original partitur: -0-
- Original parts: -0-

Minstrel Parade, The

Berlin/Berlin
Orchestrator: Unknown

Location of - Composer's manuscript: -0-
- Sheet music: IB, LoC, Y (x)
- Most complete music: IB (sm);
    LoC (sm, pv score);
    Y (sm-x, pv score)
- Most complete lyric: IB (sm);
    LoC (sm, pv score);
    Y (sm-x, pv score)
- Original partitur: -0-
- Original parts: -0-

What Is Love

Berlin/Berlin
Orchestrator: Unknown

Location of - Composer's manuscript: -0-
- Sheet music: IB, LoC, Y (x)
- Most complete music: IB (sm);
    LoC (sm, pv score);
    Y (sm-x, pv score)
- Most complete lyric: IB (sm);
    LoC (sm, pv score);
    Y (sm-x, pv score)
- Original partitur: -0-
- Original parts: -0-

Let's Go 'Round the Town

Berlin/Berlin
Orchestrator: Unknown

Location of - Composer's manuscript: -0-
- Sheet music: IB, LoC, Y (x)
- Most complete music: IB (sm);
    LoC (sm, pv score);
    Y (sm-x, pv score)
- Most complete lyric: IB (sm);
    LoC (sm, pv score);
    Y (sm-x, pv score)
- Original partitur: -0-
- Original parts: -0-

Listed in the New York programs as "Round the Town."

They Always Follow Me Around

Berlin/Berlin
Orchestrator: Unknown

Location of   - Composer's manuscript: -0-
  - Sheet music: IB, LoC, Y (x)
  - Most complete music: IB (sm);
     LoC (sm, pv score);
     Y (sm-x, pv score)
  - Most complete lyric: IB (sm);
     LoC (sm, pv score);
     Y (sm-x, pv score)
  - Original partitur: -0-
  - Original parts: -0-

Listed in the New York programs as "They Follow Me Around."

Show Us How to Do the Fox Trot

Berlin/Berlin
Orchestrator: Unknown

Location of   - Composer's manuscript: -0-
  - Sheet music: IB, LoC, Y (x)
  - Most complete music: IB (sm);
     LoC (sm, pv score);
     Y (sm-x, pv score)
  - Most complete lyric: IB (sm);
     LoC (sm, pv score);
     Y (sm-x, pv score)
  - Original partitur: -0-
  - Original parts: -0-

When I Discovered You

Berlin & Goetz/Berlin & Goetz
Orchestrator: Unknown

Location of   - Composer's manuscript: -0-
  - Sheet music: IB, LoC, Y (x)
  - Most complete music: IB (sm);
     LoC (sm, pv score);
     Y (sm-x, pv score)
  - Most complete lyric: IB (sm);
     LoC (sm, pv score);
     Y (sm-x, pv score)
  - Original partitur: -0-
  - Original parts: -0-

Syncopated Walk, The

Berlin/Berlin
Orchestrator: Unknown

Location of   - Composer's manuscript: -0-
  - Sheet music: IB, LoC, Y
  - Most complete music: LoC (pv score);
     Y (pv score)
  - Most complete lyric: LoC (pv score);
     Y (pv score)
  - Original partitur: -0-
  - Original parts: -0-

Alternate title: "Finale Act I." The patter section was not published in the sheet music.

Entr'acte I

Berlin/Berlin
Orchestrator: Unknown

Location of   - Composer's manuscript: -0-
  - Sheet music: Not published separately
  - Most complete music: LoC (pv score);
     Y (pv score)
  - Most complete lyric: INST
  - Original partitur: -0-
  - Original parts: -0-

Metropolitan Nights

Berlin/Berlin
Orchestrator: Unknown

Location of   - Composer's manuscript: -0-
  - Sheet music: Not published separately
  - Most complete music: LoC (pv score);
     Y (pv score)
  - Most complete lyric: LoC (pv score);
     Y (pv score)
  - Original partitur: -0-
  - Original parts: -0-

Irving Berlin

I Love to Have the Boys Around Me
Berlin/Berlin
Orchestrator: Unknown

Location of   - Composer's manuscript: -0-
             - Sheet music: LoC, IB (neg)
             - Most complete music: LoC (sm, pv score);
                 IB (sm-neg); Y (pv score)
             - Most complete lyric: LoC (sm, pv score);
                 IB (sm-neg); Y (pv score)
             - Original partitur: -0-
             - Original parts: -0-

Chatter Chatter
Berlin/Berlin
Orchestrator: Unknown

Location of   - Composer's manuscript: -0-
             - Sheet music: Unpublished
             - Most complete music: -0-
             - Most complete lyric: -0-
             - Original partitur: -0-
             - Original parts: -0-

Settle Down in a One-Horse Town
Berlin/Berlin
Orchestrator: Unknown

Location of   - Composer's manuscript: -0-
             - Sheet music: IB, LoC, Y
             - Most complete music: IB (sm);
                 LoC (sm, pv score);
                 Y (sm, pv score)
             - Most complete lyric: IB (sm);
                 LoC (sm, pv score);
                 Y (sm, pv score)
             - Original partitur: -0-
             - Original parts: -0-

Ragtime Opera Medley
Berlin/Berlin
Orchestrator: Unknown

Location of   - Composer's manuscript: -0-
             - Sheet music: IB, LoC, Y
             - Most complete music: IB (sm);
                 LoC (sm, pv score);
                 Y (sm, pv score)
             - Most complete lyric: IB (sm);
                 LoC (sm, pv score);
                 Y (sm, pv score)
             - Original partitur: -0-
             - Original parts: -0-

Alternate titles: "Old Operas in a New Way" and "Finale Act II."

Polka
Berlin
Orchestrator: Unknown

Location of   - Composer's manuscript: -0-
             - Sheet music: Not published separately
             - Most complete music: LoC (pv score);
                 Y (pv score)
             - Most complete lyric: INST
             - Original partitur: -0-
             - Original parts: -0-

Entr'acte II
Berlin/Berlin
Orchestrator: Unknown

Location of   - Composer's manuscript: -0-
             - Sheet music: Not published separately
             - Most complete music: LoC (pv score);
                 Y (pv score)
             - Most complete lyric: INST
             - Original partitur: -0-
             - Original parts: -0-

Watch Your Step (1914)

Homeward Bound
Berlin/Berlin
Orchestrator: Unknown

Location of - Composer's manuscript: -0-
- Sheet music: IB, LoC, Y (x)
- Most complete music: IB (sm); LoC (sm);
 Y (sm-x)
- Most complete lyric: IB (sm); LoC (sm);
 Y (sm-x)
- Original partitur: -0-
- Original parts: -0-

Included in the piano-vocal score in an instrumental version only.

Move Over
Berlin/Berlin
Orchestrator: Unknown

Location of - Composer's manuscript: -0-
- Sheet music: IB, LoC, Y (x)
- Most complete music: IB (sm);
 LoC (sm, pv score);
 Y (sm-x, pv score)
- Most complete lyric: IB (sm);
 LoC (sm, pv score);
 Y (sm-x, pv score)
- Original partitur: -0-
- Original parts: -0-

Dropped during the New York run.

High Steppers March, The
Coolman
Orchestrator: -0-

Location of - Composer's manuscript: -0-
- Sheet music: LoC
- Most complete music: LoC (sm)
- Most complete lyric: INST
- Original partitur: -0-
- Original parts: -0-

Not included in the published piano-vocal score.

Play a Simple Melody
Berlin/Berlin
Orchestrator: Unknown

Location of - Composer's manuscript: -0-
- Sheet music: IB, LoC
- Most complete music: IB (sm);
 LoC (sm, pv score); Y (pv score)
- Most complete lyric: IB (sm);
 LoC (sm, pv score); Y (pv score)
- Original partitur: -0-
- Original parts: -0-

Published under the title "Simple Melody."

Ann Eliza's Tango Tea
Author(s): Unknown
Orchestrator: Unknown

Location of - Composer's manuscript: -0-
- Sheet music: -0-
- Most complete music: -0-
- Most complete lyric: -0-
- Original partitur: -0-
- Original parts: -0-

According the New York programs, this number was dropped soon after the New York opening and then reinstated near the end of the Broadway run. It may have been a rewrite of Berlin's "Anna Liza's Wedding Day," which was published in 1913 and can be found at the New York Public Library.

One-Step, The
Author(s): Unknown
Orchestrator: Unknown

Location of - Composer's manuscript: -0-
- Sheet music: -0-
- Most complete music: -0-
- Most complete lyric: -0-
- Original partitur: -0-
- Original parts: -0-

According to the New York programs, this Castle specialty was dropped early in the New York run and then reinstated less than a month later.

Irving Berlin

Look at Them Doing It

Berlin/Berlin
Orchestrator: Unknown

Location of   - Composer's manuscript: -0-
- Sheet music: Not published separately
- Most complete music: LoC (pv score);
    Y (pv score)
- Most complete lyric: LoC (pv score);
    Y (pv score)
- Original partitur: -0-
- Original parts: -0-

Essentially a reprise of "The Syncopated Walk" with a few new lyrics.

I Hate You

Berlin/Berlin
Orchestrator: Unknown

Location of   - Composer's manuscript: -0-
- Sheet music: IB, LoC, Y (x)
- Most complete music: IB (sm); LoC (sm);
    Y (sm-x)
- Most complete lyric: IB (sm); LoC (sm);
    Y (sm-x)
- Original partitur: -0-
- Original parts: -0-

Dropped during the pre-Broadway tryout.

Come to the Land of the Argentine

Berlin/Berlin
Orchestrator: Unknown

Location of   - Composer's manuscript: -0-
- Sheet music: IB, LoC, Y (x)
- Most complete music: IB (sm); LoC (sm);
    Y (sm-x)
- Most complete lyric: IB (sm); LoC (sm);
    Y (sm-x)
- Original partitur: -0-
- Original parts: -0-

Dropped during the pre-Broadway tryout.

Lock Me in Your Harem and Throw Away the Key

Berlin/Berlin
Orchestrator: Unknown

Location of   - Composer's manuscript: -0-
- Sheet music: IB, Y (x)
- Most complete music: IB (sm); Y (sm-x)
- Most complete lyric: IB (sm); Y (sm-x)
- Original partitur: -0-
- Original parts: -0-

Dropped during the pre-Broadway tryout. Listed in the Syracuse programs as "In My Harum."

When It's Night Time in Dixie-Land

Berlin/Berlin
Orchestrator: Unknown

Location of   - Composer's manuscript: -0-
- Sheet music: LoC, Y
- Most complete music: LoC (sm); Y (sm)
- Most complete lyric: LoC (sm); Y (sm)
- Original partitur: -0-
- Original parts: -0-

Dropped during the pre-Broadway tryout.

Town Hall To-night

Berlin/Berlin
Orchestrator: Unknown

Location of   - Composer's manuscript: -0-
- Sheet music: Unpublished
- Most complete music: -0-
- Most complete lyric: -0-
- Original partitur: -0-
- Original parts: -0-

Dropped during the pre-Broadway tryout.

Lead Me to Love

Snyder/Berlin
Orchestrator: Unknown

Location of   - Composer's manuscript: -0-
             - Sheet music: IB, LoC, Y (x)
             - Most complete music: IB (sm); LoC (sm);
               Y (sm-x)
             - Most complete lyric: IB (sm); LoC (sm);
               Y (sm-x)
             - Original partitur: -0-
             - Original parts: -0-

Replaced "What Is Love" during the New York run.

I'm Sober

Author(s): Unknown
Orchestrator: Unknown

Location of   - Composer's manuscript: -0-
             - Sheet music: Unpublished
             - Most complete music: -0-
             - Most complete lyric: -0-
             - Original partitur: -0-
             - Original parts: -0-

Added during the post-Broadway tour.

I've Got-a Go Back to Texas

Berlin/Berlin
Orchestrator: Unknown

Location of   - Composer's manuscript: -0-
             - Sheet music: IB, Y (x)
             - Most complete music: IB (sm); Y (sm-x)
             - Most complete lyric: IB (sm); Y (sm-x)
             - Original partitur: -0-
             - Original parts: -0-

Added during the post-Broadway tour. Listed in some
programs as "Texas."

Watch Your Step

Berlin/Berlin
Orchestrator: Unknown

Location of   - Composer's manuscript: -0-
             - Sheet music: LoC, Y
             - Most complete music: LoC (sm); Y (sm)
             - Most complete lyric: LoC (sm): Y (sm)
             - Original partitur: -0-
             - Original parts: -0-

Probably unused.

STOP! LOOK! LISTEN!

Music   **IRVING BERLIN**
Lyrics   **IRVING BERLIN**

Musical comedy in three acts. Opened December 25, 1915 in New York and ran 105 performances (World premiere: December 1, 1925 in Philadelphia). Libretto by Harry B. Smith. Interpolated song by Henry Kailimai and G.H. Stover. Produced by Charles Dillingham. Directed by R.H. Burnside. Musical direction by Robert Bowers. Orchestration by Frank Saddler.

Synopsis and Production Information	The producers of a musical comedy are up in arms when their star, Mary Singer, runs off with millionaire Gideon Gay. Although chorus girl Gaby insists that she can take over Mary's role, the producers decide to search for a more exotic performer. A shrewd press agent, Abel Connor, is won over by Gaby's pleas and hatches a plan: He tells the producers of an undiscovered talent in far-off Hawaii; when they take the bait, he sends Gaby to Honolulu to become that girl. Several subplots woven into this story (including Gideon's efforts to prevent Mary and her mother, a comic opera star, from learning that he has a daughter) are resolved or forgotten by the final curtain, which falls as Gaby is being acclaimed an international star.
	The show requires a full singing and dancing ensemble.
Orchestration	Unknown
Comments	The original cast included Gaby Deslys as Gaby.
Location of Original Materials	Script: Missing Piano-vocal score: New York Public Library Partiturs: Missing Parts: Missing
	Although no final production script has been located, the New York Public Library has an early draft (in which the lead character is named Violette, not Gaby). Act I contains full dialogue, stage directions, and lyrics (albeit to an earlier musical running order); Acts II and III are sketchier. The piano-vocal score was prepared for publication in 1915, but never printed; it includes most of the numbers listed in the New York programs.
Rental Status	Currently unavailable for rental
Music Publisher	Irving Berlin Music Corporation
Information	Irving Berlin Music Corporation

Stop! Look! Listen! (1915)

Overture

Berlin/Berlin
Orchestrator: Unknown

Location of
- Composer's manuscript: -0-
- Sheet music: Unpublished
- Most complete music: NYPL (pv score)
- Most complete lyric: INST
- Original partitur: -0-
- Original parts: -0-

Opening Chorus Act I ["These are the costumes the manager selected..."]

Berlin/Berlin
Orchestrator: Unknown

Location of
- Composer's manuscript: -0-
- Sheet music: Unpublished
- Most complete music: NYPL (pv score)
- Most complete lyric: NYPL (pv score)
- Original partitur: -0-
- Original parts: -0-

Alternate title: "Mirror Specialty." The lyric is also in the early draft of the script at the New York Public Library.

Blow Your Horn

Berlin/Berlin
Orchestrator: Unknown

Location of
- Composer's manuscript: -0-
- Sheet music: IB, LoC, Y (x)
- Most complete music: IB (sm); LoC (sm); Y (sm-x); NYPL (pv score)
- Most complete lyric: IB (sm); LoC (sm); Y (sm-x); NYPL (pv score)
- Original partitur: -0-
- Original parts: -0-

Why Don't They Give Us a Chance?

Berlin/Berlin
Orchestrator: Unknown

Location of
- Composer's manuscript: -0-
- Sheet music: Unpublished
- Most complete music: NYPL (pv score)
- Most complete lyric: NYPL (pv score)
- Original partitur: -0-
- Original parts: -0-

Advertised but not published. Listed in the New York programs as "Give Us a Chance." The lyric is also in the early draft of the script at the New York Public Library.

I Love to Dance

Berlin/Berlin
Orchestrator: Unknown

Location of
- Composer's manuscript: -0-
- Sheet music: Not published separately
- Most complete music: NYPL (pv score)
- Most complete lyric: NYPL (pv score)
- Original partitur: -0-
- Original parts: -0-

Published in the piano selection from FOLLOW THE CROWD (the 1916 London version of STOP! LOOK! LISTEN!), which can be found at the Irving Berlin Music Corporation. The lyric is also in the early draft of the script at the New York Public Library.

And Father Wanted Me to Learn a Trade

Berlin/Berlin
Orchestrator: Unknown

Location of
- Composer's manuscript: -0-
- Sheet music: IB, LoC, Y (x)
- Most complete music: IB (sm); LoC (sm); Y (sm-x); NYPL (pv score)
- Most complete lyric: IB (sm); LoC (sm); Y (sm-x); NYPL (pv score)
- Original partitur: -0-
- Original parts: -0-

Girl on the Magazine, The
Berlin/Berlin
Orchestrator: Unknown

Location of   - Composer's manuscript: -0-
          - Sheet music: IB, LoC, NYPL, Y
          - Most complete music: IB (sm); LoC (sm);
              NYPL (sm, pv score); Y (sm)
          - Most complete lyric: IB (sm); LoC (sm);
              NYPL (sm, pv score); Y (sm)
          - Original partitur: -0-
          - Original parts: -0-

I Love a Piano
Berlin/Berlin
Orchestrator: Unknown

Location of   - Composer's manuscript: -0-
          - Sheet music: IB, LoC, NYPL, Y
          - Most complete music: IB (sm); LoC (sm);
              NYPL (sm, pv score); Y (sm)
          - Most complete lyric: IB (sm); LoC (sm);
              NYPL (sm, pv score); Y (sm)
          - Original partitur: -0-
          - Original parts: -0-

The New York Public Library piano-vocal score and script have an additional lyric (in the Act I Finale) set to the tune of "I Love a Piano" that begins, "Let's go to the movies."

Finale Act I ["I love to sit by the fire..."]
Berlin/Berlin
Orchestrator: Unknown

Location of   - Composer's manuscript: -0-
          - Sheet music: Unpublished
          - Most complete music: NYPL (pv score)
          - Most complete lyric: NYPL (pv score)
          - Original partitur: -0-
          - Original parts: -0-

Includes reprises of "I Love a Piano" (set to new lyrics) and "I Love to Dance." The lyric is also in the early draft of the script at the New York Public Library.

Entr'acte I
Berlin/Berlin
Orchestrator: Unknown

Location of   - Composer's manuscript: -0-
          - Sheet music: Unpublished
          - Most complete music: -0-
          - Most complete lyric: INST
          - Original partitur: -0-
          - Original parts: -0-

Opening Act II ["Oh, what a place is dreamy Honolulu..."]
Berlin/Berlin
Orchestrator: Unknown

Location of   - Composer's manuscript: -0-
          - Sheet music: Unpublished
          - Most complete music: NYPL (pv score)
          - Most complete lyric: NYPL (pv score, ls)
          - Original partitur: -0-
          - Original parts: -0-

That Hula Hula
Berlin/Berlin
Orchestrator: Unknown

Location of   - Composer's manuscript: -0-
          - Sheet music: IB, LoC, NYPL, Y
          - Most complete music: IB (sm); LoC (sm);
              NYPL (sm, pv score); Y (sm)
          - Most complete lyric: IB (sm); LoC (sm);
              NYPL (sm, pv score); Y (sm)
          - Original partitur: -0-
          - Original parts: -0-

Stop! Look! Listen! (1915)

Pair of Ordinary Coons, A
Berlin/Berlin
Orchestrator: Unknown

Location of - Composer's manuscript: -0-
          - Sheet music: See note
          - Most complete music: NYPL (pv score)
          - Most complete lyric: NYPL (pv score)
          - Original partitur: -0-
          - Original parts: -0-

According to Steven Suskin's <u>Show Tunes 1905-1985</u>
(Dodd, Mead & Company: 1986), this number was published
in a separate edition. No printed copy was found.

Take Off a Little Bit
Berlin/Berlin
Orchestrator: Unknown

Location of - Composer's manuscript: -0-
          - Sheet music: IB, LoC, Y (x)
          - Most complete music: IB (sm); LoC (sm);
              Y (sm-x); NYPL (pv score)
          - Most complete lyric: IB (sm); LoC (sm);
              Y (sm-x); NYPL (pv score)
          - Original partitur: -0-
          - Original parts: -0-

When I'm Out With You
Berlin/Berlin
Orchestrator: Unknown

Location of - Composer's manuscript: -0-
          - Sheet music: IB, LoC, Y
          - Most complete music: IB (sm); LoC (sm);
              Y (sm); NYPL (pv score)
          - Most complete lyric: IB (sm); LoC (sm);
              Y (sm); NYPL (pv score)
          - Original partitur: -0-
          - Original parts: -0-

Teach Me How to Love
Berlin/Berlin
Orchestrator: Unknown

Location of - Composer's manuscript: -0-
          - Sheet music: IB, LoC, Y (x)
          - Most complete music: IB (sm); LoC (sm);
              Y (sm-x); NYPL (pv score)
          - Most complete lyric: IB (sm); LoC (sm);
              Y (sm-x); NYPL (pv score)
          - Original partitur: -0-
          - Original parts: -0-

Oozums
Berlin/Berlin
Orchestrator: Unknown

Location of - Composer's manuscript: -0-
          - Sheet music: Unpublished
          - Most complete music: -0-
          - Most complete lyric: NYPL (ls)
          - Original partitur: -0-
          - Original parts: -0-

Added during the New York run.

Law Must be Obeyed, The
Berlin/Berlin
Orchestrator: Unknown

Location of - Composer's manuscript: -0-
          - Sheet music: IB, LoC, Y (x)
          - Most complete music: IB (sm); LoC (sm);
              Y (sm-x); NYPL (pv score)
          - Most complete lyric: IB (sm); LoC (sm);
              Y (sm-x); NYPL (pv score)
          - Original partitur: -0-
          - Original parts: -0-

Finale – Ragtime Melodrama
Berlin/Berlin
Orchestrator: Unknown

Location of   - Composer's manuscript: -0-
- Sheet music: Unpublished
- Most complete music: NYPL (pv score)
- Most complete lyric: NYPL (pv score)
- Original partitur: -0-
- Original parts: -0-

The lyric is also in the early draft of the script at the
New York Public Library.

Stop! Look! Listen!
Berlin/Berlin
Orchestrator: Unknown

Location of   - Composer's manuscript: -0-
- Sheet music: IB, LoC, NYPL, Y
- Most complete music: IB (sm); LoC (sm);
      NYPL (sm, pv score); Y (sm)
- Most complete lyric: IB (sm); LoC (sm);
      NYPL (sm); Y (sm)
- Original partitur: -0-
- Original parts: -0-

Entr'acte II
Berlin/Berlin
Orchestrator: Unknown

Location of   - Composer's manuscript: -0-
- Sheet music: Unpublished
- Most complete music: -0-
- Most complete lyric: INST
- Original partitur: -0-
- Original parts: -0-

I'll Be Coming Home With a Skate On
Berlin/Berlin
Orchestrator: Unknown

Location of   - Composer's manuscript: -0-
- Sheet music: Unpublished
- Most complete music: NYPL (pv score)
- Most complete lyric: NYPL (pv score, ls)
- Original partitur: -0-
- Original parts: -0-

Alternate title: "Skating Song." Advertised but not
published.

When I Get Back to the U.S.A.
Berlin/Berlin
Orchestrator: Unknown

Location of   - Composer's manuscript: -0-
- Sheet music: IB, LoC, NYPL, Y
- Most complete music: IB (sm); LoC (sm);
      NYPL (sm, pv score); Y (sm)
- Most complete lyric: IB (sm); LoC (sm);
      NYPL (sm, pv score); Y (sm)
- Original partitur: -0-
- Original parts: -0-

Everything in America Is Ragtime
Berlin/Berlin
Orchestrator: Unknown

Location of   - Composer's manuscript: -0-
- Sheet music: IB, LoC, Y (x)
- Most complete music: IB (sm); LoC (sm);
      Y (sm-x); NYPL (pv score)
- Most complete lyric: IB (sm); LoC (sm);
      Y (sm-x); NYPL (pv score)
- Original partitur: -0-
- Original parts: -0-

Finale Act III
    Berlin/Berlin
    Orchestrator: Unknown

Location of   - Composer's manuscript: -0-
             - Sheet music: -0-
             - Most complete music: -0-
             - Most complete lyric: -0-
             - Original partitur: -0-
             - Original parts: -0-

This number is listed in the New York programs, but not included in the piano-vocal score; it may have consisted solely of reprises.

On the Beach at Waiki-ki
    Kailimai/Stover
    Orchestrator: Unknown

Location of   - Composer's manuscript: -0-
             - Sheet music: NYPL
             - Most complete music: NYPL (sm)
             - Most complete lyric: NYPL (sm)
             - Original partitur: -0-
             - Original parts: -0-

This Act II specialty performed by the Hawaiian Band was dropped during the New York run. Published in 1915 by Bergstrom Music Co.

England Every Time for Me
    Berlin/Berlin
    Orchestrator: Unknown

Location of   - Composer's manuscript: -0-
             - Sheet music: JF
             - Most complete music: JF (sm)
             - Most complete lyric: JF (sm)
             - Original partitur: -0-
             - Original parts: -0-

Written for FOLLOW THE CROWD, the 1916 London version of STOP! LOOK! LISTEN!

Sailor Song
    Berlin/Berlin
    Orchestrator: Unknown

Location of   - Composer's manuscript: -0-
             - Sheet music: IB, LoC, Y (x)
             - Most complete music: IB (sm); LoC (sm);
                   Y (sm-x)
             - Most complete lyric: IB (sm); LoC (sm);
                   Y (sm-x)
             - Original partitur: -0-
             - Original parts: -0-

Dropped before the New York opening. The lyric is also in the early draft of the script at the New York Public Library.

Until I Fell in Love With You
    Berlin/Berlin
    Orchestrator: Unknown

Location of   - Composer's manuscript: -0-
             - Sheet music: LoC, NYPL, Y
             - Most complete music: LoC (sm);
                   NYPL (sm); Y (sm)
             - Most complete lyric: See note
             - Original partitur: -0-
             - Original parts: -0-

Dropped before the New York opening. The most complete lyric is in the early draft of the script at the New York Public Library.

Hunting for a Star
    Berlin/Berlin
    Orchestrator: Unknown

Location of   - Composer's manuscript: -0-
             - Sheet music: Unpublished
             - Most complete music: -0-
             - Most complete lyric: NYPL (ls)
             - Original partitur: -0-
             - Original parts: -0-

Dropped before the New York opening. The lyric is also in the early draft of the script at the New York Public Library.

Poor Mary

Berlin/Berlin

Orchestrator: Unknown

Location of - Composer's manuscript: -0-

- Sheet music: Unpublished
- Most complete music: -0-
- Most complete lyric: NYPL (ls)
- Original partitur: -0-
- Original parts: -0-

Dropped before the New York opening. The lyric is also in the early draft of the script at the New York Public Library.

THE COCOANUTS

Music   **IRVING BERLIN**
Lyrics   **IRVING BERLIN**

Musical comedy in two acts. Opened December 8, 1925 in New York and ran 276 performances (World premiere: October 27, 1925 in Boston). Libretto by George S. Kaufman. Produced by Sam H. Harris. Directed by Oscar Eagle. Choreographed by Sammy Lee. Musical direction by Frank Tours. Orchestrations by Frank Tours, Maurice B. DePackh, Stephen O. Jones.

Synopsis and Production Information

In order to prevent Robert Adams from marrying the very wealthy Polly Potter, Harvey Yates steals Mother Potter's $100,000 necklace and frames Bob. With the help of ex-criminals Willy the Wop and Silent Sam, Bob is able to prove his innocence and marry his beloved.

Other key characters include Julius, the hotel proprietor; Jamison, a hotel employee; Penelope, a singer who conspires with Harvey; and Hennesy, the detective on the scene. There is a full singing and dancing ensemble.

Orchestration

Unknown

Comments

In the original production, Julius, Sam, Willy, and Jamison were played by Groucho, Harpo, Chico, and Zeppo Marx, respectively. Margaret Dumont played Mother Potter. There was a piano specialty by Chico, a harp specialty by Harpo, and several appearances by the De Marco orchestra and dancers Antonio and Nina De Marco.

Location of Original Materials

Script: Irving Berlin Music Corporation (all lyrics), New York Public Library (all lyrics)
Piano-vocal score: See individual listings
Partiturs: Missing
Parts: Missing

Music is missing for two numbers performed in the original New York production ("The Guests" and "Why Am I a Hit With the Ladies?"), as well as for the Overture, Entr'acte, and much of the specialty material. In addition, only a melody line has been located for several others numbers. The script was published (without lyrics) in a collection of Kaufman works entitled By George (St. Martin's Press, Inc., 1979).

Rental Status

Currently unavailable for rental

Music Publisher

Irving Berlin Music Corporation

Information

Irving Berlin Music Corporation

Overture

Berlin/Berlin

Orchestrator: Unknown

Location of   - Composer's manuscript: -0-
              - Sheet music: Unpublished
              - Most complete music: -0-
              - Most complete lyric: INST
              - Original partitur: -0-
              - Original parts: -0-

Family Reputation, The

Berlin/Berlin

Orchestrator: Unknown

Location of   - Composer's manuscript: -0-
              - Sheet music: See note
              - Most complete music: LoC (m-l)
              - Most complete lyric: IB (scr); NYPL (scr)
              - Original partitur: -0-
              - Original parts: -0-

According to Steven Suskin's Show Tunes 1905-1985 (Dodd, Mead & Company: 1986), this number was issued as a professional copy (under the title "With a Family Reputation"). No printed version was found.

Guests, The

Berlin/Berlin

Orchestrator: Unknown

Location of   - Composer's manuscript: -0-
              - Sheet music: Unpublished
              - Most complete music: -0-
              - Most complete lyric: IB (scr); NYPL (scr)
              - Original partitur: -0-
              - Original parts: -0-

Alternate titles: "Opening Act I" and "So This Is Florida."

Lucky Boy

Berlin/Berlin

Orchestrator: Unknown

Location of   - Composer's manuscript: -0-
              - Sheet music: IB, LoC, NYPL, Y (x)
              - Most complete music: IB (sm);
                   LoC (sm); NYPL (sm); Y (sm-x)
              - Most complete lyric: IB (sm, scr);
                   LoC (sm); NYPL (sm, scr); Y (sm-x)
              - Original partitur: -0-
              - Original parts: -0-

Bellhops, The

Berlin/Berlin

Orchestrator: Unknown

Location of   - Composer's manuscript: -0-
              - Sheet music: Unpublished
              - Most complete music: See note
              - Most complete lyric: IB (scr); NYPL (scr)
              - Original partitur: -0-
              - Original parts: -0-

Alternate title: "Bellboy Opening." No musical manuscript has been located, but both the verse and refrain of this number can be heard as dance music in the film version (1929).

Why Am I a Hit With the Ladies?

Berlin/Berlin

Orchestrator: Unknown

Location of   - Composer's manuscript: -0-
              - Sheet music: Unpublished
              - Most complete music: -0-
              - Most complete lyric: IB (scr); NYPL (scr)
              - Original partitur: -0-
              - Original parts: -0-

Advertised but not published.

The Cocoanuts (1925)

Little Bungalow, A
Berlin/Berlin
Orchestrator: Unknown

Location of - Composer's manuscript: -0-
- Sheet music: IB, LoC, NYPL, Y
- Most complete music: IB (sm);
     LoC (sm); NYPL (sm); Y (sm)
- Most complete lyric: IB (sm, scr);
     LoC (sm); NYPL (sm, scr); Y (sm)
- Original partitur: -0-
- Original parts: -0-

Entr'acte
Berlin/Berlin
Orchestrator: Unknown

Location of - Composer's manuscript: -0-
- Sheet music: Unpublished
- Most complete music: -0-
- Most complete lyric: INST
- Original partitur: -0-
- Original parts: -0-

Florida by the Sea
Berlin/Berlin
Orchestrator: Unknown

Location of - Composer's manuscript: -0-
- Sheet music: IB, LoC, NYPL, Y
- Most complete music: IB (sm);
     LoC (sm); NYPL (sm); Y (sm)
- Most complete lyric: IB (scr); NYPL (scr)
- Original partitur: -0-
- Original parts: -0-

Tea Dance
Author(s): Unknown
Orchestrator: Unknown

Location of - Composer's manuscript: -0-
- Sheet music: Unpublished
- Most complete music: -0-
- Most complete lyric: INST
- Original partitur: -0-
- Original parts: -0-

This Act II opening (danced by "the eight Tea girls") may have been performed to the music of "Five O'Clock Tea."

Monkey Doodle-Doo, The
Berlin/Berlin
Orchestrator: Unknown

Location of - Composer's manuscript: -0-
- Sheet music: IB, LoC, NYPL, Y
- Most complete music: IB (sm);
     LoC (sm); NYPL (sm); Y (sm)
- Most complete lyric: IB (scr); NYPL (scr)
- Original partitur: -0-
- Original parts: -0-

The patter section was not published. This is not the same number as Berlin's "The Monkey Doodle Doo," which appeared in ALL ABOARD!, a musical comedy of 1913.

Five O'Clock Tea
Berlin/Berlin
Orchestrator: Unknown

Location of - Composer's manuscript: -0-
- Sheet music: IB, LoC, NYPL, Y
- Most complete music: IB (sm);
     LoC (sm); NYPL (sm); Y (sm)
- Most complete lyric: IB (sm, scr);
     LoC (sm); NYPL (sm, scr); Y (sm)
- Original partitur: -0-
- Original parts: -0-

They're Blaming the Charleston

Berlin/Berlin

Orchestrator: Unknown

Location of   - Composer's manuscript: -0-
     - Sheet music: Unpublished
     - Most complete music: LoC (pv-l)
     - Most complete lyric: IB (scr); NYPL (scr)
     - Original partitur: -0-
     - Original parts: -0-

We Should Care [second version]

Berlin/Berlin

Orchestrator: Unknown

Location of   - Composer's manuscript: -0-
     - Sheet music: IB, LoC, NYPL, Y
     - Most complete music: IB (sm);
          LoC (sm); NYPL (sm); Y (sm)
     - Most complete lyric: IB (sm, scr);
          LoC (sm); NYPL (sm, scr); Y (sm)
     - Original partitur: -0-
     - Original parts: -0-

The verse is similar to that of the first version of "We Should Care" (which was also published), as well as to that of "When My Dreams Come True," the number that replaced "We Should Care" in the film version (1929).

Minstrel Days

Berlin/Berlin

Orchestrator: Unknown

Location of   - Composer's manuscript: -0-
     - Sheet music: Unpublished
     - Most complete music: LoC (m-l)
     - Most complete lyric: IB (scr); NYPL (scr)
     - Original partitur: -0-
     - Original parts: -0-

Advertised but not published.

Specialty

Author(s): Unknown

Orchestrator: Unknown

Location of   - Composer's manuscript: -0-
     - Sheet music: -0-
     - Most complete music: -0-
     - Most complete lyric: INST
     - Original partitur: -0-
     - Original parts: -0-

Performed by the De Marco Orchestra.

Tango Melody

Berlin/Berlin

Orchestrator: Unknown

Location of   - Composer's manuscript: -0-
     - Sheet music: IB, LoC, Y
     - Most complete music: IB (sm);
          LoC (sm); Y (sm)
     - Most complete lyric: IB (sm, scr);
          LoC (sm); NYPL (scr); Y (sm)
     - Original partitur: -0-
     - Original parts: -0-

Alternate title: "Spain."

Tale of a Shirt, The

Author(s): See note

Orchestrator: Unknown

Location of   - Composer's manuscript: -0-
     - Sheet music: Unpublished
     - Most complete music: See note
     - Most complete lyric: IB (scr); NYPL (scr)
     - Original partitur: -0-
     - Original parts: -0-

Alternate title: "Shirt Number." The lyric (presumably by Berlin) is mostly set to two passages from Georges Bizet's CARMEN: the "Habanera" and the "Toreador Song."

The Cocoanuts (1925)

Piano Specialty
Author(s): Unknown
Orchestrator: Unknown

Location of   - Composer's manuscript: -0-
               - Sheet music: -0-
               - Most complete music: -0-
               - Most complete lyric: INST
               - Original partitur: -0-
               - Original parts: -0-

Performed by Chico.

Gentlemen Prefer Blondes
Berlin/Berlin
Orchestrator: Unknown

Location of   - Composer's manuscript: -0-
               - Sheet music: IB, Y (x)
               - Most complete music: IB (sm), Y (sm-x)
               - Most complete lyric: IB (sm), Y (sm-x)
               - Original partitur: -0-
               - Original parts: -0-

Replaced "Why Am I a Hit With the Ladies?" during the New York run (for the 1926 New Summer Edition). Later in the run and on tour, it in turn was replaced by "Why Am I a Hit With the Ladies?"

Harp Specialty
Author(s): Unknown
Orchestrator: Unknown

Location of   - Composer's manuscript: -0-
               - Sheet music: -0-
               - Most complete music: -0-
               - Most complete lyric: INST
               - Original partitur: -0-
               - Original parts: -0-

Performed by Harpo.

Ting-a-Ling (The Bells'll Ring)
Berlin/Berlin
Orchestrator: Unknown

Location of   - Composer's manuscript: -0-
               - Sheet music: IB, NYPL, Y
               - Most complete music: IB (sm);
                    NYPL (sm); Y (sm)
               - Most complete lyric: IB (sm);
                    NYPL (sm); Y (sm)
               - Original partitur: -0-
               - Original parts:-0-

Replaced "A Little Bungalow" during the New York run (for the 1926 New Summer Edition). Later in the run and on tour, it in turn was replaced by "A Little Bungalow."

Why Do You Want to Know Why?
Berlin/Berlin
Orchestrator: Unknown

Location of   - Composer's manuscript: -0-
               - Sheet music: IB, LoC, NYPL, Y
               - Most complete music: IB (sm);
                  LoC (sm); NYPL (sm); Y (sm)
               - Most complete lyric: IB (sm);
                  LoC (sm); NYPL (sm); Y (sm)
               - Original partitur: -0-
               - Original parts: -0-

Replaced "Family Reputation" during the New York run (for the 1926 New Summer Edition).

Everyone in the World is Doing the Charleston
Berlin/Berlin
Orchestrator: Unknown

Location of   - Composer's manuscript: -0-
               - Sheet music: See note
               - Most complete music: LoC (pv-l);
                  JF (prof)
               - Most complete lyric: LoC (pv-l);
                  JF (prof)
               - Original partitur: -0-
               - Original parts: -0-

Added during the New York run (for the 1926 New Summer Edition). Issued as a professional copy.

Irving Berlin

When We're Running a Little Hotel of Our Own
Berlin/Berlin
Orchestrator: Unknown

Location of   - Composer's manuscript: -0-
              - Sheet music: Unpublished
              - Most complete music: -0-
              - Most complete lyric: -0-
              - Original partitur: -0-
              - Original parts: -0-

Dropped during the pre-Broadway tryout. Advertised but not published.

We Should Care [first version]
Berlin/Berlin
Orchestrator: Unknown

Location of   - Composer's manuscript: -0-
              - Sheet music: LoC
              - Most complete music: LoC (sm)
              - Most complete lyric: LoC (sm)
              - Original partitur: -0-
              - Original parts: -0-

Replaced by "We Should Care" [second version].

What's There About Me?
Berlin/Berlin
Orchestrator: Unknown

Location of   - Composer's manuscript: -0-
              - Sheet music: Unpublished
              - Most complete music: LoC (m-l)
              - Most complete lyric: LoC (m-l)
              - Original partitur: -0-
              - Original parts: -0-

Replaced before the New York opening by "Why Am I a Hit With the Ladies?"

When My Dreams Come True
Berlin/Berlin
Orchestrator: Unknown

Location of   - Composer's manuscript: -0-
              - Sheet music: IB, LoC, NYPL, Y
              - Most complete music: IB (sm);
                    LoC (sm); NYPL (sm); Y (sm)
              - Most complete lyric: IB (sm);
                    LoC (sm); NYPL (sm); Y (sm)
              - Original partitur: -0-
              - Original parts: -0-

Written for the film version (1929).

Too Many Sweethearts
Berlin/Berlin
Orchestrator: Unknown

Location of   - Composer's manuscript: -0-
              - Sheet music: See note
              - Most complete music: JF (prof)
              - Most complete lyric: JF (prof)
              - Original partitur: -0-
              - Original parts: -0-

According to Steven Suskin's Show Tunes 1905-1985 (Dodd, Mead & Company: 1986), this number was issued as a professional copy in conjunction with THE COCOANUTS. The only professional copy found dates from 1923, the year Berlin wrote a song called "Too Many Sweethearts" for the third MUSIC BOX REVUE.

FACE THE MUSIC

Music	IRVING BERLIN
Lyrics	IRVING BERLIN

Musical comedy in two acts. Opened February 17, 1932 in New York and ran 165 performances (World premiere: February 8, 1932 in Philadelphia). Libretto by Moss Hart. Produced by Sam H. Harris. Directed by Hassard Short, George S. Kaufman. Choreographed by Albertina Rasch. Musical direction by Frank Tours. Orchestrations by Robert Russell Bennett, Frank Tours, Maurice B. DePackh.

Synopsis and Production Information

The Depression has reduced even the Rockefellers and Vanderbilts to dining at the automat, but members of the police force have accrued a fortune in their little tin boxes. One of these policemen, Mr. Meshbesher, spurred on by his garrulous wife, agrees to fund the latest edition of producer Hal Reisman's FOLLIES. The resulting show (RHINESTONES OF 1932) is a flop on opening night, but when the cast and crew spice it up with bathroom humor and semi-nude women, it attracts the attention of the Vice Commission and becomes Broadway's newest hit. Eventually, news of the show's illegal funding leaks out, but Reisman, ever the showman, decides to produce the investigation himself. His courtroom shenanigans, which climax with Mrs. Meshbesher riding in on an elephant, so overwhelm the judge and jury that the accused are cleared of all charges.

Other characters include Follies star Kit Baker, her pal Pat Mason, and a comic song-and-dance team. The show requires a full singing and dancing ensemble.

Orchestration

Flute; Oboe/English Horn; Clarinet/Alto Sax; Clarinet/Alto Sax; Clarinet/Tenor Sax; Trumpet I II; Trumpet III; Trombone; Percussion; Banjo/Guitar; Piano; Violin A B C D; Viola (divisi); Cello; Bass

Location of Original Materials

Script: Shubert Archive (all lyrics)
Piano-vocal score: See individual listings
Partiturs: Missing
Parts: Irving Berlin Music Corporation, Shubert Archive

All of the songs and orchestra parts survive. The Irving Berlin Music Corporation has an early draft of the script; the Library of Congress has a near-final draft (bearing the credit "additional dialogue by Morrie Ryskind"); and the New York Public Library has a final draft that is missing the last scene.

The following songs were registered for copyright during the same period in late 1931 as songs in the FACE THE MUSIC score: "Police of New York," "Two Cheers Instead of Three," "Sleep Baby" (later registered under the title, "Chase All Your Cares and Go to Sleep, Baby"), "How Can I Change My Luck," and "I'll Miss You in the Evening." Some or all of these numbers may have been, at one time, intended for FACE THE MUSIC.

Rental Status

Currently unavailable for rental

Music Publisher

Irving Berlin Music Corporation

Information

Irving Berlin Music Corporation

Irving Berlin

Overture
Berlin/Berlin
Orchestrator: Unknown

Location of - Composer's manuscript: -0-
- Sheet music: Unpublished
- Most complete music: IB (parts)
- Most complete lyric: INST
- Original partitur: -0-
- Original parts: IB

Reisman's Doing a Show
Berlin/Berlin
Orchestrator: Unknown

Location of - Composer's manuscript: -0-
- Sheet music: Unpublished
- Most complete music: IB (p); SA (p)
- Most complete lyric: IB (ls); SA (scr)
- Original partitur: -0-
- Original parts: SA

Lunching at the Automat
Berlin/Berlin
Orchestrator: Unknown

Location of - Composer's manuscript: -0-
- Sheet music: Unpublished
- Most complete music: IB (pv)
- Most complete lyric: IB (ls); SA (scr)
- Original partitur: -0-
- Original parts: IB

Alternate titles: "Automat Opening" and "Opening Act I."

Torch Song
Berlin/Berlin
Orchestrator: Unknown

Location of - Composer's manuscript: -0-
- Sheet music: Unpublished
- Most complete music: IB (p)
- Most complete lyric: IB (ls); SA (scr)
- Original partitur: -0-
- Original parts: IB

Let's Have Another Cup of Coffee
Berlin/Berlin
Orchestrator: Unknown

Location of - Composer's manuscript: -0-
- Sheet music: IB, LoC, Y
- Most complete music: IB (sm); LoC (sm);
    Y (sm)
- Most complete lyric: IB (sm, ls);
    LoC (sm); Y (sm); SA (scr)
- Original partitur: -0-
- Original parts: IB

You Must Be Born With It
Berlin/Berlin
Orchestrator: Unknown

Location of - Composer's manuscript: -0-
- Sheet music: Unpublished
- Most complete music: IB (p)
- Most complete lyric: IB (ls); SA (sm)
- Original partitur: -0-
- Original parts: IB

Face the Music (1932)

On a Roof in Manhattan
Berlin/Berlin
Orchestrator: Unknown

Location of   - Composer's manuscript: -0-
              - Sheet music: IB, Y
              - Most complete music: IB (sm); Y (sm)
              - Most complete lyric: IB (ls)
              - Original partitur: -0-
              - Original parts: IB

Alternate title: "A Roof in Manhattan."

Entr'acte
Berlin/Berlin
Orchestrator: Unknown

Location of   - Composer's manuscript: -0-
              - Sheet music: Unpublished
              - Most complete music: IB (parts)
              - Most complete lyric: INST
              - Original partitur: -0-
              - Original parts: IB

My Rhinestone Girl
Berlin/Berlin
Orchestrator: Unknown

Location of   - Composer's manuscript: -0-
              - Sheet music: Unpublished
              - Most complete music: IB (parts)
              - Most complete lyric: IB (ls); SA (scr)
              - Original partitur: -0-
              - Original parts: IB

Alternate title: "My Beautiful Rhinestone Girl."

Opening Act II ["Well of all the rotten shows..."]
Berlin/Berlin
Orchestrator: Unknown

Location of   - Composer's manuscript: -0-
              - Sheet music: Unpublished
              - Most complete music: SA (p-l); IB (p)
              - Most complete lyric: SA (p-l, scr);
                    IB (ls)
              - Original partitur: -0-
              - Original parts: IB

Soft Lights and Sweet Music
Berlin/Berlin
Orchestrator: Unknown

Location of   - Composer's manuscript: -0-
              - Sheet music: IB, LoC, Y
              - Most complete music: IB (sm); LoC (sm);
                    Y (sm)
              - Most complete lyric: IB (sm, ls);
                    LoC (sm); Y (sm); SA (scr)
              - Original partitur: -0-
              - Original parts: IB

I Say It's Spinach (and the Hell With It)
Berlin/Berlin
Orchestrator: Unknown

Location of   - Composer's manuscript: -0-
              - Sheet music: IB, LoC, Y
              - Most complete music: IB (sm); LoC (sm);
                    Y (sm)
              - Most complete lyric: IB (sm & ls)
              - Original partitur: -0-
              - Original parts: IB

Drinking Song

Berlin/Berlin
Orchestrator: Unknown

Location of - Composer's manuscript: -0-
                - Sheet music: Unpublished
                - Most complete music: IB (parts)
                - Most complete lyric: SA (scr)
                - Original partitur: -0-
                - Original parts: IB

Registered for copyright as an unpublished number in 1932 under the title "Prohibition."

Manhattan Madness

Berlin/Berlin
Orchestrator: Unknown

Location of - Composer's manuscript: -0-
                - Sheet music: IB, LoC, Y
                - Most complete music: IB (sm); LoC (sm);
                    Y (sm)
                - Most complete lyric: IB (sm, ls);
                    LoC (sm); Y (sm, ls); SA (scr)
                - Original partitur: -0-
                - Original parts: SA

Dear Old Crinoline Days

Berlin/Berlin
Orchestrator: Unknown

Location of - Composer's manuscript: -0-
                - Sheet music: Unpublished
                - Most complete music: IB (p)
                - Most complete lyric: SA (scr)
                - Original partitur: -0-
                - Original parts: IB

The tune was apparently first set to a lyric entitled "The Nudist Song," found in a lyric sheet at the Irving Berlin Music Corporation and in the script at the New York Public Library. (The parts are still entitled "The Nudist Song.") This is not the same number as Berlin's "Crinoline Days" from the 1922 MUSIC BOX REVUE.

Investigation

Berlin/Berlin
Orchestrator: Unknown

Location of - Composer's manuscript: -0-
                - Sheet music: Unpublished
                - Most complete music: IB (p)
                - Most complete lyric: IB (ls); SA (scr)
                - Original partitur: -0-
                - Original parts: IB

I Don't Want to Be Married (I Just Wanna Be Friends)

Berlin/Berlin
Orchestrator: Unknown

Location of - Composer's manuscript: -0-
                - Sheet music: Unpublished
                - Most complete music: IB (p)
                - Most complete lyric: IB (ls); SA (scr)
                - Original partitur: -0-
                - Original parts: IB

LOUISIANA PURCHASE

Music IRVING BERLIN
Lyrics IRVING BERLIN

Musical comedy in two acts. Opened May 28, 1940 in New York and ran 444 performances (World premiere: May 2, 1940 in New Haven). Libretto by Morrie Ryskind, based on a story by B.G. DeSylva. Produced by B.G. DeSylva. Directed by Edgar MacGregor. Choreographed by George Balanchine, Carl Randall. Musical direction by Robert Emmett Dolan. Orchestrations by Robert Russell Bennett; additional orchestrations by N. Lang Van Cleve. Vocal arrangements by Hugh Martin, assisted by Ralph Blane.

Synopsis and Production Information	Jimmy Taylor and his corrupt business associates in the Louisiana Purchasing Company are being indicted for fraud by Senator Oliver P. Loganberry, a straitlaced Republican from New Hampshire. With the help of his friend Mme. Bordelaise, Taylor tries to frame the Senator by catching him in a compromising position with Marina, a sweet Viennese emigrant. Unfortunately, his plan backfires when Marina decides to marry Loganberry. In the end, Marina realizes she truly loves Taylor, so the Senator weds the worldly Madame instead, and the Louisiana Purchasing Company merrily continues its wicked ways.
	The show requires a full singing and dancing ensemble.
Orchestration	Reed I (Flute, Piccolo, Clarinet, Alto Sax); Reed II (Clarinet, Bass Clarinet, Alto Sax, Flute); Reed III (Clarinet, Tenor Sax); Reed IV (Oboe, English Horn, Tenor Sax, Bass Clarinet); Reed V (Clarinet, Baritone Sax, Flute); Trumpet I II; Trumpet III; Trombone; Trombone II; Percussion I; Percussion II; Guitar; Piano; Violin A B C; Viola I II; Cello; Bass
Comments	In the original production, Taylor was played by William Gaxton, Loganberry by Victor Moore, Marina by Vera Zorina, and Mme. Bordelaise by Irene Bordoni. Carol Bruce played one of the Madame's livelier girls, Beatrice, who introduces the title song.
Location of Original Materials	Script: Irving Berlin Music Corporation (all lyrics), New York Public Library (all lyrics) Piano-vocal score: See individual listings Partiturs: Irving Berlin Music Corporation Parts: Missing
	Most of the piano-vocal material survives, but only a handful of original partiturs have surfaced.
Rental Status	Currently unavailable for rental
Music Publisher	Irving Berlin Music Corporation
Information	Irving Berlin Music Corporation

Irving Berlin

Overture
Berlin/Berlin
Orchestrator: Unknown

Location of
- Composer's manuscript: -0-
- Sheet music: Not published separately
- Most complete music: -0-
- Most complete lyric: INST
- Original partitur: -0-
- Original parts: -0-

Louisiana Purchase
Berlin/Berlin
Orchestrator: Bennett

Location of
- Composer's manuscript: -0-
- Sheet music: IB, LoC, Y
- Most complete music: IB (sm);
  LoC (sm); Y (sm)
- Most complete lyric: IB (sm, scr);
  LoC (sm); Y (sm); NYPL (scr)
- Original partitur: IB
- Original parts: -0-

Apologia
Berlin/Berlin
Orchestrator: Unknown

Location of
- Composer's manuscript: -0-
- Sheet music: Not published separately
- Most complete music: IB (v sel)
- Most complete lyric: IB (scr); NYPL (scr)
- Original partitur: -0-
- Original parts: -0-

Published in the LOUISIANA PURCHASE vocal selections
in two parts: "Opening Letter" and "Opening Chorus."

It's a Lovely Day Tomorrow
Berlin/Berlin
Orchestrator: Unknown

Location of
- Composer's manuscript: -0-
- Sheet music: IB, NYPL, Y
- Most complete music: IB (sm);
  NYPL (sm); Y (sm)
- Most complete lyric: IB (sm, scr);
  NYPL (sm, scr); Y (sm)
- Original partitur: IB
- Original parts: -0-

Scored for a string quartet.

Sex Marches On
Berlin/Berlin
Orchestrator: Unknown

Location of
- Composer's manuscript: -0-
- Sheet music: See note
- Most complete music: IB (prof); LoC (prof)
- Most complete lyric: IB (scr); NYPL (scr)
- Original partitur: -0-
- Original parts: -0-

Issued only as a professional copy.

Outside of That I Love You
Berlin/Berlin
Orchestrator: Unknown

Location of
- Composer's manuscript: -0-
- Sheet music: IB, LoC, Y
- Most complete music: IB (sm);
  LoC (sm); Y (sm)
- Most complete lyric: IB (scr); NYPL (scr)
- Original partitur: -0-
- Original parts: -0-

Louisiana Purchase (1940)

You're Lonely and I'm Lonely
Berlin/Berlin
Orchestrator: Unknown

Location of   - Composer's manuscript: -0-
      - Sheet music: IB, LoC, Y
      - Most complete music: IB (sm);
         LoC (sm); Y (sm)
      - Most complete lyric: IB (sm, scr);
         LoC (sm); Y (sm); NYPL (scr)
      - Original partitur: -0-
      - Original parts: -0-

Entr'acte
Berlin/Berlin
Orchestrator: Unknown

Location of   - Composer's manuscript: -0-
      - Sheet music: Unpublished
      - Most complete music: -0-
      - Most complete lyric: INST
      - Original partitur: -0-
      - Original parts: -0-

Dance With Me (Tonight at the Mardi Gras)
Berlin/Berlin
Orchestrator: Unknown

Location of   - Composer's manuscript: -0-
      - Sheet music: IB, LoC, NYPL, Y
      - Most complete music: IB (sm);
         LoC (sm); NYPL (sm); Y (sm)
      - Most complete lyric: IB (sm, scr);
         LoC (sm); NYPL (sm, scr); Y (sm)
      - Original partitur: IB (inc)
      - Original parts: -0-

Listed in the New York programs as "Tonight at the Mardi Gras."

Opening Act II
Berlin/Berlin
Orchestrator: Unknown

Location of   - Composer's manuscript: -0-
      - Sheet music: Unpublished
      - Most complete music: IB (ptr)
      - Most complete lyric: See note
      - Original partitur: IB
      - Original parts: -0-

This number is listed in the New York programs, but there is no lyric in the scripts; it may have been a dance number or underscoring.

Finale Act I ["What's this we hear..."]
Berlin/Berlin
Orchestrator: Unknown

Location of   - Composer's manuscript: -0-
      - Sheet music: Unpublished
      - Most complete music: See note
      - Most complete lyric: IB (scr); NYPL (scr)
      - Original partitur: -0-
      - Original parts: -0-

Consists primarily of previously introduced numbers set to new lyrics. The music for the few new passages is missing.

Latins Know How
Berlin/Berlin
Orchestrator: Unknown

Location of   - Composer's manuscript: -0-
      - Sheet music: IB, LoC, NYPL, Y
      - Most complete music: IB (sm);
         LoC (sm); NYPL (sm); Y (sm)
      - Most complete lyric: IB (sm, scr);
         LoC (sm); NYPL (sm, scr); Y (sm)
      - Original partitur: -0-
      - Original parts: -0-

What Chance Have I With Love?
Berlin/Berlin
Orchestrator: Unknown

Location of   - Composer's manuscript: -0-
             - Sheet music: IB, LoC, NYPL, Y
             - Most complete music: IB (sm);
                   LoC (sm); NYPL (sm); Y (sm)
             - Most complete lyric: IB (scr); NYPL (scr)
             - Original partitur: -0-
             - Original parts: -0-

Old Man's Darling – Young Man's Slave?
Berlin/Berlin
Orchestrator: Unknown

Location of   - Composer's manuscript: -0-
             - Sheet music: Unpublished
             - Most complete music: -0-
             - Most complete lyric: IB (scr); NYPL (scr)
             - Original partitur: -0-
             - Original parts: -0-

A ballet with dialogue and song performed by Vera Zorina.

Lord Done Fixed Up My Soul, The
Berlin/Berlin
Orchestrator: Unknown

Location of   - Composer's manuscript: -0-
             - Sheet music: IB, LoC, NYPL, Y
             - Most complete music: IB (sm);
                   LoC (sm); NYPL (sm); Y (sm)
             - Most complete lyric: IB (scr); NYPL (scr)
             - Original partitur: -0-
             - Original parts: -0-

You Can't Brush Me Off
Berlin/Berlin
Orchestrator: Unknown

Location of   - Composer's manuscript: -0-
             - Sheet music: IB, LoC, NYPL, Y
             - Most complete music: IB (sm);
                   LoC (sm); NYPL (sm); Y (sm)
             - Most complete lyric: IB (sm);
                   LoC (sm); NYPL (sm); Y (sm)
             - Original partitur: -0-
             - Original parts: -0-

The scripts at the Irving Berlin Music Corporation and the New York Public Library have the lyric to the original vocal arrangement.

Fools Fall in Love
Berlin/Berlin
Orchestrator: Unknown

Location of   - Composer's manuscript: -0-
             - Sheet music: IB, LoC, NYPL, Y
             - Most complete music: IB (sm);
                   LoC (sm); NYPL (sm); Y (sm)
             - Most complete lyric: IB (sm, scr);
                   LoC (sm); NYPL (sm, scr); Y (sm)
             - Original partitur: -0-
             - Original parts: -0-

Finale Act II ["Somebody handed us a ticket to picket..."]
Berlin/Berlin
Orchestrator: Unknown

Location of   - Composer's manuscript: -0-
             - Sheet music: Unpublished
             - Most complete music: -0-
             - Most complete lyric: IB (scr); NYPL (scr)
             - Original partitur: -0-
             - Original parts: -0-

I'd Love to Be Shot From a Cannon With You
    Berlin/Berlin
    Orchestrator: Bennett, Van Cleve

    Location of   - Composer's manuscript: -0-
                - Sheet music: See note
                - Most complete music: IB (prof);
                      LoC (prof); Y (prof)
                - Most complete lyric: IB (prof);
                      LoC (prof); Y (prof)
                - Original partitur: IB
                - Original parts: -0-

Dropped before the New York opening. Issued only as a professional copy.

Wild About You
    Berlin/Berlin
    Orchestrator: Unknown

    Location of   - Composer's manuscript: -0-
                - Sheet music: IB, LoC, NYPL, Y
                - Most complete music: IB (sm);
                      LoC (sm); NYPL (sm); Y (sm)
                - Most complete lyric: IB (sm);
                      LoC (sm); NYPL (sm); Y (sm)
                - Original partitur: -0-
                - Original parts: -0-

Dropped before the New York opening.

It'll Come to You
    Berlin/Berlin
    Orchestrator: Bennett, unknown

    Location of   - Composer's manuscript: -0-
                - Sheet music: IB, LoC, NYPL, Y
                - Most complete music: IB (sm);
                      LoC (sm); NYPL (sm); Y (sm)
                - Most complete lyric: IB (sm);
                      LoC (sm); NYPL (sm); Y (sm)
                - Original partitur: IB
                - Original parts: -0-

Dropped before the New York opening.

ANNIE GET YOUR GUN

Music	IRVING BERLIN
Lyrics	IRVING BERLIN

Musical comedy in two acts. Opened May 16, 1946 in New York and ran 1147 performances (World premiere: March 28, 1946 in New Haven). Libretto by Herbert and Dorothy Fields. Produced by Richard Rodgers and Oscar Hammerstein II. Directed by Joshua Logan. Choreographed by Helen Tamiris. Musical direction by Jay Blackton. Orchestrations by Philip J. Lang, Robert Russell Bennett, Ted Royal. Vocal arrangements by Joe Moon. Piano arrangements by Helmy Kresa.

Synopsis and Production Information
Hillbilly Annie Oakley joins Colonel Buffalo Bill's Wild West Show and is soon outshooting and outshining the handsome star, Frank Butler. A humiliated Frank defects to rival Pawnee Bill's Far East Show while Annie's career continues to soar (Chief Sitting Bull adopts her into the Sioux tribe, the monarchs of Europe hail her during a spectacular tour). But Annie has fallen in love with Frank and realizes that her skill with a rifle threatens him. Since "you can't get a hug from a mug with a slug," she deliberately loses a shooting match to Frank, restoring his pride and her own chance at happiness.

The show requires a full singing and dancing ensemble, and pair of young lovers.

Orchestration
Unknown

Comments
The original production of ANNIE GET YOUR GUN, starring Ethel Merman, was Irving Berlin's greatest stage success, winning three Donaldson Awards in the 1946-47 season, including the one for Best Score. When the show was revived in 1966 (with Merman again in the title role), Dorothy Fields revised the book a bit, deleting the young lovers (and their songs, "I'll Share It All With You" and "Who Do You Love, I Hope?"), and Berlin wrote an additional duet for Annie and Frank, "An Old-Fashioned Wedding."

Location of Original Materials
Script: Library of Congress (all lyrics), Rodgers and Hammerstein Theatre Library (all lyrics)
    (Published: Irving Berlin Music Corporation, 1952)
Piano-vocal score: Library of Congress, New York Public Library
    (Published: Irving Berlin Music Corporation, 1947)
Partiturs: Missing
Parts: Missing

Although the original orchestrations are missing, the Rodgers and Hammerstein Theatre Library has an incomplete set of parts from the original national tour. The piano-vocal score from the 1966 revival was published by the Irving Berlin Music Corporation in 1967; it can be found at the Library of Congress, the New York Public Library, and the Rodgers and Hammerstein Theatre Library. The Rodgers and Hammerstein Theatre Library has the partiturs (by Robert Russell Bennett) and parts from that production.

Rental Status
The Rodgers and Hammerstein Theatre Library rents the 1966 revival, which includes an orchestration (by Robert Russell Bennett) for 28-30 players.

Music Publisher
Irving Berlin Music Corporation

Information
Rodgers and Hammerstein Theatre Library

Annie Get Your Gun (1946)

Overture
Berlin/Berlin
Orchestrator: Unknown

Location of   - Composer's manuscript: -0-
- Sheet music: Not published separately
- Most complete music: LoC (1947 pv score);
        NYPL (1947 pv score)
- Most complete lyric: INST
- Original partitur: -0-
- Original parts: -0-

I'm a Bad, Bad Man
Berlin/Berlin
Orchestrator: Unknown

Location of   - Composer's manuscript: -0-
- Sheet music: IB, LoC, NYPL, Y
- Most complete music: IB (sm); LoC (sm,
        1947 pv score, 1967 pv score);
        NYPL (sm, 1947 pv score, 1967
        pv score); Y (sm); R&H (1967
        pv score)
- Most complete lyric: IB (sm); LoC (sm);
        NYPL (sm); Y (sm)
- Original partitur: -0-
- Original parts: -0-

Colonel Buffalo Bill
Berlin/Berlin
Orchestrator: Unknown

Location of   - Composer's manuscript: -0-
- Sheet music: IB, LoC, Y
- Most complete music: IB (sm); LoC (sm,
        1947 pv score, 1967 pv score);
        NYPL (1947 pv score, 1967 pv score);
        Y (sm); R&H (1967 pv score)
- Most complete lyric: IB (sm); LoC (sm,
        1947 pv score, 1967 pv score, scr);
        NYPL (1947 pv score, 1967 pv score);
        Y (sm); R&H (1967 pv score, scr)
- Original partitur: -0-
- Original parts: -0-

Doin' What Comes Natur'lly
Berlin/Berlin
Orchestrator: Unknown

Location of   - Composer's manuscript: -0-
- Sheet music: IB, LoC, NYPL, Y
- Most complete music: IB (sm); LoC (sm,
        1947 pv score, 1967 pv score);
        NYPL (sm, 1947 pv score, 1967
        pv score); Y (sm); R&H (1967
        pv score)
- Most complete lyric: LoC (1947 pv score,
        1967 pv score); NYPL (1947 pv score,
        1967 pv score); R&H (1967 pv score)
- Original partitur: -0-
- Original parts: -0-

Girl That I Marry, The
Berlin/Berlin
Orchestrator: Unknown

Location of - Composer's manuscript: -0-
 - Sheet music: IB, LoC, NYPL, Y
 - Most complete music: IB (sm); LoC (sm,
  1947 pv score, 1967 pv score);
  NYPL (sm, 1947 pv score, 1967
  pv score); Y (sm); R&H (1967
  pv score)
 - Most complete lyric: IB (sm); LoC (sm,
  1947 pv score, 1967 pv score, scr);
  NYPL (sm, 1947 pv score, 1967
  pv score); Y (sm); R&H (1967
  pv score, scr)
 - Original partitur: -0-
 - Original parts: -0-

There's No Business Like Show Business
Berlin/Berlin
Orchestrator: Unknown

Location of - Composer's manuscript: -0-
 - Sheet music: IB, LoC, NYPL, Y
 - Most complete music: IB (sm); LoC (sm,
  1947 pv score, 1967 pv score);
  NYPL (sm, 1947 pv score, 1967
  pv score); Y (sm); R&H (1967
  pv score)
 - Most complete lyric: LoC (sm & 1967
  pv score); NYPL (sm & 1967 pv score)
 - Original partitur: -0-
 - Original parts: -0-

You Can't Get a Man With a Gun
Berlin/Berlin
Orchestrator: Unknown

Location of - Composer's manuscript: -0-
 - Sheet music: IB, LoC, NYPL, Y
 - Most complete music: IB (sm); LoC (sm,
  1947 pv score, 1967 pv score);
  NYPL (sm, 1947 pv score, 1967
  pv score); Y (sm); R&H (1967
  pv score)
 - Most complete lyric: LoC (1947 pv score,
  1967 pv score); NYPL (1947 pv score,
  1967 pv score); R&H (1967 pv score)
 - Original partitur: -0-
 - Original parts: -0-

They Say It's Wonderful
Berlin/Berlin
Orchestrator: Unknown

Location of - Composer's manuscript: -0-
 - Sheet music: IB, LoC, NYPL, Y
 - Most complete music: IB (sm); LoC (sm,
  1947 pv score, 1967 pv score);
  NYPL (sm, 1947 pv score, 1967
  pv score); Y (sm); R&H (1967
  pv score)
 - Most complete lyric: IB (sm); LoC (sm,
  1947 pv score, 1967 pv score, scr);
  NYPL (sm, 1947 pv score, 1967
  pv score); Y (sm); R&H (1967
  pv score, scr)
 - Original partitur: -0-
 - Original parts: -0-

Annie Get Your Gun (1946)

Moonshine Lullaby

Berlin/Berlin
Orchestrator: Unknown

Location of
- Composer's manuscript: -0-
- Sheet music: IB, LoC, NYPL, Y
- Most complete music: IB (sm); LoC (sm, 1947 pv score, 1967 pv score); NYPL (sm, 1947 pv score, 1967 pv score); Y (sm); R&H (1967 pv score)
- Most complete lyric: IB (sm); LoC (sm, 1947 pv score, 1967 pv score, scr); NYPL (sm, 1947 pv score, 1967 pv score); Y (sm); R&H (1967 pv score, scr)
- Original partitur: -0-
- Original parts: -0-

Ballyhoo

Berlin/Berlin
Orchestrator: Unknown

Location of
- Composer's manuscript: -0-
- Sheet music: Not published separately
- Most complete music: LoC (1947 pv score); NYPL (1947 pv score)
- Most complete lyric: INST
- Original partitur: -0-
- Original parts: -0-

Titled "Circus Dance" in the piano-vocal score. Replaced in the 1966 revival (and the 1967 published piano-vocal score) by an extensive "Wild West Ballet."

I'll Share It All With You

Berlin/Berlin
Orchestrator: Unknown

Location of
- Composer's manuscript: -0-
- Sheet music: IB, LoC, NYPL, Y
- Most complete music: IB (sm); LoC (sm, 1947 pv score); NYPL (sm, 1947 pv score); Y (sm)
- Most complete lyric: IB (sm); LoC (sm, 1947 pv score, scr); NYPL (sm, 1947 pv score); Y (sm)
- Original partitur: -0-
- Original parts: -0-

My Defenses Are Down

Berlin/Berlin
Orchestrator: Unknown

Location of
- Composer's manuscript: -0-
- Sheet music: IB, LoC, NYPL, Y
- Most complete music: IB (sm); LoC (sm, 1947 pv score, 1967 pv score); NYPL (sm, 1947 pv score, 1967 pv score); Y (sm); R&H (1967 pv score)
- Most complete lyric: IB (sm); LoC (sm, 1947 pv score, 1967 pv score, scr); NYPL (sm, 1947 pv score, 1967 pv score); Y (sm); R&H (1967 pv score, scr)
- Original partitur: -0-
- Original parts: -0-

Irving Berlin

Wild Horse Ceremonial Dance
Berlin/Berlin
Orchestrator: Unknown

Location of
- Composer's manuscript: -0-
- Sheet music: Not published separately
- Most complete music: LoC (1947
  pv score); NYPL (1947 pv score)
- Most complete lyric: INST
- Original partitur: -0-
- Original parts: -0-

Titled "Drum Dance" in the piano-vocal score. Replaced
in the 1966 revival (and the 1967 published piano-vocal
score) by "Opening Chant," "Indian Dance," and
"Ceremonial Chant."

Adoption Dance
Berlin/Berlin
Orchestrator: Unknown

Location of
- Composer's manuscript: -0-
- Sheet music: Not published separately
- Most complete music: LoC (1947
  pv score); NYPL (1947 pv score)
- Most complete lyric: INST
- Original partitur: -0-
- Original parts: -0-

I'm an Indian Too
Berlin/Berlin
Orchestrator: Unknown

Location of
- Composer's manuscript: -0-
- Sheet music: IB, LoC, NYPL, Y
- Most complete music: IB (sm); LoC (sm,
  1947 pv score, 1967 pv score);
  NYPL (sm, 1947 pv score, 1967
  pv score); Y (sm); R&H (1967
  pv score)
- Most complete lyric: LoC (sm & either
  pv score); NYPL (sm & either
  pv score)
- Original partitur: -0-
- Original parts: -0-

Entr'acte
Berlin/Berlin
Orchestrator: Unknown

Location of
- Composer's manuscript: -0-
- Sheet music: Not published separately
- Most complete music: LoC (1947
  pv score); NYPL (1947 pv score)
- Most complete lyric: INST
- Original partitur: -0-
- Original parts: -0-

Annie Get Your Gun (1946)

I Got Lost in His Arms
Berlin/Berlin
Orchestrator: Unknown

Location of
- Composer's manuscript: -0-
- Sheet music: IB, LoC, NYPL, Y
- Most complete music: IB (sm), LoC (sm, 1947 pv score, 1967 pv score); NYPL (sm, 1947 pv score, 1967 pv score); Y (sm); R&H (1967 pv score)
- Most complete lyric: IB (sm), LoC (sm, 1947 pv score, 1967 pv score, scr); NYPL (sm, 1947 pv score, 1967 pv score); Y (sm); R&H (1967 pv score, scr)
- Original partitur: -0-
- Original parts: -0-

I Got the Sun in the Morning
Berlin/Berlin
Orchestrator: Unknown

Location of
- Composer's manuscript: -0-
- Sheet music: IB, LoC, NYPL, Y
- Most complete music: IB (sm), LoC (sm, 1947 pv score, 1967 pv score); NYPL (sm, 1947 pv score, 1967 pv score); Y (sm); R&H (1967 pv score)
- Most complete lyric: LoC (1947 pv score, 1967 pv score); NYPL (1947 pv score, 1967 pv score); R&H (1967 pv score)
- Original partitur: -0-
- Original parts: -0-

Who Do You Love, I Hope
Berlin/Berlin
Orchestrator: Unknown

Location of
- Composer's manuscript: -0-
- Sheet music: IB, LoC, NYPL, Y
- Most complete music: IB (sm), LoC (sm, 1947 pv score); NYPL (sm, 1947 pv score); Y (sm)
- Most complete lyric: IB (sm), LoC (sm, 1947 pv score, scr); NYPL (sm, 1947 pv score); Y (sm)
- Original partitur: -0-
- Original parts: -0-

Anything You Can Do
Berlin/Berlin
Orchestrator: Unknown

Location of
- Composer's manuscript: -0-
- Sheet music: IB, LoC, NYPL, Y
- Most complete music: LoC (sm & either pv score); NYPL (sm & either pv score)
- Most complete lyric: LoC (sm & either pv score); NYPL (sm & either pv score)
- Original partitur: -0-
- Original parts: -0-

Take It in Your Stride

Berlin/Berlin
Orchestrator: Unknown

Location of   - Composer's manuscript: -0-
        - Sheet music: Unpublished
        - Most complete music: -0-
        - Most complete lyric: -0-
        - Original partitur: -0-
        - Original parts: -0-

Dropped before the New York opening. Advertised but not published.

Old Fashioned Wedding, An

Berlin/Berlin
Orchestrator: Unknown

Location of   - Composer's manuscript: -0-
        - Sheet music: IB, LoC, Y
        - Most complete music: IB (sm), LoC (sm, 1967 pv score); NYPL (1967 pv score); Y (sm); R&H (1967 pv score)
        - Most complete lyric: IB (sm), LoC (sm, 1967 pv score); NYPL (1967 pv score); Y (sm); R&H (1967 pv score)
        - Original partitur: -0-
        - Original parts: -0-

Added for the 1966 revival.

Let's Go West Again

Berlin/Berlin
Orchestrator: Unknown

Location of   - Composer's manuscript: -0-
        - Sheet music: See note
        - Most complete music: LoC (prof)
        - Most complete lyric: LoC (prof)
        - Original partitur: -0-
        - Original parts: -0-

Written for the film version (1950) and issued as a professional copy.

MISS LIBERTY

Music	IRVING BERLIN
Lyrics	IRVING BERLIN

Musical comedy in two acts. Opened July 15, 1949 in New York and ran 308 performances (World premiere: June 13, 1949 in Philadelphia). Libretto by Robert E. Sherwood. Additional lyric by Emma Lazarus. Produced by Irving Berlin, Robert E. Sherwood and Moss Hart. Directed by Moss Hart. Choreographed by Jerome Robbins. Musical direction and vocal arrangements by Jay Blackton. Orchestrations by Don Walker.

Synopsis and Production Information
Horace Miller, an aspiring young photographer, tries to get an exclusive story on the arrival of the Statue of Liberty in 1885 for James Gordon Bennett's newspaper, The New York Herald. He travels to the Parisian studio of the statue's sculptor, Bartholdi, to discover Bartholdi's human inspiration, but accidentally ends up crediting the wrong girl, Monique. Monique meets great success in America as "Miss Liberty" until Joseph Pulitzer's rival newspaper, The New York World, reveals the truth. Horace and Monique seem headed for disaster until they realize they have won the hearts of the American people.

The show requires a full singing and dancing ensemble.

Orchestration
Reed I (Flute, Piccolo, Alto Sax); Reed II (Clarinet, Alto Sax); Reed III (Oboe, English Horn, Clarinet, Tenor Sax); Reed IV (Flute, Clarinet, Tenor Sax); Reed V (Clarinet, Bass Clarinet, Bassoon, Baritone Sax); Horn; Trumpet I II; Trumpet III; Percussion I II; Harp; Piano; Violin A; Violin B; Violin C; Violin D; Viola I II; Cello I II; Bass

Location of Original Materials
Script: Samuel French, Inc. (all lyrics), New York Public Library (all lyrics)
        (Published: Samuel French, Inc. 1986)
Piano-vocal score: Samuel French, Inc.
Partiturs: Irving Berlin Music Corporation
Parts: Samuel French, Inc.

Rental Status
Samuel French rents the original show. The Irving Berlin Music Corporation has stipulated that performance companies may not reinstate deleted numbers.

Music Publisher
Irving Berlin Music Corporation

Information
Samuel French, Inc.

Irving Berlin

Overture

Berlin/Berlin
Orchestrator: Walker

Location of   - Composer's manuscript: -0-
                - Sheet music: Unpublished
                - Most complete music: SF (pv score)
                - Most complete lyric: INST
                - Original partitur: IB
                - Original parts: SF

Most Expensive Statue in the World, The

Berlin/Berlin
Orchestrator: Walker

Location of   - Composer's manuscript: -0-
                - Sheet music: IB, LoC, NYPL, Y
                - Most complete music: SF (pv score)
                - Most complete lyric: SF (pv score, scr)
                - Original partitur: IB
                - Original parts: SF

Set to the same music as the first part of the deleted "Pulitzer Prize."

Extra! Extra!

Berlin/Berlin
Orchestrator: Walker

Location of   - Composer's manuscript: -0-
                - Sheet music: IB, LoC, NYPL, Y
                - Most complete music: SF (pv score)
                - Most complete lyric: SF (pv score, scr);
                      NYPL (scr)
                - Original partitur: IB
                - Original parts: SF

Opening chorus, Act I.

Little Fish in a Big Pond

Berlin/Berlin
Orchestrator: Walker

Location of   - Composer's manuscript: -0-
                - Sheet music: IB, LoC, NYPL, Y
                - Most complete music: IB (sm); LoC (sm);
                      NYPL (sm); Y (sm); SF (pv score)
                - Most complete lyric: SF (pv score, scr);
                      NYPL (scr)
                - Original partitur: IB
                - Original parts: SF

What Do I Have to Do to Get My Picture Took?

Berlin/Berlin
Orchestrator: Walker

Location of   - Composer's manuscript: -0-
                - Sheet music: Unpublished
                - Most complete music: SF (pv score)
                - Most complete lyric: SF (pv score, scr);
                      NYPL (scr)
                - Original partitur: IB (inc)
                - Original parts: SF

The last page of the partitur is missing.

Let's Take an Old-Fashioned Walk

Berlin/Berlin
Orchestrator: Walker

Location of   - Composer's manuscript: -0-
                - Sheet music: IB, LoC, Y
                - Most complete music: IB (sm); LoC (sm);
                      Y (sm); SF (pv score)
                - Most complete lyric: IB (sm); LoC (sm);
                      Y (sm); SF (pv score, scr);
                      NYPL (scr)
                - Original partitur: IB
                - Original parts: SF

Miss Liberty (1949)

Homework

Berlin/Berlin
Orchestrator: Walker

Location of
- Composer's manuscript: -0-
- Sheet music: IB, LoC, NYPL, Y
- Most complete music: IB (sm); LoC (sm);
  NYPL (sm); Y (sm); SF (pv score)
- Most complete lyric: IB (sm); LoC (sm);
  NYPL (sm); Y (sm); SF (pv score, scr)
- Original partitur: IB
- Original parts: SF

Just One Way to Say I Love You

Berlin/Berlin
Orchestrator: Walker

Location of
- Composer's manuscript: -0-
- Sheet music: IB, LoC, NYPL, Y
- Most complete music: IB (sm); LoC (sm);
  NYPL (sm); Y (sm); SF (pv score)
- Most complete lyric: SF (pv score, scr);
  NYPL (scr)
- Original partitur: IB
- Original parts: SF

Paris Wakes up and Smiles

Berlin/Berlin
Orchestrator: Walker

Location of
- Composer's manuscript: -0-
- Sheet music: IB, LoC, NYPL, Y
- Most complete music: IB (sm); LoC (sm);
  NYPL (sm); Y (sm); SF (pv score)
- Most complete lyric: IB (sm); LoC (sm);
  NYPL (sm, scr); Y (sm);
  SF (pv score, scr)
- Original partitur: IB
- Original parts: SF

Entr'acte

Berlin/Berlin
Orchestrator: Walker

Location of
- Composer's manuscript: -0-
- Sheet music: Unpublished
- Most complete music: SF (pv score)
- Most complete lyric: INST
- Original partitur: IB
- Original parts: SF

Only for Americans

Berlin/Berlin
Orchestrator: Walker

Location of
- Composer's manuscript: -0-
- Sheet music: IB, LoC, NYPL, Y
- Most complete music: IB (sm); LoC (sm);
  NYPL (sm); Y (sm); SF (pv score)
- Most complete lyric: IB (sm); LoC (sm);
  NYPL (sm, scr); Y (sm);
  SF (pv score, scr)
- Original partitur: IB
- Original parts: SF

Miss Liberty

Berlin/Berlin
Orchestrator: Walker

Location of
- Composer's manuscript: -0-
- Sheet music: IB, LoC, NYPL, Y
- Most complete music: SF (pv score)
- Most complete lyric: SF (pv score, scr);
  NYPL (scr)
- Original partitur: IB
- Original parts: SF

Train, The
Berlin/Berlin
Orchestrator: Unknown

Location of - Composer's manuscript: -0-
         - Sheet music: Unpublished
         - Most complete music: SF (pv score)
         - Most complete lyric: SF (pv score, scr);
            NYPL (scr)
         - Original partitur: IB
         - Original parts: SF

Follow the Leader Jig
Berlin/Berlin
Orchestrator: Walker

Location of - Composer's manuscript: -0-
         - Sheet music: Unpublished
         - Most complete music: SF (pv score)
         - Most complete lyric: INST
         - Original partitur: IB
         - Original parts: SF

You Can Have Him
Berlin/Berlin
Orchestrator: Walker

Location of - Composer's manuscript: -0-
         - Sheet music: IB, LoC, NYPL, Y
         - Most complete music: IB (sm); LoC (sm);
            NYPL (sm); Y (sm); SF (pv score)
         - Most complete lyric: IB (sm); LoC (sm);
            NYPL (sm, scr); Y (sm);
            SF (pv score, scr)
         - Original partitur: IB
         - Original parts: SF

Me and My Bundle
Berlin/Berlin
Orchestrator: Walker

Location of - Composer's manuscript: -0-
         - Sheet music: IB, LoC, NYPL, Y
         - Most complete music: IB (sm); LoC (sm);
            NYPL (sm); Y (sm); SF (pv score)
         - Most complete lyric: IB (sm); LoC (sm);
            NYPL (sm, scr); Y (sm);
            SF (pv score, scr)
         - Original partitur: IB
         - Original parts: SF

Policeman's Ball, The
Berlin/Berlin
Orchestrator: Walker

Location of - Composer's manuscript: -0-
         - Sheet music: IB, LoC, NYPL, Y
         - Most complete music: SF (pv score)
         - Most complete lyric: SF (pv score, scr);
            NYPL (scr)
         - Original partitur: IB
         - Original parts: SF

Falling Out of Love Can Be Fun
Berlin/Berlin
Orchestrator: Walker

Location of - Composer's manuscript: -0-
         - Sheet music: IB, LoC, NYPL, Y
         - Most complete music: IB (sm); LoC (sm);
            NYPL (sm); Y (sm); SF (pv score)
         - Most complete lyric: IB (sm); LoC (sm);
            NYPL (sm, scr); Y (sm);
            SF (pv score, scr)
         - Original partitur: IB
         - Original parts: SF

Miss Liberty (1949)

Give Me Your Tired, Your Poor
Berlin/Lazarus
Orchestrator: Walker

Location of   - Composer's manuscript: -0-
              - Sheet music: IB, LoC, Y
              - Most complete music: IB (sm); LoC (sm);
                  Y (sm); SF (pv score)
              - Most complete lyric: IB (sm); LoC (sm);
                  Y (sm); SF (pv score, scr);
                  NYPL (scr)
              - Original partitur: IB
              - Original parts: SF

Hon'rable Profession of the Fourth Estate, The
Berlin/Berlin
Orchestrator: Walker

Location of   - Composer's manuscript: -0-
              - Sheet music: IB, LoC, NYPL, Y
              - Most complete music: IB (sm); LoC (sm);
                  NYPL (sm); Y (sm)
              - Most complete lyric: IB (sm); LoC (sm);
                  NYPL (sm); Y (sm)
              - Original partitur: IB
              - Original parts: IB

Dropped during the pre-Broadway tryout. The Irving Berlin Music Corporation also has the original vocal arrangement. This number at one time was combined with the second half of "The Pulitzer Prize"; the Irving Berlin Music Corporation has a piano-vocal (with lyrics) of this version.

Next Time I Fall in Love, The
Berlin/Berlin
Orchestrator: Walker

Location of   - Composer's manuscript: -0-
              - Sheet music: Unpublished
              - Most complete music: IB (ptr)
              - Most complete lyric: -0-
              - Original partitur: IB
              - Original parts: -0-

This is probably "I'll Know Better the Next Time," which was added and dropped during the pre-Broadway tryout.

What Do I Have to Do to Get My Picture in the Paper?
Berlin/Berlin
Orchestrator: Unknown

Location of   - Composer's manuscript: -0-
              - Sheet music: IB, LoC
              - Most complete music: IB (sm); LoC (sm)
              - Most complete lyric: IB (sm); LoC (sm)
              - Original partitur: -0-
              - Original parts: IB

Replaced during the pre-Broadway tryout by "What Do I Have to Do to Get My Picture Took?"

Mrs. Monotony
Berlin/Berlin
Orchestrator: Walker

Location of   - Composer's manuscript: -0-
              - Sheet music: See note
              - Most complete music: IB (pv-l); JF (prof)
              - Most complete lyric: IB (pv-l); JF (prof)
              - Original partitur: IB
              - Original parts: IB

Written as "Mr. Monotony" for the 1948 film, EASTER PARADE, but unused. Sung during the pre-Broadway tryout of MISS LIBERTY as "Mrs. Monotony" (with different lyrics), but dropped before the New York opening. Later, "Mr. Monotony" was used in CALL ME MADAM (1950), but deleted before the Broadway opening. Sheet music for "Mr. Monotony" (with a MISS LIBERTY cover) can be found at the Irving Berlin Music Corporation, Yale University, and the Library of Congress; "Mrs. Monotony" may have been issued as sheet music as well, but only a professional copy was found.

Business for a Good Girl Is Bad
Berlin/Berlin
Orchestrator: Walker

Location of   - Composer's manuscript: -0-
              - Sheet music: See note
              - Most complete music: LoC (prof)
              - Most complete lyric: LoC (prof)
              - Original partitur: IB
              - Original parts: -0-

Dropped before the New York opening; issued only as a professional copy.

Pulitzer Prize, The

Berlin/Berlin
Orchestrator: Walker

Location of   - Composer's manuscript: -0-
           - Sheet music: Unpublished
           - Most complete music: IB (pv-l)
           - Most complete lyric: IB (pv-l)
           - Original partitur: IB
           - Original parts: IB

Dropped before the New York opening. The Irving Berlin Music Corporation also has a piano-vocal (with lyrics) to a later version, a combination of "The Honorable Profession of the Fourth Estate" (set to new lyrics) and the final section of "The Pulitzer Prize." The music to the first section was later used for "The Most Expensive Statue in the World."

Sing a Song of Sing Sing

Berlin/Berlin
Orchestrator: Unknown

Location of   - Composer's manuscript: -0-
           - Sheet music: Unpublished
           - Most complete music: IB (pv-l)
           - Most complete lyric: IB (pv-l)
           - Original partitur: -0-
           - Original parts: -0-

Dropped before the New York opening.

Entrance of Reporters

Berlin/Berlin
Orchestrator: Unknown

Location of   - Composer's manuscript: -0-
           - Sheet music: Unpublished
           - Most complete music: IB (pv-l)
           - Most complete lyric: IB (pv-l)
           - Original partitur: -0-
           - Original parts: IB

Dropped before the New York opening.

Story of Nell and the Police Gazette, The

Berlin/Berlin
Orchestrator: Unknown

Location of   - Composer's manuscript: -0-
           - Sheet music: Unpublished
           - Most complete music: IB (pv-l)
           - Most complete lyric: IB (pv-l)
           - Original partitur: -0-
           - Original parts: -0-

Dropped before the New York opening.

CALL ME MADAM

Music	IRVING BERLIN
Lyrics	IRVING BERLIN

Musical comedy in two acts. Opened October 12, 1950 in New York and ran 644 performances (World premiere: September 11, 1950 in New Haven). Libretto by Howard Lindsay and Russel Crouse. Produced by Leland Hayward. Directed by George Abbott. Choreographed by Jerome Robbins. Musical direction and vocal arrangements by Jay Blackton. Orchestrations by Don Walker. Additional orchestrations by Joe Glover. Dance music arranged by Genevieve Pitot and Jesse Meeker. Piano arrangements by Helmy Kresa.

Synopsis and Production Information

Mrs. Sally Adams, Washington's hostess with the mostes', is appointed ambassador to the Grand Duchy of Lichtenberg. Once there, she falls in love with Foreign Minister Cosmo Constantine, but her aggressive generosity with American funds wounds his old-world pride. Eventually, of course, Sally and Cosmo resolve their differences.

There is a supporting couple: Kenneth Gibson, Sally's bright and efficient young assistant, and Maria, the Princess with whom he falls in love. The show requires a full singing and dancing ensemble.

Orchestration

Reed I (Flute, Piccolo, Clarinet, Alto Sax); Reed II (Clarinet, Alto Sax, Bass Clarinet); Reed III (Oboe, English Horn, Clarinet, Tenor Sax); Reed IV (Clarinet, Tenor Sax, Flute); Reed V (Clarinet, Bass Clarinet, Bassoon, Baritone Sax, Alto Sax); Horn; Trumpet I II; Trumpet III; Trombone I; Trombone II; Percussion; Guitar; Violin A-C; Violin B-D; Viola (divisi); Cello; Bass

Comments

In the original production, Sally was played by Ethel Merman, Kenneth by Russell Nype.

Location of Original Materials

Script: New York Public Library (all lyrics)
    (Published: Irving Berlin Music Corporation, 1956)
Piano-vocal score: Music Theatre International, New York Public Library
    (Published: Irving Berlin Music Corporation, 1952)
Partiturs: Irving Berlin Music Corporation
Parts: Music Theatre International

Rental Status

Music Theatre International rents the original piano-vocal score and parts. The script is similar to the original, with minor dialogue revisions and heavy rewriting of the lyric to "They Like Ike" (retitled "They Liked Ike"). Curiously, this new lyric updates the piece to a post-Eisenhower era even though the rest of the script (like the original) is clearly set during the Truman Administration.

Music Publisher

Irving Berlin Music Corporation

Information

Music Theatre International

Irving Berlin

Overture

Berlin/Berlin
Orchestrator: Unknown

Location of
- Composer's manuscript: -0-
- Sheet music: Not published separately
- Most complete music: MTI (pv score);
    NYPL (pv score)
- Most complete lyric: INST
- Original partitur: -0-
- Original parts: MTI

Washington Square Dance

Berlin/Berlin
Orchestrator: Walker

Location of
- Composer's manuscript: -0-
- Sheet music: IB, LoC, NYPL, Y
- Most complete music: MTI (pv score);
    NYPL (pv score)
- Most complete lyric: MTI (pv score,
    scr); NYPL (pv score, scr)
- Original partitur: IB
- Original parts: MTI

The sheet music contains a few alternate words.

Mrs. Sally Adams

Berlin/Berlin
Orchestrator: Walker

Location of
- Composer's manuscript: -0-
- Sheet music: Not published separately
- Most complete music: MTI (pv score);
    NYPL (pv score)
- Most complete lyric: MTI (pv score, scr);
    NYPL (pv score, scr)
- Original partitur: IB
- Original parts: MTI

Lichtenburg

Berlin/Berlin
Orchestrator: Walker

Location of
- Composer's manuscript: -0-
- Sheet music: Not published separately
- Most complete music: MTI (pv score);
    NYPL (pv score)
- Most complete lyric: MTI (pv score,
    scr); NYPL (pv score, scr)
- Original partitur: IB
- Original parts: MTI

Includes "Cosmo's Opening."

Hostess With the Mostes' on the Ball

Berlin/Berlin
Orchestrator: Unknown

Location of
- Composer's manuscript: -0-
- Sheet music: IB, LoC, Y
- Most complete music: IB (sm); LoC (sm);
    Y (sm); MTI (pv score);
    NYPL (pv score)
- Most complete lyric: MTI (pv score, scr);
    NYPL (pv score, scr)
- Original partitur: IB
- Original parts: MTI

Can You Use Any Money Today?

Berlin/Berlin
Orchestrator: Walker

Location of
- Composer's manuscript: -0-
- Sheet music: See note
- Most complete music: IB (pv-l);
    MTI (pv score); NYPL (pv score)
- Most complete lyric: IB (pv-l);
    MTI (pv score, scr);
    NYPL (pv score, scr)
- Original partitur: IB
- Original parts: MTI

According to Steven Suskin's Show Tunes 1905-1985
(Dodd, Mead & Company: 1986), this number was issued as
sheet music upon its use in the 1953 film version. No
sheet music was found.

Call Me Madam (1950)

Marrying for Love
Berlin/Berlin
Orchestrator: Glover

Location of - Composer's manuscript: -0-
- Sheet music: IB, LoC, NYPL, Y
- Most complete music: IB (sm); LoC (sm);
    NYPL (sm, pv score); Y (sm);
    MTI (pv score)
- Most complete lyric: IB (sm); LoC (sm);
    NYPL (sm); Y (sm)
- Original partitur: IB
- Original parts: MTI

Best Thing for You, The
Berlin/Berlin
Orchestrator: Walker

Location of - Composer's manuscript: -0-
- Sheet music: IB, LoC, NYPL, Y
- Most complete music: IB (sm); LoC (sm);
    NYPL (sm, pv score); Y (sm);
    MTI (pv score)
- Most complete lyric: IB (ls)
- Original partitur: IB
- Original parts: MTI

Ocarina, The
Berlin/Berlin
Orchestrator: Walker

Location of - Composer's manuscript: -0-
- Sheet music: IB, LoC, NYPL, Y
- Most complete music: IB (sm); LoC (sm);
    NYPL (sm, pv score); Y (sm);
    MTI (pv score)
- Most complete lyric: IB (sm); LoC (sm);
    NYPL (sm, pv score, scr); Y (sm);
    MTI (pv score, scr)
- Original partitur: IB
- Original parts: MTI

The sheet music contains one lyric line that is not in the
piano-vocal score.

Entr'acte
Berlin/Berlin
Orchestrator: Glover

Location of - Composer's manuscript: -0-
- Sheet music: Not published separately
- Most complete music: NYPL (pv score);
    MTI (pv score)
- Most complete lyric: INST
- Original partitur: IB
- Original parts: MTI

It's a Lovely Day Today
Berlin/Berlin
Orchestrator: Glover

Location of - Composer's manuscript: -0-
- Sheet music: IB, LoC, Y
- Most complete music: IB (sm); LoC (sm);
    Y (sm); MTI (pv score);
    NYPL (pv score)
- Most complete lyric: MTI (pv score, scr);
    NYPL (pv score, scr)
- Original partitur: IB
- Original parts: MTI

Something to Dance About
Berlin/Berlin
Orchestrator: Glover

Location of - Composer's manuscript: -0-
- Sheet music: IB, LoC, NYPL, Y
- Most complete music: IB (sm); LoC (sm);
    NYPL (sm, pv score); Y (sm);
    MTI (pv score)
- Most complete lyric: NYPL (pv score,
    scr); MTI (pv score, scr)
- Original partitur: IB
- Original parts: MTI

Irving Berlin

Once Upon a Time Today

Berlin/Berlin

Orchestrator: Walker

Location of
- Composer's manuscript: -0-
- Sheet music: IB, LoC, NYPL, Y
- Most complete music: IB (sm); LoC (sm); NYPL (sm, pv score); Y (sm); MTI (pv score)
- Most complete lyric: IB (sm); LoC (sm); NYPL (sm); Y (sm)
- Original partitur: IB
- Original parts: MTI

You're Just in Love

Berlin/Berlin

Orchestrator: Glover

Location of
- Composer's manuscript: -0-
- Sheet music: IB, LoC, NYPL, Y
- Most complete music: IB (sm); LoC (sm); NYPL (sm, pv score); Y (sm); MTI (pv score)
- Most complete lyric: IB (sm); LoC (sm); NYPL (sm, pv score, scr); Y (sm); MTI (pv score, scr)
- Original partitur: IB
- Original parts: MTI

They Like Ike

Berlin/Berlin

Orchestrator: Walker

Location of
- Composer's manuscript: -0-
- Sheet music: IB, LoC, NYPL, Y
- Most complete music: IB (sm); LoC (sm); NYPL (sm, pv score); Y (sm); MTI (pv score)
- Most complete lyric: IB (sm); LoC (sm); NYPL (sm); Y (sm)
- Original partitur: IB
- Original parts: MTI

The Irving Berlin Music Corporation also has piano-vocals from later versions, which include "I Like Ike" and "Ike for Four More Years."

Gypsy Dance

Berlin/Berlin

Orchestrator: Unknown

Location of
- Composer's manuscript: -0-
- Sheet music: Unpublished
- Most complete music: IB (ptr)
- Most complete lyric: INST
- Original partitur: IB
- Original parts: -0-

Dropped during the pre-Broadway tryout.

Call Me Madam (1950)

Mr. Monotony

Berlin/Berlin
Orchestrator: See note

Location of - Composer's manuscript: -0-
- Sheet music: IB, LoC, Y
- Most complete music: IB (sm);
  LoC (sm); Y (sm)
- Most complete lyric: IB (sm);
  LoC (sm); Y (sm)
- Original partitur: See note
- Original parts: See note

Written for the film, EASTER PARADE, but unused. Sung during the pre-Broadway tryout of MISS LIBERTY as "Mrs. Monotony" (with different lyrics), but dropped before the New York opening. Later sung in the pre-Broadway of CALL ME MADAM (1950), but replaced by "Something to Dance About." The Irving Berlin Music Corporation has Don Walker's partitur (and parts) for "Mr. Monotony" with its MISS LIBERTY material.

Our Day of Independence

Berlin/Berlin
Orchestrator: Unknown

Location of - Composer's manuscript: -0-
- Sheet music: Unpublished
- Most complete music: NYPL (pv-l)
- Most complete lyric: NYPL (pv-l)
- Original partitur: -0-
- Original parts: -0-

Replaced "They Like Ike" during the post-Broadway tour.

Free

Berlin/Berlin
Orchestrator: Unknown

Location of - Composer's manuscript: -0-
- Sheet music: IB, LoC, Y
- Most complete music: IB (sm);
  LoC (sm); Y (sm)
- Most complete lyric: IB (sm);
  LoC (sm); Y (sm)
- Original partitur: -0-
- Original parts: -0-

Dropped during the pre-Broadway tryout. The Irving Berlin Music Corporation also has a vocal arrangement that uses "Can You Use Any Money Today?" as a countermelody.

Anthem for Presentation

Berlin/Berlin
Orchestrator: Unknown

Location of - Composer's manuscript: -0-
- Sheet music: Unpublished
- Most complete music: -0-
- Most complete lyric: -0-
- Original partitur: -0-
- Original parts: -0-

Written for the film version (1953).

MR. PRESIDENT

Music	**IRVING BERLIN**
Lyrics	**IRVING BERLIN**

Musical comedy in two acts. Opened October 20, 1962 in New York and ran 265 performances (World premiere: August 27, 1962 in Boston). Libretto by Howard Lindsay and Russel Crouse. Produced by Leland Hayward. Directed by Joshua Logan. Choreographed by Peter Gennaro. Musical direction and underscoring by Robert Emmett Dolan. Orchestrations by Philip J. Lang. Dance arrangements by Jack Elliott.

Synopsis and Production Information

MR. PRESIDENT tells the story of a simple, everyday man, Steve Henderson, who happens to be President of the United States, and his simple, American family: wife Nell, who prefers small-town life, supermarket coupons, and baking pies for country fairs; daughter Leslie, who is guy crazy; and son Larry, who likes fast cars and girls. During the family's second-term diplomatic trip to Russia, they are condemned for their "over-friendly attitude toward the Russian people," and lingering dissent costs their party the next Presidential election. After leaving the White House, the Hendersons return to their peaceful midwestern home; there they are reminded of the values that make this country great.

The show requires a full singing and dancing ensemble.

Orchestration

Reed I (Flute, Piccolo, Alto Sax); Reed II (Clarinet, Alto Sax); Reed III (Oboe, English Horn, Clarinet, Tenor Sax); Reed IV (Clarinet, Tenor Sax, Bass Clarinet); Reed V (Clarinet, Bassoon, Baritone Sax, Bass Sax); Horn I II; Trumpet I II; Trumpet III; Trombone I; Trombone II; Percussion; Harp; Guitar; Violin A B C; Viola (divisi); Cello; Bass

Location of Original Materials

Script: New York Public Library (all lyrics), Music Theatre International (most lyrics)
Piano-vocal score: Music Theatre International
Partiturs: Irving Berlin Music Corporation
Parts: Irving Berlin Music Corporation

The New York Public Library also has an early draft of the script dated June 7, 1962, and a "rehearsal version" dated July 2, 1962. Neither contains any lyrics.

Rental Status

Music Theatre International rents the original script and piano-vocal score (with an abridged Opening number) and the following orchestration reduced from the original: Reed I (Piccolo, Flute, Alto Sax, Clarinet); Reed II (Clarinet, Alto Sax); Reed III (Clarinet, Tenor Sax); Reed IV (Clarinet, Tenor Sax, Bass Clarinet); Trumpet I II; Trumpet III; Trombone I; Trombone II; Percussion; Harp; Guitar; Violin A; Violin B; Viola; Cello; Bass.

Music Publisher

Irving Berlin Music Corporation

Information

Music Theatre International

Mr. President (1962)

Overture
Berlin/Berlin
Orchestrator: Lang

Location of
- Composer's manuscript: -0-
- Sheet music: Not published separately
- Most complete music: MTI (pv score)
- Most complete lyric: INST
- Original partitur: IB
- Original parts: IB

In Our Hide-Away
Berlin/Berlin
Orchestrator: Lang

Location of
- Composer's manuscript: -0-
- Sheet music: IB, NYPL, Y
- Most complete music: IB (sm); NYPL (sm); Y (sm); LoC (pv-l); MTI (pv score)
- Most complete lyric: IB (sm); NYPL (sm, scr); Y (sm); LoC (pv-l); MTI (pv score, scr)
- Original partitur: IB
- Original parts: IB

Opening ["Just someone doing the best he can..."]
Berlin/Berlin
Orchestrator: Lang

Location of
- Composer's manuscript: -0-
- Sheet music: Unpublished
- Most complete music: IB (pv-l); MTI (pv score)
- Most complete lyric: IB (ls); NYPL (scr)
- Original partitur: IB
- Original parts: IB

First Lady, The
Berlin/Berlin
Orchestrator: Lang

Location of
- Composer's manuscript: -0-
- Sheet music: 1st version: IB, Y
  2nd version: IB, LoC
- Most complete music: IB (either sm); LoC (sm); Y (sm); MTI (pv score)
- Most complete lyric: IB (sm & sm); NYPL (scr & ls)
- Original partitur: IB
- Original parts: IB

The two versions of the sheet music differ lyrically.

Let's Go Back to the Waltz
Berlin/Berlin
Orchestrator: Lang

Location of
- Composer's manuscript: -0-
- Sheet music: IB, Y
- Most complete music: IB (sm); Y (sm); LoC (pv-l); MTI (pv score)
- Most complete lyric: IB (sm); Y (sm); LoC (pv-l); MTI (pv score, scr); NYPL (scr)
- Original partitur: IB
- Original parts: IB

Meat and Potatoes
Berlin/Berlin
Orchestrator: Lang

Location of
- Composer's manuscript: -0-
- Sheet music: IB, NYPL, Y
- Most complete music: IB (sm); NYPL (sm); Y (sm); LoC (pv-l); MTI (pv score)
- Most complete lyric: IB (sm & pv score); NYPL (scr & ls)
- Original partitur: IB
- Original parts: IB

Irving Berlin

I've Got to Be Around
Berlin/Berlin
Orchestrator: Lang

Location of - Composer's manuscript: -0-
- Sheet music: IB, NYPL, Y
- Most complete music: IB (sm); NYPL (sm);
    Y (sm); LoC (pv-l); MTI (pv score)
- Most complete lyric: IB (sm); NYPL (sm,
    scr); Y (sm); LoC (pv-l);
    MTI (pv score, scr)
- Original partitur: IB
- Original parts: IB

Is He the Only Man in the World?
Berlin/Berlin
Orchestrator: Lang

Location of - Composer's manuscript: -0-
- Sheet music: IB, NYPL, Y
- Most complete music: IB (sm); NYPL (sm);
    Y (sm); LoC (pv-l); MTI (pv score)
- Most complete lyric: MTI (pv score, scr)
- Original partitur: IB
- Original parts: IB

Secret Service, The
Berlin/Berlin
Orchestrator: Lang

Location of - Composer's manuscript: -0-
- Sheet music: IB, NYPL, Y
- Most complete music: IB (sm); NYPL (sm);
    Y (sm); LoC (pv-l); MTI (pv score)
- Most complete lyric: MTI (pv score, scr)
- Original partitur: IB
- Original parts: IB

They Love Me
Berlin/Berlin
Orchestrator: Lang

Location of - Composer's manuscript: -0-
- Sheet music: IB, NYPL, Y
- Most complete music: IB (sm, pv-l);
    NYPL (sm); Y (sm); MTI (pv score)
- Most complete lyric: IB (sm & pv-l);
    NYPL (sm & scr)
- Original partitur: IB
- Original parts: IB

It Gets Lonely in the White House
Berlin/Berlin
Orchestrator: Lang

Location of - Composer's manuscript: -0-
- Sheet music: IB, Y
- Most complete music: IB (sm, pv-l);
    Y (sm); LoC (pv-l); MTI (pv score)
- Most complete lyric: IB (sm & pv-l)
- Original partitur: IB
- Original parts: IB

Pigtails and Freckles
Berlin/Berlin
Orchestrator: Lang

Location of - Composer's manuscript: -0-
- Sheet music: IB, NYPL, Y
- Most complete music: IB (sm); NYPL (sm);
    Y (sm); LoC (pv-l); MTI (pv score)
- Most complete lyric: NYPL (scr);
    MTI (pv score, scr)
- Original partitur: -0-
- Original parts: -0-

Don't Be Afraid of Romance

Berlin/Berlin
Orchestrator: Lang

Location of
- Composer's manuscript: -0-
- Sheet music: IB, NYPL, Y
- Most complete music: IB (sm); NYPL (sm); Y (sm); LoC (pv-l); MTI (pv score)
- Most complete lyric: IB (sm); NYPL (sm, scr); Y (sm); LoC (pv-l); MTI (pv score, scr)
- Original partitur: IB
- Original parts: IB

Entr'acte

Berlin/Berlin
Orchestrator: Lang

Location of
- Composer's manuscript: -0-
- Sheet music: Unpublished
- Most complete music: MTI (pv score)
- Most complete lyric: INST
- Original partitur: IB (inc)
- Original parts: IB

Laugh It Up

Berlin/Berlin
Orchestrator: Lang

Location of
- Composer's manuscript: -0-
- Sheet music: See note
- Most complete music: IB (pv-l); LoC (pv-l); MTI (pv score)
- Most complete lyric: IB (ls & pv-l)
- Original partitur: IB
- Original parts: IB

According to Steven Suskin's Show Tunes 1905-1985 (Dodd, Mead & Company: 1986), this number was published. No sheet music was found.

Glad to Be Home

Berlin/Berlin
Orchestrator: Lang

Location of
- Composer's manuscript: -0-
- Sheet music: IB, NYPL, Y
- Most complete music: IB (sm); NYPL (sm); Y (sm); LoC (pv-l); MTI (pv score)
- Most complete lyric: IB (sm); NYPL (sm, scr); Y (sm); LoC (pv-l); MTI (pv score, scr)
- Original partitur: IB
- Original parts: IB

Empty Pockets Filled With Love

Berlin/Berlin
Orchestrator: Lang

Location of
- Composer's manuscript: -0-
- Sheet music: IB, LoC, NYPL, Y
- Most complete music: IB (sm); LoC (sm); NYPL (sm); Y (sm); MTI (pv score)
- Most complete lyric: IB (sm); LoC (sm); NYPL (sm, scr); Y (sm); MTI (pv score, scr)
- Original partitur: IB
- Original parts: IB

You Need a Hobby

Berlin/Berlin
Orchestrator: Lang

Location of
- Composer's manuscript: -0-
- Sheet music: Unpublished
- Most complete music: IB (pv-l); LoC (pv-l); MTI (pv score)
- Most complete lyric: IB (pv-l); LoC (pv-l); MTI (pv score, scr); NYPL (scr)
- Original partitur: IB
- Original parts: IB

Washington Twist, The
    Berlin/Berlin
    Orchestrator: Lang, unknown

    Location of   - Composer's manuscript: -0-
               - Sheet music: IB, Y
               - Most complete music: IB (sm); Y (sm);
                    LoC (pv-l); MTI (pv score)
               - Most complete lyric: IB (sm, ls); Y (sm)
               - Original partitur: IB
               - Original parts: IB

This Is a Great Country
    Berlin/Berlin
    Orchestrator: Lang

    Location of   - Composer's manuscript: -0-
               - Sheet music: IB, NYPL, Y
               - Most complete music: IB (sm); NYPL (sm);
                    Y (sm); LoC (pv-l); MTI (pv score)
               - Most complete lyric: IB (sm); NYPL (sm,
                    scr); Y (sm); LoC (pv-l);
                    MTI (pv score, scr)
               - Original partitur: IB
               - Original parts: IB

Song for Belly Dancer
    Berlin/Berlin
    Orchestrator: Lang, unknown

    Location of   - Composer's manuscript: -0-
               - Sheet music: IB, NYPL, Y
               - Most complete music: IB (sm); NYPL (srn);
                    Y (sm); MTI (pv score)
               - Most complete lyric: IB (sm); NYPL (sm,
                    scr); Y (sm); MTI (pv score, scr)
               - Original partitur: IB
               - Original parts: IB

Alternate title: "The Only Dance I Know."

Finale Act II ["Just someone doing the best he can..."]
    Berlin/Berlin
    Orchestrator: Lang

    Location of   - Composer's manuscript: -0-
               - Sheet music: Unpublished
               - Most complete music: IB (pv-l);
                    MTI (pv score)
               - Most complete lyric: IB (pv-l);
                    MTI (pv score, scr); NYPL (scr)
               - Original partitur: IB
               - Original parts: IB

I'm Gonna Get Him
    Berlin/Berlin
    Orchestrator: Lang

    Location of   - Composer's manuscript: -0-
               - Sheet music: IB, Y
               - Most complete music: IB (sm); Y (sm);
                    LoC (pv-l); MTI (pv score)
                - Most complete lyric: MTI (pv score, scr)
               - Original partitur: IB
               - Original parts: IB

Once Every Four Years
    Berlin/Berlin
    Orchestrator: Lang

    Location of   - Composer's manuscript: -0-
               - Sheet music: IB, Y
               - Most complete music: IB (sm); Y (sm);
                    LoC (pv-l)
               - Most complete lyric: IB (sm); Y (sm);
                    LoC (pv-l); NYPL (ls)
               - Original partitur: IB
               - Original parts: IB

Dropped during the pre-Broadway tryout.

Mr. President (1962)

Anybody Can Write

    Berlin/Berlin

    Orchestrator: Lang

    Location of   - Composer's manuscript: -0-
- Sheet music: Unpublished
- Most complete music: IB (pv-l); LoC (pv-l)
- Most complete lyric: IB (pv-l); LoC (pv-l); NYPL (ls)
- Original partitur: IB
- Original parts: IB

Dropped during the pre-Broadway tryout.

Poor Joe

    Berlin/Berlin

    Orchestrator: Unknown

    Location of   - Composer's manuscript: -0-
- Sheet music: IB
- Most complete music: IB (sm); LoC (pv-l)
- Most complete lyric: IB (sm); LoC (pv-l); NYPL (ls)
- Original partitur: -0-
- Original parts: -0-

Dropped before the New York opening.

GEORGE & IRA GERSHWIN

GEORGE GERSHWIN was born in Brooklyn on September 26, 1898, and began his musical training when he was thirteen. At sixteen he quit high school to work as a "song plugger" for a music publisher, and soon he was writing songs himself, many with lyrics by his older brother, Ira. "Swanee" (lyrics by Irving Caesar), as introduced by Al Jolson, brought George his first real fame and led to his writing a successsion of twenty-two musical comedies, among them LADY, BE GOOD! (1924), OH, KAY! (1926), FUNNY FACE (1927), STRIKE UP THE BAND (1927, revised 1930), GIRL CRAZY (1930), and the Pulitzer Prize-winning OF THEE I SING (1931). His film scores included DELICIOUS (1931), SHALL WE DANCE (1937), and A DAMSEL IN DISTRESS (1937). From his early career George had ambitions to compose serious music. When asked by Paul Whiteman to compose an original work for a special modern concert to be presented at Aeolian Hall in New York on February 12, 1924, George, though hard at work on a musical comedy, created in three short weeks one of the masterpieces of American music. RHAPSODY IN BLUE caught the public's fancy and opened a new era in American music. In 1925 the eminent conductor Walter Damrosch commissioned George to compose a piano concerto for the New York Symphony Society; many feel that the resulting CONCERTO IN F is George's finest orchestral work. Others prefer his AMERICAN IN PARIS (1928) or his SECOND RHAPSODY for piano and orchestra. In the late Twenties, Gershwin became fascinated by the DuBose Heyward novel PORGY, recognizing it as a perfect vehicle for opera using jazz and blues idioms. George's "folk opera" PORGY AND BESS opened in Boston on September 30, 1935, and had its Broadway premiere two weeks later. In addition to its 1942 and 1953 revivals and subsequent world tours, it was made into a major motion picture in 1959 and has recently been seen at Radio City Music Hall, the Metropolitan Opera, and at Glyndebourne in England. In 1937, George was at the height of his career. His three preludes for piano and his symphonic works were becoming standard repertory for recitals and concerts, and his lighter music was bringing him ever-increasing fame and fortune. In Hollywood working on the score of THE GOLDWYN FOLLIES, George collapsed and on July 11, died of a brain tumor. He was not quite 39 years old.

IRA GERSHWIN, the first songwriter to be awarded the Pulitzer Prize (along with co-librettists George S. Kaufman and Morrie Ryskind for OF THEE I SING) was born in New York City on December 6, 1896. While attending the College of New York he began contributing to the famed Conning Tower and Don Marquis' column in The Evening Sun; the latter published in 1917 his first song lyric, "You May Throw All the Rice You Desire But Please Friends, Throw No Shoes." Though the song was submitted as a joke, Marquis printed it, calling the lyric "perfect." 1918 marked the year of Ira Gershwin's first lyric to be sung from a stage, as well as the beginning of a longtime collaboration with his brother George. The song was called "The Real American Folk Song" and was interpolated into the Nora Bayes show, LADIES FIRST. Not wanting to trade on the success of his already famous brother, Ira adopted the nom de plume of Arthur Francis, combining the names of his other brother Arthur and sister Francis. It was under his pen name that Gershwin enjoyed his first major stage success, TWO LITTLE GIRLS IN BLUE, written in 1921 with another Broadway newcomer, Vincent Youmans. By 1924 it was no longer any secret that Arthur Francis was really Ira Gershwin; more important, a Gershwin lyric had become as distinctive as a Gershwin melody, so the pen name was dropped. Thus it was the Gershwin brothers who created the 1924 stage hit LADY BE GOOD, continuing their remarkable collaboration with a dozen major stage scores, including TIP TOES (1925), OH KAY! (1926), STRIKE UP THE BAND (1927 & 1930), GIRL CRAZY (1930), OF THEE I SING (1931), and the American folk opera PORGY AND BESS (written in collaboration with DuBose Heyward). In 1936, Ira accompanied his brother to Hollywood to supply the words for what became their final collaboration, three motion picture scores: SHALL WE DANCE (1937), DAMSEL IN DISTRESS (1937), and THE GOLDWYN FOLLIES (1938). Together the Gershwin brothers created dozens of "standards" but Ira was also proud of his collaborations with other composers, including Harold Arlen (LIFE BEGINS AT 8:40, A STAR IS BORN), Vernon Duke (ZIEGFELD FOLLIES OF 1936), Kurt Weill (LADY IN THE DARK, THE FIREBRAND OF FLORENCE), Aaron Copland (NORTH STAR), Harry Warren (THE BARKLEYS OF BROADWAY), Arthur Schwartz (PARK AVENUE), Burton Lane (GIVE A GIRL A BREAK), and Jerome Kern (COVER GIRL), with whom he created his greatest song hit of any one year, "Long Ago (And Far Away)." Ira Gershwin died August 17, 1983, in Beverly Hills, California.

LA-LA-LUCILLE!

Music GEORGE GERSHWIN
Lyrics ARTHUR J. JACKSON & B.G. DESYLVA

...ened May 26, 1919 in New York and ran 104 performances (World premiere:
...retto by Fred Jackson. Additional lyrics by Irving Caesar, Lou Paley, Ira
...arons.[1] Directed by Herbert Gresham. Choreographed by Julian Alfred.
...n. Orchestrations by Frank Saddler, Maurice B. DePackh.

...erit two million dollars from a spiteful aunt, John Smith is forced to divorce
...fe, Lucille. He reluctantly engages his homely janitress, Fanny, as
...and the pair retire to a hotel suite where Lucille is to discover them.
...terrupted by the house detective, newlyweds from the South, Lucille's
...ther, and Fanny's husband, a Japanese knife-thrower, but eventually, John
...cure the inheritance and remarry.

...rs include Mlle. Victorine, a saucy cabaret dancer, and her partner, Allan
...ow requires a full singing and dancing ensemble.

...; Clarinet I II; Bassoon; Horn; Trumpet I II; Trombone; Drums; Cembalo;
... I II; Cello; Bass

...rk Public Library (all lyrics)
...ore: See individual listings
...ry of Congress

...ng for seven songs performed in the New York production, as well as for the
...ntr'actes. Partiturs survive for one number in the show and three that

...ailable for rental

...rs Music

...state, George Gershwin Family Trust

...nd George B. Seitz assumed the producing chores on LA-LA-LUCILLE!

ERRATUM

On **page 374**, the music publisher of JUMBO is listed incorrectly as Chappell Music; the correct music publisher is **T.B. Harms Company, 1299 Ocean Avenue, Santa Monica, California 90401.**

Overture
    Gershwin/Jackson & DeSylva
    Orchestrator: Unknown

    Location of   - Composer's manuscript: -0-
                - Sheet music: Unpublished
                - Most complete music: -0-
                - Most complete lyric: INST
                - Original partitur: -0-
                - Original parts: -0-

Best of Everything, The
    Gershwin/Jackson & DeSylva
    Orchestrator: Unknown

    Location of   - Composer's manuscript: -0-
                - Sheet music: LoC, NYPL
                - Most complete music: LoC (sm);
                      NYPL (sm)
                - Most complete lyric: NYPL (sm & scr)
                - Original partitur: -0-
                - Original parts: -0-

Also included (with revised lyrics) in STOP FLIRTING!, the 1923 London production of the William Daly/Paul Lannin/Arthur J. Jackson musical comedy FOR GOODNESS SAKE (1922). The Ira Gershwin Estate has the "Best of Everything" sheet music from STOP FLIRTING!

Opening Act I
    Gershwin/Jackson & DeSylva
    Orchestrator: Unknown

    Location of   - Composer's manuscript: -0-
                - Sheet music: Unpublished
                - Most complete music: -0-
                - Most complete lyric: NYPL (scr)
                - Original partitur: -0-
                - Original parts: -0-

Alternate title: "Kindly Pay Us."

From Now On
    Gershwin/Jackson & DeSylva
    Orchestrator: Unknown

    Location of   - Composer's manuscript: -0-
                - Sheet music: LoC, NYPL
                - Most complete music: LoC (sm);
                      NYPL (sm)
                - Most complete lyric: LoC (sm);
                      NYPL (sm, scr)
                - Original partitur: -0-
                - Original parts: -0-

When You Live in a Furnished Flat
    Gershwin/Jackson & DeSylva
    Orchestrator: Unknown

    Location of   - Composer's manuscript: -0-
                - Sheet music: Unpublished
                - Most complete music: -0-
                - Most complete lyric: NYPL (scr)
                - Original partitur: -0-
                - Original parts: -0-

It's Hard to Tell
    Gershwin/Jackson & DeSylva
    Orchestrator: Unknown

    Location of   - Composer's manuscript: -0-
                - Sheet music: Unpublished
                - Most complete music: -0-
                - Most complete lyric: NYPL (scr)
                - Original partitur: -0-
                - Original parts: -0-

Added soon after the New York opening.

La-La-Lucille! (1919)

Tee Oodle Um Bum Bo
Gershwin/Jackson & DeSylva
Orchestrator: Unknown

Location of   - Composer's manuscript: -0-
               - Sheet music: LoC, NYPL
               - Most complete music: LoC (sm);
                   NYPL (sm)
               - Most complete lyric: LoC (sm);
                   NYPL (sm, scr)
               - Original partitur: -0-
               - Original parts: -0-

Opening Act II
Gershwin/Jackson & DeSylva
Orchestrator: Unknown

Location of   - Composer's manuscript: -0-
               - Sheet music: Unpublished
               - Most complete music: -0-
               - Most complete lyric: NYPL (scr)
               - Original partitur: -0-
               - Original parts: -0-

Alternate title: "Hotel Life."

Finale Act I ["Oh no, no! You shall not go!"]
Gershwin/Jackson & DeSylva
Orchestrator: Unknown

Location of   - Composer's manuscript: -0-
               - Sheet music: Unpublished
               - Most complete music: -0-
               - Most complete lyric: NYPL (scr)
               - Original partitur: -0-
               - Original parts: -0-

Nobody But You
Gershwin/Jackson & DeSylva
Orchestrator: Unknown

Location of   - Composer's manuscript: LoC (r), IG (sk)
               - Sheet music: LoC, NYPL
               - Most complete music: LoC (sm);
                   NYPL (sm)
               - Most complete lyric: NYPL (scr)
               - Original partitur: -0-
               - Original parts: -0-

Added soon after the New York opening.

Entr'acte I
Gershwin/Jackson & DeSylva
Orchestrator: Unknown

Location of   - Composer's manuscript: -0-
               - Sheet music: Unpublished
               - Most complete music: -0-
               - Most complete lyric: INST
               - Original partitur: -0-
               - Original parts: -0-

It's Great to Be in Love
Gershwin/Jackson & DeSylva
Orchestrator: Unknown

Location of   - Composer's manuscript: -0-
               - Sheet music: Unpublished
               - Most complete music: -0-
               - Most complete lyric: NYPL (scr)
               - Original partitur: -0-
               - Original parts: -0-

Finale Act II ["Oh! What a terrible situation."]
Gershwin/Jackson & DeSylva
Orchestrator: Unknown

Location of
- Composer's manuscript: -0-
- Sheet music: Unpublished
- Most complete music: -0-
- Most complete lyric: NYPL (scr)
- Original partitur: -0-
- Original parts: -0-

Somehow It Seldom Comes True
Gershwin/Jackson & DeSylva
Orchestrator: Unknown

Location of
- Composer's manuscript: -0-
- Sheet music: LoC, NYPL
- Most complete music: LoC (sm); NYPL (sm)
- Most complete lyric: LoC (sm); NYPL (sm, scr)
- Original partitur: -0-
- Original parts: -0-

Entr'acte II
Gershwin/Jackson & DeSylva
Orchestrator: Unknown

Location of
- Composer's manuscript: -0-
- Sheet music: Unpublished
- Most complete music: -0-
- Most complete lyric: INST
- Original partitur: -0-
- Original parts: -0-

Ten Commandments of Love, The
Gershwin/Jackson & DeSylva
Orchestrator: DePackh

Location of
- Composer's manuscript: -0-
- Sheet music: Unpublished
- Most complete music: LoC (ptr)
- Most complete lyric: NYPL (scr)
- Original partitur: LoC
- Original parts: -0-

The partitur is probably from HALF PAST EIGHT, the 1918 revue with Gershwin music in which the song was first used.

There's More to the Kiss Than the Sound
Gershwin/Caesar
Orchestrator: Unknown

Location of
- Composer's manuscript: -0-
- Sheet music: LoC
- Most complete music: LoC (sm); NYPL (sm)
- Most complete lyric: LoC (sm); NYPL (sm)
- Original partitur: -0-
- Original parts: -0-

Previously used in GOOD MORNING, JUDGE, a 1919 musical with two interpolated songs by George Gershwin, where it was titled (and published as) "There's More to the Kiss Than the X-X-X."

Money, Money, Money!
Gershwin/Jackson & DeSylva
Orchestrator: Saddler

Location of
- Composer's manuscript: -0-
- Sheet music: Unpublished
- Most complete music: LoC (ptr)
- Most complete lyric: -0-
- Original partitur: LoC
- Original parts: -0-

Dropped soon after the New York opening.

La-La-Lucille! (1919)

Oo, How I Love to Be Loved by You

    Gershwin/Paley

    Orchestrator: Unknown

Location of   - Composer's manuscript: -0-

               - Sheet music: NYPL

               - Most complete music: NYPL (sm)

               - Most complete lyric: NYPL (sm)

               - Original partitur: -0-

               - Original parts: -0-

Dropped soon after the New York opening.

Our Little Kitchenette

    Gershwin/Gershwin & DeSylva

    Orchestrator: Saddler

Location of   - Composer's manuscript: -0-

               - Sheet music: Unpublished

               - Most complete music: LoC (ptr)

               - Most complete lyric: IG (ls)

               - Original partitur: LoC

               - Original parts: -0-

Dropped during the pre-Broadway tryout. Later rewritten for SWEET LITTLE DEVIL (1924), but dropped before the pre-Broadway tryout. Alternate title: "Kitchenette."

Love of a Wife, The

    Gershwin/Jackson & DeSylva

    Orchestrator: Saddler

Location of   - Composer's manuscript: -0-

               - Sheet music: LoC, NYPL

               - Most complete music: LoC (sm);

                      NYPL (sm)

               - Most complete lyric: LoC (sm);

                      NYPL (sm)

               - Original partitur: LoC

               - Original parts: -0-

Dropped during the pre-Broadway tryout, although a passage from it remained in the Act II Finale.

A DANGEROUS MAID

Music	GEORGE GERSHWIN
Lyrics	ARTHUR FRANCIS [IRA GERSHWIN][2]

Musical comedy in three acts. Closed out of town (World premiere: March 21, 1921 in Atlantic City). Libretto by Charles W. Bell, based on his play A DISLOCATED HONEYMOON. Produced and directed by Edgar MacGregor. Choreographed by Julian Alfred. Musical direction by Harold Vicars. Orchestrations by Frank Saddler.

Synopsis and Production Information
Mr. and Mrs. Phillip Hammond are determined to break up the marriage of their son Harry and chorus girl Elsie Crofton. They arrange a job for Harry at a construction camp where no women are allowed, and lure Elsie to their summer home on Long Island. But a sly Elsie, working her feminine wiles on every man in sight, manages to create such a stir that the Hammonds banish her from their home. Elsie and Harry are happily reunited.

The show includes a full singing and dancing ensemble.

Orchestration
Flute; Oboe; Clarinet I II; Bassoon; Horn; Trumpet I II; Drums; Violin I Desk 1; Violin I Desk 2; Violin II; Viola; Cello; Bass

Comments
The Pittsburg Press reported on April 12, 1921: "The show is on its way to New York, where it will be presented under the name of ELSIE." ELSIE finally premiered on Broadway in 1923, with the same librettist, but with a score now split between the team of Noble Sissle and Eubie Blake and that of Monte Carlo and Alma Sanders. It lasted only 40 performances.

Location of Original Materials
Script: Missing
Piano-vocal score: See individual listings
Partiturs: Library of Congress
Parts: Missing

Although the script is missing, the Shubert Archive has a copy of A DISLOCATED HONEYMOON, the play on which A DANGEROUS MAID was based; it contains the same characters and plot as the musical version. Of the songs performed during the pre-Broadway tryout, one is missing ("True Love") and another incomplete ("Anything for You"). Partiturs have survived for the Overture, Entr'acte I, and two of the published songs.

Rental Status
Currently unavailable for rental

Music Publisher
Warner Brothers Music

Information
Ira Gershwin Estate, George Gershwin Family Trust

---

[2] At this point in his career, Ira Gershwin was writing under the pseudonym "Arthur Francis."

A Dangerous Maid (1921)

Overture
Gershwin/Gershwin
Orchestrator: Saddler

Location of - Composer's manuscript: -0-
            - Sheet music: Unpublished
            - Most complete music: LoC (ptr)
            - Most complete lyric: INST
            - Original partitur: LoC (inc)
            - Original parts: -0-

The partitur contains only the introduction and the links between numbers.

Just to Know You Are Mine
Gershwin/Gershwin
Orchestrator: Unknown

Location of - Composer's manuscript: -0-
            - Sheet music: LoC, NYPL
            - Most complete music: LoC (sm);
               NYPL (sm)
            - Most complete lyric: LoC (sm);
               NYPL (sm)
            - Original partitur: -0-
            - Original parts: -0-

Musical Preface
Gershwin/Gershwin
Orchestrator: Unknown

Location of - Composer's manuscript: -0-
            - Sheet music: Unpublished
            - Most complete music: -0-
            - Most complete lyric: INST
            - Original partitur: -0-
            - Original parts: -0-

Entr'acte I
Gershwin/Gershwin
Orchestrator: Saddler

Location of - Composer's manuscript: -0-
            - Sheet music: Unpublished
            - Most complete music: LoC (ptr)
            - Most complete lyric: INST
            - Original partitur: LoC
            - Original parts: -0-

Anything for You
Gershwin/Gershwin
Orchestrator: Unknown

Location of - Composer's manuscript: IG (sk)
            - Sheet music: Unpublished
            - Most complete music: IG (sk)
            - Most complete lyric: -0-
            - Original partitur: -0-
            - Original parts: -0-

Boy Wanted
Gershwin/Gershwin
Orchestrator: Saddler

Location of - Composer's manuscript: -0-
            - Sheet music: LoC
            - Most complete music: LoC (sm)
            - Most complete lyric: IG (ls)
            - Original partitur: LoC
            - Original parts: -0-

With a revised lyric (by Ira Gershwin and Desmond Carter), this number was later used in PRIMROSE (1924).

Simple Life, The

Gershwin/Gershwin

Orchestrator: Unknown

Location of
- Composer's manuscript: -0-
- Sheet music: LoC, NYPL
- Most complete music: LoC (sm); NYPL (sm)
- Most complete lyric: LoC (sm); NYPL (sm)
- Original partitur: -0-
- Original parts: -0-

True Love

Gershwin/Gershwin

Orchestrator: Unknown

Location of
- Composer's manuscript: -0-
- Sheet music: Unpublished
- Most complete music: -0-
- Most complete lyric: -0-
- Original partitur: -0-
- Original parts: -0-

Sirens, The

Gershwin/Gershwin

Orchestrator: Unknown

Location of
- Composer's manuscript: -0-
- Sheet music: Not published separately
- Most complete music: IG (pv)
- Most complete lyric: IG (ls)
- Original partitur: -0-
- Original parts: -0-

Later used in PRIMROSE (1924) under the title "Four Little Sirens." A complete version was published in the PRIMROSE piano-vocal score, which can be found at the Library of Congress and the New York Public Library.

Entr'acte II

Gershwin/Gershwin

Orchestrator: Unknown

Location of
- Composer's manuscript: -0-
- Sheet music: Unpublished
- Most complete music: -0-
- Most complete lyric: INST
- Original partitur: -0-
- Original parts: -0-

Dancing Shoes

Gershwin/Gershwin

Orchestrator: Unknown

Location of
- Composer's manuscript: -0-
- Sheet music: NYPL
- Most complete music: NYPL (sm)
- Most complete lyric: NYPL (sm)
- Original partitur: -0-
- Original parts: -0-

Some Rain Must Fall

Gershwin/Gershwin

Orchestrator: Saddler

Location of
- Composer's manuscript: -0-
- Sheet music: LoC, NYPL
- Most complete music: LoC (sm); NYPL (sm)
- Most complete lyric: LoC (sm); NYPL (sm)
- Original partitur: LoC
- Original parts: -0-

A Dangerous Maid (1921)

Pidgie Woo

Gershwin/Gershwin

Orchestrator: Unknown

Location of - Composer's manuscript: -0-
- Sheet music: Unpublished
- Most complete music: -0-
- Most complete lyric: -0-
- Original partitur: -0-
- Original parts: -0-

Unused.

Every Girl Has a Way

Gershwin/Gershwin

Orchestrator: Unknown

Location of - Composer's manuscript: -0-
- Sheet music: Unpublished
- Most complete music: -0-
- Most complete lyric: IG (ls)
- Original partitur: -0-
- Original parts: -0-

Unused.

OUR NELL

Music   GEORGE GERSHWIN & WILLIAM DALY
Lyrics   BRIAN HOOKER

Musical melodrama in two acts. Opened December 4, 1922 in New York and ran 40 performances (World premiere: November 20, 1922 in Stamford, Connecticut). Libretto by A.E. Thomas and Brian Hooker. Produced by Ed Davidow and Rufus LeMaire. Directed by W.H. Gilmore and Edgar MacGregor. Choreographed by Julian Mitchell. Musical direction by Charles Sieger.

Synopsis and Production Information	A dark secret has forced Helen Ford to leave her job in New York and return to her little country home at Hensfoot Corners (where she is known as plain old Nell). She arrives to discover that her kindly grandfather and aunt can't meet their mortgage payments. To save them, Helen makes the ultimate sacrifice: She gives up the decent farmhand who loves her in order to marry the rich city slicker who done her wrong. Luckily, at the eleventh hour, everyone finally does right by Our Nell.
	Supporting characters include Chris and Myrtle, two rural aspirants for motion picture glory, and Mrs. Rogers, the big-city vamp. The show requires a full singing and dancing ensemble.
Orchestration	Unknown
Comments	OUR NELL combines elements of 19th-century rural melodrama and 1920's musical comedy and simultaneously satirizes both forms. The show's pre-Broadway title, HAYSEED, appears on early editions of the sheet music.
Location of Original Materials	Script: Library of Congress (no lyrics) Piano-vocal score: See individual listings Partiturs: Missing Parts: Missing
	The script (entitled HAYSEED) dates from the pre-Broadway tryout, but its plot, characters, and musical running order are similar to those of the New York show. Only five songs from the original production have surfaced.
Rental Status	Currently unavailable for rental
Music Publisher	Warner Brothers Music
Information	Ira Gershwin Estate, George Gershwin Family Trust

Our Nell (1922)

Overture
Gershwin & Daly/Hooker
Orchestrator: Unknown

Location of   - Composer's manuscript: -0-
               - Sheet music: Unpublished
               - Most complete music: -0-
               - Most complete lyric: INST
               - Original partitur: -0-
               - Original parts: -0-

Innocent Ingenue Baby
Daly & Gershwin/Hooker
Orchestrator: Unknown

Location of   - Composer's manuscript: -0-
               - Sheet music: LoC, NYPL
               - Most complete music: LoC (sm);
                    NYPL (sm)
               - Most complete lyric: LoC (sm);
                    NYPL (sm)
               - Original partitur: -0-
               - Original parts: -0-

Opening
Gershwin & Daly/Hooker
Orchestrator: Unknown

Location of   - Composer's manuscript: -0-
               - Sheet music: Unpublished
               - Most complete music: -0-
               - Most complete lyric: -0-
               - Original partitur: -0-
               - Original parts: -0-

Old New England Home
Daly/Hooker
Orchestrator: Unknown

Location of   - Composer's manuscript: -0-
               - Sheet music: LoC
               - Most complete music: LoC (sm)
               - Most complete lyric: LoC (sm)
               - Original partitur: -0-
               - Original parts: -0-

Gol-Dum!
Gershwin & Daly/Hooker
Orchestrator: Unknown

Location of   - Composer's manuscript: -0-
               - Sheet music: Unpublished
               - Most complete music: -0-
               - Most complete lyric: -0-
               - Original partitur: -0-
               - Original parts: -0-

Cooney County Fair, The
Gershwin/Hooker
Orchestrator: Unknown

Location of   - Composer's manuscript: -0-
               - Sheet music: Unpublished
               - Most complete music: -0-
               - Most complete lyric: -0-
               - Original partitur: -0-
               - Original parts: -0-

George & Ira Gershwin

Names I Love to Hear
    Gershwin & Daly/Hooker
    Orchestrator: Unknown

    Location of   - Composer's manuscript: -0-
                - Sheet music: Unpublished
                - Most complete music: -0-
                - Most complete lyric: -0-
                - Original partitur: -0-
                - Original parts: -0-

Madrigal
    Gershwin & Daly/Hooker
    Orchestrator: Unknown

    Location of   - Composer's manuscript: -0-
                - Sheet music: Unpublished
                - Most complete music: -0-
                - Most complete lyric: -0-
                - Original partitur: -0-
                - Original parts: -0-

By and By
    Gershwin/Hooker
    Orchestrator: Unknown

    Location of   - Composer's manuscript: IG (sk)
                - Sheet music: LoC, NYPL
                - Most complete music: LoC (sm); NYPL (sm)
                - Most complete lyric: LoC (sm); NYPL (sm)
                - Original partitur: -0-
                - Original parts: -0-

We Go to Church on Sunday
    Gershwin/Hooker
    Orchestrator: Unknown

    Location of   - Composer's manuscript: -0-
                - Sheet music: Unpublished
                - Most complete music: -0-
                - Most complete lyric: -0-
                - Original partitur: -0-
                - Original parts: -0-

Entr'acte
    Gershwin & Daly/Hooker
    Orchestrator: Unknown

    Location of   - Composer's manuscript: -0-
                - Sheet music: Unpublished
                - Most complete music: -0-
                - Most complete lyric: -0-
                - Original partitur: -0-
                - Original parts: -0-

Walking Home With Angeline
    Gershwin/Hooker
    Orchestrator: Unknown

    Location of   - Composer's manuscript: IG (sk)
                - Sheet music: LoC, NYPL
                - Most complete music: LoC (sm); NYPL (sm)
                - Most complete lyric: LoC (sm); NYPL (sm)
                - Original partitur: -0-
                - Original parts: -0-

The critic for the The New York Telegram, in a review dated December 5, 1922, quotes a few lyrics from this number that are not found in the published sheet music.

Our Nell (1922)

Oh, You Lady!
Gershwin & Daly/Hooker
Orchestrator: Unknown

Location of   - Composer's manuscript: -0-
- Sheet music: Unpublished
- Most complete music: -0-
- Most complete lyric: -0-
- Original partitur: -0-
- Original parts: -0-

Barn Dance
Gershwin and/or Daly
Orchestrator: Unknown

Location of   - Composer's manuscript: -0-
- Sheet music: Unpublished
- Most complete music: -0-
- Most complete lyric: -0-
- Original partitur: -0-
- Original parts: -0-

Little Villages
Gershwin & Daly/Hooker
Orchestrator: Unknown

Location of   - Composer's manuscript: -0-
- Sheet music: Unpublished
- Most complete music: LoC (pv-I)
- Most complete lyric: LoC (pv-I, ls)
- Original partitur: -0-
- Original parts: -0-

Alternate titles: "All the Little Villages" and "Wedding Trip."

Custody of the Child, The
Gershwin/Hooker
Orchestrator: Unknown

Location of   - Composer's manuscript: -0-
- Sheet music: Unpublished
- Most complete music: -0-
- Most complete lyric: -0-
- Original partitur: -0-
- Original parts: -0-

Dropped during the pre-Broadway tryout.

[unspecified duet for Helen and Frank]
Author(s): Unknown
Orchestrator: Unknown

Location of   - Composer's manuscript: -0-
- Sheet music: Unpublished
- Most complete music: -0-
- Most complete lyric: -0-
- Original partitur: -0-
- Original parts: -0-

The New York programs give no further information.

SWEET LITTLE DEVIL

Music	GEORGE GERSHWIN
Lyrics	B.G. DESYLVA

Musical comedy in three acts. Opened January 21, 1924 in New York and ran 120 performances (World premiere: December 20, 1923 in Boston). Libretto by Frank Mandel and Laurence Schwab. Additional lyric by Ira Gershwin. Produced by Laurence Schwab. Directed by Edgar MacGregor. Choreographed by Sammy Lee. Musical direction by Ivan Rudisill.

Synopsis and Production Information	Virginia Culpepper lives in New York with her cousin, Follies star Joyce West. When Tom Nesbitt, an American engineer in Peru, sends Joyce a fan letter, Virginia intercepts it and begins a correspondence with him, pretending to be her cousin. Soon Tom and his friend Fred come to New York to complete a lucrative business deal, and Tom decides to call on the famous Miss West. To Virginia's horror, Joyce -- who has learned of Tom's imminent fortune -- takes credit for the letters. As Virginia struggles to reveal the truth, Joyce, her friend May, and her press agent Sam merrily conspire to swindle Tom and Fred. Eventually everyone ends up in Peru, where Tom finally realizes that he loves Virginia.
	SWEET LITTLE DEVIL has minimal set requirements: The first two acts take place entirely on Joyce's roof. There is a full singing and dancing ensemble.
Orchestration	Flute I II; Oboe; Clarinet I II; Bassoon; Horn I II; Trumpet I II; Trombone; Percussion; Harp; Violin I Desk 1; Violin I Desk 2; Violin I Desk 3; Viola I; Viola II; Cello; Bass
Comments	The show's pre-Broadway title, A PERFECT LADY, appears on early editions of the sheet music.
Location of Original Materials	Script: Amherst College (most lyrics), Library of Congress (no lyrics) Piano-vocal score: See individual listings Partiturs: Missing Parts: Tams-Witmark Music Library & Amherst College
	All of the songs survive (except for two that were dropped after the New York opening), but a piano-vocal score has not been assembled. Tams-Witmark has an incomplete set of parts from the post-Broadway tour; the missing parts, which form a reduced orchestration for nine players, are at Amherst College. The Amherst script, derived from the post-Broadway tour, is missing a few numbers; the song cues may be found in the libretto at the Library of Congress.
Rental Status	Currently unavailable for rental
Music Publisher	Warner Brothers Music
Information	Ira Gershwin Estate, George Gershwin Family Trust

Sweet Little Devil (1924)

Overture
Gershwin/DeSylva
Orchestrator: Unknown

Location of   - Composer's manuscript: -0-
              - Sheet music: Unpublished
              - Most complete music: TW (parts)
              - Most complete lyric: INST
              - Original partitur: -0-
              - Original parts: TW

Virginia
Gershwin/DeSylva
Orchestrator: Unknown

Location of   - Composer's manuscript: LoC (sk)
              - Sheet music: LoC, NYPL
              - Most complete music: LoC (sm);
                  NYPL (sm)
              - Most complete lyric: LoC (sm);
                  NYPL (sm); AC (ls, scr)
              - Original partitur: -0-
              - Original parts: TW & AC

Strike, Strike, Strike
Gershwin/DeSylva
Orchestrator: Unknown

Location of   - Composer's manuscript: -0-
              - Sheet music: Unpublished
              - Most complete music: AC (p-l)
              - Most complete lyric: AC (p-l, ls, scr);
                  IG (ls)
              - Original partitur: -0-
              - Original parts: TW & AC

Some One Who Believes in You
Gershwin/DeSylva
Orchestrator: Unknown

Location of   - Composer's manuscript: -0-
              - Sheet music: LoC, NYPL
              - Most complete music: LoC (sm);
                  NYPL (sm)
              - Most complete lyric: LoC (sm);
                  NYPL (sm); AC (ls, scr)
              - Original partitur: -0-
              - Original parts: TW & AC

You're Mighty Lucky
Gershwin/DeSylva
Orchestrator: Unknown

Location of   - Composer's manuscript: -0-
              - Sheet music: Unpublished
              - Most complete music: IG (pv)
              - Most complete lyric: IG (ls); AC (ls, scr)
              - Original partitur: -0-
              - Original parts: TW & AC

Added by the post-Broadway tour.

Jijibo, The
Gershwin/DeSylva
Orchestrator: Unknown

Location of   - Composer's manuscript: -0-
              - Sheet music: LoC, NYPL
              - Most complete music: LoC (sm);
                  NYPL (sm); AC (pv-l)
              - Most complete lyric: LoC (sm);
                  NYPL (sm); AC (pv-l, ls)
              - Original partitur: -0-
              - Original parts: TW & AC

George & Ira Gershwin

Entr'acte I

Gershwin/DeSylva
Orchestrator: Unknown

Location of
- Composer's manuscript: -0-
- Sheet music: Unpublished
- Most complete music: TW (parts)
- Most complete lyric: INST
- Original partitur: -0-
- Original parts: TW

Flirtation Ballet

Gershwin/DeSylva
Orchestrator: Unknown

Location of
- Composer's manuscript: -0-
- Sheet music: Unpublished
- Most complete music: TW (parts)
- Most complete lyric: INST
- Original partitur: -0-
- Original parts: TW

Quite a Party

Gershwin/DeSylva
Orchestrator: Unknown

Location of
- Composer's manuscript: -0-
- Sheet music: Unpublished
- Most complete music: AC (pv-I)
- Most complete lyric: AC (pv-I, ls, scr)
- Original partitur: -0-
- Original parts: TW & AC

Alternate title: "Opening Act II."

Matrimonial Handicap, The

Gershwin/DeSylva
Orchestrator: Unknown

Location of
- Composer's manuscript: LoC (sk)
- Sheet music: Unpublished
- Most complete music: TW (parts)
- Most complete lyric: IG (ls)
- Original partitur: -0-
- Original parts: TW

Under a One-Man Top

Gershwin/DeSylva
Orchestrator: Unknown

Location of
- Composer's manuscript: -0-
- Sheet music: LoC, NYPL
- Most complete music: LoC (sm); NYPL (sm)
- Most complete lyric: LoC (sm); NYPL (sm)
- Original partitur: -0-
- Original parts: TW

Just Supposing

Gershwin/DeSylva
Orchestrator: Unknown

Location of
- Composer's manuscript: -0-
- Sheet music: Unpublished
- Most complete music: AC (p)
- Most complete lyric: AC (ls, scr)
- Original partitur: -0-
- Original parts: TW & AC

Sweet Little Devil (1924)

Hey! Hey!

Gershwin/DeSylva
Orchestrator: Unknown

Location of
- Composer's manuscript: LoC
- Sheet music: LoC, NYPL
- Most complete music: LoC (sm);
    NYPL (sm); AC (pv)
- Most complete lyric: LoC (sm);
    NYPL (sm); AC (ls)
- Original partitur: -0-
- Original parts: TW & AC

Alternate titles: "Hey! Hey! Let 'Er Go!" and "Be the Life of the Crowd."

Hooray for the U.S.A.

Gershwin/DeSylva
Orchestrator: Unknown

Location of
- Composer's manuscript: -0-
- Sheet music: Unpublished
- Most complete music: AC (p)
- Most complete lyric: AC (ls) & IG (ls)
- Original partitur: -0-
- Original parts: TW & AC

Entr'acte II

Gershwin/DeSylva
Orchestrator: Unknown

Location of
- Composer's manuscript: -0-
- Sheet music: Unpublished
- Most complete music: TW (parts)
- Most complete lyric: INST
- Original partitur: -0-
- Original parts: TW (inc)

Sweet Little Devil

Gershwin/DeSylva
Orchestrator: Unknown

Location of
- Composer's manuscript: -0-
- Sheet music: Unpublished
- Most complete music: AC (p)
- Most complete lyric: AC (ls, scr)
- Original partitur: -0-
- Original parts: TW & AC

Added by the post-Broadway tour.

Rosita

Gershwin/DeSylva
Orchestrator: Unknown

Location of
- Composer's manuscript: -0-
- Sheet music: LoC
- Most complete music: LoC (sm)
    & AC (pv-I)
- Most complete lyric: LoC (sm) & AC (scr)
- Original partitur: -0-
- Original parts: TW & AC

Alternate titles: "Opening Act III" and "Pepita." The piano-vocal and parts contain only the verse and an instrumental tag, apparently all that was performed in the original production. The sheet music, entitled "Pepita," includes the refrain.

System

Gershwin/DeSylva
Orchestrator: Unknown

Location of
- Composer's manuscript: -0-
- Sheet music: Unpublished
- Most complete music: -0-
- Most complete lyric: -0-
- Original partitur: -0-
- Original parts: -0-

Dropped by the post-Broadway tour.

Same Old Story, The

Gershwin/DeSylva
Orchestrator: Unknown

Location of - Composer's manuscript: -0-
- Sheet music: Unpublished
- Most complete music: -0-
- Most complete lyric: -0-
- Original partitur: -0-
- Original parts: -0-

Dropped by the post-Broadway tour.

Mah-Jongg

Gershwin/DeSylva
Orchestrator: Unknown

Location of - Composer's manuscript: -0-
- Sheet music: LoC
- Most complete music: LoC (sm)
- Most complete lyric: LoC (sm)
- Original partitur: -0-
- Original parts: -0-

Unused. Later included in GEORGE WHITE'S SCANDALS (1924).

Our Little Kitchenette

Gershwin/Gershwin & DeSylva
Orchestrator: See note

Location of - Composer's manuscript: -0-
- Sheet music: Unpublished
- Most complete music: See note
- Most complete lyric: IG (ls)
- Original partitur: See note
- Original parts: -0-

Dropped before the pre-Broadway tryout. Performed during the pre-Broadway tryout of LA-LA-LUCILLE! (1919); the lyric was later rewritten for SWEET LITTLE DEVIL. The only known music manuscript is Frank Saddler's partitur from LA-LA-LUCILLE!, which is at the Library of Congress.

PRIMROSE

Music	GEORGE GERSHWIN
Lyrics	DESMOND CARTER & IRA GERSHWIN

Musical comedy in three acts. Opened September 11, 1924 in London and ran 255 performances. Libretto by George Grossmith and Guy Bolton. Additional lyric by B.G. DeSylva. Produced by George Grossmith and J.A.E. Malone. Directed by Charles A. Maynard. Choreographed by Laddie Cliff and Carl Hyson. Musical direction by John Ansell. Orchestrations by George Gershwin, Frank Saddler.

Synopsis and Production Information

Joan lives with her guardian, Sir Barnaby Falls, and his son, Freddie, in a mansion on the Thames. Nearby, novelist Hilary Vane has moored his houseboat, where he is currently entertaining his friend, Tony Mopham, the son of an ancient family, and Tony's girl, Pinkie Peach, a beauty specialist. Joan fancies Hilary, but becomes so disillusioned when she finds Pinkie in his arms that she runs off to London, determined to become a wild woman.

The show requires a full singing and dancing ensemble.

Orchestration

Flute I II; Oboe: Clarinet I II; Bassoon; Horn I II; Trumpet I II; Trombone I II; Drums; Harp; Violin I II; Viola I II; Cello; Bass

Comments

This was the first show in which Ira Gershwin used his own name instead of the pseudonym "Arthur Francis."

Location of Original Materials

Script: Missing
Piano-vocal score: Library of Congress, New York Public Library
    (Published: Harms, Inc. 1924)
Partiturs: Library of Congress
Parts: Missing

The published piano-vocal score lacks the Overture, Entr'actes, "That New-Fangled Mother of Mine" and "Mary, Queen of Scots." Most of the original partiturs have survived; parts were extracted from them in 1987 and sent to the Library of Congress. In 1987, Larry Moore scored the four songs for which partiturs were missing; his orchestrations are also at the Library of Congress.

Rental Status

Currently unavailable for rental

Music Publisher

Warner Brothers Music

Information

Ira Gershwin Estate, George Gershwin Family Trust

Overture

    Gershwin/Carter & Gershwin
    Orchestrator: Unknown

    Location of   - Composer's manuscript: -0-
                  - Sheet music: Unpublished
                  - Most complete music: LoC (ptr)
                  - Most complete lyric: INST
                  - Original partitur: LoC (inc)
                  - Original parts: LoC (1987)

The partitur contains only the introduction, the links between numbers, and two of the songs. In 1987, Larry Moore orchestrated the missing numbers; the partitur and parts are at the Library of Congress.

Isn't It Wonderful?

    Gershwin/Gershwin & Carter
    Orchestrator: Gershwin

    Location of   - Composer's manuscript: LoC
                  - Sheet music: LoC
                  - Most complete music: LoC (sm, pv score);
                     NYPL (pv score)
                  - Most complete lyric: LoC (sm
                     & pv score)
                  - Original partitur: LoC
                  - Original parts: LoC (1987)

Opening Chorus Act I

    Gershwin/Carter
    Orchestrator: Unknown

    Location of   - Composer's manuscript: -0-
                  - Sheet music: Not published separately
                  - Most complete music: LoC (ptr & pv score)
                  - Most complete lyric: IG (ls)
                  - Original partitur: LoC
                  - Original parts: LoC (1987)

Alternate title: "Leaving Town While We May."

This Is the Life for a Man

    Gershwin/Carter
    Orchestrator: Unknown

    Location of   - Composer's manuscript: -0-
                  - Sheet music: LoC
                  - Most complete music: LoC (sm, pv score);
                     NYPL (pv score)
                  - Most complete lyric: LoC (sm, pv score);
                     NYPL (pv score)
                  - Original partitur: LoC
                  - Original parts: LoC (1987)

Alternate title: "The Countryside."

Till I Meet Someone Like You

    Gershwin/Carter
    Orchestrator: Unknown

    Location of   - Composer's manuscript: -0-
                  - Sheet music: Not published separately
                  - Most complete music: LoC (pv score);
                     NYPL (pv score)
                  - Most complete lyric: LoC (pv score);
                     NYPL (pv score)
                  - Original partitur: -0-
                  - Original parts: -0-

Orchestrated for performance in 1987; the partitur and parts are at the Library of Congress.

When Toby Is Out of Town

    Gershwin/Carter
    Orchestrator: Unknown

    Location of   - Composer's manuscript: LoC (sk)
                  - Sheet music: Not published separately
                  - Most complete music: LoC (pv score);
                     NYPL (pv score)
                  - Most complete lyric: LoC (pv score);
                     NYPL (pv score)
                  - Original partitur: LoC
                  - Original parts: LoC (1987)

Primrose (1924)

Some Far-Away Someone

Gershwin/Gershwin & DeSylva

Orchestrator: Unknown

Location of
- Composer's manuscript: -0-
- Sheet music: LoC
- Most complete music: LoC (sm, pv score);
  NYPL (pv score)
- Most complete lyric: LoC (sm, pv score);
  NYPL (pv score)
- Original partitur: LoC
- Original parts: -0-

The music was originally used for "At Half Past Seven"
(lyrics by B.G. DeSylva) in the revue NIFTIES OF 1923.
The arrangement in the piano-vocal score includes a brief
tag.

Mophams, The

Gershwin/Carter

Orchestrator: Unknown

Location of
- Composer's manuscript: -0-
- Sheet music: Not published separately
- Most complete music: LoC (pv score);
  NYPL (pv score)
- Most complete lyric: LoC (pv score);
  NYPL (pv score)
- Original partitur: LoC
- Original parts: LoC (1987)

Finale Act I ["Can we do anything..."]

Gershwin/Gershwin & Carter

Orchestrator: Unknown

Location of
- Composer's manuscript: -0-
- Sheet music: Not published separately
- Most complete music: LoC (pv score);
  NYPL (pv score)
- Most complete lyric: LoC (pv score);
  NYPL (pv score)
- Original partitur: LoC
- Original parts: LoC (1987)

Entr'acte I

Gershwin/Carter & Gershwin

Orchestrator: Unknown

Location of
- Composer's manuscript: -0-
- Sheet music: Unpublished
- Most complete music: -0-
- Most complete lyric: INST
- Original partitur: -0-
- Original parts: -0-

Opening Chorus Act II

Gershwin/Carter

Orchestrator: Unknown

Location of
- Composer's manuscript: -0-
- Sheet music: Not published separately
- Most complete music: LoC (pv score);
  NYPL (pv score)
- Most complete lyric: LoC (pv score);
  NYPL (pv score)
- Original partitur: LoC
- Original parts: LoC (1987)

Alternate title: "Roses of France."

Four Little Sirens

Gershwin/Gershwin

Orchestrator: Unknown

Location of
- Composer's manuscript: -0-
- Sheet music: Not published separately
- Most complete music: LoC (pv score);
  NYPL (pv score)
- Most complete lyric: LoC (pv score);
  NYPL (pv score)
- Original partitur: LoC
- Original parts: LoC (1987)

Originally used in A DANGEROUS MAID (1921) under the
title "The Sirens."

79

Berkeley Square and Kew
    Gershwin/Carter
    Orchestrator: Gershwin

    Location of - Composer's manuscript: -0-
              - Sheet music: Not published separately
              - Most complete music: LoC (pv score);
                 NYPL (pv score)
              - Most complete lyric: LoC (pv score);
                 NYPL (pv score)
              - Original partitur: LoC
              - Original parts: LoC (1987)

Wait a Bit, Susie
    Gershwin/Gershwin & Carter
    Orchestrator: Unknown

    Location of - Composer's manuscript: -0-
              - Sheet music: LoC
              - Most complete music: LoC (sm, pv score);

                 NYPL (pv score)
              - Most complete lyric: LoC (sm, pv score);
                 NYPL (pv score)
              - Original partitur: -0-
              - Original parts: -0-

Orchestrated for performance in 1987; the partitur and parts are at the Library of Congress. The music was later used for "Beautiful Gypsy," intended for ROSALIE (1928).

Boy Wanted
    Gershwin/Gershwin & Carter
    Orchestrator: Saddler

    Location of - Composer's manuscript: -0-
              - Sheet music: LoC
              - Most complete music: LoC (sm, pv score);
                 NYPL (pv score)
              - Most complete lyric: IG (ls)
              - Original partitur: LoC
              - Original parts: LoC (1987)

Carter rewrote Gershwin's lyrics from A DANGEROUS MAID (1921), and the Saddler orchestration from the earlier show was used.

Mary Queen of Scots
    Gershwin/Carter
    Orchestrator: Unknown

    Location of - Composer's manuscript: -0-
              - Sheet music: Unpublished
              - Most complete music: See note
              - Most complete lyric: See note
              - Original partitur: -0-
              - Original parts: -0-

In 1987, Larry Moore created a piano-vocal from the recording by original cast members Leslie Henson and Claude Hulbert (English Columbia 9001) and then orchestrated the number for performance. The piano-vocal, partitur and parts are at the Library of Congress.

Primrose (1924)

Naughty Baby

Gershwin/Gershwin & Carter

Orchestrator: Gershwin

Location of
- Composer's manuscript: LoC (sk) &
  IG (sk)
- Sheet music: LoC
- Most complete music: LoC (pv score);
  NYPL (pv score)
- Most complete lyric: LoC (pv score);
  NYPL (pv score)
- Original partitur: LoC
- Original parts: -0-

The manuscript of the verse is at the Library of Congress; the refrain, dating from 1921, is at the Ira Gershwin Estate. The version published in the sheet music does not include the countermelody. The partitur, dated April 19, 1922, is believed to be the earliest surviving orchestration by George Gershwin.

Finale Act II

Gershwin/Carter

Orchestrator: Unknown

Location of
- Composer's manuscript: -0-
- Sheet music: Not published separately
- Most complete music: LoC (pv score);
  NYPL (pv score)
- Most complete lyric: LoC (pv score);
  NYPL (pv score)
- Original partitur: LoC
- Original parts: LoC (1987)

Alternate title: "The Fourteenth of July."

Entr'acte II

Gershwin/Carter & Gershwin

Orchestrator: -0-

Location of
- Composer's manuscript: -0-
- Sheet music: Unpublished
- Most complete music: -0-
- Most complete lyric: INST
- Original partitur: -0-
- Original parts: -0-

Ballet

Gershwin

Orchestrator: Unknown

Location of
- Composer's manuscript: -0-
- Sheet music: Not published separately
- Most complete music: LoC (pv score);
  NYPL (pv score)
- Most complete lyric: INST
- Original partitur: LoC
- Original parts: LoC (1987)

I Make Hay While the Sun Shines

Gershwin/Carter

Orchestrator: Unknown

Location of
- Composer's manuscript: -0-
- Sheet music: Not published separately
- Most complete music: LoC (pv score);
  NYPL (pv score)
- Most complete lyric: LoC (pv score);
  NYPL (pv score)
- Original partitur: -0-
- Original parts: -0-

Orchestrated for performance in 1987; the partitur and parts are at the Library of Congress.

That New-Fangled Mother of Mine

Gershwin/Carter

Orchestrator: Unknown

Location of
- Composer's manuscript: -0-
- Sheet music: LoC
- Most complete music: LoC (sm)
- Most complete lyric: LoC (sm)
- Original partitur: LoC
- Original parts: LoC (1987)

Beau Brummel

Gershwin/Carter

Orchestrator: Unknown

Location of   - Composer's manuscript: -0-
- Sheet music: Not published separately
- Most complete music: LoC (pv score);
    NYPL (pv score)
- Most complete lyric: LoC (pv score);
    NYPL(pv score)
- Original partitur: LoC
- Original parts: LoC (1987)

When You're Not at Your Best

Gershwin/Carter

Orchestrator: Unknown

Location of   - Composer's manuscript: -0-
- Sheet music: Unpublished
- Most complete music: -0-
- Most complete lyric: IG (ls)
- Original partitur: -0-
- Original parts: -0-

Unused.

Pep! Zip! And Punch!

Gershwin/Carter

Orchestrator: Unknown

Location of   - Composer's manuscript: -0-
- Sheet music: Unpublished
- Most complete music: -0-
- Most complete lyric: IG (ls)
- Original partitur: -0-
- Original parts: -0-

Unused. Alternate title: "The Live Wire."

LADY, BE GOOD!

Music	**GEORGE GERSHWIN**
Lyrics	**IRA GERSHWIN**

Musical comedy in two acts. Opened December 1, 1924 in New York and ran 330 performances (World premiere: November 17, 1924 in Philadelphia). Book by Guy Bolton and Fred Thompson. Additional lyrics by Arthur Jackson, Desmond Carter, Lou Paley. Produced by Alex A. Aarons and Vinton Freedley. Directed by Felix Edwards. Choreographed by Sammy Lee. Musical direction by Paul Lannin. Orchestrations by Robert Russell Bennett, Charles N. Grant, Paul Lannin, Stephen O. Jones, Max Steiner, William Daly.

Synopsis and Production Information

Dick and Susie Trevor are a penniless brother and sister evicted from their Rhode Island home. Dick plans to restore the family fortune by offering himself to the wealthy (and vapid) Josephine Vanderwater; Susie, desperate to save him from a loveless marriage, poses as a Spanish widow in order to procure a substantial inheritance. Complications arise when the "dead" husband turns out to be Susie's current boyfriend, Jack.

Other characters include lawyer Watty Watkins (the chief comic), Dick's love interest (Shirley), an eccentric supporting couple (Bertie and Daisy), and a strolling ukulele player. The show requires a full singing and dancing ensemble, and strong dancers in the roles of Dick and Susie.

Orchestration

Flute I II; Oboe; Clarinet I II; Bassoon; Horn I II; Trumpet I II; Trombone I II; Percussion; Harp; Piano I; Piano II; Violin I II; Viola; Cello; Bass

Comments

LADY, BE GOOD! marked the Gershwins' first successful full-length collaboration. The original cast included Fred and Adele Astaire as Dick and Susie, Walter Catlett as Watty Watkins, and Cliff ("Ukulele Ike") Edwards essentially playing himself. Victor Arden and Phil Ohman provided two-piano specialties. LADY, BE GOOD! also fared well on its post-Broadway tour and in London, where it opened on April 14, 1926 and ran 326 performances.

Location of Original Materials

Script: Library of Congress (all lyrics)
Piano-vocal score: Tams-Witmark Music Library
Partiturs: Library of Congress
Parts: Missing

Only eight of the original partiturs have been found; none of these contain Arden and Ohman's two-piano routines.

Rental Status

In 1986, Tommy Krasker compiled a new LADY, BE GOOD! libretto that uses the original script as a foundation, but reinforces it with material from the post-Broadway tour and the London production. Tams-Witmark Music Library currently rents this script, along with the original piano-vocal score and the following orchestration adapted from the original: Flute; Oboe; Clarinet; Alto Sax; Bassoon; Trumpet I II; Trombone; Percussion; Piano; Violin I; Violin II; Viola; Cello; Bass.

Music Publisher

Warner Brothers Music

Information

Tams-Witmark Music Library

Overture

Gershwin/Gershwin
Orchestrator: Unknown

Location of   - Composer's manuscript: -0-
          - Sheet music: Unpublished
          - Most complete music: LoC (ptr)
             & TW (pv score)
          - Most complete lyric: INST
          - Original partitur: LoC (inc)
          - Original parts: -0-

The partitur contains only the introduction and the links between numbers.

Hang On to Me

Gershwin/Gershwin
Orchestrator: Unknown

Location of   - Composer's manuscript: LoC (sk)
          - Sheet music: LoC, NYPL
          - Most complete music: LoC (sm);
             NYPL (sm); TW (pv score)
          - Most complete lyric: LoC (sm);
             TW (pv score, 1986 scr)
          - Original partitur: -0-
          - Original parts: -0-

The British edition of the sheet music, issued at the time of the 1926 London production, contains additional lyrics (for a second verse) that are probably not by Ira Gershwin.

Wonderful Party, A

Gershwin/Gershwin
Orchestrator: Jones

Location of   - Composer's manuscript: -0-
          - Sheet music: Unpublished
          - Most complete music: TW (pv score)
          - Most complete lyric: TW (pv score,
             1986 scr); LoC (1924 scr)
          - Original partitur: LoC
          - Original parts: -0-

End of a String, The

Gershwin/Gershwin
Orchestrator: Lannin

Location of   - Composer's manuscript: LoC (sk)
          - Sheet music: Unpublished
          - Most complete music: TW (pv score)
          - Most complete lyric: TW (1986 scr)
          - Original partitur: LoC
          - Original parts: -0-

We're Here Because

Gershwin/Gershwin
Orchestrator: Lannin

Location of   - Composer's manuscript: IG (sk)
          - Sheet music: Unpublished
          - Most complete music: TW (pv score)
          - Most complete lyric: TW (1987 scr);
             LoC (1924 scr)
          - Original partitur: LoC
          - Original parts: -0-

Fascinating Rhythm

Gershwin/Gershwin
Orchestrator: Unknown

Location of   - Composer's manuscript: LoC
          - Sheet music: LoC, NYPL
          - Most complete music: LoC (sm);
             NYPL (sm); TW (pv score)
          - Most complete lyric: IG (ls)
          - Original partitur: -0-
          - Original parts: -0-

The British edition of the sheet music, issued at the time of the 1926 London production, contains additional lyrics (for a second verse) that are probably not by Ira Gershwin.

Lady, Be Good! (1924)

So Am I

Gershwin/Gershwin
Orchestrator: Unknown

Location of - Composer's manuscript: LoC
  - Sheet music: LoC, NYPL
  - Most complete music: LoC (sm);
      NYPL (sm); TW (pv score)
  - Most complete lyric: IG (ls)
  - Original partitur: -0-
  - Original parts: -0-

The British edition of the sheet music, issued at the time of the 1926 London production, contains additional lyrics (for a second verse) that are probably not by Ira Gershwin.

Entr'acte

Gershwin/Gershwin
Orchestrator: Unknown

Location of - Composer's manuscript: -0-
  - Sheet music: Unpublished
  - Most complete music: -0-
  - Most complete lyric: INST
  - Original partitur: -0-
  - Original parts: -0-

Oh, Lady Be Good!

Gershwin/Gershwin
Orchestrator: Unknown

Location of - Composer's manuscript: LoC
  - Sheet music: LoC, NYPL
  - Most complete music: LoC (sm);
      NYPL (sm); TW (pv score)
  - Most complete lyric: IG (ls)
  - Original partitur: -0-
  - Original parts: -0-

Linger in the Lobby

Gershwin/Gershwin
Orchestrator: Bennett

Location of - Composer's manuscript: -0-
  - Sheet music: Unpublished
  - Most complete music: TW (pv score)
  - Most complete lyric: IG (ls)
  - Original partitur: LoC (inc)
  - Original parts: -0-

Added soon after the New York opening, replacing "Weather Man" and "Rainy Afternoon Girls." The first page of the partitur is missing.

Finale Act I ["Ting-a-ling, the wedding bells..."]

Gershwin/Gershwin
Orchestrator: Steiner

Location of - Composer's manuscript: -0-
  - Sheet music: Unpublished
  - Most complete music: TW (pv score)
  - Most complete lyric: TW (1986 scr)
  - Original partitur: LoC (inc)
  - Original parts: -0-

Half of It, Dearie, Blues, The

Gershwin/Gershwin
Orchestrator: Unknown

Location of - Composer's manuscript: -0-
  - Sheet music: LoC, NYPL
  - Most complete music: TW (pv score)
  - Most complete lyric: IG (ls)
  - Original partitur: -0-
  - Original parts: -0-

George & Ira Gershwin

Juanita

Gershwin/Gershwin
Orchestrator: Unknown

Location of - Composer's manuscript: IG (sk)
- Sheet music: Unpublished
- Most complete music: TW (pv score)
- Most complete lyric: TW (pv score,
     1986 scr); LoC (1924 scr)
- Original partitur: -0-
- Original parts: -0-

I'd Rather Charleston

Gershwin/Carter
Orchestrator: Unknown

Location of - Composer's manuscript: -0-
- Sheet music: LoC
- Most complete music: LoC (sm);
     TW (pv score)
- Most complete lyric: TW (1986 scr)
- Original partitur: -0-
- Original parts: -0-

This number, which was added for the London production,
is part of the current rental package.

Little Jazz Bird

Gershwin/Gershwin
Orchestrator: Unknown

Location of - Composer's manuscript: LoC
- Sheet music: LoC, NYPL, TW (x)
- Most complete music: LoC (sm);
     NYPL (sm); TW (sm-x)
- Most complete lyric: LoC (sm, 1924 scr);
     NYPL (sm); TW (sm-x, 1986 scr)
- Original partitur: -0-
- Original parts: -0-

The British edition of the sheet music, issued at the time
of the 1926 London production, contains additional lyrics
(for a second verse) that are probably not by Ira
Gershwin.

Carnival Time

Gershwin
Orchestrator: Grant

Location of - Composer's manuscript: -0-
- Sheet music: Unpublished
- Most complete music: TW (pv score)
- Most complete lyric: INST
- Original partitur: LoC
- Original parts: -0-

Swiss Miss

Gershwin/Gershwin & Jackson
Orchestrator: Unknown

Location of - Composer's manuscript: -0-
- Sheet music: LoC
- Most complete music: TW (pv score)
- Most complete lyric: TW (1986 scr)
- Original partitur: -0-
- Original parts: -0-

Published only as an instrumental piece.

Finale Act II ["Fascinating wedding..."]

Gershwin/Gershwin
Orchestrator: Unknown

Location of - Composer's manuscript: -0-
- Sheet music: Unpublished
- Most complete music: TW (pv score)
- Most complete lyric: TW (pv score,
     1986 scr); LoC (1924 scr)
- Original partitur: -0-
- Original parts: -0-

A reprise of "Fascinating Rhythm," set to new lyrics.

Lady, Be Good! (1924)

Weather Man

Gershwin/Gershwin

Orchestrator: Unknown

Location of
- Composer's manuscript: LoC
- Sheet music: Unpublished
- Most complete music: LoC (pv)
- Most complete lyric: IG (ls)
- Original partitur: -0-
- Original parts: -0-

Replaced soon after the New York opening by "Linger in the Lobby."

Man I Love, The

Gershwin/Gershwin

Orchestrator: See note

Location of
- Composer's manuscript: LoC
- Sheet music: LoC
- Most complete music: LoC (sm)
- Most complete lyric: LoC (sm)
  & NYPL (ls)
- Original partitur: See note
- Original parts: See note

Dropped during the pre-Broadway tryout. Later used in the 1927 STRIKE UP THE BAND; the Library of Congress has William Daly's partitur from that production, as well as parts that were extracted from it in 1986. The Library of Congress also has a piano-vocal that contains the music for a discarded verse.

Rainy Afternoon Girls

Gershwin/Gershwin

Orchestrator: Unknown

Location of
- Composer's manuscript: LoC
- Sheet music: Unpublished
- Most complete music: LoC (pv)
- Most complete lyric: IG (ls)
- Original partitur: -0-
- Original parts: -0-

Replaced soon after the New York opening by "Linger in the Lobby."

Seeing Dickie Home

Gershwin/Gershwin

Orchestrator: Daly

Location of
- Composer's manuscript: -0-
- Sheet music: Unpublished
- Most complete music: LoC (ptr)
- Most complete lyric: IG (ls)
- Original partitur: LoC
- Original parts: -0-

Part of the Act I opening, this number was dropped during the pre-Broadway tryout.

Leave It to Love

Gershwin/Gershwin

Orchestrator: Unknown

Location of
- Composer's manuscript: IG
- Sheet music: Unpublished
- Most complete music: IG (pv)
- Most complete lyric: -0-
- Original partitur: -0-
- Original parts: -0-

Added and dropped during the pre-Broadway tryout.

Will You Remember Me?

Gershwin/Gershwin

Orchestrator: Unknown

Location of
- Composer's manuscript: -0-
- Sheet music: Unpublished
- Most complete music: IG (pv-l)
- Most complete lyric: IG (pv-l)
- Original partitur: -0-
- Original parts: -0-

An unused duet intended for Jack and Susie, apparently replaced by "So Am I."

George & Ira Gershwin

Singin' Pete

Gershwin/Gershwin
Orchestrator: Unknown

Location of
- Composer's manuscript: -0-
- Sheet music: Unpublished
- Most complete music: LoC (p sk)
- Most complete lyric: IG (ls)
- Original partitur: -0-
- Original parts: -0-

An unused number intended for Ukulele Ike.

Buy a Little Button From Us

Gershwin/Carter
Orchestrator: Unknown

Location of
- Composer's manuscript: -0-
- Sheet music: Unpublished
- Most complete music: TW (pv score)
- Most complete lyric: TW (pv score)
- Original partitur: -0-
- Original parts: -0-

Added for the London production.

Evening Star

Gershwin/Gershwin
Orchestrator: Unknown

Location of
- Composer's manuscript: See note
- Sheet music: Unpublished
- Most complete music: IG (pv-I)
- Most complete lyric: IG (pv-I)
- Original partitur: -0-
- Original parts: -0-

Unused, intended for Shirley. The Library of Congress has a Gershwin manuscript for a male vocal arrangement written to accompany the song.

Something About Love

Gershwin/Paley
Orchestrator: Unknown

Location of
- Composer's manuscript: -0-
- Sheet music: LoC
- Most complete music: LoC (sm)
- Most complete lyric: LoC (sm)
- Original partitur: -0-
- Original parts: -0-

Originally used in THE LADY IN RED, a 1919 musical comedy with two interpolated Gershwin songs, this number was added for the London production of LADY, BE GOOD!

Bad Bad Men, The

Gershwin/Gershwin
Orchestrator: Unknown

Location of
- Composer's manuscript: IG
- Sheet music: Unpublished
- Most complete music: IG (p)
- Most complete lyric: IG (ls)
- Original partitur: -0-
- Original parts: -0-

An unused trio, with a lyric originally set to music by Vincent Youmans for TWO LITTLE GIRLS IN BLUE (1921).

TELL ME MORE

Music   GEORGE GERSHWIN
Lyrics   B.G. DESYLVA & IRA GERSHWIN

Musical comedy in two acts. Opened April 13, 1925 in New York and ran 100 performances (World premiere: April 6, 1925 in Atlantic City). Libretto by Fred Thompson and William K. Wells. Additional music and lyrics by William Daly, Lou Holtz, Desmond Carter, Claude Hulbert. Produced by Alfred E. Aarons. Directed by John Harwood. Choreographed by Sammy Lee. Musical direction by Max Steiner.

Synopsis and Production Information	Peg, a shopgirl, meets Kenneth, a polo player, at a masked ball, but is crushed to discover that he is soon leaving for his summer home in Viewport. Her debutante friend Jane is also vacationing in Viewport, and invites Peg to join her -- under one condition: Peg must allow Jane's boyfriend, a poor Jewish clerk named Monty, to pose as her brother. Second act misunderstandings abound, but all is resolved through a subplot that reunites Peg with her real brother, Kenneth's ne'er-do-well pal Billy.
	The only other key character is Peg's shopgirl pal, Bonnie, who pairs off with Billy by the Act II curtain. The show requires a full singing and dancing ensemble.
Orchestration	Unknown[3]
Comments	In the original production, Monty was played by comic Lou Holtz. Although TELL ME MORE had a brief tenure on Broadway, it enjoyed greater success in London, where it opened less than a month after the New York premiere and achieved a run of 263 performances.
	The show's pre-Broadway title, MY FAIR LADY, appears on early editions of the sheet music.
Location of Original Materials	Script: Ira Gershwin Estate (most lyrics) Piano-vocal score: See individual listings Partiturs: Missing Parts: Missing
	Most of the piano-vocal material performed in the original New York production survives, but it has not been assembled or edited.
Rental Status	Currently unavailable for rental
Music Publisher	Warner Brothers Music
Information	Ira Gershwin Estate, George Gershwin Family Trust

---

[3] A Gershwin manuscript from TELL ME MORE (at the Library of Congress) lists the following instrumentation: Flute; Oboe/English Horn; Clarinet; Clarinet/Bass Clarinet; Bassoon; Horn; Trumpet I II; Trombone; Drums; Harp; Violin I II; Viola; Cello; Bass. Since no orchestrations survive, this list cannot be verified.

Overture

Gershwin/DeSylva & Gershwin
Orchestrator: Unknown

Location of   - Composer's manuscript: -0-
          - Sheet music: Unpublished
          - Most complete music: -0-
          - Most complete lyric: INST
          - Original partitur: -0-
          - Original parts: -0-

Mr. and Mrs. Sipkin

Gershwin/DeSylva & Gershwin
Orchestrator: Unknown

Location of   - Composer's manuscript: -0-
          - Sheet music: Unpublished
          - Most complete music: LoC (pv)
          - Most complete lyric: IG (ls)
          - Original partitur: -0-
          - Original parts: -0-

The piano-vocal is entitled "Monty, Their Only Child."

Tell Me More

Gershwin/DeSylva & Gershwin
Orchestrator: Unknown

Location of   - Composer's manuscript: LoC
          - Sheet music: LoC, NYPL
          - Most complete music: LoC (sm); NYPL (sm)
          - Most complete lyric: IG (ls)
          - Original partitur: -0-
          - Original parts: -0-

When the Debbies Go By

Gershwin/DeSylva & Gershwin
Orchestrator: Unknown

Location of   - Composer's manuscript: LoC
          - Sheet music: Unpublished
          - Most complete music: LoC (pv)
          - Most complete lyric: IG (ls)
          - Original partitur: -0-
          - Original parts: -0-

Shop-Girls and Mannequins

Gershwin/DeSylva & Gershwin
Orchestrator: Unknown

Location of   - Composer's manuscript: -0-
          - Sheet music: Not published separately
          - Most complete music: LoC (pv)
          - Most complete lyric: IG (ls)
          - Original partitur: -0-
          - Original parts: -0-

Alternate titles: "Opening Act I" and "Opening Ensemble."
(It was indeed the first number performed by the
Ensemble, although it was the second number in the
show.) Published only in the British piano selection
(issued at the time of the London production), which can
be found at the Ira Gershwin Estate. The lyric is not in
the script.

Three Times a Day

Gershwin/DeSylva & Gershwin
Orchestrator: Unknown

Location of   - Composer's manuscript: -0-
          - Sheet music: LoC, NYPL
          - Most complete music: LoC (sm);
             NYPL (sm)
          - Most complete lyric: LoC (sm);
             NYPL (sm); IG (ls)
          - Original partitur: -0-
          - Original parts: -0-

Tell Me More (1925)

Why Do I Love You?
Gershwin/DeSylva & Gershwin
Orchestrator: Unknown

Location of   - Composer's manuscript: LoC
        - Sheet music: LoC, NYPL
        - Most complete music: LoC (sm); NYPL (sm)
        - Most complete lyric: LoC (sm);
            NYPL (sm); IG (scr, ls)
        - Original partitur: -0-
        - Original parts: -0-

The Ira Gershwin Estate also has a lyric sheet with an
unused countermelody.

Entr'acte
Gershwin/DeSylva & Gershwin
Orchestrator: Unknown

Location of   - Composer's manuscript: -0-
        - Sheet music: Unpublished
        - Most complete music: -0-
        - Most complete lyric: INST
        - Original partitur: -0-
        - Original parts: -0-

How Can I Win You Now?
Gershwin/DeSylva & Gershwin
Orchestrator: Unknown

Location of   - Composer's manuscript: LoC
        - Sheet music: Unpublished
        - Most complete music: LoC (p)
        - Most complete lyric: IG (ls)
        - Original partitur: -0-
        - Original parts: -0-

Replaced soon after the New York opening by "Once."

Love Is in the Air
Gershwin/DeSylva & Gershwin
Orchestrator: Unknown

Location of   - Composer's manuscript: LoC
        - Sheet music: Unpublished
        - Most complete music: LoC (pv)
        - Most complete lyric: IG (scr, ls)
        - Original partitur: -0-
        - Original parts: -0-

Alternate title: "Opening Act II."

Kickin' the Clouds Away
Gershwin/DeSylva & Gershwin
Orchestrator: Unknown

Location of   - Composer's manuscript: -0-
        - Sheet music: LoC, NYPL
        - Most complete music: LoC (sm)
        - Most complete lyric: LoC (sm);
            NYPL (sm); IG (scr, ls)
        - Original partitur: -0-
        - Original parts: -0-

The Library of Congress also has a piano-vocal with the
original dance arrangement.

My Fair Lady
Gershwin/DeSylva & Gershwin
Orchestrator: Unknown

Location of   - Composer's manuscript: -0-
        - Sheet music: LoC, NYPL
        - Most complete music: LoC (sm);
            NYPL (sm)
        - Most complete lyric: LoC (sm);
            NYPL (sm); IG (scr, ls)
        - Original partitur: -0-
        - Original parts: -0-

In the script, the number is entitled "Lady Fair."

In Sardinia

Gershwin/DeSylva & Gershwin
Orchestrator: Unknown

Location of - Composer's manuscript: LoC
  - Sheet music: Not published separately
  - Most complete music: LoC (pv)
  - Most complete lyric: IG (ls)
  - Original partitur: -0-
  - Original parts: -0-

A spoof of Jerome Kern and Clifford Grey's "The Schnitza Komisski" from SALLY (1920). The refrain was published in the piano selection from the New York production of TELL ME MORE (under the title "Where the Delicatessen Flows"); this selection can be found at the Ira Gershwin Estate.

Finaletto ["Kenneth won the yachting race..."]

Gershwin/DeSylva & Gershwin
Orchestrator: Unknown

Location of - Composer's manuscript: -0-
  - Sheet music: Unpublished
  - Most complete music: LoC (pv)
  - Most complete lyric: IG (scr, ls)
  - Original partitur: -0-
  - Original parts: -0-

Baby!

Gershwin/DeSylva & Gershwin
Orchestrator: Unknown

Location of - Composer's manuscript: -0-
  - Sheet music: LoC, NYPL
  - Most complete music: LoC (sm); NYPL (sm)
  - Most complete lyric: IG (scr, ls)
  - Original partitur: -0-
  - Original parts: -0-

The music, set to Clifford Grey lyric entitled "Sweetheart," was initially intended for an unproduced 1922 musical, FLYING ISLAND. "Sweetheart" was eventually used in the 1923 Gershwin/Grey London revue, THE RAINBOW, and published with THE RAINBOW sheet music. For TELL ME MORE, Ira Gershwin and B.G. DeSylva wrote a new lyric to the music of "Sweetheart," and the resulting song, "Baby," was introduced in TELL ME MORE and published. Finally, when TELL ME MORE played London, George Gershwin set the "Baby" lyric to new music (since London audiences had already heard the tune in THE RAINBOW). The second version of "Baby" was also published and can be found at the Library of Congress.

Poetry of Motion, The

Author(s): Unknown
Orchestrator: Unknown

Location of - Composer's manuscript: -0-
  - Sheet music: -0-
  - Most complete music: -0-
  - Most complete lyric: -0-
  - Original partitur: -0-
  - Original parts: -0-

A specialty number performed by blackface dancers Willie Covan and Leonard Ruffin.

Tell Me More (1925)

Ukulele Lorelei

Gershwin/DeSylva & Gershwin
Orchestrator: Unknown

Location of - Composer's manuscript: LoC
- Sheet music: Unpublished
- Most complete music: LoC (pv)
- Most complete lyric: IG (ls)
- Original partitur: -0-
- Original parts: -0-

Oh Sole, Oh Me!

Holtz/Holtz
Orchestrator: Unknown

Location of - Composer's manuscript: -0-
- Sheet music: Unpublished
- Most complete music: LoC (p)
- Most complete lyric: See note
- Original partitur: -0-
- Original parts: -0-

Listed in the New York programs as "Oh, So La Mi." Lou Holtz's specialty number, which he had been performing in vaudeville for a number of years, was based on "O Sole Mio!", the 19th-century Neopolitan song by Edoardo di Capua and Giovanni Capurro. Holtz recorded the song twice on Victor, first in the spring of 1923 (Victor 19079) and then (with different lyrics) a year later (Victor 19403).

Once

Daly/Gershwin
Orchestrator: Unknown

Location of - Composer's manuscript: -0-
- Sheet music: Unpublished
- Most complete music: LoC (p)
- Most complete lyric: IG (ls)
- Original partitur: -0-
- Original parts: -0-

Replaced "How Can I Win You Now?" soon after the New York opening. George Gershwin later set the lyric to new music for FUNNY FACE (1927); Tams-Witmark Music Library has a piano-vocal of that version, which contains a few alternate lyrics.

I'm Somethin' on Avenue A

Gershwin/DeSylva & Gershwin
Orchestrator: Unknown

Location of - Composer's manuscript: -0-
- Sheet music: Unpublished
- Most complete music: -0-
- Most complete lyric: IG (ls)
- Original partitur: -0-
- Original parts: -0-

Dropped during the pre-Broadway tryout.

He-Man, The

Gershwin/DeSylva & Gershwin
Orchestrator: Unknown

Location of - Composer's manuscript: LoC
- Sheet music: Unpublished
- Most complete music: LoC (pv)
- Most complete lyric: IG (ls)
- Original partitur: -0-
- Original parts: -0-

Dropped during the pre-Broadway tryout.

Gushing

Gershwin/Gershwin
Orchestrator: Unknown

Location of - Composer's manuscript: LoC
- Sheet music: Unpublished
- Most complete music: LoC (pv)
- Most complete lyric: IG (ls)
- Original partitur: -0-
- Original parts: -0-

Unused. Later intended for ROSALIE (1928), but again unused.

Murderous Monty (and Light Fingered Jane)

Gershwin/Carter

Orchestrator: Unknown

Location of   - Composer's manuscript: -0-
- Sheet music: LoC
- Most complete music: LoC (sm)
- Most complete lyric: LoC (sm)
- Original partitur: -0-
- Original parts: -0-

Added for the London production.

Have You Heard?

Gershwin/Hulbert

Orchestrator: Unknown

Location of   - Composer's manuscript: -0-
- Sheet music: Unpublished
- Most complete music: -0-
- Most complete lyric: -0-
- Original partitur: -0-
- Original parts: -0-

Added for the London production.

Love, I Never Knew

Gershwin/Carter

Orchestrator: Unknown

Location of   - Composer's manuscript: -0-
- Sheet music: Not published separately
- Most complete music: IG (p sel)
- Most complete lyric: -0-
- Original partitur: -0-
- Original parts: -0-

Added for the London production. Published only in the British piano selection, which can be found at the Ira Gershwin Estate.

TIP-TOES

Music **GEORGE GERSHWIN**
Lyrics **IRA GERSHWIN**

Musical comedy in two acts. Opened December 28, 1925 in New York and ran 194 performances (World premiere: November 24, 1925 in Washington, D.C.). Libretto by Guy Bolton and Fred Thompson. Produced by Alex A. Aarons and Vinton Freedley. Directed by John Harwood. Choreographed by Sammy Lee. Musical direction by William Daly.

Synopsis and Production Information	"Tip-Toes" Kaye, a vaudeville dancer, is persuaded by her partners, Al and Uncle Hen, to masquerade as a lady of wealth in Florida in order to snare a rich husband. Tip-Toes lands a wealthy glue magnate, Steve Metcalf, but their courtship is cut short when she's hit by a car and loses her memory. Steve is furious when he discovers Tip-Toes' deception,[4] but she finally convinces him that he means more to her than his money.
	The show requires a full singing and dancing ensemble.
Orchestration	Flute; Oboe; Clarinet I II; Bassoon; Horn I II; Trumpet I II; Trombone; Percussion; Piano I; Piano II; Violin I Desk 1; Violin I Desk 2; Violin I Desk 3; Viola I; Viola II; Cello; Bass
Comments	The original production included the two-piano team of Victor Arden and Phil Ohman. TIP-TOES also enjoyed a successful London run in 1926.
Location of Original Materials	Script: Tams-Witmark Music Library (all lyrics), Library of Congress (all lyrics) Piano-vocal score: Tams-Witmark Music Library Partiturs: Missing Parts: Library of Congress
	Roughly 85 percent of the original parts have been located, but they have not been edited or corrected.
Rental Status	Tams-Witmark Music Library rents the original book and piano-vocal score, along with the following 1947 orchestration loosely based on the original: Flute/Piccolo (optional); Reed I (Clarinet, Alto Sax); Reed II (Clarinet, Alto Sax); Reed III (Flute, Tenor Sax); Reed IV (Clarinet, Tenor Sax); Trumpet I II; Trombone I; Trombone II; Percussion; Piano I; Piano II; Violin AB; Violin CD; Viola; Cello; Bass.
Music Publisher	Warner Brothers Music
Information	Tams-Witmark Music Library

---

4   Strangely, he never notices that she has amnesia.

Overture

Gershwin/Gershwin
Orchestrator: Unknown

Location of - Composer's manuscript: -0-
               - Sheet music: Unpublished
               - Most complete music: LoC (parts)
               - Most complete lyric: INST
               - Original partitur: -0-
               - Original parts: LoC

Looking for a Boy

Gershwin/Gershwin
Orchestrator: Unknown

Location of - Composer's manuscript: -0-
               - Sheet music: LoC, NYPL
               - Most complete music: LoC (sm);
                    NYPL (sm); TW (pv score)
               - Most complete lyric: IG (ls)
               - Original partitur: -0-
               - Original parts: LoC (inc)

The British edition of the sheet music, issued at the time of the London production, contains additional lyrics (for a second verse) that are probably not by Ira Gershwin.

Waiting for the Train

Gershwin/Gershwin
Orchestrator: Unknown

Location of - Composer's manuscript: -0-
               - Sheet music: Not published separately
               - Most complete music: TW (pv score)
               - Most complete lyric: TW (scr); LoC (scr)
               - Original partitur: -0-
               - Original parts: LoC (inc)

Alternate titles: "Florida" and "Opening Act I." A section of this number was published in the piano selection from the New York production; this selection can be found at the Ira Gershwin Estate.

Lady Luck

Gershwin/Gershwin
Orchestrator: Unknown

Location of - Composer's manuscript: -0-
               - Sheet music: Unpublished
               - Most complete music: TW (pv score)
               - Most complete lyric: TW (pv score, scr);
                    LoC (scr)
               - Original partitur: -0-
               - Original parts: LoC

Nice Baby

Gershwin/Gershwin
Orchestrator: Unknown

Location of - Composer's manuscript: -0-
               - Sheet music: LoC, NYPL
               - Most complete music: LoC (sm);
                    NYPL (sm); TW (pv score)
               - Most complete lyric: LoC (sm, scr);
                    NYPL (sm); TW (pv score, scr)
               - Original partitur: -0-
               - Original parts: LoC (inc)

When Do We Dance?

Gershwin/Gershwin
Orchestrator: Unknown

Location of - Composer's manuscript: -0-
               - Sheet music: LoC, NYPL
               - Most complete music: LoC (sm);
                    NYPL (sm); TW (pv score)
               - Most complete lyric: LoC (sm, scr);
                    NYPL (sm); TW (pv score, scr)
               - Original partitur: -0-
               - Original parts: LoC (inc)

Tip-Toes (1925)

These Charming People
Gershwin/Gershwin
Orchestrator: Unknown

Location of   - Composer's manuscript: -0-
             - Sheet music: LoC, NYPL
             - Most complete music: LoC (sm);
                NYPL (sm), TW (pv score)
             - Most complete lyric: IG (ls)
             - Original partitur: -0-
             - Original parts: LoC

The British edition of the sheet music, issued at the time of the London production, contains alternate lyrics to the second verse that are probably not by Ira Gershwin.

That Certain Feeling
Gershwin/Gershwin
Orchestrator: Unknown

Location of   - Composer's manuscript: LoC (r)
             - Sheet music: LoC, NYPL
             - Most complete music: LoC (sm);
                NYPL (sm); TW (pv score)
             - Most complete lyric: IG (ls)
             - Original partitur: -0-
             - Original parts: LoC

Sweet and Low-Down
Gershwin/Gershwin
Orchestrator: Unknown

Location of   - Composer's manuscript: LoC (r)
             - Sheet music: LoC, NYPL
             - Most complete music: LoC (sm);
                NYPL (sm); TW (pv score)
             - Most complete lyric: LoC (sm, scr);
                NYPL (sm); TW (pv score, scr); LOSO
             - Original partitur: -0-
             - Original parts: LoC (inc)

Finale Act I ["Oh, what was that noise?"]
Gershwin/Gershwin
Orchestrator: Unknown

Location of   - Composer's manuscript: -0-
             - Sheet music: Unpublished
             - Most complete music: TW (pv score)
             - Most complete lyric: TW (scr); LoC (scr)
             - Original partitur: -0-
             - Original parts: LoC (inc)

Entr'acte
Gershwin/Gershwin
Orchestrator: Unknown

Location of   - Composer's manuscript: -0-
             - Sheet music: Unpublished
             - Most complete music: LoC (parts)
             - Most complete lyric: INST
             - Original partitur: -0-
             - Original parts: LoC (inc)

Our Little Captain
Gershwin/Gershwin
Orchestrator: Unknown

Location of   - Composer's manuscript: -0-
             - Sheet music: Unpublished
             - Most complete music: TW (pv score)
             - Most complete lyric: TW (scr); LoC (scr)
             - Original partitur: -0-
             - Original parts: LoC (inc)

The lyric is not in the piano-vocal score. There are no orchestra parts for this number in the Tams-Witmark rental package.

It's a Great Little World

Gershwin/Gershwin
Orchestrator: Unknown

Location of - Composer's manuscript: LoC
- Sheet music: IG
- Most complete music: IG (sm);
    TW (pv score)
- Most complete lyric: IG (sm);
    TW (pv score, scr); LoC (scr)
- Original partitur: -0-
- Original parts: LoC

Alternate title: "Give In." Some copies of the British edition of the sheet music, which was issued at the time of the London production, contain additional lyrics (for a second verse and refrain) that are probably not by Ira Gershwin.

Nightie-Night

Gershwin/Gershwin
Orchestrator: Unknown

Location of - Composer's manuscript: -0-
- Sheet music: LoC
- Most complete music: LoC (sm)
- Most complete lyric: IG (ls)
- Original partitur: -0-
- Original parts: LoC (inc)

The verse, which was not performed in the original production, is not included in the piano-vocal score.

Tip-Toes

Gershwin/Gershwin
Orchestrator: Unknown

Location of - Composer's manuscript: -0-
- Sheet music: Unpublished
- Most complete music: TW (pv score)
- Most complete lyric: TW (scr); LoC (scr)
- Original partitur: -0-
- Original parts: LoC (inc)

There are no orchestra parts for this number in the Tams-Witmark rental package; instead there are parts for a song entitled "Stamp Your Worries Away." The authorship of "Stamp Your Worries Away" is unknown.

Finale Act II ["I've learned my lesson..."]

Gershwin/Gershwin
Orchestrator: Unknown

Location of - Composer's manuscript: -0-
- Sheet music: Unpublished
- Most complete music: TW (pv score)
- Most complete lyric: TW (pv score, scr)
- Original partitur: -0-
- Original parts: LoC (inc)

A reprise of "That Certain Feeling," set to new lyrics.

Harlem River Chanty

Gershwin/Gershwin
Orchestrator: Unknown

Location of - Composer's manuscript: -0-
- Sheet music: See note
- Most complete music: See note
- Most complete lyric: LOSO
- Original partitur: -0-
- Original parts: -0-

Dropped during the pre-Broadway tryout. Initial publication in 1968 in a choral arrangement, which can be found at the Ira Gershwin Estate.

Harbor of Dreams

Gershwin/Gershwin
Orchestrator: Unknown

Location of - Composer's manuscript: -0-
- Sheet music: Unpublished
- Most complete music: -0-
- Most complete lyric: IG (ls)
- Original partitur: -0-
- Original parts: -0-

Dropped during the pre-Broadway tryout.

Tip-Toes (1925)

Dancing Hour

    Gershwin/Gershwin

    Orchestrator: Unknown

    Location of   - Composer's manuscript: -0-

                 - Sheet music: Unpublished

                 - Most complete music: -0-

                 - Most complete lyric: -0-

                 - Original partitur: -0-

                 - Original parts: -0-

Dropped during the pre-Broadway tryout. Later used in FUNNY FACE (1927), but again dropped before the New York opening.

Gather Ye Rosebuds

    Gershwin/Gershwin

    Orchestrator: Unknown

    Location of   - Composer's manuscript: -0-

                 - Sheet music: Unpublished

                 - Most complete music: IG (pv-I)

                 - Most complete lyric: IG (pv-I)

                 - Original partitur: -0-

                 - Original parts: -0-

Dropped during the pre-Broadway tryout.

Life's Too Short to Be Blue

    Gershwin/Gershwin

    Orchestrator: Unknown

    Location of   - Composer's manuscript: -0-

                 - Sheet music: Unpublished

                 - Most complete music: -0-

                 - Most complete lyric: IG (ls)

                 - Original partitur: -0-

                 - Original parts: -0-

Dropped during the pre-Broadway tryout.

We

    Gershwin/Gershwin

    Orchestrator: Unknown

    Location of   - Composer's manuscript: -0-

                 - Sheet music: Unpublished

                 - Most complete music: -0-

                 - Most complete lyric: IG (ls)

                 - Original partitur: -0-

                 - Original parts: -0-

Unused.

SONG OF THE FLAME

Music	GEORGE GERSHWIN & HERBERT STOTHART
Lyrics	OTTO HARBACH & OSCAR HAMMERSTEIN II

Operetta in two acts. Opened December 30, 1925 in New York and ran 219 performances (World premiere: December 9, 1925 in Wilmington, Delaware). Libretto by Otto Harbach and Oscar Hammerstein II. Produced by Arthur Hammerstein. Directed by Frank Reicher. Choreographed by Jack Haskell. Musical direction by Herbert Stothart. Orchestrations by Robert Russell Bennett.

Synopsis and Production Information

Konstantin and Aniuta are leaders in the Communist uprising in Russia. Though Aniuta (a.k.a. "The Flame") loves Volodya, a Prince of the old establishment, and vows to do him no harm, Konstantin plunders his palace anyway. The principals then flee to Paris, where Aniuta learns that Konstanin has used the Prince's stolen money for his own personal gain. Konstantin is banished to Siberia, Volodya gets his wealth back, and Volodya and Aniuta decide to return to Russia to fight for the ideals they once shared.

Others characters include Count Boris, a landowner who is neither good-looking, bright, nor popular with the ladies; Nicholas, one of Boris' workers; and Tartar, a tough peasant woman. There is a full singing and dancing ensemble.

Orchestration

Flute I II; Oboe (English Horn); Clarinet I II; Bassoon; Horn I II; Trumpet I II; Trumpet III; Trombone; Tuba; Percussion I II; Harp (Celeste); Violin I II; Viola I; Viola II; Cello; Bass

Comments

The original cast of two hundred included the Russian Art Choir and the American Ballet.

Location of Original Materials

Script: Tams-Witmark Music Library (few lyrics), New York Public Library (few lyrics), Library of Congress (few lyrics)
Piano-vocal score: Tams-Witmark Music Library
Partiturs: Missing
Parts: Tams-Witmark Music Library

In the original production, the Russian Art Choir sang several traditional Russian folks songs. Some of these are in the piano-vocal score; four were published separately ("The Field," "In the Village," "The Pines of the Village," and "I Was There") and can be found at the New York Public Library and at Tams-Witmark Music Library.

Rental Status

Currently unavailable for rental

Music Publisher

Warner Brothers Music

Information

Ira Gershwin Estate, George Gershwin Family Trust

Song of the Flame (1925)

Overture

Gershwin & Stothart/Harbach & Hammerstein
Orchestrator: Unknown

Location of   - Composer's manuscript: -0-
              - Sheet music: Unpublished
              - Most complete music: TW (pv score)
              - Most complete lyric: INST
              - Original partitur: -0-
              - Original parts: TW

Song of the Flame, The

Gershwin & Stothart/Harbach & Hammerstein
Orchestrator: Unknown

Location of   - Composer's manuscript: -0-
              - Sheet music: LoC, NYPL, TW
              - Most complete music: LoC (sm);
                    NYPL (sm); TW (sm, pv score)
              - Most complete lyric: LoC (sm);
                    NYPL (sm); TW (sm, pv score)
              - Original partitur: -0-
              - Original parts: TW

Prelude

Gershwin & Stothart/Harbach & Hammerstein
Orchestrator: Unknown

Location of   - Composer's manuscript: -0-
              - Sheet music: Unpublished
              - Most complete music: TW (pv score)
              - Most complete lyric: TW (pv score)
              - Original partitur: -0-
              - Original parts: TW

Woman's Work Is Never Done

Gershwin & Stothart/Harbach & Hammerstein
Orchestrator: Unknown

Location of   - Composer's manuscript: -0-
              - Sheet music: Unpublished
              - Most complete music: TW (pv score)
              - Most complete lyric: TW (pv score)
              - Original partitur: -0-
              - Original parts: TW

Far Away

Gershwin & Stothart/Harbach & Hammerstein
Orchestrator: Unknown

Location of   - Composer's manuscript: -0-
              - Sheet music: Unpublished
              - Most complete music: TW (pv score)
              - Most complete lyric: TW (pv score)
              - Original partitur: -0-
              - Original parts: TW

Great Big Bear

Stothart/Harbach & Hammerstein
Orchestrator: Unknown

Location of   - Composer's manuscript: -0-
              - Sheet music: LoC, NYPL, TW
              - Most complete music: LoC (sm);
                    NYPL (sm); TW (sm, pv score)
              - Most complete lyric: LoC (sm);
                    NYPL (sm); TW (sm, pv score)
              - Original partitur: -0-
              - Original parts: TW

Signal, The
Gershwin/Harbach & Hammerstein
Orchestrator: Unknown

Location of   - Composer's manuscript: -0-
            - Sheet music: LoC, NYPL, TW
            - Most complete music: LoC (sm);
                NYPL (sm); TW (sm, pv score)
            - Most complete lyric: LoC (sm);
                NYPL (sm); TW (sm, pv score)
            - Original partitur: -0-
            - Original parts: TW

You May Wander Away
Stothart/Harbach & Hammerstein
Orchestrator: Unknown

Location of   - Composer's manuscript: -0-
            - Sheet music: LoC, NYPL, TW
            - Most complete music: LoC (sm);
                NYPL (sm); TW (sm, pv score)
            - Most complete lyric: LoC (sm);
                NYPL (sm); TW (sm, pv score)
            - Original partitur: -0-
            - Original parts: TW

Cossack's Love Song, The
Gershwin & Stothart/Harbach & Hammerstein
Orchestrator: Unknown

Location of   - Composer's manuscript: -0-
            - Sheet music: LoC, NYPL, TW
            - Most complete music: LoC (sm);
                NYPL (sm); TW (sm, pv score)
            - Most complete lyric: LoC (sm);
                NYPL (sm); TW (sm, pv score)
            - Original partitur: -0-
            - Original parts: TW

Finaletto ["You may wander away..."]
Gershwin & Stothart/Harbach & Hammerstein
Orchestrator: Unknown

Location of   - Composer's manuscript: -0-
            - Sheet music: Unpublished
            - Most complete music: TW (pv score)
            - Most complete lyric: TW (pv score)
            - Original partitur: -0-
            - Original parts: TW

Tartar!
Gershwin & Stothart/Harbach & Hammerstein
Orchestrator: Unknown

Location of   - Composer's manuscript: -0-
            - Sheet music: Not published separately
            - Most complete music: TW (pv score)
            - Most complete lyric: TW (pv score)
            - Original partitur: -0-
            - Original parts: TW

Published only in the piano selection, which can be found
at the Ira Gershwin Estate.

Vodka
Gershwin & Stothart/Harbach & Hammerstein
Orchestrator: Unknown

Location of   - Composer's manuscript: -0-
            - Sheet music: LoC, NYPL, TW
            - Most complete music: LoC (sm);
                NYPL (sm); TW (sm, pv score)
            - Most complete lyric: LoC (sm);
                NYPL (sm); TW (sm, pv score)
            - Original partitur: -0-
            - Original parts: TW

Finale Act I ["You dogs! You pack of drunken libertines!"]
    Gershwin & Stothart/Harbach & Hammerstein
    Orchestrator: Unknown

    Location of   - Composer's manuscript: -0-
               - Sheet music: Unpublished
               - Most complete music: TW (pv score)
               - Most complete lyric: TW (pv score)
               - Original partitur: -0-
               - Original parts: TW

Entr'acte
    Gershwin & Stothart/Harbach & Hammerstein
    Orchestrator: Unknown

    Location of   - Composer's manuscript: -0-
               - Sheet music: Unpublished
               - Most complete music: TW (parts)
               - Most complete lyric: INST
               - Original partitur: -0-
               - Original parts: TW

I Want Two Husbands
    Stothart/Harbach & Hammerstein
    Orchestrator: Bennett

    Location of   - Composer's manuscript: -0-
               - Sheet music: Unpublished
               - Most complete music: TW (ptr)
               - Most complete lyric: -0-
               - Original partitur: TW
               - Original parts: TW

Dropped soon after the New York opening.

Midnight Bells
    Gershwin/Harbach & Hammerstein
    Orchestrator: Unknown

    Location of   - Composer's manuscript: -0-
               - Sheet music: NYPL, TW
               - Most complete music: NYPL (sm);
                  TW (sm)
               - Most complete lyric: NYPL (sm);
                  TW (sm)
               - Original partitur: -0-
               - Original parts: -0-

Dropped soon after the New York opening.

Ballet – The First Blossom
    Gershwin & Stothart/Harbach & Hammerstein
    Orchestrator: Unknown

    Location of   - Composer's manuscript: -0-
               - Sheet music: Unpublished
               - Most complete music: TW (pv score)
               - Most complete lyric: TW (pv score)
               - Original partitur: -0-
               - Original parts: TW

Alternate title: "The Snow Ballet."

Finaletto Act II
    Gershwin & Stothart/Harbach & Hammerstein
    Orchestrator: Unknown

    Location of   - Composer's manuscript: -0-
               - Sheet music: Unpublished
               - Most complete music: -0-
               - Most complete lyric: -0-
               - Original partitur: -0-
               - Original parts: TW

Finale Ultimo ["Far away, too far away..."]

Gershwin & Stothart/Harbach & Hammerstein
Orchestrator: Unknown

Location of   - Composer's manuscript: -0-
- Sheet music: Unpublished
- Most complete music: TW (pv score)
- Most complete lyric: TW (pv score)
- Original partitur: -0-
- Original parts: TW

You and You and Me

Stothart/Harbach & Hammerstein
Orchestrator: Unknown

Location of   - Composer's manuscript: -0-
- Sheet music: Unpublished
- Most complete music: -0-
- Most complete lyric: -0-
- Original partitur: -0-
- Original parts: -0-

Dropped during the pre-Broadway tryout.

You Are You

Gershwin & Stothart/Harbach & Hammerstein
Orchestrator: Unknown

Location of   - Composer's manuscript: -0-
- Sheet music: LoC, NYPL
- Most complete music: LoC (sm); NYPL (sm)
- Most complete lyric: LoC (sm); NYPL (sm)
- Original partitur: -0-
- Original parts: -0-

Dropped during the pre-Broadway tryout.

OH, KAY!

Music   **GEORGE GERSHWIN**
Lyrics   **IRA GERSHWIN**

Musical comedy in two acts. Opened November 8, 1926 in New York and ran 256 performances (World premiere: October 18, 1926 in Philadelphia). Libretto by Guy Bolton and P.G. Wodehouse. Additional lyrics by Howard Dietz. Produced by Alex A. Aarons and Vinton Freedley. Directed by John Harwood. Choreographed by Sammy Lee. Musical direction by William Daly. Orchestrations by Hilding Anderson.

Synopsis and Production Information	Three charming bootleggers -- Larry, Shorty and the Duke -- have secretly used Jimmy Winter's summer home as a storage space for liquor while he was off getting married. When Jimmy arrives with his new bride, Constance, the trio arrange for Shorty to pose as the new family butler. Soon Jimmy discovers that his marriage is invalid; Constance storms out, and in comes Kay, the Duke's sister, who is hiding from a Revenue officer. Kay convinces Jimmy to let her pose as his new wife, and then, when Constance returns, as Shorty's wife, a cockney cook. After numerous masquerades, misundertandings, and denouements, Jimmy claims Kay as the next Mrs. Winter.
	The only other key characters are Constance's stuffy father and a distaff pair of twins. The show requires a full singing and dancing ensemble. Constance, her father, Shorty, and the Duke are non-singing roles.
Orchestration	Flute I II; Oboe: Clarinet I II; Bassoon; Horn I II; Trumpet I II; Trombone; Drums; Piano I; Piano II; Harp; Violin I II III; Viola I II; Cello; Bass
Comments	In the original production, Kay was played by Gertrude Lawrence, Shorty by Victor Moore. Victor Arden and Phil Ohman provided two-piano specialties.
Location of Original Materials	Script: Library of Congress (all lyrics) Piano-vocal score: Tams-Witmark Music Library Partiturs: Library of Congress Parts: Missing
	All of the piano-vocal material performed in the original New York production survives except the music to the "Finaletto Act I." Original orchestrations are missing for all numbers except the Overture. The Library of Congress has an early draft of the script with an opening scene that was eventually cut; it contains an exchange between Kay and Shorty that appears to have been Ira Gershwin's inspiration for "Someone to Watch Over Me."
Rental Status	Tams-Witmark rents the original script and songs (minus the missing passage), along with the following orchestration loosely based on the original: Flute; Oboe; Clarinet I II; Bassoon; Horn I II; Trumpet I II; Trombone; Percussion; Piano; Violin I; Violin II; Viola; Cello; Bass.
Music Publisher	Warner Brothers Music
Information	Tams-Witmark Music Library

Overture

Gershwin/Gershwin & Dietz
Orchestrator: Anderson

Location of - Composer's manuscript: LoC (sk)
          - Sheet music: Unpublished
          - Most complete music: LoC (ptr)
          - Most complete lyric: INST
          - Original partitur: LoC (inc)
          - Original parts: -0-

The partitur contains only the introduction and the links between numbers. In 1986, Larry Moore orchestrated the missing songs; the new partitur and parts are at the Ira Gershwin Estate. The Tams-Witmark piano-vocal score contains an entirely different Overture, one based on an OH, KAY! piano selection.

Woman's Touch, The

Gershwin/Gershwin
Orchestrator: Unknown

Location of - Composer's manuscript: -0-
          - Sheet music: Not published separately
          - Most complete music: TW (pv score)
          - Most complete lyric: TW (pv score);
             LoC (scr)
          - Original partitur: -0-
          - Original parts: -0-

Initial publication in the OH, KAY! vocal selections (Warner Brothers: 1984).

Don't Ask

Gershwin/Gershwin
Orchestrator: Unknown

Location of - Composer's manuscript: -0-
          - Sheet music: Not published separately
          - Most complete music: TW (pv score)
          - Most complete lyric: TW (pv score);
             LoC (scr)
          - Original partitur: -0-
          - Original parts: -0-

Initial publication in the OH, KAY! vocal selections (Warner Brothers: 1984). The Ira Gershwin Estate also has the lyrics for an early version entitled "Guess Who?"

Dear Little Girl

Gershwin/Gershwin
Orchestrator: Unknown

Location of - Composer's manuscript: -0-
          - Sheet music: LoC, NYPL
          - Most complete music: LoC (sm);
             NYPL (sm); TW (pv score)
          - Most complete lyric: IG (ls)
          - Original partitur: -0-
          - Original parts: -0-

Initial publication following the song's inclusion in the 1968 film, STAR!

Maybe

Gershwin/Gershwin
Orchestrator: Unknown

Location of - Composer's manuscript: -0-
          - Sheet music: LoC, NYPL
          - Most complete music: LoC (sm);
             NYPL (sm); TW (pv score)
          - Most complete lyric: LoC (scr);
             TW (pv score)
          - Original partitur: -0-
          - Original parts: -0-

The Ira Gershwin Estate has a lyric sheet with an unused second act reprise.

Clap Yo' Hands

Gershwin/Gershwin
Orchestrator: Unknown

Location of - Composer's manuscript: LoC (r)
          - Sheet music: LoC, NYPL
          - Most complete music: LoC (sm);
             NYPL (sm); TW (pv score)
          - Most complete lyric: LoC (sm, scr);
             NYPL (sm); TW (pv score); LOSO
          - Original partitur: -0-
          - Original parts: -0-

Oh, Kay! (1926)

Do-Do-Do
Gershwin/Gershwin
Orchestrator: Unknown

Location of   - Composer's manuscript: LoC (r)
    - Sheet music: LoC, NYPL
    - Most complete music: LoC (sm);
        NYPL (sm); TW (pv score)
    - Most complete lyric: LoC (sm, scr);
        NYPL (sm); TW (pv score)
    - Original partitur: -0-
    - Original parts: -0-

The lyrics in the Tams-Witmark script are incomplete.

Finaletto ["Yes, we heard a noise..."]
Gershwin/Gershwin
Orchestrator: Unknown

Location of   - Composer's manuscript: -0-
    - Sheet music: Unpublished
    - Most complete music: See note
    - Most complete lyric: LoC (scr); IG (ls)
    - Original partitur: -0-
    - Original parts: -0-

These passages, which weave in and out of dialogue, are not included in the Tams-Witmark rental package. The music to the one section ("Oh, it's perfectly grand...") was printed in the OH, KAY! piano selection that Tams-Witmark uses as an Overture; the music to the remainder of the Finaletto is missing.

Finale Act I ["Isn't it grand. Clap-a yo' hand!"]
Gershwin/Gershwin
Orchestrator: Unknown

Location of   - Composer's manuscript: -0-
    - Sheet music: Unpublished
    - Most complete music: TW (pv score)
    - Most complete lyric: TW (pv score);
        LoC (scr)
    - Original partitur: -0-
    - Original parts: -0-

Essentially "Clap Yo' Hands" set to new lyrics.

Entr'acte
Gershwin/Gershwin
Orchestrator: Unknown

Location of   - Composer's manuscript: -0-
    - Sheet music: Unpublished
    - Most complete music: -0-
    - Most complete lyric: INST
    - Original partitur: -0-
    - Original parts: -0-

Bride and Groom
Gershwin/Gershwin
Orchestrator: Unknown

Location of   - Composer's manuscript: -0-
    - Sheet music: Not published separately
    - Most complete music: TW (pv score)
    - Most complete lyric: TW (pv score);
        LoC (scr)
    - Original partitur: -0-
    - Original parts: -0-

Initial publication in the OH, KAY! vocal selections (Warner Brothers: 1984). Alternate titles: "Opening Act II" and "Never Too Late to Mend-elssohn." The Ira Gershwin Estate has a lyric sheet with an unused second act reprise.

Someone to Watch Over Me
Gershwin/Gershwin
Orchestrator: Unknown

Location of   - Composer's manuscript: -0-
    - Sheet music: LoC, NYPL
    - Most complete music: LoC (sm);
        NYPL (sm); TW (pv score)
    - Most complete lyric: IG (ls)
    - Original partitur: -0-
    - Original parts: -0-

Fidgety Feet

Gershwin/Gershwin
Orchestrator: Unknown

Location of - Composer's manuscript: -0-
- Sheet music: LoC, NYPL
- Most complete music: LoC (sm);
  NYPL (sm); TW (pv score)
- Most complete lyric: LoC (sm, scr);
  NYPL (sm); TW (pv score)
- Original partitur: -0-
- Original parts: -0-

Show Me the Town

Gershwin/Gershwin
Orchestrator: See note

Location of - Composer's manuscript: -0-
- Sheet music: LoC, NYPL
- Most complete music: LoC (sm);
  NYPL (sm)
- Most complete lyric: IG (ls)
- Original partitur: See note
- Original parts: See note

Replaced before the New York opening by "Dear Little Girl." Later used (with a different verse) in ROSALIE (1928). Tams-Witmark has the later version in its ROSALIE piano-vocal score. The Library of Congress has a Hans Spialek partitur for the ROSALIE "Show Me the Town"; Tams-Witmark has the corresponding parts.

Heaven on Earth

Gershwin/Gershwin & Dietz
Orchestrator: Unknown

Location of - Composer's manuscript: -0-
- Sheet music: LoC, NYPL
- Most complete music: LoC (sm);
  NYPL (sm); TW (pv score)
- Most complete lyric: LoC (sm, scr);
  NYPL (sm); TW (pv score)
- Original partitur: -0-
- Original parts: -0-

What's the Use?

Gershwin/Gershwin
Orchestrator: Unknown

Location of - Composer's manuscript: -0-
- Sheet music: Unpublished
- Most complete music: -0-
- Most complete lyric: IG (ls)
- Original partitur: -0-
- Original parts: -0-

Unused.

Oh, Kay!

Gershwin/Gershwin & Dietz
Orchestrator: Unknown

Location of - Composer's manuscript: -0-
- Sheet music: LoC, NYPL
- Most complete music: LoC (sm);
  NYPL (sm); TW (pv score)
- Most complete lyric: LoC (sm, scr);
  NYPL (sm); TW (pv score)
- Original partitur: -0-
- Original parts: -0-

Moon Is on the Sea, The

Gershwin/Gershwin
Orchestrator: Unknown

Location of - Composer's manuscript: -0-
- Sheet music: Unpublished
- Most complete music: -0-
- Most complete lyric: IG (ls)
- Original partitur: -0-
- Original parts: -0-

Unused. Alternate title: "The Sun Is on the Sea."

Oh, Kay! (1926)

Stepping With Baby
Gershwin/Gershwin
Orchestrator: Unknown

Location of   - Composer's manuscript: -0-
            - Sheet music: Unpublished
            - Most complete music: -0-
            - Most complete lyric: IG (ls)
            - Original partitur: -0-
            - Original parts: -0-

Unused.

When Our Ship Comes Sailing In
Gershwin/Gershwin & Dietz
Orchestrator: Unknown

Location of   - Composer's manuscript: -0-
            - Sheet music: Unpublished
            - Most complete music: IG (pv)
            - Most complete lyric: IG (ls)
            - Original partitur: -0-
            - Original parts: -0-

Unused.

Ain't It Romantic?
Gershwin/Gershwin
Orchestrator: Unknown

Location of   - Composer's manuscript: -0-
            - Sheet music: Unpublished
            - Most complete music: IG (pv-l)
            - Most complete lyric: IG (ls)
            - Original partitur: -0-
            - Original parts: -0-

An unused duet for Kay and Shorty.

Finaletto Act II, Scene 1 ["On single life today the curtain's falling..."]
Gershwin/Gershwin
Orchestrator: Unknown

Location of   - Composer's manuscript: -0-
            - Sheet music: Unpublished
            - Most complete music: -0-
            - Most complete lyric: IG (ls)
            - Original partitur: -0-
            - Original parts: -0-

Unused.

Bring On the Ding Dong Dell
Gershwin/Gershwin
Orchestrator: Unknown

Location of   - Composer's manuscript: -0-
            - Sheet music: Unpublished
            - Most complete music: -0-
            - Most complete lyric: IG (ls)
            - Original partitur: -0-
            - Original parts: -0-

Unused. Later rewritten for the 1927 STRIKE UP THE BAND, but again unused.

If a Bootlegger Thinks of His Mother
Author(s): Unknown
Orchestrator: Unknown

Location of   - Composer's manuscript: -0-
            - Sheet music: Unpublished
            - Most complete music: -0-
            - Most complete lyric: See note
            - Original partitur: -0-
            - Original parts: -0-

Unused. The lyric is in the early draft of the script at the Library of Congress.

STRIKE UP THE BAND (1927)

Music	GEORGE GERSHWIN
Lyrics	IRA GERSHWIN

Musical satire in two acts. Closed out of town (World premiere: August 29, 1927 in Long Branch, New Jersey). Libretto by George S. Kaufman. Produced by Edgar Selwyn. Directed by R.H. Burnside. Choreographed by John Boyle. Musical direction and orchestrations by William Daly.

Synopsis and Production Information

When Switzerland protests a U.S. tariff on imported cheese, Horace J. Fletcher, proud owner of the Fletcher American Cheese Company, decides to finance a war against the Swiss, offering the U.S. Government 25 percent of the profits. Newspaperman Jim Townsend, who is infatuated with Fletcher's daughter Joan, discovers that Fletcher's cheese is made from Grade-B milk and vocally opposes the war. Jim is conscripted and eventually leads the American forces to victory.

Other characters include C. Edgar Sloane, Fletcher's shifty manager; Col. Holmes, the President's confidential adviser ("The Unofficial Spokesman of the U.S.A."); George Spelvin of the U.S. Secret Service, who appears in various comic disguises throughout the evening; Mrs. Draper, a formidable lady looking for a husband; and Mrs. Draper's spunky daughter Anne, who pairs up with Fletcher's young foreman Timothy for several numbers. There is a full singing and dancing ensemble.

Orchestration

Flute I II; Oboe; Clarinet I II; Bassoon; Horn I II; Trumpet I II; Trombone; Drums; Harp; Violin I; Violin II; Violin III; Viola I; Viola II; Cello; Bass

Comments

STRIKE UP THE BAND finally reached Broadway in 1930 with a revised book (by Morrie Ryskind) and several new Gershwin songs. The 1930 production is also included in this catalog.

Location of Original Materials

Script: New York Public Library (no lyrics)
Piano-vocal score: See individual listings
Partiturs: Library of Congress
Parts: Library of Congress

All of the piano-vocal material performed during the pre-Broadway tryout survives, with the following exceptions: the Overture, the Entr'acte, and the music to the verse of "Meadow Serenade." Although no piano-vocal score has been assembled, the score from the 1930 production, which contains some of the 1927 songs, was published. One partitur survives, as do parts for three numbers.

Rental Status

Currently unavailable for rental

Music Publisher

Warner Brothers Music

Information

Ira Gershwin Estate, George Gershwin Family Trust

Strike Up the Band (1927)

Overture

Gershwin/Gershwin
Orchestrator: Unknown

Location of   - Composer's manuscript: -0-
             - Sheet music: Unpublished
             - Most complete music: -0-
             - Most complete lyric: INST
             - Original partitur: -0-
             - Original parts: -0-

Typical Self-Made American, A

Gershwin/Gershwin
Orchestrator: Unknown

Location of   - Composer's manuscript: -0-
             - Sheet music: Not published separately
             - Most complete music: LoC (1930 pv
                score); NYPL (1930 pv score)
             - Most complete lyric: LoC (1930 pv
                score); NYPL (1930 pv score)
             - Original partitur: -0-
             - Original parts: -0-

Also included in the 1930 production.

Fletcher's American Cheese Choral Society

Gershwin/Gershwin
Orchestrator: Unknown

Location of   - Composer's manuscript: -0-
             - Sheet music: Unpublished
             - Most complete music: LoC (1930 pv score);
                NYPL (1930 pv score)
             - Most complete lyric: NYPL (ls)
             - Original partitur: -0-
             - Original parts: -0-

With a few altered lyrics, this number was included in the 1930 production as "Fletcher's American Chocolate Choral Society."

Meadow Serenade

Gershwin/Gershwin
Orchestrator: Unknown

Location of   - Composer's manuscript: -0-
             - Sheet music: Unpublished
             - Most complete music: IG (pv-l)
             - Most complete lyric: IG (ls)
             - Original partitur: -0-
             - Original parts: -0-

The music to the refrain was reconstructed from memory by Kay Swift; the music to the verse is missing.

17 and 21

Gershwin/Gershwin
Orchestrator: Unknown

Location of   - Composer's manuscript: -0-
             - Sheet music: LoC, NYPL
             - Most complete music: LoC (sm); NYPL (sm)
             - Most complete lyric: LoC (sm);
                NYPL (sm, ls)
             - Original partitur: -0-
             - Original parts: -0-

Unofficial Spokesman, The

Gershwin/Gershwin
Orchestrator: Unknown

Location of   - Composer's manuscript: -0-
             - Sheet music: Unpublished
             - Most complete music: LoC (pv-l)
             - Most complete lyric: NYPL (ls)
             - Original partitur: -0-
             - Original parts: -0-

Includes "The Wizard of the Age," which was not included in the 1930 production and, therefore, not published in the piano-vocal score. The 1930 piano-vocal score, which can be found at the Library of Congress and the New York Public Library, contains a few alternate lyrics.

111

Patriotic Rally
 Gershwin/Gershwin
 Orchestrator: Unknown

 Location of - Composer's manuscript: -0-
       - Sheet music: Not published separately
       - Most complete music: LoC (1930 pv score);
         NYPL (1930 pv score)
       - Most complete lyric: NYPL (ls
         & 1930 pv score)
       - Original partitur: -0-
       - Original parts: LoC

Also included in the 1930 production.

Man I Love, The
 Gershwin/Gershwin
 Orchestrator: Daly

 Location of - Composer's manuscript: LoC
       - Sheet music: LoC
       - Most complete music: LoC (sm)
       - Most complete lyric: LoC (sm) & NYPL (ls)
       - Original partitur: LoC
       - Original parts: LoC (1986)

Originally intended for LADY, BE GOOD! (1924); later intended for ROSALIE (1928), but dropped before the pre-Broadway tryout. The Library of Congress also has a piano-vocal with music for a discarded verse.

Yankee Doodle Rhythm
 Gershwin/Gershwin
 Orchestrator: Unknown

 Location of - Composer's manuscript: -0-
       - Sheet music: LoC, NYPL
       - Most complete music: LoC (sm); NYPL (sm)
       - Most complete lyric: LoC (sm);
         NYPL (sm, ls)
       - Original partitur: -0-
       - Original parts: -0-

Ensemble ["Stop! What is this mischief you're doing!"]
 Gershwin/Gershwin
 Orchestrator: Unknown

 Location of - Composer's manuscript: -0-
       - Sheet music: Unpublished
       - Most complete music: LoC (1930 pv
         score); NYPL (1930 pv score)
       - Most complete lyric: NYPL (ls)
       - Original partitur: -0-
       - Original parts: -0-

Included in the 1930 production under the title "He Knows Milk"; the 1930 piano-vocal score, which can be found at the Library of Congress and the New York Public Library, contains a few alternate lyrics used in that version. One four-bar phrase in this number became the basis for "Soon," the principal love song in the 1930 production.

Strike Up the Band
 Gershwin/Gershwin
 Orchestrator: Unknown

 Location of - Composer's manuscript: LoC (r)
       - Sheet music: LoC, NYPL
       - Most complete music: LoC (sm, 1930 pv
         score); NYPL (sm, 1930 pv score)
       - Most complete lyric: IG (ls)
       - Original partitur: -0-
       - Original parts: -0-

Also included in the 1930 production.

Entr'acte
 Gershwin/Gershwin
 Orchestrator: Unknown

 Location of - Composer's manuscript: -0-
       - Sheet music: Unpublished
       - Most complete music: -0-
       - Most complete lyric: INST
       - Original partitur: -0-
       - Original parts: -0-

Oh, This Is Such a Lovely War

Gershwin/Gershwin
Orchestrator: Unknown

Location of   - Composer's manuscript: -0-
               - Sheet music: Unpublished
               - Most complete music: LoC (parts)
                    & IG (pv)
               - Most complete lyric: NYPL (ls)
                    & IG (ls)
               - Original partitur: -0-
               - Original parts: LoC

Includes "The Knitting Song." Two sections were dropped either in rehearsal or in performance: a 32-bar interlude sung by the Swiss Girls (which is in the parts and the New York Public Library lyric sheet) and a number for the Red, White and Blue Nurses (which is at the Ira Gershwin Estate).

Military Dancing Drill

Gershwin/Gershwin
Orchestrator: Unknown

Location of   - Composer's manuscript: -0-
               - Sheet music: LoC, NYPL
               - Most complete music: LoC (sm & 1930
                    pv score); NYPL (sm & 1930 pv score)
               - Most complete lyric: NYPL (sm & ls &
                    1930 pv score)
               - Original partitur: -0-
               - Original parts: LoC

This number has two entirely different verses: The verse written for the 1927 production is published in the sheet music, although the lyric sheet at the New York Public Library suggests that it was revised slightly in rehearsal; the verse performed in 1930 is published in the piano-vocal score.

Hoping That Someday You'd Care

Gershwin/Gershwin
Orchestrator: Unknown

Location of   - Composer's manuscript: -0-
               - Sheet music: Unpublished
               - Most complete music: IG (pv-I)
               - Most complete lyric: IG (pv-I)
               - Original partitur: -0-
               - Original parts: -0-

The music to the verse was used in the 1930 production for the verse of "Soon."

How About a Man?

Gershwin/Gershwin
Orchestrator: Unknown

Location of   - Composer's manuscript: -0-
               - Sheet music: Unpublished
               - Most complete music: LoC (pv)
               - Most complete lyric: IG (ls)
               - Original partitur: -0-
               - Original parts: -0-

This is not the same song as "How About a Boy Like Me?" from the 1930 production.

Finaletto Act II, Scene 1 ["Jim, consider what you are doing!"]
Gershwin/Gershwin
Orchestrator: Unknown

Location of
- Composer's manuscript: -0-
- Sheet music: Unpublished
- Most complete music: LoC (pv)
- Most complete lyric: NYPL (ls)
- Original partitur: -0-
- Original parts: -0-

Come-Look-at-the-War-Choral-Society
Gershwin/Gershwin
Orchestrator: Unknown

Location of
- Composer's manuscript: -0-
- Sheet music: Unpublished
- Most complete music: See note
- Most complete lyric: NYPL (ls)
- Original partitur: -0-
- Original parts: -0-

This number, set to music from "Fletcher's American Cheese Choral Society" and "Patriotic Rally," may have been dropped before the New York opening.

Homeward Bound
Gershwin/Gershwin
Orchestrator: Unknown

Location of
- Composer's manuscript: -0-
- Sheet music: Unpublished
- Most complete music: LoC (pv)
- Most complete lyric: NYPL (ls)
- Original partitur: -0-
- Original parts: -0-

Sing Carry On!
Gershwin/Gershwin
Orchestrator: Unknown

Location of
- Composer's manuscript: LoC
- Sheet music: Unpublished
- Most complete music: LoC (pv); IG (pv)
- Most complete lyric: -0-
- Original partitur: -0-
- Original parts: -0-

Unused.

War That Ended War, The
Gershwin/Gershwin
Orchestrator: Unknown

Location of
- Composer's manuscript: LoC
- Sheet music: Unpublished
- Most complete music: LoC (pv)
- Most complete lyric: IG (ls)
- Original partitur: -0-
- Original parts: -0-

The piano-vocal is entitled "Opening Act III, Scene I."

Bring On the Ding Dong Dell
Gershwin/Gershwin
Orchestrator: Unknown

Location of
- Composer's manuscript: -0-
- Sheet music: Unpublished
- Most complete music: -0-
- Most complete lyric: IG (ls)
- Original partitur: -0-
- Original parts: -0-

Unused. A revision of a song previously intended for OH, KAY! (1926).

FUNNY FACE

Music   GEORGE GERSHWIN
Lyrics   IRA GERSHWIN

Musical comedy in two acts. Opened November 22, 1927 in New York and ran 244 performances (World premiere: October 11, 1927 in Philadelphia). Libretto by Fred Thompson and Paul Gerard Smith. Produced by Alex A. Aarons and Vinton Freedley. Directed by Edgar MacGregor. Choreographed by Bobby Connolly. Musical direction by Alfred Newman. Orchestrations by Robert Russell Bennett, George Gershwin.

Synopsis and Production Information	Jimmy Reeve has three wards: Frankie, June, and Dora. When Jimmy takes Frankie's diary (she has been filling it with nasty lies about him), Frankie enlists a pilot she worships (Peter) and Dora's boyfriend (Dugsie) to steal it back. But while Peter and Dugsie are carrying out their mission, two real crooks -- Chester and Herbert -- break into Jimmy's home to purloin the family jewels. The diary and the jewels (both kept in blue envelopes) get switched; second-act mayhem is the result.
	The show requires a full singing and dancing ensemble, and strong dancers in the roles of Jimmy and Frankie. Chester and Herbert are non-singing roles.
Orchestration	Flute; Oboe; Clarinet I II; Bassoon; Horn I II; Trumpet I II; Trombone; Drums; Piano I; Piano II; Violin I; Violin II; Viola I II; Cello I II; Bass
Comments	FUNNY FACE premiered in Philadelphia as SMARTY, with a book by Fred Thompson and Robert Benchley and eight numbers that were eventually dropped; the title SMARTY appears on early editions of the sheet music. In the original New York production, Fred and Adele Astaire played Jimmy and Frankie, Victor Moore played Herbert, and Victor Arden and Phil Ohman were on hand to provide two-piano specialties. The 1983 Broadway musical MY ONE AND ONLY included six numbers from FUNNY FACE ("High Hat," "'S Wonderful," "In the Swim," "He Loves and She Loves," "My One and Only," and the title song) and one that had been dropped out of town ("How Long Has This Been Going On?").
Location of Original Materials	Script: Tams-Witmark Music Library (most lyrics) Piano-vocal score: Tams-Witmark Music Library Partiturs: Ira Gershwin Estate Parts: Missing
	Partiturs survive for two numbers that were dropped before the New York opening. The Library of Congress has a script to SMARTY; it includes a lengthy opening scene (with three numbers) that was deleted before the show reached New York.
Rental Status	Along with the original book and piano-vocal score, Tams-Witmark has parts for the following orchestration adapted from the original: Flute; Oboe; Clarinet; Bassoon; Alto Sax (doubling Clarinet, Soprano Sax and Baritone Sax); Tenor Sax (doubling Clarinet and Soprano Sax); Horn I II; Trumpet I II; Trombone; Drums; Piano; Violin A; Violin B; Violin C; Viola; Cello; Bass. This material is not currently available for rental.
Music Publisher	Warner Brothers Music
Information	Tams-Witmark Music Library

Overture

Gershwin/Gershwin
Orchestrator: Unknown

Location of   - Composer's manuscript: -0-
      - Sheet music: Unpublished
      - Most complete music: TW (pv score)
      - Most complete lyric: INST
      - Original partitur: -0-
      - Original parts: -0-

Funny Face

Gershwin/Gershwin
Orchestrator: Unknown

Location of   - Composer's manuscript: LoC
      - Sheet music: LoC, NYPL
      - Most complete music: LoC (sm);
           NYPL (sm); TW (pv score)
      - Most complete lyric: IG (ls)
      - Original partitur: -0-
      - Original parts: -0-

Birthday Party

Gershwin/Gershwin
Orchestrator: Unknown

Location of   - Composer's manuscript: LoC
      - Sheet music: Unpublished
      - Most complete music: TW (pv score)
      - Most complete lyric: TW (pv score, scr)
      - Original partitur: -0-
      - Original parts: -0-

High Hat

Gershwin/Gershwin
Orchestrator: Unknown

Location of   - Composer's manuscript: LoC
      - Sheet music: LoC, NYPL
      - Most complete music: LoC (sm);
           NYPL (sm); TW (pv score)
      - Most complete lyric: LoC (sm);
           NYPL (sm); TW (pv score, scr)
      - Original partitur: -0-
      - Original parts: -0-

On the original London recording of "Tell the Doc"
(English Columbia 9592, reissused on Monmouth-Evergreen
MES-7037), Leslie Henson sings additional "High Hat"
lyrics; there is no evidence that these are by Ira
Gershwin.

Once

Gershwin/Gershwin
Orchestrator: Unknown

Location of   - Composer's manuscript: LoC
      - Sheet music: Unpublished
      - Most complete music: TW (pv-l)
      - Most complete lyric: TW (pv-l, scr)
      - Original partitur: -0-
      - Original parts: -0-

This lyric was initially set to music by William Daly and
used in TELL ME MORE (1925). The Ira Gershwin Estate
has a lyric sheet from TELL ME MORE with a few
alternate lines.

'S Wonderful

Gershwin/Gershwin
Orchestrator: Unknown

Location of   - Composer's manuscript: LoC (r)
      - Sheet music: LoC, NYPL
      - Most complete music: LoC (sm);
           NYPL (sm); TW (pv score)
      - Most complete lyric: IG (ls)
      - Original partitur: -0-
      - Original parts: -0-

On the original London recording of "Tell the Doc"
(English Columbia 9592, reissused on Monmouth-Evergreen
MES-7037), Leslie Henson sings additional "'S Wonderful"
lyrics; there is no evidence that these are by Ira
Gershwin.

Funny Face (1927)

Let's Kiss and Make Up
Gershwin/Gershwin
Orchestrator: Unknown

Location of   - Composer's manuscript: LoC (v)
- Sheet music: LoC, NYPL
- Most complete music: LoC (sm);
      NYPL (sm); TW (pv score)
- Most complete lyric: IG (ls)
- Original partitur: -0-
- Original parts: -0-

The Ira Gershwin Estate also has a lyric sheet for an early version entitled "Come! Come! Come Closer!"

In the Swim
Gershwin/Gershwin
Orchestrator: Unknown

Location of   - Composer's manuscript: -0-
- Sheet music: Not published separately
- Most complete music: TW (pv score)
- Most complete lyric: TW (pv score, scr)
- Original partitur: -0-
- Original parts: -0-

Initial publication in the MY ONE AND ONLY vocal selections (Warner Brothers: 1983).

Finale Act I ["Good heavens, they're gone!"]
Gershwin/Gershwin
Orchestrator: Unknown

Location of   - Composer's manuscript: -0-
- Sheet music: Unpublished
- Most complete music: TW (pv score)
- Most complete lyric: TW (pv score, scr)
- Original partitur: -0-
- Original parts: -0-

He Loves and She Loves
Gershwin/Gershwin
Orchestrator: Unknown

Location of   - Composer's manuscript: LoC
- Sheet music: LoC, NYPL
- Most complete music: LoC (sm);
      NYPL (sm); TW (pv score)
- Most complete lyric: IG (ls)
- Original partitur: -0-
- Original parts: -0-

Entr'acte
Gershwin/Gershwin
Orchestrator: Unknown

Location of   - Composer's manuscript: -0-
- Sheet music: Unpublished
- Most complete music: TW (pv score)
- Most complete lyric: INST
- Original partitur: -0-
- Original parts: -0-

Tell The Doc
Gershwin/Gershwin
Orchestrator: Unknown

Location of   - Composer's manuscript: LoC
- Sheet music: See note
- Most complete music: TW (pv score)
- Most complete lyric: TW (scr)
- Original partitur: -0-
- Original parts: -0-

Published only in a vocal arrangement, which can be found at the Library of Congress. On the original London recording of "Tell the Doc" (English Columbia 9592, reissused on Monmouth-Evergreen MES-7037), Leslie sings additional lyrics to this number; there is no evidence that these are by Ira Gershwin.

My One and Only

Gershwin/Gershwin
Orchestrator: Unknown

Location of
- Composer's manuscript: LoC (r)
- Sheet music: LoC, NYPL
- Most complete music: LoC (sm);
  NYPL (sm); TW (pv score)
- Most complete lyric: LoC (sm);
  NYPL (sm); TW (pv score)
- Original partitur: -0-
- Original parts: -0-

Finale Ultimo ["I love your funny face..."]

Gershwin/Gershwin
Orchestrator: Unknown

Location of
- Composer's manuscript: -0-
- Sheet music: Unpublished
- Most complete music: TW (pv score)
- Most complete lyric: TW (scr)
- Original partitur: -0-
- Original parts: -0-

Sing a Little Song

Gershwin/Gershwin
Orchestrator: Unknown

Location of
- Composer's manuscript: -0-
- Sheet music: Unpublished
- Most complete music: TW (pv score)
- Most complete lyric: TW (pv score)
- Original partitur: -0-
- Original parts: -0-

A specialty number (consisting mostly of reprises) for Ohman and Arden, the Ritz Quartet and sixteen singers.

Blue Hullaballoo

Gershwin/Gershwin
Orchestrator: Unknown

Location of
- Composer's manuscript: -0-
- Sheet music: Unpublished
- Most complete music: -0-
- Most complete lyric: IG (ls)
- Original partitur: -0-
- Original parts: -0-

Dropped soon after the New York opening.

Babbitt and the Bromide, The

Gershwin/Gershwin
Orchestrator: Unknown

Location of
- Composer's manuscript: -0-
- Sheet music: LoC, NYPL
- Most complete music: LoC (sm);
  NYPL (sm); TW (pv score)
- Most complete lyric: LoC (sm);
  NYPL (sm); TW (pv score, scr); LOSO
- Original partitur: -0-
- Original parts: -0-

Aviator

Gershwin/Gershwin
Orchestrator: Unknown

Location of
- Composer's manuscript: -0-
- Sheet music: Unpublished
- Most complete music: LoC (pv)
- Most complete lyric: IG (ls)
- Original partitur: -0-
- Original parts: -0-

Dropped during the pre-Broadway tryout. Alternate titles: "Opening Act I," "We're All A-Worry, All Agog," and "Flying Fete."

When You're Single

Gershwin/Gershwin

Orchestrator: Bennett

Location of - Composer's manuscript: LoC
           - Sheet music: Unpublished
           - Most complete music: LoC (pv)
           - Most complete lyric: IG (ls)
           - Original partitur: IG
           - Original parts: -0-

Dropped during the pre-Broadway tryout.

World Is Mine, The

Gershwin/Gershwin

Orchestrator: Unknown

Location of - Composer's manuscript: LoC
           - Sheet music: LoC, NYPL
           - Most complete music: LoC (sm);
              NYPL (sm)
           - Most complete lyric: LoC (sm);
              NYPL (sm)
           - Original partitur: -0-
           - Original parts: -0-

Dropped during the pre-Broadway tryout. Alternate title: "Toddling Along." Later used in the 9:15 REVUE (1930).

Your Eyes! Your Smile!

Gershwin/Gershwin

Orchestrator: Unknown

Location of - Composer's manuscript: -0-
           - Sheet music: Unpublished
           - Most complete music: IG (pv-l)
           - Most complete lyric: IG (pv-l)
           - Original partitur: -0-
           - Original parts: -0-

Alternate title: "Those Eyes." This duet for Frankie and Peter was dropped during the pre-Broadway tryout. The music to the verse was later used for the verse of "You Started It," intended for both GIRL CRAZY (1930) and the film DELICIOUS (1931); the music to the release became the release of "You've Got What Gets Me," written for and used in the first film version of GIRL CRAZY (1932).

How Long Has This Been Going On?

Gershwin/Gershwin

Orchestrator: Unknown

Location of - Composer's manuscript: -0-
           - Sheet music: LoC, NYPL
           - Most complete music: LoC (sm);
              NYPL (sm)
           - Most complete lyric: IG (ls)
           - Original partitur: -0-
           - Original parts: See note

Replaced during the pre-Broadway tryout by "He Loves and She Loves." Later used (with revised lyrics) in ROSALIE (1928); Tams-Witmark Music Library has a set of parts for "How Long Has This Been Going On?" with its ROSALIE material. The 1957 film version of FUNNY FACE includes alternate lyrics; there is no evidence that these are by Ira Gershwin.

Finest of the Finest

Gershwin/Gershwin
Orchestrator: Unknown

Location of - Composer's manuscript: IG
           - Sheet music: Unpublished
           - Most complete music: IG (pv)
           - Most complete lyric: IG (ls)
           - Original partitur: -0-
           - Original parts: -0-

Dropped during the pre-Broadway tryout.

Dancing Hour

Gershwin/Gershwin
Orchestrator: Unknown

Location of - Composer's manuscript: -0-
           - Sheet music: Unpublished
           - Most complete music: -0-
           - Most complete lyric: -0-
           - Original partitur: -0-
           - Original parts: -0-

Dropped during the pre-Broadway tryout. Also dropped during the pre-Broadway tryout of TIP-TOES (1925).

Dance Alone With You

Gershwin/Gershwin
Orchestrator: Unknown

Location of - Composer's manuscript: LoC
           - Sheet music: LoC, NYPL
           - Most complete music: LoC (sm);
               NYPL (sm)
           - Most complete lyric: LoC (sm);
               NYPL (sm)
           - Original partitur: -0-
           - Original parts: See note

Dropped during the pre-Broadway tryout. Alternate title: "Why Does Everybody Have to Cut In?" The music was later used for "Ev'rybody Knows I Love Somebody" in ROSALIE (1928); Tams-Witmark Music Library has a set of parts for "Ev'rybody Knows I Love Somebody" with its ROSALIE material.

Come Along, Let's Gamble

Gershwin/Gershwin
Orchestrator: Unknown

Location of - Composer's manuscript: -0-
           - Sheet music: Unpublished
           - Most complete music: -0-
           - Most complete lyric: IG (ls)
           - Original partitur: -0-
           - Original parts: -0-

An unused Act I Finale.

Acrobats

Gershwin/Gershwin
Orchestrator: Unknown

Location of - Composer's manuscript: IG
           - Sheet music: Unpublished
           - Most complete music: IG (pv)
           - Most complete lyric: IG (ls)
           - Original partitur: -0-
           - Original parts: -0-

Unused.

Bluebeard

Gershwin/Gershwin
Orchestrator: Unknown

Location of - Composer's manuscript: -0-
           - Sheet music: Unpublished
           - Most complete music: -0-
           - Most complete lyric: IG (ls)
           - Original partitur: -0-
           - Original parts: -0-

An unused trio.

Funny Face (1927)

Invalid Entrance

    Gershwin/Gershwin

    Orchestrator: Unknown

Location of   - Composer's manuscript: -0-

              - Sheet music: Unpublished

              - Most complete music: -0-

              - Most complete lyric: IG (ls)

              - Original partitur: -0-

              - Original parts: -0-

Unused.

Look at the Damn Thing Now

    Gershwin/Gershwin

    Orchestrator: Unknown

Location of   - Composer's manuscript: -0-

              - Sheet music: Unpublished

              - Most complete music: -0-

              - Most complete lyric: -0-

              - Original partitur: -0-

              - Original parts: -0-

Added for the London production (1928).

Astaire's Nut Dance

    Gershwin

    Orchestrator: Gershwin

Location of   - Composer's manuscript: -0-

              - Sheet music: Unpublished

              - Most complete music: IG (ptr)

              - Most complete lyric: INST

              - Original partitur: IG

              - Original parts: -0-

Dropped before the New York opening.

ROSALIE

Music GEORGE GERSHWIN & SIGMUND ROMBERG
Lyrics P.G. WODEHOUSE & IRA GERSHWIN

Musical comedy/extravaganza in two acts. Opened January 10, 1928 in New York and ran 335 performances (World premiere: December 5, 1927 in Boston). Libretto by William Anthony McGuire and Guy Bolton. Additional song by Bert Kalmar and Harry Ruby. Produced by Florenz Ziegfeld. Directed by William Anthony McGuire. Choreographed by Seymour Felix. Musical direction by Oscar Bradley. Orchestrations by Hans Spialek, Emil Gerstenberger, Max Steiner, Maurice B. DePackh, William Daly, Hilding Anderson.

Synopsis and Production Information	While visiting West Point, Princess Rosalie of Romanza falls in love with an American flyer, but the Queen, unwilling to let her daughter wed a commoner, holds Rosalie prisoner aboard a ship. Eventually, Rosalie escapes (disguised as a cadet) and reunites with her handsome flyer. Everyone then travels to Paris, where, after the Princess dances a ballet, her befuddled father is prompted to simplify everyone's life by abdicating.
	The enormous cast includes a lead comic and his demanding girlfriend, as well as captains, lieutenants, cadets, flunkeys, show girls, and a full singing and dancing ensemble.
Orchestration	Flute I II; Oboe; Clarinet I II; Bassoon; Horn I II; Trumpet I II; Trumpet III; Trombone I II; Percussion; Harp; Stage Bugle; Piano; Violin I, Stand 1; Violin I, Stand 2; Viola I; Viola II; Cello I II; Bass
Comments	ROSALIE was designed primarily as a showcase for Marilyn Miller, who played the Princess.
Location of Original Materials	Script: Tams-Witmark Music Library (most lyrics) Piano-vocal score: Tams-Witmark Music Library Partiturs: Library of Congress Parts: Tams-Witmark Music Library
Rental Status	Tams-Witmark rents a version that approximates the original show; however, the musical material does not precisely match the script.
Music Publisher	Warner Brothers Music
Information	Tams-Witmark Music Library

Rosalie (1928)

Overture
Gershwin & Romberg/Wodehouse & Gershwin
Orchestrator: Spialek

Location of - Composer's manuscript: -0-
              - Sheet music: Unpublished
              - Most complete music: TW (pv score)
              - Most complete lyric: INST
              - Original partitur: LoC (inc)
              - Original parts: TW

Entrance of the Hussars
Romberg/Wodehouse
Orchestrator: Gerstenberger

Location of - Composer's manuscript: -0-
              - Sheet music: Unpublished
              - Most complete music: TW (pv score)
              - Most complete lyric: TW (pv score, scr)
              - Original partitur: LoC
              - Original parts: TW

Here They Are
Romberg/Wodehouse
Orchestrator: Gerstenberger

Location of - Composer's manuscript: -0-
              - Sheet music: Unpublished
              - Most complete music: TW (pv score)
              - Most complete lyric: TW (pv score, scr)
              - Original partitur: LoC
              - Original parts: TW

Alternate title: "Opening Act I."

Hussar March
Romberg/Wodehouse
Orchestrator: Spialek

Location of - Composer's manuscript: -0-
              - Sheet music: LoC
              - Most complete music: TW (pv score)
              - Most complete lyric: LoC (sm)
                  & TW (pv score)
              - Original partitur: -0-
              - Original parts: TW

Show Me the Town
Gershwin/Gershwin
Orchestrator: Spialek

Location of - Composer's manuscript: -0-
              - Sheet music: LoC, NYPL
              - Most complete music: See note
              - Most complete lyric: IG (ls)
              - Original partitur: LoC
              - Original parts: TW

Published with the sheet music from OH, KAY! (1926), for which it was originally intended. This number has two different verses: One is published in the sheet music, the other is in the ROSALIE piano-vocal score at Tams-Witmark.

Say So!
Gershwin/Wodehouse & Gershwin
Orchestrator: Gerstenberger

Location of - Composer's manuscript: -0-
              - Sheet music: LoC, NYPL
              - Most complete music: LoC (sm);
                  NYPL (sm); TW (pv score)
              - Most complete lyric: LoC (sm);
                  NYPL (sm); TW (pv score)
              - Original partitur: LoC (inc)
              - Original parts: TW

The Ira Gershwin Estate has a lyric sheet for an early version (apparently intended for FUNNY FACE) entitled "When the Right One Comes Along."

Finaletto

Romberg/Wodehouse
Orchestrator: Unknown

Location of   - Composer's manuscript: -0-
           - Sheet music: Unpublished
           - Most complete music: TW (pv score)
           - Most complete lyric: TW (pv score, scr)
           - Original partitur: -0-
           - Original parts: TW

Alternate title: "Just One Little Kiss."

West Point March

Romberg
Orchestrator: Gerstenberger

Location of   - Composer's manuscript: -0-
           - Sheet music: Unpublished
           - Most complete music: TW (pv score)
           - Most complete lyric: INST
           - Original partitur: LoC
           - Original parts: TW

Let Me Be a Friend to You

Gershwin/Gershwin
Orchestrator: Unknown

Location of   - Composer's manuscript: -0-
           - Sheet music: Unpublished
           - Most complete music: -0-
           - Most complete lyric: IG (ls)
           - Original partitur: -0-
           - Original parts: -0-

This number is not in the Tams-Witmark rental package.

Oh Gee! Oh Joy!

Gershwin/Wodehouse & Gershwin
Orchestrator: Unknown

Location of   - Composer's manuscript: -0-
           - Sheet music: LoC, NYPL
           - Most complete music: LoC (sm);
               NYPL (sm); TW (pv score)
           - Most complete lyric: IG (ls)
           - Original partitur: -0-
           - Original parts: TW

The Ira Gershwin Estate also has a lyric sheet for an early version titled "What Could I Do?"

West Point Song

Romberg/Wodehouse
Orchestrator: Gerstenberger

Location of   - Composer's manuscript: -0-
           - Sheet music: LoC, NYPL
           - Most complete music: TW (pv score)
           - Most complete lyric: IG (ls)
           - Original partitur: LoC
           - Original parts: TW

Alternate title: "West Point Bugle."

Finale Act I

Romberg/Wodehouse & Gershwin
Orchestrator: Anderson

Location of   - Composer's manuscript: -0-
           - Sheet music: NYPL
           - Most complete music: NYPL (sm)
               & TW (pv score)
           - Most complete lyric: NYPL (sm)
               & TW (pv score) & IG (ls)
           - Original partitur: LoC
           - Original parts: TW

Alternate titles: "Kingdom of Dreams" and "Castle of Dreams." Only the Romberg/Wodehouse "Why Must We Always Be Dreaming?" (part of which is sung in the Finale Act I) was published.

Rosalie (1928)

Entr'acte

Gershwin & Romberg/Wodehouse & Gershwin

Orchestrator: Unknown

Location of
- Composer's manuscript: -0-
- Sheet music: Unpublished
- Most complete music: TW (pv score)
- Most complete lyric: INST
- Original partitur: LoC (inc)
- Original parts: TW

King Can Do No Wrong, The

Romberg/Wodehouse & Gershwin

Orchestrator: Unknown

Location of
- Composer's manuscript: -0-
- Sheet music: Unpublished
- Most complete music: TW (pv score)
- Most complete lyric: IG (ls)
- Original partitur: -0-
- Original parts: TW

Opening Valse

Romberg/Wodehouse

Orchestrator: Steiner

Location of
- Composer's manuscript: -0-
- Sheet music: Unpublished
- Most complete music: TW (pv score)
- Most complete lyric: TW (pv score)
- Original partitur: LoC
- Original parts: TW

The lyric is not in the script.

Ev'rybody Knows I Love Somebody

Gershwin/Gershwin

Orchestrator: Unknown

Location of
- Composer's manuscript: -0-
- Sheet music: LoC, NYPL
- Most complete music: LoC (sm);
    NYPL (sm); TW (pv score)
- Most complete lyric: LoC (sm);
    NYPL (sm); TW (pv score, scr)
- Original partitur: -0-
- Original parts: TW

Added after the New York opening. The music was previously used for "Dance Alone With You" in the pre-Broadway tryout of FUNNY FACE (1927).

New York Serenade

Gershwin/Gershwin

Orchestrator: DePackh

Location of
- Composer's manuscript: -0-
- Sheet music: Unpublished
- Most complete music: TW (pv score)
- Most complete lyric: TW (pv score, scr)
- Original partitur: LoC
- Original parts: TW

Follow the Drum

Gershwin/Gershwin

Orchestrator: Unknown

Location of
- Composer's manuscript: -0-
- Sheet music: Not published separately
- Most complete music: TW (pv score)
- Most complete lyric: IG (ls)
- Original partitur: -0-
- Original parts: TW

Added after the New York opening. The refrain was published in the piano selection, which can be found at the Ira Gershwin Estate.

How Long Has This Been Going On?
Gershwin/Gershwin
Orchestrator: Unknown

Location of - Composer's manuscript: -0-
- Sheet music: LoC, NYPL
- Most complete music: LoC (sm);
    NYPL (sm); TW (pv score)
- Most complete lyric: IG (ls)
- Original partitur: -0-
- Original parts: TW

Originally intended for FUNNY FACE (1927). The lyric to the verse was rewritten for ROSALIE. The 1957 film version of FUNNY FACE includes alternate lyrics to "How Long Has This Been Going On?"; there is no evidence that these were written by Ira Gershwin.

Setting Up Exercises
Gershwin
Orchestrator: Daly

Location of - Composer's manuscript: -0-
- Sheet music: See note
- Most complete music: TW (pv score)
- Most complete lyric: INST
- Original partitur: LoC
- Original parts: TW

Published in a separate edition under the title "Merry Andrew."

Tho' Today We Are Flunkeys Merely
Romberg/Wodehouse
Orchestrator: Spialek

Location of - Composer's manuscript: -0-
- Sheet music: Unpublished
- Most complete music: TW (pv score)
- Most complete lyric: TW (pv score)
- Original partitur: LoC
- Original parts: TW

The lyric is not in the script.

Ballet
Romberg
Orchestrator: Gerstenberger

Location of - Composer's manuscript: -0-
- Sheet music: Unpublished
- Most complete music: TW (pv score)
- Most complete lyric: INST
- Original partitur: LoC
- Original parts: TW

Ace, Jack and King
Ruby/Kalmar
Orchestrator: DePackh

Location of - Composer's manuscript: -0-
- Sheet music: Unpublished
- Most complete music: LoC (ptr)
- Most complete lyric: -0-
- Original partitur: LoC
- Original parts: -0-

Dropped during the pre-Broadway tryout.

Beautiful Gypsy
Gershwin/Gershwin
Orchestrator: Unknown

Location of - Composer's manuscript: -0-
- Sheet music: LoC
- Most complete music: LoC (sm)
- Most complete lyric: IG (ls)
- Original partitur: -0-
- Original parts: -0-

Dropped during the pre-Broadway tryout. The music was previously used for "Wait a Bit, Susie" in PRIMROSE (1924).

Rosalie (1928)

Rosalie

Gershwin/Gershwin
Orchestrator: Unknown

Location of - Composer's manuscript: -0-
- Sheet music: LoC, NYPL
- Most complete music: LoC (sm);
    NYPL (sm)
- Most complete lyric: IG (ls)
- Original partitur: -0-
- Original parts: -0-

Dropped during the pre-Broadway tryout. The Ira Gershwin Estate also has a piano-vocal and lyric sheet for an early version.

Goodbye to the One Girl

Author(s): Unknown
Orchestrator: Unknown

Location of - Composer's manuscript: -0-
- Sheet music: Unpublished
- Most complete music: -0-
- Most complete lyric: IG (ls)
- Original partitur: -0-
- Original parts: -0-

Dropped during the pre-Broadway tryout.

I Forgot What I Started to Say

Gershwin/Gershwin
Orchestrator: Unknown

Location of - Composer's manuscript: LoC
- Sheet music: Unpublished
- Most complete music: LoC (p)
- Most complete lyric: IG (ls)
- Original partitur: -0-
- Original parts: -0-

Dropped during the pre-Broadway tryout.

Trio: Dick, King, Delroy

Author(s): Unknown
Orchestrator: Gerstenberger

Location of - Composer's manuscript: -0-
- Sheet music: Unpublished
- Most complete music: LoC (pv-l)
- Most complete lyric: LoC (pv-l)
- Original partitur: LoC
- Original parts: -0-

Dropped before the New York opening.

Yankee Doodle Rhythm

Gershwin/Gershwin
Orchestrator: Unknown

Location of - Composer's manuscript: -0-
- Sheet music: LoC, NYPL
- Most complete music: LoC (sm);
    NYPL (sm)
- Most complete lyric: LoC (sm);
    NYPL (sm)
- Original partitur: -0-
- Original parts: -0-

Dropped during the pre-Broadway tryout. Originally used in STRIKE UP THE BAND (1927).

When Cadets Parade

Gershwin/Gershwin
Orchestrator: Unknown

Location of - Composer's manuscript: -0-
- Sheet music: Unpublished
- Most complete music: LoC (pv)
- Most complete lyric: IG (ls)
- Original partitur: -0-
- Original parts: -0-

Unused. The music was originally set to a Clifford Grey lyric entitled "When the Mites Go By."

You Know How It Is

Gershwin/Wodehouse & Gershwin
Orchestrator: Unknown

Location of   - Composer's manuscript: -0-
              - Sheet music: Unpublished
              - Most complete music: -0-
              - Most complete lyric: IG (ls)
              - Original partitur: -0-
              - Original parts: -0-

Unused.

Man I Love, The

Gershwin/Gershwin
Orchestrator: See note

Location of   - Composer's manuscript: LoC
              - Sheet music: LoC
              - Most complete music: LoC (sm)
              - Most complete lyric: LoC (sm) & NYPL (ls)
              - Original partitur: See note
              - Original parts: See note

Dropped before the pre-Broadway tryout. Previously dropped during the pre-Broadway tryout of LADY, BE GOOD! (1924); performed in STRIKE UP THE BAND (1927). The Library of Congress has William Daly's partitur from STRIKE UP THE BAND, as well as parts that were extracted from it in 1986. The Library of Congress also has a piano-vocal that contains the music for a discarded verse.

True to Them All

Gershwin/Gershwin
Orchestrator: Unknown

Location of   - Composer's manuscript: -0-
              - Sheet music: Unpublished
              - Most complete music: -0-
              - Most complete lyric: IG (ls)
              - Original partitur: -0-
              - Original parts: -0-

Unused.

Under the Furlough Moon

Gershwin & Romberg/Gershwin
Orchestrator: Unknown

Location of   - Composer's manuscript: -0-
              - Sheet music: Unpublished
              - Most complete music: LoC (pv-l)
              - Most complete lyric: LoC (pv-l, ls);
                IG (ls)
              - Original partitur: -0-
              - Original parts: -0-

Unused.

Head Waiter

Author(s): Unknown
Orchestrator: Unknown

Location of   - Composer's manuscript: -0-
              - Sheet music: Unpublished
              - Most complete music: LoC (ptr)
              - Most complete lyric: -0-
              - Original partitur: LoC
              - Original parts: -0-

Unused.

At the Ex-King's Club

Gershwin/Gershwin
Orchestrator: Unknown

Location of   - Composer's manuscript: -0-
              - Sheet music: Unpublished
              - Most complete music: LoC (ptr)
              - Most complete lyric: IG (ls)
              - Original partitur: LoC
              - Original parts: -0-

Unused.

Rosalie (1928)

Cadet Song
　　Author(s): Unknown
　　Orchestrator: Unknown

　　Location of　- Composer's manuscript: -0-
　　　　　　　　- Sheet music: Unpublished
　　　　　　　　- Most complete music: -0-
　　　　　　　　- Most complete lyric: IG (ls)
　　　　　　　　- Original partitur: -0-
　　　　　　　　- Original parts: -0-

　　Unused.

TREASURE GIRL

Music   **GEORGE GERSHWIN**
Lyrics   **IRA GERSHWIN**

Musical comedy in two acts. Opened November 8, 1928 in New York and ran 68 performances (World premiere: October 15, 1928 in Philadelphia). Libretto by Fred Thompson and Vincent Lawrence. Produced by Alex A. Aarons and Vinton Freedley. Directed by Bertram Harrison. Choreographed by Bobby Connolly. Musical direction by Alfred Newman. Orchestrations by William Daly.

Synopsis and Production Information	Ann Wainwright is a spoiled and willful young woman who has lost both her fortune and her boyfriend, Neil. While participating in a treasure hunt for a $20,000 prize, she is forced to come to terms with her selfish behavior and fear of commitment. In the process, she wins back her money and her man.
	In addition to Ann and Neil, the cast includes a supporting couple (Nat and Polly), a comic (Larry), and a full singing and dancing ensemble.
Orchestration	Flute I II; Oboe; Clarinet I II; Bassoon; Horn I II; 2nd Horn; Trumpet I II; Trumpet III; Trombone; Drums; Piano I; Piano II; Harp; Violin I; Violin II; Viola I; Viola II; Cello; Bass
Comments	In the original production, Ann was played by Gertrude Lawrence, Nat and Polly by Clifton Webb and Mary Hay, and Larry by Walter Catlett. Victor Arden and Phil Ohman provided two-piano specialties.
Location of Original Materials	Script: Library of Congress (all lyrics), New York Public Library (all lyrics) Piano-vocal score: See individual listings Partiturs: Library of Congress Parts: Missing
	Only one partitur has surfaced; in addition, music is missing for four numbers performed in the original New York production, as well as for the Overture and Entr'acte.
Rental Status	Currently unavailable for rental
Music Publisher	Warner Brothers Music
Information	Ira Gershwin Estate, George Gershwin Family Trust

Treasure Girl (1928)

Overture
Gershwin/Gershwin
Orchestrator: Unknown

Location of
- Composer's manuscript: -0-
- Sheet music: Unpublished
- Most complete music: -0-
- Most complete lyric: INST
- Original partitur: -0-
- Original parts: -0-

According to Mr. Grimes
Gershwin/Gershwin
Orchestrator: Unknown

Location of
- Composer's manuscript: -0-
- Sheet music: Unpublished
- Most complete music: -0-
- Most complete lyric: LoC (scr);
  NYPL (scr)
- Original partitur: -0-
- Original parts: -0-

Skull and Bones
Gershwin/Gershwin
Orchestrator: Unknown

Location of
- Composer's manuscript: -0-
- Sheet music: Unpublished
- Most complete music: -0-
- Most complete lyric: LoC (scr);
  NYPL (scr)
- Original partitur: -0-
- Original parts: -0-

Place in the Country
Gershwin/Gershwin
Orchestrator: Unknown

Location of
- Composer's manuscript: -0-
- Sheet music: Unpublished
- Most complete music: LoC (pv)
- Most complete lyric: LoC (scr);
  NYPL (scr)
- Original partitur: -0-
- Original parts: -0-

I've Got a Crush on You
Gershwin/Gershwin
Orchestrator: Unknown

Location of
- Composer's manuscript: LoC (lead)
- Sheet music: LoC
- Most complete music: LoC (sm)
- Most complete lyric: IG (ls)
- Original partitur: -0-
- Original parts: -0-

This number was not published until its inclusion in the
Gershwins' 1930 revision of STRIKE UP THE BAND. Also
published in the piano-vocal score of STRIKE UP THE
BAND, which can be found at the Library of Congress and
the New York Public Library.

K-ra-zy for You
Gershwin/Gershwin
Orchestrator: Unknown

Location of
- Composer's manuscript: -0-
- Sheet music: LoC, NYPL
- Most complete music: LoC (sm);
  NYPL (sm)
- Most complete lyric: LoC (sm, scr);
  NYPL (sm, scr)
- Original partitur: -0-
- Original parts: -0-

I Don't Think I'll Fall in Love Today

Gershwin/Gershwin

Orchestrator: Unknown

Location of   - Composer's manuscript: -0-
- Sheet music: LoC, NYPL
- Most complete music: LoC (sm); NYPL (sm)
- Most complete lyric: IG (ls)
- Original partitur: -0-
- Original parts: -0-

Finale Act I ["We're looking for the treasure..."]

Gershwin/Gershwin

Orchestrator: Unknown

Location of   - Composer's manuscript: -0-
- Sheet music: Unpublished
- Most complete music: -0-
- Most complete lyric: LoC (scr);
     NYPL (scr)
- Original partitur: -0-
- Original parts: -0-

Got a Rainbow

Gershwin/Gershwin

Orchestrator: Unknown

Location of   - Composer's manuscript: -0-
- Sheet music: LoC, NYPL
- Most complete music: LoC (sm); NYPL (sm)
- Most complete lyric: LoC (sm, scr);
     NYPL (sm, scr)
- Original partitur: -0-
- Original parts: -0-

Entr'acte

Gershwin/Gershwin

Orchestrator: Unknown

Location of   - Composer's manuscript: -0-
- Sheet music: Unpublished
- Most complete music: -0-
- Most complete lyric: INST
- Original partitur: -0-
- Original parts: -0-

Feeling I'm Falling

Gershwin/Gershwin

Orchestrator: Unknown

Location of   - Composer's manuscript: LoC
- Sheet music: LoC, NYPL
- Most complete music: LoC (sm); NYPL (sm)
- Most complete lyric: LoC (sm, scr);
     NYPL (sm, scr)
- Original partitur: -0-
- Original parts: -0-

Treasure Island

Gershwin/Gershwin

Orchestrator: Unknown

Location of   - Composer's manuscript: -0-
- Sheet music: Unpublished
- Most complete music: -0-
- Most complete lyric: LoC (scr);
     NYPL (scr)
- Original partitur: -0-
- Original parts: -0-

Alternate title: "Opening Act II."

What Causes That?

Gershwin/Gershwin
Orchestrator: Unknown

Location of   - Composer's manuscript: LoC (r)
               - Sheet music: Unpublished
               - Most complete music: LoC (pv)
               - Most complete lyric: LoC (scr);
                    NYPL (scr)
               - Original partitur: -0-
               - Original parts: -0-

A-Hunting We Will Go

Gershwin/Gershwin
Orchestrator: Unknown

Location of   - Composer's manuscript: -0-
               - Sheet music: Unpublished
               - Most complete music: LoC (pv)
               - Most complete lyric: IG (ls)
               - Original partitur: -0-
               - Original parts: -0-

Although the bulk of this song was dropped prior to the New York opening, the second half of the refrain remained in the show. Alternate title: "Tally-Ho."

What Are We Here For?

Gershwin/Gershwin
Orchestrator: Unknown

Location of   - Composer's manuscript: -0-
               - Sheet music: LoC, NYPL
               - Most complete music: LoC (sm); NYPL (sm)
               - Most complete lyric: LoC (sm, scr);
                    NYPL (sm, scr)
               - Original partitur: -0-
               - Original parts: -0-

Oh, So Nice!

Gershwin/Gershwin
Orchestrator: Daly

Location of   - Composer's manuscript: -0-
               - Sheet music: LoC, NYPL
               - Most complete music: LoC (sm);
                    NYPL (sm)
               - Most complete lyric: LoC (sm);
                    NYPL (sm)
               - Original partitur: LoC
               - Original parts: -0-

This Act I duet for Ann and Neil was dropped soon after the New York opening.

Where's the Boy? Here's the Girl!

Gershwin/Gershwin
Orchestrator: Unknown

Location of   - Composer's manuscript: -0-
               - Sheet music: LoC, NYPL, IG
               - Most complete music: LoC (sm);
                    NYPL (sm); IG (sm)
               - Most complete lyric: IG (sm & ls)
               - Original partitur: -0-
               - Original parts: -0-

Dead Men Tell No Tales

Gershwin/Gershwin
Orchestrator: Unknown

Location of   - Composer's manuscript: -0-
               - Sheet music: Unpublished
               - Most complete music: LoC (pv)
               - Most complete lyric: IG (ls)
               - Original partitur: -0-
               - Original parts: -0-

Dropped during the pre-Broadway tryout.

I Want to Marry a Marionette
  Gershwin/Gershwin
  Orchestrator: Unknown

  Location of   - Composer's manuscript: LoC (r)
              - Sheet music: Unpublished
              - Most complete music: LoC (pv)
              - Most complete lyric: LoC (ls); IG (ls)
              - Original partitur: -0-
              - Original parts: -0-

This number for Ann and the male ensemble was dropped during the pre-Broadway tryout.

This Particular Party
  Gershwin/Gershwin
  Orchestrator: Unknown

  Location of   - Composer's manuscript: -0-
              - Sheet music: Unpublished
              - Most complete music: -0-
              - Most complete lyric: IG (ls)
              - Original partitur: -0-
              - Original parts: -0-

An unused Act I opening.

Goodbye to the Old Love
  Gershwin/Gershwin
  Orchestrator: Unknown

  Location of   - Composer's manuscript: -0-
              - Sheet music: Unpublished
              - Most complete music: LoC (p)
              - Most complete lyric: IG (ls)
              - Original partitur: -0-
              - Original parts: -0-

This Act I quartet was dropped during the pre-Broadway tryout.

SHOW GIRL

Music   **GEORGE GERSHWIN**
Lyrics   **GUS KAHN & IRA GERSHWIN**

Musical comedy/extravaganza in two acts. Opened July 2, 1929 in New York and ran 111 performances (World premiere: June 24, 1929 in Boston). Libretto by William Anthony McGuire, based on the novel by J.P. McEvoy. Additional music and lyrics by Jimmy Durante, William H. Farrell, Vincent Youmans and J. Russel Robinson. Produced by Florenz Ziegfeld. Directed by William Anthony McGuire. Choreographed by Bobby Connolly, Albertina Rasch. Musical direction by William Daly. Orchestrations by Maurice B. DePackh, William Daly.

Synopsis and Production Information	Dixie Dugan is a brash, inexperienced dancer who lies and flirts her way to a leading role in Ziegfeld's latest show. On opening night, she dumps her current boyfriend (a sweet guy who sells greeting cards) to elope with an up-and-coming playwright whom she hardly knows. The show requires a full singing and dancing ensemble, and a slew of specialty acts.
Orchestration	Flute; Oboe; Clarinet I II; Alto Sax I II; Tenor Sax; Horn; Trumpet I II; Trombone; Drums; Harp; Violin I II; Viola; Cello; Bass
Comments	SHOW GIRL was as much an edition of the ZIEGFELD FOLLIES as a musical comedy: Act I opened with a twenty-minute excerpt from a fictitious Ziegfeld production, MAGNOLIAS, a Civil War musical; Act II began with a ballet set to Gershwin's AN AMERICAN IN PARIS. In addition to specialty performances by the Albertina Rasch dancers, ballerina/contortionist Harriet Hoctor, singer/guitarist Nick Lucas, and Duke Ellington's orchestra, Jimmy Durante -- backed up by Lou Clayton and Eddie Jackson -- sang at least five of his own numbers. There was not much room left for the plot.
Location of Original Materials	Script: Ira Gershwin Estate (most lyrics) Piano-vocal score: See individual listings Partiturs: Yale University Parts: Missing Partiturs for only three numbers in the New York production are known to survive; however, most of the Gershwin songs have surfaced, as have many of Durante's.
Rental Status	Currently unavailable for rental
Music Publisher	Warner Brothers Music
Information	Ira Gershwin Estate, George Gershwin Family Trust

Overture

Gershwin/Kahn & Gershwin
Orchestrator: DePackh

Location of - Composer's manuscript: -0-
        - Sheet music: Unpublished
        - Most complete music: Y (ptr)
        - Most complete lyric: INST
        - Original partitur: Y (inc)
        - Original parts: -0-

The partitur contains only the introduction and the links between numbers. In 1987, Larry Moore orchestrated the missing songs; the new partitur and parts are at the Ira Gershwin Estate.

Happy Birthday

Gershwin/Kahn & Gershwin
Orchestrator: Unknown

Location of - Composer's manuscript: -0-
        - Sheet music: Unpublished
        - Most complete music: LoC (pv) & IG (pv)
        - Most complete lyric: IG (ls)
        - Original partitur: -0-
        - Original parts: -0-

The piano-vocal is in two sections: Part A is at the Library of Congress; part B is at the Ira Gershwin Estate.

My Sunday Fella

Gershwin/Kahn & Gershwin
Orchestrator: DePackh

Location of - Composer's manuscript: -0-
        - Sheet music: Unpublished
        - Most complete music: LoC (pv)
        - Most complete lyric: IG (scr)
        - Original partitur: Y
        - Original parts: -0-

Yale University also has a nine-page DePackh partitur for the "My Sunday Fella" Ballet.

Finaletto Act I, Scene 1 ["Tell me, what has happened?"]

Gershwin/Kahn & Gershwin
Orchestrator: Unknown

Location of - Composer's manuscript: -0-
        - Sheet music: Unpublished
        - Most complete music: LoC (pv)
        - Most complete lyric: IG (scr, ls)
        - Original partitur: -0-
        - Original parts: -0-

How Could I Forget?

Gershwin/Kahn & Gershwin
Orchestrator: Unknown

Location of - Composer's manuscript: LoC
        - Sheet music: Unpublished
        - Most complete music: LoC (pv)
        - Most complete lyric: IG (ls)
        - Original partitur: -0-
        - Original parts: -0-

Magnolia Finale

Gershwin/Kahn & Gershwin
Orchestrator: Daly

Location of - Composer's manuscript: -0-
        - Sheet music: Unpublished
        - Most complete music: IG (ptr)
        - Most complete lyric: IG (ls)
        - Original partitur: IG
        - Original parts: -0-

The lyric is not in the script.

Mississippi Dry

Youmans/Robinson

Orchestrator: Unknown

Location of   - Composer's manuscript: -0-
- Sheet music: LoC
- Most complete music: LoC (sm)
- Most complete lyric: LoC (sm); IG (scr)
- Original partitur: -0-
- Original parts: -0-

Added after the New York opening.

Lolita, My Love

Gershwin/Kahn & Gershwin

Orchestrator: Unknown

Location of   - Composer's manuscript: LoC (r)
- Sheet music: Unpublished
- Most complete music: LoC (pv)
- Most complete lyric: IG (ls)
- Original partitur: -0-
- Original parts: -0-

Although this number is listed in the opening night program, it does not appear in the script and may have been dropped after the New York opening.

Can Broadway Do Without Me?

Durante/Durante

Orchestrator: Unknown

Location of   - Composer's manuscript: -0-
- Sheet music: Not published separately
- Most complete music: See note
- Most complete lyric: See note
- Original partitur: -0-
- Original parts: -0-

Published as "I Know Darn Well I Can Do Without Broadway" in Jimmy (Schnozzle) Durante's Jumbo Song Book (Harry Engel, Inc.: 1936), which can be found at the Library of Congress. Durante's off-the-cuff renditions of this number defy a "most complete" listing; versions worth examining include the printed music, the lyric in the script (at the Ira Gershwin Estate), and Durante's own recording on Columbia 1860-D (reissued on Epic LN-3234).

Do What You Do

Gershwin/Kahn & Gershwin

Orchestrator: Unknown

Location of   - Composer's manuscript: LoC (v)
- Sheet music: LoC, NYPL
- Most complete music: LoC (sm); NYPL (sm)
- Most complete lyric: LoC (sm); NYPL (sm); IG (scr)
- Original partitur: -0-
- Original parts: -0-

The Ira Gershwin Estate also has additional lyrics for a second act reprise.

Spain

Durante/Durante
Orchestrator: Unknown

Location of   - Composer's manuscript: -0-
     - Sheet music: Unpublished
     - Most complete music: LoC (p)
     - Most complete lyric: -0-
     - Original partitur: -0-
     - Original parts: -0-

Although this number is listed in the opening night program, it does not appear in the script and may have been dropped after the New York opening.

One Man

Gershwin/Kahn & Gershwin
Orchestrator: Unknown

Location of   - Composer's manuscript: -0-
     - Sheet music: Unpublished
     - Most complete music: LoC (p)
     - Most complete lyric: IG (ls)
     - Original partitur: -0-
     - Original parts: -0-

So Are You

Gershwin/Kahn & Gershwin
Orchestrator: Unknown

Location of   - Composer's manuscript: -0-
     - Sheet music: LoC, NYPL
     - Most complete music: LoC (sm);
       NYPL (sm)
     - Most complete lyric: LoC (sm);
       NYPL (sm); IG (scr)
     - Original partitur: -0-
     - Original parts: -0-

The Ira Gershwin Estate also has additional lyrics for a second act reprise.

I Must Be Home By Twelve O'Clock

Gershwin/Kahn & Gershwin
Orchestrator: Unknown

Location of   - Composer's manuscript: LoC (v)
     - Sheet music: LoC, NYPL
     - Most complete music: LoC (sm);
       NYPL (sm)
     - Most complete lyric: LoC (sm);
       NYPL (sm); IG (scr)
     - Original partitur: -0-
     - Original parts: -0-

The Ira Gershwin Estate also has additional lyrics for a second act reprise.

Black and White

Author(s): Unknown
Orchestrator: Unknown

Location of   - Composer's manuscript: -0-
     - Sheet music: -0-
     - Most complete music: -0-
     - Most complete lyric: -0-
     - Original partitur: -0-
     - Original parts: -0-

African Daisies

Author(s): Unknown
Orchestrator: Unknown

Location of   - Composer's manuscript: -0-
     - Sheet music: -0-
     - Most complete music: -0-
     - Most complete lyric: -0-
     - Original partitur: -0-
     - Original parts: -0-

A dance number performed by the Albertina Rasch Girls.

Show Girl (1929)

Jimmy the Well Dressed Man

Durante/Durante
Orchestrator: Unknown

Location of - Composer's manuscript: -0-
- Sheet music: Not published separately
- Most complete music: See note
- Most complete lyric: See note
- Original partitur: -0-
- Original parts: -0-

Published as "I'm Jimmy That Well Dressed Man" in <u>Jimmy (Schnozzle) Durante's Jumbo Song Book</u> (Harry Engel, Inc.: 1936), which can be found at the Library of Congress. Durante's off-the-cuff renditions of this number defy a "most complete" listing; versions worth examining include the printed music and Durante's recording on Decca 23568.

Who Will Be With You

Farrell & Durante/Farrell & Durante
Orchestrator: Unknown

Location of - Composer's manuscript: -0-
- Sheet music: LoC, NYPL
- Most complete music: LoC (sm);
  NYPL (sm)
- Most complete lyric: LoC (sm);
  NYPL (sm)
- Original partitur: -0-
- Original parts: -0-

Published in 1913 by F.B. Haviland Music. Renewed in 1955 by Leo Feist, Inc. Also recommended: Durante's recording on Decca 23567.

Harlem Serenade

Gershwin/Kahn & Gershwin
Orchestrator: Unknown

Location of - Composer's manuscript: -0-
- Sheet music: LoC, NYPL
- Most complete music: LoC (sm);
  NYPL (sm)
- Most complete lyric: LoC (sm);
  NYPL (sm); IG (scr)
- Original partitur: -0-
- Original parts: -0-

Entr'acte

Gershwin/Kahn & Gershwin
Orchestrator: Unknown

Location of - Composer's manuscript: -0-
- Sheet music: Unpublished
- Most complete music: -0-
- Most complete lyric: INST
- Original partitur: -0-
- Original parts: -0-

American in Paris – Blues Ballet, An

Gershwin
Orchestrator: Unknown

Location of - Composer's manuscript: LoC
- Sheet music: See note
- Most complete music: See note
- Most complete lyric: INST
- Original partitur: -0-
- Original parts: -0-

Gershwin's 1928 tone poem, AN AMERICAN IN PARIS, is published in several ways, including a piano transcription by William Daly (which can be found at the Library of Congress). The Library of Congress also has Gershwin's original partitur of AN AMERICAN IN PARIS; however, the partitur and parts used for SHOW GIRL's substantially smaller pit orchestra are missing.

Home Blues

Gershwin/Kahn & Gershwin
Orchestrator: Unknown

Location of - Composer's manuscript: LoC
- Sheet music: Unpublished
- Most complete music: LoC (pv)
- Most complete lyric: IG (scr)
- Original partitur: -0-
- Original parts: -0-

A song based on the blues section of AN AMERICAN IN PARIS. The music to the verse is missing.

Broadway, My Street
Durante/Durante
Orchestrator: Unknown

Location of   - Composer's manuscript: -0-
              - Sheet music: Unpublished
              - Most complete music: LoC (p)
              - Most complete lyric: IG (scr)
              - Original partitur: -0-
              - Original parts: -0-

I Ups to Him
Durante/Durante
Orchestrator: Unknown

Location of   - Composer's manuscript: -0-
              - Sheet music: Unpublished
              - Most complete music: See note
              - Most complete lyric: See note
              - Original partitur: -0-
              - Original parts: -0-

Registered for copyright as an unpublished song in 1929 by Jimmy Durante. The Library of Congress has a piano arrangement, and the Ira Gershwin Estate has a lyric in the SHOW GIRL script. Durante performs different lyrics on his recordings for Columbia (1860-D) and Decca (23567).

Follow the Minstrel Band
Gershwin/Kahn & Gershwin
Orchestrator: Unknown

Location of   - Composer's manuscript: LoC (r)
              - Sheet music: Unpublished
              - Most complete music: LoC (pv)
              - Most complete lyric: IG (scr)
              - Original partitur: -0-
              - Original parts: -0-

Liza
Gershwin/Kahn & Gershwin
Orchestrator: Unknown

Location of   - Composer's manuscript: LoC
              - Sheet music: LoC, NYPL
              - Most complete music: LoC (sm);
                  NYPL (sm)
              - Most complete lyric: LoC (sm);
                  NYPL (sm); IG (scr)
              - Original partitur: -0-
              - Original parts: -0-

Feeling Sentimental
Gershwin/Kahn & Gershwin
Orchestrator: Unknown

Location of   - Composer's manuscript: -0-
              - Sheet music: LoC
               - Most complete music: LoC (sm)
              - Most complete lyric: LoC (sm)
              - Original partitur: -0-
              - Original parts: -0-

Dropped during the pre-Broadway tryout.

I Couldn't Be Good
Author(s): Unknown
Orchestrator: Unknown

Location of   - Composer's manuscript: -0-
              - Sheet music: Unpublished
              - Most complete music: LoC (pv-I)
              - Most complete lyric: LoC (pv-I)
              - Original partitur: -0-
              - Original parts: -0-

Dropped during the pre-Broadway tryout.

Show Girl (1929)

At Mrs. Simpkin's Finishing School
Gershwin/Kahn & Gershwin
Orchestrator: Unknown

Location of - Composer's manuscript: -0-
           - Sheet music: Unpublished
           - Most complete music: LoC (pv)
           - Most complete lyric: IG (ls)
           - Original partitur: -0-
           - Original parts: -0-

Unused.

Adored One
Gershwin/Kahn & Gershwin
Orchestrator: Unknown

Location of - Composer's manuscript: -0-
           - Sheet music: Unpublished
           - Most complete music: IG (pv-l)
           - Most complete lyric: IG (pv-l)
           - Original partitur: -0-
           - Original parts: -0-

Unused.

Tonight's the Night
Gershwin/Kahn & Gershwin
Orchestrator: DePackh

Location of - Composer's manuscript: -0-
           - Sheet music: Unpublished
           - Most complete music: LoC (p)
           - Most complete lyric: IG (ls)
           - Original partitur: LoC
           - Original parts: -0-

Dropped before the New York opening.

I Just Looked At You
Gershwin/Kahn & Gershwin
Orchestrator: Unknown

Location of - Composer's manuscript: -0-
           - Sheet music: Unpublished
           - Most complete music: See note
           - Most complete lyric: IG (ls)
           - Original partitur: -0-
           - Original parts: -0-

The music, set to a lyric by Ira entitled "Lady of the Moon," was composed for EAST IS WEST, an unproduced Gershwin musical from 1928. For SHOW GIRL, Kahn and Gershwin wrote this new lyric, but the song was never used. Later, Ira wrote yet another lyric to the same tune, and the resulting song, "Blah, Blah, Blah," was sung in the film DELICIOUS (1931) and published. Sheet music for "Blah, Blah, Blah" can be found at the Library of Congress and the New York Public Library.

I'm Just a Bundle of Sunshine
Gershwin/Kahn & Gershwin
Orchestrator: Unknown

Location of - Composer's manuscript: -0-
           - Sheet music: Unpublished
           - Most complete music: -0-
           - Most complete lyric: IG (ls)
           - Original partitur: -0-
           - Original parts: -0-

Unused.

Somebody Stole My Heart Away
Gershwin/Kahn & Gershwin
Orchestrator: Unknown

Location of - Composer's manuscript: -0-
           - Sheet music: Unpublished
           - Most complete music: LoC (p)
           - Most complete lyric: IG (ls)
           - Original partitur: -0-
           - Original parts: -0-

Unused.

Someone's Always Calling a Rehearsal
Gershwin/Kahn & Gershwin
Orchestrator: Unknown

Location of - Composer's manuscript: -0-
     - Sheet music: Unpublished
     - Most complete music: -0-
     - Most complete lyric: IG (Is)
     - Original partitur: -0-
     - Original parts: -0-

Unused.

Home Lovin' Gal
Gershwin/Kahn & Gershwin
Orchestrator: Unknown

Location of - Composer's manuscript: -0-
     - Sheet music: Unpublished
     - Most complete music: -0-
     - Most complete lyric: IG (Is)
     - Original partitur: -0-
     - Original parts: -0-

Unused. Alternate title: "Home Lovin' Man."

I'm Out for No Good Reason Tonight
Gershwin/Kahn & Gershwin
Orchestrator: Unknown

Location of - Composer's manuscript: -0-
     - Sheet music: Unpublished
     - Most complete music: -0-
     - Most complete lyric: IG (Is)
     - Original partitur: -0-
     - Original parts: -0-

Unused.

STRIKE UP THE BAND (1930)

Music **GEORGE GERSHWIN**
Lyrics **IRA GERSHWIN**

Musical satire in two acts. Opened January 14, 1930 in New York and ian 191 performances (World premiere: December 25, 1929 in Boston). Libretto by Morrie Ryskind, based on the 1927 STRIKE UP THE BAND libretto by George S. Kaufman. Produced by Edgar Selwyn. Directed by Alexander Leftwich. Choreographed by George Hale. Musical direction by Hilding Anderson.

Synopsis and Production Information	When Switzerland protests a U.S. tariff on imported chocolate, Horace J. Fletcher, proud owner of the Fletcher American Chocolate Company, is outraged; when his daughter Joan announces plans to marry newspaperman Jim Townsend, who has publicly criticized Fletcher's operation, he becomes downright hysterical and suffers a mild stroke. While unconscious, Fletcher dreams that he finances a war against Switzerland, during which Jim proves his worth. When he awakens, he gives Joan and Jim his blessing.
	Other characters include C. Edgar Sloane, Fletcher's shifty manager; Col. Holmes, the President's confidential adviser ("The Unofficial Spokesman of the U.S.A."); Holmes' right-hand man, Gideon; Mrs. Draper, a formidable lady looking for a husband; and Mrs. Draper's spunky daughter Anne, who pairs up with Fletcher's young foreman Timothy for several numbers. There is a full singing and dancing ensemble.
Orchestration	Flute I II; Oboe; Clarinet I II; Bassoon; Horn I II; Trumpet I II; Trumpet III; Trombone; Drums; Harp; Violin I; Violin II; Violin III; Viola I; Viola II; Cello; Bass
Comments	After STRIKE UP THE BAND closed out of town in 1927, it was revised with a semi-new book and several new songs and presented on Broadway in this version, with Bobby Clark and Paul McCullough in the roles of Holmes and Gideon. The 1927 production is also included in this catalog.
Location of Original Materials	Script: Missing Piano-vocal score: Library of Congress, New York Public Library (Published: New World Music, 1930) Partiturs: Missing Parts: Library of Congress
	Although no final production script has been located, the Ira Gershwin Estate has a draft dated November, 1929. It contains no lyrics. Parts to four numbers survive.
Rental Status	Currently unavailable for rental
Music Publisher	Warner Brothers Music
Information	Ira Gershwin Estate, George Gershwin Family Trust

Overture
    Gershwin/Gershwin
    Orchestrator: Unknown

    Location of   - Composer's manuscript: -0-
              - Sheet music: Not published separately
              - Most complete music: LoC (pv score);
                  NYPL (pv score)
              - Most complete lyric: INST
              - Original partitur: -0-
              - Original parts: -0-

I Mean to Say
    Gershwin/Gershwin
    Orchestrator: Unknown

    Location of   - Composer's manuscript: -0-
              - Sheet music: LoC, NYPL
              - Most complete music: LoC (sm, pv score);
                  NYPL (sm, pv score)
              - Most complete lyric: LoC (sm, pv score);
                  NYPL (sm, pv score)
              - Original partitur: -0-
              - Original parts: LoC (inc)

Fletcher's American Chocolate Choral Society
    Gershwin/Gershwin
    Orchestrator: Unknown

    Location of   - Composer's manuscript: -0-
              - Sheet music: Not published separately
              - Most complete music: LoC (pv score);
                  NYPL (pv score)
              - Most complete lyric: LoC (pv score);
                  NYPL (pv score)
              - Original partitur: -0-
              - Original parts: -0-

Previously used in the 1927 production with a slightly different lyric entitled "Fletcher's American Cheese Choral Society"; the earlier lyric can be found in a lyric sheet at the New York Public Library.

Typical Self-Made American, A
    Gershwin/Gershwin
    Orchestrator: Unknown

    Location of   - Composer's manuscript: -0-
              - Sheet music: Not published separately
              - Most complete music: LoC (pv score);
                  NYPL (pv score)
              - Most complete lyric: LoC (pv score);
                  NYPL (pv score)
              - Original partitur: -0-
              - Original parts: -0-

Previously used in the 1927 production.

Strike Up the Band (1930)

Soon

Gershwin/Gershwin
Orchestrator: Unknown

Location of   - Composer's manuscript: -0-
     - Sheet music: LoC, NYPL
     - Most complete music: LoC (sm, pv score);
       NYPL (sm, pv score)
     - Most complete lyric: LoC (sm, pv score);
       NYPL (sm, pv score)
     - Original partitur: -0-
     - Original parts: -0-

The music to the verse came from the verse of "Hoping That Someday You'd Care" in the 1927 production; the music to the refrain grew out of a phrase in the 1927 Ensemble number (retitled "He Knows Milk" in 1930).

Patriotic Rally

Gershwin/Gershwin
Orchestrator: Unknown

Location of   - Composer's manuscript: -0-
     - Sheet music: Not published separately
     - Most complete music: LoC (pv score);
       NYPL (pv score)
     - Most complete lyric: NYPL (pv score
       & ls)
     - Original partitur: -0-
     - Original parts: LoC

Previously used in the 1927 production.

Unofficial Spokesman, The

Gershwin/Gershwin
Orchestrator: Unknown

Location of   - Composer's manuscript: -0-
     - Sheet music: Not published separately
     - Most complete music: LoC (pv score);
       NYPL (pv score)
     - Most complete lyric: LoC (pv score);
       NYPL (pv score)
     - Original partitur: -0-
     - Original parts: -0-

"The Wizard of the Age," which book-ended this number in the 1927 production, was not used in 1930 and, therefore, was not published in the piano-vocal score. The lyrics to "Wizard" are in a lyric sheet at the New York Public Library (which also contains a few earlier lyrics for "The Unofficial Spokesman"); the music is in a piano-vocal at the Library of Congress.

If I Became the President

Gershwin/Gershwin
Orchestrator: Unknown

Location of   - Composer's manuscript: -0-
     - Sheet music: Not published separately
     - Most complete music: LoC (pv score);
       NYPL (pv score)
     - Most complete lyric: LoC (pv score);
       NYPL (pv score)
     - Original partitur: -0-
     - Original parts: LoC

The Ira Gershwin Estate also has three pages of lyrics that Bobby Clark suggested as alternates.

Hangin' Around With You

Gershwin/Gershwin
Orchestrator: Unknown

Location of   - Composer's manuscript: -0-
     - Sheet music: LoC, NYPL
     - Most complete music: LoC (sm, pv score);
        NYPL (sm, pv score)
     - Most complete lyric: IG (ls)
     - Original partitur: -0-
     - Original parts: -0-

In the Rattle of the Battle

Gershwin/Gershwin
Orchestrator: Unknown

Location of   - Composer's manuscript: -0-
     - Sheet music: Not published separately
     - Most complete music: LoC (pv score);
        NYPL (pv score)
     - Most complete lyric: LoC (pv score);
        NYPL (pv score)
     - Original partitur: -0-
     - Original parts: -0-

He Knows Milk

Gershwin/Gershwin
Orchestrator: Unknown

Location of   - Composer's manuscript: -0-
     - Sheet music: Not published separately
     - Most complete music: LoC (pv score);
        NYPL (pv score)
     - Most complete lyric: LoC (pv score);
        NYPL (pv score)
     - Original partitur: -0-
     - Original parts: -0-

This number is virtually identical to the Ensemble number at this spot in the 1927 production, with a few altered lyrics and one section deleted at the end. The lyrics used in 1927 are in a lyric sheet at the New York Public Library.

Military Dancing Drill

Gershwin/Gershwin
Orchestrator: Unknown

Location of   - Composer's manuscript: -0-
     - Sheet music: LoC, NYPL
     - Most complete music: LoC (sm
        & pv score); NYPL (sm & pv score)
     - Most complete lyric: NYPL (sm & ls
        & pv score)
     - Original partitur: -0-
     - Original parts: LoC

This number has two entirely different verses: The verse written for the 1927 production is published in the sheet music, although the lyric sheet at the New York Public Library suggests that it was revised slightly in rehearsal; the verse performed in 1930 is published in the piano-vocal score.

Strike Up the Band

Gershwin/Gershwin
Orchestrator: Unknown

Location of   - Composer's manuscript: LoC (r)
     - Sheet music: LoC, NYPL
     - Most complete music: LoC (sm, pv score);
        NYPL (sm, pv score)
     - Most complete lyric: IG (ls)
     - Original partitur: -0-
     - Original parts: -0-

Mademoiselle in New Rochelle

Gershwin/Gershwin
Orchestrator: Unknown

Location of   - Composer's manuscript: -0-
     - Sheet music: LoC, NYPL
     - Most complete music: LoC (sm, pv score);
        NYPL (sm, pv score)
     - Most complete lyric: LoC (sm, pv score);
        NYPL (sm, pv score)
     - Original partitur: -0-
     - Original parts: -0-

Strike Up the Band (1930)

I've Got a Crush on You
Gershwin/Gershwin
Orchestrator: Unknown

Location of   - Composer's manuscript: LoC (lead)
              - Sheet music: LoC
              - Most complete music: LoC (sm, pv score);
                 NYPL (pv score)
              - Most complete lyric: IG (ls)
              - Original partitur: -0-
              - Original parts: -0-

Previously used in TREASURE GIRL (1928).

Ring a Ding a Ding Dong Dell
Gershwin/Gershwin
Orchestrator: Unknown

Location of   - Composer's manuscript: -0-
              - Sheet music: Not published separately
              - Most complete music: LoC (pv score);
                 NYPL (pv score)
              - Most complete lyric: LoC (pv score);
                 NYPL (pv score)
              - Original partitur: -0-
              - Original parts: -0-

How About a Boy Like Me?
Gershwin/Gershwin
Orchestrator: Unknown

Location of   - Composer's manuscript: -0-
              - Sheet music: Not published separately
              - Most complete music: LoC (pv score);
                 NYPL (pv score)
              - Most complete lyric: LoC (pv score);
                 NYPL (pv score)
              - Original partitur: -0-
              - Original parts: -0-

This is not the same song as "How About a Man?" from the 1927 production.

I Want to Be a War Bride
Gershwin/Gershwin
Orchestrator: Unknown

Location of   - Composer's manuscript: -0-
              - Sheet music: LoC
              - Most complete music: LoC (sm)
              - Most complete lyric: LoC (sm)
              - Original partitur: -0-
              - Original parts: -0-

Dropped soon after the New York opening.

Official Resume
Gershwin/Gershwin
Orchestrator: Unknown

Location of   - Composer's manuscript: -0-
              - Sheet music: Not published separately
              - Most complete music: LoC (pv score);
                 NYPL (pv score)
              - Most complete lyric: LoC (pv score);
                 NYPL (pv score)
              - Original partitur: -0-
              - Original parts: -0-

There Never Was Such a Charming War
Gershwin/Gershwin
Orchestrator: Unknown

Location of   - Composer's manuscript: -0-
              - Sheet music: Unpublished
              - Most complete music: -0-
              - Most complete lyric: IG (ls)
              - Original partitur: -0-
              - Original parts: -0-

Unused.

Thanks to You
Gershwin/Gershwin
Orchestrator: Unknown

Location of   - Composer's manuscript: -0-
             - Sheet music: Unpublished
             - Most complete music: LoC (pv-l)
             - Most complete lyric: LoC (pv-l)
             - Original partitur: -0-
             - Original parts: -0-

An unused duet for Jim and Joan. Prepared for
publication, but never printed.

GIRL CRAZY

Music   **GEORGE GERSHWIN**
Lyrics   **IRA GERSHWIN**

Musical comedy in two acts. Opened October 14, 1930 in New York and ran 272 performances (World premiere: September 29, 1930 in Philadelphia). Libretto by Guy Bolton and John McGowan. Additional lyric (unused) by Lou Paley. Produced by Alex A. Aarons and Vinton Freedley. Directed by Alexander Leftwich. Choreographed by George Hale. Musical direction by Earl Busby. Orchestrations by Robert Russell Bennett.

Synopsis and Production Information	Danny Churchill, a New York playboy, is sent by his father to an Arizona ranch far from the evils of the big city. During his stay there, he sets up a dude ranch, fights his old New York rival (Sam) for the hand of the local post-girl (Molly), and fends off the town thugs.
	Additional principals include Gieber, the chief comic, and Kate, a saloon singer. The show requires a full singing and dancing ensemble.
Orchestration	Flute; Oboe (English Horn); Alto Sax I (Clarinet & Baritone Sax); Alto Sax II (Clarinet & Baritone Sax); Tenor Sax (Flute & Clarinet); Trumpet I II; Trumpet III; Trombone I II; Percussion; Piano; Violin I; Violin II; Viola I; Viola II; Cello; Bass
Comments	In the original production, Molly was played by Ginger Rogers, Kate by Ethel Merman, and Gieber by Willie Howard. The orchestra included Benny Goodman, Glenn Miller, Red Nichols, Jimmy Dorsey, Jack Teagarden, and Gene Krupa.
Location of Original Materials	Script: Tams-Witmark Music Library (all lyrics)
	Piano-vocal score: Tams-Witmark Music Library, Library of Congress, New York Public Library (Published: New World Music, 1954)
	Partiturs: Missing
	Parts: Tams-Witmark Music Library
	The Ira Gershwin Estate has an early draft of the script.
Rental Status	Tams-Witmark rents both the original show and a Guy Bolton update (c. 1960) with a few interpolated Gershwin numbers from other shows and an new orchestration for 22 players.
Music Publisher	Warner Brothers Music
Information	Tams-Witmark Music Library

Overture
Gershwin/Gershwin
Orchestrator: Unknown

Location of - Composer's manuscript: -0-
              - Sheet music: Not published separately
              - Most complete music: LoC (pv score);
                    NYPL (pv score); TW (pv score)
              - Most complete lyric: INST
              - Original partitur: -0-
              - Original parts: TW

Could You Use Me?
Gershwin/Gershwin
Orchestrator: Unknown

Location of - Composer's manuscript: LoC
              - Sheet music: LoC, NYPL
              - Most complete music: LoC (sm, pv score);
                    NYPL (sm, pv score); TW (pv score)
              - Most complete lyric: IG (ls)
              - Original partitur: -0-
              - Original parts: TW

Bidin' My Time
Gershwin/Gershwin
Orchestrator: Unknown

Location of - Composer's manuscript: LoC
              - Sheet music: LoC, NYPL
              - Most complete music: LoC (sm, pv score);
                    NYPL (sm, pv score); TW (pv score)
              - Most complete lyric: LoC (pv score);
                    NYPL (pv score); TW (pv score, scr);
                  LOSO
              - Original partitur: -0-
              - Original parts: TW

Bronco Busters
Gershwin/Gershwin
Orchestrator: Unknown

Location of - Composer's manuscript: -0-
              - Sheet music: Not published separately
              - Most complete music: LoC (pv score);
                    NYPL (pv score); TW (pv score)
              - Most complete lyric: LoC (pv score);
                    NYPL (pv score); TW (pv score, scr)
              - Original partitur: -0-
              - Original parts: TW

Lonesome Cowboy, The
Gershwin/Gershwin
Orchestrator: Unknown

Location of - Composer's manuscript: -0-
              - Sheet music: Not published separately
              - Most complete music: LoC (pv score);
                    NYPL (pv score); TW (pv score)
              - Most complete lyric: LoC (pv score);
                    NYPL (pv score); TW (pv score, scr)
              - Original partitur: -0-
              - Original parts: TW

Barbary Coast
Gershwin/Gershwin
Orchestrator: Unknown

Location of - Composer's manuscript: -0-
              - Sheet music: Not published separately
              - Most complete music: LoC (pv score);
                    NYPL (pv score); TW (pv score)
              - Most complete lyric: LoC (pv score);
                    NYPL (pv score); TW (pv score, scr)
              - Original partitur: -0-
              - Original parts: TW

Girl Crazy (1930)

Embraceable You

Gershwin/Gershwin

Orchestrator: Unknown

Location of   - Composer's manuscript: -0-
- Sheet music: LoC, NYPL
- Most complete music: LoC (sm, pv score);
      NYPL (sm, pv score); TW (pv score)
- Most complete lyric: IG (ls)
- Original partitur: -0-
- Original parts: TW

Originally written for EAST IS WEST, an unproduced
Gershwin operetta from 1928.

I Got Rhythm

Gershwin/Gershwin

Orchestrator: Unknown

Location of   - Composer's manuscript: LoC
- Sheet music: LoC, NYPL
- Most complete music: LoC (sm, pv score);
      NYPL (sm, pv score); TW (pv score)
- Most complete lyric: LoC (sm, pv score);
      NYPL (sm, pv score);
      TW (pv score, scr); LOSO
- Original partitur: -0-
- Original parts: TW

Goldfarb! That's I'm!

Gershwin/Gershwin

Orchestrator: Unknown

Location of   - Composer's manuscript: -0-
- Sheet music: Not published separately
- Most complete music: LoC (pv score);
      NYPL (pv score); TW (pv score)
- Most complete lyric: LoC (pv score);
      NYPL (pv score); TW (pv score, scr)
- Original partitur: -0-
- Original parts: TW

Alternate title: "Finaletto."

Finale Act I [He's a bronco buster..."]

Gershwin/Gershwin

Orchestrator: Unknown

Location of   - Composer's manuscript: IG
- Sheet music: Not published separately
- Most complete music: LoC (pv score);
      NYPL (pv score); TW (pv score)
- Most complete lyric: LoC (pv score);
      NYPL (pv score); TW (pv score)
- Original partitur: -0-
- Original parts: TW

Sam and Delilah

Gershwin/Gershwin

Orchestrator: Unknown

Location of   - Composer's manuscript: LoC
- Sheet music: LoC, NYPL
- Most complete music: LoC (sm, pv score);
      NYPL (sm, pv score); TW (pv score)
- Most complete lyric: LoC (sm, pv score);
      NYPL (sm, pv score);
      TW (pv score, scr); LOSO
- Original partitur: -0-
- Original parts: TW

Entr'acte

Gershwin/Gershwin

Orchestrator: Unknown

Location of   - Composer's manuscript: -0-
- Sheet music: Not published separately
- Most complete music: LoC (pv score);
      NYPL (pv score); TW (pv score)
- Most complete lyric: LoC (pv score);
      NYPL (pv score); TW (pv score)
- Original partitur: -0-
- Original parts: TW

Portions of the Entr'acte were sung.

Land of the Gay Caballero

Gershwin/Gershwin

Orchestrator: Unknown

Location of   - Composer's manuscript: IG
- Sheet music: Not published separately
- Most complete music: LoC (pv score);
    NYPL (pv score); TW (pv score)
- Most complete lyric: LoC (pv score);
    NYPL (pv score); TW (pv score, scr)
- Original partitur: -0-
- Original parts: TW

Alternate title: "Opening Act II."

Boy! What Love Has Done to Me

Gershwin/Gershwin

Orchestrator: Unknown

Location of   - Composer's manuscript: -0-
- Sheet music: LoC, NYPL
- Most complete music: LoC (sm, pv score);
    NYPL (sm, pv score); TW (pv score)
- Most complete lyric: LoC (sm, pv score);
    NYPL (sm, pv score);
    TW (pv score, scr)
- Original partitur: -0-
- Original parts: TW

But Not for Me

Gershwin/Gershwin

Orchestrator: Unknown

Location of   - Composer's manuscript: LoC
- Sheet music: LoC
- Most complete music: LoC (sm, pv score);
    NYPL (pv score); TW (pv score)
- Most complete lyric: LoC (pv score);
    NYPL (pv score); TW (pv score)
- Original partitur: -0-
- Original parts: TW

When It's Cactus Time In Arizona

Gershwin/Gershwin

Orchestrator: Unknown

Location of   - Composer's manuscript: -0-
- Sheet music: Not published separately
- Most complete music: LoC (pv score);
    NYPL (pv score); TW (pv score)
- Most complete lyric: LoC (pv score);
    NYPL (pv score); TW (pv score, scr)
- Original partitur: -0-
- Original parts: TW

Treat Me Rough

Gershwin/Gershwin

Orchestrator: Unknown

Location of   - Composer's manuscript: -0-
- Sheet music: LoC
- Most complete music: LoC (sm, pv score);
    NYPL (pv score); TW (pv score)
- Most complete lyric: IG (ls)
- Original partitur: -0-
- Original parts: TW

You Can't Unscramble Scrambled Eggs

Gershwin/Gershwin

Orchestrator: Unknown

Location of   - Composer's manuscript: -0-
- Sheet music: Unpublished
- Most complete music: IG (pv)
- Most complete lyric: IG (ls)
- Original partitur: -0-
- Original parts: -0-

Dropped before the New York opening.

Girl Crazy (1930)

And I Have You
Gershwin/Gershwin
Orchestrator: Unknown

Location of
- Composer's manuscript: -0-
- Sheet music: Unpublished
- Most complete music: -0-
- Most complete lyric: IG (ls)
- Original partitur: -0-
- Original parts: -0-

Dropped before the New York opening.

Are You Dancing?
Gershwin/Gershwin
Orchestrator: Unknown

Location of
- Composer's manuscript: IG
- Sheet music: Unpublished
- Most complete music: IG (pv)
- Most complete lyric: IG (ls)
- Original partitur: -0-
- Original parts: -0-

Unused.

Something Peculiar
Gershwin/Gershwin & Paley
Orchestrator: Unknown

Location of
- Composer's manuscript: -0-
- Sheet music: Unpublished
- Most complete music: IG (pv)
- Most complete lyric: IG (ls)
- Original partitur: -0-
- Original parts: -0-

Unused. This number may have been written as early as 1921 and also intended for LADY, BE GOOD! (1924).

You've Got What Gets Me
Gershwin/Gershwin
Orchestrator: Unknown

Location of
- Composer's manuscript: -0-
- Sheet music: LoC, NYPL
- Most complete music: LoC (sm); NYPL (sm)
- Most complete lyric: LoC (sm); NYPL (sm)
- Original partitur: -0-
- Original parts: -0-

Written for the 1932 film version. The release was previously used as the release of "Your Eyes! Your Smile!", which was dropped during the pre-Broadway of FUNNY FACE (1927).

Gambler of the West, The
Gershwin/Gershwin
Orchestrator: Unknown

Location of
- Composer's manuscript: -0-
- Sheet music: Unpublished
- Most complete music: -0-
- Most complete lyric: IG (ls)
- Original partitur: -0-
- Original parts: -0-

Dropped before the New York opening.

OF THEE I SING

Music GEORGE GERSHWIN
Lyrics IRA GERSHWIN

Musical satire in two acts. Opened December 26, 1931 in New York and ran 441 performances (World premiere: December 8, 1931 in Boston). Libretto by George S. Kaufman and Morrie Ryskind. Produced by Sam H. Harris. Directed by George S. Kaufman. Choreographed by George Hale. Musical direction by Charles Previn. Orchestrations by Robert Russell Bennett, William Daly, George Gershwin.

Synopsis and Production Information	The National Party, deciding that its Presidential nominee, John P. Wintergreen, will run on a platform of love, sponsors a beauty pageant in Atlantic City to choose Wintergreen a bride. As luck (and love) would have it, John falls for a secretary at the pageant, Mary Turner, who makes incomparable corn muffins. The pageant winner, Diana Devereaux (the fairest flower of the South), seeks revenge, and when the inflammatory French Ambassador joins her cause, a newly-elected Wintergreen finds himself threatened with impeachment. The power of love, of course, saves the day.
	Other characters include befuddled Vice-President Throttlebottom, who wanders through the White House unrecognized by his own staff, and secretaries Sam Jenkins and Miss Benson, who lead the chorus in two numbers. There is a full singing and dancing ensemble.
Orchestration	Reed I (Flute, Piccolo); Reed II (Oboe); Reed III (Alto Sax, Clarinet, Bass Clarinet); Reed IV (Alto Sax, Clarinet); Reed V (Tenor Sax, Clarinet); Horn; Trumpet I II; Trumpet III; Trombone; Percussion; Piano; Violin A B C; Viola; Cello; Bass
Comments	OF THEE I SING won the Pulitzer Prize for Drama in 1932. In the original production, Wintergreen was played by William Gaxton, Throttlebottom by Victor Moore.

Location of Original Materials	Script: Samuel French, Inc. (most lyrics)
	     (Published: Alfred A. Knopf, Inc., 1932)
	Piano-vocal score: Library of Congress, New York Public Library, Samuel French, Inc.
	     (Published: New World Music, 1932)
	Partiturs: Library of Congress
	Parts: Ira Gershwin Estate

	Only one partitur has surfaced. All of the original parts survive; partiturs reconstructed from them in 1986 are at the Ira Gershwin Estate.
Rental Status	Samuel French currently rents the original book and piano-vocal score with a reduced orchestration for 18 players. Inquiries regarding performance of the original orchestrations should be directed to the Ira Gershwin Estate.
Music Publisher	Warner Brothers Music
Information	Ira Gershwin Estate, George Gershwin Family Trust

Of Thee I Sing (1931)

Overture

Gershwin/Gershwin
Orchestrator: Unknown

Location of
- Composer's manuscript: -0-
- Sheet music: Not published separately
- Most complete music: LoC (pv score); NYPL (pv score); SF (pv score)
- Most complete lyric: INST
- Original partitur: IG (1987)
- Original parts: IG

Finaletto Act I, Scene IV ["As the chairman of the committee..."]

Gershwin/Gershwin
Orchestrator: Unknown

Location of
- Composer's manuscript: LoC
- Sheet music: Not published separately
- Most complete music: LoC (pv score); NYPL (pv score); SF (pv score)
- Most complete lyric: LoC (pv score); NYPL (pv score); SF (pv score, scr)
- Original partitur: IG (1987)
- Original parts: IG

Includes "Some Girls Can Bake a Pie."

Wintergreen for President

Gershwin/Gershwin
Orchestrator: Unknown

Location of
- Composer's manuscript: LoC
- Sheet music: WB
- Most complete music: LoC (pv score); NYPL (pv score); SF (pv score)
- Most complete lyric: LoC (pv score); NYPL (pv score); SF (pv score)
- Original partitur: IG (1987)
- Original parts: IG

Love Is Sweeping the Country

Gershwin/Gershwin
Orchestrator: Unknown

Location of
- Composer's manuscript: LoC
- Sheet music: LoC
- Most complete music: LoC (pv score); NYPL (pv score); SF (pv score)
- Most complete lyric: LoC (pv score); NYPL (pv score); SF (pv score); LOSO
- Original partitur: IG (1987)
- Original parts: IG

The sheet music does not include the patter. The partitur and parts contain a dance arrangement that is not found in the piano-vocal score.

Who Is The Lucky Girl to Be?/Because, Because

Gershwin/Gershwin
Orchestrator: Unknown

Location of
- Composer's manuscript: LoC
- Sheet music: LoC
- Most complete music: LoC (pv score); NYPL (pv score); SF (pv score)
- Most complete lyric: LoC (pv score); NYPL (pv score), SF (pv score, scr)
- Original partitur: IG (1987)
- Original parts: IG

Only "Because, Because" was published as sheet music.

Of Thee I Sing

Gershwin/Gershwin
Orchestrator: Unknown

Location of
- Composer's manuscript: -0-
- Sheet music: LoC
- Most complete music: LoC (pv score); NYPL (pv score); SF (pv score)
- Most complete lyric: LoC (pv score); NYPL (pv score); SF (pv score)
- Original partitur: IG (1987)
- Original parts: IG

The verse, which was not performed in the original production, is not in the published script.

Finale Act I
　　Gershwin/Gershwin
　　Orchestrator: Unknown

　　Location of　- Composer's manuscript: -0-
　　　　　　　- Sheet music: Not published separately
　　　　　　　- Most complete music: LoC (pv score);
　　　　　　　　　NYPL (pv score); SF (pv score)
　　　　　　　- Most complete lyric: LoC (pv score);
　　　　　　　　　NYPL (pv score); SF (pv score, scr)
　　　　　　　- Original partitur: IG (1987)
　　　　　　　- Original parts: IG

Includes "A Kiss for Cinderella." The Library of Congress also has a piano-vocal for an early version containing additional music and lyrics. For the 1952 Broadway revival of OF THEE I SING, Ira Gershwin updated some of the lyrics to this song; these are published in his <u>Lyrics on Several Occasions</u>.

Entr'acte
　　Gershwin/Gershwin
　　Orchestrator: Unknown

　　Location of　- Composer's manuscript: -0-
　　　　　　　- Sheet music: Unpublished
　　　　　　　- Most complete music: IG (parts)
　　　　　　　- Most complete lyric: INST
　　　　　　　- Original partitur: IG (1987)
　　　　　　　- Original parts: IG

Hello, Good Morning
　　Gershwin/Gershwin
　　Orchestrator: Gershwin

　　Location of　- Composer's manuscript: -0-
　　　　　　　- Sheet music: Not published separately
　　　　　　　- Most complete music: LoC (pv score);
　　　　　　　　　NYPL (pv score); SF (pv score)
　　　　　　　- Most complete lyric: LoC (pv score);
　　　　　　　　　NYPL (pv score); SF (pv score, scr)
　　　　　　　- Original partitur: LoC
　　　　　　　- Original parts: IG

Alternate title: "Opening Act II."

Who Cares?
　　Gershwin/Gershwin
　　Orchestrator: Unknown

　　Location of　- Composer's manuscript: LoC
　　　　　　　- Sheet music: LoC, NYPL
　　　　　　　- Most complete music: LoC (sm
　　　　　　　　　& pv score); NYPL (sm & pv score)
　　　　　　　- Most complete lyric: LoC (sm
　　　　　　　　　& pv score); NYPL (sm & pv score)
　　　　　　　- Original partitur: IG (1987)
　　　　　　　- Original parts: IG

The verse published in the sheet music was not performed in the original production. The Library of Congress manuscript also contains a sketch for an unused 18-bar verse. For the 1952 Broadway revival of OF THEE I SING, Ira Gershwin updated some of the lyrics to this song; these are published in his <u>Lyrics on Several Occasions</u>.

Illegitimate Daughter, The
　　Gershwin/Gershwin
　　Orchestrator: Unknown

　　Location of　- Composer's manuscript: LoC
　　　　　　　- Sheet music: LoC
　　　　　　　- Most complete music: LoC (pv score);
　　　　　　　　　NYPL (pv score); SF (pv score)
　　　　　　　- Most complete lyric: LoC (pv score);
　　　　　　　　　NYPL (pv score); SF (pv score, scr)
　　　　　　　- Original partitur: IG (1987)
　　　　　　　- Original parts: IG

Senator From Minnesota, The
　　Gershwin/Gershwin
　　Orchestrator: Unknown

　　Location of　- Composer's manuscript: LoC
　　　　　　　- Sheet music: Not published separately
　　　　　　　- Most complete music: LoC (pv score);
　　　　　　　　　NYPL (pv score); SF (pv score)
　　　　　　　- Most complete lyric: LoC (pv score);
　　　　　　　　　NYPL (pv score); SF (pv score)
　　　　　　　- Original partitur: IG (1987)
　　　　　　　- Original parts: IG

Of Thee I Sing (1931)

Senate, The
Gershwin/Gershwin
Orchestrator: Unknown

Location of   - Composer's manuscript: LoC
    - Sheet music: Not published separately
    - Most complete music: LoC (pv &
      pv score)
    - Most complete lyric: LoC (pv &
      pv score)
    - Original partitur: IG (1987)
    - Original parts: IG

Includes "Jilted, Jilted!" The Library of Congress
manuscript contains 20 measures that were dropped before
the New York opening.

Trumpeter Blow Your Golden Horn
Gershwin/Gershwin
Orchestrator: Unknown

Location of   - Composer's manuscript: LoC
    - Sheet music: Not published separately
    - Most complete music: LoC (pv score);
      NYPL (pv score); SF (pv score)
    - Most complete lyric: LoC (pv score);
      NYPL (pv score); SF (pv score, scr)
    - Original partitur: IG (1987)
    - Original parts: IG

Posterity Is Just Around the Corner
Gershwin/Gershwin
Orchestrator: Unknown

Location of   - Composer's manuscript: LoC
    - Sheet music: Not published separately
    - Most complete music: LoC (pv score);
      NYPL (pv score); SF (pv score)
    - Most complete lyric: LoC (pv score);
      NYPL (pv score); SF (pv score)
    - Original partitur: IG (1987)
    - Original parts: IG

Finale Ultimo ["On that matter no one budges..."]
Gershwin/Gershwin
Orchestrator: Unknown

Location of   - Composer's manuscript: -0-
    - Sheet music: Not published separately
    - Most complete music: LoC (pv score);
      NYPL (pv score); SF (pv score)
    - Most complete lyric: LoC (pv score);
      NYPL (pv score); SF (pv score)
    - Original partitur: IG (1987)
    - Original parts: IG

PARDON MY ENGLISH

Music	GEORGE GERSHWIN
Lyrics	IRA GERSHWIN

Musical comedy in two acts. Opened January 20, 1933 in New York and ran 46 performances (World premiere: December 2, 1932 in Philadelphia). Libretto by Herbert Fields. Produced by Alex A. Aarons and Vinton Freedley. Directed by John McGowan. Choreographed by George Hale. Musical direction by Earl Busby. Orchestrations by William Daly, Robert Russell Bennett, Adolph Deutsch.

Synopsis and Production Information	Golo and Gita, international jewel thieves, arrive in Dresden after stealing the Crown Prince's monocle. Golo complicates matters by falling in love with the Police Commissioner's daughter Ilse. After numerous false arrests, an aborted wedding, and a kidnapping, Golo receives a blow to the head that cures him of his kleptomaniac tendencies and restores him to his civilian identity, Michael Bramleigh.
	The cast includes an American dance team and a full singing and dancing ensemble.
Orchestration	Reed I (Oboe, English Horn); Reed II (Alto Sax, Clarinet, Baritone Sax); Reed III (Alto Sax, Clarinet, Flute, Piccolo); Reed IV (Tenor Sax, Clarinet); Horn I II; Trumpet I II; Trombone; Percussion; Piano; Violin I; Violin II; Viola; Cello; Bass
Comments	PARDON MY ENGLISH went through several librettists (including Morrie Ryskind and Jack McGowan) and directors (including George S. Kaufman and Ernst Lubitsch) en route to Broadway. Characters were added, subplots deleted, and the leading character's affliction changed from a split personality to kleptomania. The show's eventual failure broke up the producing team of Aarons and Freedley.
Location of Original Materials	Script: Missing Piano-vocal score: See individual listings Partiturs: Library of Congress Parts: Library of Congress
	The Library of Congress has an early draft by Fields and Ryskind that approximates the show performed in Philadelphia, but in no way represents the final production script. All of the songs from the show survive, as do most of the partiturs and parts.
Rental Status	Currently unavailable for rental
Music Publisher	Warner Brothers Music
Information	Ira Gershwin Estate, George Gershwin Family Trust

Pardon My English (1933)

Overture
Gershwin/Gershwin
Orchestrator: Daly

Location of   - Composer's manuscript: LoC
               - Sheet music: Unpublished
               - Most complete music: LoC (parts)
               - Most complete lyric: INST
               - Original partitur: LoC (inc), LoC (1987)
               - Original parts: LoC

Pardon My English
Gershwin/Gershwin
Orchestrator: Daly

Location of   - Composer's manuscript: -0-
               - Sheet music: Unpublished
               - Most complete music: LoC (ptr)
               - Most complete lyric: IG (ls)
               - Original partitur: LoC
               - Original parts: LoC (1987)

In Three-Quarter Time
Gershwin/Gershwin
Orchestrator: Bennett

Location of   - Composer's manuscript: LoC
               - Sheet music: Unpublished
               - Most complete music: LoC (pv-l)
               - Most complete lyric: LOSO
               - Original partitur: LoC
               - Original parts: LoC (1987)

The Library of Congress also has the original vocal arrangement.

Dancing in the Streets
Gershwin/Gershwin
Orchestrator: Bennett

Location of   - Composer's manuscript: -0-
               - Sheet music: Unpublished
               - Most complete music: LoC (pv-l)
               - Most complete lyric: IG (ls)
               - Original partitur: LoC
               - Original parts: LoC

The Library of Congress also has the original chorus parts.

Lorelei, The
Gershwin/Gershwin
Orchestrator: Unknown

Location of   - Composer's manuscript: LoC
               - Sheet music: NYPL
               - Most complete music: NYPL (sm);
                          LoC (pv-l)
               - Most complete lyric: NYPL (sm);
                          LoC (pv-l); LOSO
               - Original partitur: LoC (1987)
               - Original parts: LoC

The Library of Congress also has the original vocal arrangement.

So What?
Gershwin/Gershwin
Orchestrator: Bennett

Location of   - Composer's manuscript: LoC
               - Sheet music: LoC, NYPL; IG
               - Most complete music: LoC (sm);
                          NYPL (sm); IG (sm)
               - Most complete lyric: IG (sm & ls)
               - Original partitur: LoC
               - Original parts: LoC

A duet in the show, the lyric was reworked into a solo for the sheet music. The Library of Congress also has the original male chorus parts.

159

Isn't It a Pity?

Gershwin/Gershwin
Orchestrator: Bennett

Location of   - Composer's manuscript: LoC (v)
          - Sheet music: LoC, NYPL
          - Most complete music: LoC (sm);
              NYPL (sm)
          - Most complete lyric: IG (ls)
          - Original partitur: LoC
          - Original parts: LoC, LoC (1987)

My Cousin in Milwaukee

Gershwin/Gershwin
Orchestrator: Deutsch

Location of   - Composer's manuscript: -0-
          - Sheet music: LoC, NYPL
          - Most complete music: LoC (sm);
              NYPL (sm)
          - Most complete lyric: LoC (sm);
              NYPL (sm)
          - Original partitur: LoC
          - Original parts: LoC, LoC (1987)

Hail the Happy Couple

Gershwin/Gershwin
Orchestrator: Unknown

Location of   - Composer's manuscript: -0-
          - Sheet music: Unpublished
          - Most complete music: LoC (parts)
          - Most complete lyric: IG (ls)
          - Original partitur: -0-
          - Original parts: LoC

Alternate title: "Bride and Groom." The parts are entitled "Opening Garden Scene." The music to the refrain was taken from the refrain of the deleted "Watch Your Head," and was later used for "Comes the Revolution" in LET 'EM EAT CAKE (1933).

Dresden Northwest Mounted, The

Gershwin/Gershwin
Orchestrator: Daly

Location of   - Composer's manuscript: -0-
          - Sheet music: Unpublished
          - Most complete music: LoC (pv-l)
          - Most complete lyric: IG (ls)
          - Original partitur: LoC
          - Original parts: LoC (1987)

The Library of Congress also has the original male chorus parts.

Luckiest Man In the World

Gershwin/Gershwin
Orchestrator: Bennett

Location of   - Composer's manuscript: LoC
          - Sheet music: LoC, NYPL
          - Most complete music: LoC (sm);
              NYPL (sm)
          - Most complete lyric: LoC (sm);
              NYPL (sm)
          - Original partitur: LoC
          - Original parts: LoC

This is not the same number as the deleted "Luckiest Boy in the World."

Finale Act I

Gershwin/Gershwin
Orchestrator: Daly

Location of   - Composer's manuscript: LoC
          - Sheet music: Unpublished
          - Most complete music: LoC (pv-l)
          - Most complete lyric: IG (ls)
          - Original partitur: LoC
          - Original parts: LoC

Alternate title: "What Sort of Wedding Is This?"

Pardon My English (1933)

Entr'acte

Gershwin/Gershwin

Orchestrator: Unknown

Location of — Composer's manuscript: -0-
— Sheet music: Unpublished
— Most complete music: LoC (parts)
— Most complete lyric: INST
— Original partitur: -0-
— Original parts: LoC

Tonight

Gershwin/Gershwin

Orchestrator: Daly

Location of — Composer's manuscript: LoC
— Sheet music: See note
— Most complete music: LoC (pv)
— Most complete lyric: IG (ls)
— Original partitur: LoC
— Original parts: LoC

Published without lyrics in 1971 under the title "Two Waltzes in C."

Where You Go, I Go

Gershwin/Gershwin

Orchestrator: Unknown

Location of — Composer's manuscript: LoC
— Sheet music: LoC, NYPL
— Most complete music: LoC (sm); NYPL (sm)
— Most complete lyric: LoC (sm); NYPL (sm)
— Original partitur: LoC (1987)
— Original parts: LoC

I've Got to Be There

Gershwin/Gershwin

Orchestrator: Deutsch

Location of — Composer's manuscript: -0-
— Sheet music: LoC, NYPL
— Most complete music: LoC (sm); NYPL (sm)
— Most complete lyric: LoC (sm); NYPL (sm)
— Original partitur: LoC
— Original parts: LoC

The Library of Congress also has the original male chorus parts and a pencil sketch of the original vocal arrangement.

Finaletto ["Open in the name of the law!"]

Gershwin/Gershwin

Orchestrator: Bennett

Location of — Composer's manuscript: -0-
— Sheet music: Unpublished
— Most complete music: LoC (pv-l)
— Most complete lyric: IG (ls)
— Original partitur: LoC
— Original parts: LoC

Finale Act II

Gershwin/Gershwin

Orchestrator: Bennett

Location of — Composer's manuscript: -0-
— Sheet music: Unpublished
— Most complete music: LoC (pv-l)
— Most complete lyric: IG (ls)
— Original partitur: LoC (inc)
— Original parts: LoC

Alternate titles: "He's Not Himself" and "Poor Michael! Poor Golo!"

Freud and Jung and Adler

Gershwin/Gershwin

Orchestrator: Unknown

Location of
- Composer's manuscript: -0-
- Sheet music: Unpublished
- Most complete music: IG (pv-l)
- Most complete lyric: IG (ls)
- Original partitur: -0-
- Original parts: -0-

Dropped before the New York opening. The piano-vocal was reconstructed from memory by Kay Swift. Russell Warner orchestrated this numbers for performance in 1987; the partitur and parts are at the Library of Congress.

He's Oversexed

Gershwin/Gershwin

Orchestrator: Unknown

Location of
- Composer's manuscript: -0-
- Sheet music: Unpublished
- Most complete music: IG (pv-l)
- Most complete lyric: IG (ls)
- Original partitur: -0-
- Original parts: -0-

Dropped before the New York opening. The piano-vocal was reconstructed from memory by Kay Swift. Russell Warner orchestrated this numbers for performance in 1987; the partitur and parts are at the Library of Congress.

Watch Your Head

Gershwin/Gershwin

Orchestrator: Bennett

Location of
- Composer's manuscript: -0-
- Sheet music: Unpublished
- Most complete music: LoC (ptr)
- Most complete lyric: IG (ls)
- Original partitur: LoC
- Original parts: LoC (1987)

Dropped before the New York opening. The partitur is entitled "Nurses." The music of the refrain was used for the refrain of "Hail the Happy Couple," and later for "Comes the Revolution" in LET 'EM EAT CAKE (1933).

Together at Last

Gershwin/Gershwin

Orchestrator: Daly

Location of
- Composer's manuscript: LoC
- Sheet music: Unpublished
- Most complete music: LoC (pv-l)
- Most complete lyric: LoC (pv-l, ls)
- Original partitur: LoC
- Original parts: LoC (1987)

Dropped before the New York opening. Prepared for publication, but never printed.

Luckiest Boy in the World

Gershwin/Gershwin

Orchestrator: Bennett

Location of
- Composer's manuscript: -0-
- Sheet music: Unpublished
- Most complete music: LoC (ptr)
- Most complete lyric: IG (ls)
- Original partitur: LoC
- Original parts: LoC (1987)

Dropped before the New York opening.

Fatherland, Mother of the Band

Gershwin/Gershwin

Orchestrator: Daly

Location of
- Composer's manuscript: -0-
- Sheet music: Unpublished
- Most complete music: LoC (pv-l)
- Most complete lyric: IG (ls)
- Original partitur: LoC
- Original parts: LoC

Dropped before the New York opening. Alternate title: "Drink, Drink, Drink." The Library of Congress also has the original vocal arrangement.

No Tickee, No Washee
    Gershwin/Gershwin
    Orchestrator: Daly

    Location of   - Composer's manuscript: LoC
                - Sheet music: Unpublished
                - Most complete music: LoC (ptr
                     & 1987 parts)
                - Most complete lyric: IG (ls)
                - Original partitur: LoC
                - Original parts: LoC (inc), LoC (1987)

This Act II Opening was dropped before the New York premiere. Much of it was reworked into an Act I Finale, the result being "What Sort of Wedding Is This?"

LET 'EM EAT CAKE

Music	**GEORGE GERSHWIN**
Lyrics	**IRA GERSHWIN**

Musical satire in two acts. Opened October 21, 1933 in New York and ran 90 performances (World premiere: October 2, 1933 in Boston). Libretto by George S. Kaufman and Morrie Ryskind. Produced by Sam H. Harris. Directed by George S. Kaufman. Choreographed by Von Gruna and Ned McGurn. Musical direction by William Daly. Orchestrations by Edward Powell.

Synopsis and Production Information

U.S. President John P. Wintergreen, defeated by John P. Tweedledee in his campaign for reelection, moves to New York with his wife Mary and opens a modest clothing store. Business is slow until Wintergreen, attuned to the voice of the people, devises an irresistible marketing strategy: He promises with the sale of each blue shirt "a revolution or your money back." The success of this ploy allows Wintergreen to maneuver a government takeover and establish a dictatorship of the proletariat. But the increasingly power-mad Army rebels and threatens Wintergreen and his cronies with the guillotine. At the eleventh hour, Mary saves the day with a tactic that appeals to the vanity and greed of the American public.

Other characters include the bumbling ex-Vice-President Throttlebottom, malcontent Kruger, the libidinous General Snookfield, and Snookfield's tarty playmate Trixie. There is a full singing ensemble and few dances.

Orchestration

Unknown

Comments

LET 'EM EAT CAKE was a sequel to OF THEE I SING (1931); Wintergreen and Throttlebottom were again played by William Gaxton and Victor Moore.

Location of Original Materials

Script: Samuel French, Inc. (some lyrics)
    (Published: Alfred A. Knopf, Inc., 1933)
Piano-vocal score: Ira Gershwin Estate
Partiturs: Missing
Parts: Missing

The piano-vocal score was reconstructed by John McGlinn in 1986. Russell Warner then created a new orchestration for 24 players, for which partiturs and parts are available. The Library of Congress has an early draft of the script.

Rental Status

Currently unavailable for rental

Music Publisher

Warner Brothers Music

Information

Ira Gershwin Estate, George Gershwin Family Trust

Let 'Em Eat Cake (1933)

Overture

Gershwin/Gershwin
Orchestrator: Unknown

Location of   - Composer's manuscript: LoC
- Sheet music: Unpublished
- Most complete music: IG (pv score)
- Most complete lyric: INST
- Original partitur: -0-
- Original parts: -0-

Store Scene

Gershwin/Gershwin
Orchestrator: Unknown

Location of   - Composer's manuscript: LoC
- Sheet music: LoC, NYPL
- Most complete music: IG (pv score)
- Most complete lyric: IG (pv score)
- Original partitur: -0-
- Original parts: -0-

Includes "Shirts by the Millions," "Comes the Revolution," and "Mine." There is no Gershwin manuscript for "Comes the Revolution," which was reconstructed in the 1960's by Ira Gershwin and Kay Swift and is musically similar to the refrains of "Hail the Happy Couple" and "Watch Your Head" from PARDON MY ENGLISH (1933). Only "Mine" is published.

Tweedledee for President

Gershwin/Gershwin
Orchestrator: Unknown

Location of   - Composer's manuscript: LoC
- Sheet music: Unpublished
- Most complete music: IG (pv score)
- Most complete lyric: IG (pv score)
- Original partitur: -0-
- Original parts: -0-

Climb Up the Social Ladder

Gershwin/Gershwin
Orchestrator: Unknown

Location of   - Composer's manuscript: LoC
- Sheet music: Unpublished
- Most complete music: IG (pv score)
- Most complete lyric: IG (pv score)
- Original partitur: -0-
- Original parts: -0-

Although this number was dropped soon after the New York opening, it has been included in the piano-vocal score. The Library of Congress also has a lyric sheet with an early version.

Union Square

Gershwin/Gershwin
Orchestrator: Unknown

Location of   - Composer's manuscript: LoC
- Sheet music: LoC, NYPL
- Most complete music: IG (pv score)
- Most complete lyric: LOSO
- Original partitur: -0-
- Original parts: -0-

Union League

Gershwin/Gershwin
Orchestrator: Unknown

Location of   - Composer's manuscript: LoC (lead)
- Sheet music: Unpublished
- Most complete music: IG (pv score)
- Most complete lyric: LOSO
- Original partitur: -0-
- Original parts: -0-

Kay Swift harmonized the number from Gershwin's leadsheet. Alternate title: "Cloistered From the Noisy City."

165

On and On and On

Gershwin/Gershwin
Orchestrator: Unknown

Location of - Composer's manuscript: LoC
 - Sheet music: LoC, NYPL
 - Most complete music: IG (pv score)
 - Most complete lyric: IG (pv score) & LOSO
 - Original partitur: -0-
 - Original parts: -0-

Opening Act II

Gershwin/Gershwin
Orchestrator: Unknown

Location of - Composer's manuscript: LoC
 - Sheet music: LoC, NYPL
 - Most complete music: IG (pv score)
 - Most complete lyric: IG (pv score)
 - Original partitur: -0-
 - Original parts: -0-

Includes "Blue, Blue, Blue" and "Who's the Greatest?"
Only "Blue, Blue, Blue" was published.

Finale Act I

Gershwin/Gershwin
Orchestrator: Unknown

Location of - Composer's manuscript: LoC
 - Sheet music: LoC, NYPL
 - Most complete music: IG (pv score)
 - Most complete lyric: IG (pv score)
 - Original partitur: -0-
 - Original parts: -0-

Includes "I've Brushed My Teeth," "Double Dummy Drill,"
"The General's Gone to a Party," "All the Mothers of the
Nation," and the title song. Only the title song was
published.

League of Nations, The

Gershwin/Gershwin
Orchestrator: Unknown

Location of - Composer's manuscript: LoC
 - Sheet music: Unpublished
 - Most complete music: IG (pv score)
 - Most complete lyric: IG (pv score)
 - Original partitur: -0-
 - Original parts: -0-

Includes "No Comprenez, No Capish, No Versteh!" and
"Why Speak of Money?" Although "Why Speak of Money?"
was dropped before the New York opening, it has been
included in the piano-vocal score.

Entr'acte

Gershwin/Gershwin
Orchestrator: Unknown

Location of - Composer's manuscript: -0-
 - Sheet music: Unpublished
 - Most complete music: -0-
 - Most complete lyric: INST
 - Original partitur: -0-
 - Original parts: -0-

Up and At 'Em

Gershwin/Gershwin
Orchestrator: Unknown

Location of - Composer's manuscript: LoC
 - Sheet music: Unpublished
 - Most complete music: IG (pv score)
 - Most complete lyric: IG (pv score)
 - Original partitur: -0-
 - Original parts: -0-

Let 'Em Eat Cake (1933)

Trial of Throttlebottom, The
Gershwin/Gershwin
Orchestrator: Unknown

Location of   - Composer's manuscript: LoC
            - Sheet music: Unpublished
            - Most complete music: IG (pv score)
            - Most complete lyric: IG (pv score)
            - Original partitur: -0-
            - Original parts: -0-

Includes "That's What He Did," "I Know a Foul Ball," and "Throttle Throttlebottom".

Hanging Throttlebottom in the Morning
Gershwin/Gershwin
Orchestrator: Unknown

Location of   - Composer's manuscript: LoC
            - Sheet music: Unpublished
            - Most complete music: IG (pv score)
            - Most complete lyric: IG (pv score)
            - Original partitur: -0-
            - Original parts: -0-

Trial of Wintergreen, The
Gershwin/Gershwin
Orchestrator: Unknown

Location of   - Composer's manuscript: LoC
            - Sheet music: Unpublished
            - Most complete music: IG (pv score)
            - Most complete lyric: IG (pv score)
            - Original partitur: -0-
            - Original parts: -0-

Includes "A Hell of a Hole" and "It Isn't What You Did."

First Lady and First Gent
Gershwin/Gershwin
Orchestrator: Unknown

Location of   - Composer's manuscript: LoC (frag)
            - Sheet music: Unpublished
            - Most complete music: IG (pv score)
            - Most complete lyric: IG (pv score)
            - Original partitur: -0-
            - Original parts: -0-

This unused number, reconstructed largely by Kay Swift, has replaced the missing "Let 'Em Eat Caviar" in the piano-vocal score.

Let 'Em Eat Caviar
Gershwin/Gershwin
Orchestrator: Unknown

Location of   - Composer's manuscript: -0-
            - Sheet music: Unpublished
            - Most complete music: -0-
            - Most complete lyric: -0-
            - Original partitur: -0-
            - Original parts: -0-

This number, which has apparently not survived, has been replaced in the piano-vocal score by the unused "First Lady and First Gent."

Oyez! Oyez! Oyez!
Gershwin/Gershwin
Orchestrator: Unknown

Location of   - Composer's manuscript: LoC
            - Sheet music: Unpublished
            - Most complete music: IG (pv score)
            - Most complete lyric: IG (pv score)
            - Original partitur: -0-
            - Original parts: -0-

Although this number was dropped before the New York opening, it has been included in the piano-vocal score.

COLE PORTER

COLE PORTER was born in 1891 in Peru, Indiana, and wrote his first composition, the instrumental "Song of the Birds," at the age of ten. His earliest published musical composition was "The Bobolink Waltz" (1902). He attended Worcester Academy in Massachusetts from 1905 to 1909, graduating as valedictorian. At Yale (1909-1913), he wrote the college's now famous football songs, "Bingo Eli Yale" and "Bull Dog." While at Yale he wrote several musical comedies: CORA (1911), AND THE VILLAIN STILL PURSUED HER (1912), THE POT OF GOLD (1912), and THE KALEIDOSCOPE (1913). While attending Harvard Law School (1913-1914), he teamed with T. Lawrason Riggs to write the musical PARANOIA (1914). In 1914 he transferred to the Harvard School of Music. "Esmeralda" (titled "As I Love You" in THE KALEIDOSCOPE) was the first Porter song to appear in a Broadway show (HANDS UP, July 22, 1915). In the summer of 1917 he sailed for Europe to participate in the work of the Duryea Relief Organization in France. In April 1918 he enlisted in the French Foreign Legion. During most of the next decade (1918-1929), he lived primarily in Europe. In 1920 and 1921 he studied counterpoint, harmony, and orchestration at the Schola Cantorum in Paris. During the summer of 1923 he collaborated with Gerald Murphy on the ballet WITHIN THE QUOTA, a satire on American life in the 1920's.

By the end of the 1920's Porter achieved success writing for the theater. His work includes music and lyrics for these shows: SEE AMERICA FIRST (1916), HITCHY-KOO OF 1919 and 1922, GREENWICH VILLAGE FOLLIES (1924), PARIS (1928), WAKE UP AND DREAM (1929), THE NEW YORKERS (1930), GAY DIVORCE (1932), NYMPH ERRANT (1933), ANYTHING GOES (1934), JUBILEE (1935), BORN TO DANCE (film, 1936), RED, HOT AND BLUE! (1936), ROSALIE (film, 1937), YOU NEVER KNOW (1938), LEAVE IT TO ME (1938), BROADWAY MELODY OF 1940 (film, 1939), DU BARRY WAS A LADY (1939), PANAMA HATTIE (1940), YOU'LL NEVER GET RICH (film, 1941), LET'S FACE IT (1941), SOMETHING FOR THE BOYS (1942), SOMETHING TO SHOUT ABOUT (film, 1941), MEXICAN HAYRIDE (1943), SEVEN LIVELY ARTS (1944), AROUND THE WORLD IN EIGHTY DAYS (1946), THE PIRATE (film, 1948), KISS ME, KATE (1948), OUT OF THIS WORLD (1950), CAN-CAN (1953), SILK STOCKINGS (1955), HIGH SOCIETY (film, 1956), LES GIRLS (film, 1957) and ALADDIN (television, 1958). His hits include "I've a Shooting Box in Scotland," "An Old-Fashioned Garden," "I'm in Love Again," "Two Little Babes in the Wood," "Let's Do It, Let's Fall In Love," "The Laziest Gal in Town," "Let's Misbehave," "You Do Something To Me," "What Is This Thing Called Love," "Love For Sale," "Night and Day," "Experiment," "Miss Otis Regrets," "I Get a Kick Out of You," "All Through the Night," "You're the Top," "Anything Goes," "Blow, Gabriel, Blow," "Begin the Beguine," "Just One of Those Things," "It's De-Lovely," "Ridin' High," "Easy to Love," "I've Got You Under My Skin," "In the Still of the Night," "Rosalie," "At Long Last Love," "My Heart Belongs to Daddy," "Do I Love You?," "Well, Did You Evah!," "Friendship," "I Concentrate on You," "Let's Be Buddies," "Don't Fence Me In," "You'd Be So Nice to Come Home To," "Hey Good-Lookin'," "Ev'rytime We Say Goodbye," "Be a Clown," "Another Op'nin, Another Show," "Wunderbar," "So In Love," "Were Thine That Special Face," "Why Can't You Behave," "Too Darn Hot," "Brush Up Your Shakespeare," "Always True to You in My Fashion," "I Am Loved," "From This Moment On," "Use Your Imagination," "It's All Right With Me," "I Love Paris," "C'est Magnifique," "All of You," "You're Sensational," and "True Love. Cole Porter died in Santa Monica, California, on October 15, 1964.

SEE AMERICA FIRST

Music   **COLE PORTER**
Lyrics   **COLE PORTER & T. LAWRASON RIGGS**

Comic opera in two acts. Opened March 28, 1916 in New York and ran 15 performances (World premiere: February 22, 1916 in Schenectady). Libretto by T. Lawrason Riggs and Cole Porter. Produced by Elizabeth Marbury. Directed by J.H. Benrimo.

Synopsis and Production Information	Wealthy East Coast Senator Huggins sends his daughter Polly out west to a "back-to-nature" finishing school in hope that she'll find a "real man" for a husband. Polly, however, has designs on a Duke with whom she once exchanged glances at the opera in London. The Duke turns up on the western scene disguised as a cowboy, and after a few musical numbers, he and Polly decide to get hitched. Happily, Polly's father forgoes his rigid doctrines when he falls in love with Sarah, the provincial chaperone at Polly's school.

Other characters include a dancing couple and Indian Chief Blood-in-his-Eye (specialty comic). There is a full singing and dancing ensemble. |
| **Orchestration** | Unknown |
| **Comments** | SEE AMERICA FIRST was an attempt at an Americanized Gilbert and Sullivan musical. |
| **Location of Original Materials** | Script: Missing
Piano-vocal score: See individual listings
Partiturs: Missing
Parts: Missing

Most of the piano-vocal score survives, but it has not been assembled or edited.

SEE AMERICA FIRST underwent numerous revisions between its "completion" in the autumn of 1915 and its New York opening. To best demonstrate these changes, we have departed from our usual practice of listing songs in the New York running order and consigning deleted material to the back; instead, we have reconstructed as closely as possible the original sequence of numbers. |
Rental Status	Currently unavailable for rental
Music Publisher	G. Schirmer, Inc.
Information	Cole Porter Trusts

Overture

Porter/Porter & Riggs
Orchestrator: Unknown

Location of - Composer's manuscript: -0-
 - Sheet music: Unpublished
 - Most complete music: -0-
 - Most complete lyric: INST
 - Original partitur: -0-
 - Original parts: -0-

Younger Sons of Peers

Porter/Porter & Riggs
Orchestrator: Unknown

Location of - Composer's manuscript: LoC
 - Sheet music: Unpublished
 - Most complete music: LoC (pv-I);
  CPT (pv-I); Y (pv-I)
 - Most complete lyric: LoC (pv-I);
  CPT (pv-I); Y (pv-I); CLCP
 - Original partitur: -0-
 - Original parts: -0-

May have been deleted before the New York opening.

Dawn Music

Porter
Orchestrator: Unknown

Location of - Composer's manuscript: -0-
 - Sheet music: Unpublished
 - Most complete music: -0-
 - Most complete lyric: INST
 - Original partitur: -0-
 - Original parts: -0-

Greetings, Gentlemen

Porter/Porter & Riggs
Orchestrator: Unknown

Location of - Composer's manuscript: Y
 - Sheet music: Unpublished
 - Most complete music: Y (pv-I);
  CPT (pv-I)
 - Most complete lyric: Y (pv-I);
  CPT (pv-I); CLCP
 - Original partitur: -0-
 - Original parts: -0-

Not listed in the New York programs.

Badmen

Porter/Porter & Riggs
Orchestrator: Unknown

Location of - Composer's manuscript: LoC
 - Sheet music: Unpublished
 - Most complete music: LoC (pv-I);
  CPT (pv-I); Y (pv-I)
 - Most complete lyric: LoC (pv-I);
  CPT (pv-I); Y (pv-I); CLCP
 - Original partitur: -0-
 - Original parts: -0-

To Follow Every Fancy

Porter/Porter & Riggs
Orchestrator: Unknown

Location of - Composer's manuscript: LoC & Y
 - Sheet music: Unpublished
 - Most complete music: LoC (pv-I)
  & Y (pv-I)
 - Most complete lyric: LoC (pv-I)
  & Y (pv-I); CLCP
 - Original partitur: -0-
 - Original parts: -0-

See America First (1916)

See America First [first version]
Porter/Porter & Riggs
Orchestrator: Unknown

Location of   - Composer's manuscript: LoC, Y
              - Sheet music: Unpublished
              - Most complete music: LoC (pv-l); Y (pv-l)
              - Most complete lyric: LoC (pv-l); Y (pv-l);
                 CLCP
              - Original partitur: -0-
              - Original parts: -0-

Discarded in favor of "See America First" [second version].

See America First [second version]
Porter/Porter & Riggs
Orchestrator: Unknown

Location of   - Composer's manuscript: -0-
              - Sheet music: CPT, LoC, NYPL, Y
              - Most complete music: CPT (sm); LoC (sm);
                 NYPL (sm); Y (sm)
              - Most complete lyric: CPT (sm); LoC (sm);
                 NYPL (sm); Y (sm); CLCP
              - Original partitur: -0-
              - Original parts: -0-

Well, It's Good to Be Here Again
Porter/Porter & Riggs
Orchestrator: Unknown

Location of   - Composer's manuscript: LoC
              - Sheet music: Unpublished
              - Most complete music: LoC (pv-l);
                 CPT (pv-l); Y (pv-l)
              - Most complete lyric: LoC (pv-l);
                 CPT (pv-l); Y (pv-l); CLCP
              - Original partitur: -0-
              - Original parts: -0-

May have been deleted before the New York opening.

Hold-Up Ensemble
Porter/Porter & Riggs
Orchestrator: Unknown

Location of   - Composer's manuscript: LoC & Y
              - Sheet music: Unpublished
              - Most complete music: LoC (pv-l)
                 & Y (pv-l)
              - Most complete lyric: LoC (pv-l)
                 & Y (pv-l); CLCP
              - Original partitur: -0-
              - Original parts: -0-

Language of Flowers, The
Porter/Porter & Riggs
Orchestrator: Unknown

Location of   - Composer's manuscript: LoC & Y
              - Sheet music: CPT, LoC, Y
              - Most complete music: CPT (sm); LoC (sm);
                 Y (sm)
              - Most complete lyric: CLCP
              - Original partitur: -0-
              - Original parts: -0-

Written for Porter and Riggs' 1914 college show PARANOIA, where it was known as "Flower Song."

Entrance of Indian Maidens
Porter/Porter & Riggs
Orchestrator: Unknown

Location of   - Composer's manuscript: LoC
              - Sheet music: Unpublished
              - Most complete music: LoC (pv-l);
                 CPT (pv-l); Y (pv-l)
              - Most complete lyric: LoC (pv-l);
                 CPT (pv-l); Y (pv-l); CLCP
              - Original partitur: -0-
              - Original parts: -0-

This may be the number titled "Indian Girls' Chant" in the New York programs.

If In Spite of Our Attempts
Porter/Porter & Riggs
Orchestrator: Unknown

Location of   - Composer's manuscript: Y
- Sheet music: Unpublished
- Most complete music: Y (pv-l); CPT (pv-l)
- Most complete lyric: Y (pv-l); CPT (pv-l);
  CLCP
- Original partitur: -0-
- Original parts: -0-

This might be the "Indian Maidens' Chorus" listed in the
New York programs.

Social Coach of All the Fashionable Future Debutantes, The
Porter/Porter & Riggs
Orchestrator: Unknown

Location of   - Composer's manuscript: LoC
- Sheet music: Unpublished
- Most complete music: LoC (pv-l);
  CPT (pv-l); Y (pv-l)
- Most complete lyric: LoC (pv-l);
  CPT (pv-l); Y (pv-l); CLCP
- Original partitur: -0-
- Original parts: -0-

Replaced by "Something's Got to Be Done" before the
show went into production.

Something's Got to Be Done
Porter/Porter & Riggs
Orchestrator: Unknown

Location of   - Composer's manuscript: Y
- Sheet music: CPT, LoC, Y
- Most complete music: CPT (sm); LoC (sm);
  Y (sm)
- Most complete lyric: CPT (sm); LoC (sm);
  Y (sm); CLCP
- Original partitur: -0-
- Original parts: -0-

Replaced "The Social Coach of All the Fashionable Future
Debutantes" before the show went into production.

Pity Me, Please
Porter/Porter & Riggs
Orchestrator: Unknown

Location of   - Composer's manuscript: Y, LoC
- Sheet music: CPT, LoC, Y
- Most complete music: CPT (sm); LoC (sm);
  Y (sm)
- Most complete lyric: CPT (sm); LoC (sm);
  Y (sm); CLCP
- Original partitur: -0-
- Original parts: -0-

Replaced before the New York opening by "I've Got an
Awful Lot to Learn."

I've Got an Awful Lot to Learn
Porter/Porter & Riggs
Orchestrator: Unknown

Location of   - Composer's manuscript: -0-
- Sheet music: CPT, LoC, Y
- Most complete music: CPT (sm); LoC (sm);
  Y (sm)
- Most complete lyric: CPT (sm); LoC (sm);
  Y (sm); CLCP
- Original partitur: -0-
- Original parts: -0-

Replaced "Pity Me, Please" just prior to the New York
opening.

Dinner
Porter/Porter & Riggs
Orchestrator: Unknown

Location of   - Composer's manuscript: Y, LoC
- Sheet music: Unpublished
- Most complete music: Y (pv-l); LoC (pv-l)
- Most complete lyric: Y (pv-l);
  LoC (pv-l); CLCP
- Original partitur: -0-
- Original parts: -0-

Dropped before the New York opening.

Hail, Ye Indian Maidens
    Porter/Porter & Riggs
    Orchestrator: Unknown

    Location of - Composer's manuscript: Y
               - Sheet music: Unpublished
               - Most complete music: Y (pv-l); CPT (pv-l)
               - Most complete lyric: Y (pv-l); CPT (pv-l);
                    CLCP
               - Original partitur: -0-
               - Original parts: -0-

Not listed in the New York programs.

Fascinating Females
    Porter/Porter & Riggs
    Orchestrator: Unknown

    Location of - Composer's manuscript: Y
               - Sheet music: Unpublished
               - Most complete music: Y (pv-l); CPT (pv-l)
               - Most complete lyric: Y (pv-l); CPT (pv-l);
                    CLCP
               - Original partitur: -0-
               - Original parts: -0-

Not listed in the New York programs.

Beautiful, Primitive Indian Girls
    Porter/Porter & Riggs
    Orchestrator: Unknown

    Location of - Composer's manuscript: Y
               - Sheet music: Unpublished
               - Most complete music: Y (pv-l); CPT (pv-l)
               - Most complete lyric: Y (pv-l); CPT (pv-l);
                    CLCP
               - Original partitur: -0-
               - Original parts: -0-

Lady I've Vowed to Wed, The
    Porter/Porter & Riggs
    Orchestrator: Unknown

    Location of - Composer's manuscript: LoC
               - Sheet music: Unpublished
               - Most complete music: LoC (pv-l);
                    CPT (pv-l); Y (pv-l)
               - Most complete lyric: LoC (pv-l);
                    CPT (pv-l); Y (pv-l); CLCP
               - Original partitur: -0-
               - Original parts: -0-

Alternate titles: "Announcement Ensemble" and
"Engagement Ensemble."

Prithee, Come Crusading With Me
    Porter/Porter & Riggs
    Orchestrator: Unknown

    Location of - Composer's manuscript: Y
               - Sheet music: CPT, LoC, NYPL, Y
               - Most complete music: CPT (sm); LoC (sm);
                    NYPL (sm); Y (sm)
               - Most complete lyric: CLCP
               - Original partitur: -0-
               - Original parts: -0-

Listed in the New York programs as "Damsel, Damsel."
Originally written for Porter and Riggs' 1914 college show
PARANOIA (under the title "Won't You Come Crusading
With Me") and later expanded for SEE AMERICA FIRST.

Finale Act I ["Strolling quite fancy free..."]
    Porter/Porter & Riggs
    Orchestrator: Unknown

    Location of - Composer's manuscript: Y & LoC
               - Sheet music: Unpublished
               - Most complete music: Y (pv-l)
                    & LoC (pv-l)
               - Most complete lyric: Y (pv-l)
                    & LoC (pv-l); CLCP
               - Original partitur: -0-
               - Original parts: -0-

There are at least two versions of this extended ensemble
number. Some of the material at the end is missing and
presumed lost.

Entr'acte

Porter/Porter & Riggs

Orchestrator: Unknown

Location of
- Composer's manuscript: -0-
- Sheet music: Unpublished
- Most complete music: -0-
- Most complete lyric: INST
- Original partitur: -0-
- Original parts: -0-

Ever and Ever Yours

Porter/Porter & Riggs

Orchestrator: Unknown

Location of
- Composer's manuscript: -0-
- Sheet music: CPT, LoC, Y
- Most complete music: CPT (sm); LoC (sm); Y (sm, pv-l)
- Most complete lyric: CPT (sm); LoC (sm); Y (sm, pv-l); CLCP
- Original partitur: -0-
- Original parts: -0-

Replaced "Oh, Bright, Fair Dream" just before the New York opening.

Mirror, Mirror

Porter/Porter & Riggs

Orchestrator: Unknown

Location of
- Composer's manuscript: LoC
- Sheet music: Unpublished
- Most complete music: LoC (pv-l); CPT (pv-l); Y (pv-l)
- Most complete lyric: LoC (pv-l); CPT (pv-l); Y (pv-l); CLCP
- Original partitur: -0-
- Original parts: -0-

Opening chorus of Act II.

Wake, Love, Wake

Porter/Porter & Riggs

Orchestrator: Unknown

Location of
- Composer's manuscript: -0-
- Sheet music: Unpublished
- Most complete music: -0-
- Most complete lyric: -0-
- Original partitur: -0-
- Original parts: -0-

Dropped during the pre-Broadway tryout.

Oh, Bright, Fair Dream

Porter/Porter & Riggs

Orchestrator: Unknown

Location of
- Composer's manuscript: -0-
- Sheet music: CPT, LoC, Y
- Most complete music: CPT (sm); LoC (sm); Y (sm)
- Most complete lyric: CPT (sm); LoC (sm); Y (sm); CLCP
- Original partitur: -0-
- Original parts: -0-

Replaced during the pre-Broadway tryout by "Ever and Ever Yours."

Lady Fair, Lady Fair

Porter/Porter & Riggs

Orchestrator: Unknown

Location of
- Composer's manuscript: LoC
- Sheet music: Unpublished
- Most complete music: LoC (pv-l); CPT (pv-l); Y (pv-l)
- Most complete lyric: LoC (pv-l); CPT (pv-l); Y (pv-l); CLCP
- Original partitur: -0-
- Original parts: -0-

Dropped before the New York opening.

See America First (1916)

Love Came and Crowned Me
    Porter/Porter & Riggs
    Orchestrator: Unknown

    Location of - Composer's manuscript: LoC
              - Sheet music: Unpublished
              - Most complete music: LoC (pv-l);
                  CPT (pv-l); Y (pv-l)
              - Most complete lyric: LoC (pv-l);
                  CPT (pv-l); Y (pv-l); CLCP
              - Original partitur: -0-
              - Original parts: -0-

Dropped just before the New York opening. This number was derived from "Idyll," a song Porter and Riggs wrote for the 1914 college show PARANOIA. The lyric for "Idyll" is in The Complete Lyrics of Cole Porter.

Woodland Dance
    Porter
    Orchestrator: Unknown

    Location of - Composer's manuscript: -0-
              - Sheet music: Unpublished
              - Most complete music: -0-
              - Most complete lyric: INST
              - Original partitur: -0-
              - Original parts: -0-

Lima
    Porter/Porter & Riggs
    Orchestrator: Unknown

    Location of - Composer's manuscript: -0-
              - Sheet music: CPT, LoC, Y
              - Most complete music: CPT (sm); LoC (sm);
                  Y (sm)
              - Most complete lyric: CPT (sm); LoC (sm);
                  Y (sm); CLCP
              - Original partitur: -0-
              - Original parts: -0-

Added just before the New York opening.

When a Body's in Love
    Porter/Porter & Riggs
    Orchestrator: Unknown

    Location of - Composer's manuscript: LoC
              - Sheet music: Unpublished
              - Most complete music: LoC (pv-l);
                  CPT (pv-l); Y (pv-l)
              - Most complete lyric: LoC (pv-l);
                  CPT (pv-l); Y (pv-l); CLCP
              - Original partitur: -0-
              - Original parts: -0-

Dropped during the pre-Broadway tryout.

Will You Love Me When My Flivver Is a Wreck?
    Author(s): Unknown
    Orchestrator: Unknown

    Location of - Composer's manuscript: -0-
              - Sheet music: -0-
              - Most complete music: -0-
              - Most complete lyric: -0-
              - Original partitur: -0-
              - Original parts: -0-

Revelation Ensemble
    Porter/Porter & Riggs
    Orchestrator: Unknown

    Location of - Composer's manuscript: LoC
              - Sheet music: Unpublished
              - Most complete music: LoC (pv-l);
                  CPT (pv-l); Y (pv-l)
              - Most complete lyric: LoC (pv-l);
                  CPT (pv-l); Y (pv-l); CLCP
              - Original partitur: -0-
              - Original parts: -0-

Dropped during the pre-Broadway tryout.

Slow Sinks the Sun
Porter/Porter & Riggs
Orchestrator: Unknown

Location of - Composer's manuscript: -0-
- Sheet music: CPT, LoC, Y
- Most complete music: CPT (sm);
    LoC (sm); Y (sm)
- Most complete lyric: CPT (sm, ls);
    LoC (sm); Y (sm); CLCP
- Original partitur: -0-
- Original parts: -0-

Dropped before the New York opening. Written for Porter and Riggs' 1914 college show PARANOIA.

I've a Shooting Box in Scotland
Porter/Porter & Riggs
Orchestrator: Unknown

Location of - Composer's manuscript: -0-
- Sheet music: CPT, LoC, NYPL, Y
- Most complete music: CPT (sm); LoC (sm);
    NYPL (sm); Y (sm)
- Most complete lyric: CLCP
- Original partitur: -0-
- Original parts: -0-

Written for and introduced in Porter and Riggs' 1914 college show PARANOIA. The number then appeared with revised lyrics in SEE AMERICA FIRST. The Complete Lyrics of Cole Porter also has "I've Had Shooting Pains in Scotland," the parody version to which Porter often humorously referred.

Step We Grandly
Porter/Porter & Riggs
Orchestrator: Unknown

Location of - Composer's manuscript: Y
- Sheet music: Unpublished
- Most complete music: Y (pv-l); CPT (pv-l)
- Most complete lyric: Y (pv-l); CPT (pv-l);
    CLCP
- Original partitur: -0-
- Original parts: -0-

Dropped before the New York opening.

Buy Her a Box at the Opera
Porter/Porter & Riggs
Orchestrator: Unknown

Location of - Composer's manuscript: -0-
- Sheet music: CPT, LoC, Y
- Most complete music: CPT (sm); LoC (sm);
    Y (sm)
- Most complete lyric: CPT (sm); LoC (sm);
    Y (sm); CLCP
- Original partitur: -0-
- Original parts: -0-

A late addition to the score, this number replaced "Step We Grandly" and "Sweet Simplicity."

Sweet Simplicity
Porter/Porter & Riggs
Orchestrator: Unknown

Location of - Composer's manuscript: Y
- Sheet music: Unpublished
- Most complete music: Y (pv-l); CPT (pv-l)
- Most complete lyric: Y (pv-l);
    CPT (pv-l); CLCP
- Original partitur: -0-
- Original parts: -0-

Dropped during the pre-Broadway tryout.

When I Used to Lead the Ballet
Porter/Porter
Orchestrator: Unknown

Location of - Composer's manuscript: -0-
- Sheet music: CPT, LoC, Y
- Most complete music: CPT (sm); LoC (sm);
    Y (sm)
- Most complete lyric: CPT (sm); LoC (sm);
    Y (sm); CLCP
- Original partitur: -0-
- Original parts: -0-

Written for THE POT OF GOLD (1912), the fall initiation play at the Delta Kappa Epsilon fraternity house at Yale.

178

See America First (1916)

Finale Act II

Porter/Porter & Riggs

Orchestrator: Unknown

Location of - Composer's manuscript: -0-
- Sheet music: -0-
- Most complete music: -0-
- Most complete lyric: -0-
- Original partitur: -0-
- Original parts: -0-

Bichloride of Mercury

Porter/Porter & Riggs

Orchestrator: Unknown

Location of - Composer's manuscript: -0-
- Sheet music: Unpublished
- Most complete music: -0-
- Most complete lyric: -0-
- Original partitur: -0-
- Original parts: -0-

Dropped before the New York opening.

Serenade

Porter/Porter & Riggs

Orchestrator: Unknown

Location of - Composer's manuscript: -0-
- Sheet music: Unpublished
- Most complete music: -0-
- Most complete lyric: -0-
- Original partitur: -0-
- Original parts: -0-

Dropped before the New York opening.

Je Vous Comprends

Porter/Porter & Riggs

Orchestrator: Unknown

Location of - Composer's manuscript: Y
- Sheet music: Unpublished
- Most complete music: Y (pv-l); CPT (pv-l)
- Most complete lyric: Y (pv-l);
    CPT (pv-l); CLCP
- Original partitur: -0-
- Original parts: -0-

Unused.

179

PARIS

Music	COLE PORTER
Lyrics	COLE PORTER

Comedy with music in three acts. Opened October 8, 1928 in New York and ran 195 performances (World premiere: February 6, 1928 in Atlantic City). Libretto by Martin Brown. Additional music and lyrics by E. Ray Goetz, Walter Kollo, Louis Alter. Produced by Gilbert Miller in association with E. Ray Goetz. Directed by W.H. Gilmore. Choreographed by "Red" Stanley.

Synopsis and Production Information

Mrs. Cora Sabbott, an imperious Massachusetts matron, is summoned to Paris by the impending marriage of her son Andrew to Vivienne Rolland, the darling of the Paris stage. Scheming to terminate the engagement, Cora pretends to succumb to the uninhibiting influence of alcohol and to the roguish charms of Guy Pennel, Vivienne's devoted dancing partner. Her plans succeed: By the final curtain, Vivienne and Guy recognize their love, and Andrew realizes that marriage to the equally dim-witted Brenda Kaley would be more suitable.

The only other characters are Harriet (Vivienne's maid), Marcel (Vivienne's press agent), a valet, and a porter. There is no ensemble. All of the action takes place in the salon of Vivienne's flat at a smart Parisian hotel; the orchestra is onstage as part of the show Vivienne is currently rehearsing.

Orchestration

Unknown

Comments

In the original production, Vivienne was played by Irene Bordoni. Irving Aaronson and the Commanders were the onstage orchestra.

Location of Original Materials

Script: Cole Porter Trusts (no lyrics), New York Public Library (no lyrics), Library of Congress (no lyrics)
Piano-vocal score: See individual listings
Partiturs: Missing
Parts: Missing

All of the songs performed in the original New York production have surfaced with the exception of the title number, which is not by Porter.

Rental Status

Currently unavailable for rental

Music Publisher

Warner Brothers Music

Information

Cole Porter Trusts

Paris (1928)

Land of Going to Be, The
Goetz & Kollo/Goetz & Kollo
Orchestrator: Unknown

Location of - Composer's manuscript: -0-
   - Sheet music: CPT, LoC, NYPL
   - Most complete music: CPT (sm);
      LoC (sm); NYPL (sm)
   - Most complete lyric: CPT (sm);
      LoC (sm); NYPL (sm)
   - Original partitur: -0-
   - Original parts: -0-

Don't Look at Me That Way
Porter/Porter
Orchestrator: Unknown

Location of - Composer's manuscript: -0-
   - Sheet music: CPT, LoC, NYPL, Y
   - Most complete music: CPT (sm);
      LoC (sm); NYPL (sm); Y (sm)
   - Most complete lyric: CPT (sm);
      LoC (sm); NYPL (sm); Y (sm); CLCP
   - Original partitur: -0-
   - Original parts: -0-

Paris
Goetz & Alter/Goetz & Alter
Orchestrator: Unknown

Location of - Composer's manuscript: -0-
   - Sheet music: -0-
   - Most complete music: -0-
   - Most complete lyric: -0-
   - Original partitur: -0-
   - Original parts: -0-

Let's Do It, Let's Fall in Love
Porter/Porter
Orchestrator: Unknown

Location of - Composer's manuscript: Y
   - Sheet music: CPT, LoC, NYPL, Y
   - Most complete music: CPT (sm);
      LoC (sm); NYPL (sm); Y (sm)
   - Most complete lyric: CPT (ls); CLCP
   - Original partitur: -0-
   - Original parts: -0-

Replaced "Let's Misbehave" before the New York opening.

Two Little Babes in the Woods
Porter/Porter
Orchestrator: Unknown

Location of - Composer's manuscript: Y
   - Sheet music: CPT, LoC, NYPL, Y
   - Most complete music: Y (pv-l)
   - Most complete lyric: Y (pv-l); CLCP
   - Original partitur: -0-
   - Original parts: -0-

Introduced in the 1924 GREENWICH VILLAGE FOLLIES; a
shorter version was performed four years later in PARIS
and published.

Vivienne
Porter/Porter
Orchestrator: Unknown

Location of - Composer's manuscript: Y
   - Sheet music: CPT, LoC, NYPL, Y
   - Most complete music: CPT (sm);
      LoC (sm); NYPL (sm); Y (sm)
   - Most complete lyric: CPT (sm);
      LoC (sm); NYPL (sm); Y (sm); CLCP
   - Original partitur: -0-
   - Original parts: -0-

Heaven Hop, The

Porter/Porter

Orchestrator: Unknown

Location of
- Composer's manuscript: -0-
- Sheet music: CPT, LoC, NYPL, Y
- Most complete music: CPT (sm);
    LoC (sm); NYPL (sm); Y (sm)
- Most complete lyric: CPT (sm);
    LoC (sm); NYPL (sm); Y (sm); CLCP
- Original partitur: -0-
- Original parts: -0-

Which?

Porter/Porter

Orchestrator: Unknown

Location of
- Composer's manuscript: -0-
- Sheet music: CPT, NYPL, Y
- Most complete music: CPT (sm);
    NYPL (sm); Y (sm)
- Most complete lyric: CPT (sm);
    NYPL (sm); Y (sm); CLCP
- Original partitur: -0-
- Original parts: -0-

Dropped in rehearsal. The Complete Lyrics of Cole Porter also has a later version used in Porter's 1929 revue, WAKE UP AND DREAM.

Quelque-Chose

Porter/Porter

Orchestrator: Unknown

Location of
- Composer's manuscript: -0-
- Sheet music: CPT, LoC, NYPL, Y
- Most complete music: CPT (sm);
    LoC (sm); NYPL (sm); Y (sm)
- Most complete lyric: CLCP
- Original partitur: -0-
- Original parts: -0-

Dropped before the New York opening. Alternate title: "I've Got Quelque-Chose."

Dizzy Baby

Porter/Porter

Orchestrator: Unknown

Location of
- Composer's manuscript: -0-
- Sheet music: Unpublished
- Most complete music: CPT (pv-l);
    LoC (pv-l)
- Most complete lyric: CPT (pv-l);
    LoC (pv-l); CLCP
- Original partitur: -0-
- Original parts: -0-

Dropped in rehearsal.

Let's Misbehave

Porter/Porter

Orchestrator: Unknown

Location of
- Composer's manuscript: -0-
- Sheet music: CPT, LoC, NYPL, Y
- Most complete music: CPT (sm);
    LoC (sm); NYPL (sm); Y (sm)
- Most complete lyric: CPT (sm);
    LoC (sm); NYPL (sm); Y (sm); CLCP
- Original partitur: -0-
- Original parts: -0-

Replaced before the New York opening by "Let's Do It, Let's Fall in Love."

Bad Girl in Paree

Porter/Porter

Orchestrator: Unknown

Location of
- Composer's manuscript: -0-
- Sheet music: Unpublished
- Most complete music: CPT (pv-l);
    Y (pv-l)
- Most complete lyric: CPT (pv-l)
    Y (pv-l); CLCP
- Original partitur: -0-
- Original parts: -0-

Unused.

When I Found You

Porter/Porter

Orchestrator: Unknown

Location of   - Composer's manuscript: -0-

             - Sheet music: Unpublished

             - Most complete music: CPT (pv-l);

                    Y (pv-l)

             - Most complete lyric: CPT (pv-l);

                    Y (pv-l); CLCP

             - Original partitur: -0-

             - Original parts: -0-

Unused.

FIFTY MILLION FRENCHMEN

Music   COLE PORTER
Lyrics   COLE PORTER

Musical comedy in two acts. Opened November 27, 1929 in New York and ran 254 performances (World premiere: November 14, 1929 in Boston). Book by Herbert Fields. Produced by E. Ray Goetz. Directed by Monty Woolley. Choreographed by Larry Ceballos. Musical direction by Gene Salzer. Orchestrations by Hans Spialek, F. Henri Klickmann, Robert Russell Bennett, Maurice B. DePackh, Charles Miller.

Synopsis and Production Information	Peter Forbes, a young American millionaire in Paris, bets his friend Billy Baxter that he can survive a month without his line of credit and -- in that time -- win the hand of Looloo Carroll, a young girl he fancies. He becomes a tour guide, a gigolo, and a magician -- enduring countless humiliations -- before winning the bet and the girl.
	Other characters include Peter's friend Michael and Looloo's friend Joyce, who team up for a couple of numbers. Much of the comedy is provided by Violet Hildegarde, a New York tourist looking to be shocked, and Fay De Vere, a cabaret artist seeking a man primitive enough to satisfy her needs. Parisian locations include the bar at the Ritz, the race track at Longchamps, the Hotel Claridge, and the Chateau Madrid. There is a full singing and dancing ensemble.
Orchestration	Flute; Oboe; Reed I (Clarinet, Alto Sax); Reed II (Clarinet, Alto Sax); Reed III (Clarinet, Tenor Sax); Horn; Trumpet I II; Trumpet III; Trombone; Percussion; Banjo; Piano; Violin I II III IV; Viola I II; Cello; Bass
Comments	FIFTY MILLION FRENCHMEN marked Porter's first successful musical comedy.[5] In the original production, Peter was played by William Gaxton, Violet by Helen Broderick.
Location of Original Materials	Script: Cole Porter Trusts (all lyrics), Tams-Witmark Music Library (all lyrics) Piano-vocal score: See individual listings Partiturs: Tams-Witmark Music Library, Yale University Parts: Tams-Witmark Music Library
	All of the songs performed in the New York production survive, as do most of the partiturs and roughly half of the parts. Early drafts of the script can be found at the Library of Congress and New York Public Library.
Rental Status	Currently unavailable for rental
Music Publisher	Warner Brothers Music
Information	Cole Porter Trusts

---

[5]   Porter's 1928 hit, PARIS, was more a comedy with songs than a musical comedy.

Fifty Million Frenchmen (1929)

Overture
Porter/Porter
Orchestrator: Klickmann

Location of - Composer's manuscript: -0-
            - Sheet music: Unpublished
            - Most complete music: CPT (p); TW (p)
            - Most complete lyric: INST
            - Original partitur: TW
            - Original parts: TW (1988)

American Express, The
Porter/Porter
Orchestrator: Klickmann

Location of - Composer's manuscript: -0-
            - Sheet music: Unpublished
            - Most complete music: CPT (p) &
                TW (ptr)
            - Most complete lyric: CPT (scr); TW (scr);
                CLCP
            - Original partitur: TW
            - Original parts: -0-

Alternate title: "Opening, American Express Scene."

Toast to Volstead, A
Porter/Porter
Orchestrator: Klickmann

Location of - Composer's manuscript: -0-
            - Sheet music: Unpublished
            - Most complete music: CPT (pv-l)
            - Most complete lyric: CPT (scr); TW (scr);
                CLCP
            - Original partitur: TW
            - Original parts: -0-

Dropped by January 6, 1930. Alternate title: "Opening, Ritz Bar."

You've Got That Thing
Porter/Porter
Orchestrator: Spialek

Location of - Composer's manuscript: -0-
            - Sheet music: CPT, LoC, Y
            - Most complete music: CPT (sm, pv-l);
                LoC (sm); Y (sm), TW (pv-l)
            - Most complete lyric: CPT (pv-l);
                TW (pv-l); CLCP
            - Original partitur: TW
            - Original parts: TW

Tams-Witmark Music Library also has a Bennett partitur that was apparently unused.

You Do Something to Me
Porter/Porter
Orchestrator: Spialek, Bennett

Location of - Composer's manuscript: -0-
            - Sheet music: CPT, LoC, NYPL, Y
            - Most complete music: CPT (sm);
                LoC (sm); NYPL (sm); Y (sm);
                TW (pv-l)
            - Most complete lyric: CPT (sm);
                LoC (sm); NYPL (sm); Y (sm);
                CLCP
            - Original partitur: TW
            - Original parts: TW

Tams-Witmark Music Library also has a Klickmann partitur that was apparently unused.

Find Me a Primitive Man
Porter/Porter
Orchestrator: Bennett

Location of - Composer's manuscript: -0-
            - Sheet music: CPT, LoC, NYPL, Y
            - Most complete music: CPT (sm);
                LoC (sm); NYPL (sm); Y (sm)
            - Most complete lyric: CPT (scr);
                TW (scr); CLCP
            - Original partitur: TW
            - Original parts: TW

Tams-Witmark Music Library also has a sixty-page Spialek partitur that was apparently unused. Yale University has music for an early version.

Where Would You Get Your Coat?

Porter/Porter

Orchestrator: Miller

Location of
- Composer's manuscript: -0-
- Sheet music: Unpublished
- Most complete music: CPT (lead);
  LoC (lead)
- Most complete lyric: CPT (ls, scr);
  TW (scr); CLCP
- Original partitur: Y
- Original parts: TW (1988)

Do You Want to See Paris?

Porter/Porter

Orchestrator: Spialek

Location of
- Composer's manuscript: -0-
- Sheet music: Unpublished
- Most complete music: CPT (pv-l);
  TW (pv-l)
- Most complete lyric: CPT (pv-l, scr);
  TW (pv-l, scr); CLCP
- Original partitur: TW
- Original parts: -0-

A revised version of "Omnibus," introduced in Porter's 1928 show, "La Revue des Ambassadeurs." The Complete Lyrics of Cole Porter also includes the earlier version.

At Longchamps Today

Porter/Porter

Orchestrator: Klickmann

Location of
- Composer's manuscript: -0-
- Sheet music: Unpublished
- Most complete music: CPT (pv-l)
- Most complete lyric: CPT (pv-l); CLCP
- Original partitur: TW
- Original parts: TW (inc)

Yankee Doodle

Porter/Porter

Orchestrator: Unknown

Location of
- Composer's manuscript: -0-
- Sheet music: Unpublished
- Most complete music: CPT (pv-l)
- Most complete lyric: CPT (pv-l); CLCP
- Original partitur: TW
- Original parts: TW

Happy Heaven of Harlem, The

Porter/Porter

Orchestrator: DePackh

Location of
- Composer's manuscript: -0-
- Sheet music: LoC, NYPL, TW, CPT (x)
- Most complete music: LoC (sm);
  NYPL (sm); TW (sm); CPT (sm-x)
- Most complete lyric: LoC (sm);
  NYPL (sm); TW (sm, scr);
  CPT (sm-x, scr); CLCP
- Original partitur: TW
- Original parts: TW

The partitur and parts are titled "My Harlem Wench," an early version of "The Happy Heaven of Harlem," Since the two numbers are musically almost identical, the "Harlem Wench" partitur was probably for "Happy Heaven."

Why Shouldn't I Have You?

Porter/Porter

Orchestrator: Klickmann

Location of
- Composer's manuscript: -0-
- Sheet music: Unpublished
- Most complete music: CPT (pv-l);
  TW (pv-l)
- Most complete lyric: CPT (pv-l, scr);
  TW (pv-l, scr); CLCP
- Original partitur: TW
- Original parts: -0-

Replaced "Down With Everybody But Us" during the pre-Broadway tryout.

Fifty Million Frenchmen (1929)

Entr'acte
Porter/Porter
Orchestrator: Klickmann

Location of   - Composer's manuscript: -0-
          - Sheet music: Unpublished
          - Most complete music: CPT (p)
          - Most complete lyric: INST
          - Original partitur: TW
          - Original parts: TW (inc)

I'm in Love
Porter/Porter
Orchestrator: Klickmann

Location of   - Composer's manuscript: -0-
          - Sheet music: CPT, LoC, NYPL, Y
          - Most complete music: CPT (sm);
               LoC (sm); NYPL (sm); Y (sm)
          - Most complete lyric: CPT (sm, scr);
               LoC (sm); NYPL (sm); Y (sm);
               TW (scr); CLCP
          - Original partitur: TW
          - Original parts: -0-

Added after the Boston opening.

Somebody's Going to Throw a Big Party
Porter/Porter
Orchestrator: Spialek

Location of   - Composer's manuscript: -0-
          - Sheet music: Unpublished
          - Most complete music: CPT (pv-l)
          - Most complete lyric: CPT (pv-l); CLCP
          - Original partitur: TW
          - Original parts: TW

Part 1 of the "Opening, Claridge Scene."

Let's Step Out
Porter/Porter
Orchestrator: Spialek

Location of   - Composer's manuscript: -0-
          - Sheet music: LoC, NYPL, Y, CPT (x)
          - Most complete music: LoC (sm);
               NYPL (sm); Y (sm); CPT (sm-x)
          - Most complete lyric: LoC (sm);
               NYPL (sm); Y (sm); CPT (sm-x); CLCP
          - Original partitur: TW
          - Original parts: TW

Added to the show by March 24, 1930, replacing "The Boy Friend Back Home."

It Isn't Done
Porter/Porter
Orchestrator: Spialek

Location of   - Composer's manuscript: -0-
          - Sheet music: Unpublished
          - Most complete music: CPT (pv-l)
          - Most complete lyric: CPT (pv-l); CLCP
          - Original partitur: TW
          - Original parts: TW

Part 2 of the "Opening, Claridge Scene."

Specialty
Author(s): Unknown
Orchestrator: Unknown

Location of   - Composer's manuscript: -0-
          - Sheet music: -0-
          - Most complete music: -0-
          - Most complete lyric: -0-
          - Original partitur: -0-
          - Original parts: -0-

Performed by Peter and the California Collegians.

Paree, What Did You Do to Me?
    Porter/Porter
    Orchestrator: Spialek

    Location of - Composer's manuscript: -0-
              - Sheet music: CPT, LoC, NYPL, Y
              - Most complete music: CPT (sm);
                  LoC (sm); NYPL (sm); Y (sm)
              - Most complete lyric: CPT (sm, scr);
                  LoC (sm); NYPL (sm); Y (sm);
                  TW (scr); CLCP
              - Original partitur: TW
              - Original parts: -0-

You Don't Know Paree
    Porter/Porter
    Orchestrator: Unknown

    Location of - Composer's manuscript: -0-
              - Sheet music: CPT, LoC, NYPL, Y
              - Most complete music: CPT (sm);
                  LoC (sm); NYPL (sm); Y (sm)
              - Most complete lyric: CPT (sm, scr);
                  LoC (sm); NYPL (sm); Y (sm);
                  TW (scr); CLCP
              - Original partitur: TW
              - Original parts: TW (inc), TW (1988)

Replaced "The Snake in the Grass" ballet during the pre-Broadway tryout.

I'm Unlucky at Gambling
    Porter/Porter
    Orchestrator: DePackh

    Location of - Composer's manuscript: -0-
              - Sheet music: CPT, LoC, NYPL, Y
              - Most complete music: CPT (sm);
                  LoC (sm); NYPL (sm); Y (sm)
              - Most complete lyric: CPT (scr);
                  TW (scr); CLCP
              - Original partitur: TW
              - Original parts: TW (1988)

Tale of the Oyster, The
    Porter/Porter
    Orchestrator: Unknown

    Location of - Composer's manuscript: -0-
              - Sheet music: Not published separately
              - Most complete music: CPT (pv-l);
                  TW (pv-l)
              - Most complete lyric: CPT (pv-l);
                  TW (pv-l); CLCP
              - Original partitur: -0-
              - Original parts: TW

Dropped from the show by January 6, 1930. Initial publication in The Unpublished Cole Porter (Simon & Schuster: 1975). The Complete Lyrics of Cole Porter also has an early version entitled "The Scampi."

Boy Friend Back Home, The
    Porter/Porter
    Orchestrator: Unknown

    Location of - Composer's manuscript: -0-
              - Sheet music: Unpublished
              - Most complete music: CPT (pv);
                  TW (pv)
              - Most complete lyric: CPT (scr);
                  TW (scr); CLCP
              - Original partitur: -0-
              - Original parts: -0-

Added after the New York opening and replaced by March 24, 1930 by "Let's Step Out."

Emigrants, The
    Porter/Porter
    Orchestrator: Klickmann

    Location of - Composer's manuscript: -0-
              - Sheet music: Unpublished
              - Most complete music: CPT (pv-l)
              - Most complete lyric: CPT (pv-l); CLCP
              - Original partitur: TW
              - Original parts: TW

Dropped during the pre-Broadway tryout.

Fifty Million Frenchmen (1929)

Watching the World Go By

Porter/Porter
Orchestrator: Unknown

Location of - Composer's manuscript: -0-
 - Sheet music: Unpublished
 - Most complete music: CPT (lead)
 - Most complete lyric: CPT (ls); CLCP
 - Original partitur: -0-
 - Original parts: -0-

Dropped during the pre-Broadway tryout.

I Worship You

Porter/Porter
Orchestrator: Spialek

Location of - Composer's manuscript: Y (x)
 - Sheet music: CPT, NYPL, Y
 - Most complete music: CPT (sm);
   NYPL (sm); Y (sm)
 - Most complete lyric: CPT (sm);
   NYPL (sm); Y (sm); CLCP
 - Original partitur: Y
 - Original parts: TW

Dropped during the pre-Broadway tryout.

Down With Everybody But Us

Porter/Porter
Orchestrator: Unknown

Location of - Composer's manuscript: -0-
 - Sheet music: Unpublished
 - Most complete music: CPT (pv-l);
   TW (pv-l)
 - Most complete lyric: CPT (pv-l);
   TW (pv-l); CLCP
 - Original partitur: -0-
 - Original parts: TW

Replaced during the pre-Broadway tryout by "Why
Shouldn't I Have You?"

Please Don't Make Me Be Good

Porter/Porter
Orchestrator: Klickmann

Location of - Composer's manuscript: -0-
 - Sheet music: CPT, LoC, NYPL, Y
 - Most complete music: CPT (sm);
   LoC (sm); NYPL (sm); Y (sm)
 - Most complete lyric: CPT (sm);
   LoC (sm); NYPL (sm); Y (sm); CLCP
 - Original partitur: TW (inc)
 - Original parts: TW

Dropped during the pre-Broadway tryout.

Queen of Terre Haute, The

Porter/Porter
Orchestrator: Unknown

Location of - Composer's manuscript: -0-
 - Sheet music: CPT, LoC, Y
 - Most complete music: CPT (sm);
   LoC (sm); Y (sm)
 - Most complete lyric: CPT (sm);
   LoC (sm); Y (sm); CLCP
 - Original partitur: -0-
 - Original parts: TW

Dropped during the pre-Broadway tryout. Yale University
also has an early version entitled "A Girl From Terra
Haute."

Snake in the Grass, The

Porter
Orchestrator: Unknown

Location of - Composer's manuscript: Y (x)
 - Sheet music: Unpublished
 - Most complete music: CPT (p); TW (p)
 - Most complete lyric: INST
 - Original partitur: -0-
 - Original parts: TW

This Act II ballet choreographed by Leonide Massine was
replaced during the pre-Broadway tryout by "You Don't
Know Paree."

Why Don't We Try Staying Home?

Porter/Porter

Orchestrator: Unknown

Location of
- Composer's manuscript: -0-
- Sheet music: Not published separately
- Most complete music: CPT (pv-l);
  LoC (pv-l); TW (pv-l)
- Most complete lyric: CPT (pv-l);
  LoC (pv-l); TW (pv-l); CLCP
- Original partitur: -0-
- Original parts: -0-

Dropped in rehearsal. Initial publication in The Unpublished Cole Porter (Simon & Schuster: 1975).

My Harlem Wench

Porter/Porter

Orchestrator: DePackh

Location of
- Composer's manuscript: -0-
- Sheet music: Unpublished
- Most complete music: CPT (pv-l);
  TW (pv-l)
- Most complete lyric: CPT (pv-l);
  TW (pv-l); CLCP
- Original partitur: TW
- Original parts: TW

This number is musically almost identical to "The Happy Heaven of Harlem."

That's Why I Love You

Porter/Porter

Orchestrator: Unknown

Location of
- Composer's manuscript: -0-
- Sheet music: Unpublished
- Most complete music: CPT (pv-l);
  LoC (pv-l); TW (pv-l)
- Most complete lyric: CPT (pv-l);
  LoC (pv-l); TW (pv-l); CLCP
- Original partitur: -0-
- Original parts: -0-

Dropped in rehearsal. This number is musically similar to "You've Got That Thing."

Let's Turn On the Love Interest

Porter/Porter

Orchestrator: Unknown

Location of
- Composer's manuscript: -0-
- Sheet music: Unpublished
- Most complete music: TW (pv); Y (pv)
- Most complete lyric: -0-
- Original partitur: -0-
- Original parts: -0-

Unused.

Heaven of Harlem, The

Porter/Porter

Orchestrator: Unknown

Location of
- Composer's manuscript: -0-
- Sheet music: Unpublished
- Most complete music: -0-
- Most complete lyric: CPT (nb); CLCP
- Original partitur: -0-
- Original parts: -0-

Unused.

THE NEW YORKERS

Music   COLE PORTER
Lyrics   COLE PORTER

Musical comedy/revue in two acts. Opened December 8, 1930 in New York and ran 168 performances (World premiere: November 12, 1930 in Philadelphia). Libretto by Herbert Fields, based on a story by E. Ray Goetz and Peter Arno. Additional music and lyrics by Jimmy Durante, Chas. Henderson and Fred Waring. Produced by E. Ray Goetz. Directed by Monty Woolley. Choreographed by George Hale, Fred Waring. Musical direction by Al Goodman. Orchestrations by Hans Spialek.

Synopsis and Production Information	During socialite Alice Wentworth's fling with bootlegger Al Spanish, she joins in a subterranean escape from the police, visits a bootlegging factory, arranges a raid on a speakeasy she's running out of her home, and masterminds a jailbreak. A character named Jimmy Deegan is on hand to offer musical salutes to money, wood, data, and the Hot Patata; to invent an alcoholic tonic called Licquor Lax; to murder his archrival Feet McGeehan four times; and to preside over the wedding of Al and Alice, for which the bridemaids carry bouquets of bombs and the maid-of-honor wields a pistol.
	Other characters include songstress Mona and her boyfriend James. The show requires a full singing and dancing ensemble.
Comments	In the original production, Jimmy Deegan was played by Jimmy Durante, who was backed up by Lou Clayton and Eddie Jackson.
Orchestration	Unknown
Location of Original Materials	Script: Cole Porter Trusts (most lyrics) Piano-vocal score: See individual listings Partiturs: Missing Parts: Missing
	Most of the Porter songs performed in the New York production have survived; however, much of the music by other songwriters is still missing.
Rental Status	Currently unavailable for rental
Music Publisher	Warner Brothers Music
Information	Cole Porter Trusts

Cole Porter

Overture

Author(s): Unknown

Orchestrator: Unknown

Location of
- Composer's manuscript: -0-
- Sheet music: Unpublished
- Most complete music: -0-
- Most complete lyric: INST
- Original partitur: -0-
- Original parts: -0-

Where Have You Been?

Porter/Porter

Orchestrator: Unknown

Location of
- Composer's manuscript: Y (v)
- Sheet music: CPT, LoC, NYPL, Y
- Most complete music: CPT (sm);
    LoC (sm); NYPL (sm); Y (sm)
- Most complete lyric: CPT (sm, scr);
    LoC (sm); NYPL (sm); Y (sm); CLCP
- Original partitur: -0-
- Original parts: -0-

Go Into Your Dance

Porter/Porter

Orchestrator: Unknown

Location of
- Composer's manuscript: -0-
- Sheet music: Unpublished
- Most complete music: CPT (pv-I);
    LoC (pv-I)
- Most complete lyric: CPT (scr); CLCP
- Original partitur: -0-
- Original parts: -0-

The music to the verse is missing.

Say It With Gin

Porter/Porter

Orchestrator: Unknown

Location of
- Composer's manuscript: -0-
- Sheet music: Unpublished
- Most complete music: CPT (pv); LoC (pv)
- Most complete lyric: CPT (scr); CLCP
- Original partitur: -0-
- Original parts: -0-

Alternate title: "Opening Chorus to Bootleg Scene".

Hot Patata, The

Durante/Durante

Orchestrator: Unknown

Location of
- Composer's manuscript: -0-
- Sheet music: Unpublished
- Most complete music: See note
- Most complete lyric: CPT (scr)
- Original partitur: -0-
- Original parts: -0-

Durante recorded this number for Columbia (36732); his rendition includes some lyrics that are not in the script.

Venice

Porter/Porter

Orchestrator: Unknown

Location of
- Composer's manuscript: -0-
- Sheet music: Unpublished
- Most complete music: -0-
- Most complete lyric: CPT (scr); CLCP
- Original partitur: -0-
- Original parts: -0-

Love for Sale
 Porter/Porter
 Orchestrator: Unknown

Location of - Composer's manuscript: Y (v)
  - Sheet music: CPT, LoC, NYPL, Y
  - Most complete music: CPT (sm);
    LoC (sm); NYPL (sm); Y (sm)
  - Most complete lyric: CPT (sm, scr);
    LoC (sm); NYPL (sm); Y (sm); CLCP
  - Original partitur: -0-
  - Original parts: -0-

The script also contains an introductory rhymed passage
that may have been sung.

Great Indoors, The
 Porter/Porter
 Orchestrator: Unknown

Location of - Composer's manuscript: -0-
  - Sheet music: CPT, LoC, NYPL, Y
  - Most complete music: CPT (sm);
    LoC (sm); NYPL (sm); Y (sm)
  - Most complete lyric: CPT (sm, scr);
    LoC (sm); NYPL (sm); Y (sm); CLCP
  - Original partitur: -0-
  - Original parts: -0-

I'm Getting Myself Ready for You
 Porter/Porter
 Orchestrator: Unknown

Location of - Composer's manuscript: -0-
  - Sheet music: CPT, NYPL, Y
  - Most complete music: CPT (sm);
    NYPL (sm); Y (sm)
  - Most complete lyric: CPT (scr); CLCP
  - Original partitur: -0-
  - Original parts: -0-

Money!
 Durante/Durante
 Orchestrator: Unknown

Location of - Composer's manuscript: -0-
  - Sheet music: Unpublished
  - Most complete music: -0-
  - Most complete lyric: CPT (scr)
  - Original partitur: -0-
  - Original parts: -0-

Drinking Song
 Henderson & Waring/Henderson & Waring
 Orchestrator: Unknown

Location of - Composer's manuscript: -0-
  - Sheet music: See note
  - Most complete music: See note
  - Most complete lyric: See note
  - Original partitur: -0-
  - Original parts: -0-

Apparently published in the early Thirties, with rights
now controlled by Warner Brothers Music. No copy was
found.

Wood!
 Durante/Durante
 Orchestrator: Unknown

Location of - Composer's manuscript: -0-
  - Sheet music: Unpublished
  - Most complete music: LoC (m-l)
  - Most complete lyric: LoC (m-l);
    CPT (scr)
  - Original partitur: -0-
  - Original parts: -0-

Registered for copyright as an unpublished song in 1952.

Entr'acte

Author(s): Unknown
Orchestrator: Unknown

Location of
- Composer's manuscript: -0-
- Sheet music: Unpublished
- Most complete music: -0-
- Most complete lyric: INST
- Original partitur: -0-
- Original parts: -0-

Sheikin Fool

Durante/Durante
Orchestrator: Unknown

Location of
- Composer's manuscript: -0-
- Sheet music: Unpublished
- Most complete music: -0-
- Most complete lyric: -0-
- Original partitur: -0-
- Original parts: -0-

[unspecified song for Three Girl Friends]

Author(s): Unknown
Orchestrator: Unknown

Location of
- Composer's manuscript: -0-
- Sheet music: -0-
- Most complete music: -0-
- Most complete lyric: -0-
- Original partitur: -0-
- Original parts: -0-

Neither the script nor the New York programs give any additional information.

Let's Fly Away

Porter/Porter
Orchestrator: Unknown

Location of
- Composer's manuscript: -0-
- Sheet music: CPT, LoC, NYPL, Y
- Most complete music: CPT (sm);
      LoC (sm); NYPL (sm); Y (sm)
- Most complete lyric: CPT (sm, scr);
      LoC (sm); NYPL (sm); Y (sm); CLCP
- Original partitur: -0-
- Original parts: -0-

[unspecified song for Mona]

Author(s): Unknown
Orchestrator: Unknown

Location of
- Composer's manuscript: -0-
- Sheet music: -0-
- Most complete music: -0-
- Most complete lyric: -0-
- Original partitur: -0-
- Original parts: -0-

Neither the script nor the New York programs give any additional information.

I Happen to Like New York

Porter/Porter
Orchestrator: Unknown

Location of
- Composer's manuscript: -0-
- Sheet music: CPT, LoC, Y
- Most complete music: CPT (sm);
      LoC (sm); Y (sm)
- Most complete lyric: CPT (sm, scr);
      LoC (sm); Y (sm); CLCP
- Original partitur: -0-
- Original parts: -0-

Added within six weeks of the New York opening. In the script, the title changes in the final line to "I happen to love New York."

The New Yorkers (1930)

Sing Sing for Sing Sing
Porter/Porter
Orchestrator: Unknown

Location of   - Composer's manuscript: -0-
  - Sheet music: Unpublished
  - Most complete music: Y (pv-l)
  - Most complete lyric: Y (pv-l);
      CPT (scr); CLCP
  - Original partitur: -0-
  - Original parts: -0-

Data
Durante/Durante
Orchestrator: Unknown

Location of   - Composer's manuscript: -0-
  - Sheet music: Unpublished
  - Most complete music: -0-
  - Most complete lyric: CPT (scr)
  - Original partitur: -0-
  - Original parts: -0-

Take Me Back to Manhattan
Porter/Porter
Orchestrator: Unknown

Location of   - Composer's manuscript: Y (sk)
  - Sheet music: CPT, LoC, NYPL, Y
  - Most complete music: CPT (sm);
      LoC (sm); NYPL (sm); Y (sm)
  - Most complete lyric: CPT (sm, scr);
      LoC (sm); NYPL (sm); Y (sm); CLCP
  - Original partitur: -0-
  - Original parts: -0-

Replaced "Just One of Those Things" during the pre-Broadway tryout.

Just One of Those Things
Porter/Porter
Orchestrator: Unknown

Location of   - Composer's manuscript: Y
  - Sheet music: CPT, LoC, Y
  - Most complete music: CPT (sm);
      LoC (sm); Y (sm)
  - Most complete lyric: CPT (sm);
      LoC (sm); Y (sm); CLCP
  - Original partitur: -0-
  - Original parts: -0-

Although this song was replaced during the pre-Broadway tryout by "Take Me Back to Manhattan," some of the lyrics remain in the script, including a couplet that is not found in The Complete Lyrics of Cole Porter. This is not the famous Porter song with the same title from JUBILEE (1935).

Poor Rich, The
Porter/Porter
Orchestrator: Unknown

Location of   - Composer's manuscript: -0-
  - Sheet music: Unpublished
  - Most complete music: -0-
  - Most complete lyric: CLCP
  - Original partitur: -0-
  - Original parts: -0-

Dropped between the Philadelphia and New Haven tryouts. Alternate titles: "Help the Poor Rich" and "Please Help the Poor Rich."

Flit Drill
Author(s): Unknown
Orchestrator: Unknown

Location of   - Composer's manuscript: -0-
  - Sheet music: Unpublished
  - Most complete music: -0-
  - Most complete lyric: -0-
  - Original partitur: -0-
  - Original parts: -0-

Dropped before the New York opening.

Opening Scene 1
Porter/Porter
Orchestrator: Unknown

Location of - Composer's manuscript: -0-
- Sheet music: Unpublished
- Most complete music: CPT (pv-l);
    LoC (pv-l); Y (pv-l)
- Most complete lyric: CPT (pv-l);
    LoC (pv-l); Y (pv-l); CLCP
- Original partitur: -0-
- Original parts: -0-

Unused. Alternate title: "We've Been Spending the Summer With Our Families."

Opening Reuben's Scene
Porter/Porter
Orchestrator: Unknown

Location of - Composer's manuscript: -0-
- Sheet music: Unpublished
- Most complete music: CPT (pv-l);
    Y (pv-l)
- Most complete lyric: CPT (pv-l);
    Y (pv-l); CLCP
- Original partitur: -0-
- Original parts: -0-

Unused. Alternate title: "Where Can One Powder One's Nose?"

It Only Happens in Dreams
Porter/Porter
Orchestrator: Unknown

Location of - Composer's manuscript: Y
- Sheet music: Unpublished
- Most complete music: Y (pv); CPT (pv)
- Most complete lyric: CLCP
- Original partitur: -0-
- Original parts: -0-

Unused.

You're Too Far Away
Porter/Porter
Orchestrator: Unknown

Location of - Composer's manuscript: -0-
- Sheet music: CPT, LoC, Y
- Most complete music: CPT (sm);
    LoC (sm); Y (sm)
- Most complete lyric: CPT (sm);
    LoC (sm); Y (sm); CLCP
- Original partitur: -0-
- Original parts: -0-

Unused. Later sung in the Manchester performances of NYMPH ERRANT (1933) and published as an independent song in 1934.

I've Got You on My Mind
Porter/Porter
Orchestrator: Unknown

Location of - Composer's manuscript: LoC (sk)
- Sheet music: See note
- Most complete music: LoC (sk)
- Most complete lyric: -0-
- Original partitur: -0-
- Original parts: -0-

Unused. A later version was peformed in GAY DIVORCE (1932) and published.

But He Never Says He Loves Me
Porter/Porter
Orchestrator: Unknown

Location of - Composer's manuscript: -0-
- Sheet music: See note
- Most complete music: LoC (pv-l)
- Most complete lyric: LoC (pv-l)
- Original partitur: -0-
- Original parts: -0-

Dropped during the pre-Broadway tryout. Reworked for NYMPH ERRANT (1933), where it was introduced (and published) as "The Physician."

The New Yorkers (1930)

Why Talk About Sex?
  Porter/Porter
  Orchestrator: Unknown

  Location of   - Composer's manuscript: -0-
        - Sheet music: Unpublished
        - Most complete music: -0-
        - Most complete lyric: -0-
        - Original partitur: -0-
        - Original parts: -0-

  Unused.

I'm Haunted By You
  Porter/Porter
  Orchestrator: Unknown

  Location of   - Composer's manuscript: LoC (sk)
        - Sheet music: Unpublished
        - Most complete music: LoC (sk)
        - Most complete lyric: -0-
        - Original partitur: -0-
        - Original parts: -0-

  Unused.

My Louisa
  Porter/Porter
  Orchestrator: Unknown

  Location of   - Composer's manuscript: -0-
        - Sheet music: Unpublished
        - Most complete music: CPT (pv-l)
        - Most complete lyric: CLCP
        - Original partitur: -0-
        - Original parts: -0-

  Unused. Previously intended for WAKE UP AND DREAM,
  Porter's 1929 London revue.

I've Got to Be Psychoanalyzed By You
  Porter/Porter
  Orchestrator: Unknown

  Location of   - Composer's manuscript: LoC (sk)
        - Sheet music: Unpublished
        - Most complete music: LoC (sk)
        - Most complete lyric: -0-
        - Original partitur: -0-
        - Original parts: -0-

  Unused.

You've Got to Be Hard-Boiled
  Porter/Porter
  Orchestrator: Unknown

  Location of   - Composer's manuscript: Y (frag)
        - Sheet music: Unpublished
        - Most complete music: Y (frag)
        - Most complete lyric: -0-
        - Original partitur: -0-
        - Original parts: -0-

  Unused.

Mona and Her Kiddies
  Author(s): Unknown
  Orchestrator: Unknown

  Location of   - Composer's manuscript: -0-
        - Sheet music: Unpublished
        - Most complete music: -0-
        - Most complete lyric: -0-
        - Original partitur: -0-
        - Original parts: -0-

  Dropped during the pre-Broadway tryout.

GAY DIVORCE

Music   COLE PORTER
Lyrics   COLE PORTER

Musical comedy in two acts. Opened November 29, 1932 in New York and ran 248 performances (World premiere: November 7, 1932 in Boston). Libretto by Dwight Taylor, musical adaptation by Kenneth Webb and Samuel Hoffenstein. Produced by Dwight Deere Wiman and Tom Weatherly. Directed by Howard Lindsay. Choreographed by Carl Randall and Barbara Newberry. Musical direction by Gene Salzer. Orchestrations by Hans Spialek, Robert Russell Bennett.

Synopsis and Production Information

While traveling abroad, American novelist Guy Holden falls in love with a beautiful lady named Mimi, who mysteriously disappears after their initial meeting. When he later runs into her a seaside resort, she mistakes him for the paid corespondent she has hired to facilitate her divorce.

Other characters include Guy's lawyer friend, Egbert; Mimi's oft-divorced friend and protectress, Hortense; and the idiot corespondent Tonetti, whose motto is "Your wife is safe with Tonetti -- he prefers spaghetti." The show requires a full singing and dancing ensemble.

Orchestration

Reed I (Flute, Clarinet, Alto Sax); Reed II (Clarinet, Alto Sax); Reed III (Oboe, Clarinet, Tenor Sax); Trumpet I II; Trumpet III; Trombone; Percussion; Piano; Violin I; Violin II; Violin III (dbl. Banjo); Cello; Bass

Comments

In the original production, Guy was played by Fred Astaire. Astaire repeated his role in the 1933 London production and in the 1934 film version, GAY DIVORCEE, which co-starred Ginger Rogers. Of the songs in GAY DIVORCE, only "Night and Day" was retained for the film. Additional numbers by other songwriters were added; one of these, "The Continental" (by Con Conrad and Herb Magidson), won the first Academy Award given for Best Song.

Location of Original Materials

Script: Cole Porter Trusts (all lyrics)
Piano-vocal score: See individual listings
Partiturs: Shubert Archive
Parts: Yale University

All of the songs and partiturs from the original New York production survive, as do most of the parts. Tams-Witmark Music Library has a bound piano-vocal score that is missing the Overture, the Entr'acte, the vocal to "What Will Become of Our England?", and "Mister and Missus Fitch."

Rental Status

Tams-Witmark will lease the original script and their piano-vocal score to theatrical companies interested in performing the show with piano accompaniment. Inquiries regarding performance of the show with its original orchestrations should be directed to the Cole Porter Trusts.

Music Publisher   Warner Brothers Music

Information   Cole Porter Trusts, Tams-Witmark Music Library

Gay Divorce (1932)

Overture
Porter/Porter
Orchestrator: Spialek, Bennett

Location of - Composer's manuscript: -0-
 - Sheet music: Unpublished
 - Most complete music: Y (parts)
 - Most complete lyric: INST
 - Original partitur: SA (inc)
 - Original parts: Y

Salt Air
Porter/Porter
Orchestrator: Bennett

Location of - Composer's manuscript: -0-
 - Sheet music: Unpublished
 - Most complete music: CPT (pv-l);
  LoC (pv-l)
 - Most complete lyric: CPT (scr); CLCP
 - Original partitur: SA
 - Original parts: Y

After You, Who?
Porter/Porter
Orchestrator: Bennett

Location of - Composer's manuscript: Y (sk)
 - Sheet music: CPT, LoC, NYPL, Y
 - Most complete music: CPT (sm);
  LoC (sm); NYPL (sm); Y (sm)
 - Most complete lyric: CPT (sm, scr);
  LoC (sm); NYPL (sm); Y (sm); CLCP
 - Original partitur: SA
 - Original parts: Y

I Still Love the Red, White and Blue
Porter/Porter
Orchestrator: Spialek

Location of - Composer's manuscript: -0-
 - Sheet music: Unpublished
 - Most complete music: CPT (pv-l)
 - Most complete lyric: CPT (scr); CLCP
 - Original partitur: SA
 - Original parts: Y

Why Marry Them?
Porter/Porter
Orchestrator: Spialek

Location of - Composer's manuscript: -0-
 - Sheet music: Unpublished
 - Most complete music: CPT (pv-l)
 - Most complete lyric: CPT (pv-l, scr);
  CLCP
 - Original partitur: SA
 - Original parts: Y

Night and Day
Porter/Porter
Orchestrator: Bennett

Location of - Composer's manuscript: -0-
 - Sheet music: CPT, LoC, NYPL, Y
 - Most complete music: CPT (sm);
  LoC 'sm); NYPL (sm); Y (sm)
 - Most complete lyric: CPT (sm, scr);
  LoC (sm); NYPL (sm); Y (sm); CLCP
 - Original partitur: SA
 - Original parts: Y

The Shubert Archive also has an unused Spialek partitur.

How's Your Romance?

Porter/Porter

Orchestrator: Spialek

Location of
- Composer's manuscript: -0-
- Sheet music: CPT, LoC, NYPL, Y
- Most complete music: CPT (sm);
      LoC (sm); NYPL (sm); Y (sm)
- Most complete lyric: CLCP
- Original partitur: SA
- Original parts: Y

I've Got You on My Mind

Porter/Porter

Orchestrator: Spialek

Location of
- Composer's manuscript: LoC (sk)
- Sheet music: CPT, LoC, NYPL, Y
- Most complete music: CPT (sm);
      LoC (sm); NYPL (sm); Y (sm)
- Most complete lyric: CPT (sm);
      LoC (sm); NYPL (sm); Y (sm); CLCP
- Original partitur: SA (inc)
- Original parts: Y

Previously intended for THE NEW YORKERS (1930).

Entr'acte

Porter/Porter

Orchestrator: Spialek

Location of
- Composer's manuscript: -0-
- Sheet music: Unpublished
- Most complete music: Y (parts)
- Most complete lyric: INST
- Original partitur: SA (inc)
- Original parts: Y

Mister and Missus Fitch

Porter/Porter

Orchestrator: Spialek

Location of
- Composer's manuscript: -0-
- Sheet music: LoC, Y, CPT (x)
- Most complete music: LoC (sm); Y (sm);
      CPT (sm-x)
- Most complete lyric: CPT (scr); CLCP
- Original partitur: SA
- Original parts: Y (inc)

The orchestra piano part is missing.

What Will Become of Our England?

Porter/Porter

Orchestrator: Spialek

Location of
- Composer's manuscript: -0-
- Sheet music: Unpublished
- Most complete music: CPT (pv-l);
      Y (pv-l)
- Most complete lyric: CPT (scr); CLCP
- Original partitur: SA
- Original parts: Y

You're in Love

Porter/Porter

Orchestrator: Bennett

Location of
- Composer's manuscript: -0-
- Sheet music: CPT, LoC, NYPL, Y
- Most complete music: CPT (sm & pv-l)
- Most complete lyric: CPT (sm & pv-l,
      scr); CLCP
- Original partitur: SA
- Original parts: Y

The introductory patter was not published.

Gay Divorce (1932)

Fate

Porter/Porter

Orchestrator: Unknown

Location of
- Composer's manuscript: -0-
- Sheet music: Unpublished
- Most complete music: CPT (pv-l);
  LoC (pv-l)
- Most complete lyric: CPT (pv-l);
  LoC (pv-l); CLCP
- Original partitur: -0-
- Original parts: -0-

Unused.

In Case You Don't Know

Porter/Porter

Orchestrator: Unknown

Location of
- Composer's manuscript: -0-
- Sheet music: Unpublished
- Most complete music: CPT (pv); TW (pv)
- Most complete lyric: -0-
- Original partitur: -0-
- Original parts: -0-

Unused.

Weekend Affair, A

Porter/Porter

Orchestrator: Unknown

Location of
- Composer's manuscript: -0-
- Sheet music: Unpublished
- Most complete music: CPT (pv-l)
- Most complete lyric: CPT (pv-l); CLCP
- Original partitur: -0-
- Original parts: -0-

Unused.

Never Say No

Porter/Porter

Orchestrator: Unknown

Location of
- Composer's manuscript: -0-
- Sheet music: Unpublished
- Most complete music: Y (sk)
- Most complete lyric: -0-
- Original partitur: -0-
- Original parts: -0-

Written for the London production.

Never Give In to Love

Porter/Porter

Orchestrator: Unknown

Location of
- Composer's manuscript: -0-
- Sheet music: Unpublished
- Most complete music: CPT (pv); TW (pv)
- Most complete lyric: -0-
- Original partitur: -0-
- Original parts: -0-

Unused.

Waiters v. Waitresses

Porter/Porter

Orchestrator: Unknown

Location of
- Composer's manuscript: -0-
- Sheet music: Unpublished
- Most complete music: -0-
- Most complete lyric: -0-
- Original partitur: -0-
- Original parts: -0-

Written for the London production.

I Love Only You
> Porter/Porter
> Orchestrator: Unknown

> Location of   - Composer's manuscript: -0-
>   - Sheet music: Not published separately
>   - Most complete music: CPT (p sel)
>   - Most complete lyric: CLCP
>   - Original partitur: -0-
>   - Original parts: -0-

Written for the London production. Published in the British piano selection.

NYMPH ERRANT

Music	COLE PORTER
Lyrics	COLE PORTER

Musical comedy in two acts. Opened October 6, 1933 in London and ran 154 performances (World premiere: September 11, 1933 in Manchester). Libretto by Romney Brent, based on the novel by James Laver. Produced by Charles B. Cochran. Directed by Romney Brent.

Synopsis and Production Information	Fresh out of boarding school, pretty young Evangeline is looking to lose her innocence. Her quest takes her to the beach at Neauville, the Cafe du Dome in Paris, a palazzo in Venice, and a harem in Turkey -- without an ounce of success. Returning home dejected and defeated, she receives an unexpected and welcome proposition from the family gardener. The show requires a full singing and dancing ensemble.
Orchestration	Flute; Oboe; Clarinet I; Clarinet II; Clarinet III; Alto Sax I; Alto Sax II; Tenor Sax; Trumpet I; Trumpet II III; Trombone; Drums; Piano; Violin I II; Viola I II; Cello; Bass
Comments	In the original production, Evangeline was played by Gertrude Lawrence.
Location of Original Materials	Script: Cole Porter Trusts (all lyrics) Piano-vocal score: See individual listings Partiturs: Cole Porter Trusts Parts: Missing All of the piano-vocal material survives, but only one partitur.
Rental Status	Currently unavailable for rental
Music Publisher	Warner Brothers Music
Information	Cole Porter Trusts

Cole Porter

Overture

Porter/Porter
Orchestrator: Unknown

Location of — Composer's manuscript: -0-
— Sheet music: Unpublished
— Most complete music: CPT (p sk)
— Most complete lyric: INST
— Original partitur: -0-
— Original parts: -0-

Experiment

Porter/Porter
Orchestrator: Unknown

Location of — Composer's manuscript: -0-
— Sheet music: CPT, LoC, Y
— Most complete music: CPT (sm);
    LoC (sm); Y (sm)
— Most complete lyric: CPT (sm, ls, scr);
    LoC (sm); Y (sm); CLCP
— Original partitur: -0-
— Original parts: -0-

The Complete Lyrics of Cole Porter also has a revised
lyric intended for the unproduced film MISSISSIPPI BELLE
(1943-44).

It's Bad for Me

Porter/Porter
Orchestrator: Unknown

Location of — Composer's manuscript: -0-
— Sheet music: CPT, LoC, Y
— Most complete music: CPT (sm);
    LoC (sm); Y (sm)
— Most complete lyric: CPT (sm, ls, scr);
    LoC (sm); Y (sm); CLCP
— Original partitur: -0-
— Original parts: -0-

Neauville-Sur-Mer

Porter/Porter
Orchestrator: Unknown

Location of — Composer's manuscript: -0-
— Sheet music: Not published separately
— Most complete music: CPT (pv-l)
— Most complete lyric: CPT (pv-l, ls, scr);
    CLCP
— Original partitur: -0-
— Original parts: -0-

Published in the piano selection. Originally titled
"Deauville-Sur-Mer."

Cocotte, The

Porter/Porter
Orchestrator: Unknown

Location of — Composer's manuscript: -0-
— Sheet music: Not published separately
— Most complete music: CPT (pv-l);
    LoC (pv-l)
— Most complete lyric: CPT (ls, scr); CLCP
— Original partitur: -0-
— Original parts: -0-

Published in the piano selection.

How Could We Be Wrong?

Porter/Porter
Orchestrator: Unknown

Location of — Composer's manuscript: -0-
— Sheet music: CPT, LoC, Y
— Most complete music: CPT (sm);
    LoC (sm); Y (sm)
— Most complete lyric: CPT (sm, ls, scr);
    LoC (sm); Y (sm); CLCP
— Original partitur: -0-
— Original parts: -0-

Nymph Errant (1933)

They're Always Entertaining

Porter/Porter

Orchestrator: Unknown

Location of   - Composer's manuscript: -0-
- Sheet music: Unpublished
- Most complete music: CPT (pv-l);
  - LoC (pv-l)
- Most complete lyric: CPT (pv-l, ls, scr);
  - LoC (pv-l); CLCP
- Original partitur: -0-
- Original parts: -0-

Entr'acte

Porter/Porter

Orchestrator: Unknown

Location of   - Composer's manuscript: -0-
- Sheet music: Unpublished
- Most complete music: -0-
- Most complete lyric: INST
- Original partitur: -0-
- Original parts: -0-

Cazanova

Porter/Porter

Orchestrator: Unknown

Location of   - Composer's manuscript: -0-
- Sheet music: Unpublished
- Most complete music: CPT (pv)
- Most complete lyric: CPT (scr); CLCP
- Original partitur: -0-
- Original parts: -0-

Replaced "Georgia Sand" soon after the London opening.

Ruins

Porter/Porter

Orchestrator: Unknown

Location of   - Composer's manuscript: -0-
- Sheet music: Unpublished
- Most complete music: CPT (pv)
- Most complete lyric: CPT (ls, scr); CLCP
- Original partitur: -0-
- Original parts: -0-

Nymph Errant

Porter/Porter

Orchestrator: Unknown

Location of   - Composer's manuscript: -0-
- Sheet music: CPT, LoC, Y
- Most complete music: CPT (sm);
  - LoC (sm); Y (sm)
- Most complete lyric: CPT (sm, scr);
  - LoC (sm); Y (sm); CLCP
- Original partitur: -0-
- Original parts: -0-

Replaced "When Love Comes Your Way" before the London opening.

Physician, The

Porter/Porter

Orchestrator: Unknown

Location of   - Composer's manuscript: -0-
- Sheet music: CPT, LoC, Y
- Most complete music: CPT (sm);
  - LoC (sm); Y (sm)
- Most complete lyric: CPT (scr) & CLCP
- Original partitur: -0-
- Original parts: -0-

An earlier version, "But He Never Says He Loves Me," was sung during the pre-Broadway tryout of THE NEW YORKERS (1930). The Complete Lyrics of Cole Porter and the script contain different lyrics for the third refrain.

Solomon

Porter/Porter

Orchestrator: Unknown

Location of   - Composer's manuscript: -0-
      - Sheet music: CPT, LoC, Y
      - Most complete music: CPT (sm);
           LoC (sm); Y (sm)
      - Most complete lyric: CPT (sm, ls, scr);
           LoC (sm); Y (sm); CLCP
      - Original partitur: -0-
      - Original parts: -0-

Back to Nature With You

Porter/Porter

Orchestrator: Unknown

Location of   - Composer's manuscript: -0-
      - Sheet music: Not published separately
      - Most complete music: CPT (pv-l)
      - Most complete lyric: CPT (pv-l, ls, scr);
           CLCP
      - Original partitur: -0-
      - Original parts: -0-

Published in the piano selection.

Plumbing

Porter/Porter

Orchestrator: Unknown

Location of   - Composer's manuscript: -0-
      - Sheet music: Unpublished
      - Most complete music: CPT (pv-l)
      - Most complete lyric: CPT (pv-l, ls, scr);
           CLCP
      - Original partitur: -0-
      - Original parts: -0-

Si Vous Aimez les Poitrines

Porter/Porter

Orchestrator: Unknown

Location of   - Composer's manuscript: -0-
      - Sheet music: Unpublished
      - Most complete music: CPT (pv)
      - Most complete lyric: CPT (ls); CLCP
      - Original partitur: -0-
      - Original parts: -0-

Alternate title: "If You Like les Belles Poitrines."

You're Too Far Away

Porter/Porter

Orchestrator: Unknown

Location of   - Composer's manuscript: -0-
      - Sheet music: CPT, LoC, Y
      - Most complete music: CPT (sm);
           LoC (sm); Y (sm)
      - Most complete lyric: CPT (sm);
           LoC (sm); Y (sm); CLCP
      - Original partitur: -0-
      - Original parts: -0-

Originally intended for THE NEW YORKERS (1930), this number was sung in the Manchester performances of NYMPH ERRANT under the title "I Look at You." After it was dropped from NYMPH ERRANT, it was published as an independent song in 1934.

When Love Comes Your Way

Porter/Porter

Orchestrator: Unknown

Location of   - Composer's manuscript: -0-
      - Sheet music: CPT, LoC, NYPL, Y
      - Most complete music: CPT (sm);
           LoC (sm); NYPL (sm); Y (sm)
      - Most complete lyric: CPT (sm);
           LoC (sm); NYPL (sm); Y (sm); CLCP
      - Original partitur: -0-
      - Original parts: -0-

Dropped before the London opening. Later used in JUBILEE (1935).

Nymph Errant (1933)

Sweet Nudity

Porter/Porter

Orchestrator: Unknown

Location of
- Composer's manuscript: -0-
- Sheet music: Unpublished
- Most complete music: CPT (pv-I)
- Most complete lyric: CPT (pv-I); CLCP
- Original partitur: CPT
- Original parts: -0-

Dropped in rehearsal. Alternate title: "Nudity, Sweet Nudity."

French Colonial Exposition Scene

Porter/Porter

Orchestrator: Unknown

Location of
- Composer's manuscript: -0-
- Sheet music: Unpublished
- Most complete music: -0-
- Most complete lyric: CLCP
- Original partitur: -0-
- Original parts: -0-

Unused.

Georgia Sand

Porter/Porter

Orchestrator: Unknown

Location of
- Composer's manuscript: -0-
- Sheet music: Not published separately
- Most complete music: CPT (pv)
- Most complete lyric: CLCP
- Original partitur: -0-
- Original parts: -0-

Replaced soon after the London opening by "Cazanova."
Published in the piano selection.

ANYTHING GOES

Music	COLE PORTER
Lyrics	COLE PORTER

Musical comedy in two acts. Opened November 21, 1934 in New York and ran 420 performances (World premiere: November 5, 1934 in Boston). Libretto by Guy Bolton and P.G. Wodehouse, revised by Howard Lindsay and Russel Crouse. Produced by Vinton Freedley. Directed by Howard Lindsay. Choreographed by Robert Alton. Musical direction by Earl Busby. Orchestrations by Hans Spialek, Robert Russell Bennett, Menotti Salta.

Synopsis and Production Information	In order to prevent the marriage of pretty Hope Harcourt to Sir Evelyn Oakleigh, Billy Crocker stows away on a ship bound for London. He is assisted in his mission by his pal Reno Sweeney, evangelist turned nightclub singer, and by Moon Face Martin, Public Enemy Number Thirteen, who has come aboard disguised as a clergyman.

The show requires a full singing and dancing ensemble. |
| Orchestration | Reed I (Oboe, English Horn, Bass Oboe, Celeste); Reed II (Alto Sax, Clarinet, Baritone Sax, Bass Clarinet, Flute); Reed III (Alto Sax, Clarinet, Bass Clarinet, Flute, Piccolo, Oboe); Reed IV (Tenor Sax, Clarinet, Flute); Trumpet I II; Trumpet III; Trombone; Percussion I II; Piano; Violin A B C D; Viola; Cello (divisi); Bass |
| Comments | In the original production, Billy was played by William Gaxton, Reno by Ethel Merman, and Moon Face by Victor Moore. |
| Location of Original Material | Script: Tams-Witmark Music Library (all lyrics), Cole Porter Trusts (all lyrics)
Piano-vocal score: Tams-Witmark Music Library, Cole Porter Trusts
Partiturs: Tams-Witmark Music Library
Parts: Tams-Witmark Music Library

In 1983, Hans Spialek and John McGlinn restored most of the original orchestrations from surviving material at Tams-Witmark Music Library; these materials, which are virtually complete, are now at Tams-Witmark.

When ANYTHING GOES played London in 1935, musical routines and lyrics were altered; the London version was then published the following year, the score by Harms, Inc. and the script by Samuel French, Inc. The London script is at Tams-Witmark, the London score at the New York Public Library. Because this version does not match the New York production, it has largely been excluded from the song listings on the following pages. |
Rental Status	Tams-Witmark rents the 1934 book and piano-vocal score with the following orchestration reduced from the original: Reed I (Flute, Clarinet, Alto Sax); Reed II (Oboe, English Horn, Clarinet, Alto Sax); Reed III (Clarinet, Bass Clarinet, Tenor Sax); Trumpet I II; Trombone; Percussion I II; Piano; Violin I; Violin II; Viola; Cello; Bass. Tams-Witmark also rents a 1962 version with a revised book, several interpolated Porter songs from other shows, and a new orchestration for 22 players (also available in a reduced version for eight players).
Music Publisher	Warner Brothers Music
Information	Tams-Witmark Music Library

Anything Goes (1934)

Overture

Porter/Porter
Orchestrator: Spialek

Location of
- Composer's manuscript: -0-
- Sheet music: Unpublished
- Most complete music: CPT (pv score); TW (pv score)
- Most complete lyric: INST
- Original partitur: TW (1983)
- Original parts: TW (1983)

The full orchestration was restored in 1983 from the reduced Tams-Witmark parts.

Bon Voyage/There's No Cure Like Travel

Porter/Porter
Orchestrator: Spialek

Location of
- Composer's manuscript: -0-
- Sheet music: Not published separately
- Most complete music: CPT (pv-l)
- Most complete lyric: CPT (pv-l); CLCP
- Original partitur: TW
- Original parts: TW (1983)

Published in the piano-vocal score from the London production. These two numbers function as countermelodies and together make up the "Opening Act I, Scene 2." "There's No Cure Like Travel" was not performed in the original New York production.

I Get a Kick Out of You

Porter/Porter
Orchestrator: Bennett

Location of
- Composer's manuscript: -0-
- Sheet music: CPT, LoC, Y
- Most complete music: CPT (sm, pv score); LoC (sm); Y (sm); TW (pv score)
- Most complete lyric: CPT (sm, pv score, scr); LoC (sm); Y (sm); TW (pv score, scr); CLCP
- Original partitur: TW
- Original parts: TW (1983)

The Complete Lyrics of Cole Porter also contains an early version of the lyric.

All Through the Night

Porter/Porter
Orchestrator: Bennett, Salta

Location of
- Composer's manuscript: -0-
- Sheet music: CPT, LoC, NYPL, Y
- Most complete music: CPT (pv-l)
- Most complete lyric: CLCP
- Original partitur: TW (inc)
- Original parts: TW (1983 inc)

The verse, which was not performed in the original production, is not in the script or piano-vocal score. It was apparently scored in 1934, but the partitur (and parts) are missing.

There'll Always Be a Lady Fair

Porter/Porter

Orchestrator: Unknown

Location of — Composer's manuscript: -0-
— Sheet music: CPT, LoC, NYPL, Y
— Most complete music: CPT (sm, pv score);
     LoC (sm); NYPL (sm); Y (sm);
     TW (sm, pv score)
— Most complete lyric: CLCP
— Original partitur: TW (1983)
— Original parts: TW (1983)

Alternate title: "Sailor's Chantey." The full orchestration was restored in 1983 from the reduced Tams-Witmark parts.

Where Are the Men?

Porter/Porter

Orchestrator: Unknown

Location of — Composer's manuscript: Y
— Sheet music: Not published separately
— Most complete music: CPT (pv score);
     TW (pv score)
— Most complete lyric: CPT (pv score, scr);
     TW (pv score, scr); CLCP
— Original partitur: TW (1983)
— Original parts: TW (1983)

Published in the piano-vocal score from the London production. The full orchestration was restored in 1983 from the reduced Tams-Witmark parts.

You're the Top

Porter/Porter

Orchestrator: Unknown

Location of — Composer's manuscript: -0-
— Sheet music: CPT, LoC, NYPL, Y
— Most complete music: CPT (sm, pv score);
     LoC (sm); NYPL (sm); Y (sm);
     TW (pv score)
— Most complete lyric: CLCP
— Original partitur: TW (inc)
— Original parts: TW (1983)

P.G. Wodehouse wrote additional lyrics for the 1935 London production.

Anything Goes

Porter/Porter

Orchestrator: Bennett, Salta

Location of — Composer's manuscript: -0-
— Sheet music: CPT, LoC, NYPL, Y
— Most complete music: CPT (sm, pv score);
     LoC (sm); NYPL (sm); Y (sm);
     TW (pv score)
— Most complete lyric: CLCP
— Original partitur: TW (inc), TW (1983)
— Original parts: TW (1983)

P.G. Wodehouse wrote additional lyrics for the 1935 London production.

Entr'acte

Porter/Porter

Orchestrator: Spialek

Location of — Composer's manuscript: -0-
— Sheet music: Unpublished
— Most complete music: CPT (pv score);
     TW (pv score)
— Most complete lyric: INST
— Original partitur: TW (1983)
— Original parts: TW (1983)

The full orchestration was restored in 1983 from the reduced Tams-Witmark parts.

Public Enemy Number One

Porter/Porter

Orchestrator: Spialek

Location of — Composer's manuscript: -0-
— Sheet music: Not published separately
— Most complete music: CPT (pv score);
     TW (pv score)
— Most complete lyric: CPT (pv score, scr);
     TW (pv score, scr); CLCP
— Original partitur: TW
— Original parts: TW (1983)

Published in the piano-vocal score from the London production.

Anything Goes (1934)

Blow, Gabriel, Blow
Porter/Porter
Orchestrator: Bennett

Location of — Composer's manuscript: -0-
— Sheet music: CPT, LoC, NYPL, Y
— Most complete music: CPT (sm, pv score);
       LoC (sm); NYPL (sm); Y (sm);
       TW (pv score)
— Most complete lyric: CPT (sm, pv score,
       scr); LoC (sm); NYPL (sm); Y (sm);
       TW (pv score, scr); CLCP
— Original partitur: TW
— Original parts: TW (1983)

Be Like the Bluebird
Porter/Porter
Orchestrator: Unknown

Location of — Composer's manuscript: -0-
— Sheet music: CPT, LoC, Y
— Most complete music: CPT (sm, pv score);
       LoC (sm); Y (sm); TW (pv score)
— Most complete lyric: CPT (sm, pv score,
       scr); LoC (sm); Y (sm);
       TW (pv score, scr); CLCP
— Original partitur: TW (1983)
— Original parts: TW (1983)

The full orchestration was restored in 1983 from the
reduced Tams-Witmark parts. Cole Porter recorded a
second refrain on Victor 24843.

Gypsy in Me, The
Porter/Porter
Orchestrator: Spialek

Location of — Composer's manuscript: -0-
— Sheet music: CPT, LoC, NYPL, Y
— Most complete music: CPT (sm, pv score);
       LoC (sm); NYPL (sm); Y (sm);
       TW (pv score)
— Most complete lyric: CPT (sm, pv score,
       scr); LoC (sm); NYPL (sm); Y (sm);
       TW (pv score, scr); CLCP
— Original partitur: TW
— Original parts: TW (1983)

Buddie, Beware
Porter/Porter
Orchestrator: Unknown

Location of — Composer's manuscript: -0-
— Sheet music: CPT, LoC, NYPL, Y
— Most complete music: CPT (sm);
       LoC (sm); NYPL (sm); Y (sm)
— Most complete lyric: CLCP
— Original partitur: -0-
— Original parts: -0-

Introduced in New York by Ethel Merman, but replaced by
December 10, 1934 with a reprise of "I Get a Kick Out of
You."

Waltz Down the Aisle
Porter/Porter
Orchestrator: Unknown

Location of — Composer's manuscript: -0-
— Sheet music: CPT, LoC, NYPL, Y
— Most complete music: CPT (pv-l)
— Most complete lyric: CPT (pv-l); CLCP
— Original partitur: -0-
— Original parts: -0-

This unused number was subsequently lengthened for
JUBILEE (1935), but dropped before the New York
opening.

What a Joy to Be Young
Porter/Porter
Orchestrator: Unknown

Location of — Composer's manuscript: -0-
— Sheet music: Unpublished
— Most complete music: CPT (pv-l)
— Most complete lyric: CPT (pv-l); CLCP
— Original partitur: -0-
— Original parts: -0-

Dropped before the New York opening. Listed in the
Boston programs as "To Be in Love and Young."

Kate the Great

Porter/Porter

Orchestrator: See note

Location of   - Composer's manuscript: -0-
                - Sheet music: Not published separately
                - Most complete music: CPT (pv-l)
                - Most complete lyric: CPT (pv-l); CLCP
                - Original partitur: -0-
                - Original parts: -0-

Unused. Initial publication in Music & Lyrics by Cole
Porter, Volume II (Chappell). The release was later used
as the principal theme in "So Near and Yet So Far" in
Porter's 1941 film, YOU'LL NEVER GET RICH. Hans
Spialek orchestrated "Kate the Great" in 1983 (it was
dropped from the original production before being scored);
the partitur and parts are at Tams-Witmark.

JUBILEE

Music   **COLE PORTER**
Lyrics   **COLE PORTER**

Musical comedy in two acts. Opened October 12, 1935 in New York and ran 169 performances (World premiere: September 21, 1935 in Boston). Libretto by Moss Hart. Produced by Sam H. Harris and Max Gordon. Directed by Hassard Short, Monty Woolley. Choreographed by Albertina Rasch. Musical direction by Frank Tours. Orchestrations by Robert Russell Bennett.

Synopsis and Production Information	The Royal Family of a fictional European country use the threat posed by an impending revolution as an excuse to abandon the throne and pursue their private dreams. The King meets up with party-giver extraordinaire Eva Standing; the Queen chases after swimmer-turned-actor Charles Rausmiller (a.k.a Mowgli); the Prince woos songstress Karen O'Kane; and the Princess wins the admiration and affection of playwright/composer/actor Eric Dare. When the revolutionary threat is revealed to be a hoax, the family members are forced to return to power, but they manage to incorporate their newfound friends into their royal lives.
	The show requires a full singing and dancing ensemble. Karen and the Prince are dancing as well as singing roles. Settings include the Royal Palace, a movie theatre (a scene that includes a film excerpt from MOWGLI AND THE WHITE GODDESS), the swank Cafe Martinique, and the beach at Rockwell.
Orchestration	Unknown
Location of Original Materials	Script: Cole Porter Trusts (all lyrics) Piano-vocal score: Cole Porter Trusts Partiturs: Missing Parts: Missing
	All of the piano-vocal material performed in the original New York production has survived except the music to "Gather Ye Autographs." Early drafts of the script can be found at the Library of Congress and the New York Public Library.
Rental Status	The Cole Porter Trusts has a rental property that was prepared in 1984; it consists of the original book (with the addition of some dialogue and stage directions from early drafts), the original score (with "There's Nothing Like Swimming" reinstated and the missing "Gather Ye Autographs" deleted), and a new orchestration by Larry Moore for 24 players.
Music Publisher	Warner Brothers Music
Information	Cole Porter Trusts

Overture

Porter/Porter
Orchestrator: Unknown

Location of   - Composer's manuscript: -0-
         - Sheet music: Unpublished
         - Most complete music: -0-
         - Most complete lyric: INST
         - Original partitur: -0-
         - Original parts: -0-

The rental material includes a newly arranged Overture.

Why Shouldn't I?

Porter/Porter
Orchestrator: Unknown

Location of   - Composer's manuscript: -0-
         - Sheet music: CPT, LoC, NYPL, Y
         - Most complete music: CPT (pv-l)
         - Most complete lyric: CPT (pv-l); CLCP
         - Original partitur: -0-
         - Original parts: -0-

The piano-vocal contains an unpublished interlude that was not performed in the original production.

Our Crown

Porter/Porter
Orchestrator: Unknown

Location of   - Composer's manuscript: -0-
         - Sheet music: Unpublished
         - Most complete music: CPT (pv score, pv-l)
         - Most complete lyric: CPT (pv score, pv-l,
              1935 scr, 1984 scr); CLCP
         - Original partitur: -0-
         - Original parts: -0-

Alternate title: "National Anthem."

Entrance of Eric

Porter/Porter
Orchestrator: Unknown

Location of   - Composer's manuscript: -0-
         - Sheet music: Unpublished
         - Most complete music: CPT (pv score,
              pv-l)
         - Most complete lyric: CPT (pv score,
              pv-l, 1935 scr, 1984 scr); CLCP
         - Original partitur: -0-
         - Original parts: -0-

We're Off to Feathermore

Porter/Porter
Orchestrator: Unknown

Location of   - Composer's manuscript: -0-
         - Sheet music: Unpublished
         - Most complete music: CPT (pv score, pv-l)
         - Most complete lyric: CPT (pv score, pv-l,
              1984 scr); CLCP
         - Original partitur: -0-
         - Original parts: -0-

Alternate title: "Feathermore." An additional lyric can be found in the early draft at the Library of Congress.

Kling-Kling Bird on the Divi-Divi Tree, The

Porter/Porter
Orchestrator: Unknown

Location of   - Composer's manuscript: -0-
         - Sheet music: CPT, LoC, NYPL, Y
         - Most complete music: CPT (pv score,
              pv-l)
         - Most complete lyric: CPT (pv score,
              pv-l, 1984 scr); CLCP
         - Original partitur: -0-
         - Original parts: -0-

Jubilee (1935)

When Love Comes Your Way
Porter/Porter
Orchestrator: Unknown

Location of
- Composer's manuscript: -0-
- Sheet music: CPT, LoC, NYPL, Y
- Most complete music: CPT (sm, pv score);
    LoC (sm); NYPL (sm); Y (sm)
- Most complete lyric: CPT (sm, pv score,
    1935 scr, 1984 scr); LoC (sm); NYPL
    (sm); Y (sm); CLCP
- Original partitur: -0-
- Original parts: -0-

Originally performed during the pre-London tryout of
NYMPH ERRANT (1933). The scripts include a variation
on the last line.

Gather Ye Autographs While Ye May
Porter/Porter
Orchestrator: Unknown

Location of
- Composer's manuscript: -0-
- Sheet music: Unpublished
- Most complete music: -0-
- Most complete lyric: CPT (1935 scr);
    CLCP
- Original partitur: -0-
- Original parts: -0-

What a Nice Municipal Park
Porter/Porter
Orchestrator: Unknown

Location of
- Composer's manuscript: -0-
- Sheet music: Unpublished
- Most complete music: CPT (pv score,
    pv-l)
- Most complete lyric: CPT (pv score,
    pv-l, 1935 scr, 1984 scr); CLCP
- Original partitur: -0-
- Original parts: -0-

My Loulou
Porter/Porter
Orchestrator: Unknown

Location of
- Composer's manuscript: -0-
- Sheet music: Unpublished
- Most complete music: CPT (pv score,
    pv-l)
- Most complete lyric: CPT (pv score,
    pv-l, 1935 scr, 1984 scr); CLCP
- Original partitur: -0-
- Original parts: -0-

When Me, Mowgli, Love
Porter/Porter
Orchestrator: Unknown

Location of
- Composer's manuscript: -0-
- Sheet music: Unpublished
- Most complete music: CPT (pv score,
    pv-l)
- Most complete lyric: CPT (pv score,
    pv-l, 1935 scr, 1984 scr); CLCP
- Original partitur: -0-
- Original parts: -0-

Begin the Beguine
Porter/Porter
Orchestrator: Unknown

Location of
- Composer's manuscript: -0-
- Sheet music: CPT, LoC, NYPL, Y
- Most complete music: CPT (sm, pv score);
    LoC (sm); NYPL (sm); Y (sm)
- Most complete lyric: CPT (sm, pv score,
    1935 scr, 1984 scr); LoC (sm);
    NYPL (sm); Y (sm); CLCP
- Original partitur: -0-
- Original parts: -0-

Good Morning, Miss Standing
    Porter/Porter
    Orchestrator: Unknown

    Location of   - Composer's manuscript: -0-
               - Sheet music: Unpublished
               - Most complete music: CPT (pv score,
                  pv-l); LoC (pv-l)
               - Most complete lyric: CPT (pv score, pv-l,
                  1935 scr, 1984 scr); LoC (pv-l); CLCP
               - Original partitur: -0-
               - Original parts: -0-

Listed in the New York programs as "Recitative."

My Most Intimate Friend
    Porter/Porter
    Orchestrator: Unknown

    Location of   - Composer's manuscript: -0-
               - Sheet music: Unpublished
               - Most complete music: CPT (pv score,
                  pv-l)
               - Most complete lyric: CPT (1935 scr &
                  1984 scr); CLCP
               - Original partitur: -0-
               - Original parts: -0-

Picture of Me Without You, A
    Porter/Porter
    Orchestrator: Unknown

    Location of   - Composer's manuscript: -0-
               - Sheet music: CPT, LoC, NYPL, Y
               - Most complete music: CPT (pv score,
                  pv-l)
                - Most complete lyric: CPT (pv score);
                  CLCP
               - Original partitur: -0-
               - Original parts: -0-

Ev'rybod-ee Who's Anybod-ee
    Porter/Porter
    Orchestrator: Unknown

    Location of   - Composer's manuscript: -0-
               - Sheet music: Unpublished
               - Most complete music: CPT (pv score,
                  pv-l)
               - Most complete lyric: CPT (pv score,
                  pv-l, 1935 scr, 1984 scr); CLCP
               - Original partitur: -0-
               - Original parts: -0-

Masque: The Judgement of Paris
    Porter/Porter
    Orchestrator: Unknown

    Location of   - Composer's manuscript: -0-
               - Sheet music: Unpublished
               - Most complete music: CPT (pv score)
               - Most complete lyric: CPT (pv score,
                  1935 scr, 1984 scr); CLCP
               - Original partitur: -0-
               - Original parts: -0-

Consists of "Entrance of Paris," "Hera's Dance," "Pallas Athene's Dance," and "Aphrodite's Dance."

Swing That Swing
    Porter/Porter
    Orchestrator: Unknown

    Location of   - Composer's manuscript: -0-
               - Sheet music: Unpublished
               - Most complete music: CPT (pv score,
                  pv-l); LoC (pv-l)
               - Most complete lyric: CPT (pv score,
                  pv-l, 1935 scr, 1984 scr); LoC (pv-l);
                  CLCP
               - Original partitur: -0-
               - Original parts: -0-

The Complete Lyrics of Cole Porter also has a few additional lyrics.

Jubilee (1935)

Entr'acte
Porter/Porter
Orchestrator: Unknown

Location of
- Composer's manuscript: -0-
- Sheet music: Unpublished
- Most complete music: -0-
- Most complete lyric: INST
- Original partitur: -0-
- Original parts: -0-

The rental material includes a newly arranged Entr'acte.

Six Little Wives
Porter/Porter
Orchestrator: Unknown

Location of
- Composer's manuscript: -0-
- Sheet music: Unpublished
- Most complete music: CPT (pv score, pv-I)
- Most complete lyric: CPT (pv score, pv-I); CLCP
- Original partitur: -0-
- Original parts: -0-

Includes "To Get Away." In the original production, the title was changed to "Gay Little Wives" when a seventh wife was added to the number. An earlier title had been "Tired Little Wives."

Sunday Morning Breakfast Time
Porter/Porter
Orchestrator: Unknown

Location of
- Composer's manuscript: -0-
- Sheet music: Unpublished
- Most complete music: CPT (pv score, pv-I)
- Most complete lyric: CPT (pv score, pv-I, 1935 scr, 1984 scr); CLCP
- Original partitur: -0-
- Original parts: -0-

Beach Dance
Porter
Orchestrator: Unknown

Location of
- Composer's manuscript: -0-
- Sheet music: Unpublished
- Most complete music: CPT (pv score, pv); LoC (pv)
- Most complete lyric: INST
- Original partitur: -0-
- Original parts: -0-

Mr. and Mrs. Smith
Porter/Porter
Orchestrator: Unknown

Location of
- Composer's manuscript: -0-
- Sheet music: Unpublished
- Most complete music: CPT (pv score, pv-I)
- Most complete lyric: CPT (pv score, pv-I, 1935 scr, 1984 scr); CLCP
- Original partitur: -0-
- Original parts: -0-

Me and Marie
Porter/Porter
Orchestrator: Unknown

Location of
- Composer's manuscript: -0-
- Sheet music: CPT, LoC, NYPL, Y
- Most complete music: CPT (pv score, pv-I)
- Most complete lyric: CPT (pv score, pv-I, 1935 scr, 1984 scr); CLCP
- Original partitur: -0-
- Original parts: -0-

The patter section was not published.

Just One of Those Things

Porter/Porter

Orchestrator: Unknown

Location of
- Composer's manuscript: -0-
- Sheet music: CPT, LoC, NYPL, Y
- Most complete music: CPT (sm, pv score); LoC (sm); NYPL (sm); Y (sm)
- Most complete lyric: CPT (sm, pv score, 1984 scr); LoC (sm); NYPL (sm); Y (sm); CLCP
- Original partitur: -0-
- Original parts: -0-

I'm Yours

Porter/Porter

Orchestrator: Unknown

Location of
- Composer's manuscript: -0-
- Sheet music: Unpublished
- Most complete music: CPT (pv-l)
- Most complete lyric: CPT (pv-l); CLCP
- Original partitur: -0-
- Original parts: -0-

Unused. Written for Porter's unproduced musical, EVER YOURS (1933-34). Later rewritten for YOU NEVER KNOW (1938), but dropped during the pre-Broadway tryout. Alternate title: "Yours."

Jubilee Presentation

Porter

Orchestrator: Unknown

Location of
- Composer's manuscript: -0-
- Sheet music: Unpublished
- Most complete music: CPT (pv score, pv)
- Most complete lyric: INST
- Original partitur: -0-
- Original parts: -0-

Sing Jubilee

Porter/Porter

Orchestrator: Unknown

Location of
- Composer's manuscript: -0-
- Sheet music: Unpublished
- Most complete music: CPT (pv-l)
- Most complete lyric: CPT (pv-l); CLCP
- Original partitur: -0-
- Original parts: -0-

Unused.

There's Nothing Like Swimming

Porter/Porter

Orchestrator: Unknown

Location of
- Composer's manuscript: -0-
- Sheet music: Unpublished
- Most complete music: CPT (pv score, pv-l)
- Most complete lyric: CPT (pv score, pv-l, 1984 scr); CLCP
- Original partitur: -0-
- Original parts: -0-

Dropped during the pre-Broadway tryout, but included in the current rental package.

Waltz Down the Aisle

Porter/Porter

Orchestrator: Unknown

Location of
- Composer's manuscript: -0-
- Sheet music: CPT, LoC, NYPL, Y
- Most complete music: CPT (pv-l)
- Most complete lyric: CPT (pv-l); CLCP
- Original partitur: -0-
- Original parts: -0-

Originally intended for ANYTHING GOES (1934), this number was considerably lengthened for JUBILEE, but not used. The early draft at the Library of Congress contains a few alternate lyrics.

RED, HOT AND BLUE!

Music	COLE PORTER
Lyrics	COLE PORTER

Musical comedy in two acts. Opened October 29, 1936 in New York and ran 183 performances (World premiere: October 7, 1936 in Boston). Libretto by Howard Lindsay and Russel Crouse. Produced by Vinton Freedley. Directed by Howard Lindsay. Choreographed by George Hale. Musical direction by Frank Tours. Orchestrations by Robert Russell Bennett.

Synopsis and Production Information	Former manicurist "Nails" Duquesne is now a wealthy widow determined to fill her time with philanthropic ventures. With the aid of her assistant, ex-convict "Policy" Pinkle, she takes up the case of lawyer Bob Hale, who lost the love of his life at age six when he shoved her into a waffle iron and branded her on the rear. When "Nails" starts a national lottery to find the girl, the Senate Finance Committee, hoping to use the contest money to balance the national budget, complicates an already messy situation. The show includes a secondary couple, a specialty dance team (optional), and a full singing and dancing ensemble.
Orchestration	Unknown
Comments	In the original production, "Nails" was played by Ethel Merman, Pinkle by Jimmy Durante, and Bob Hale by Bob Hope.
Location of Original Materials	Script: Cole Porter Trusts (all lyrics) Piano-vocal score: See individual listings Partiturs: Missing Parts: Missing
Comments	All of the songs performed in the original production survive, but they have not been assembled into a piano-vocal score.
Rental Status	Currently unavailable for rental
Music Publisher	Chappell Music
Information	Cole Porter Trusts

Overture

Porter/Porter

Orchestrator: Unknown

Location of   - Composer's manuscript: -0-
- Sheet music: Unpublished
- Most complete music: -0-
- Most complete lyric: INST
- Original partitur: -0-
- Original parts: -0-

Perennial Debutantes

Porter/Porter

Orchestrator: Unknown

Location of   - Composer's manuscript: -0-
- Sheet music: Not published separately
- Most complete music: CPT (pv-l)
- Most complete lyric: CPT (pv-l, scr);
  CLCP
- Original partitur: -0-
- Original parts: -0-

Published in a limited edition of RED, HOT AND BLUE! songs (issued by Random House in November, 1936), which can be found at the Library of Congress.

At Ye Olde Coffee Shoppe in Cheyenne

Porter/Porter

Orchestrator: Unknown

Location of   - Composer's manuscript: -0-
- Sheet music: Unpublished
- Most complete music: CPT (pv-l);
  LoC (pv-l)
- Most complete lyric: CPT (pv-l, scr);
  LoC (pv-l); CLCP
- Original partitur: -0-
- Original parts: -0-

Ours

Porter/Porter

Orchestrator: Unknown

Location of   - Composer's manuscript: -0-
- Sheet music: CPT, LoC, Y
- Most complete music: CPT (pv-l)
- Most complete lyric: CPT (pv-l); CLCP
- Original partitur: -0-
- Original parts: -0-

The published sheet music and script do not include the patter.

It's a Great Life

Porter/Porter

Orchestrator: Unknown

Location of   - Composer's manuscript: -0-
- Sheet music: Unpublished
- Most complete music: CPT (pv-l)
- Most complete lyric: CPT (pv-l, scr);
  CLCP
- Original partitur: -0-
- Original parts: -0-

Down in the Depths

Porter/Porter

Orchestrator: Unknown

Location of   - Composer's manuscript: -0-
- Sheet music: CPT, LoC, NYPL, Y
- Most complete music: CPT (sm);
  LoC (sm); NYPL (sm); Y (sm)
- Most complete lyric: CLCP
- Original partitur: -0-
- Original parts: -0-

Added during the Boston tryout, replacing "Goodbye, Little Dream, Goodbye." Listed in the New Haven programs as "On the 90th Floor."

Red, Hot and Blue! (1936)

Carry On
Porter/Porter
Orchestrator: Unknown

Location of   - Composer's manuscript: -0-
- Sheet music: Unpublished
- Most complete music: CPT (pv-l);
     LoC (pv-l)
- Most complete lyric: CPT (pv-l, scr);
     LoC (pv-l); CLCP
- Original partitur: -0-
- Original parts: -0-

Little Skipper From Heaven Above, A
Porter/Porter
Orchestrator: Unknown

Location of   - Composer's manuscript: -0-
- Sheet music: CPT, LoC, NYPL, Y
- Most complete music: CPT (pv-l)
- Most complete lyric: CPT (pv-l); CLCP
- Original partitur: -0-
- Original parts: -0-

You've Got Something
Porter/Porter
Orchestrator: Unknown

Location of   - Composer's manuscript: -0-
- Sheet music: CPT, LoC, NYPL, Y
- Most complete music: CPT (sm);
     LoC (sm); NYPL (sm); Y (sm)
- Most complete lyric: CPT (sm);
     LoC (sm); NYPL (sm); Y (sm); CLCP
- Original partitur: -0-
- Original parts: -0-

Five Hundred Million
Porter/Porter
Orchestrator: Unknown

Location of   - Composer's manuscript: -0-
- Sheet music: Unpublished
- Most complete music: CPT (pv-l)
- Most complete lyric: CPT (pv-l); CLCP
- Original partitur: -0-
- Original parts: -0-

It's De-Lovely
Porter/Porter
Orchestrator: Unknown

Location of   - Composer's manuscript: -0-
- Sheet music: CPT, LoC, NYPL, Y
- Most complete music: CPT (sm);
     LoC (sm); NYPL (sm); Y (sm)
- Most complete lyric: CLCP
- Original partitur: -0-
- Original parts: -0-

Ridin' High
Porter/Porter
Orchestrator: Unknown

Location of   - Composer's manuscript: -0-
- Sheet music: CPT, LoC, NYPL, Y
- Most complete music: CPT (sm & pv-l)
- Most complete lyric: CPT (scr); CLCP
- Original partitur: -0-
- Original parts: -0-

The sheet music does not include the patter.

Entr'acte
    Porter/Porter
    Orchestrator: Unknown

    Location of   - Composer's manuscript: -0-
                  - Sheet music: Unpublished
                  - Most complete music: -0-
                  - Most complete lyric: INST
                  - Original partitur: -0-
                  - Original parts: -0-

We're About to Start Big Rehearsin'
    Porter/Porter
    Orchestrator: Unknown

    Location of   - Composer's manuscript: -0-
                  - Sheet music: Unpublished
                  - Most complete music: CPT (pv-l)
                  - Most complete lyric: CPT (pv-l, scr);
                      CLCP
                  - Original partitur: -0-
                  - Original parts: -0-

Hymn to Hymen
    Porter/Porter
    Orchestrator: Unknown

    Location of   - Composer's manuscript: -0-
                  - Sheet music: Unpublished
                  - Most complete music: CPT (pv-l)
                  - Most complete lyric: CPT (pv-l, scr);
                      CLCP
                  - Original partitur: -0-
                  - Original parts: -0-

What a Great Pair We'll Be
    Porter/Porter
    Orchestrator: Unknown

    Location of   - Composer's manuscript: -0-
                  - Sheet music: Not published separately
                  - Most complete music: CPT (pv-l)
                  - Most complete lyric: CPT (pv-l, scr);
                      CLCP
                  - Original partitur: -0-
                  - Original parts: -0-

Published in a limited edition of RED, HOT AND BLUE! songs (issued by Random House in November, 1936), which can be found at the Library of Congress.

You're a Bad Influence on Me
    Porter/Porter
    Orchestrator: Unknown

    Location of   - Composer's manuscript: -0-
                  - Sheet music: CPT, LoC, NYPL, Y
                  - Most complete music: CPT (sm);
                      LoC (sm); NYPL (sm); Y (sm)
                  - Most complete lyric: CLCP
                  - Original partitur: -0-
                  - Original parts: -0-

Replaced during the New York run by "The Ozarks Are Callin' Me Home."

Red, Hot and Blue
    Porter/Porter
    Orchestrator: Unknown

    Location of   - Composer's manuscript: -0-
                  - Sheet music: CPT, LoC, NYPL, Y
                  - Most complete music: CPT (sm);
                      LoC (sm); NYPL (sm); Y (sm)
                  - Most complete lyric: CPT (scr); CLCP
                  - Original partitur: -0-
                  - Original parts: -0-

Red, Hot and Blue! (1936)

Ozarks Are Callin' Me Home, The
Porter/Porter
Orchestrator: Unknown

Location of   - Composer's manuscript: -0-
           - Sheet music: CPT, LoC, Y
           - Most complete music: CPT (sm);
               LoC (sm); Y (sm)
           - Most complete lyric: CPT (sm);
               LoC (sm); Y (sm); CLCP
           - Original partitur: -0-
           - Original parts: -0-

Added to the New York production by November 30, 1936, replacing "You're a Bad Influence on Me."

When Your Troubles Have Started
Porter/Porter
Orchestrator: Unknown

Location of   - Composer's manuscript: -0-
           - Sheet music: Not published separately
           - Most complete music: CPT (pv-l);
               LoC (pv-l)
           - Most complete lyric: CPT (pv-l);
               LoC (pv-l); CLCP
           - Original partitur: -0-
           - Original parts: -0-

Dropped during the Boston tryout. Initial publication in The Unpublished Cole Porter (Simon & Schuster: 1975).

Goodbye, Little Dream, Goodbye
Porter/Porter
Orchestrator: Unknown

Location of   - Composer's manuscript: -0-
           - Sheet music: CPT, LoC, NYPL, Y
           - Most complete music: CPT (sm);
               LoC (sm); NYPL (sm); Y (sm)
           - Most complete lyric: CPT (sm);
               LoC (sm); NYPL (sm); Y (sm); CLCP
           - Original partitur: -0-
           - Original parts: -0-

Written for Porter's 1936 film BORN TO DANCE, but not used. Replaced during the Boston tryout of RED, HOT AND BLUE! by "Down in the Depths."

Bertie and Gertie
Porter/Porter
Orchestrator: Unknown

Location of   - Composer's manuscript: -0-
           - Sheet music: Unpublished
           - Most complete music: CPT (pv-l);
               LoC (pv-l)
           - Most complete lyric: CPT (pv-l);
               LoC (pv-l); CLCP
           - Original partitur: -0-
           - Original parts: -0-

Dropped in rehearsal.

Who But You?
Porter/Porter
Orchestrator: Unknown

Location of   - Composer's manuscript: -0-
           - Sheet music: Unpublished
           - Most complete music: Y (pv-l);
               LoC (pv-l)
           - Most complete lyric: Y (pv-l);
               LoC (pv-l); CLCP
           - Original partitur: -0-
           - Original parts: -0-

Unused. Also dropped from Porter's 1936 film BORN TO DANCE.

That's the News I'm Waiting to Hear
Porter/Porter
Orchestrator: Unknown

Location of   - Composer's manuscript: -0-
           - Sheet music: Unpublished
           - Most complete music: CPT (pv-l);
               LoC (pv-l)
           - Most complete lyric: CPT (pv-l);
               LoC (pv-l); CLCP
           - Original partitur: -0-
           - Original parts: -0-

Unused.

Lonely Star

Porter/Porter

Orchestrator: Unknown

Location of   - Composer's manuscript: -0-
- Sheet music: Unpublished
- Most complete music: -0-
- Most complete lyric: CPT (ls); CLCP
- Original partitur: -0-
- Original parts: -0-

Unused.

Where?

Porter/Porter

Orchestrator: Unknown

Location of   - Composer's manuscript: -0-
- Sheet music: Unpublished
- Most complete music: -0-
- Most complete lyric: CLCP
- Original partitur: -0-
- Original parts: -0-

Unused.

YOU NEVER KNOW

Music	COLE PORTER, ROBERT KATSCHER
Lyrics	COLE PORTER, ROWLAND LEIGH

Musical comedy in two acts. Opened September 21, 1938 in New York and ran 78 performances (World premiere: March 3, 1938 in New Haven). Libretto by Rowland Leigh, from the musical play BY CANDLELIGHT by Robert Katscher, Siegfried Geyer, and Karl Farkas. Additional songs by Alex Fogarty and Edwin Gilbert, Dana Suesse. Produced by Lee and J.J. Shubert, in association with John Shubert. Directed by Rowland Leigh. Choreographed by Robert Alton. Musical direction by John McManus. Orchestrations by Hans Spialek. Additional orchestrations by Claude Austin, Maurice B. DePackh, Eli Jacobi, Menotti Salta, Don Walker, Max Hoffman.

Synopsis and Production Information	Maria, maid to Mme. Baltin, impersonates her mistress while carrying out an assignation with the Baron de Romer's valet Gaston, whom she believes to be the Baron himself. The Baron discovers the pair, but, being a good sport, he assumes the role of his servant in order to assist Gaston in his romantic pursuit. When Mme. Baltin discovers her maid's deceit, she is less of a good sport and exposes the masquerade. All ends happily, though, as the foursome sup by candlelight.
	Other characters include the Baron's gregarious friend Ida Courtney (who learned at an early age always to say, "Yes, yes, yes") and Mme. Baltin's cheating husband, Henri, the dry goods king of France ("12 branches in Paris -- 52 throughout the entire country"). There is a full singing and dancing ensemble.
Orchestration	Reed I (Flute, Piccolo); Reed II (Oboe, English Horn); Reed III (Clarinet, Alto Sax); Reed IV (Clarinet, Alto Sax); Reed V (Bass Clarinet, Tenor Sax); Trumpet I II; Trumpet III; Trombone; Percussion; Violin I II; Viola; Cello; Bass
Comments	In the original production, Gaston was played by Clifton Webb, Maria by Lupe Velez, and Mme. Baltin by Libby Holman.
Location of Original Materials	Script: Shubert Archive (most lyrics) Piano-vocal score: See individual listings Partiturs: Shubert Archive Parts: Shubert Archive
	Most of the piano-vocal material and parts survive, as do many of the partiturs, but they have not been assembled or edited. The Shubert Archive also has early drafts of the script from October 1937, April 1938, and August 22, 1938.
Rental Status	Currently unavailable for rental
Music Publisher	Chappell Music
Information	Cole Porter Trusts

Cole Porter

Overture

Porter/Porter

Orchestrator: Spialek, unknown

Location of - Composer's manuscript: -0-
- Sheet music: Unpublished
- Most complete music: SA (ptr & parts)
- Most complete lyric: INST
- Original partitur: SA (inc)
- Original parts: SA (inc)

By Candlelight

Katscher/Leigh

Orchestrator: Unknown

Location of - Composer's manuscript: -0-
- Sheet music: CPT, LoC, NYPL
- Most complete music: CPT (sm);
      LoC (sm); NYPL (sm)
- Most complete lyric: CPT (sm);
      LoC (sm); NYPL (sm); CLCP
- Original partitur: -0-
- Original parts: -0-

The Shubert Archive has a partitur and incomplete set of parts for an instrumental version entitled "Candlelight Waltz."

I Am Gaston

Porter/Porter

Orchestrator: Spialek

Location of - Composer's manuscript: -0-
- Sheet music: Unpublished
- Most complete music: CPT (pv-l);
      SA (pv-l)
- Most complete lyric: CPT (pv-l);
      SA (pv-l); CLCP
- Original partitur: SA
- Original parts: SA

Added to the show during its pre-Broadway tryout. Alternate title: "Prologue."

Maria

Porter/Porter

Orchestrator: Spialek, DePackh

Location of - Composer's manuscript: -0-
- Sheet music: CPT, LoC, NYPL, Y
- Most complete music: CPT (sm);
      LoC (sm); NYPL (sm); Y (sm);
      SA (pv-l)
- Most complete lyric: SA (pv-l & scr)
- Original partitur: SA
- Original parts: SA

Au Revoir, Cher Baron

Porter/Porter

Orchestrator: Unknown

Location of - Composer's manuscript: -0-
- Sheet music: Unpublished
- Most complete music: CPT (pv-l);
      LoC (pv-l)
- Most complete lyric: SA (scr)
- Original partitur: -0-
- Original parts: -0-

Added to the show during its pre-Broadway tryout.

You Never Know

Porter/Porter

Orchestrator: Spialek

Location of - Composer's manuscript: -0-
- Sheet music: CPT, NYPL, Y
- Most complete music: CPT (sm);
      NYPL (sm); Y (sm)
- Most complete lyric: SA (scr) & CLCP
- Original partitur: SA
- Original parts: SA

Added to the show during its pre-Broadway tryout. The Complete Lyrics of Cole Porter also has an early version.

You Never Know (1938)

Ladies' Room
Fogerty/Gilbert
Orchestrator: Unknown

Location of
- Composer's manuscript: -0-
- Sheet music: Unpublished
- Most complete music: -0-
- Most complete lyric: SA (scr)
- Original partitur: -0-
- Original parts: -0-

What Is That Tune?
Porter/Porter
Orchestrator: Spialek

Location of
- Composer's manuscript: -0-
- Sheet music: LoC, NYPL, Y, CPT (x)
- Most complete music: LoC (sm);
  NYPL (sm); Y (sm); CPT (sm-x)
- Most complete lyric: LoC (sm);
  NYPL (sm); Y (sm); CPT (sm-x);
  SA (scr); CLCP
- Original partitur: SA
- Original parts: SA

Added to the show during its pre-Broadway tryout. The Shubert Archive also has a partitur for "That Tune (Rhumba)."

For No Rhyme or Reason
Porter/Porter
Orchestrator: Austin

Location of
- Composer's manuscript: -0-
- Sheet music: CPT, LoC, NYPL, Y
- Most complete music: CPT (sm);
  LoC (sm); NYPL (sm); Y (sm);
  SA (pv-l)
- Most complete lyric: CPT (sm);
  LoC (sm); NYPL (sm); Y (sm);
  SA (pv-l, scr); CLCP
- Original partitur: SA
- Original parts: SA

The Shubert Archive also has a Spialek partitur for "Hartmans' Rhyme or Reason."

From Alpha to Omega
Porter/Porter
Orchestrator: Walker

Location of
- Composer's manuscript: -0-
- Sheet music: CPT, LoC, NYPL, Y
- Most complete music: CPT (sm);
  LoC (sm); NYPL (sm); Y (sm);
  SA (pv-l)
- Most complete lyric: CLCP
- Original partitur: SA
- Original parts: SA

Don't Let It Get You Down
Porter/Porter
Orchestrator: Spialek, Austin

Location of
- Composer's manuscript: -0-
- Sheet music: Unpublished
- Most complete music: CPT (pv-l)
- Most complete lyric: CPT (pv-l);
  SA (scr); CLCP
- Original partitur: SA
- Original parts: -0-

Written for the 1938 Rene Clair film BREAK THE NEWS, but unused. Added to YOU NEVER KNOW during its pre-Broadway tryout. The Shubert Archive also has a DePackh partitur (and corresponding parts) for "Preiser Dance (Don't Let It Get You Down)."

What Shall I Do?
Porter/Porter & Leigh
Orchestrator: Unknown

Location of
- Composer's manuscript: -0-
- Sheet music: LoC, NYPL, Y, CPT (x)
- Most complete music: SA (parts)
- Most complete lyric: SA (scr) & CLCP
- Original partitur: -0-
- Original parts: SA

Porter's lyric was augmented with special material by Leigh in which Velez did impressions of Tallulah Bankhead, Katharine Hepburn, Vera Zorina, Shirley Temple, Gloria Swanson and Dolores Del Rio.

Entr'acte
Porter/Porter
Orchestrator: Spialek

Location of - Composer's manuscript: -0-
- Sheet music: Unpublished
- Most complete music: SA (ptr & parts)
- Most complete lyric: INST
- Original partitur: SA (inc)
- Original parts: SA (inc)

Take Yourself a Trip
Fogerty/Gilbert
Orchestrator: Unknown

Location of - Composer's manuscript: -0-
- Sheet music: Unpublished
- Most complete music: SA (pv)
- Most complete lyric: SA (scr)
- Original partitur: -0-
- Original parts: SA

Alternate title: "Go South."

Let's Put It to Music
Fogerty/Gilbert
Orchestrator: Unknown

Location of - Composer's manuscript: -0-
- Sheet music: Unpublished
- Most complete music: SA (pv)
- Most complete lyric: SA (scr)
- Original partitur: -0-
- Original parts: SA (inc)

Yes, Yes, Yes
Porter/Porter
Orchestrator: Unknown

Location of - Composer's manuscript: -0-
- Sheet music: Unpublished
- Most complete music: CPT (pv) &
SA (parts)
- Most complete lyric: SA (scr); CLCP
- Original partitur: -0-
- Original parts: SA

At Long Last Love
Porter/Porter
Orchestrator: Unknown

Location of - Composer's manuscript: -0-
- Sheet music: CPT, LoC, NYPL, Y
- Most complete music: CPT (sm);
LoC (sm); NYPL (sm); Y (sm);
SA (pv-l)
- Most complete lyric: CLCP
- Original partitur: -0-
- Original parts: SA

The Shubert Archive also has chorus parts with the original vocal arrangment.

Gendarme
Katscher/Leigh
Orchestrator: Unknown

Location of - Composer's manuscript: -0-
- Sheet music: Unpublished
- Most complete music: SA (pv)
- Most complete lyric: SA (scr)
- Original partitur: -0-
- Original parts: SA

You Never Know (1938)

No

Suesse/Suesse
Orchestrator: Unknown

Location of - Composer's manuscript: -0-
- Sheet music: LoC, NYPL
- Most complete music: LoC (sm);
  NYPL (sm)
- Most complete lyric: SA (scr)
- Original partitur: -0-
- Original parts: SA

I'm Yours

Porter/Porter
Orchestrator: Spialek

Location of - Composer's manuscript: -0-
- Sheet music: Unpublished
- Most complete music: CPT (pv-l);
  SA (pv-l)
- Most complete lyric: CLCP
- Original partitur: SA
- Original parts: -0-

Dropped by March 28, 1938, this number was a reworking
of "I'm Yours" from JUBILEE (1935).

Good Evening, Princess

Porter/Porter
Orchestrator: Unknown

Location of - Composer's manuscript: Y (frag)
- Sheet music: Unpublished
- Most complete music: CPT (pv-l);
  SA (pv-l)
- Most complete lyric: CPT (pv-l);
  SA (pv-l); CLCP
- Original partitur: -0-
- Original parts: SA

The parts are from the pre-Broadway tryout. The lyric is
not in the script.

What a Priceless Pleasure

Porter/Porter
Orchestrator: Unknown

Location of - Composer's manuscript: -0-
- Sheet music: Unpublished
- Most complete music: CPT (pv-l);
  LoC (pv-l)
- Most complete lyric: CPT (pv-l);
  LoC (pv-l); CLCP
- Original partitur: -0-
- Original parts: SA

Dropped during the pre-Broadway tryout. Alternate title:
"The Waiters."

I'll Black His Eyes

Porter/Porter
Orchestrator: Unknown

Location of - Composer's manuscript: -0-
- Sheet music: Unpublished
- Most complete music: CPT (pv-l);
  SA (pv-l)
- Most complete lyric: CPT (pv-l);
  SA (pv-l); CLCP
- Original partitur: -0-
- Original parts: SA

Dropped during the pre-Broadway tryout.

Just One Step Ahead of Love

Porter/Porter
Orchestrator: Unknown

Location of - Composer's manuscript: -0-
- Sheet music: Unpublished
- Most complete music: CPT (pv-l)
- Most complete lyric: CLCP
- Original partitur: -0-
- Original parts: SA

Added and deleted during the pre-Broadway tryout.
Alternate title: "One Step Ahead of Love."

Finale Act I ["Ha, ha, ha..."]
Porter/Porter
Orchestrator: Unknown

Location of - Composer's manuscript: -0-
- Sheet music: Unpublished
- Most complete music: CPT (pv-I);
  SA (pv-I)
- Most complete lyric: CPT (pv-I);
  SA (pv-I); CLCP
- Original partitur: -0-
- Original parts: SA

Dropped during the pre-Broadway tryout.

Cafe Society Set, The
Author(s): Unknown
Orchestrator: Unknown

Location of - Composer's manuscript: -0-
- Sheet music: Unpublished
- Most complete music: SA (pv)
- Most complete lyric: See note
- Original partitur: -0-
- Original parts: SA

Dropped during the pre-Broadway tryout. The lyric is in the April, 1938 draft of the script at the Shubert Archive.

By Candlelight
Porter/Porter
Orchestrator: Unknown

Location of - Composer's manuscript: -0-
- Sheet music: Unpublished
- Most complete music: CPT (pv-I)
- Most complete lyric: CPT (pv-I); CLCP
- Original partitur: -0-
- Original parts: -0-

Unused.

I'm Back in Circulation
Porter/Porter
Orchestrator: Unknown

Location of - Composer's manuscript: -0-
- Sheet music: Unpublished
- Most complete music: CPT (pv-I);
  LoC (pv-I)
- Most complete lyric: CPT (pv-I);
  LoC (pv-I); CLCP
- Original partitur: -0-
- Original parts: -0-

Probably unused.

I'm Going In For Love
Porter/Porter
Orchestrator: Unknown

Location of - Composer's manuscript: -0-
- Sheet music: Not published separately
- Most complete music: CPT (pv-I)
- Most complete lyric: CPT (pv-I); CLCP
- Original partitur: -0-
- Original parts: -0-

Probably unused. Initial publication in The Unpublished Cole Porter (Simon & Schuster: 1975).

It's No Laughing Matter
Porter/Porter
Orchestrator: Unknown

Location of - Composer's manuscript: -0-
- Sheet music: Unpublished
- Most complete music: CPT (pv-I);
  LoC (pv-I)
- Most complete lyric: CPT (pv-I);
  LoC (pv-I); CLCP
- Original partitur: -0-
- Original parts: -0-

Unused.

LEAVE IT TO ME

Music   COLE PORTER
Lyrics   COLE PORTER

Musical comedy in two acts. Opened November 9, 1938 in New York and ran 307 performances (World premiere: October 13, 1938 in New Haven). Libretto by Bella and Samuel Spewack, suggested by their play CLEAR ALL WIRES. Produced by Vinton Freedley. Directed by Samuel Spewack. Choreographed by Robert Alton. Musical direction by Max Meth. Orchestrations by Don Walker, W.C. Lindenmann.

Synopsis and Production Information	When bathtub manufacturer Alonzo P. Goodhue is appointed U.S. Ambassador to Russia, an envious J.H. Brody, publisher of the <u>Paris and Chicago World-Tribune,</u> orders his best correspondent, Buckley Thomas, to see that Goodhue is disgraced and recalled. As it turns out, the unassuming Goodhue is himself anxious to be shipped home, and so he and Thomas join forces. Goodhue delivers an antagonistic speech, kicks the German Ambassador in the belly, and attempts to assassinate a Prince -- and in each case he is proclaimed a hero. Finally, Thomas, realizing that only <u>good</u> deeds go unrewarded, has Goodhue deliver an optimistic speech expressing hope for a united world. Goodhue is promptly recalled.
	Other characters include Colette, Thomas' old flame; Dolly, an incorrigible flirt; and the robust Mrs. Goodhue, who delivers several spirited musical numbers. There is a full singing and dancing ensemble.
Orchestration	Reed I (Flute, Piccolo, Clarinet, Alto Sax); Reed II (Flute, Clarinet, Bass Clarinet, Alto Sax); Reed III (Clarinet, Tenor Sax); Reed IV (Clarinet, Tenor Sax); Trumpet I II; Trumpet III; Trombone I; Trombone II; Percussion; Harp; Guitar; Piano; Violin I II; Viola I II; Cello; Bass
Comments	The original cast included William Gaxton as Thomas, Victor Moore as Goodhue, Sophie Tucker as Mrs. Goodhue, Tamara as Colette, and Mary Martin as Dolly.
Location of Original Materials	Script: Cole Porter Trusts (all lyrics), Tams-Witmark Music Library (all lyrics) (Published in <u>Great Musicals of the American Theatre</u>: Chilton Book Company, 1976) Piano-vocal score: Tams-Witmark Music Library Partiturs: Tams-Witmark Music Library Parts: Tams-Witmark Music Library
	All of the songs survive, but partiturs and parts are missing for most numbers.
Rental Status	Tams-Witmark Music Library will lease the script and piano-vocal score to theatrical companies interested in performing the show with piano accompaniment.
Music Publisher	Chappell Music
Information	Tams-Witmark Music Library, Cole Porter Trusts

Overture

Porter/Porter

Orchestrator: Walker

Location of
- Composer's manuscript: -0-
- Sheet music: Unpublished
- Most complete music: TW (ptr)
- Most complete lyric: INST
- Original partitur: TW
- Original parts: -0-

How Do You Spell Ambassador?

Porter/Porter

Orchestrator: Unknown

Location of
- Composer's manuscript: Y (frag)
- Sheet music: Unpublished
- Most complete music: CPT (pv-l);
  TW (pv score)
- Most complete lyric: CPT (pv-l);
  TW (pv score); CLCP
- Original partitur: -0-
- Original parts: -0-

We Drink to You, J.H. Brody

Porter/Porter

Orchestrator: Unknown

Location of
- Composer's manuscript: -0-
- Sheet music: Unpublished
- Most complete music: CPT (pv-l);
  TW (pv score)
- Most complete lyric: CPT (pv-l);
  TW (pv score); CLCP
- Original partitur: -0-
- Original parts: -0-

Vite, Vite, Vite

Porter/Porter

Orchestrator: Unknown

Location of
- Composer's manuscript: -0-
- Sheet music: Not published separately
- Most complete music: CPT (pv-l);
  TW (pv score)
- Most complete lyric: CPT (pv-l);
  TW (pv score); CLCP
- Original partitur: -0-
- Original parts: -0-

Initial publication in vocal selections from the 1982 film EVIL UNDER THE SUN.

I'm Taking the Steps to Russia

Porter/Porter

Orchestrator: Unknown

Location of
- Composer's manuscript: -0-
- Sheet music: CPT, LoC, NYPL, Y
- Most complete music: TW (pv score)
- Most complete lyric: CLCP
- Original partitur: -0-
- Original parts: -0-

The patter section was not published.

Get Out of Town

Porter/Porter

Orchestrator: Unknown

Location of
- Composer's manuscript: -0-
- Sheet music: CPT, LoC, NYPL, Y
- Most complete music: CPT (sm); LoC (sm);
  NYPL (sm); Y (sm); TW (pv score)
- Most complete lyric: CPT (sm); LoC (sm);
  NYPL (sm); Y (sm); TW (pv score);
  CLCP
- Original partitur: -0-
- Original parts: -0-

Leave It to Me (1938)

When All's Said and Done
Porter/Porter
Orchestrator: Unknown

Location of
- Composer's manuscript: -0-
- Sheet music: Unpublished
- Most complete music: CPT (pv-l);
  TW (pv score)
- Most complete lyric: CLCP
- Original partitur: -0-
- Original parts: -0-

Entr'acte
Porter/Porter
Orchestrator: Unknown

Location of
- Composer's manuscript: -0-
- Sheet music: Unpublished
- Most complete music: -0-
- Most complete lyric: INST
- Original partitur: -0-
- Original parts: -0-

Most Gentlemen Don't Like Love
Porter/Porter
Orchestrator: Unknown

Location of
- Composer's manuscript: -0-
- Sheet music: CPT, LoC, NYPL, Y
- Most complete music: CPT (sm); LoC (sm);
  NYPL (sm); Y (sm); TW (pv score)
- Most complete lyric: TW (ls); CLCP
- Original partitur: -0-
- Original parts: -0-

From Now On
Porter/Porter
Orchestrator: Unknown

Location of
- Composer's manuscript: -0-
- Sheet music: CPT, LoC, NYPL, Y
- Most complete music: CPT (sm); LoC (sm);
  NYPL (sm); Y (sm); TW (pv score)
- Most complete lyric: CPT (ls); CLCP
- Original partitur: -0-
- Original parts: -0-

The music to the patter section is missing.

Comrade Alonzo
Porter/Porter
Orchestrator: Unknown

Location of
- Composer's manuscript: -0-
- Sheet music: Unpublished
- Most complete music: CPT (pv-l);
  TW (pv score)
- Most complete lyric: CPT (pv-l);
  TW (pv score); CLCP
- Original partitur: -0-
- Original parts: -0-

I Want to Go Home
Porter/Porter
Orchestrator: Unknown

Location of
- Composer's manuscript: -0-
- Sheet music: CPT, LoC, Y
- Most complete music: CPT (sm); LoC (sm);
  Y (sm); TW (pv score)
- Most complete lyric: TW (ls); CLCP
- Original partitur: -0-
- Original parts: -0-

My Heart Belongs to Daddy

Porter/Porter

Orchestrator: Unknown

Location of
- Composer's manuscript: -0-
- Sheet music: CPT, LoC, NYPL, Y
- Most complete music: CPT (sm); LoC (sm); NYPL (sm); Y (sm); TW (pv score)
- Most complete lyric: CPT (sm & ls)
- Original partitur: -0-
- Original parts: -0-

The lyric sheet and The Complete Lyrics of Cole Porter have the version performed in the show; the sheet music has different lyrics to the verse.

To the U.S.A. From the U.S.S.R.

Porter/Porter

Orchestrator: Unknown

Location of
- Composer's manuscript: -0-
- Sheet music: Unpublished
- Most complete music: CPT (pv-l); TW (pv score)
- Most complete lyric: CLCP
- Original partitur: -0-
- Original parts: -0-

Tomorrow

Porter/Porter

Orchestrator: Unknown

Location of
- Composer's manuscript: -0-
- Sheet music: CPT, LoC, NYPL, Y
- Most complete music: CPT (sm); LoC (sm); NYPL (sm); Y (sm); TW (pv score)
- Most complete lyric: CLCP
- Original partitur: -0-
- Original parts: -0-

When the Hen Stops Laying

Porter/Porter

Orchestrator: Unknown

Location of
- Composer's manuscript: -0-
- Sheet music: Unpublished
- Most complete music: CPT (pv-l); LoC (pv-l); TW (pv-l)
- Most complete lyric: CPT (pv-l); LoC (pv-l); TW (ls); CLCP
- Original partitur: -0-
- Original parts: TW

Replaced during the pre-Broadway tryout by "When All's Said and Done."

Far Away

Porter/Porter

Orchestrator: Lindenmann

Location of
- Composer's manuscript: -0-
- Sheet music: CPT, LoC, NYPL, Y
- Most complete music: CPT (sm); LoC (sm); NYPL (sm); Y (sm); TW (pv score)
- Most complete lyric: CPT (sm); LoC (sm); NYPL (sm); Y (sm); TW (pv score); CLCP
- Original partitur: -0-
- Original parts: -0-

Recall Goodhue

Porter/Porter

Orchestrator: Unknown

Location of
- Composer's manuscript: -0-
- Sheet music: Unpublished
- Most complete music: CPT (pv-l) TW (pv-l)
- Most complete lyric: CPT (pv-l); TW (pv-l); CLCP
- Original partitur: -0-
- Original parts: TW

Probably dropped before the New York opening.

Leave It to Me (1938)

Just Another Page in Your Diary

Porter/Porter

Orchestrator: Unknown

Location of - Composer's manuscript: -0-
- Sheet music: Unpublished
- Most complete music: CPT (pv-I);
    LoC (pv-I); TW (pv-I)
- Most complete lyric: CLCP
- Original partitur: -0-
- Original parts: -0-

Unused. Introduced in 1941 in the revue TWO WEEKS
WITH PAY. There are two versions of this song.

As Long As It's Not About Love

Porter/Porter

Orchestrator: Unknown

Location of - Composer's manuscript: -0-
- Sheet music: Unpublished
- Most complete music: -0-
- Most complete lyric: LoC (ls); CLCP
- Original partitur: -0-
- Original parts: -0-

Unused.

Information, Please

Porter/Porter

Orchestrator: Unknown

Location of - Composer's manuscript: -0-
- Sheet music: Unpublished
- Most complete music: CPT (pv-I);
    LoC (pv-I); TW (pv-I)
- Most complete lyric: TW (ls); CLCP
- Original partitur: -0-
- Original parts: -0-

Unused.

Why Can't I Forget You?

Porter/Porter

Orchestrator: Unknown

Location of - Composer's manuscript: -0-
- Sheet music: Unpublished
- Most complete music: -0-
- Most complete lyric: LoC (ls); CLCP
- Original partitur: -0-
- Original parts: -0-

Unused.

There's a Fan

Porter/Porter

Orchestrator: Unknown

Location of - Composer's manuscript: -0-
- Sheet music: Unpublished
- Most complete music: CPT (pv-I);
    LoC (pv-I); TW (pv-I)
- Most complete lyric: CPT (pv-I);
    LoC (pv-I); TW (pv-I, ls); CLCP
- Original partitur: -0-
- Original parts: -0-

Unused.

DU BARRY WAS A LADY

Music   COLE PORTER
Lyrics   COLE PORTER

Musical comedy in two acts. Opened December 6, 1939 in New York and ran 408 performances (World premiere: November 9, 1939 in New Haven). Libretto by Herbert Fields and B.G. DeSylva. Produced by B.G. DeSylva. Directed by Edgar MacGregor. Choreographed by Robert Alton. Musical direction by Gene Salzer. Orchestrations by Hans Spialek; additional orchestrations by Robert Russell Bennett, Ted Royal, Walter Paul, F. Marks. Vocal arrangements by Hugh Martin.

Synopsis and Production Information	Louis Blore, washroom attendent at the Club Petite, is in love with songstress May Daly. Louis accidentally drinks a Mickey Finn that he had intended for May's boyfriend, Alex, and dreams for an act and a half that he is King Louis XV and May, the Comtesse DuBarry. When he awakens, he realizes that he has no chance with May and will have to settle for her friendship.
	Other characters include a singing/dancing couple (Alice and Harry) and a secondary comic (Charley) who plays the Dauphin in the dream sequence. The show requires a full singing and dancing ensemble. Sets and costumes must evoke first a Thirties nightspot and then an imagined 18th century Versailles.
Orchestration	Oboe; Reed I (Flute, Clarinet, Alto Sax); Reed II (Oboe, Clarinet); Reed III (Clarinet, Alto Sax); Reed IV (Flute, Clarinet, Bassoon, Tenor Sax, Bari Sax); Horn; Trumpet I II; Trumpet III; Trombone; Percussion; Harp; Piano; Violin I II; Violin III; Cello; Bass
Comments	In the original production, Louis was played by Bert Lahr, May by Ethel Merman, and Alice and Harry by Betty Grable and Charles Walters.
Location of Original Materials	Script: Cole Porter Trusts (all lyrics), New York Public Library (all lyrics), Tams-Witmark Music Library (all lyrics) Piano-vocal score: Tams-Witmark Music Library, Cole Porter Trusts Partiturs: Tams-Witmark Music Libary Parts: Tams-Witmark Music Library
	All of the piano-vocals and parts survive, as do most of the partiturs. Early drafts of the script can be found at the Library of Congress and the New York Public Library.
Rental Status	Tams-Witmark rents the original show.
Music Publisher	Chappell Music
Information	Tams-Witmark Music Library

Du Barry Was a Lady (1939)

Overture

Porter/Porter

Orchestrator: Spialek, Paul

Location of - Composer's manuscript: -0-
- Sheet music: Unpublished
- Most complete music: TW (pv score);
    CPT (pv score)
- Most complete lyric: INST
- Original partitur: TW (inc)
- Original parts: TW

Opening

Porter/Porter

Orchestrator: Royal

Location of - Composer's manuscript: -0-
- Sheet music: Unpublished
- Most complete music: TW (pv score);
    CPT (pv score, pv-I)
- Most complete lyric: TW (pv score, scr);
    CPT (pv score, pv-I, scr); NYPL (scr);
    CLCP
- Original partitur: TW
- Original parts: TW

Alternate titles: "Where's Louie?" and "Prologue Opening No. 1."

Ev'ry Day a Holiday

Porter/Porter

Orchestrator: Bennett

Location of - Composer's manuscript: -0-
- Sheet music: CPT, LoC, NYPL, Y
- Most complete music: CPT (pv-I)
- Most complete lyric: CPT (ls); CLCP
- Original partitur: TW
- Original parts: TW

Neither the sheet music nor the piano-vocal score includes the patter section. The piano-vocal score does contain Hugh Martin's original vocal arrangement.

It Ain't Etiquette

Porter/Porter

Orchestrator: Unknown

Location of - Composer's manuscript: -0-
- Sheet music: Not published separately
- Most complete music: TW (pv score);
    CPT (pv score)
- Most complete lyric: TW (scr);
    CPT (scr, ls); NYPL (scr); CLCP
- Original partitur: -0-
- Original parts: TW

Initial publication in Music and Lyrics by Cole Porter, Volume II (Chappell).

When Love Beckoned (on 52nd Street)

Porter/Porter

Orchestrator: Spialek, Royal

Location of - Composer's manuscript: -0-
- Sheet music: CPT, LoC, NYPL, Y
- Most complete music: CPT (sm, pv score);
    LoC (sm); NYPL (sm); Y (sm);
    TW (pv score)
- Most complete lyric: CPT (ls); CLCP
- Original partitur: TW (inc)
- Original parts: TW

Neither the piano-vocal score nor the sheet music contains the lyrics to the second act reprise, which was replaced by "Give Him the Oo-La-La" prior to the New York opening. Tams-Witmark also has a Marks partitur for the encore.

Come On In

Porter/Porter

Orchestrator: Royal

Location of - Composer's manuscript: -0-
- Sheet music: CPT, LoC, NYPL, Y
- Most complete music: CPT (sm, pv score);
    LoC (sm); NYPL (sm); Y (sm);
    TW (pv score)
- Most complete lyric: CPT (scr, ls);
    TW (scr); NYPL (scr); CLCP
- Original partitur: TW
- Original parts: TW

Dream Song

Porter/Porter

Orchestrator: Paul

Location of   - Composer's manuscript: -0-
- Sheet music: Unpublished
- Most complete music: TW (pv score);
    CPT (pv score, pv-l)
- Most complete lyric: TW (pv score, scr);
    CPT (pv score, pv-l, scr); NYPL (scr);
    CLCP
- Original partitur: TW
- Original parts: TW

But in the Morning, No

Porter/Porter

Orchestrator: Spialek

Location of   - Composer's manuscript: -0-
- Sheet music: CPT, LoC, NYPL, Y
- Most complete music: CPT (sm);
    LoC (sm); NYPL (sm); Y (sm)
- Most complete lyric: CLCP
- Original partitur: TW
- Original parts: TW

Although the verse was not performed in the show (and is therefore not in the piano-vocal score and parts), it is included in the partitur.

Mesdames et Messieurs

Porter/Porter

Orchestrator: Bennett

Location of   - Composer's manuscript: -0-
- Sheet music: Unpublished
- Most complete music: TW (pv score);
    CPT (pv score)
- Most complete lyric: TW (pv score, scr);
    CPT (pv score, scr); NYPL (scr);
    CLCP
- Original partitur: TW
- Original parts: TW

Do I Love You?

Porter/Porter

Orchestrator: Spialek, Royal

Location of   - Composer's manuscript: -0-
- Sheet music: CPT, LoC, NYPL, Y
- Most complete music: CPT (sm, pv score);
    LoC (sm); NYPL (sm); Y (sm);
    TW (pv score)
- Most complete lyric: CPT (sm, pv score,
    scr); LoC (sm); NYPL (sm, scr);
    Y (sm); TW (pv score, scr); CLCP
- Original partitur: TW
- Original parts: TW

Gavotte, The

Porter/Porter

Orchestrator: Unknown

Location of   - Composer's manuscript: -0-
- Sheet music: Unpublished
- Most complete music: TW (pv score);
    CPT (pv score)
- Most complete lyric: INST
- Original partitur: -0-
- Original parts: TW

A dance based on "Mesdames et Messieurs."

Danse Victoire

Porter/Porter

Orchestrator: Royal

Location of   - Composer's manuscript: -0-
- Sheet music: Unpublished
- Most complete music: TW (pv score);
    CPT (pv score)
- Most complete lyric: INST
- Original partitur: TW
- Original parts: TW

Uses themes from "Come On In" and "Well, Did You Evah!" Alternate title: "Rhythm Dance."

Du Barry Was a Lady (1939)

Danse Erotique
Porter/Porter
Orchestrator: Unknown

Location of   - Composer's manuscript: -0-
         - Sheet music: Unpublished
         - Most complete music: TW (pv score);
            CPT (pv score)
         - Most complete lyric: INST
         - Original partitur: -0-
         - Original parts: TW

Utilizes passages from "It Was Written In the Stars."

Danse Tzigane
Porter
Orchestrator: Spialek

Location of   - Composer's manuscript: -0-
         - Sheet music: Unpublished
         - Most complete music: TW (pv score);
            CPT (pv score)
         - Most complete lyric: INST
         - Original partitur: TW
         - Original parts: TW

Alternate title: "Opening Act II."

Du Barry Was a Lady
Porter/Porter
Orchestrator: Spialek, Paul

Location of   - Composer's manuscript: -0-
         - Sheet music: Unpublished
         - Most complete music: TW (pv score);
            CPT (pv score, pv-l)
         - Most complete lyric: TW (pv score);
            CPT (pv score, pv-l); CLCP
         - Original partitur: TW
         - Original parts: TW

Alternate title: "Finale Act I."

Give Him the Oo-La-La
Porter/Porter
Orchestrator: Spialek

Location of   - Composer's manuscript: -0-
         - Sheet music: CPT, LoC, NYPL, Y
         - Most complete music: TW (pv score);
            CPT (pv score)
         - Most complete lyric: TW (scr);
            CPT (scr, ls); NYPL (scr); CLCP
         - Original partitur: TW
         - Original parts: TW

Added during the Boston tryout.

Entr'acte
Porter/Porter
Orchestrator: Unknown

Location of   - Composer's manuscript: -0-
         - Sheet music: Unpublished
         - Most complete music: -0-
         - Most complete lyric: INST
         - Original partitur: -0-
         - Original parts: -0-

Well, Did You Evah!
Porter/Porter
Orchestrator: Paul

Location of   - Composer's manuscript: -0-
         - Sheet music: CPT, LoC, NYPL
         - Most complete music: CPT (pv score, sm);
            LoC (sm); NYPL (sm); TW (pv score)
         - Most complete lyric: CPT (ls); CLCP
         - Original partitur: TW
         - Original parts: TW

Porter later revised the lyric for the 1956 film HIGH
SOCIETY; The Complete Lyrics of Cole Porter also has
the movie version.

Cole Porter

It Was Written in the Stars
Porter/Porter
Orchestrator: Spialek

Location of - Composer's manuscript: -0-
      - Sheet music: CPT, LoC, NYPL, Y
      - Most complete music: CPT (pv score, sm);
          LoC (sm); NYPL (sm); Y (sm);
          TW (pv score)
      - Most complete lyric: CPT (pv score, sm,
          scr); LoC (sm); NYPL (sm, scr);
          Y (sm); TW (pv score, scr); CLCP
      - Original partitur: TW
      - Original parts: TW

Friendship
Porter/Porter
Orchestrator: Royal

Location of - Composer's manuscript: -0-
      - Sheet music: CPT, LoC, NYPL, Y
      - Most complete music: CPT (pv score, sm);
          LoC (sm); NYPL (sm); Y (sm);
          TW (pv score)
      - Most complete lyric: CLCP
      - Original partitur: TW
      - Original parts: TW

L'Apres Midi D'un Boeuf
Porter
Orchestrator: Royal

Location of - Composer's manuscript: -0-
      - Sheet music: Unpublished
      - Most complete music: TW (pv score);
          CPT (pv score)
      - Most complete lyric: INST
      - Original partitur: TW
      - Original parts: TW

Added between the Boston and Philadelphia tryouts.

What Have I?
Porter/Porter
Orchestrator: Spialek

Location of - Composer's manuscript: -0-
      - Sheet music: Unpublished
      - Most complete music: CPT (pv-l);
          LoC (pv-l)
      - Most complete lyric: CPT (ls); CLCP
      - Original partitur: TW
      - Original parts: TW

Intended for Louie (Bert Lahr), but dropped in rehearsal. The instrumental introduction is still in the piano-vocal score.

Katie Went to Haiti
Porter/Porter
Orchestrator: Unknown

Location of - Composer's manuscript: -0-
      - Sheet music: CPT, LoC, NYPL, Y
      - Most complete music: TW (pv score);
          CPT (pv score)
      - Most complete lyric: CPT (ls); CLCP
      - Original partitur: TW (inc)
      - Original parts: TW

Includes the "Zombie Dance," the only section for which a partitur has been found.

In the Big Money
Porter/Porter
Orchestrator: Unknown

Location of - Composer's manuscript: -0-
      - Sheet music: Unpublished
      - Most complete music: CPT (pv-l);
          LoC (pv-l)
      - Most complete lyric: CPT (pv-l);
          LoC (pv-l); CLCP
      - Original partitur: -0-
      - Original parts: -0-

Unused; intended for May (Ethel Merman).

PANAMA HATTIE

Music   COLE PORTER
Lyrics   COLE PORTER

Musical comedy in two acts. Opened October 30, 1940 in New York and ran 501 performances (World premiere: October 3, 1940 in New Haven). Libretto by Herbert Fields and B.G. DeSylva. Produced by B.G. DeSylva. Directed by Edgar MacGregor. Choreographed by Robert Alton. Musical direction by Gene Salzer. Orchestrations by Robert Russell Bennett, Hans Spialek, Don Walker.

Synopsis and Production Information	Hattie Maloney, a brassy nightclub singer in Panama, tries to fit into the upper-crust world of her fiance, Nick Bullett, an officer in the armed forces. In Act I, she charms Nick's no-nonsense daughter Geraldine by adopting a more conservative style of dressing. In Act II, she wins over Nick's boss, Whitney Randolph, by foiling a plot to blow up the canal.
	Other characters include three comic sailors (Windy, Woozy, and Skat), the Bulletts' British butler (Budd), Hattie's frantic friend (Florrie), and a specialty dance team. There is a full singing and dancing ensemble.
Orchestration	Flute; Clarinet; Reed I (Flute, Piccolo, Clarinet, Alto Sax); Reed II (Flute, Clarinet, Alto Sax); Reed III (Oboe, Clarinet, Tenor Sax); Reed IV (Flute, Clarinet, Bass Clarinet, Tenor Sax, Baritone Sax); Trumpet I II; Trumpet III; Trombone I; Trombone II; Percussion; Piano; Guitar; Violin A B C; Viola; Cello; Bass
Comments	In the original production, Hattie was played by Ethel Merman, Florrie by Betty Hutton, and Budd by Arthur Treacher.
Location of Original Materials	Script: Tams-Witmark Music Library (all lyrics), Cole Porter Trusts (all lyrics) Piano-vocal score: Tams-Witmark Music Library Partiturs: Missing Parts: Tams-Witmark Music Library
Rental Status	Tams-Witmark rents the original show.
Music Publisher	Chappell Music
Information	Tams-Witmark Music Library

Overture

Porter/Porter

Orchestrator: Unknown

Location of   - Composer's manuscript: -0-
- Sheet music: Unpublished
- Most complete music: TW (pv score);
      CPT (pv)
- Most complete lyric: INST
- Original partitur: -0-
- Original parts: TW

Visit Panama

Porter/Porter

Orchestrator: Unknown

Location of   - Composer's manuscript: Y (sk)
- Sheet music: NYPL, Y, CPT (x)
- Most complete music: TW (pv score)
- Most complete lyric: TW (pv score, scr);
      CPT (scr); CLCP
- Original partitur: -0-
- Original parts: TW

The patter section was not published.

Opening Act I, Scene 1

Porter/Porter

Orchestrator: Unknown

Location of   - Composer's manuscript: Y (sk)
- Sheet music: Unpublished
- Most complete music: TW (pv score);
      CPT (pv-l)
- Most complete lyric: TW (pv score, scr);
      CPT (pv-l, scr); CLCP
- Original partitur: -0-
- Original parts: TW

Alternate title: "A Stroll on the Plaza Sant'Ana."

My Mother Would Love You

Porter/Porter

Orchestrator: Unknown

Location of   - Composer's manuscript: -0-
- Sheet music: NYPL, CPT (x), Y
- Most complete music: NYPL (sm);
      CPT (sm-x); Y (sm); TW (pv score)
- Most complete lyric: CLCP
- Original partitur: -0-
- Original parts: TW

Join It Right Away

Porter/Porter

Orchestrator: Unknown

Location of   - Composer's manuscript: -0-
- Sheet music: Unpublished
- Most complete music: TW (pv score);
      CPT (pv)
- Most complete lyric: TW (scr); CPT (scr);
      CLCP
- Original partitur: -0-
- Original parts: TW

I've Still Got My Health

Porter/Porter

Orchestrator: Unknown

Location of   - Composer's manuscript: -0-
- Sheet music: CPT, NYPL, Y
- Most complete music: CPT (sm);
      NYPL (sm); Y (sm); TW (pv score)
- Most complete lyric: TW (scr); CPT (scr);
      CLCP
- Original partitur: -0-
- Original parts: TW

Panama Hattie (1940)

Fresh as a Daisy
Porter/Porter
Orchestrator: Unknown

Location of   - Composer's manuscript: -0-
            - Sheet music: CPT, NYPL, Y
            - Most complete music: CPT (sm);
                NYPL (sm); Y (sm); TW (pv score)
            - Most complete lyric: CLCP
            - Original partitur: -0-
            - Original parts: TW

The piano-vocal score also includes an extensive dance section.

Welcome to Jerry
Porter/Porter
Orchestrator: Unknown

Location of   - Composer's manuscript: -0-
            - Sheet music: Unpublished
            - Most complete music: CPT (pv-I)
            - Most complete lyric: CPT (pv-I, scr);
                TW (scr); CLCP
            - Original partitur: -0-
            - Original parts: -0-

Although this number is listed in all New York programs, it was evidently dropped during the Broadway run or the post-Broadway tour as it does not appear in the piano-vocal score and parts.

Carmen's Dance
Author(s): Unknown
Orchestrator: Unknown

Location of   - Composer's manuscript: -0-
            - Sheet music: Unpublished
            - Most complete music: TW (pv score);
                CPT (pv)
            - Most complete lyric: INST
            - Original partitur: -0-
            - Original parts: TW

A specialty dance originally performed by Carmen D'Antonio.

Let's Be Buddies
Porter/Porter
Orchestrator: Unknown

Location of   - Composer's manuscript: -0-
            - Sheet music: NYPL, CPT (x), Y
            - Most complete music: See note
            - Most complete lyric: CLCP
            - Original partitur: -0-
            - Original parts: TW

The piano-vocal score (at Tams-Witmark Music Library) contains the version performed in the original production; the sheet music has a different verse and no patter section.

I'm Throwing a Ball Tonight
Porter/Porter
Orchestrator: Unknown

Location of   - Composer's manuscript: -0-
            - Sheet music: Not published separately
            - Most complete music: TW (pv score)
            - Most complete lyric: CLCP
            - Original partitur: -0-
            - Original parts: TW

Initial publication in The Unpublished Cole Porter (Simon & Schuster: 1975). In the piano-vocal score and parts, the number is followed by an extensive dance entitled "Throwing a Conga."

Entr'acte
Porter/Porter
Orchestrator: Unknown

Location of   - Composer's manuscript: -0-
            - Sheet music: Unpublished
            - Most complete music: TW (pv score);
                CPT (pv)
            - Most complete lyric: INST
            - Original partitur: -0-
            - Original parts: TW

We Detest a Fiesta

Porter/Porter

Orchestrator: Unknown

Location of   - Composer's manuscript: -0-
       - Sheet music: Unpublished
       - Most complete music: CPT (pv-l)
       - Most complete lyric: CPT (pv-l); CLCP
       - Original partitur: -0-
       - Original parts: TW

The piano-vocal score contains only half the number.

All I've Got to Get Now Is My Man

Porter/Porter

Orchestrator: Unknown

Location of   - Composer's manuscript: -0-
       - Sheet music: CPT, NYPL, Y
       - Most complete music: TW (pv score)
       - Most complete lyric: TW (scr); CPT (scr);
          CLCP
       - Original partitur: -0-
       - Original parts: TW

Who Would Have Dreamed?

Porter/Porter

Orchestrator: Unknown

Location of   - Composer's manuscript: -0-
       - Sheet music: CPT, NYPL, Y
       - Most complete music: TW (pv score)
       - Most complete lyric: TW (pv score, scr);
          CPT (scr), CLCP
       - Original partitur: -0-
       - Original parts: TW

You Said It

Porter/Porter

Orchestrator: Unknown

Location of   - Composer's manuscript: -0-
       - Sheet music: Unpublished
       - Most complete music: TW (pv score)
       - Most complete lyric: TW (scr);
          CPT (scr, ls); CLCP
       - Original partitur: -0-
       - Original parts: TW

Make It Another Old-Fashioned, Please

Porter/Porter

Orchestrator: Unknown

Location of   - Composer's manuscript: -0-
       - Sheet music: CPT, NYPL, Y
       - Most complete music: CPT (sm);
          NYPL (sm); Y (sm); TW (pv score)
       - Most complete lyric: CLCP
       - Original partitur: -0-
       - Original parts: TW

God Bless the Women

Porter/Porter

Orchestrator: Unknown

Location of   - Composer's manuscript: -0-
       - Sheet music: Unpublished
       - Most complete music: TW (pv score);
          CPT (pv-l)
       - Most complete lyric: TW (scr);
          CPT (pv-l, scr); CLCP
       - Original partitur: -0-
       - Original parts: TW

Panama Hattie (1940)

They Ain't Done Right by Our Nell

Porter/Porter

Orchestrator: Unknown

Location of — Composer's manuscript: -0-
— Sheet music: Unpublished
— Most complete music: CPT (pv-l)
— Most complete lyric: CLCP
— Original partitur: -0-
— Original parts: -0-

Dropped within a week of the New York opening.

Americans All Drink Coffee

Porter/Porter

Orchestrator: Unknown

Location of — Composer's manuscript: -0-
— Sheet music: Unpublished
— Most complete music: CPT (pv-l)
— Most complete lyric: CLCP
— Original partitur: -0-
— Original parts: -0-

Dropped during the pre-Broadway tryout.

Here's to Panama Hattie

Porter/Porter

Orchestrator: Unknown

Location of — Composer's manuscript: -0-
— Sheet music: Unpublished
— Most complete music: CPT (pv-l)
— Most complete lyric: CPT (pv-l); CLCP
— Original partitur: -0-
— Original parts: -0-

Dropped during the pre-Broadway tryout.

LET'S FACE IT

Music   COLE PORTER
Lyrics   COLE PORTER

Musical comedy in two acts. Opened October 29, 1941 in New York and ran 547 performances (World premiere: October 6, 1941 in Boston). Libretto by Herbert and Dorothy Fields, based on the play CRADLE SNATCHERS by Russell Medcraft and Norma Mitchell. Additional songs by Sylvia Fine and Max Liebman. Produced by Vinton Freedley. Directed by Edgar MacGregor. Choreographed by Charles Walters. Musical direction by Max Meth. Orchestrations by Hans Spialek, Don Walker, Ted Royal, Walter Paul.

Synopsis and Production Information	To make their husbands jealous, Maggie Watson, Nancy Collister, and Cornelia Pidgeon invite three young Army inductees to Maggie's summer home at Southampton. The inductees' girlfriends get wind of the scheme and decide to crash the party. In addition to the twelve principals, the show requires a full singing and dancing ensemble.
Orchestration	Unknown
Comments	In the original production, the lead inductee was played by Danny Kaye, Maggie Watson by Eve Arden.
Location of Original Materials	Script: Cole Porter Trusts (all lyrics) Piano-vocal score: See individual listings Partiturs: Missing Parts: Missing All of the Porter songs performed in the original New York production survive.
Rental Status	Currently unavailable for rental
Music Publisher	Chappell Music
Information	Cole Porter Trusts

Let's Face It (1941)

Overture

Porter/Porter

Orchestrator: Unknown

Location of   - Composer's manuscript: -0-
       - Sheet music: Unpublished
       - Most complete music: -0-
       - Most complete lyric: INST
       - Original partitur: -0-
       - Original parts: -0-

Jerry, My Soldier Boy

Porter/Porter

Orchestrator: Unknown

Location of   - Composer's manuscript: -0-
       - Sheet music: CPT, LoC, NYPL, Y
       - Most complete music: CPT (sm);
           LoC (sm); NYPL (sm); Y (sm)
       - Most complete lyric: CPT (ls, scr); CLCP
       - Original partitur: -0-
       - Original parts: -0-

Milk, Milk, Milk

Porter/Porter

Orchestrator: Unknown

Location of   - Composer's manuscript: -0-
       - Sheet music: Unpublished
       - Most complete music: CPT (pv-l)
       - Most complete lyric: CPT (pv-l, scr); CLCP
       - Original partitur: -0-
       - Original parts: -0-

Alternate title: "Opening Act I, Scene 1."

Let's Face It

Porter/Porter

Orchestrator: Unknown

Location of   - Composer's manuscript: -0-
       - Sheet music: Unpublished
       - Most complete music: CPT (pv-l)
       - Most complete lyric: CPT (pv-l, scr);
           CLCP
       - Original partitur: -0-
       - Original parts: -0-

Lady Needs a Rest, A

Porter/Porter

Orchestrator: Unknown

Location of   - Composer's manuscript: -0-
       - Sheet music: Unpublished
       - Most complete music: CPT (pv-l);
           LoC (pv-l)
       - Most complete lyric: CPT (ls, scr); CLCP
       - Original partitur: -0-
       - Original parts: -0-

Farming

Porter/Porter

Orchestrator: Unknown

Location of   - Composer's manuscript: -0-
       - Sheet music: CPT, LoC, NYPL, Y
       - Most complete music: CPT (sm);
           LoC (sm); NYPL (sm); Y (sm)
       - Most complete lyric: CLCP
       - Original partitur: -0-
       - Original parts: -0-

Ev'rything I Love

Porter/Porter

Orchestrator: Unknown

Location of   - Composer's manuscript: -0-
- Sheet music: CPT, LoC, NYPL, Y
- Most complete music: CPT (sm);
      LoC (sm); NYPL (sm); Y (sm)
- Most complete lyric: CPT (ls, scr); CLCP
- Original partitur: -0-
- Original parts: -0-

The music to the tag is missing.

Baby Games

Porter/Porter

Orchestrator: Unknown

Location of   - Composer's manuscript: -0-
- Sheet music: Unpublished
- Most complete music: CPT (pv-l);
      LoC (pv-l)
- Most complete lyric: CPT (ls, scr);
      CLCP
- Original partitur: -0-
- Original parts: -0-

In the original production, Danny Kaye performed Fine and Liebman's "A Fairy Tale" during "Baby Games." The Cole Porter Trusts have a piano-vocal for "A Fairy Tale" that includes dialogue and lyrics.

Ace in the Hole

Porter/Porter

Orchestrator: Unknown

Location of   - Composer's manuscript: -0-
- Sheet music: CPT, LoC, NYPL
- Most complete music: CPT (pv-l)
- Most complete lyric: CPT (scr); CLCP
- Original partitur: -0-
- Original parts: -0-

Rub Your Lamp

Porter/Porter

Orchestrator: Unknown

Location of   - Composer's manuscript: -0-
- Sheet music: CPT, LoC, NYPL, Y
- Most complete music: CPT (sm);
      LoC (sm); NYPL (sm); Y (sm)
- Most complete lyric: CPT (sm, scr);
      LoC (sm); NYPL (sm); Y (sm); CLCP
- Original partitur: -0-
- Original parts: -0-

You Irritate Me So

Porter/Porter

Orchestrator: Unknown

Location of   - Composer's manuscript: -0-
- Sheet music: CPT, LoC, NYPL, Y
- Most complete music: CPT (pv-l)
- Most complete lyric: CPT (ls, scr); CLCP
- Original partitur: -0-
- Original parts: -0-

Entr'acte

Porter/Porter

Orchestrator: Unknown

Location of   - Composer's manuscript: -0-
- Sheet music: Unpublished
- Most complete music: -0-
- Most complete lyric: INST
- Original partitur: -0-
- Original parts: -0-

248

Let's Face It (1941)

I've Got Some Unfinished Business With You
Porter/Porter
Orchestrator: Unknown

Location of   - Composer's manuscript: -0-
          - Sheet music: Unpublished
          - Most complete music: CPT (pv-I);
               LoC (pv-I)
          - Most complete lyric: CPT (pv-I, scr);
               LoC (pv-I); CLCP
          - Original partitur: -0-
          - Original parts: -0-

I Hate You, Darling
Porter/Porter
Orchestrator: Unknown

Location of   - Composer's manuscript: -0-
          - Sheet music: CPT, LoC, NYPL, Y
          - Most complete music: CPT (pv-I)
          - Most complete lyric: CPT (pv-I); CLCP
          - Original partitur: -0-
          - Original parts: -0-

Let's Not Talk About Love
Porter/Porter
Orchestrator: Unknown

Location of   - Composer's manuscript: -0-
          - Sheet music: CPT, LoC, NYPL, Y
          - Most complete music: CPT (sm);
               LoC (sm); NYPL (sm); Y (sm)
          - Most complete lyric: CLCP
          - Original partitur: -0-
          - Original parts: -0-

Eve Arden's refrain ("Let's Talk About Love") was probably not performed in the original production.

Melody in Four F
Fine & Liebman/Fine & Liebman
Orchestrator: Unknown

Location of   - Composer's manuscript: -0-
          - Sheet music: See note
          - Most complete music: See note
          - Most complete lyric: See note
          - Original partitur: -0-
          - Original parts: -0-

Apparently published by Chappell; no copy was found. Danny Kaye later performed this number in the 1944 film UP IN ARMS; the movie soundtrack has been released by Sunbeam Records on Sountrak STK-113.

Little Rumba Numba, A
Porter/Porter
Orchestrator: Unknown

Location of   - Composer's manuscript: -0-
          - Sheet music: CPT, LoC, NYPL, Y
          - Most complete music: CPT (sm);
               LoC (sm); NYPL (sm); Y (sm)
          - Most complete lyric: CPT (sm, scr);
               LoC (sm); NYPL (sm); Y (sm); CLCP
          - Original partitur: -0-
          - Original parts: -0-

Get Yourself a Girl
Porter/Porter
Orchestrator: Unknown

Location of   - Composer's manuscript: -0-
          - Sheet music: Unpublished
          - Most complete music: CPT (pv-I);
               LoC (pv-I)
          - Most complete lyric: CLCP
          - Original partitur: -0-
          - Original parts: -0-

Most of this number was dropped during the pre-Broadway tryout; only a few lines remain in the script.

Revenge

Porter/Porter

Orchestrator: Unknown

Location of
- Composer's manuscript: -0-
- Sheet music: Unpublished
- Most complete music: CPT (pv-l);
    LoC (pv-l)
- Most complete lyric: CLCP
- Original partitur: -0-
- Original parts: -0-

Dropped in rehearsal.

Make a Date With a Great Psychoanalyst

Porter/Porter

Orchestrator: Unknown

Location of
- Composer's manuscript: -0-
- Sheet music: Unpublished
- Most complete music: CPT (pv-l);
    LoC (pv-l)
- Most complete lyric: See note
- Original partitur: -0-
- Original parts: -0-

Unused; written for Eve Arden. There are two versions of the lyric to the verse: One is in the piano-vocals, the other is in The Complete Lyrics of Cole Porter.

What Are Little Husbands Made Of?

Porter/Porter

Orchestrator: Unknown

Location of
- Composer's manuscript: -0-
- Sheet music: Unpublished
- Most complete music: CPT (pv-l)
- Most complete lyric: CLCP
- Original partitur: -0-
- Original parts: -0-

Dropped in rehearsal.

You Can't Beat My Bill

Porter/Porter

Orchestrator: Unknown

Location of
- Composer's manuscript: -0-
- Sheet music: Unpublished
- Most complete music: -0-
- Most complete lyric: CPT (ls); CLCP
- Original partitur: -0-
- Original parts: -0-

Unused.

Pets

Porter/Porter

Orchestrator: -0-

Location of
- Composer's manuscript: -0-
- Sheet music: Unpublished
- Most complete music: CPT (pv-l);
    LoC (pv-l)
- Most complete lyric: CLCP
- Original partitur: -0-
- Original parts: -0-

Dropped in rehearsal.

Up to His Old Tricks Again

Porter/Porter

Orchestrator: Unknown

Location of
- Composer's manuscript: -0-
- Sheet music: Unpublished
- Most complete music: -0-
- Most complete lyric: CLCP
- Original partitur: -0-
- Original parts: -0-

Unused.

SOMETHING FOR THE BOYS

Music   **COLE PORTER**
Lyrics   **COLE PORTER**

Musical comedy in two acts. Opened January 7, 1943 in New York and ran 422 performances (World premiere: December 18, 1942 in Boston). Libretto by Herbert and Dorothy Fields. Produced by Michael Todd. Directed by Hassard Short, Herbert Fields. Choreographed by Jack Cole, Lew Kessler. Musical direction by William Parson. Orchestrations by Robert Russell Bennett, Hans Spialek, Don Walker, Ted Royal, Walter Paul.

Synopsis and Production Information

A defense worker (Blossom), a pitchman (Harry), and a burlesque queen (Chiquita) inherit equal shares of a Texas ranch near Kelly flying field. They successfully transform it into a boarding house for soldiers' wives, but Lieutenant Grubbs, convinced that they're running a different sort of house, tries to put them out of business. Eventually, Blossom, aided by a carborundum-coated filling on her tooth that allows her to hear radio signals, manages to clear her family name.

Other characters include bandleader Sgt. Rocky Fulton (the romantic lead), Rocky's snobbish fiance Melanie, squatter Tobias Twitch (comic role), and two of Rocky's admirers: Mary-Frances (singer) and Betty-Jean (dancer). The show includes a full singing and dancing ensemble.

Orchestration

Pit Orchestra: Reed I (Flute, Piccolo, Clarinet, Alto Sax); Reed II (Clarinet, Alto Sax, Baritone Sax, Flute); Reed III (Oboe, English Horn, Tenor Sax, Clarinet); Reed IV (Clarinet, Tenor Sax); Reed V (Clarinet, Alto Sax, Bass Clarinet); Trumpet I II; Trombone I II; Percussion; Piano; Violin A B C; Cello; Bass

Stage Band: Trumpet I; Trumpet II; Trombone; Tuba (dbl. Bass); Bass Drum; Glockenspiel

Comments

In the original production, Blossom was played by Ethel Merman, Chiquita by Paula Laurence, Mary-Frances by Betty Garrett, and Betty-Jean by Betty Bruce.

Location of Original Materials

Script: Cole Porter Trusts (all lyrics), Tams-Witmark Music Library (all lyrics)
Piano-vocal score: Cole Porter Trusts
Partiturs: Cole Porter Trusts
Parts: Missing

The partiturs at the Cole Porter Trusts are miniature photocopies of the originals.

Rental Status

Currently unavailable for rental

Music Publisher

Chappell Music

Information

Cole Porter Trusts

Cole Porter

Overture
Porter/Porter
Orchestrator: Spialek, Paul

Location of - Composer's manuscript: -0-
            - Sheet music: Unpublished
            - Most complete music: CPT (pv score)
            - Most complete lyric: INST
            - Original partitur: CPT (x)
            - Original parts: -0-

When My Baby Goes to Town
Porter/Porter
Orchestrator: Walker

Location of - Composer's manuscript: -0-
            - Sheet music: CPT, LoC, NYPL, Y
            - Most complete music: CPT (sm, pv score);
                LoC (sm); NYPL (sm); Y (sm)
            - Most complete lyric: CPT (ls); CLCP
            - Original partitur: CPT (x)
            - Original parts: -0-

Prologue
Porter/Porter
Orchestrator: Bennett

Location of - Composer's manuscript: -0-
            - Sheet music: Unpublished
            - Most complete music: CPT (pv-l, pv score)
            - Most complete lyric: CPT (scr, ls);
                TW (scr); CLCP
            - Original partitur: CPT (x)
            - Original parts: -0-

Alternate title: "Announcement of Inheritance."

Something for the Boys
Porter/Porter
Orchestrator: Walker

Location of - Composer's manuscript: -0-
            - Sheet music: CPT, LoC, NYPL, Y
            - Most complete music: CPT (sm, pv score);
                LoC (sm); NYPL (sm); Y (sm)
            - Most complete lyric: CPT (ls); CLCP
            - Original partitur: CPT (x)
            - Original parts: -0-

See That You're Born in Texas
Porter/Porter
Orchestrator: Spialek, Paul

Location of - Composer's manuscript: -0-
            - Sheet music: CPT, LoC, NYPL, Y
            - Most complete music: CPT (sm, pv score);
                LoC (sm); NYPL (sm); Y (sm)
            - Most complete lyric: CPT (sm, ls, scr);
                LoC (sm); NYPL (sm); Y (sm);
                TW (scr); CLCP
            - Original partitur: CPT (x)
            - Original parts: -0-

The original stage band parts are at the Cole Porter Trusts.

When We're Home on the Range
Porter/Porter
Orchestrator: Spialek

Location of - Composer's manuscript: -0-
            - Sheet music: Unpublished
            - Most complete music: CPT (pv-l,
                pv score)
            - Most complete lyric: CPT (ls, scr);
                TW (scr); CLCP
            - Original partitur: CPT (x)
            - Original parts: -0-

Something for the Boys (1943)

Could It Be You?
Porter/Porter
Orchestrator: Bennett

Location of
- Composer's manuscript: -0-
- Sheet music: CPT, LoC, NYPL, Y
- Most complete music: CPT (sm & pv)
- Most complete lyric: CPT (sm & scr);
    CLCP
- Original partitur: CPT (x)
- Original parts: -0-

The piano-vocal and script have the version performed in the show; the sheet music contains a different verse.

Assembly Line
Porter/Porter
Orchestrator: Royal

Location of
- Composer's manuscript: -0-
- Sheet music: Unpublished
- Most complete music: CPT (pv-l,
    pv score)
- Most complete lyric: CPT (pv-l, ls);
    CLCP
- Original partitur: CPT (x)
- Original parts: -0-

Alternate title: "Opening Act I, Scene 5." The lyric, which was not performed in the original production, is not included in the piano-vocal score.

Hey, Good-Lookin'
Porter/Porter
Orchestrator: Walker, Paul

Location of
- Composer's manuscript: -0-
- Sheet music: CPT, LoC, NYPL, Y
- Most complete music: CPT (sm, pv score);
    LoC (sm); NYPL (sm); Y (sm)
- Most complete lyric: CPT (ls, scr);
    TW (scr); CLCP
- Original partitur: CPT (x)
- Original parts: -0-

Leader of a Big-Time Band, The
Porter/Porter
Orchestrator: Walker

Location of
- Composer's manuscript: -0-
- Sheet music: CPT, LoC, NYPL, Y
- Most complete music: CPT (sm, pv score);
    LoC (sm); NYPL (sm); Y (sm)
- Most complete lyric: CPT (ls); CLCP
- Original partitur: CPT (x)
- Original parts: -0-

He's a Right Guy
Porter/Porter
Orchestrator: Spialek

Location of
- Composer's manuscript: -0-
- Sheet music: CPT, LoC, NYPL, Y
- Most complete music: CPT (sm, pv score);
    LoC (sm); NYPL (sm); Y (sm)
- Most complete lyric: CPT (sm, scr, ls);
    LoC (sm); NYPL (sm); Y (sm); CLCP
- Original partitur: -0-
- Original parts: -0-

Entr'acte
Porter/Porter
Orchestrator: Unknown

Location of
- Composer's manuscript: -0-
- Sheet music: Unpublished
- Most complete music: CPT (pv score)
- Most complete lyric: CPT (pv score)
- Original partitur: CPT (x)
- Original parts: -0-

Parts of the Entr'acte were sung by a male chorus; the original vocal arrangement is at the Cole Porter Trusts.

I'm in Love With a Soldier Boy

Porter/Porter

Orchestrator: Unknown

Location of   - Composer's manuscript: -0-
- Sheet music: CPT, LoC, NYPL, Y
- Most complete music: CPT (sm & pv score)
- Most complete lyric: CPT (sm & scr, ls); CLCP
- Original partitur: CPT (x)
- Original parts: -0-

The piano-vocal score has the version performed in the original production; the sheet music contains different lyrics and a revised ending.

There's a Happy Land in the Sky

Porter/Porter

Orchestrator: Walker

Location of   - Composer's manuscript: -0-
- Sheet music: Unpublished
- Most complete music: CPT (pv-l, pv score)
- Most complete lyric: CPT (pv-l, scr, ls); TW (scr); CLCP
- Original partitur: CPT (x)
- Original parts: -0-

By the Mississinewah

Porter/Porter

Orchestrator: Spialek

Location of   - Composer's manuscript: -0-
- Sheet music: CPT, LoC, NYPL, Y
- Most complete music: CPT (pv-l, pv score)
- Most complete lyric: CPT (ls); CLCP
- Original partitur: CPT (x)
- Original parts: -0-

A duet in the show, the song was published as a solo. The music to the patter section is missing.

Square Dance

Porter/Porter

Orchestrator: Walker

Location of   - Composer's manuscript: -0-
- Sheet music: Unpublished
- Most complete music: CPT (pv score)
- Most complete lyric: See note
- Original partitur: CPT (x)
- Original parts: -0-

In addition to some new material, this dance contains two choruses of "See That You're Born in Texas," the second being a vocal reprise. The original stage band parts are at the Cole Porter Trusts.

Specialty

Porter/Porter

Orchestrator: Royal

Location of   - Composer's manuscript: -0-
- Sheet music: Unpublished
- Most complete music: CPT (pv score)
- Most complete lyric: INST
- Original partitur: CPT (x)
- Original parts: -0-

Betty-Jean's specialty dance consists primarily of "See That You're Born in Texas" and "When My Baby Goes to Town."

So Long, San Antonio

Porter/Porter

Orchestrator: Spialek

Location of   - Composer's manuscript: -0-
- Sheet music: Unpublished
- Most complete music: CPT (pv-l); LoC (pv-l)
- Most complete lyric: CPT (ls); CLCP
- Original partitur: -0-
- Original parts: -0-

This Act II opening was replaced by "I'm in Love With a Soldier Boy" during the Boston tryout.

Something for the Boys (1943)

Riddle-Diddle Me This
Porter/Porter
Orchestrator: Unknown

Location of   - Composer's manuscript: -0-
             - Sheet music: Unpublished
             - Most complete music: CPT (pv-l);
                LoC (pv-l)
             - Most complete lyric: CPT (ls)
             - Original partitur: -0-
             - Original parts: -0-

This Act II duet for Blossom and Harry was dropped during the Boston tryout.

Texas Will Make You a Man
Porter/Porter
Orchestrator: Unknown

Location of   - Composer's manuscript: -0-
             - Sheet music: Unpublished
             - Most complete music: -0-
             - Most complete lyric: CPT (ls); CLCP
             - Original partitur: -0-
             - Original parts: -0-

Unused.

Washington, D.C.
Porter/Porter
Orchestrator: Unknown

Location of   - Composer's manuscript: -0-
             - Sheet music: Unpublished
             - Most complete music: CPT (pv-l);
                LoC (pv-l)
             - Most complete lyric: CPT (pv-l, ls);
                LoC (pv-l); CLCP
             - Original partitur: -0-
             - Original parts: -0-

Dropped in rehearsal.

Well, I Just Wouldn't Know
Porter/Porter
Orchestrator: Unknown

Location of   - Composer's manuscript: -0-
             - Sheet music: Unpublished
             - Most complete music: -0-
             - Most complete lyric: CLCP
             - Original partitur: -0-
             - Original parts: -0-

Unused.

Oh, How I Could Go For You
Porter/Porter
Orchestrator: Unknown

Location of   - Composer's manuscript: CPT (sk)
             - Sheet music: Unpublished
             - Most complete music: CPT (sk)
             - Most complete lyric: CPT (ls); CLCP
             - Original partitur: -0-
             - Original parts: -0-

Unused.

Wouldn't It Be Crazy?
Porter/Porter
Orchestrator: Unknown

Location of   - Composer's manuscript: -0-
             - Sheet music: Unpublished
             - Most complete music: -0-
             - Most complete lyric: CPT (ls); CLCP
             - Original partitur: -0-
             - Original parts: -0-

Unused.

MEXICAN HAYRIDE

Music	COLE PORTER
Lyrics	COLE PORTER

Musical comedy in two acts. Opened January 28, 1944 in New York and ran 481 performances (World premiere: December 29, 1943 in Boston). Libretto by Herbert and Dorothy Fields. Produced by Michael Todd. Directed by Hassard Short, John Kennedy. Choreographed by Paul Haakon. Musical direction by Harry Levant. Orchestrations by Robert Russell Bennett, Ted Royal.

Synopsis and Production Information

Joe Bascom, an American numbers racket king on the lam in Mexico, eludes the local authorities (and his wife) by hiding in a hoopskirt, playing flute in a Mariachi band, and selling tortillas as a buck-toothed squaw.

Other characters include female bullfighter Montana, her manager Lombo, David Winthrop of the American Embassy, and Latin singer Lolita. The show requires a full singing and dancing ensemble. Settings include the Plaza de Toros, the bar at Ciro's, the Palace at Chepultepec, and Xochimilco.

Orchestration

Unknown

Comments

MEXICAN HAYRIDE was primarily a showcase for Bobby Clark, who played Joe Bascom. The original cast also included June Havoc as Montana.

Location of Original Materials

Script: Cole Porter Trusts (all lyrics)
Piano-vocal score: See individual listings
Partiturs: Missing
Parts: Missing

Music is missing for one song performed in the New York production, as well as for the Overture and the Entr'acte. The Library of Congress has an early draft of the script.

Rental Status

Currently unavailable for rental

Music Publisher

Chappell Music

Information

Cole Porter Trusts

Mexican Hayride (1944)

Overture

Porter/Porter
Orchestrator: Unknown

Location of
- Composer's manuscript: -0-
- Sheet music: Unpublished
- Most complete music: -0-
- Most complete lyric: INST
- Original partitur: -0-
- Original parts: -0-

Good-Will Movement, The

Porter/Porter
Orchestrator: Unknown

Location of
- Composer's manuscript: -0-
- Sheet music: CPT, NYPL, LoC, Y
- Most complete music: CPT (sm);
      NYPL (sm); LoC (sm); Y (sm)
- Most complete lyric: CPT (sm, scr);
      NYPL (sm); LoC (sm); Y (sm); CLCP
- Original partitur: -0-
- Original parts: -0-

The music to the Trio is missing.

Entrance of Montana

Porter/Porter
Orchestrator: Unknown

Location of
- Composer's manuscript: -0-
- Sheet music: Unpublished
- Most complete music: -0-
- Most complete lyric: CLCP
- Original partitur: -0-
- Original parts: -0-

Alternate title: "Opening Act I."

I Love You

Porter/Porter
Orchestrator: Unknown

Location of
- Composer's manuscript: -0-
- Sheet music: CPT, NYPL, LoC, Y
- Most complete music: CPT (sm);
      NYPL (sm); LoC (sm); Y (sm)
- Most complete lyric: CPT (sm, scr);
      NYPL (sm); LoC (sm); Y (sm); CLCP
- Original partitur: -0-
- Original parts: -0-

Sing to Me, Guitar

Porter/Porter
Orchestrator: Unknown

Location of
- Composer's manuscript: -0-
- Sheet music: CPT, NYPL, LoC, Y
- Most complete music: CPT (sm);
      NYPL (sm); LoC (sm); Y (sm)
- Most complete lyric: CPT (sm, scr);
      NYPL (sm); LoC (sm); Y (sm); CLCP
- Original partitur: -0-
- Original parts: -0-

The Complete Lyrics of Cole Porter also contains a brief
tag.

There Must Be Someone for Me

Porter/Porter
Orchestrator: Unknown

Location of
- Composer's manuscript: -0-
- Sheet music: CPT, NYPL, LoC, Y
- Most complete music: CPT (sm);
      NYPL (sm); LoC (sm); Y (sm)
- Most complete lyric: CPT (ls)
- Original partitur: -0-
- Original parts: -0-

Carlotta

Porter/Porter
Orchestrator: Unknown

Location of - Composer's manuscript: -0-
           - Sheet music: CPT, NYPL, LoC, Y
           - Most complete music: CPT (sm);
                 NYPL (sm); LoC (sm); Y (sm)
           - Most complete lyric: CPT (sm, scr);
                 NYPL (sm); LoC (sm); Y (sm); CLCP
           - Original partitur: -0-
           - Original parts: -0-

What a Crazy Way to Spend Sunday

Porter/Porter
Orchestrator: Unknown

Location of - Composer's manuscript: -0-
           - Sheet music: Unpublished
           - Most complete music: See note
           - Most complete lyric: CPT (scr); CLCP
           - Original partitur: -0-
           - Original parts: -0-

The music survives only on the original cast recording (Decca DL-5232).

Girls

Porter/Porter
Orchestrator: Unknown

Location of - Composer's manuscript: -0-
           - Sheet music: CPT, NYPL, LoC, Y
           - Most complete music: CPT (sm & pv-l)
           - Most complete lyric: CPT (ls); CLCP
           - Original partitur: -0-
           - Original parts: -0-

The sheet music contains no patter.

Abracadabra

Porter/Porter
Orchestrator: Unknown

Location of - Composer's manuscript: -0-
           - Sheet music: CPT, NYPL, LoC, Y
           - Most complete music: CPT (sm);
                 NYPL (sm); LoC (sm); Y (sm)
           - Most complete lyric: CPT (scr); CLCP
           - Original partitur: -0-
           - Original parts: -0-

Entr'acte

Porter/Porter
Orchestrator: Unknown

Location of - Composer's manuscript: -0-
           - Sheet music: Unpublished
           - Most complete music: -0-
           - Most complete lyric: INST
           - Original partitur: -0-
           - Original parts: -0-

Count Your Blessings

Porter/Porter
Orchestrator: Unknown

Location of - Composer's manuscript: -0-
           - Sheet music: CPT, NYPL, LoC, Y
           - Most complete music: CPT (sm);
                 NYPL (sm); LoC (sm); Y (sm)
           - Most complete lyric: CLCP
           - Original partitur: -0-
           - Original parts: -0-

The script also contains a few alternate lyrics.

Mexican Hayride (1944)

Hereafter
Porter/Porter
Orchestrator: Unknown

Location of   - Composer's manuscript: -0-
          - Sheet music: Unpublished
          - Most complete music: CPT (pv-l)
          - Most complete lyric: CPT (pv-l); CLCP
          - Original partitur: -0-
          - Original parts: -0-

This Act I duet for Joe and Montana was dropped during the Boston tryout.

Tequila
Porter/Porter
Orchestrator: Unknown

Location of   - Composer's manuscript: -0-
          - Sheet music: Unpublished
          - Most complete music: CPT (pv-l);
             LoC (pv-l)
          - Most complete lyric: CPT (pv-l);
             LoC (pv-l); CLCP
          - Original partitur: -0-
          - Original parts: -0-

Dropped during the Boston tryout.

It Must Be Fun to Be You
Porter/Porter
Orchestrator: Unknown

Location of   - Composer's manuscript: -0-
          - Sheet music: CPT, NYPL, LoC, Y
          - Most complete music: CPT (pv-l)
          - Most complete lyric: CPT (pv-l); CLCP
          - Original partitur: -0-
          - Original parts: -0-

This Act I trio was dropped during the Boston tryout.

We're Off for a Hayride in Mexico
Porter/Porter
Orchestrator: Unknown

Location of   - Composer's manuscript: -0-
          - Sheet music: Unpublished
          - Most complete music: CPT (pv-l);
             LoC (pv-l)
          - Most complete lyric: CPT (pv-l);
             LoC (pv-l); CLCP
          - Original partitur: -0-
          - Original parts: -0-

Alternate title: "Prologue Act I." This opening number was dropped in rehearsal.

Opening Act I, Scene 3 ["Here's a cheer for dear old Ciro's..."]
Porter/Porter
Orchestrator: Unknown

Location of   - Composer's manuscript: -0-
          - Sheet music: Unpublished
          - Most complete music: CPT (pv-l)
          - Most complete lyric: CPT (pv); CLCP
          - Original partitur: -0-
          - Original parts: -0-

Dropped during the Boston tryout.

He Certainly Kills the Women
Porter/Porter
Orchestrator: Unknown

Location of   - Composer's manuscript: -0-
          - Sheet music: Unpublished
          - Most complete music: CPT (pv-l);
             LoC (pv-l)
          - Most complete lyric: CPT (pv-l, ls);
             LoC (pv-l); CLCP
          - Original partitur: -0-
          - Original parts: -0-

Dropped in rehearsal.

Humble Hollywood Executive, A
Porter/Porter
Orchestrator: Unknown

Location of   - Composer's manuscript: -0-
       - Sheet music: Unpublished
       - Most complete music: CPT (pv-l);
           LoC (pv-l)
       - Most complete lyric: CPT (ls); CLCP
       - Original partitur: -0-
       - Original parts: -0-

Unused.

It's a Big Night
Porter/Porter
Orchestrator: Unknown

Location of   - Composer's manuscript: -0-
       - Sheet music: Unpublished
       - Most complete music: CPT (pv-l);
           LoC (pv-l)
       - Most complete lyric: CPT (pv-l);
           LoC (pv-l); CLCP
       - Original partitur: -0-
       - Original parts: -0-

Unused.

It's Just Like the Good Old Days
Porter/Porter
Orchestrator: Unknown

Location of   - Composer's manuscript: -0-
       - Sheet music: Unpublished
       - Most complete music: CPT (pv-l);
           LoC (pv-l)
       - Most complete lyric: CPT (pv-l, ls);
           LoC (pv-l); CLCP
       - Original partitur: -0-
       - Original parts: -0-

An unused duet intended for Joe and Montana.

It's Just Yours
Porter/Porter
Orchestrator: Unknown

Location of   - Composer's manuscript: -0-
       - Sheet music: Not published separately
       - Most complete music: CPT (pv-l)
       - Most complete lyric: CLCP
       - Original partitur: -0-
       - Original parts: -0-

Unused. Initial publication in The Unpublished Cole Porter (Simon & Schuster: 1975).

Octet
Porter/Porter
Orchestrator: Unknown

Location of   - Composer's manuscript: -0-
       - Sheet music: Unpublished
       - Most complete music: CPT (pv-l);
           LoC (pv-l)
       - Most complete lyric: CPT (pv-l);
           LoC (pv-l); CLCP
       - Original partitur: -0-
       - Original parts: -0-

An unused Act II Finale.

Put a Sack Over Their Heads
Porter/Porter
Orchestrator: Unknown

Location of   - Composer's manuscript: -0-
       - Sheet music: Unpublished
       - Most complete music: CPT (pv-l)
       - Most complete lyric: CPT (pv-l); CLCP
       - Original partitur: -0-
       - Original parts: -0-

An unused number intended for Joe (Bobby Clark).

Mexican Hayride (1944)

Sightseeing Tour, A
Porter/Porter
Orchestrator: Unknown

Location of   - Composer's manuscript: -0-
           - Sheet music: Unpublished
           - Most complete music: CPT (pv-l);
               LoC (pv-l)
           - Most complete lyric: CPT (pv-l);
               LoC (pv-l); CLCP
           - Original partitur: -0-
           - Original parts: -0-

Unused.

I'm So Glahd to Meet You
Porter/Porter
Orchestrator: Unknown

Location of   - Composer's manuscript: CPT (sk)
           - Sheet music: Unpublished
           - Most complete music: CPT (sk)
           - Most complete lyric: CPT (ls); CLCP
           - Original partitur: -0-
           - Original parts: -0-

Unused.

That's What You Mean to Me
Porter/Porter
Orchestrator: Unknown

Location of   - Composer's manuscript: -0-
           - Sheet music: Unpublished
           - Most complete music: CPT (pv-l)
           - Most complete lyric: CPT (pv-l); CLCP
           - Original partitur: -0-
           - Original parts: -0-

Unused.

C.P. Theme
Porter/Porter
Orchestrator: Unknown

Location of   - Composer's manuscript: -0-
           - Sheet music: Unpublished
           - Most complete music: CPT (sk)
           - Most complete lyric: -0-
           - Original partitur: -0-
           - Original parts: -0-

Unused.

I'm Afraid I Love You
Porter/Porter
Orchestrator: Unknown

Location of   - Composer's manuscript: -0-
           - Sheet music: Unpublished
           - Most complete music: CPT (pv-l);
               LoC (pv-l)
           - Most complete lyric: CPT (pv-l);
               LoC (pv-l); CLCP
           - Original partitur: -0-
           - Original parts: -0-

Unused.

AROUND THE WORLD IN EIGHTY DAYS

Music	COLE PORTER
Lyrics	COLE PORTER

Musical comedy in two acts. Opened May 31, 1946 in New York and ran 75 performances (World premiere: April 28, 1946 in Boston). Libretto by Orson Welles, from the novel by Jules Verne. Produced by Orson Welles as a Mercury Theatre Production. Directed by Orson Welles. Choreographed by Nelson Barclift. Musical direction by Harry Levant. Orchestrations by Robert Russell Bennett, Ted Royal.

Synopsis and Production Information

Mr. Phileas Fogg, a bachelor of means and exact habits, bets London's Whist Club that he can travel around the world in eighty days. Accompanied by Pat Passepartout, his Yankee valet, and Missus Aouda, an Indian maiden -- and pursued by Detective Inspector Fix of Scotland Yard and Pat's Irish girlfriend Molly -- he journeys to Paris, Madrid, Brindisi, Suez, Bombay, Calcutta, Hong Kong, California, the Rocky Mountains, and New York before returning to London and winning the wager.

Film sequences are used throughout to bridge the eighty-odd scenes. The show requires a full singing and dancing ensemble.

Orchestration

Flute I II; Oboe; Clarinet I II; Horn I II; Trumpet I II; Trumpet III; Trombone I; Trombone II; Percussion; Piano; Harp; Violin A B C D; Viola I II; Cello; Bass

Location of Original Materials

Script: Cole Porter Trusts (most lyrics), New York Public Library (most lyrics)
Piano-vocal score: See individual listings
Partiturs: Library of Congress
Parts: Missing

The script dates from the rehearsal period, but its plot, characters, and musical running order are similar to those of the New York show. Although all of the songs survive, only two of the orchestrations have been located.

Rental Status

Currently unavailable for rental

Music Publisher

Chappell Music

Information

Cole Porter Trusts

Around the World in Eighty Days (1946)

Overture
Porter/Porter
Orchestrator: Unknown

Location of - Composer's manuscript: -0-
           - Sheet music: Unpublished
           - Most complete music: -0-
           - Most complete lyric: INST
           - Original partitur: -0-
           - Original parts: -0-

Mee-rah-lah
Porter/Porter
Orchestrator: Unknown

Location of - Composer's manuscript: -0-
           - Sheet music: Unpublished
           - Most complete music: CPT (pv-l)
           - Most complete lyric: CPT (pv-l); CLCP
           - Original partitur: -0-
           - Original parts: -0-

Alternate title: "Suez Dance."

Look What I Found
Porter/Porter
Orchestrator: Bennett

Location of - Composer's manuscript: -0-
           - Sheet music: CPT, LoC, NYPL, Y
           - Most complete music: CPT (sm);
               LoC (sm); NYPL (sm); Y (sm)
           - Most complete lyric: CPT (sm, scr);
               LoC (sm); NYPL (sm, scr); Y (sm);
               CLCP
           - Original partitur: LoC
           - Original parts: -0-

Suttee Procession and Dance
Porter/Porter
Orchestrator: Unknown

Location of - Composer's manuscript: -0-
           - Sheet music: Unpublished
           - Most complete music: CPT (pv-l);
               LoC (pv-l)
           - Most complete lyric: CPT (pv-l);
               LoC (pv-l)
           - Original partitur: -0-
           - Original parts: -0-

There He Goes, Mr. Phileas Fogg
Porter/Porter
Orchestrator: Bennett

Location of - Composer's manuscript: -0-
           - Sheet music: CPT, LoC, Y
           - Most complete music: CPT (sm); LoC (sm);
               Y (sm)
           - Most complete lyric: CPT (sm, scr);
               LoC (sm); Y (sm); NYPL (scr); CLCP
           - Original partitur: LoC
           - Original parts: -0-

Sea Chanty
Porter/Porter
Orchestrator: Unknown

Location of - Composer's manuscript: -0-
           - Sheet music: Unpublished
           - Most complete music: CPT (pv-l)
           - Most complete lyric: CPT (pv-l); CLCP
           - Original partitur: -0-
           - Original parts: -0-

Should I Tell You I Love You?
Porter/Porter
Orchestrator: Unknown

Location of   - Composer's manuscript: -0-
            - Sheet music: CPT, LoC, NYPL, Y
            - Most complete music: CPT (pv-I)
            - Most complete lyric: CPT (pv-I); CLCP
            - Original partitur: -0-
            - Original parts: -0-

Entr'acte
Porter/Porter
Orchestrator: Unknown

Location of   - Composer's manuscript: -0-
            - Sheet music: Unpublished
            - Most complete music: -0-
            - Most complete lyric: INST
            - Original partitur: -0-
            - Original parts: -0-

Pipe Dreaming
Porter/Porter
Orchestrator: Unknown

Location of   - Composer's manuscript: -0-
            - Sheet music: CPT, LoC, NYPL, Y
            - Most complete music: CPT (sm);
                LoC (sm); NYPL (sm); Y (sm)
            - Most complete lyric: CPT (sm, scr);
                LoC (sm); NYPL (sm, scr); Y (sm);
                CLCP
            - Original partitur: -0-
            - Original parts: -0-

Act II Opening California Scene
Porter/Porter
Orchestrator: Unknown

Location of   - Composer's manuscript: -0-
            - Sheet music: Unpublished
            - Most complete music: CPT (pv)
            - Most complete lyric: INST
            - Original partitur: -0-
            - Original parts: -0-

Oka Saka Circus
Porter/Porter
Orchestrator: Unknown

Location of   - Composer's manuscript: -0-
            - Sheet music: Unpublished
            - Most complete music: CPT (pv); LoC (pv)
            - Most complete lyric: INST
            - Original partitur: -0-
            - Original parts: -0-

Alternate title: "Japanese Circus Scene."

If You Smile At Me
Porter/Porter
Orchestrator: Unknown

Location of   - Composer's manuscript: -0-
            - Sheet music: CPT, LoC, NYPL, Y
            - Most complete music: CPT (sm);
                LoC (sm); NYPL (sm); Y (sm)
            - Most complete lyric: CPT (sm);
                LoC (sm); NYPL (sm); Y (sm); CLCP
            - Original partitur: -0-
            - Original parts: -0-

Around the World in Eighty Days (1946)

Wherever They Fly the Flag of England
Porter/Porter
Orchestrator: Unknown

Location of - Composer's manuscript: -0-
- Sheet music: CPT, LoC, Y
- Most complete music: CPT (sm);
    LoC (sm); Y (sm)
- Most complete lyric: CPT (sm, scr);
    LoC (sm); Y (sm); NYPL (scr); CLCP
- Original partitur: -0-
- Original parts: -0-

Slave Auction
Porter/Porter
Orchestrator: Unknown

Location of - Composer's manuscript: -0-
- Sheet music: Unpublished
- Most complete music: -0-
- Most complete lyric: CPT (ls); CLCP
- Original partitur: -0-
- Original parts: -0-

Unused.

Missus Aouda
Porter/Porter
Orchestrator: Unknown

Location of - Composer's manuscript: -0-
- Sheet music: Unpublished
- Most complete music: CPT (pv-l);
    LoC (pv-l)
- Most complete lyric: CPT (scr, ls);
    NYPL (scr); CLCP
- Original partitur: -0-
- Original parts: -0-

Dropped before the New York opening.

Snagtooth Gertie
Porter/Porter
Orchestrator: Unknown

Location of - Composer's manuscript: -0-
- Sheet music: Unpublished
- Most complete music: CPT (pv-l);
    LoC (pv-l)
- Most complete lyric: CPT (pv-l);
    LoC (pv-l); CLCP
- Original partitur: -0-
- Original parts: -0-

Unused.

KISS ME, KATE

Music   COLE PORTER
Lyrics   COLE PORTER

Musical play in two acts. Opened December 30, 1948 in New York and ran 1077 performances (World premiere: December 2, 1948 in Philadelphia). Libretto by Sam and Bella Spewack, based on the play THE TAMING OF THE SHREW by William Shakespeare. Produced by Saint Subber and Lemuel Ayers. Directed by John C. Wilson. Choreographed by Hanya Holm. Musical direction by Pembroke Davenport. Orchestrations by Robert Russell Bennett. Incidental ballet music arranged by Genevieve Pitot.

Synopsis and Production Information	Sparks fly when impresario Fred Graham and his ex-wife, Lilli Vanessi, reunite to perform a musical version of THE TAMING OF THE SHREW in Baltimore. Their feuding spills from the backstage dressing rooms onto the stage, fueling their performances as Petruchio and Katherine. Finally, Lilli comes to accept the depth of her love for Fred and commits to a future with him.
	Other characters include flirtatious starlet Lois Lane and her ne'er-do-well dancing beau, Bill Calhoun (Bianca and Lucentio in the SHREW scenes), and a pair of comic gangsters. The show requires a full singing and dancing ensemble. Settings and costumes must alternately convey the gritty life of a Forties theatrical troupe and the pageantry of a Shakespearean epic set to music.
Orchestration	Reed I (Flute II, Clarinet, Alto Sax); Reed II (Clarinet, Bass Clarinet, Alto Sax); Reed III (Oboe, English Horn, Clarinet, Tenor Sax); Reed IV (Flute I, Piccolo, Clarinet, Tenor Sax); Reed V (Clarinet, Bassoon, Baritone Sax); Horn; Trumpet I II; Trumpet III; Percussion; Harp; Piano/Celeste; Guitar/Mandolin (doubles Violin); Violin I; Violin II; Viola; Cello; Bass
Comments	KISS ME, KATE won five Antoinette Perry Awards in 1949, including the award for Best Musical.
Location of Original Materials	Script: Cole Porter Trusts (all lyrics), Tams-Witmark Music Library (all lyrics) (Published: Alfred A. Knopf, Inc., 1953; reprinted in <u>Ten Great Musicals of the American Theatre</u>: Chilton Book Company, 1973) Piano-vocal score: Cole Porter Trusts, Library of Congress, New York Public Library, Tams-Witmark Music Library (Published: T.B. Harms, 1951) Partiturs: Missing Parts: Tams-Witmark Music Library The Library of Congress has a large collection of Porter's lyric worksheets and sketches from KISS ME, KATE.
Rental Status	Tams-Witmark rents the original show.
Music Publisher	Chappell Music
Information	Tams-Witmark Music Library

Kiss Me, Kate (1948)

Overture
Porter/Porter
Orchestrator: Unknown

Location of
- Composer's manuscript: -0-
- Sheet music: Not published separately
- Most complete music: CPT (pv score); LoC (pv score); NYPL (pv score); TW (pv score)
- Most complete lyric: INST
- Original partitur: -0-
- Original parts: TW

Another Op'nin', Another Show
Porter/Porter
Orchestrator: Unknown

Location of
- Composer's manuscript: -0-
- Sheet music: CPT, LoC, NYPL, Y
- Most complete music: CPT (sm, pv score); LoC (sm, pv score); NYPL (sm, pv score); Y (sm); TW (pv score)
- Most complete lyric: CPT (sm, pv score, scr); LoC (sm, pv score); NYPL (sm, pv score); Y (sm); TW (pv score, scr); CLCP
- Original partitur: -0-
- Original parts: TW

Why Can't You Behave?
Porter/Porter
Orchestrator: Unknown

Location of
- Composer's manuscript: -0-
- Sheet music: CPT, LoC, NYPL, Y
- Most complete music: CPT (pv score); LoC (pv score); NYPL (pv score); TW (pv score)
- Most complete lyric: CPT (pv score, scr); LoC (pv score); NYPL (pv score); TW (pv score, scr); CLCP
- Original partitur: -0-
- Original parts: TW

Wunderbar
Porter/Porter
Orchestrator: Unknown

Location of
- Composer's manuscript: -0-
- Sheet music: CPT, LoC, NYPL, Y
- Most complete music: CPT (pv score); LoC (pv score); NYPL (pv score); TW (pv score)
- Most complete lyric: CPT (pv score, scr); LoC (pv score); NYPL (pv score); CPT (pv score, scr); CLCP
- Original partitur: -0-
- Original parts: TW

So in Love
Porter/Porter
Orchestrator: Unknown

Location of
- Composer's manuscript: -0-
- Sheet music: CPT, LoC, NYPL, Y
- Most complete music: CPT (sm, pv score); LoC (sm, pv score); NYPL (sm, pv score); Y (sm); TW (pv score)
- Most complete lyric: CPT (sm, pv score, scr); LoC (sm, pv score); NYPL (sm, pv score); Y (sm); TW (pv score, scr); CLCP
- Original partitur: -0-
- Original parts: TW

We Open in Venice
Porter/Porter
Orchestrator: Unknown

Location of
- Composer's manuscript: -0-
- Sheet music: CPT, LoC, NYPL, Y
- Most complete music: CPT (pv score); LoC (pv score); NYPL (pv score); TW (pv score)
- Most complete lyric: CPT (pv score, scr); LoC (pv score); NYPL (pv score); TW (pv score, scr); CLCP
- Original partitur: -0-
- Original parts: TW

Includes "Padua Street Scene."

Dance: End Padua Street Scene
Porter
Orchestrator: Unknown

Location of   - Composer's manuscript: -0-
       - Sheet music: Not published separately
       - Most complete music: CPT (pv score);
          LoC (pv score); NYPL (pv score);
          TW (pv score)
       - Most complete lyric: INST
       - Original partitur: -0-
       - Original parts: TW

I've Come to Wive It Wealthily in Padua
Porter/Porter
Orchestrator: Unknown

Location of   - Composer's manuscript: -0-
       - Sheet music: CPT, LoC, NYPL, Y
       - Most complete music: CPT (sm, pv score);
          LoC (sm, pv score); NYPL (sm,
          pv score); Y (sm); TW (pv score)
       - Most complete lyric: CPT (sm, pv score,
          scr); LoC (sm, pv score); NYPL (sm,
          pv score); Y (sm); TW (pv score, scr);
          CLCP
       - Original partitur: -0-
       - Original parts: TW

Tom, Dick or Harry
Porter/Porter
Orchestrator: Unknown

Location of   - Composer's manuscript: -0-
       - Sheet music: CPT, LoC, NYPL, Y
       - Most complete music: CPT (sm, pv score);
          LoC (sm, pv score); NYPL (sm,
          pv score); Y (sm); TW (pv score)
       - Most complete lyric: CPT (sm, pv score,
          scr); LoC (sm, pv score); NYPL (sm,
          pv score); Y (sm); TW (pv score, scr);
          CLCP
       - Original partitur: -0-
       - Original parts: TW

I Hate Men
Porter/Porter
Orchestrator: Unknown

Location of   - Composer's manuscript: -0-
       - Sheet music: CPT, LoC, NYPL, Y
       - Most complete music: CPT (sm, pv score,
          pv-l); LoC (sm, pv score); NYPL (sm,
          pv score); Y (sm); TW (pv score)
       - Most complete lyric: CPT (pv-l); CLCP
       - Original partitur: -0-
       - Original parts: TW

Rose Dance
Porter
Orchestrator: Unknown

Location of   - Composer's manuscript: -0-
       - Sheet music: Not published separately
       - Most complete music: CPT (pv score);
          LoC (pv score); NYPL (pv score);
          TW (pv score)
       - Most complete lyric: INST
       - Original partitur: -0-
       - Original parts: TW

Were Thine That Special Face
Porter/Porter
Orchestrator: Unknown

Location of   - Composer's manuscript: -0-
       - Sheet music: CPT, LoC, NYPL, Y
       - Most complete music: CPT (sm, pv score);
          LoC (sm, pv score); NYPL (sm,
          pv score); Y (sm); TW (pv score)
       - Most complete lyric: CPT (sm, pv score,
          scr); LoC (sm, pv score); NYPL (sm,
          pv score); Y (sm); TW (pv score, scr);
          CLCP
       - Original partitur: -0-
       - Original parts: TW

Kiss Me, Kate (1948)

I Sing of Love
Porter/Porter
Orchestrator: Unknown

Location of
- Composer's manuscript: -0-
- Sheet music: CPT, LoC, NYPL, Y
- Most complete music: CPT (pv score, pv-l); LoC (pv score); NYPL (pv score); TW (pv score)
- Most complete lyric: CPT (pv-l); CLCP
- Original partitur: -0-
- Original parts: TW

In the show, the song is entitled "We Sing of Love."

Entr'acte
Porter/Porter
Orchestrator: Unknown

Location of
- Composer's manuscript: -0-
- Sheet music: Not published separately
- Most complete music: CPT (pv score); LoC (pv score); NYPL (pv score); TW (pv score)
- Most complete lyric: INST
- Original partitur: -0-
- Original parts: TW

Tarantella
Porter
Orchestrator: Unknown

Location of
- Composer's manuscript: -0-
- Sheet music: Not published separately
- Most complete music: CPT (pv score); LoC (pv score); NYPL (pv score); TW (pv score)
- Most complete lyric: INST
- Original partitur: -0-
- Original parts: TW

Too Darn Hot
Porter/Porter
Orchestrator: Unknown

Location of
- Composer's manuscript: -0-
- Sheet music: CPT, LoC, NYPL, Y
- Most complete music: CPT (pv score, pv-l); LoC (pv score); NYPL (pv score); TW (pv score)
- Most complete lyric: CPT (pv score, pv-l, scr); LoC (pv score); NYPL (pv score); TW (pv score); CLCP
- Original partitur: -0-
- Original parts: TW

Finale Act I ["So kiss me, Kate, thou lovely loon..."]
Porter/Porter
Orchestrator: Unknown

Location of
- Composer's manuscript: -0-
- Sheet music: Not published separately
- Most complete music: CPT (pv score); LoC (pv score); NYPL (pv score); TW (pv score)
- Most complete lyric: CPT (pv score); LoC (pv score); NYPL (pv score); TW (pv score); CLCP
- Original partitur: -0-
- Original parts: TW

Where Is the Life That Late I Led?
Porter/Porter
Orchestrator: Unknown

Location of
- Composer's manuscript: -0-
- Sheet music: CPT, LoC, NYPL, Y
- Most complete music: CPT (pv score); LoC (pv score); NYPL (pv score); TW (pv score)
- Most complete lyric: CPT (pv score, scr); LoC (pv score); NYPL (pv score); TW (pv score, scr); CLCP
- Original partitur: -0-
- Original parts: TW

Cole Porter

Always True to You in My Fashion

Porter/Porter
Orchestrator: Unknown

Location of   - Composer's manuscript: -0-
- Sheet music: CPT, LoC, NYPL, Y
- Most complete music: CPT (pv score
  & sm); LoC (pv score & sm);
  NYPL (pv score & sm)
- Most complete lyric: CPT (pv score
  & sm); LoC (pv score & sm);
  NYPL (pv score & sm)
- Original partitur: -0-
- Original parts: TW

The piano-vocal score has the show version, which begins
with a reprise of "Why Can't You Behave?"; the sheet
music has an entirely different verse.

Bianca

Porter/Porter
Orchestrator: Unknown

Location of   - Composer's manuscript: -0-
- Sheet music: CPT, LoC, NYPL, Y
- Most complete music: CPT (sm, pv score,
  pv-l); LoC (sm, pv score); NYPL (sm,
  pv score); Y (sm); TW (pv score)
- Most complete lyric: CPT (pv score
  & pv-l)
- Original partitur: -0-
- Original parts: TW

Brush Up Your Shakespeare

Porter/Porter
Orchestrator: Unknown

Location of   - Composer's manuscript: -0-
- Sheet music: LoC, NYPL, Y, CPT (x)
- Most complete music: CPT (pv score);
  LoC (pv score); NYPL (pv score);
  TW (pv score)
- Most complete lyric: CPT (pv score, scr);
  LoC (pv score); NYPL (pv score);
  TW (pv score, scr); CLCP
- Original partitur: -0-
- Original parts: TW

I Am Ashamed That Women Are So Simple

Porter/Shakespeare & Porter
Orchestrator: Unknown

Location of   - Composer's manuscript: -0-
- Sheet music: CPT, LoC, NYPL, Y
- Most complete music: CPT (sm, pv score);
  LoC (sm, pv score); NYPL (sm,
  pv score); Y (sm); TW (pv score)
- Most complete lyric: CPT (sm, pv score,
  scr); LoC (sm, pv score); NYPL (sm,
  pv score); Y (sm); TW (pv score, scr);
  CLCP
- Original partitur: -0-
- Original parts: TW

Finale Act II ["So kiss me, Kate, and twice and thrice..."]

Porter/Porter
Orchestrator: Unknown

Location of   - Composer's manuscript: -0-
- Sheet music: Not published separately
- Most complete music: CPT (pv score);
  LoC (pv score); NYPL (pv score);
  TW (pv score)
- Most complete lyric: CPT (pv score, scr);
  LoC (pv score); NYPL (pv score);
  TW (pv score, scr); CLCP
- Original partitur: -0-
- Original parts: TW

It Was Great Fun the First Time

Porter/Porter
Orchestrator: Unknown

Location of   - Composer's manuscript: -0-
- Sheet music: Unpublished
- Most complete music: CPT (pv-l);
  LoC (pv-l)
- Most complete lyric: CPT (pv-l);
  LoC (pv-l); CLCP
- Original partitur: -0-
- Original parts: -0-

Dropped in rehearsal.

Kiss Me, Kate (1948)

We Shall Never Be Younger

Porter/Porter

Orchestrator: Unknown

Location of
- Composer's manuscript: -0-
- Sheet music: Unpublished
- Most complete music: CPT (pv-l)
- Most complete lyric: CPT (pv-l); CLCP
- Original partitur: -0-
- Original parts: -0-

Unused. The music to the release was later used for the release of "No Lover" in OUT OF THIS WORLD (1950).

I'm Afraid, Sweetheart, I Love You

Porter/Porter

Orchestrator: Unknown

Location of
- Composer's manuscript: -0-
- Sheet music: Not published separately
- Most complete music: CPT (pv-l); LoC (pv-l)
- Most complete lyric: CPT (pv-l); LoC (pv-l); CLCP
- Original partitur: -0-
- Original parts: -0-

Unused. Initial publication in The Unpublished Cole Porter (Simon & Schuster: 1975).

Woman's Career, A

Porter/Porter

Orchestrator: Unknown

Location of
- Composer's manuscript: -0-
- Sheet music: Unpublished
- Most complete music: CPT (pv-l); LoC (pv-l)
- Most complete lyric: CPT (pv-l); LoC (pv-l); CLCP
- Original partitur: -0-
- Original parts: -0-

Dropped in rehearsal.

If Ever Married I'm

Porter/Porter

Orchestrator: Unknown

Location of
- Composer's manuscript: -0-
- Sheet music: Unpublished
- Most complete music: CPT (pv-l); LoC (pv-l)
- Most complete lyric: CPT (pv-l); LoC (pv-l); CLCP
- Original partitur: -0-
- Original parts: -0-

Dropped in rehearsal.

What Does Your Servant Dream About?

Porter/Porter

Orchestrator: Unknown

Location of
- Composer's manuscript: -0-
- Sheet music: Unpublished
- Most complete music: CPT (pv-l)
- Most complete lyric: CPT (pv-l); CLCP
- Original partitur: -0-
- Original parts: -0-

Unused.

Harlequin Ballerina

Porter

Orchestrator: Bennett

Location of
- Composer's manuscript: -0-
- Sheet music: Unpublished
- Most complete music: TW (ptr)
- Most complete lyric: INST
- Original partitur: TW
- Original parts: -0-

A deleted section of the "We Open in Venice" dance.

OUT OF THIS WORLD

Music	COLE PORTER
Lyrics	COLE PORTER

Musical comedy in two acts. Opened December 21, 1950 in New York and ran 157 performances (World premiere: November 4, 1950 in Philadelphia). Libretto by Dwight Taylor and Reginald Lawrence. Produced by Saint Subber and Lemuel Ayers. Directed by Agnes de Mille. Choreographed by Hanya Holm. Musical direction by Pembroke Davenport. Orchestrations by Robert Russell Bennett. Dance music arranged by Genevieve Pitot. Incidental music arranged by Trudi Rittman.

Synopsis and Production Information

Jupiter, father of the gods, picks Helen Kenyon, a fair American mortal, as his latest conquest. His son Mercury escorts her to an inn near Athens, where Jupiter woos her in the guise of Helen's husband, Art. The next day, Helen realizes she has been deceived; meeting the god face to face, she rejects his offer of immortality, insisting that her husband's love is all she needs.

The largest role in the show is that of Juno, Jupiter's wife, who traipses about the Greek countryside in various ineffectual mortal disguises searching for her cheating husband. Other characters include Niki Scolianos, American gangster turned innkeeper, Niki's ambitious niece Chloe, and Night, a female dancer. There is a full singing and dancing ensemble.

Comments

In the original production, Juno was played by Charlotte Greenwood.

Orchestration

Reed I (Clarinet, Alto Sax); Reed II (Clarinet, Alto Sax, Bass Clarinet); Reed III (Flute, Piccolo, Clarinet, Tenor Sax); Reed IV (Oboe, English Horn, Clarinet, Tenor Sax); Reed V (Clarinet, Bassoon, Baritone Sax); Horn I II; Trumpet I II; Trombone I; Trombone II; Percussion; Harp I; Harp II; Guitar I; Guitar II; Piano; Violin A; Violin B; Violin C; Violin D; Viola; Cello; Bass

Location of Original Materials

Script: Cole Porter Trusts
Piano-vocal score: Tams-Witmark Music Library
Partiturs: Missing
Parts: Tams-Witmark Music Library

Rental Status

Tams-Witmark currently rents a 1956 revision; it consists of a skeletal book, the original score (reinstating "From This Moment On" and "You Don't Remind Me"), and the original parts (minus the Harp II, Guitar II, and Violin D books).

Music Publisher

Chappell Music

Information

Tams Witmark Music Library, Cole Porter Trusts

Out of This World (1950)

Overture

Porter/Porter

Orchestrator: Unknown

Location of
- Composer's manuscript: -0-
- Sheet music: Unpublished
- Most complete music: TW (pv score)
- Most complete lyric: INST
- Original partitur: -0-
- Original parts: TW

Prologue ["Ladies and gentlemen, this costume may strike you as odd..."]

Porter/Porter

Orchestrator: Unknown

Location of
- Composer's manuscript: -0-
- Sheet music: Unpublished
- Most complete music: TW (pv score)
- Most complete lyric: TW (pv score);
     CPT (scr); CLCP
- Original partitur: -0-
- Original parts: TW

I Jupiter, I Rex

Porter/Porter

Orchestrator: Unknown

Location of
- Composer's manuscript: Y
- Sheet music: Unpublished
- Most complete music: TW (pv score)
- Most complete lyric: TW (pv score);
     CPT (scr); CLCP
- Original partitur: -0-
- Original parts: TW

Use Your Imagination

Porter/Porter

Orchestrator: Unknown

Location of
- Composer's manuscript: -0-
- Sheet music: CPT, LoC, NYPL, Y
- Most complete music: CPT (sm);
     LoC (sm); NYPL (sm); Y (sm)
- Most complete lyric: CLCP
- Original partitur: -0-
- Original parts: TW

The verse, which was not performed in the original production, is not included in the script, piano-vocal score, or parts.

Hail, Hail, Hail

Porter/Porter

Orchestrator: Unknown

Location of
- Composer's manuscript: -0-
- Sheet music: Unpublished
- Most complete music: TW (pv score)
- Most complete lyric: TW (pv score);
     CPT (scr); CLCP
- Original partitur: -0-
- Original parts: TW

I Got Beauty

Porter/Porter

Orchestrator: Unknown

Location of
- Composer's manuscript: -0-
- Sheet music: Unpublished
- Most complete music: TW (pv score)
- Most complete lyric: TW (pv score);
     CPT (scr); CLCP
- Original partitur: -0-
- Original parts: TW

Maiden Fair
Porter/Porter
Orchestrator: Unknown

Location of - Composer's manuscript: -0-
- Sheet music: Unpublished
- Most complete music: TW (pv score);
CPT (pv-l)
- Most complete lyric: CLCP
- Original partitur: -0-
- Original parts: TW

They Couldn't Compare to You
Porter/Porter
Orchestrator: Unknown

Location of - Composer's manuscript: -0-
- Sheet music: Unpublished
- Most complete music: TW (pv score)
- Most complete lyric: TW (pv score);
CPT (scr); CLCP
- Original partitur: -0-
- Original parts: TW

Where, Oh Where?
Porter/Porter
Orchestrator: Unknown

Location of - Composer's manuscript: -0-
- Sheet music: CPT, LoC, NYPL, Y
- Most complete music: CPT (sm);
LoC (sm); NYPL (sm); Y (sm);
TW (pv score)
- Most complete lyric: CLCP
- Original partitur: -0-
- Original parts: TW

The lyric to the second refrain was not performed in the original production.

What Do You Think About Men?
Porter/Porter
Orchestrator: Unknown

Location of - Composer's manuscript: -0-
- Sheet music: Unpublished
- Most complete music: TW (pv score);
CPT (pv-l)
- Most complete lyric: TW (pv score);
CPT (pv-l, scr); CLCP
- Original partitur: -0-
- Original parts: TW

I Am Loved
Porter/Porter
Orchestrator: Unknown

Location of - Composer's manuscript: -0-
- Sheet music: CPT, LoC, NYPL, Y
- Most complete music: CPT (sm);
LoC (sm); NYPL (sm); Y (sm);
TW (pv score)
- Most complete lyric: CPT (sm, scr);
LoC (sm); NYPL (sm); Y (sm);
TW (pv score); CLCP
- Original partitur: -0-
- Original parts: TW

Dance of Night
Porter & Pitot
Orchestrator: Unknown

Location of - Composer's manuscript: -0-
- Sheet music: Unpublished
- Most complete music: TW (pv score)
- Most complete lyric: INST
- Original partitur: -0-
- Original parts: TW

Out of This World (1950)

I Sleep Easier Now

Porter/Porter
Orchestrator: Unknown

Location of   - Composer's manuscript: -0-
              - Sheet music: Unpublished
              - Most complete music: TW (pv score);
                  CPT (pv-l)
              - Most complete lyric: TW (pv score);
                  CPT (scr); CLCP
              - Original partitur: -0-
              - Original parts: TW

Added during the pre-Broadway tryout.

Climb Up the Mountain

Porter/Porter
Orchestrator: Unknown

Location of   - Composer's manuscript: -0-
              - Sheet music: Unpublished
              - Most complete music: TW (pv score)
              - Most complete lyric: TW (pv score);
                  CPT (scr); CLCP
              - Original partitur: -0-
              - Original parts: TW

Ballet

Porter & Pitot
Orchestrator: Unknown

Location of   - Composer's manuscript: -0-
              - Sheet music: Unpublished
              - Most complete music: TW (pv score)
              - Most complete lyric: INST
              - Original partitur: -0-
              - Original parts: TW

No Lover

Porter/Porter
Orchestrator: Unknown

Location of   - Composer's manuscript: -0-
              - Sheet music: CPT, LoC, NYPL, Y
              - Most complete music: CPT (sm);
                  LoC (sm); NYPL (sm); Y (sm);
                  TW (pv score)
              - Most complete lyric: CLCP
              - Original partitur: -0-
              - Original parts: TW

Entr'acte

Porter/Porter
Orchestrator: Unknown

Location of   - Composer's manuscript: -0-
              - Sheet music: Unpublished
              - Most complete music: TW (pv score)
              - Most complete lyric: INST
              - Original partitur: -0-
              - Original parts: TW

Cherry Pies Ought to Be You

Porter/Porter
Orchestrator: Unknown

Location of   - Composer's manuscript: -0-
              - Sheet music: CPT, LoC, NYPL, Y
              - Most complete music: CPT (sm);
                  LoC (sm); NYPL (sm); Y (sm)
              - Most complete lyric: CLCP
              - Original partitur: -0-
              - Original parts: TW

The verse, which was not performed in the original
production, is not included in the script, piano-vocal
score, or parts.

Hark to the Song of the Night
Porter/Porter
Orchestrator: Unknown

Location of   - Composer's manuscript: -0-
    - Sheet music: CPT, LoC, NYPL, Y
    - Most complete music: CPT (sm);
        LoC (sm); NYPL (sm); Y (sm);
        TW (pv score)
    - Most complete lyric: CPT (sm, scr);
        LoC (sm); NYPL (sm); Y (sm);
        TW (pv score); CLCP
    - Original partitur: -0-
    - Original parts: TW

From This Moment On
Porter/Porter
Orchestrator: Unknown

Location of   - Composer's manuscript: -0-
    - Sheet music: CPT, LoC, NYPL, Y
    - Most complete music: TW (pv score)
    - Most complete lyric: TW (pv score);
        CPT (scr); CLCP
    - Original partitur: -0-
    - Original parts: TW

Dropped during the pre-Broadway tryout, but later used in the 1953 film version of KISS ME, KATE. The patter section was not published.

Peasant Dance
Porter & Pitot/Porter
Orchestrator: Unknown

Location of   - Composer's manuscript: -0-
    - Sheet music: Unpublished
    - Most complete music: TW (pv score)
    - Most complete lyric: TW (pv score)
    - Original partitur: -0-
    - Original parts: TW

Based primarily on "Maiden Fair."

We're On the Road to Athens
Porter/Porter
Orchestrator: Unknown

Location of   - Composer's manuscript: -0-
    - Sheet music: Unpublished
    - Most complete music: CPT (pv-l)
    - Most complete lyric: CPT (pv-l); CLCP
    - Original partitur: -0-
    - Original parts: -0-

Dropped during the pre-Broadway tryout.

Nobody's Chasing Me
Porter/Porter
Orchestrator: Unknown

Location of   - Composer's manuscript: -0-
    - Sheet music: CPT, LoC, NYPL, Y
    - Most complete music: CPT (sm);
        LoC (sm); NYPL (sm); Y (sm);
        TW (pv score)
    - Most complete lyric: CLCP
    - Original partitur: -0-
    - Original parts: TW

You Don't Remind Me
Porter/Porter
Orchestrator: Unknown

Location of   - Composer's manuscript: -0-
    - Sheet music: CPT, LoC, NYPL, Y
    - Most complete music: CPT (sm);
        LoC (sm); NYPL (sm); Y (sm)
    - Most complete lyric: CPT (sm);
        LoC (sm); NYPL (sm); Y (sm); CLCP
    - Original partitur: -0-
    - Original parts: TW

Dropped during the pre-Broadway tryout. The verse was not performed in the original production.

Out of This World (1950)

Hush, Hush, Hush
    Porter/Porter
    Orchestrator: Unknown

    Location of   - Composer's manuscript: -0-
               - Sheet music: Unpublished
               - Most complete music: CPT (pv-I)
               - Most complete lyric: CPT (pv-I); CLCP
               - Original partitur: -0-
               - Original parts: -0-

Dropped during the pre-Broadway tryout.

Away From It All
    Porter/Porter
    Orchestrator: Unknown

    Location of   - Composer's manuscript: -0-
               - Sheet music: Unpublished
               - Most complete music: CPT (pv-I)
               - Most complete lyric: CPT (pv-I); CLCP
               - Original partitur: -0-
               - Original parts: -0-

Unused.

Midsummer Night
    Porter/Porter
    Orchestrator: Unknown

    Location of   - Composer's manuscript: -0-
               - Sheet music: Unpublished
               - Most complete music: CPT (pv-I);
                    LoC (pv-I)
               - Most complete lyric: CPT (pv-I);
                    LoC (pv-I); CLCP
               - Original partitur: -0-
               - Original parts: -0-

Unused.

Oh, It Must Be Fun
    Porter/Porter
    Orchestrator: Unknown

    Location of   - Composer's manuscript: -0-
               - Sheet music: Not published separately
               - Most complete music: CPT (pv-I);
                    LoC (pv-I)
               - Most complete lyric: CPT (pv-I);
                    LoC (pv-I); CLCP
               - Original partitur: -0-
               - Original parts: -0-

Unused. Initial publication in The Unpublished Cole Porter (Simon & Schuster: 1975).

To Hell With Ev'rything But Us
    Porter/Porter
    Orchestrator: Unknown

    Location of   - Composer's manuscript: -0-
               - Sheet music: Unpublished
               - Most complete music: CPT (pv-I)
               - Most complete lyric: CLCP
               - Original partitur: -0-
               - Original parts: -0-

Unused.

Tonight I Love You More
    Porter/Porter
    Orchestrator: Unknown

    Location of   - Composer's manuscript: -0-
               - Sheet music: Unpublished
               - Most complete music: CPT (pv-I)
               - Most complete lyric: CPT (pv-I); CLCP
               - Original partitur: -0-
               - Original parts: -0-

Unused.

Why Do You Wanta Hurt Me So?
    Porter/Porter
    Orchestrator: Unknown

    Location of   - Composer's manuscript: -0-
                 - Sheet music: See note
                 - Most complete music: CPT (pv-l);
                    LoC (prof)
                 - Most complete lyric: CLCP
                 - Original partitur: -0-
                 - Original parts: -0-

Unused. Issued only as a professional copy.

Lock Up Your Chickens
    Porter/Porter
    Orchestrator: Unknown

    Location of   - Composer's manuscript: -0-
                 - Sheet music: Unpublished
                 - Most complete music: -0-
                 - Most complete lyric: CLCP
                 - Original partitur: -0-
                 - Original parts: -0-

Unused. Only a lyric fragment survives.

CAN-CAN

Music COLE PORTER
Lyrics COLE PORTER

Musical comedy in two acts. Opened May 7, 1953 in New York and ran 892 performances (World premiere: March 23, 1953 in Philadelphia). Libretto by Abe Burrows. Produced by Cy Feuer and Ernest Martin. Directed by Abe Burrows. Choreographed by Michael Kidd. Musical direction by Milton Rosenstock. Orchestrations by Philip J. Lang. Dance music arranged by Genevieve Pitot.

Synopsis and Production Information	In turn-of-the-century Paris, Pistache, proud owner of the infamous Bal du Paradis, spars with Aristide Forestiere, a self-righteous judge determined to close all Parisian dancehalls. Eventually, the pair fall in love, and Aristide concedes that "obscenity is in the eye of the beholder."
	Other principals include Claudine (a dancer) and her cowardly boyfriend, Boris. The show requires a full singing and dancing ensemble.
Orchestration	Reed I (Flute, Piccolo, Clarinet); Reed II (Oboe, English Horn); Reed III (Eb Clarinet, Bb Clarinet, Bass Clarinet, Alto Sax); Reed IV (Flute, Clarinet); Reed V (Clarinet, Bassoon); Horn I II; Horn III; Trumpet I II; Trombone (Euphonium opt.); Percussion; Guitar; Piano/Celeste; Violin A/C (dbl. Accordion); Violin B/D; Viola; Cello; Bass (Tuba opt.)
Comments	In the original production, Pistache was played by Lilo, Claudine by Gwen Verdon.
Location of Original Materials	Script: Tams-Witmark Music Library (all lyrics), Cole Porter Trusts (all lyrics) Piano-vocal score: Tams-Witmark Music Library, Cole Porter Trusts, Library of Congress, New York Public Library (Published: Chappell & Co., 1954) Partiturs: Missing Parts: Tams-Witmark Music Library
Rental Status	Tams-Witmark rents the original show.
Music Publisher	Chappell Music
Information	Tams-Witmark Music Library

Overture

Porter/Porter

Orchestrator: Unknown

Location of
- Composer's manuscript: -0-
- Sheet music: Not published separately
- Most complete music: CPT (pv score); LoC (pv score); NYPL (pv score); TW (pv score)
- Most complete lyric: INST
- Original partitur: -0-
- Original parts: TW

C'est Magnifique

Porter/Porter

Orchestrator: Unknown

Location of
- Composer's manuscript: -0-
- Sheet music: CPT, LoC, NYPL, Y
- Most complete music: CPT (sm, pv score); LoC (sm, pv score); NYPL (sm, pv score); Y (sm); TW (pv score)
- Most complete lyric: CPT (sm, pv score, scr); LoC (sm, pv score); NYPL (sm, pv score); Y (sm); TW (pv score, scr); CLCP
- Original partitur: -0-
- Original parts: TW

Maidens Typical of France

Porter/Porter

Orchestrator: Unknown

Location of
- Composer's manuscript: -0-
- Sheet music: Not published separately
- Most complete music: CPT (pv score); LoC (pv score); NYPL (pv score); TW (pv score)
- Most complete lyric: CLCP
- Original partitur: -0-
- Original parts: TW

Quadrille

Porter & Pitot/Porter

Orchestrator: Unknown

Location of
- Composer's manuscript: -0-
- Sheet music: Not published separately
- Most complete music: CPT (pv score); LoC (pv score); NYPL (pv score); TW (pv score)
- Most complete lyric: INST
- Original partitur: -0-
- Original parts: TW

Never Give Anything Away

Porter/Porter

Orchestrator: Unknown

Location of
- Composer's manuscript: -0-
- Sheet music: CPT, LoC, NYPL, Y
- Most complete music: CPT (sm, pv score); LoC (sm, pv score); NYPL (sm, pv score); Y (sm); TW (pv score)
- Most complete lyric: CPT (pv score, scr); LoC (pv score); NYPL (pv score); TW (pv score, scr); CLCP
- Original partitur: -0-
- Original parts: TW

Come Along With Me

Porter/Porter

Orchestrator: Unknown

Location of
- Composer's manuscript: -0-
- Sheet music: CPT, LoC, NYPL, Y
- Most complete music: CPT (sm, pv score); LoC (sm, pv score); NYPL (sm, pv score); Y (sm); TW (pv score)
- Most complete lyric: CPT (pv score, scr); LoC (pv score); NYPL (pv score); TW (pv score, scr); CLCP
- Original partitur: -0-
- Original parts: TW

Can-Can (1953)

Live and Let Live
Porter/Porter
Orchestrator: Unknown

Location of — Composer's manuscript: -0-
— Sheet music: CPT, LoC, NYPL, Y
— Most complete music: CPT (sm, pv score);
    LoC (sm, pv score); NYPL (sm,
    pv score); Y (sm); TW (pv score)
— Most complete lyric: CLCP
— Original partitur: -0-
— Original parts: TW

Montmart'
Porter/Porter
Orchestrator: Unknown

Location of — Composer's manuscript: -0-
— Sheet music: CPT, LoC, NYPL, Y
— Most complete music: CPT (sm, pv score);
    LoC (sm, pv score); NYPL (sm,
    pv score); Y (sm); TW (pv score)
— Most complete lyric: CLCP
— Original partitur: -0-
— Original parts: TW

I Am in Love
Porter/Porter
Orchestrator: Unknown

Location of — Composer's manuscript: -0-
— Sheet music: CPT, LoC, NYPL, Y
— Most complete music: CPT (sm);
    LoC (sm); NYPL (sm); Y (sm)
— Most complete lyric: CPT (sm);
    LoC (sm); NYPL (sm); Y (sm); CLCP
— Original partitur: -0-
— Original parts: TW

The verse was not performed in the original production.

Garden of Eden Ballet
Porter & Pitot
Orchestrator: Unknown

Location of — Composer's manuscript: -0-
— Sheet music: Not published separately
— Most complete music: CPT (pv score);
    LoC (pv score); NYPL (pv score);
    TW (pv score)
— Most complete lyric: INST
— Original partitur: -0-
— Original parts: TW

If You Loved Me Truly
Porter/Porter
Orchestrator: Unknown

Location of — Composer's manuscript: -0-
— Sheet music: CPT, LoC, NYPL, Y
— Most complete music: CPT (pv score
    & pv-l)
— Most complete lyric: CPT (pv score
    & pv-l); CLCP
— Original partitur: -0-
— Original parts: TW

The published piano-vocal score is missing a passage at
the top of the number.

Eve's Dance
Porter & Pitot
Orchestrator: Unknown

Location of — Composer's manuscript: -0-
— Sheet music: Not published separately
— Most complete music: CPT (pv score);
    LoC (pv score); NYPL (pv score);
    TW (pv score)
— Most complete lyric: INST
— Original partitur: -0-
— Original parts: TW

Allez-Vous-En
Porter/Porter
Orchestrator: Unknown

Location of - Composer's manuscript: -0-
- Sheet music: CPT, LoC, NYPL, Y
- Most complete music: CPT (sm);
    LoC (sm); NYPL (sm); Y (sm)
- Most complete lyric: CPT (sm);
    LoC (sm); NYPL (sm); Y (sm); CLCP
- Original partitur: -0-
- Original parts: TW

The verse was not performed in the original production.

Entr'acte
Porter/Porter
Orchestrator: Unknown

Location of - Composer's manuscript: -0-
- Sheet music: Not published separately
- Most complete music: CPT (pv score);
    LoC (pv score); NYPL (pv score);
    TW (pv score)
- Most complete lyric: INST
- Original partitur: -0-
- Original parts: TW

Never, Never Be an Artist
Porter/Porter
Orchestrator: Unknown

Location of - Composer's manuscript: -0-
- Sheet music: Not published separately
- Most complete music: CPT (pv score);
    LoC (pv score); NYPL (pv score);
    TW (pv score)
- Most complete lyric: CPT (pv score, scr);
    LoC (pv score); NYPL (pv score);
    TW (pv score, scr); CLCP
- Original partitur: -0-
- Original parts: TW

It's All Right With Me
Porter/Porter
Orchestrator: Unknown

Location of - Composer's manuscript: -0-
- Sheet music: CPT, LoC, NYPL, Y
- Most complete music: CPT (sm, pv score);
    LoC (sm, pv score); NYPL (sm,
    pv score); Y (sm); TW (pv score)
- Most complete lyric: CPT (sm, pv score,
    scr); LoC (sm, pv score); NYPL (sm,
    pv score); Y (sm); TW (pv score, scr);
    CLCP
- Original partitur: -0-
- Original parts: TW

Ev'ry Man Is a Stupid Man
Porter/Porter
Orchestrator: Unknown

Location of - Composer's manuscript: -0-
- Sheet music: Not published separately
- Most complete music: CPT (pv score,
    pv-l); LoC (pv score);
    NYPL (pv score); TW (pv score)
- Most complete lyric: CPT (pv score
    & pv-l); CLCP
- Original partitur: -0-
- Original parts: TW

Apache Dance
Porter & Pitot
Orchestrator: Unknown

Location of - Composer's manuscript: -0-
- Sheet music: Not published separately
- Most complete music: CPT (pv score);
    LoC (pv score); NYPL (pv score);
    TW (pv score)
- Most complete lyric: INST
- Original partitur: -0-
- Original parts: TW

Can-Can (1953)

I Love Paris
    Porter/Porter
    Orchestrator: Unknown

    Location of   - Composer's manuscript: -0-
                - Sheet music: CPT, LoC, NYPL, Y
                - Most complete music: CPT (sm, pv score);
                    LoC (sm, pv score); NYPL (sm,
                    pv score); Y (sm); TW (pv score)
                - Most complete lyric: CPT (sm, pv score,
                    scr); LoC (sm, pv score); NYPL (sm,
                    pv score); Y (sm); TW (pv score, scr);
                    CLCP
                - Original partitur: -0-
                - Original parts: TW

I Shall Positively Pay You Next Monday
    Porter/Porter
    Orchestrator: Unknown

    Location of   - Composer's manuscript: -0-
                - Sheet music: Unpublished
                - Most complete music: CPT (pv-l)
                - Most complete lyric: CPT (pv-l); CLCP
                - Original partitur: -0-
                - Original parts: -0-

Dropped during the Philadelphia tryout.

Can-Can
    Porter/Porter
    Orchestrator: Unknown

    Location of   - Composer's manuscript: -0-
                - Sheet music: CPT, LoC, NYPL, Y
                - Most complete music: CPT (sm);
                    LoC (sm); NYPL (sm); Y (sm)
                - Most complete lyric: CLCP
                - Original partitur: -0-
                - Original parts: TW

The verse was not performed in the original production.

Man Must His Honor Defend, A
    Porter/Porter
    Orchestrator: Unknown

    Location of   - Composer's manuscript: -0-
                - Sheet music: Unpublished
                - Most complete music: CPT (pv-l)
                - Most complete lyric: CPT (pv-l); CLCP
                - Original partitur: -0-
                - Original parts: -0-

Dropped during the Philadelphia tryout.

Law, The
    Porter/Porter
    Orchestrator: Unknown

    Location of   - Composer's manuscript: -0-
                - Sheet music: Unpublished
                - Most complete music: CPT (pv-l)
                - Most complete lyric: CLCP
                - Original partitur: -0-
                - Original parts: -0-

Dropped during the Philadephia tryout.

Nothing to Do But Work
    Porter/Porter
    Orchestrator: Unknown

    Location of   - Composer's manuscript: -0-
                - Sheet music: Unpublished
                - Most complete music: CPT (pv-l)
                - Most complete lyric: CPT (pv-l); CLCP
                - Original partitur: -0-
                - Original parts: -0-

Unused.

Opening Laundry Scene
Porter/Porter
Orchestrator: Unknown

Location of   - Composer's manuscript: -0-
          - Sheet music: Unpublished
          - Most complete music: CPT (pv-l)
          - Most complete lyric: CPT (pv-l); CLCP
          - Original partitur: -0-
          - Original parts: -0-

Unused.

What a Fair Thing Is a Woman
Porter/Porter
Orchestrator: Unknown

Location of   - Composer's manuscript: -0-
          - Sheet music: Unpublished
          - Most complete music: CPT (pv-l)
          - Most complete lyric: CPT (pv-l); CLCP
          - Original partitur: -0-
          - Original parts: -0-

Unused.

Her Heart Was in Her Work
Porter/Porter
Orchestrator: Unknown

Location of   - Composer's manuscript: -0-
          - Sheet music: Unpublished
          - Most complete music: CPT (pv-l)
          - Most complete lyric: CLCP
          - Original partitur: -0-
          - Original parts: -0-

Unused.

Am I in Love?
Porter/Porter
Orchestrator: Unknown

Location of   - Composer's manuscript: -0-
          - Sheet music: Unpublished
          - Most complete music: -0-
          - Most complete lyric: CLCP
          - Original partitur: -0-
          - Original parts: -0-

Unused.

Who Said Gay Paree?
Porter/Porter
Orchestrator: Unknown

Location of   - Composer's manuscript: -0-
          - Sheet music: Not published separately
          - Most complete music: CPT (pv-l)
          - Most complete lyric: CPT (pv-l); CLCP
          - Original partitur: -0-
          - Original parts: -0-

Unused. Initial publication in The Unpublished Cole Porter (Simon & Schuster: 1975).

To Think That This Could Happen to Me
Porter/Porter
Orchestrator: Unknown

Location of   - Composer's manuscript: -0-
          - Sheet music: Not published separately
          - Most complete music: CPT (pv-l)
          - Most complete lyric: CPT (pv-l); CLCP
          - Original partitur: -0-
          - Original parts: -0-

Unused. Initial publication in The Unpublished Cole Porter (Simon & Schuster: 1975).

Can-Can (1953)

I Do

Porter/Porter
Orchestrator: Unknown

Location of
- Composer's manuscript: -0-
- Sheet music: Unpublished
- Most complete music: CPT (pv-l)
- Most complete lyric: CLCP
- Original partitur: -0-
- Original parts: -0-

Unused.

I Like the Ladies

Porter/Porter
Orchestrator: Unknown

Location of
- Composer's manuscript: -0-
- Sheet music: Unpublished
- Most complete music: -0-
- Most complete lyric: LoC (ls);
  CLCP
- Original partitur: -0-
- Original parts: -0-

Unused.

When Love Comes to Call

Porter/Porter
Orchestrator: Unknown

Location of
- Composer's manuscript: -0-
- Sheet music: Not published separately
- Most complete music: CPT (pv-l)
- Most complete lyric: CPT (pv-l); CLCP
- Original partitur: -0-
- Original parts: -0-

Unused. Initial publication in The Unpublished Cole Porter (Simon & Schuster: 1975).

If Only You Could Love Me

Porter/Porter
Orchestrator: Unknown

Location of
- Composer's manuscript: Y
- Sheet music: Unpublished
- Most complete music: CPT (pv); Y (pv)
- Most complete lyric: -0-
- Original partitur: -0-
- Original parts: -0-

Unused.

SILK STOCKINGS

Music	COLE PORTER
Lyrics	COLE PORTER

Musical comedy in two acts. Opened February 24, 1955 in New York and ran 477 performances (World premiere: November 26, 1954 in Philadelphia). Libretto by George S. Kaufman, Leueen MacGrath and Abe Burrows, suggested by the screenplay NINOTCHKA by Charles Brackett, Billy Wilder, Walter Reisch, and Ernst Lubitsch, based on an original story by Melchior Lengyel. Produced by Cy Feuer and Ernest Martin. Directed by Cy Feuer. Choreographed by Eugene Loring. Musical direction and vocal arrangements by Herbert Greene. Orchestrations by Don Walker, Irwin Kostal. Dance music arranged by Genevieve Pitot.

Synopsis and Production Information	Special envoy Nina Yaschenko is dispatched from the Soviet Union to rescue three foolish commissars who have been seduced by the pleasures of Paris. She is romanced by theatrical agent Steven Canfield and eventually comes to recognize the virtues of capitalist indulgence.
	Other characters include Peter Boroff, Russia's greatest composer, and Janice Dayton, America's swimming sweetheart, who has come to Paris to star in her first serious, non-swimming picture, WAR AND PEACE.[6] The show requires a full singing and dancing ensemble.
Orchestration	Reed I (Clarinet, Bass Clarinet, Alto Sax); Reed II (Flute, Piccolo, Clarinet, Alto Sax); Reed III (Clarinet, Bass Clarinet, Tenor Sax, Bass Sax); Reed IV (Clarinet, Bass Clarinet, Tenor Sax); Reed V (Oboe, English Horn, Clarinet, Bass Clarinet, Alto Sax, Bari Sax); Horn; Trumpet I II; Trumpet III; Trombone I; Trombone II; Trombone III; Percussion; Piano; Harp; Guitar; Violin A B C D; Viola; Cello; Bass
Comments	The 1957 film version of SILK STOCKINGS, directed by Rouben Mamoulian, starred Fred Astaire, Cyd Charisse, Janis Paige, and Peter Lorre. The screenplay, which retained most of Porter's score, combined passages from NINOTCHKA and the 1955 stage musical.
Location of Original Materials	Script: Tams-Witmark Music Library (all lyrics), Cole Porter Trusts (all lyrics) Piano-vocal score: Tams-Witmark Music Library Partiturs: Library of Congress Parts: Tams-Witmark Music Library
	The partiturs at the Library of Congress are ozalid copies of the originals; the Library of Congress also has a large collection of Porter's lyric worksheets and sketches from SILK STOCKINGS.
Rental Status	Tams-Witmark rents the original show.
Music Publisher	Chappell Music
Information	Tams-Witmark Music Library

---

[6] As she puts it, "It's going to make a great picture when it's boiled down." Eventually, she boils it down to a musical about the Empress Josephine entitled NOT TONIGHT.

Silk Stockings (1955)

Overture

Porter/Porter
Orchestrator: Walker, Kostal

Location of - Composer's manuscript: -0-
- Sheet music: Unpublished
- Most complete music: TW (pv score)
- Most complete lyric: INST
- Original partitur: LoC (x)
- Original parts: TW

Stereophonic Sound

Porter/Porter
Orchestrator: Walker

Location of - Composer's manuscript: -0-
- Sheet music: CPT, NYPL, Y
- Most complete music: CPT (sm);
    NYPL (sm); Y (sm); TW (pv score)
- Most complete lyric: TW (pv score, scr);
    CPT (scr)
- Original partitur: LoC (x)
- Original parts: TW

Replaced "There's a Hollywood That's Good" during the
pre-Broadway tryout. Fred Astaire and Janis Paige
perform additional lyrics in the film version (1957).

Too Bad

Porter/Porter
Orchestrator: Walker

Location of - Composer's manuscript: -0-
- Sheet music: Unpublished
- Most complete music: TW (pv score)
    & CPT (pv-l)
- Most complete lyric: CLCP
- Original partitur: LoC (x)
- Original parts: TW

The piano-vocal at the Cole Porter Trusts contains a
verse that was not used in the original production.

It's a Chemical Reaction, That's All

Porter/Porter
Orchestrator: Walker

Location of - Composer's manuscript: -0-
- Sheet music: CPT, LoC, NYPL, Y
- Most complete music: CPT (sm);
    LoC (sm); NYPL (sm); Y (sm);
    TW (pv score)
- Most complete lyric: CPT (sm, scr);
    LoC (sm); NYPL (sm); Y (sm);
    TW (pv score, scr); CLCP
- Original partitur: LoC (x)
- Original parts: TW

Paris Loves Lovers

Porter/Porter
Orchestrator: Walker

Location of - Composer's manuscript: -0-
- Sheet music: CPT, LoC, NYPL, Y
- Most complete music: CPT (sm);
    LoC (sm); NYPL (sm); Y (sm);
    TW (pv score)
- Most complete lyric: TW (pv score, scr);
    CPT (sm, scr); LoC (sm); NYPL (sm);
    Y (sm); CLCP
- Original partitur: LoC (x)
- Original parts: TW

All of You

Porter/Porter
Orchestrator: Walker

Location of - Composer's manuscript: -0-
- Sheet music: CPT, NYPL, Y
- Most complete music: CPT (sm);
    NYPL (sm); Y (sm); TW (pv score)
- Most complete lyric: CPT (sm, scr);
    NYPL (sm); Y (sm);
    TW (pv score, scr); CLCP
- Original partitur: LoC (x)
- Original parts: TW

Cole Porter

Satin and Silk

Porter/Porter

Orchestrator: Walker

Location of
- Composer's manuscript: -0-
- Sheet music: LoC, NYPL, Y, CPT (x)
- Most complete music: LoC (sm); NYPL (sm); Y (sm); CPT (sm-x); TW (pv score)
- Most complete lyric: LoC (sm); NYPL (sm); Y (sm); CPT (sm-x, scr); TW (pv score, scr); CLCP
- Original partitur: LoC (x)
- Original parts: TW

Without Love

Porter/Porter

Orchestrator: Walker

Location of
- Composer's manuscript: -0-
- Sheet music: CPT, LoC, NYPL, Y
- Most complete music: CPT (sm); LoC (sm); NYPL (sm); Y (sm); TW (pv score)
- Most complete lyric: CPT (sm, scr); LoC (sm); NYPL (sm); Y (sm); TW (pv score, scr); CLCP
- Original partitur: LoC (x)
- Original parts: TW

Entr'acte

Porter/Porter

Orchestrator: Walker, Kostal

Location of
- Composer's manuscript: -0-
- Sheet music: Unpublished
- Most complete music: TW (pv score)
- Most complete lyric: INST
- Original partitur: LoC (x)
- Original parts: TW

Hail Bibinski

Porter/Porter

Orchestrator: Walker

Location of
- Composer's manuscript: -0-
- Sheet music: Unpublished
- Most complete music: TW (pv score); CPT (pv-l)
- Most complete lyric: TW (pv score, scr); CPT (pv-l, scr); CLCP
- Original partitur: LoC (x)
- Original parts: TW

As On Through the Seasons We Sail

Porter/Porter

Orchestrator: Walker

Location of
- Composer's manuscript: -0-
- Sheet music: CPT, LoC, NYPL, Y
- Most complete music: CPT (sm); LoC (sm); NYPL (sm); Y (sm); TW (pv score)
- Most complete lyric: CPT (sm & scr); CLCP
- Original partitur: LoC (x)
- Original parts: TW

Josephine

Porter/Porter

Orchestrator: Walker

Location of
- Composer's manuscript: -0-
- Sheet music: CPT, LoC, NYPL, Y
- Most complete music: CPT (sm); LoC (sm); NYPL (sm); Y (sm); TW (pv score)
- Most complete lyric: CPT (sm, scr); LoC (sm); NYPL (sm); Y (sm); TW (pv score, scr); CLCP
- Original partitur: LoC (x)
- Original parts: TW

The Complete Lyrics of Cole Porter also contains a refrain for the movie-within-a-show.

Silk Stockings (1955)

Siberia

Porter/Porter
Orchestrator: Kostal

Location of
- Composer's manuscript: -0-
- Sheet music: CPT, LoC, NYPL, Y
- Most complete music: CPT (sm);
    LoC (sm); NYPL (sm); Y (sm);
    TW (pv score)
- Most complete lyric: CLCP
- Original partitur: LoC (x)
- Original parts: TW

Silk Stockings

Porter/Porter
Orchestrator: Walker

Location of
- Composer's manuscript: -0-
- Sheet music: CPT, LoC, NYPL, Y
- Most complete music: CPT (sm);
    LoC (sm); NYPL (sm); Y (sm)
- Most complete lyric: CPT (sm);
    LoC (sm); NYPL (sm); Y (sm); CLCP
- Original partitur: LoC (x)
- Original parts: TW

The verse, which was not performed in the original
production, is not included in the piano-vocal score.

Red Blues, The

Porter/Porter
Orchestrator: Walker

Location of
- Composer's manuscript: -0-
- Sheet music: Unpublished
- Most complete music: TW (pv score);
    CPT (pv-l)
- Most complete lyric: TW (pv score, scr);
    CPT (pv-l, scr); CLCP
- Original partitur: LoC (x)
- Original parts: TW

Fated to Be Mated

Porter/Porter
Orchestrator: Unknown

Location of
- Composer's manuscript: -0-
- Sheet music: CPT, LoC, NYPL, Y
- Most complete music: CPT (sm);
    LoC (sm); NYPL (sm); Y (sm)
- Most complete lyric: CPT (sm);
    LoC (sm); NYPL (sm); Y (sm); CLCP
- Original partitur: -0-
- Original parts: -0-

Written for the film version (1957), which was scored by
Conrad Salinger, with additional orchestrations by Skip
Martin and Al Woodbury.

Ritz Roll and Rock, The

Porter/Porter
Orchestrator: Unknown

Location of
- Composer's manuscript: -0-
- Sheet music: CPT, LoC, Y
- Most complete music: CPT (sm);
    LoC (sm); Y (sm)
- Most complete lyric: CPT (sm);
    LoC (sm); Y (sm); CLCP
- Original partitur: -0-
- Original parts: -0-

Written for the film version (1957), which was scored by
Conrad Salinger, with additional orchestrations by Skip
Martin and Al Woodbury.

Ode to a Tractor

Porter
Orchestrator: Unknown

Location of
- Composer's manuscript: -0-
- Sheet music: Unpublished
- Most complete music: See note
- Most complete lyric: INST
- Original partitur: -0-
- Original parts: -0-

Dropped during the pre-Broadway tryout. The Cole Porter
Trusts have piano arrangements of "Boroff's Ode" and
"Theme of Ode to a Tractor"; either of these may have
been used in this spot.

Art
    Porter/Porter
    Orchestrator: Unknown

    Location of   - Composer's manuscript: -0-
                - Sheet music: Unpublished
                - Most complete music: CPT (pv-l)
                - Most complete lyric: CPT (pv-l); CLCP
                - Original partitur: -0-
                - Original parts: -0-

Dropped during the pre-Broadway tryout.

If Ever We Get Out of Jail
    Porter/Porter
    Orchestrator: Unknown

    Location of   - Composer's manuscript: -0-
                - Sheet music: Unpublished
                - Most complete music: CPT (pv-l)
                - Most complete lyric: CPT (pv-l); CLCP
                - Original partitur: -0-
                - Original parts: -0-

This early version of "As On Through the Seasons We Sail" was dropped in rehearsal.

There's a Hollywood That's Good
    Porter/Porter
    Orchestrator: Unknown

    Location of   - Composer's manuscript: -0-
                - Sheet music: Unpublished
                - Most complete music: CPT (pv-l)
                - Most complete lyric: CLCP
                - Original partitur: -0-
                - Original parts: -0-

Replaced during the pre-Broadway tryout by "Stereophonic Sound."

Let's Make It a Night
    Porter/Porter
    Orchestrator: Unknown

    Location of   - Composer's manuscript: -0-
                - Sheet music: Unpublished
                - Most complete music: CPT (pv-l)
                - Most complete lyric: CPT (pv-l); CLCP
                - Original partitur: -0-
                - Original parts: -0-

Unused.

Give Me the Land
    Porter/Porter
    Orchestrator: Unknown

    Location of   - Composer's manuscript: -0-
                - Sheet music: Not published separately
                - Most complete music: CPT (pv-l);
                    LoC (pv-l)
                - Most complete lyric: CLCP
                - Original partitur: -0-
                - Original parts: -0-

Unused. Initial publication in The Unpublished Cole Porter (Simon & Schuster: 1975).

Under the Dress
    Porter/Porter
    Orchestrator: Unknown

    Location of   - Composer's manuscript: -0-
                - Sheet music: Unpublished
                - Most complete music: CPT (pv-l)
                - Most complete lyric: CPT (pv-l); CLCP
                - Original partitur: -0-
                - Original parts: -0-

Unused. Replaced by "The Perfume of Love," which was then replaced by "Satin and Silk."

Silk Stockings (1955)

Perfume of Love, The
Porter/Porter
Orchestrator: Unknown

Location of - Composer's manuscript: -0-
              - Sheet music: Unpublished
              - Most complete music: CPT (pv-l)
              - Most complete lyric: CPT (pv-l); CLCP
              - Original partitur: -0-
              - Original parts: -0-

Unused. Replaced by "Satin and Silk."

Bebe of Gay Paree
Porter/Porter
Orchestrator: Unknown

Location of - Composer's manuscript: -0-
              - Sheet music: Unpublished
              - Most complete music: LoC (sk)
              - Most complete lyric: CLCP
              - Original partitur: -0-
              - Original parts: -0-

Unused.

What a Ball
Porter/Porter
Orchestrator: Unknown

Location of - Composer's manuscript: -0-
              - Sheet music: Unpublished
              - Most complete music: CPT (pv-l)
              - Most complete lyric: CPT (pv-l); CLCP
              - Original partitur: -0-
              - Original parts: -0-

Unused.

I'm the Queen Thamar
Porter/Porter
Orchestrator: Unknown

Location of - Composer's manuscript: -0-
              - Sheet music: Unpublished
              - Most complete music: -0-
              - Most complete lyric: -0-
              - Original partitur: -0-
              - Original parts: -0-

Unused.

Why Should I Trust You?
Porter/Porter
Orchestrator: Unknown

Location of - Composer's manuscript: -0-
              - Sheet music: Unpublished
              - Most complete music: CPT (pv-l)
              - Most complete lyric: CPT (pv-l); CLCP
              - Original partitur: -0-
              - Original parts: -0-

Unused.

Keep Your Chin Up
Porter/Porter
Orchestrator: Unknown

Location of - Composer's manuscript: -0-
              - Sheet music: Unpublished
              - Most complete music: -0-
              - Most complete lyric: -0-
              - Original partitur: -0-
              - Original parts: -0-

Unused.

RICHARD RODGERS & LORENZ HART

RICHARD RODGERS was born in New York City on June 28, 1902, and received his undergraduate education at Columbia University, where he met his first partner, Lorenz Hart. With Hart, he wrote 750 songs over a period of nearly twenty-five years. Among the shows to which Rodgers and Hart contributed songs are THE GARRICK GAIETIES (1925 & 1926), DEAREST ENEMY (1925), PEGGY-ANN (1926), A CONNECTICUT YANKEE (1927), PRESENT ARMS (1928), ON YOUR TOES (1936), I'D RATHER BE RIGHT (1937), I MARRIED AN ANGEL (1938), THE BOYS FROM SYRACUSE (1938), TOO MANY GIRLS (1939), and PAL JOEY (1941). Their works also included a nightclub revue, a non-musical play, and nine films. After Lorenz Hart died, Rodgers began an extraordinary collaboration with Oscar Hammerstein II. Together they created some of Broadway's classic musicals, including OKLAHOMA! (1943), CAROUSEL (1945), SOUTH PACIFIC (1949), and THE KING AND I (1951). They were responsible for the 1945 musical film, STATE FAIR, and the 1957 television musical, CINDERELLA. As producers, Rodgers and Hammerstein presented the original production of John van Druten's I REMEMBER MAMA as well as Irving Berlin's ANNIE GET YOUR GUN and Samuel Taylor's THE HAPPY TIME. After Hammerstein's death in 1960, Rodgers wrote both lyrics and music for NO STRINGS (1962) and the television adaptation of ANDROCLES AND THE LION (1967). He collaborated with Stephen Sondheim on DO I HEAR A WALTZ? (1965), with Martin Charnin on TWO BY TWO (1971), and with Sheldon Harnick on REX (1976). His last Broadway show was I REMEMBER MAMA (1979), with lyrics by Martin Charnin and Raymond Jessel. During his career, he received two Oscars, two Pulitzer Prizes, two Emmy Awards, three New York Drama Critics Circle Awards, and seven Tony Awards. Rodgers died in New York on December 30, 1979.

LORENZ HART was born in New York City on May 2, 1895. His earliest surviving verse (1911) was written for The Columbia News, the newspaper-literary magazine of the Columbia Grammar School in New York City, where he was a student. In 1914 he graduated from Columbia Grammar and began studies at the Columbia School of Journalism. During the summers of 1918-1920 he wrote lyrics while working as a dramatics counselor at Brant Lake Camp in the Adirondack Mountains, New York. He first met Richard Rodgers in 1919, when Rodgers was a sixteen-year-old freshman at Columbia University. Hart, who graduated some years earlier, was living in a brownstone house on 119th Street, piecing out a living by translating German plays and musical comedies into English for the Shuberts. "Any Old Place With You," Rodgers and Hart's first published song and their first song in a Broadway show, was introduced in A LONELY ROMEO in August, 1919. Their first major collaboration was YOU'D BE SURPRISED, an amateur show presented in 1920. During the next five years they wrote no fewer than fifteen musical comedies, but their financial rewards were slim. Then, in 1925, the tide turned with their score for THE GARRICK GAIETIES. During the next six years Rodgers and Hart were represented by thirteen musical comedies in New York and three in London. After a brief sojourn to Hollywood, they returned to Broadway in 1935 with an astonishing string of successes including ON YOUR TOES (1936), BABES IN ARMS (1937), I MARRIED AN ANGEL (1938), THE BOYS FROM SYRACUSE (1938), and TOO MANY GIRLS (1939) capped by the brilliantly innovative PAL JOEY (1940). Rodgers and Hart's songs include such standards as "Manhattan," "My Heart Stood Still," "Thou Swell," "Where or When," "Lover," "Isn't It Romantic," "This Can't Be Love," "There's A Small Hotel," "Falling in Love with Love," and others far too numerous to cite. Lorenz Hart died on November 22, 1943, in New York.

DEAREST ENEMY

Music   **RICHARD RODGERS**
Lyrics   **LORENZ HART**

Musical comedy in three acts. Opened September 18, 1925 in New York and ran 286 performances (World premiere: July 20, 1925 in Akron, Ohio). Libretto by Herbert Fields. Produced by George Ford. Directed by John Murray Anderson, Charles Sinclair and Harry Ford. Choreographed by Carl Hemmer. Musical direction by Richard Rodgers. Orchestrations by Emil Gerstenberger, Harold Sanford.

Synopsis and Production Information

Mrs. Robert Murray is asked to assist the American Revolutionary War effort by detaining British troops overnight in her Murray Hill mansion (so that the American forces can gain ground). She throws a magnificent ball for the enemy soldiers, and soon her debutantes find themselves torn between loyalty to their country and to the Redcoats with whom they've fallen in love. The English soon discover that they've been tricked by wine, women, and songs, but by then, an American victory has been assured. After the war, countries separate, but hearts reunite.

The romantic leads are British officer Sir John Copeland and Mrs. Murray's niece Betsy, who first appears wearing only a barrel. Comedic support is provided by Captain Harry Tryon and Mrs. Murray's daughter Jane. There is a full singing and dancing ensemble.

Orchestration

Flute; Oboe; Clarinet I II; Bassoon; Horn I II; Trumpet I II; Trombone I II; Percussion; Harp; Violin I II; Viola I II; Cello; Bass

Comments

In its early stages, the show was known as SWEET REBEL.

Location of Original Materials

Script: Rodgers and Hammerstein Theatre Library (most lyrics),
       New York Public Library (most lyrics)
Piano-vocal score: See individual listings
Partiturs: Rodgers and Hammerstein Theatre Library
Parts: Rodgers and Hammerstein Theatre Library

Most of the songs performed in the New York production survive, but original partiturs and parts are missing for all but one number. The Rodgers and Hammerstein Theatre Library has a set of parts for an eleven-piece orchestration reduced from the original; it includes all the songs from the New York production except "I Beg Your Pardon", the Entr'actes, and the Act III Opening. The Library of Congress has an early draft of the script under the title SWEET REBEL.

Rental Status

Currently unavailable for rental

Music Publisher

Marlin Enterprises and Lorenz Hart Publishing Co., c/o Warner Brothers Music

Information

Rodgers and Hammerstein Theatre Library

Overture

Rodgers/Hart
Orchestrator: Unknown

Location of   - Composer's manuscript: -0-
    - Sheet music: Unpublished
    - Most complete music: R&H (reduced parts)
    - Most complete lyric: INST
    - Original partitur: -0-
    - Original parts: -0-

I Beg Your Pardon

Rodgers/Hart
Orchestrator: Unknown

Location of   - Composer's manuscript: -0-
    - Sheet music: Unpublished
    - Most complete music: -0-
    - Most complete lyric: CLLH
    - Original partitur: -0-
    - Original parts: -0-

Heigh-Ho, Lackaday

Rodgers/Hart
Orchestrator: Unknown

Location of   - Composer's manuscript: LoC
    - Sheet music: Unpublished
    - Most complete music: R&H (p-l)
    - Most complete lyric: R&H (p-l, scr);
        NYPL (scr); CLLH
    - Original partitur: -0-
    - Original parts: -0-

Alternate title: "Opening Act I."

Cheerio

Rodgers/Hart
Orchestrator: Unknown

Location of   - Composer's manuscript: -0-
    - Sheet music: LoC, NYPL
    - Most complete music: LoC (sm);
        NYPL (sm); R&H (pv-l)
    - Most complete lyric: LoC (sm);
        NYPL (sm, scr); R&H (scr, pv-l);
        CLLH
    - Original partitur: -0-
    - Original parts: -0-

War Is War

Rodgers/Hart
Orchestrator: Sanford

Location of   - Composer's manuscript: -0-
    - Sheet music: Unpublished
    - Most complete music: R&H (p-l)
    - Most complete lyric: R&H (scr);
        NYPL (scr); CLLH
    - Original partitur: R&H
    - Original parts: R&H

Full-Blown Roses

Rodgers/Hart
Orchestrator: Unknown

Location of   - Composer's manuscript: -0-
    - Sheet music: Unpublished
    - Most complete music: R&H (p-l)
    - Most complete lyric: R&H (p-l, scr);
        NYPL (scr); CLLH
    - Original partitur: -0-
    - Original parts: -0-

Dearest Enemy (1925)

Hermits, The
Rodgers/Hart
Orchestrator: Unknown

Location of - Composer's manuscript: -0-
           - Sheet music: Unpublished
           - Most complete music: R&H (p-l)
           - Most complete lyric: CLLH
           - Original partitur: -0-
           - Original parts: -0-

Originally intended for WINKLE TOWN, an unproduced
Rodgers and Hart musical from 1922.

Entr'acte I
Rodgers/Hart
Orchestrator: Unknown

Location of - Composer's manuscript: -0-
           - Sheet music: Unpublished
           - Most complete music: -0-
           - Most complete lyric: INST
           - Original partitur: -0-
           - Original parts: -0-

Here In My Arms
Rodgers/Hart
Orchestrator: Unknown

Location of - Composer's manuscript: -0-
           - Sheet music: LoC, NYPL
           - Most complete music: LoC (sm);
               NYPL (sm); R&H (pv-l)
           - Most complete lyric: CLLH
           - Original partitur: -0-
           - Original parts: -0-

Also used in LIDO LADY (1926). The scripts at the New
York Public Library and the Rodgers and Hammerstein
Theatre Library contain an additional quatrain.

Gavotte
Rodgers/Hart
Orchestrator: Unknown

Location of - Composer's manuscript: -0-
           - Sheet music: Unpublished
           - Most complete music: R&H (p-l)
           - Most complete lyric: R&H (p-l); CLLH
           - Original partitur: -0-
           - Original parts: -0-

Finale Act I ["Tho' we've no authentic reason..."]
Rodgers/Hart
Orchestrator: Unknown

Location of - Composer's manuscript: -0-
           - Sheet music: Unpublished
           - Most complete music: R&H (p-l)
           - Most complete lyric: R&H (p-l, scr);
               NYPL (scr); CLLH
           - Original partitur: -0-
           - Original parts: -0-

I'd Like to Hide It
Rodgers/Hart
Orchestrator: Unknown

Location of - Composer's manuscript: -0-
           - Sheet music: Unpublished
           - Most complete music: R&H (p-l)
           - Most complete lyric: R&H (p-l, scr);
               NYPL (scr); CLLH
           - Original partitur: -0-
           - Original parts: -0-

Where the Hudson River Flows

Rodgers/Hart
Orchestrator: Unknown

Location of - Composer's manuscript: -0-
- Sheet music: Unpublished
- Most complete music: R&H (p-l)
- Most complete lyric: R&H (p-l, scr);
  NYPL (scr); CLLH
- Original partitur: -0-
- Original parts: -0-

Old Enough to Love

Rodgers/Hart
Orchestrator: Unknown

Location of - Composer's manuscript: LoC
- Sheet music: Unpublished
- Most complete music: R&H (p-l); LoC (pv)
- Most complete lyric: R&H (p-l, scr);
  NYPL (scr); CLLH
- Original partitur: -0-
- Original parts: -0-

Originally intended for WINKLE TOWN, an unproduced
Rodgers and Hart musical from 1922.

Bye and Bye

Rodgers/Hart
Orchestrator: Unknown

Location of - Composer's manuscript: LoC (x)
- Sheet music: NYPL
- Most complete music: NYPL (sm);
  R&H (pv-l); LoC (pv)
- Most complete lyric: NYPL (sm); CLLH
- Original partitur: -0-
- Original parts: -0-

Here's a Kiss

Rodgers/Hart
Orchestrator: Unknown

Location of - Composer's manuscript: -0-
- Sheet music: LoC, NYPL
- Most complete music: LoC (sm);
  NYPL (sm); R&H (pv-l)
- Most complete lyric: LoC (sm);
  NYPL (sm); R&H (pv-l); CLLH
- Original partitur: -0-
- Original parts: -0-

The lyric is not in either script.

Sweet Peter

Rodgers/Hart
Orchestrator: Unknown

Location of - Composer's manuscript: -0-
- Sheet music: LoC, NYPL
- Most complete music: LoC (sm);
  NYPL (sm); R&H (p-l)
- Most complete lyric: LoC (sm);
  NYPL (sm, scr); R&H (p-l, scr); CLLH
- Original partitur: -0-
- Original parts: -0-

Entr'acte II

Rodgers/Hart
Orchestrator: Unknown

Location of - Composer's manuscript: -0-
- Sheet music: Unpublished
- Most complete music: -0-
- Most complete lyric: INST
- Original partitur: -0-
- Original parts: -0-

Dearest Enemy (1925)

Opening Act III

Rodgers/Hart

Orchestrator: Unknown

Location of
- Composer's manuscript: -0-
- Sheet music: Unpublished
- Most complete music: -0-
- Most complete lyric: -0-
- Original partitur: -0-
- Original parts: -0-

Ale, Ale, Ale

Rodgers/Hart

Orchestrator: Unknown

Location of
- Composer's manuscript: -0-
- Sheet music: Unpublished
- Most complete music: -0-
- Most complete lyric: -0-
- Original partitur: -0-
- Original parts: -0-

Dropped before the New York opening.

Pipes of Pansy, The

Rodgers/Hart

Orchestrator: See note

Location of
- Composer's manuscript: -0-
- Sheet music: Unpublished
- Most complete music: R&H (pv-I)
- Most complete lyric: R&H (pv-I, ls); CLLH
- Original partitur: See note
- Original parts: -0-

Intended for DEAREST ENEMY, THE GIRL FRIEND (1926), PEGGY-ANN (1926), and SHE'S MY BABY (1928), but dropped from all four shows before their New York openings. The New York Public Library has two partiturs for "The Pipes of Pansy" (by Roy Webb and F. Henri Klickmann) in its SHE'S MY BABY collection.

Oh Dear

Rodgers/Hart

Orchestrator: Unknown

Location of
- Composer's manuscript: LoC
- Sheet music: Unpublished
- Most complete music: LoC (pv)
- Most complete lyric: -0-
- Original partitur: -0-
- Original parts: -0-

Dropped before the New York opening.

Girls Do Not Tempt Me

Rodgers/Hart

Orchestrator: Unknown

Location of
- Composer's manuscript: -0-
- Sheet music: Unpublished
- Most complete music: -0-
- Most complete lyric: CLLH
- Original partitur: -0-
- Original parts: -0-

Dropped before the New York opening. The lyric can also be found in the early draft of the script at the Library of Congress.

Dear Me

Rodgers/Hart

Orchestrator: Unknown

Location of
- Composer's manuscript: -0-
- Sheet music: Unpublished
- Most complete music: -0-
- Most complete lyric: -0-
- Original partitur: -0-
- Original parts: -0-

Dropped before the New York opening.

Dearest Enemy

Rodgers/Hart

Orchestrator: Unknown

Location of - Composer's manuscript: -0-
             - Sheet music: Unpublished
             - Most complete music: -0-
             - Most complete lyric: -0-
             - Original partitur: -0-
             - Original parts: -0-

Unused.

How Can We Help But Miss You

Rodgers/Hart

Orchestrator: Unknown

Location of - Composer's manuscript: -0-
             - Sheet music: Unpublished
             - Most complete music: -0-
             - Most complete lyric: -0-
             - Original partitur: -0-
             - Original parts: -0-

Unused.

THE GIRL FRIEND

Music   **RICHARD RODGERS**
Lyrics   **LORENZ HART**

Musical comedy in two acts. Opened March 17, 1926 in New York and ran 301 performances (World premiere: March 8, 1926 in Atlantic City). Libretto by Herbert Fields. Produced by Lew Fields. Directed by John Harwood. Choreographed by Jack Haskell. Musical direction by Paul Lannin. Orchestrations by Maurice B. DePackh.

Synopsis and Production Information	Leonard Silver, a dairy farmer from Long Island, gets a chance to compete in a six-day bicycle race. His girlfriend Mollie, who has helped train him, is not allowed to attend the race because Wynn, the sister of Lenny's sponsor, has designs on Lenny. Despite jealousies and complications, Lenny wins the race and marries Mollie.

Other characters include prominent sport promoter Arthur Spencer, Wynn's upper-class fiance Thomas Larson, Lenny's bicycle partner Donald, and Donald's girlfriend Irene. The show requires a full singing and dancing ensemble. |
| **Orchestration** | Unknown |
| **Location of Original Materials** | Script: Rodgers and Hammerstein Theatre Library (all lyrics)
Piano-vocal score: See individual listings
Partiturs: Missing
Parts: Missing

Music is missing for three songs performed in the original New York production, as well as for the Overture and the Entr'acte. Early drafts of the script can be found at the Rodgers and Hammerstein Theatre Library and the Library of Congress. |
Rental Status	Currently unavailable for rental
Music Publisher	Marlin Enterprises and Lorenz Hart Publishing Co., c/o Warner Brothers Music
Information	Rodgers and Hammerstein Theatre Library

Overture

Rodgers/Hart

Orchestrator: Unknown

Location of - Composer's manuscript: -0-
- Sheet music: Unpublished
- Most complete music: -0-
- Most complete lyric: INST
- Original partitur: -0-
- Original parts: -0-

Girl Friend, The

Rodgers/Hart

Orchestrator: Unknown

Location of - Composer's manuscript: LoC (x)
- Sheet music: LoC, NYPL
- Most complete music: LoC (sm);
     NYPL (sm); R&H (pv-l)
- Most complete lyric: R&H (scr); CLLH
- Original partitur: -0-
- Original parts: -0-

Hey! Hey!

Rodgers/Hart

Orchestrator: Unknown

Location of - Composer's manuscript: LoC (sk)
- Sheet music: Unpublished
- Most complete music: LoC (sk); R&H (sk)
- Most complete lyric: R&H (scr); CLLH
- Original partitur: -0-
- Original parts: -0-

Goodbye, Lenny

Rodgers/Hart

Orchestrator: Unknown

Location of - Composer's manuscript: -0-
- Sheet music: Unpublished
- Most complete music: -0-
- Most complete lyric: R&H (scr); CLLH
- Original partitur: -0-
- Original parts: -0-

Simple Life, The

Rodgers/Hart

Orchestrator: Unknown

Location of - Composer's manuscript: -0-
- Sheet music: Unpublished
- Most complete music: R&H (pv)
- Most complete lyric: R&H (scr); CLLH
- Original partitur: -0-
- Original parts: -0-

Blue Room, The

Rodgers/Hart

Orchestrator: Unknown

Location of - Composer's manuscript: LoC (x)
- Sheet music: LoC, NYPL
- Most complete music: LoC (sm);
     NYPL (sm); R&H (pv-l)
- Most complete lyric: R&H (pv-l, scr)
- Original partitur: -0-
- Original parts: -0-

Cabarets

Rodgers/Hart

Orchestrator: Unknown

Location of   - Composer's manuscript: -0-
             - Sheet music: Unpublished
             - Most complete music: -0-
             - Most complete lyric: R&H (scr); CLLH
             - Original partitur: -0-
             - Original parts: -0-

He's a Winner

Rodgers/Hart

Orchestrator: Unknown

Location of   - Composer's manuscript: -0-
             - Sheet music: Unpublished
             - Most complete music: -0-
             - Most complete lyric: R&H (scr); CLLH
             - Original partitur: -0-
             - Original parts: -0-

Why Do I?

Rodgers/Hart

Orchestrator: Unknown

Location of   - Composer's manuscript: LoC (x)
             - Sheet music: LoC, NYPL
             - Most complete music: LoC (sm);
                 NYPL (sm); R&H (pv-l)
             - Most complete lyric: LoC (sm);
                 NYPL (sm); R&H (ls, scr); CLLH
             - Original partitur: -0-
             - Original parts: -0-

Town Hall Tonight

Rodgers/Hart

Orchestrator: Unknown

Location of   - Composer's manuscript: LoC
             - Sheet music: Unpublished
             - Most complete music: LoC (pv); R&H (pv)
             - Most complete lyric: CLLH
             - Original partitur: -0-
             - Original parts: -0-

Damsel Who Done All the Dirt, The

Rodgers/Hart

Orchestrator: Unknown

Location of   - Composer's manuscript: LoC
             - Sheet music: Not published separately
             - Most complete music: LoC (pv); R&H (pv)
             - Most complete lyric: R&H (scr); CLLH
             - Original partitur: -0-
             - Original parts: -0-

Published only in the piano selection, which can be found at the Rodgers and Hammerstein Theatre Library and at the Library of Congress.

Good Fellow Mine

Rodgers/Hart

Orchestrator: Unknown

Location of   - Composer's manuscript: LoC
             - Sheet music: LoC, NYPL
             - Most complete music: LoC (sm);
                 NYPL (sm); R&H (pv-l)
             - Most complete lyric: LoC (sm);
                 NYPL (sm); R&H (pv-l, scr); CLLH
             - Original partitur: -0-
             - Original parts: -0-

Entr'acte
Rodgers/Hart
Orchestrator: Unknown

Location of - Composer's manuscript: -0-
- Sheet music: Unpublished
- Most complete music: -0-
- Most complete lyric: INST
- Original partitur: -0-
- Original parts: -0-

What Is It?
Rodgers/Hart
Orchestrator: Unknown

Location of - Composer's manuscript: -0-
- Sheet music: Not published separately
- Most complete music: R&H (p sel);
LoC (p sel)
- Most complete lyric: R&H (scr); CLLH
- Original partitur: -0-
- Original parts: -0-

Published only in the piano selection.

Creole Crooning Song
Rodgers/Hart
Orchestrator: Unknown

Location of - Composer's manuscript: LoC
- Sheet music: Unpublished
- Most complete music: LoC (pv); R&H (pv)
- Most complete lyric: R&H (scr); CLLH
- Original partitur: -0-
- Original parts: -0-

Two of a Kind
Rodgers/Hart
Orchestrator: Unknown

Location of - Composer's manuscript: LoC
- Sheet music: Unpublished
- Most complete music: LoC (pv); R&H (pv)
- Most complete lyric: -0-
- Original partitur: -0-
- Original parts: -0-

Dropped during the pre-Broadway tryout.

I'd Like to Take You Home
Rodgers/Hart
Orchestrator: Unknown

Location of - Composer's manuscript: LoC
- Sheet music: Unpublished
- Most complete music: LoC (pv); R&H (pv)
- Most complete lyric: R&H (scr)
- Original partitur: -0-
- Original parts: -0-

The Complete Lyrics of Lorenz Hart has an earlier version
that was used in BAD HABITS OF 1925, a revue with
songs by Rodgers and Hart.

Turkey in the Straw
Rodgers/Hart
Orchestrator: Unknown

Location of - Composer's manuscript: LoC
- Sheet music: Unpublished
- Most complete music: LoC (pv); R&H (pv)
- Most complete lyric: -0-
- Original partitur: -0-
- Original parts: -0-

Dropped during the pre-Broadway tryout.

The Girl Friend (1926)

Sleepyhead
Rodgers/Hart
Orchestrator: Unknown

Location of   - Composer's manuscript: LoC
              - Sheet music: LoC, NYPL
              - Most complete music: LoC (sm);
                  NYPL (sm); R&H (pv-l)
              - Most complete lyric: LoC (sm);
                  NYPL (sm); R&H (pv-l); CLLH
              - Original partitur: -0-
              - Original parts: -0-

Dropped during the pre-Broadway tryout. Later used in THE GARRICK GAIETIES (1926), a revue with songs by Rodgers and Hart.

In New Orleans
Rodgers/Hart
Orchestrator: Unknown

Location of   - Composer's manuscript: -0-
              - Sheet music: Unpublished
              - Most complete music: -0-
              - Most complete lyric: R&H (ls); CLLH
              - Original partitur: -0-
              - Original parts: -0-

Replaced in rehearsal by "Creole Crooning Song."

Hum To
Rodgers/Hart
Orchestrator: Unknown

Location of   - Composer's manuscript: LoC (lead)
              - Sheet music: Unpublished
              - Most complete music: LoC (lead);
                  R&H (lead)
              - Most complete lyric: -0-
              - Original partitur: -0-
              - Original parts: -0-

Dropped in rehearsal. Alternate title: "To Hum."

Pipes of Pansy, The
Rodgers/Hart
Orchestrator: See note

Location of   - Composer's manuscript: -0-
              - Sheet music: Unpublished
              - Most complete music: R&H (pv-l)
              - Most complete lyric: R&H (pv-l, ls);
                  CLLH
              - Original partitur: See note
              - Original parts: -0-

Unused. Also intended for DEAREST ENEMY (1925), PEGGY-ANN (1926), and SHE'S MY BABY (1928). The New York Public Library has two partiturs for "The Pipes of Pansy" (by Roy Webb and F. Henri Klickmann) in its SHE'S MY BABY collection.

LIDO LADY

Music   **RICHARD RODGERS**
Lyrics   **LORENZ HART**

Musical comedy in three acts. Opened December 1, 1926 in London and ran 259 performances (World premiere: October 4, 1926 in Bradford). Libretto by Ronald Jeans, based on the script by Guy Bolton, Bert Kalmar and Harry Ruby. Additional songs by Jean Boyer, Vincent Scotto, Con Conrad, Desmond Carter, Ray Henderson, Lew Brown, B.G. DeSylva. Produced by Jack Hulbert and Paul Murray. Directed by Jack Hulbert. Musical direction by Sydney Baynes.

Synopsis and Production Information	Harry Bassett, an English dandy, is in passionate pursuit of the lovely, athletic Fay Blake, who lives on the Lido in Venice with her father, a wealthy sporting goods manufacturer. Harry's efforts to prove his love through sporting events fail to impress Fay, but when he discovers that the slick and charming Luis Valeze (a guest at the Blake villa and supposed South American tennis champion) is really an imposter out to steal Father Blake's secret new tennis ball formula, he wins Fay's heart and her father's approval. Other characters include inventor Spencer Weldon, famous American movie star Peggy Bassett, and family friend "Peaches" Stone. There is a full singing ensemble, and several male specialty dancers.
Orchestration	Unknown
Comments	In its early stages, the show was known as THE LOVE CHAMPION.
Location of Original Materials	Script: New York Public Library (most lyrics) Piano-vocal score: See individual listings Partiturs: Missing Parts: Missing Music is missing for the Overture, the Act I Opening ("A Cup of Tea"), both Entr'actes, and most of the specialty material; one lyric is missing as well ("I Must Be Going"). The script at the New York Public Library is credited to Bolton, Kalmar and Ruby -- with no mention of Ronald Jeans. According to two British reviews (in The Era and The Stage), Jeans was responsible for "special scenes."
Rental Status	Currently unavailable for rental
Music Publisher	Marlin Enterprises and Lorenz Hart Publishing Co., c/o Warner Brothers Music
Information	Rodgers and Hammerstein Theatre Library

Lido Lady (1926)

Overture

Author(s): Unknown
Orchestrator: Unknown

Location of   - Composer's manuscript: -0-
              - Sheet music: Unpublished
              - Most complete music: -0-
              - Most complete lyric: INST
              - Original partitur: -0-
              - Original parts: -0-

Lido Lady

Rodgers/Hart
Orchestrator: Unknown

Location of   - Composer's manuscript: -0-
              - Sheet music: LoC, NYPL
              - Most complete music: LoC (sm);
                    NYPL (sm)
              - Most complete lyric: LoC (sm);
                    NYPL (sm, scr); CLLH
              - Original partitur: -0-
              - Original parts: -0-

Cup of Tea, A

Rodgers/Hart
Orchestrator: Unknown

Location of   - Composer's manuscript: -0-
              - Sheet music: Unpublished
              - Most complete music: -0-
              - Most complete lyric: CLLH
              - Original partitur: -0-
              - Original parts: -0-

Alternate title: "Lido Lady, Opening."

Tiny Flat Near Soho, A

Rodgers/Hart
Orchestrator: Unknown

Location of   - Composer's manuscript: LoC
              - Sheet music: LoC, NYPL
              - Most complete music: LoC (sm);
                    NYPL (sm)
              - Most complete lyric: CLLH
              - Original partitur: -0-
              - Original parts: -0-

Under the title "A Little House in Soho" (with a few revised lyrics), this song was later used in SHE'S MY BABY (1928). The New York Public Library has Stephen O. Jones' partitur (and parts) for "A Little House in Soho" in its SHE'S MY BABY collection.

You're on the Lido Now

Rodgers/Hart
Orchestrator: Unknown

Location of   - Composer's manuscript: -0-
              - Sheet music: LoC
              - Most complete music: LoC (sm); R&H (pv)
              - Most complete lyric: LoC (sm); CLLH
              - Original partitur: -0-
              - Original parts: -0-

But Not Today

Boyer, Scotto & Conrad/Carter
Orchestrator: Unknown

Location of   - Composer's manuscript: -0-
              - Sheet music: LoC
              - Most complete music: LoC (sm)
              - Most complete lyric: NYPL (scr)
              - Original partitur: -0-
              - Original parts: -0-

Here in My Arms

Rodgers/Hart
Orchestrator: Unknown

Location of - Composer's manuscript: -0-
 - Sheet music: LoC, NYPL
 - Most complete music: LoC (sm);
   NYPL (sm); R&H (pv-l)
 - Most complete lyric: CLLH
 - Original partitur: -0-
 - Original parts: -0-

Originally used in DEAREST ENEMY (1925). An additional quatrain can be found in the DEAREST ENEMY scripts at the New York Public Library and the Rodgers and Hammerstein Theatre Library.

Beauty of Another Day, The

Rodgers/Hart
Orchestrator: Unknown

Location of - Composer's manuscript: LoC
 - Sheet music: Unpublished
 - Most complete music: LoC (pv)
 - Most complete lyric: NYPL (scr);
   CLLH
 - Original partitur: -0-
 - Original parts: -0-

Finale Act I ["Good old Harry..."]

Rodgers, Boyer, Scotto & Conrad/Hart & Carter
Orchestrator: Unknown

Location of - Composer's manuscript: -0-
 - Sheet music: Unpublished
 - Most complete music: R&H (pv)
 - Most complete lyric: NYPL (scr) & CLLH
 - Original partitur: -0-
 - Original parts: -0-

My Heart Is Sheba Bound

Rodgers/Hart
Orchestrator: Unknown

Location of - Composer's manuscript: R&H
 - Sheet music: Not published separately
 - Most complete music: R&H (pv)
 - Most complete lyric: CLLH
 - Original partitur: -0-
 - Original parts: -0-

The refrain was published in the piano selection, which can be found at the Rodgers and Hammerstein Theatre Library. The Complete Lyrics of Lorenz Hart also contains an earlier version of the lyric.

Entr'acte I

Author(s): Unknown
Orchestrator: Unknown

Location of - Composer's manuscript: -0-
 - Sheet music: Unpublished
 - Most complete music: -0-
 - Most complete lyric: INST
 - Original partitur: -0-
 - Original parts: -0-

Dancer, The

Author(s): Unknown
Orchestrator: Unknown

Location of - Composer's manuscript: -0-
 - Sheet music: -0-
 - Most complete music: -0-
 - Most complete lyric: -0-
 - Original partitur: -0-
 - Original parts: -0-

A specialty number for dancer Dave Fitzgibbon.

It All Depends on You

Henderson/DeSylva & Brown

Orchestrator: Unknown

Location of   - Composer's manuscript: -0-
                 - Sheet music: NYPL
                 - Most complete music: NYPL (sm)
                 - Most complete lyric: NYPL (scr)
                 - Original partitur: -0-
                 - Original parts: -0-

Finale Act II ["Do you really mean to go?"]

Rodgers & Henderson/Hart, DeSylva & Brown

Orchestrator: Unknown

Location of   - Composer's manuscript: LoC
                 - Sheet music: Unpublished
                 - Most complete music: R&H (pv)
                 - Most complete lyric: NYPL (scr) & CLLH
                 - Original partitur: -0-
                 - Original parts: -0-

Charleston, The

Author(s): Unknown

Orchestrator: Unknown

Location of   - Composer's manuscript: -0-
                 - Sheet music: -0-
                 - Most complete music: -0-
                 - Most complete lyric: -0-
                 - Original partitur: -0-
                 - Original parts: -0-

This number may have been the famous "Charleston," written by James P. Johnson and Cecil Mack for the 1923 musical comedy RUNNIN' WILD.

Entr'acte II

Author(s): Unknown

Orchestrator: Unknown

Location of   - Composer's manuscript: -0-
                 - Sheet music: Unpublished
                 - Most complete music: -0-
                 - Most complete lyric: INST
                 - Original partitur: -0-
                 - Original parts: -0-

Try Again Tomorrow

Rodgers/Hart

Orchestrator: See note

Location of   - Composer's manuscript: -0-
                 - Sheet music: LoC, NYPL
                 - Most complete music: LoC (sm);
                     NYPL (sm); R&H (pv)
                 - Most complete lyric: CLLH
                 - Original partitur: See note
                 - Original parts: See note

Also used in SHE'S MY BABY. The New York Public Library has Charles N. Grant's partitur (and parts) for "Try Again Tomorrow" in its SHE'S MY BABY collection.

What's the Use?

Rodgers/Hart

Orchestrator: Unknown

Location of   - Composer's manuscript: -0-
                 - Sheet music: LoC, NYPL
                 - Most complete music: LoC (sm);
                     NYPL (sm)
                 - Most complete lyric: CLLH
                 - Original partitur: -0-
                 - Original parts: -0-

The music was first used for "Who's That Little Girl?" in Rodgers and Hart's 1926 musical revue, THE FIFTH AVENUE FOLLIES.

Cheri-Beri

Pestalozza/Thaler

Orchestrator: Unknown

Location of - Composer's manuscript: -0-
- Sheet music: See note
- Most complete music: See note
- Most complete lyric: See note
- Original partitur: -0-
- Original parts: -0-

The script contains no lyric, but this number was probably "Ciribiribin" by A. Pestalozza and Rudolf Thaler, published in 1909. Sheet music for "Ciribiribin" can be found at the New York Public Library.

Atlantic Blues

Rodgers/Hart

Orchestrator: Unknown

Location of - Composer's manuscript: LoC
- Sheet music: LoC, NYPL
- Most complete music: LoC (sm);
    NYPL (sm)
- Most complete lyric: LoC (sm);
    NYPL (sm, scr); CLLH
- Original partitur: -0-
- Original parts: -0-

For PRESENT ARMS (1928), Hart rewrote the lyric slightly and the number was published as "Blue Ocean Blues." The Rodgers and Hammerstein Theatre Library has Hans Spialek's partitur for "Blue Ocean Blues" with its PRESENT ARMS material.

Letter Dance

Author(s): Unknown

Orchestrator: Unknown

Location of - Composer's manuscript: -0-
- Sheet music: -0-
- Most complete music: -0-
- Most complete lyric: -0-
- Original partitur: -0-
- Original parts: -0-

A specialty number performed by Jack Hulbert, who played Harry.

Finale Ultimo

Rodgers & Henderson/Hart, DeSylva & Brown

Orchestrator: Unknown

Location of - Composer's manuscript: -0-
- Sheet music: Unpublished
- Most complete music: See note
- Most complete lyric: NYPL (scr)
- Original partitur: -0-
- Original parts: -0-

Reprises of "A Tiny Flat Near Soho" and "It All Depends on You," both set to new lyrics. Both numbers are published (see individual listings above). The Complete Lyrics of Lorenz Hart also has the Hart lyric.

I Must Be Going

Rodgers/Hart

Orchestrator: Unknown

Location of - Composer's manuscript: -0-
- Sheet music: Not published separately
- Most complete music: R&H (p sel)
- Most complete lyric: -0-
- Original partitur: -0-
- Original parts: -0-

Published only in the piano selection.

Exercise

Rodgers/Hart

Orchestrator: Unknown

Location of - Composer's manuscript: LoC
- Sheet music: Unpublished
- Most complete music: LoC (pv)
- Most complete lyric: R&H (ls); CLLH
- Original partitur: -0-
- Original parts: -0-

Dropped before the London opening.

Lido Lady (1926)

I Want a Man

Rodgers/Hart

Orchestrator: Unknown

Location of   - Composer's manuscript: LoC
- Sheet music: LoC, R&H
- Most complete music: LoC (sm); R&H (sm)
- Most complete lyric: LoC (sm);
      R&H (sm); CLLH
- Original partitur: -0-
- Original parts: -0-

Dropped before the London opening. An earlier version was intended for WINKLE TOWN, an unproduced Rodgers and Hart musical comedy from 1922; a later version was used in AMERICA'S SWEETHEART (1931). The verse changed each time; the refrain remained musically the same. Tams-Witmark Music Library has Robert Russell Bennett's partitur (and parts) for the AMERICA'S SWEETHEART version.

Two to Eleven

Rodgers/Hart

Orchestrator: Unknown

Location of   - Composer's manuscript: LoC
- Sheet music: Unpublished
- Most complete music: LoC (pv)
- Most complete lyric: R&H (ls); CLLH
- Original partitur: -0-
- Original parts: -0-

Unused.

Chuck It!

Rodgers/Hart

Orchestrator: Unknown

Location of   - Composer's manuscript: LoC
- Sheet music: Not published separately
- Most complete music: R&H (pv-l)
- Most complete lyric: R&H (pv-l, ls); CLLH
- Original partitur: -0-
- Original parts: -0-

Dropped before the London opening. The refrain is published in the piano selection of PEGGY-ANN (1926), the show in which the song was finally used. The material at the Rodgers and Hammerstein Theatre Library is in the PEGGY-ANN collection.

Morning Is Midnight

Rodgers/Hart

Orchestrator: See note

Location of   - Composer's manuscript: -0-
- Sheet music: LoC, NYPL
- Most complete music: LoC (sm);
      NYPL (sm); R&H (pv-l)
- Most complete lyric: CLLH
- Original partitur: See note
- Original parts: See note

Dropped before the London opening. Later intended for SHE'S MY BABY (1928), but again dropped. The New York Public Library has Hans Spialek's partitur (and the orchestra piano part) for "Morning is Midnight" in its SHE'S MY BABY collection.

Ever-Ready Freddie

Rodgers/Hart

Orchestrator: Unknown

Location of   - Composer's manuscript: LoC
- Sheet music: Unpublished
- Most complete music: LoC (pv); R&H (pv)
- Most complete lyric: R&H (ls); CLLH
- Original partitur: -0-
- Original parts: -0-

Dropped before the London opening.

Camera Shoot

Rodgers/Hart

Orchestrator: See note

Location of   - Composer's manuscript: LoC (sk),
      NYPL (sk)
- Sheet music: Unpublished
- Most complete music: R&H (pv);
      NYPL (pv)
- Most complete lyric: R&H (ls); CLLH
- Original partitur: See note
- Original parts: -0-

Dropped before the London opening. Later used in SHE'S MY BABY (1928). The New York Public Library has Stephen O. Jones' partitur for "Camera Shoot" in its SHE'S MY BABY collection.

PEGGY-ANN

Music   **RICHARD RODGERS**
Lyrics   **LORENZ HART**

Musical comedy in two acts. Opened December 27, 1926 in New York and ran 333 performances (World premiere: December 13, 1926 in Philadelphia). Libretto by Herbert Fields, suggested by the musical comedy TILLIE'S NIGHTMARE by A. Baldwin Sloane, Alex Gerber, and Edgar Smith. Produced by Lew Fields and Lyle D. Andrews. Directed by Robert Milton. Choreographed by Seymour Felix. Musical direction and orchestrations by Roy Webb.

Synopsis and Production Information	In a small boarding house in upstate New York, Peggy-Ann Barnes, feeling that life is passing her by, starts an argument with her boyfriend, Guy. He walks out on her, and soon after, she falls asleep and dreams of adventures in New York and Cuba -- complete with talking fish and singing pirates, fake ministers and drunk notary publics, nightclub raids and foiled weddings. Through her dream, Peggy comes to realize how much Guy means to her; when he returns, they kiss and make up.
	Other characters (appearing in both the boarding house and Peggy's dream) include vaudevillians Mr. and Mrs. Frost, their precocious daughter Alice, Peggy's snobbish sister Dolores, Dolores' conceited boyfriend Mr. Small, and the inevitable supporting couple, Pat and Fred. There is a full singing and dancing ensemble.
Orchestration	Unknown
Location of Original Materials	Script: New York Public Library (all lyrics), Rodgers and Hammerstein Theatre Library (all lyrics) Piano-vocal score: See individual listings Partiturs: Missing Parts: Missing
	All of the songs performed in the original New York production have survived. Although the partiturs and parts are still missing, Amherst College has parts to an eleven-piece orchestration based on the original.
Rental Status	Currently unavailable for rental
Music Publisher	Marlin Enterprises and Lorenz Hart Publishing Co., c/o Warner Brothers Music
Information	Rodgers and Hammerstein Theatre Library

Peggy-Ann (1926)

Overture

Rodgers/Hart

Orchestrator: Unknown

Location of   - Composer's manuscript: -0-
               - Sheet music: Unpublished
               - Most complete music: AC (reduced parts)
               - Most complete lyric: INST
               - Original partitur: -0-
               - Original parts: -0-

Howdy to Broadway

Rodgers/Hart

Orchestrator: Unknown

Location of   - Composer's manuscript: LoC
               - Sheet music: LoC
               - Most complete music: LoC (sm);
                    R&H (pv-l)
               - Most complete lyric: NYPL (scr);
                    R&H (scr); CLLH
               - Original partitur: -0-
               - Original parts: -0-

For the London production (1927), the title was changed to "Howdy, London."

Hello!

Rodgers/Hart

Orchestrator: Unknown

Location of   - Composer's manuscript: -0-
               - Sheet music: LoC
               - Most complete music: LoC (sm);
                    R&H (pv-l)
               - Most complete lyric: LoC (sm);
                    R&H (pv-l, scr); NYPL (scr); CLLH
               - Original partitur: -0-
               - Original parts: -0-

Little Birdie Told Me So, A

Rodgers/Hart

Orchestrator: Unknown

Location of   - Composer's manuscript: LoC (sk)
               - Sheet music: LoC, NYPL
               - Most complete music: LoC (sm);
                    NYPL (sm); R&H (pv-l)
               - Most complete lyric: LoC (sm);
                    NYPL (sm, scr); R&H (pv-l, scr); CLLH
               - Original partitur: -0-
               - Original parts: -0-

During the 1927 London run, the lyric to this number (which had been labeled "not suitable," "lacking in good taste," and "sniggering" by the London critics) was rewritten by Desmond Carter, and the song was published as "The Country Mouse."

Tree in the Park, A

Rodgers/Hart

Orchestrator: Unknown

Location of   - Composer's manuscript: LoC (sk)
               - Sheet music: LoC, NYPL
               - Most complete music: LoC (sm);
                    NYPL (sm); R&H (pv-l)
               - Most complete lyric: LoC (sm);
                    NYPL (sm, scr); R&H (pv-l, scr); CLLH
               - Original partitur: -0-
               - Original parts: -0-

Charming, Charming

Rodgers/Hart

Orchestrator: Unknown

Location of   - Composer's manuscript: LoC
               - Sheet music: Unpublished
               - Most complete music: R&H (pv-l)
               - Most complete lyric: R&H (pv-l, scr);
                    NYPL (scr); CLLH
               - Original partitur: -0-
               - Original parts: -0-

Alternate title: "Store Opening."

Where's That Rainbow?
Rodgers/Hart
Orchestrator: Unknown

Location of
- Composer's manuscript: LoC (sk)
- Sheet music: LoC, NYPL
- Most complete music: LoC (sm);
  NYPL (sm); R&H (pv-l)
- Most complete lyric: LoC (sm)
  NYPL (sm); R&H (pv-l); CLLH
- Original partitur: -0-
- Original parts: -0-

The piano-vocal also includes dance music and an encore.

Finale Act I ["Here's that wedding you hear about..."]
Rodgers/Hart
Orchestrator: Unknown

Location of
- Composer's manuscript: LoC
- Sheet music: Unpublished
- Most complete music: R&H (pv)
- Most complete lyric: R&H (ls, scr);
  NYPL (scr); CLLH
- Original partitur: -0-
- Original parts: -0-

Alternate title: "Wedding Procession."

Entr'acte
Rodgers/Hart
Orchestrator: Unknown

Location of
- Composer's manuscript: -0-
- Sheet music: Unpublished
- Most complete music: -0-
- Most complete lyric: INST
- Original partitur: -0-
- Original parts: -0-

Opening Act II ["Stop! What is it? A pirate ship!"]
Rodgers/Hart
Orchestrator: Unknown

Location of
- Composer's manuscript: -0-
- Sheet music: Unpublished
- Most complete music: R&H (pv)
- Most complete lyric: NYPL (scr);
  R&H (scr); CLLH
- Original partitur: -0-
- Original parts: -0-

Alternate title: "We Pirates from Weehawken." For the London production (1927), the title was changed to "We Pirates from Wee Dorkin."

Chuck It!
Rodgers/Hart
Orchestrator: Unknown

Location of
- Composer's manuscript: LoC
- Sheet music: Not published separately
- Most complete music: R&H (pv-l)
- Most complete lyric: R&H (pv-l, ls, scr);
  NYPL (scr); CLLH
- Original partitur: -0-
- Original parts: -0-

The refrain was published in the piano selection, which can be found at the Rodgers and Hammerstein Theatre Library.

Havana
Rodgers/Hart
Orchestrator: Unknown

Location of
- Composer's manuscript: -0-
- Sheet music: Not published separately
- Most complete music: R&H (pv-l)
- Most complete lyric: R&H (pv-l, scr);
  NYPL (scr); CLLH
- Original partitur: -0-
- Original parts: -0-

The verse was published in the piano selection, which can be found at the Rodgers and Hammerstein Theatre Library.

Maybe It's Me

Rodgers/Hart

Orchestrator: Unknown

Location of   - Composer's manuscript: -0-
- Sheet music: LoC, NYPL
- Most complete music: LoC (sm);
     NYPL (sm); R&H (pv-l)
- Most complete lyric: LoC (sm);
     NYPL (sm); R&H (pv-l); CLLH
- Original partitur: -0-
- Original parts: -0-

Originally used in Rodgers and Hart's 1926 musical revue, THE FIFTH AVENUE FOLLIES. The PEGGY-ANN scripts contain an alternate line in the first verse.

Give This Little Girl a Hand

Rodgers/Hart

Orchestrator: Unknown

Location of   - Composer's manuscript: LoC (sk)
- Sheet music: LoC
- Most complete music: R&H (pv-l)
- Most complete lyric: R&H (pv-l); CLLH
- Original partitur: -0-
- Original parts: -0-

The Complete Lyrics of Lorenz Hart also has an early version.

Peggy, Peggy

Rodgers/Hart

Orchestrator: Unknown

Location of   - Composer's manuscript: LoC
- Sheet music: Unpublished
- Most complete music: R&H (pv-l)
- Most complete lyric: R&H (pv-l, scr);
     NYPL (scr); CLLH
- Original partitur: -0-
- Original parts: -0-

The Complete Lyrics of Lorenz Hart also has an early version.

In His Arms

Rodgers/Hart

Orchestrator: Unknown

Location of   - Composer's manuscript: -0-
- Sheet music: Unpublished
- Most complete music: -0-
- Most complete lyric: -0-
- Original partitur: -0-
- Original parts: -0-

Dropped during the New York run.

Pipes of Pansy, The

Rodgers/Hart

Orchestrator: See note

Location of   - Composer's manuscript: -0-
- Sheet music: Unpublished
- Most complete music: R&H (pv-l)
- Most complete lyric: R&H (pv-l, ls);
     CLLH
- Original partitur: See note
- Original parts: -0-

Unused. Also intended for DEAREST ENEMY (1925), THE GIRL FRIEND (1926), and SHE'S MY BABY (1928), but dropped from all four productions. The New York Public Library has two partiturs for "The Pipes of Pansy" (by Roy Webb and F. Henri Klickmann) in its SHE'S MY BABY collection. The lyric is also in the early draft of the PEGGY-ANN script at the Library of Congress.

Trampin' Along

Rodgers/Hart

Orchestrator: Unknown

Location of   - Composer's manuscript: -0-
- Sheet music: Unpublished
- Most complete music: R&H (pv)
- Most complete lyric: R&H (ls); CLLH
- Original partitur: -0-
- Original parts: -0-

Replaced during the pre-Broadway tryout by "Howdy to Broadway."

315

Paris Is Really Divine

Rodgers/Hart

Orchestrator: Unknown

Location of   - Composer's manuscript: -0-
- Sheet music: Unpublished
- Most complete music: R&H (pv-I);
      LoC (pv)
- Most complete lyric: R&H (ls); CLLH
- Original partitur: -0-
- Original parts: -0-

Dropped during the pre-Broadway tryout. Later used in ONE DAM THING AFTER ANOTHER, Rodgers and Hart's 1927 London revue.

I'm So Humble

Rodgers/Hart

Orchestrator: Unknown

Location of   - Composer's manuscript: -0-
- Sheet music: Unpublished
- Most complete music: R&H (pv-I)
- Most complete lyric: R&H (pv-I); CLLH
- Original partitur: -0-
- Original parts: -0-

Dropped soon after the New York opening. The lyric is also in the early draft of the script at the Library of Congress under the title "Inferiority Complex."

Come and Tell Me

Rodgers/Hart

Orchestrator: Unknown

Location of   - Composer's manuscript: -0-
- Sheet music: LoC, NYPL
- Most complete music: LoC (sm);
      NYPL (sm); R&H (pv-I)
- Most complete lyric: LoC (sm);
      NYPL (sm); R&H (ls); CLLH
- Original partitur: -0-
- Original parts: -0-

Dropped during the pre-Broadway tryout. Published with the sheet music from BETSY (1926), for which it was also intended, although the singers on the printed music are Peggy and Guy, the lead characters in PEGGY-ANN. The piano-vocal and lyric sheet at the Rodgers and Hammerstein Theatre Library are with the BETSY material. The lyric is also in the early draft of the PEGGY-ANN script at the Library of Congress.

BETSY

Music	RICHARD RODGERS
Lyrics	LORENZ HART

Musical comedy in two acts. Opened December 28, 1926 in New York and ran 39 performances (World premiere: December 20, 1926 in Washington, D.C.). Libretto by Irving Caesar and David Freedman, revised by William Anthony McGuire. Additional music and lyrics by Irving Berlin, Irving Caesar, Jacques Offenbach, A. Segal, M. Siegel. Produced by Florenz Ziegfeld. Directed by William Anthony McGuire. Choreographed by Sammy Lee. Musical direction by Victor Baravalle.

Synopsis and Production Information	Betsy Kitzel's three brothers (Louie, Moe, and Joe) are engaged to rich, pretty women (Winnie, May, and Flora), but Mama Kitzel will not let them marry until they find a husband for Betsy. They try to turn Archie, an idler and bird fancier, into someone suitable, but he falls for Betsy's younger sister, Ruth. Luckily, Betsy's dreams of performing on the stage lead to a happy ending for everybody.
	The show includes a full singing and dancing ensemble, and numerous specialty acts.
Orchestration	Unknown
Comments	BETSY was primarily a showcase for vaudeville performer Belle Baker, who played the title role. The original production also included two appearances by Borrah Minevitch and his Harmonica Symphony Orchestra, a balloon number, and a song in which the chorus girls tossed hot dogs into the audience.
Location of Original Materials	Script: Missing Piano-vocal score: See individual listings Partiturs: Missing Parts: Missing
	Although no final production script has been located, the Rodgers and Hammerstein Theatre Library has an early draft by Caesar and Freedman entitled BUY BUY BETTY. Three songs performed in the New York production are still missing, as are the Overture, the Entr'acte, and most of the specialty material.
Rental Status	Currently unavailable for rental
Music Publisher	Marlin Enterprises and Lorenz Hart Publishing Co., c/o Warner Brothers Music
Information	Rodgers and Hammerstein Theatre Library

Overture

Author(s): Unknown
Orchestrator: Unknown

Location of   - Composer's manuscript: -0-
                - Sheet music: Unpublished
                - Most complete music: -0-
                - Most complete lyric: INST
                - Original partitur: -0-
                - Original parts: -0-

Stonewall Moskowitz March

Rodgers/Hart & Caesar
Orchestrator: Unknown

Location of   - Composer's manuscript: R&H
                - Sheet music: LoC, NYPL
                - Most complete music: LoC (sm);
                    NYPL (sm); R&H (pv-l)
                - Most complete lyric: R&H (ls); CLLH
                - Original partitur: -0-
                - Original parts: -0-

Kitzel Engagement, The

Rodgers/Hart
Orchestrator: Unknown

Location of   - Composer's manuscript: LoC
                - Sheet music: Unpublished
                - Most complete music: R&H (pv); LoC (pv)
                - Most complete lyric: R&H (ls); CLLH
                - Original partitur: -0-
                - Original parts: -0-

Alternate title: "Opening Ensemble."

One of Us Should Be Two

Rodgers/Hart
Orchestrator: Unknown

Location of   - Composer's manuscript: -0-
                - Sheet music: Unpublished
                - Most complete music: R&H (pv)
                - Most complete lyric: R&H (ls); CLLH
                - Original partitur: -0-
                - Original parts: -0-

My Missus

Rodgers/Hart
Orchestrator: Unknown

Location of   - Composer's manuscript: -0-
                - Sheet music: Unpublished
                - Most complete music: R&H (pv-l)
                - Most complete lyric: CLLH
                - Original partitur: -0-
                - Original parts: -0-

Sing

Rodgers/Hart
Orchestrator: Unknown

Location of   - Composer's manuscript: LoC
                - Sheet music: LoC, NYPL
                - Most complete music: LoC (sm);
                    NYPL (sm); R&H (pv-l)
                - Most complete lyric: LoC (sm);
                    NYPL (sm); R&H (pv-l, ls); CLLH
                - Original partitur: -0-
                - Original parts: -0-

Also sung in the London musical LADY LUCK (1927) and in the Broadway musical LADY FINGERS (1929).

Betsy (1926)

In Our Parlor on the Third Floor Back
Rodgers/Hart
Orchestrator: Unknown

Location of - Composer's manuscript: -0-
- Sheet music: Unpublished
- Most complete music: -0-
- Most complete lyric: -0-
- Original partitur: -0-
- Original parts: -0-

Follow On
Rodgers/Hart
Orchestrator: Unknown

Location of - Composer's manuscript: -0-
- Sheet music: Unpublished
- Most complete music: -0-
- Most complete lyric: -0-
- Original partitur: -0-
- Original parts: -0-

This Funny World
Rodgers/Hart
Orchestrator: Unknown

Location of - Composer's manuscript: -0-
- Sheet music: LoC, NYPL
- Most complete music: LoC (sm);
  NYPL (sm); R&H (pv-I)
- Most complete lyric: LoC (sm);
  NYPL (sm); R&H (pv-I); CLLH
- Original partitur: -0-
- Original parts: -0-

National Dances
Rodgers/Hart
Orchestrator: Unknown

Location of - Composer's manuscript: LoC
- Sheet music: Unpublished
- Most complete music: LoC (pv) &
  R&H (pv)
- Most complete lyric: -0-
- Original partitur: -0-
- Original parts: -0-

The piano-vocals are entitled "Nations Patter."

Don't Believe
Caesar & Siegel/Caesar & Siegel
Orchestrator: Unknown

Location of - Composer's manuscript: -0-
- Sheet music: Unpublished
- Most complete music: -0-
- Most complete lyric: -0-
- Original partitur: -0-
- Original parts: -0-

Replaced before the New York opening by "The Tales of
Hoffman," then reinstated during the run when "The Tales
of Hoffman" was dropped.

Push Around
Rodgers/Hart
Orchestrator: Unknown

Location of - Composer's manuscript: -0-
- Sheet music: Unpublished
- Most complete music: -0-
- Most complete lyric: -0-
- Original partitur: -0-
- Original parts: -0-

Bugle Blow

    Rodgers/Hart

    Orchestrator: Unknown

    Location of   - Composer's manuscript: -0-

                  - Sheet music: Unpublished

                  - Most complete music: R&H (pv)

                  - Most complete lyric: CLLH

                  - Original partitur: -0-

                  - Original parts: -0-

The music to the patter section is missing.

Cradle of the Deep

    Rodgers/Hart

    Orchestrator: Unknown

    Location of   - Composer's manuscript: -0-

                  - Sheet music: Unpublished

                  - Most complete music: R&H (pv)

                  - Most complete lyric: R&H (ls); CLLH

                  - Original partitur: -0-

                  - Original parts: -0-

Finale Act I ["I guess I should be satisfied..."]

    Rodgers/Hart

    Orchestrator: Unknown

    Location of   - Composer's manuscript: -0-

                  - Sheet music: Unpublished

                  - Most complete music: R&H (pv)

                  - Most complete lyric: R&H (ls); CLLH

                  - Original partitur: -0-

                  - Original parts: -0-

If I Were You

    Rodgers/Hart

    Orchestrator: See note

    Location of   - Composer's manuscript: -0-

                  - Sheet music: LoC

                  - Most complete music: LoC (sm);

                      R&H (pv-l)

                  - Most complete lyric: CLLH

                  - Original partitur: See note

                  - Original parts: -0-

Also used in SHE'S MY BABY (1928), with a different lyric to the verse. The New York Public Library has two partiturs for "If I Were You" (by Stephen O. Jones and Hans Spialek) in its SHE'S MY BABY collection.

Entr'acte

    Author(s): Unknown

    Orchestrator: Unknown

    Location of   - Composer's manuscript: -0-

                  - Sheet music: Unpublished

                  - Most complete music: -0-

                  - Most complete lyric: INST

                  - Original partitur: -0-

                  - Original parts: -0-

Blue Skies

    Berlin/Berlin

    Orchestrator: Unknown

    Location of   - Composer's manuscript: -0-

                  - Sheet music: LoC, NYPL, IB, Y

                  - Most complete music: LoC (sm);

                      NYPL (sm); IB (sm); Y (sm)

                  - Most complete lyric: LoC (sm);

                      NYPL (sm); IB (sm); Y (sm)

                  - Original partitur: -0-

                  - Original parts: -0-

Added to the show on opening night in New York.

Leave It to Levy

Rodgers/Caesar

Orchestrator: Unknown

Location of   - Composer's manuscript: -0-
                - Sheet music: Unpublished
                - Most complete music: R&H (pv)
                - Most complete lyric: See note
                - Original partitur: -0-
                - Original parts: -0-

The lyric is the early draft of the script at the Rodgers and Hammerstein Theatre Library.

Finaletto, Act II Scene 1 ["First we throw Moe out"]

Rodgers/Hart

Orchestrator: Unknown

Location of   - Composer's manuscript: -0-
                - Sheet music: Unpublished
                - Most complete music: See note
                - Most complete lyric: R&H (ls); CLLH
                - Original partitur: -0-
                - Original parts: -0-

A new lyric set to the music of "Sing." The Library of Congress and the New York Public Library have sheet music for "Sing"; the Rodgers and Hammerstein Theatre Library has a piano-vocal.

Birds Up High

Rodgers/Hart

Orchestrator: Unknown

Location of   - Composer's manuscript: -0-
                - Sheet music: Unpublished
                - Most complete music: R&H (pv)
                - Most complete lyric: R&H (ls); CLLH
                - Original partitur: -0-
                - Original parts: -0-

Shuffle

Rodgers/Hart

Orchestrator: Unknown

Location of   - Composer's manuscript: LoC
                - Sheet music: Not published separately
                - Most complete music: R&H (pv); LoC (pv)
                - Most complete lyric: CLLH
                - Original partitur: -0-
                - Original parts: -0-

Also used in ONE DAM THING AFTER ANOTHER, Rodgers and Hart's 1927 London revue. The refrain was published in the ONE DAM THING AFTER ANOTHER piano selection, which can be found at the Rodgers and Hammerstein Theatre Library.

Dance Specialty

Author(s): Unknown

Orchestrator: Unknown

Location of   - Composer's manuscript: -0-
                - Sheet music: Unpublished
                - Most complete music: -0-
                - Most complete lyric: -0-
                - Original partitur: -0-
                - Original parts: -0-

A dance specialty for Evelyn Law, who played Flora.

Song Specialty

Author(s): Unknown

Orchestrator: Unknown

Location of   - Composer's manuscript: -0-
                - Sheet music: -0-
                - Most complete music: -0-
                - Most complete lyric: -0-
                - Original partitur: -0-
                - Original parts: -0-

Belle Baker's eleven o'clock spot.

Tales of Hoffman, The
  Caesar & Offenbach/Caesar & Segal
  Orchestrator: Unknown

  Location of - Composer's manuscript: -0-
               - Sheet music: Unpublished
               - Most complete music: R&H (pv-I)
               - Most complete lyric: R&H (pv-I)
               - Original partitur: -0-
               - Original parts: -0-

Replaced during the New York run by "Don't Believe."

In Variety
  Rodgers/Hart
  Orchestrator: Unknown

  Location of - Composer's manuscript: -0-
               - Sheet music: Unpublished
               - Most complete music: -0-
               - Most complete lyric: -0-
               - Original partitur: -0-
               - Original parts: -0-

Dropped before the New York opening.

At the Saskatchewan
  Rodgers/Hart
  Orchestrator: Unknown

  Location of - Composer's manuscript: R&H
               - Sheet music: Unpublished
               - Most complete music: R&H (pv)
               - Most complete lyric: R&H (ls); CLLH
               - Original partitur: -0-
               - Original parts: -0-

Dropped before the New York opening.

Is My Girl Refined?
  Rodgers/Hart
  Orchestrator: Unknown

  Location of - Composer's manuscript: LoC
               - Sheet music: Unpublished
               - Most complete music: R&H (pv); LoC (pv)
               - Most complete lyric: R&H (ls); CLLH
               - Original partitur: -0-
               - Original parts: -0-

Dropped before the New York opening.

You're the Mother Type
  Rodgers/Hart
  Orchestrator: Unknown

  Location of - Composer's manuscript: -0-
               - Sheet music: LoC, NYPL
               - Most complete music: LoC (sm);
                   NYPL (sm); R&H (pv-I)
               - Most complete lyric: LoC (sm);
                   NYPL (sm); R&H (pv-I); CLLH
               - Original partitur: -0-
               - Original parts: -0-

Dropped before the New York opening.

Six Little Kitzels
  Rodgers/Hart
  Orchestrator: Unknown

  Location of - Composer's manuscript: -0-
               - Sheet music: Unpublished
               - Most complete music: R&H (pv)
               - Most complete lyric: R&H (ls); CLLH
               - Original partitur: -0-
               - Original parts: -0-

Dropped before the New York opening.

Transformation

Rodgers/Hart

Orchestrator: Unknown

Location of - Composer's manuscript: -0-
           - Sheet music: Unpublished
           - Most complete music: -0-
           - Most complete lyric: R&H (ls); CLLH
           - Original partitur: -0-
           - Original parts: -0-

Dropped before the New York opening.

Come and Tell Me

Rodgers/Hart

Orchestrator: Unknown

Location of - Composer's manuscript: -0-
           - Sheet music: LoC, NYPL
           - Most complete music: LoC (sm);
              NYPL (sm); R&H (pv-l)
           - Most complete lyric: LoC (sm);
              NYPL (sm); R&H (ls); CLLH
           - Original partitur: -0-
           - Original parts: -0-

Although this number was dropped before the New York
opening, a passage from it remained in the Act I Finale.
Also intended for PEGGY-ANN (1926). The singers listed
in the BETSY sheet music for this song are Peggy and
Guy, the lead characters from PEGGY-ANN.

Ladies' Home Companion, A

Rodgers/Hart

Orchestrator: Unknown

Location of - Composer's manuscript: -0-
           - Sheet music: Unpublished
           - Most complete music: -0-
           - Most complete lyric: CLLH
           - Original partitur: -0-
           - Original parts: -0-

Dropped during the pre-Broadway tryout; later used in A
CONNECTICUT YANKEE (1927). The lyric is also in the
1927 CONNECTICUT YANKEE scripts at the Rodgers and
Hammerstein Theatre Library and the New York Public
Library.

Show Me How to Make Love

Rodgers/Hart

Orchestrator: Unknown

Location of - Composer's manuscript: -0-
           - Sheet music: Unpublished
           - Most complete music: -0-
           - Most complete lyric: -0-
           - Original partitur: -0-
           - Original parts: -0-

Dropped before the New York opening.

Burn Up

Rodgers/Hart

Orchestrator: Unknown

Location of - Composer's manuscript: R&H
           - Sheet music: Unpublished
           - Most complete music: R&H (pv)
           - Most complete lyric: R&H (ls); CLLH
           - Original partitur: -0-
           - Original parts: -0-

Unused.

Social Work

Rodgers/Hart

Orchestrator: Unknown

Location of - Composer's manuscript: -0-
           - Sheet music: Unpublished
           - Most complete music: R&H (pv)
           - Most complete lyric: R&H (ls); CLLH
           - Original partitur: -0-
           - Original parts: -0-

Unused.

Viva Italia

Rodgers/Hart

Orchestrator: Unknown

Location of - Composer's manuscript: -0-
            - Sheet music: Unpublished
            - Most complete music: -0-
            - Most complete lyric: R&H (ls); CLLH
            - Original partitur: -0-
            - Original parts: -0-

Unused.

Melican Man, A

Rodgers/Hart

Orchestrator: Unknown

Location of - Composer's manuscript: -0-
            - Sheet music: Unpublished
            - Most complete music: -0-
            - Most complete lyric: R&H (ls); CLLH
            - Original partitur: -0-
            - Original parts: -0-

Unused.

A CONNECTICUT YANKEE (1927)

Music **RICHARD RODGERS**
Lyrics **LORENZ HART**

Musical comedy in two acts. Opened November 3, 1927 in New York and ran 418 performances (World premiere: September 30, 1927 in Stamford, Connecticut). Libretto by Herbert Fields, adapted from the novel A CONNECTICUT YANKEE IN KING ARTHUR'S COURT by Mark Twain. Produced by Lew Fields and Lyle D. Andrews. Directed by Alexander Leftwich. Choreographed by Busby Berkeley. Musical direction by Roy Webb. Orchestrations by Roy Webb, Robert Russell Bennett.

Synopsis and Production Information	Martin's old girlfriend Alice turns up at the bachelor party celebrating his impending marriage to Fay Morgan. Fay appears and, upon seeing the two together, knocks Martin out with a bottle. An unconscious Martin then dreams that he is back in the court of King Arthur, wooing the lovely lady-in-waiting Alisande while the King's jealous sister, Morgan Le Fay, tries to separate them. As the kingdom goes into an uproar over these conflicts, Martin wakes up and realizes he truly wants to marry Alice.
	Other characters include Sir Galahad and lady-in-waiting Evelyn, who team up for a couple of numbers. There is a full singing and dancing ensemble.
Orchestration	Reed 1 (Flute, Piccolo); Reed 2 (Oboe, English Horn); Reed 3 (Clarinet, Flute); Reed 4 (Clarinet, Bass Clarinet); Reed 5 (Clarinet, Bassoon); Horn; Trumpet I II; Trombone; Percussion; Piano/Celeste; Violin A B; Violin C D; Viola; Cello; Bass
Comments	In 1943, Richard Rodgers presented a revival of A CONNECTICUT YANKEE, with a partly revised book and several new Rodgers and Hart songs. That production is also included in this catalog.
Location of Original Materials	Script: New York Public Library (most lyrics), Rodgers and Hammerstein Theatre Library (most lyrics) Piano-vocal score: See individual listings Partiturs: Rodgers and Hammerstein Theatre Library, Tams-Witmark Music Library Parts: Missing
	Music and/or lyrics to four numbers performed in the New York production are missing, as are the Overture and the Entr'acte. Only two partiturs have surfaced.
Rental Status	Currently unavailable for rental. Tams-Witmark Music Library rents the 1943 revision.
Music Publisher	Marlin Enterprises and Lorenz Hart Publishing Co., c/o Warner Brothers Music
Information	Rodgers and Hammerstein Theatre Library

Overture
Rodgers/Hart
Orchestrator: Unknown

Location of   - Composer's manuscript: -0-
          - Sheet music: Unpublished
          - Most complete music: -0-
          - Most complete lyric: INST
          - Original partitur: -0-
          - Original parts: -0-

Ladies' Home Companion, A
Rodgers/Hart
Orchestrator: Unknown

Location of   - Composer's manuscript: -0-
          - Sheet music: Unpublished
          - Most complete music: -0-
          - Most complete lyric: R&H (scr);
               NYPL (scr); CLLH
          - Original partitur: -0-
          - Original parts: -0-

My Heart Stood Still
Rodgers/Hart
Orchestrator: Unknown

Location of   - Composer's manuscript: -0-
          - Sheet music: LoC, NYPL
          - Most complete music: LoC (sm);
               NYPL (sm); R&H (pv-l);
               TW (1943 pv score)
          - Most complete lyric: LoC (sm);
               NYPL (sm, scr); R&H (pv-l, scr);
               CLLH
          - Original partitur: -0-
          - Original parts: -0-

The lyric was updated for the 1943 production; this later
version is in the Tams-Witmark piano-vocal score and
early drafts of the 1943 script at the Rodgers and
Hammerstein Theatre Library and the New York Public
Library.

Thou Swell
Rodgers/Hart
Orchestrator: Unknown

Location of   - Composer's manuscript: -0-
          - Sheet music: LoC, NYPL
          - Most complete music: LoC (sm);
               NYPL (sm); R&H (pv-l);
               TW (1943 pv score)
          - Most complete lyric: LoC (sm);
               NYPL (sm, scr); R&H (pv-l, scr);
               TW (1943 pv score), CLLH
          - Original partitur: -0-
          - Original parts: -0-

At the Round Table
Rodgers/Hart
Orchestrator: Unknown

Location of   - Composer's manuscript: -0-
          - Sheet music: Not published separately
          - Most complete music: TW (1943 pv score)
          - Most complete lyric: CLLH
          - Original partitur: -0-
          - Original parts: -0-

Alternate title: "Knights' Opening." The refrain was
published in the piano selection.

On a Desert Island With Thee
Rodgers/Hart
Orchestrator: Webb

Location of   - Composer's manuscript: -0-
          - Sheet music: LoC, NYPL
          - Most complete music: LoC (sm);
               NYPL (sm); R&H (pv-l);
               TW (1943 pv score)
          - Most complete lyric: LoC (sm);
               NYPL (sm, scr); R&H (pv-l, scr);
               TW (1943 pv score); CLLH
          - Original partitur: R&H
          - Original parts: -0-

A Connecticut Yankee (1927)

Finale Act I ["Ibbidi bibbidi sibbidi sab!"]
Rodgers/Hart
Orchestrator: Bennett

Location of
- Composer's manuscript: -0-
- Sheet music: Unpublished
- Most complete music: R&H (lead-l)
  & TW (1943 pv score)
- Most complete lyric: R&H (scr);
  NYPL (scr); CLLH
- Original partitur: TW
- Original parts: -0-

The Complete Lyrics of Lorenz Hart also contains
alternate lyrics used in the 1943 production.

I Feel at Home With You
Rodgers/Hart
Orchestrator: Unknown

Location of
- Composer's manuscript: -0-
- Sheet music: LoC, NYPL
- Most complete music: LoC (sm);
  NYPL (sm); R&H (pv-l);
  TW (1943 pv score)
- Most complete lyric: LoC (sm);
  NYPL (sm, scr); R&H (scr, ls); CLLH
- Original partitur: -0-
- Original parts: -0-

Entr'acte
Rodgers/Hart
Orchestrator: Unknown

Location of
- Composer's manuscript: -0-
- Sheet music: Unpublished
- Most complete music: -0-
- Most complete lyric: INST
- Original partitur: -0-
- Original parts: -0-

Sandwich Men, The
Rodgers/Hart
Orchestrator: Unknown

Location of
- Composer's manuscript: -0-
- Sheet music: Unpublished
- Most complete music: -0-
- Most complete lyric: R&H (scr);
  NYPL (scr); CLLH
- Original partitur: -0-
- Original parts: -0-

Nothing's Wrong
Rodgers/Hart
Orchestrator: Unknown

Location of
- Composer's manuscript: LoC
- Sheet music: Not published separately
- Most complete music: LoC (pv)
- Most complete lyric: -0-
- Original partitur: -0-
- Original parts: -0-

The refrain was published in the piano selection.

Evelyn, What Do You Say?
Rodgers/Hart
Orchestrator: Unknown

Location of
- Composer's manuscript: -0-
- Sheet music: Unpublished
- Most complete music: -0-
- Most complete lyric: R&H (scr);
  NYPL (scr); CLLH
- Original partitur: -0-
- Original parts: -0-

The Rodgers and Hammerstein Theatre Library has a lyric
sheet for an earlier version of the song, "Morgan Le Fay,"
which has virtually the same lyric as "Evelyn, What Do
You Say?" and was probably set to the same music.

I Blush

    Rodgers/Hart

    Orchestrator: Unknown

Location of   - Composer's manuscript: -0-
                 - Sheet music: LoC, NYPL
                 - Most complete music: LoC (sm);
                     NYPL (sm); R&H (pv-l)
                 - Most complete lyric: LoC (sm);
                     NYPL (sm); R&H (pv-l, ls); CLLH
                 - Original partitur: -0-
                 - Original parts: -0-

Replaced during the pre-Broadway tryout by "Nothing's Wrong."

Someone Should Tell Them

    Rodgers/Hart

    Orchestrator: See note

Location of   - Composer's manuscript: -0-
                 - Sheet music: LoC, NYPL
                 - Most complete music: LoC (sm);
                     NYPL (sm); R&H (pv-l)
                 - Most complete lyric: LoC (sm);
                     NYPL (sm); R&H (pv-l); CLLH
                 - Original partitur: See note
                 - Original parts: See note

Dropped during the pre-Broadway tryout. The music was later used for "There's So Much More" in AMERICA'S SWEETHEART (1931); Tams-Witmark Music Library has Robert Russell Bennett's partitur (and parts) for "Someone Should Tell Them" with its AMERICA'S SWEETHEART material.

You're What I Need

    Rodgers/Hart

    Orchestrator: See note

Location of   - Composer's manuscript: -0-
                 - Sheet music: LoC, NYPL
                 - Most complete music: LoC (sm);
                     NYPL (sm); R&H (pv-l)
                 - Most complete lyric: LoC (sm);
                     NYPL (sm); R&H (ls); CLLH
                 - Original partitur: See note
                 - Original parts: -0-

Dropped during the pre-Broadway tryout. Published with the sheet music from SHE'S MY BABY (1928), in which the song was later used. The New York Public Library has two partiturs for "You're What I Need" (by Stephen O. Jones and F. Henri Klickmann) in its SHE'S MY BABY collection.

Britain's Own Ambassadors

    Rodgers/Hart

    Orchestrator: Unknown

Location of   - Composer's manuscript: -0-
                 - Sheet music: Unpublished
                 - Most complete music: -0-
                 - Most complete lyric: -0-
                 - Original partitur: -0-
                 - Original parts: -0-

Dropped in rehearsal.

SHE'S MY BABY

Music   **RICHARD RODGERS**
Lyrics   **LORENZ HART**

Musical farce in two acts. Opened January 3, 1928 in New York and ran 71 performances (World premiere: December 12, 1927 in Washington, D.C.). Libretto by Guy Bolton, Bert Kalmar and Harry Ruby. Additional song by Ivor Novello and Douglas Furber. Produced by Charles Dillingham. Directed by Edward Royce. Choreographed by Mary Read. Musical direction by Gene Salzer. Orchestrations by Hans Spialek, Robert Russell Bennett, Roy Webb, Stephen O. Jones, Carl F. Williams, F. Henri Klickmann, Charles N. Grant, Charles Miller.

Synopsis and Production Information	Bob Martin needs money to produce a show starring his girlfriend, Polly. His uncle, Mr. Hemingway, will give him the money provided that he has a wife and baby. A plan to enact this scenario using Tilly, a friend's maid who's trying to break into show business, creates comic complications.
	Musical support is provided by Clyde Parker (Bob's author friend) and Josie (a performer). There is a full singing and dancing ensemble.
Orchestration	Reed I (Flute, Piccolo, Alto Sax); Reed II (Oboe, Tenor Sax, Baritone Sax); Reed III (Clarinet, Alto Sax); Reed IV (Clarinet, Alto Sax); Horn I II; Trumpet I II; Trombone; Percussion; Piano; Guitar/Banjo; Violin I II; Viola I; Viola II; Cello; Bass
Comments	In the original production, Tilly was played by Beatrice Lillie.
Location of Original Materials	Script: Missing Piano-vocal score: See individual listings Partiturs: New York Public Library Parts: New York Public Library
	Although the final production script is missing, the Rodgers and Hammerstein Theatre Library has an early draft with no lyrics. Most of the piano-vocal material and partiturs survive, as do parts for several numbers.
Rental Status	Currently unavailable for rental
Music Publisher	Marlin Enterprises and Lorenz Hart Publishing Co., c/o Warner Brothers Music
Information	Rodgers and Hammerstein Theatre Library

Overture

Rodgers/Hart
Orchestrator: Jones, Spialek

Location of
- Composer's manuscript: -0-
- Sheet music: Unpublished
- Most complete music: NYPL (ptr)
- Most complete lyric: INST
- Original partitur: NYPL
- Original parts: -0-

You're What I Need

Rodgers/Hart
Orchestrator: Jones, Klickmann

Location of
- Composer's manuscript: -0-
- Sheet music: LoC, NYPL
- Most complete music: LoC (sm); NYPL (sm); R&H (pv-l)
- Most complete lyric: LoC (sm); NYPL (sm); R&H (ls); CLLH
- Original partitur: NYPL
- Original parts: -0-

Previously used in the pre-Broadway tryout of A CONNECTICUT YANKEE (1927).

This Goes Up

Rodgers/Hart
Orchestrator: Jones, Spialek

Location of
- Composer's manuscript: NYPL (sk)
- Sheet music: Unpublished
- Most complete music: R&H (pv-l)
- Most complete lyric: R&H (pv-l, ls); CLLH
- Original partitur: NYPL
- Original parts: NYPL

Here She Comes

Rodgers/Hart
Orchestrator: Jones

Location of
- Composer's manuscript: NYPL (sk)
- Sheet music: Unpublished
- Most complete music: NYPL (sk & ptr)
- Most complete lyric: CLLH
- Original partitur: NYPL
- Original parts: -0-

Alternate titles: "All Set! Let's Go" and "Musical Entrance -- Tilly."

My Lucky Star

Rodgers/Hart
Orchestrator: Webb

Location of
- Composer's manuscript: -0-
- Sheet music: NYPL
- Most complete music: R&H (pv-l)
- Most complete lyric: R&H (pv-l); CLLH
- Original partitur: NYPL
- Original parts: NYPL

The Complete Lyrics of Lorenz Hart also contains earlier lyrics used in Rodgers and Hart's 1927 London revue, ONE DAM THING AFTER ANOTHER.

Swallows, The

Author(s): Unknown
Orchestrator: Unknown

Location of
- Composer's manuscript: -0-
- Sheet music: Unpublished
- Most complete music: -0-
- Most complete lyric: -0-
- Original partitur: -0-
- Original parts: -0-

She's My Baby (1928)

When I Go on the Stage

Rodgers/Hart
Orchestrator: Jones

Location of
- Composer's manuscript: NYPL (sk)
- Sheet music: LoC
- Most complete music: LoC (sm);
  R&H (pv-l)
- Most complete lyric: CLLH
- Original partitur: NYPL
- Original parts: -0-

Camera Shoot

Rodgers/Hart
Orchestrator: Jones

Location of
- Composer's manuscript: NYPL (sk);
  LoC (sk)
- Sheet music: Unpublished
- Most complete music: R&H (pv);
  NYPL (pv)
- Most complete lyric: R&H (ls); CLLH
- Original partitur: NYPL
- Original parts: -0-

Intended for LIDO LADY (1926).

Try Again Tomorrow

Rodgers/Hart
Orchestrator: Grant

Location of
- Composer's manuscript: -0-
- Sheet music: LoC, NYPL
- Most complete music: LoC (sm);
  NYPL (sm); R&H (pv)
- Most complete lyric: CLLH
- Original partitur: NYPL
- Original parts: NYPL

Previously used in LIDO LADY (1926).

Smart People

Rodgers/Hart
Orchestrator: Spialek

Location of
- Composer's manuscript: -0-
- Sheet music: Unpublished
- Most complete music: NYPL (pv)
- Most complete lyric: CLLH
- Original partitur: NYPL
- Original parts: NYPL (inc)

Of the orchestra parts, only the piano part survives.

Tiller Girls Dances

Author(s): Unknown
Orchestrator: Unknown

Location of
- Composer's manuscript: -0-
- Sheet music: -0-
- Most complete music: -0-
- Most complete lyric: -0-
- Original partitur: NYPL
- Original parts: -0-

The New York programs for SHE'S MY BABY list three untitled dance specialties performed by the John Tiller Girls. The New York Public Library has partiturs for "Toe Dance (Tiller Girls)," "Drum Dance (Tiller Girls)," "Tiller Girls Dance," and "Tiller Girls Encore," with nothing to indicate which of these were actually used.

Finale Act I ["When I saw him last..."]

Rodgers/Hart
Orchestrator: Jones

Location of
- Composer's manuscript: NYPL (sk)
- Sheet music: Unpublished
- Most complete music: R&H (pv)
- Most complete lyric: CLLH
- Original partitur: NYPL
- Original parts: -0-

Entr'acte

Rodgers/Hart
Orchestrator: Unknown

Location of   - Composer's manuscript: -0-
               - Sheet music: Unpublished
               - Most complete music: NYPL (ptr)
               - Most complete lyric: INST
               - Original partitur: NYPL
               - Original parts: NYPL (inc)

Of the orchestra parts, only the piano part survives.

Where Can the Baby Be?

Rodgers/Hart
Orchestrator: Miller

Location of   - Composer's manuscript: -0-
               - Sheet music: Unpublished
               - Most complete music: R&H (pv)
               - Most complete lyric: CLLH
               - Original partitur: NYPL
               - Original parts: -0-

The piano-vocal is entitled "Opening Act II."

I Need Some Cooling Off

Rodgers/Hart
Orchestrator: Spialek, Klickmann

Location of   - Composer's manuscript: -0-
               - Sheet music: NYPL
               - Most complete music: NYPL (sm);
                    R&H (pv)
               - Most complete lyric: NYPL (sm);
                    CLLH
               - Original partitur: NYPL
               - Original parts: -0-

Previously used in Rodgers and Hart's 1927 London revue, ONE DAM THING AFTER ANOTHER.

Little House in Soho, A

Rodgers/Hart
Orchestrator: Jones

Location of   - Composer's manuscript: NYPL
               - Sheet music: LoC, NYPL
               - Most complete music: LoC (sm);
                    NYPL (sm); R&H (pv)
               - Most complete lyric: LoC (sm);
                    NYPL (sm); CLLH
               - Original partitur: NYPL
               - Original parts: NYPL

Originally published as "A Tiny Flat Near Soho" from LIDO LADY (1926). The Complete Lyrics of Lorenz Hart has additional lyrics used in the earlier show. The New York Public Library has the SHE'S MY BABY vocal arrangement.

Baby's Best Friend, A

Rodgers/Hart
Orchestrator: Spialek

Location of   - Composer's manuscript: -0-
               - Sheet music: LoC
               - Most complete music: R&H (pv-I)
               - Most complete lyric: R&H (pv-I, ls);
                    CLLH
               - Original partitur: NYPL
               - Original parts: -0-

Beatrice Lillie's comic recitation following the verse and refrain was not published.

Whoopsie

Rodgers/Hart
Orchestrator: Spialek

Location of   - Composer's manuscript: -0-
               - Sheet music: LoC, NYPL
               - Most complete music: LoC (sm);
                    NYPL (sm); R&H (pv-I)
               - Most complete lyric: LoC (sm);
                    NYPL (sm); R&H (pv-I, ls); CLLH
               - Original partitur: NYPL
               - Original parts: -0-

Dropped soon after the New York opening.

She's My Baby (1928)

Trio

Author(s): Unknown
Orchestrator: Williams

Location of
- Composer's manuscript: -0-
- Sheet music: -0-
- Most complete music: R&H (pv)
- Most complete lyric: -0-
- Original partitur: NYPL
- Original parts: NYPL

The partitur and parts are also titled "Nick Long's Dance," but the identity of this number remains unclear.

March With Me

Novello/Furber
Orchestrator: Unknown

Location of
- Composer's manuscript: -0-
- Sheet music: NYPL
- Most complete music: NYPL (sm)
- Most complete lyric: NYPL (sm)
- Original partitur: -0-
- Original parts: -0-

Added during the New York run. Originally in ANDRE CHARLOT'S REVUE OF 1924.

Wasn't It Great?

Rodgers/Hart
Orchestrator: Bennett

Location of
- Composer's manuscript: -0-
- Sheet music: Unpublished
- Most complete music: NYPL (ptr)
- Most complete lyric: CLLH
- Original partitur: NYPL
- Original parts: -0-

Dropped soon after the New York opening.

Morning Is Midnight

Rodgers/Hart
Orchestrator: Spialek

Location of
- Composer's manuscript: -0-
- Sheet music: LoC, NYPL
- Most complete music: LoC (sm); NYPL (sm); R&H (pv-l)
- Most complete lyric: CLLH
- Original partitur: NYPL
- Original parts: NYPL (inc)

Dropped before the New York opening. Originally intended for LIDO LADY (1926), from which it was also dropped. Of the orchestra parts, only the piano part survives.

If I Were You

Rodgers/Hart
Orchestrator: Jones, Spialek

Location of
- Composer's manuscript: -0-
- Sheet music: LoC
- Most complete music: LoC (sm); R&H (pv-l)
- Most complete lyric: CLLH
- Original partitur: NYPL
- Original parts: -0-

Dropped during the pre-Broadway tryout, then restored to the score soon after the opening. Published with the sheet music from BETSY (1926), in which it was first performed.

Pipes of Pansy, The

Rodgers/Hart
Orchestrator: Webb, Klickmann

Location of
- Composer's manuscript: -0-
- Sheet music: Unpublished
- Most complete music: R&H (pv-l)
- Most complete lyric: R&H (pv-l, ls); CLLH
- Original partitur: NYPL
- Original parts: -0-

Dropped before the New York opening. Previously intended for DEAREST ENEMY (1925), THE GIRL FRIEND (1926), and PEGGY-ANN (1926).

How Was I to Know?
Rodgers/Hart
Orchestrator: Jones, Klickmann

Location of   - Composer's manuscript: -0-
                - Sheet music: LoC, NYPL
                - Most complete music: LoC (sm);
                        NYPL (sm); R&H (pv-l)
                - Most complete lyric: LoC (sm);
                        NYPL (sm); R&H (pv-l, ls)
                - Original partitur: NYPL
                - Original parts: -0-

Dropped before the New York opening. The music was used later for "Why Do You Suppose?" in HEADS UP (1929).

PRESENT ARMS

Music   RICHARD RODGERS
Lyrics   LORENZ HART

Musical comedy in two acts. Opened April 26, 1928 in New York and ran 155 performances (World premiere: April 9, 1928 in Wilmington, Delaware). Libretto by Herbert Fields. Produced by Lew Fields. Directed by Alexander Leftwich. Choreographed by Busby Berkeley. Musical direction by Roy Webb. Orchestrations by Roy Webb, Hans Spialek.

Synopsis and Production Information	Chick Evans, "just a lousy leatherneck" marine from Brooklyn, is stationed at "Poil Harbor," where he falls in love with Lady Delphine Witherspoon, daughter of a wealthy English plantation owner. He fools her into believing he's a high-ranking captain, his slang part of a new school of poets who abandon grammatical regulations -- until his lowbrow shipmates blow his cover. A betrayed Delphine almost marries her father's humorless German business associate, Herr Ludwig Von Richter, but in the end, she realizes she truly loves her no-frills marine.
	Other characters include Sergeant Douglas Atwell and his ex-wife Edna, who team up for a few numbers. There is a full singing and dancing ensemble.
Orchestration	Flute; Oboe; Clarinet I II; Bassoon; Horn I II; Trumpet I II; Trombone; Percussion; Dulcitone; Piano; Violin I II; Viola I II; Cello; Bass
Location of Original Materials	Script: Rodgers and Hammerstein Theatre Library (all lyrics) Piano-vocal score: See individual listings Partiturs: Rodgers and Hammerstein Theatre Library Parts: Missing
	Although most of the piano-vocal material survives, it has not been assembled or edited. Partiturs are missing only for the Overture and Entr'acte. The Rodgers and Hammerstein Theatre Library and the Library of Congress have early drafts of the script.
Rental Status	Currently unavailable for rental
Music Publisher	Marlin Enterprises and Lorenz Hart Publishing Co., c/o Warner Brothers Music
Information	Rodgers and Hammerstein Theatre Library

Overture

Rodgers/Hart
Orchestrator: Unknown

Location of
- Composer's manuscript: -0-
- Sheet music: Unpublished
- Most complete music: -0-
- Most complete lyric: INST
- Original partitur: -0-
- Original parts: -0-

Do I Hear You Saying, "I Love You"?

Rodgers/Hart
Orchestrator: Webb, Spialek

Location of
- Composer's manuscript: LoC (sk)
- Sheet music: LoC, NYPL
- Most complete music: LoC (sm);
  NYPL (sm); R&H (pv-l)
- Most complete lyric: LoC (sm);
  NYPL (sm); R&H (scr); CLLH
- Original partitur: R&H
- Original parts: -0-

Tell It to the Marines

Rodgers/Hart
Orchestrator: Webb

Location of
- Composer's manuscript: -0-
- Sheet music: Not published separately
- Most complete music: R&H (pv)
- Most complete lyric: R&H (ls, scr); CLLH
- Original partitur: R&H
- Original parts: -0-

Alternate title: "A Lot of Nuts." The refrain was
published in the piano selection, which can be found at
the Rodgers and Hammerstein Theatre Library.

Kiss for Cinderella, A

Rodgers/Hart
Orchestrator: Webb

Location of
- Composer's manuscript: LoC (sk)
- Sheet music: LoC, NYPL
- Most complete music: LoC (sm);
  NYPL (sm); R&H (pv-l)
- Most complete lyric: R&H (scr); CLLH
- Original partitur: R&H
- Original parts: -0-

You Took Advantage of Me

Rodgers/Hart
Orchestrator: Webb, Spialek

Location of
- Composer's manuscript: -0-
- Sheet music: LoC, NYPL
- Most complete music: LoC (sm);
  NYPL (sm); R&H (pv-l)
- Most complete lyric: LoC (sm);
  NYPL (sm); R&H (pv-l, scr); CLLH
- Original partitur: R&H
- Original parts: -0-

Is It the Uniform?

Rodgers/Hart
Orchestrator: Webb

Location of
- Composer's manuscript: LoC (sk)
- Sheet music: Unpublished
- Most complete music: R&H (pv-l)
- Most complete lyric: R&H (pv-l, ls);
  CLLH
- Original partitur: R&H
- Original parts: -0-

Present Arms (1928)

Crazy Elbows
Rodgers/Hart
Orchestrator: Unknown

Location of   - Composer's manuscript: LoC (sk)
    - Sheet music: LoC, NYPL
    - Most complete music: LoC (sm);
       NYPL (sm); R&H (pv-l)
    - Most complete lyric: LoC (sm);
       NYPL (sm); R&H (pv-l, ls, scr); CLLH
    - Original partitur: R&H
    - Original parts: -0-

Down By the Sea
Rodgers/Hart
Orchestrator: Webb, Spialek

Location of   - Composer's manuscript: LoC (sk)
    - Sheet music: LoC, NYPL
    - Most complete music: LoC (sm);
       NYPL (sm); R&H (pv-l)
    - Most complete lyric: LoC (sm);
       NYPL (sm); R&H (pv-l, scr); CLLH
    - Original partitur: R&H
    - Original parts: -0-

Finale Act I ["Nuts, he travels with us nuts..."]
Rodgers/Hart
Orchestrator: Webb

Location of   - Composer's manuscript: -0-
    - Sheet music: Unpublished
    - Most complete music: R&H (pv)
    - Most complete lyric: R&H (ls); CLLH
    - Original partitur: R&H
    - Original parts: -0-

I'm a Fool, Little One
Rodgers/Hart
Orchestrator: Webb

Location of   - Composer's manuscript: -0-
    - Sheet music: LoC
    - Most complete music: LoC (sm);
       R&H (pv-l)
    - Most complete lyric: R&H (scr); CLLH
    - Original partitur: R&H
    - Original parts: -0-

Entr'acte
Rodgers/Hart
Orchestrator: Unknown

Location of   - Composer's manuscript: -0-
    - Sheet music: Unpublished
    - Most complete music: -0-
    - Most complete lyric: INST
    - Original partitur: -0-
    - Original parts: -0-

Finaletto Act II, Scene 3 ["This rescue is a terrible calamity!"]
Rodgers/Hart
Orchestrator: Webb

Location of   - Composer's manuscript: LoC (sk)
    - Sheet music: Unpublished
    - Most complete music: R&H (pv)
    - Most complete lyric: R&H (scr); CLLH
    - Original partitur: R&H
    - Original parts: -0-

The Rodgers and Hammerstein Theatre Library also has a lyric sheet for an early version that includes part of "I Love You More Than Yesterday."

Blue Ocean Blues

Rodgers/Hart

Orchestrator: Spialek

Location of - Composer's manuscript: LoC (sk)
- Sheet music: NYPL
- Most complete music: NYPL (sm);
  R&H (pv-I)
- Most complete lyric: NYPL (sm);
  R&H (pv-I, scr); CLLH
- Original partitur: R&H
- Original parts: -0-

With a slightly different lyric, this number was first used in LIDO LADY (1926), where it was entitled "Atlantic Blues."

I Love You More Than Yesterday

Rodgers/Hart

Orchestrator: Unknown

Location of - Composer's manuscript: LoC (sk)
- Sheet music: LoC
- Most complete music: LoC (sm)
- Most complete lyric: LoC (sm); CLLH
- Original partitur: -0-
- Original parts: -0-

Dropped before the New York opening. Later used in the 1929 Broadway musical LADY FINGERS.

Hawaii

Rodgers/Hart

Orchestrator: Webb

Location of - Composer's manuscript: -0-
- Sheet music: Unpublished
- Most complete music: R&H (pv)
- Most complete lyric: R&H (ls, scr); CLLH
- Original partitur: R&H
- Original parts: -0-

What Price Love

Rodgers/Hart

Orchestrator: Unknown

Location of - Composer's manuscript: -0-
- Sheet music: Unpublished
- Most complete music: R&H (pv)
- Most complete lyric: -0-
- Original partitur: -0-
- Original parts: -0-

Unused.

Kohala, Welcome

Rodgers/Hart

Orchestrator: Spialek

Location of - Composer's manuscript: -0-
- Sheet music: Unpublished
- Most complete music: R&H (pv)
- Most complete lyric: -0-
- Original partitur: R&H
- Original parts: -0-

CHEE-CHEE

Music   RICHARD RODGERS
Lyrics   LORENZ HART

Musical narrative in two acts. Opened September 25, 1928 in New York and ran 31 performances (World premiere: August 27, 1928 in Philadelphia). Libretto by Herbert Fields, adapted from Charles Petit's novel THE SON OF THE GRAND EUNUCH. Produced by Lew Fields. Directed by Alexander Leftwich. Choreographed by Jack Haskell. Musical direction by Roy Webb. Orchestrations by Roy Webb, F. Henri Klickmann, Hilding Anderson, Stephen O. Jones.

Synopsis and Production Information	Li Pi Tchou, son of the Grand Eunuch at the Court of the Holy Emperor of Peking, has great qualms about inheriting the throne from his father. Li Pi and his dutiful wife, Chee-Chee, flee the court and learn about life in the real world, where Chee-Chee is propositioned and Li Pi is wounded by the great Tartar Chief, sworn enemy of all the eunuchs. Eventually, the couple is forced to return to court, but happily, Li Pi escapes his fate.
	The supporting couple is Li-Li Wee, daughter of the grand Eunuch, and her fiance, Prince Tao-Tee, son of his Majesty, son of Heaven. The show requires a full singing and dancing ensemble, and scenery and costumes of colorful Oriental splendor.
Orchestration	Flute; Oboe; Clarinet I II; Bassoon; Horn I II; Trumpet I II; Trombone I II; Percussion; Dulcitone; Harp; Violin I II; Viola I II; Cello; Bass
Location of Original Materials	Script: Rodgers and Hammerstein Theatre Library (some lyrics) Piano-vocal score: See individual listings Partiturs: Rodgers and Hammerstein Theatre Library Parts: Rodgers and Hammerstein Theatre Library Many of the numbers survive in piano-vocal form; others can be reconstructed from the partiturs, which are virtually complete. Few of the parts survive.
Rental Status	Currently unavailable for rental
Music Publisher	Marlin Enterprises and Lorenz Hart Publishing Co., c/o Warner Brothers Music
Information	Rodgers and Hammerstein Theatre Library

Overture

Rodgers/Hart

Orchestrator: Webb

Location of - Composer's manuscript: -0-
        - Sheet music: Unpublished
        - Most complete music: R&H (ptr)
        - Most complete lyric: INST
        - Original partitur: R&H
        - Original parts: -0-

I Am a Prince

Rodgers/Hart

Orchestrator: Webb

Location of - Composer's manuscript: -0-
        - Sheet music: Unpublished
        - Most complete music: R&H (ptr)
        - Most complete lyric: R&H (scr); CLLH
        - Original partitur: R&H (inc)
        - Original parts: -0-

Prelude

Rodgers/Hart

Orchestrator: Webb

Location of - Composer's manuscript: -0-
        - Sheet music: Unpublished
        - Most complete music: R&H (p, ptr)
        - Most complete lyric: INST
        - Original partitur: R&H
        - Original parts: -0-

In a Great Big Way

Rodgers/Hart

Orchestrator: Webb

Location of - Composer's manuscript: -0-
        - Sheet music: Unpublished
        - Most complete music: R&H (ptr)
        - Most complete lyric: R&H (scr); CLLH
        - Original partitur: R&H
        - Original parts: -0-

We're Men of Brains

Rodgers/Hart

Orchestrator: Webb

Location of - Composer's manuscript: -0-
        - Sheet music: Unpublished
        - Most complete music: R&H (ptr & p)
        - Most complete lyric: R&H (scr); CLLH
        - Original partitur: R&H
        - Original parts: R&H (inc)

Alternate title: "Eunuch's Chorus." Of the orchestra parts, only the piano part survives.

Most Majestic of Domestic Officials, The

Rodgers/Hart

Orchestrator: Webb

Location of - Composer's manuscript: -0-
        - Sheet music: Unpublished
        - Most complete music: R&H (pv)
        - Most complete lyric: R&H (scr); CLLH
        - Original partitur: R&H
        - Original parts: R&H (inc)

Alternate title: "Entrance of the Grand Eunuch." Of the orchestra parts, only the piano part survives.

Chee-Chee (1928)

Holy of Holies
Rodgers/Hart
Orchestrator: Webb

Location of - Composer's manuscript: -0-
            - Sheet music: Unpublished
            - Most complete music: R&H (ptr)
            - Most complete lyric: R&H (scr); CLLH
            - Original partitur: R&H
            - Original parts: -0-

The partitur is entitled "Prayer."

Await Your Love
Rodgers/Hart
Orchestrator: Webb

Location of - Composer's manuscript: -0-
            - Sheet music: Unpublished
            - Most complete music: R&H (ptr)
            - Most complete lyric: R&H (scr); CLLH
            - Original partitur: R&H
            - Original parts: R&H (inc)

Alternate title: "Concubines' Song." Of the orchestra parts, only the piano part survives.

Her Hair Is Black as Licorice
Rodgers/Hart
Orchestrator: Webb

Location of - Composer's manuscript: -0-
            - Sheet music: Unpublished
            - Most complete music: R&H (ptr)
            - Most complete lyric: R&H (scr); CLLH
            - Original partitur: R&H
            - Original parts: R&H (inc)

The partitur is entitled "Food Solo." Of the orchestra parts, only the piano part survives.

Joy Is Mine
Rodgers/Hart
Orchestrator: Webb

Location of - Composer's manuscript: -0-
            - Sheet music: Unpublished
            - Most complete music: R&H (ptr)
            - Most complete lyric: R&H (scr); CLLH
            - Original partitur: R&H
            - Original parts: -0-

This may have been dropped before the New York opening.

Dear, Oh Dear
Rodgers/Hart
Orchestrator: Webb

Location of - Composer's manuscript: -0-
            - Sheet music: LoC, NYPL
            - Most complete music: LoC (sm);
               NYPL (sm); R&H (pv)
            - Most complete lyric: LoC (sm);
               NYPL (sm); R&H (ls); CLLH
            - Original partitur: R&H
            - Original parts: -0-

I Wake at Morning
Rodgers/Hart
Orchestrator: Webb

Location of - Composer's manuscript: -0-
            - Sheet music: Unpublished
            - Most complete music: R&H (ptr)
            - Most complete lyric: R&H (scr); CLLH
            - Original partitur: R&H
            - Original parts: -0-

The Rodgers and Hammerstein Theatre Library also has a partitur for "A Prelude to I Wake at Morning."

I Grovel to the Earth
Rodgers/Hart
Orchestrator: Webb

Location of - Composer's manuscript: -0-
- Sheet music: Unpublished
- Most complete music: R&H (ptr)
- Most complete lyric: R&H (scr); CLLH
- Original partitur: R&H
- Original parts: -0-

Alternate title: "Chee-Chee's First Entrance".

Opening Scene 2
Rodgers/Hart
Orchestrator: Webb

Location of - Composer's manuscript: -0-
- Sheet music: Unpublished
- Most complete music: R&H (pv)
- Most complete lyric: -0-
- Original partitur: R&H
- Original parts: -0-

Just a Little Thing
Rodgers/Hart
Orchestrator: Webb

Location of - Composer's manuscript: -0-
- Sheet music: Unpublished
- Most complete music: R&H (prt)
- Most complete lyric: R&H (scr); CLLH
- Original partitur: R&H
- Original parts: -0-

I Must Love You
Rodgers/Hart
Orchestrator: Webb

Location of - Composer's manuscript: -0-
- Sheet music: LoC, NYPL
- Most complete music: LoC (sm);
    NYPL (sm); R&H (pv-I)
- Most complete lyric: LoC (sm);
    NYPL (sm); R&H (pv-I, ls); CLLH
- Original partitur: R&H
- Original parts: R&H (inc)

Of the orchestra parts, only the piano part and the 1st violin, 2nd desk survive. The music was later used for "Send for Me" in SIMPLE SIMON (1930).

Finaletto Act I, Scene 1 ["You are both agreed..."]
Rodgers/Hart
Orchestrator: Webb

Location of - Composer's manuscript: -0-
- Sheet music: Unpublished
- Most complete music: R&H (pv)
- Most complete lyric: R&H (scr); CLLH
- Original partitur: R&H
- Original parts: R&H (inc)

Of the orchestra parts, only the 2nd violin part survives.

Owl Song
Rodgers/Hart
Orchestrator: Unknown

Location of - Composer's manuscript: -0-
- Sheet music: Unpublished
- Most complete music: -0-
- Most complete lyric: R&H (ls); CLLH
- Original partitur: -0-
- Original parts: -0-

342

Chee-Chee (1928)

I Bow a Glad Good Day
Rodgers/Hart
Orchestrator: Webb

Location of - Composer's manuscript: -0-
- Sheet music: Unpublished
- Most complete music: R&H (ptr)
- Most complete lyric: R&H (scr); CLLH
- Original partitur: R&H
- Original parts: -0-

The partitur is entitled "Tavern Opening."

Chee-Chee's Second Entrance
Rodgers/Hart
Orchestrator: Unknown

Location of - Composer's manuscript: -0-
- Sheet music: Unpublished
- Most complete music: -0-
- Most complete lyric: -0-
- Original partitur: -0-
- Original parts: -0-

Better Be Good to Me
Rodgers/Hart
Orchestrator: Webb, Klickmann

Location of - Composer's manuscript: LoC (sk)
- Sheet music: LoC, NYPL
- Most complete music: LoC (sm);
    NYPL (sm); R&H (pv-l)
- Most complete lyric: LoC (sm);
    NYPL (sm); R&H (pv-l, ls); CLLH
- Original partitur: R&H
- Original parts: -0-

Finale Act I
Rodgers/Hart
Orchestrator: Webb

Location of - Composer's manuscript: -0-
- Sheet music: Unpublished
- Most complete music: R&H (pv)
- Most complete lyric: -0-
- Original partitur: R&H
- Original parts: -0-

Tartar Song, The
Rodgers/Hart
Orchestrator: Webb

Location of - Composer's manuscript: -0-
- Sheet music: LoC, NYPL
- Most complete music: LoC (sm);
    NYPL (sm); R&H (pv)
- Most complete lyric: LoC (sm);
    NYPL (sm); R&H (ls); CLLH
- Original partitur: R&H
- Original parts: -0-

The Rodgers and Hammerstein Theatre Library also has a
partitur for the "Tartar March."

Entr'acte
Rodgers/Hart
Orchestrator: Webb

Location of - Composer's manuscript: -0-
- Sheet music: Unpublished
- Most complete music: R&H (ptr)
- Most complete lyric: INST
- Original partitur: R&H
- Original parts: -0-

Knonghouse Song

Rodgers/Hart

Orchestrator: Webb

Location of
- Composer's manuscript: -0-
- Sheet music: Unpublished
- Most complete music: R&H (ptr)
- Most complete lyric: R&H (scr); CLLH
- Original partitur: R&H
- Original parts: -0-

Monastery Opening

Rodgers/Hart

Orchestrator: Anderson

Location of
- Composer's manuscript: -0-
- Sheet music: Unpublished
- Most complete music: R&H (pv)
- Most complete lyric: -0-
- Original partitur: R&H
- Original parts: -0-

Sleep, Weary Head

Rodgers/Hart

Orchestrator: Webb

Location of
- Composer's manuscript: -0-
- Sheet music: Unpublished
- Most complete music: R&H (ptr)
- Most complete lyric: R&H (scr); CLLH
- Original partitur: R&H
- Original parts: -0-

Chinese Dance

Rodgers/Hart

Orchestrator: Unknown

Location of
- Composer's manuscript: -0-
- Sheet music: Unpublished
- Most complete music: -0-
- Most complete lyric: INST
- Original partitur: -0-
- Original parts: -0-

Singing a Love Song

Rodgers/Hart

Orchestrator: Webb

Location of
- Composer's manuscript: -0-
- Sheet music: LoC, NYPL
- Most complete music: LoC (sm); NYPL (sm); R&H (pv)
- Most complete lyric: LoC (sm); NYPL (sm); CLLH
- Original partitur: R&H
- Original parts: -0-

The music was later used for "I Still Believe in You" in SIMPLE SIMON (1930).

Living Buddha

Rodgers/Hart

Orchestrator: Unknown

Location of
- Composer's manuscript: -0-
- Sheet music: Unpublished
- Most complete music: R&H (ptr)
- Most complete lyric: R&H (scr); CLLH
- Original partitur: R&H
- Original parts: -0-

Alternate title: "Impassive Buddha."

Chee-Chee (1928)

Moon of My Delight
Rodgers/Hart
Orchestrator: Webb

Location of   - Composer's manuscript: -0-
        - Sheet music: LoC, NYPL
        - Most complete music: LoC (sm);
             NYPL (sm); R&H (pv)
        - Most complete lyric: LoC (sm);
             NYPL (sm); R&H (ls); CLLH
        - Original partitur: R&H
        - Original parts: R&H (inc)

Of the orchestra parts, only the piano part survives. The refrain has the same melody as "Thank You in Advance," written in 1931-1932. The Rodgers and Hammerstein Theatre Library also has a partitur for the "Dance to Moon of My Delight."

I Grovel to Your Cloth
Rodgers/Hart
Orchestrator: Webb

Location of   - Composer's manuscript: -0-
        - Sheet music: Unpublished
        - Most complete music: R&H (ptr)
        - Most complete lyric: R&H (scr); CLLH
        - Original partitur: R&H
        - Original parts: -0-

Musically the same as "I Grovel to the Earth." Alternate title: "Chee-Chee's Third Entrance."

We Are the Horrors of Deadliest Woe
Rodgers/Hart
Orchestrator: Unknown

Location of   - Composer's manuscript: -0-
        - Sheet music: Unpublished
        - Most complete music: -0-
        - Most complete lyric: R&H (scr); CLLH
        - Original partitur: -0-
        - Original parts: -0-

Alternate title: "Chorus of Torments."

Oh, Gala Day, Red-Letter Day
Rodgers/Hart
Orchestrator: Unknown

Location of   - Composer's manuscript: -0-
        - Sheet music: Unpublished
        - Most complete music: R&H (pv)
        - Most complete lyric: CLLH
        - Original partitur: -0-
        - Original parts: -0-

Alternate titles: "Palace Opening" and "Finale Palace Opening."

Finale Act II ["Farewell, Oh life!"]
Rodgers/Hart
Orchestrator: Unknown

Location of   - Composer's manuscript: -0-
        - Sheet music: Unpublished
        - Most complete music: -0-
        - Most complete lyric: R&H (scr); CLLH
        - Original partitur: -0-
        - Original parts: -0-

I'll Never Share You
Rodgers/Hart
Orchestrator: Jones

Location of   - Composer's manuscript: -0-
        - Sheet music: Unpublished
        - Most complete music: R&H (pv)
        - Most complete lyric: CLLH
        - Original partitur: R&H
        - Original parts: -0-

Apparently replaced by "Dear, Oh Dear" before the New York opening. Alternate title: "If You Were My Concubine."

SPRING IS HERE

Music   RICHARD RODGERS
Lyrics   LORENZ HART

Musical comedy in two acts. Opened March 11, 1929 in New York and ran 104 performances (World premiere: February 25, 1929 in Philadelphia). Libretto by Owen Davis, adapted from his play SHOTGUN WEDDING. Produced by Alex A. Aarons and Vinton Freedley. Directed by Alexander Leftwich. Choreographed by Bobby Connolly. Musical direction by Alfred Newman. Orchestrations by Maurice B. DePackh.

Synopsis and Production Information	Terry is madly in love with Betty, but she intends to elope with Stacy, a mysterious older man she finds more thrilling. Her family and friends advise Terry to flirt with other women to make Betty jealous. He does. It works. Musical support is provided by Betty's sister Mary Jane, Mary Jane's friends Steve and Maude, and Betty's crazy Uncle Willie. There is a full singing and dancing ensemble.
Orchestration	Flute; Oboe; Clarinet I II; Horn I II; Trumpet I II; Trombone; Percussion; Piano I; Piano II; Violin I II; Viola I II; Cello; Bass
Comments	The original production included the two-piano team of Victor Arden and Phil Ohman.
Location of Original Materials	Script: Missing Piano-vocal score: See individual listings Partiturs: Rodgers and Hammerstein Theatre Library Parts: Missing Although no final production script has been located, there is an early draft at the Library of Congress containing some lyrics, and a still earlier version at the Rodgers and Hammerstein Theatre Library with no lyrics. Nearly all of the piano-vocal material survives, but only one partitur.
Rental Status	Currently unavailable for rental
Music Publisher	Marlin Enterprises and Lorenz Hart Publishing Co., c/o Warner Brothers Music
Information	Rodgers and Hammerstein Theatre Library

Spring Is Here (1929)

Overture

Rodgers/Hart
Orchestrator: Unknown

Location of   - Composer's manuscript: -0-
            - Sheet music: Unpublished
            - Most complete music: -0-
            - Most complete lyric: INST
            - Original partitur: -0-
            - Original parts: -0-

Yours Sincerely

Rodgers/Hart
Orchestrator: Unknown

Location of   - Composer's manuscript: -0-
            - Sheet music: NYPL
            - Most complete music: NYPL (sm);
               R&H (pv-l)
            - Most complete lyric: NYPL (sm);
               CLLH
            - Original partitur: -0-
            - Original parts: -0-

Opening Act I

Rodgers/Hart
Orchestrator: Unknown

Location of   - Composer's manuscript: -0-
            - Sheet music: Unpublished
            - Most complete music: R&H (pv)
            - Most complete lyric: R&H (ls); CLLH
            - Original partitur: -0-
            - Original parts: -0-

Alternate title: "A Cup of Tea."

Finaletto Scene 1

Rodgers/Hart
Orchestrator: Unknown

Location of   - Composer's manuscript: -0-
            - Sheet music: Unpublished
            - Most complete music: R&H (pv)
            - Most complete lyric: R&H (ls); CLLH
            - Original partitur: -0-
            - Original parts: -0-

Alternate title: "We're Gonna Raise Hell."

Spring Is Here In Person

Rodgers/Hart
Orchestrator: Unknown

Location of   - Composer's manuscript: -0-
            - Sheet music: Unpublished
            - Most complete music: R&H (pv)
            - Most complete lyric: CLLH
            - Original partitur: -0-
            - Original parts: -0-

You Never Say Yes

Rodgers/Hart
Orchestrator: Unknown

Location of   - Composer's manuscript: -0-
            - Sheet music: LoC, NYPL
            - Most complete music: LoC (sm);
               NYPL (sm); R&H (pv-l)
            - Most complete lyric: LoC (sm);
               NYPL (sm); R&H (pv-l, ls); CLLH
            - Original partitur: -0-
            - Original parts: -0-

With a Song in My Heart
Rodgers/Hart
Orchestrator: DePackh

Location of   - Composer's manuscript: -0-
              - Sheet music: LoC, NYPL
              - Most complete music: LoC (sm);
                  NYPL (sm); R&H (pv-l)
              - Most complete lyric: LoC (sm);
                  NYPL (sm); CLLH
              - Original partitur: R&H
              - Original parts: -0-

Entr'acte
Rodgers/Hart
Orchestrator: Unknown

Location of   - Composer's manuscript: -0-
              - Sheet music: Unpublished
              - Most complete music: -0-
              - Most complete lyric: INST
              - Original partitur: -0-
              - Original parts: -0-

Baby's Awake Now
Rodgers/Hart
Orchestrator: Unknown

Location of   - Composer's manuscript: -0-
              - Sheet music: NYPL
              - Most complete music: NYPL (sm);
                  R&H (pv-l)
              - Most complete lyric: NYPL (sm);
                  R&H (pv-l, ls); CLLH
              - Original partitur: -0-
              - Original parts: -0-

Opening Act II
Rodgers/Hart
Orchestrator: Unknown

Location of   - Composer's manuscript: -0-
              - Sheet music: Unpublished
              - Most complete music: R&H (pv)
              - Most complete lyric: CLLH
              - Original partitur: -0-
              - Original parts: -0-

Alternate title: "This Is Not Long Island."

Finale Act I ["Oh, look! It's a note!"]
Rodgers/Hart
Orchestrator: Unknown

Location of   - Composer's manuscript: -0-
              - Sheet music: Unpublished
              - Most complete music: R&H (pv)
              - Most complete lyric: R&H (ls); CLLH
              - Original partitur: -0-
              - Original parts: -0-

Red-Hot Trumpet
Rodgers/Hart
Orchestrator: Unknown

Location of   - Composer's manuscript: -0-
              - Sheet music: Unpublished
              - Most complete music: See note
              - Most complete lyric: R&H (ls); CLLH
              - Original partitur: -0-
              - Original parts: -0-

This number was recorded by the Edisongsters on Edison 14043. No musical manuscript was found.

What a Girl!

Rodgers/Hart
Orchestrator: Unknown

Location of - Composer's manuscript: -0-
 - Sheet music: Unpublished
 - Most complete music: R&H (pv)
 - Most complete lyric: R&H (ls); CLLH
 - Original partitur: -0-
 - Original parts: -0-

Why Can't I?

Rodgers/Hart
Orchestrator: Unknown

Location of - Composer's manuscript: -0-
 - Sheet music: LoC, NYPL
 - Most complete music: LoC (sm);
   NYPL (sm); R&H (pv-l)
 - Most complete lyric: LoC (sm);
   NYPL (sm); R&H (ls); CLLH
 - Original partitur: -0-
 - Original parts: -0-

Rich Man! Poor Man!

Rodgers/Hart
Orchestrator: Unknown

Location of - Composer's manuscript: -0-
 - Sheet music: LoC, NYPL
 - Most complete music: LoC (sm);
   NYPL (sm); R&H (pv-l)
 - Most complete lyric: LoC (sm);
   NYPL (sm); CLLH
 - Original partitur: -0-
 - Original parts: -0-

Word in Edgeways, A

Rodgers/Hart
Orchestrator: Unknown

Location of - Composer's manuscript: -0-
 - Sheet music: Unpublished
 - Most complete music: R&H (pv)
 - Most complete lyric: CLLH
 - Original partitur: -0-
 - Original parts: -0-

Dropped during the pre-Broadway tryout.

Specialty Dance

Author(s): Unknown
Orchestrator: Unknown

Location of - Composer's manuscript: -0-
 - Sheet music: -0-
 - Most complete music: -0-
 - Most complete lyric: -0-
 - Original partitur: -0-
 - Original parts: -0-

A specialty number performed by Cy Landry.

Color of Her Eyes, The

Rodgers/Hart
Orchestrator: Unknown

Location of - Composer's manuscript: LoC
 - Sheet music: LoC
 - Most complete music: LoC (sm); R&H (pv)
 - Most complete lyric: CLLH
 - Original partitur: -0-
 - Original parts: -0-

Dropped during the pre-Broadway tryout. Published with
the sheet music from EVER GREEN (1930), the show in
which the song was finally used.

Lady Luck Is Grinning

Rodgers/Hart

Orchestrator: Unknown

Location of   - Composer's manuscript: -0-

                 - Sheet music: Unpublished

                 - Most complete music: -0-

                 - Most complete lyric: R&H (ls); CLLH

                 - Original partitur: -0-

                 - Original parts: -0-

Dropped before the New York opening. The lyric is also in the early draft of the script at the Library of Congress.

HEADS UP!

Music   **RICHARD RODGERS**
Lyrics   **LORENZ HART**

Musical comedy in two acts. Opened November 11, 1929 in New York and ran 144 performances (World premiere: October 25, 1929 in Philadelphia). Libretto by John McGowan and Paul Gerard Smith. Produced by Alex A. Aarons and Vinton Freedley. Directed and choreographed by George Hale. Musical direction by Alfred Newman. Orchestrations by Robert Russell Bennett, Charles Miller.

Synopsis and Production Information	Mrs. Martha Trumbull disapproves of her daughter Mary's boyfriend, Jack Mason, a recent graduate of the Naval Academy. But Jack proves himself by helping to arrest the evil captain who is using the Trumbull yacht to smuggle alcohol.
	Other characters include Skippy, a meek reformed convict who is now a hand on Mrs. Trumbull's yacht; Mary's friend Peggy; and a comic supporting couple, Betty and Georgie. There is a full singing and dancing ensemble.
Orchestration	Flute; Oboe; Clarinet/Alto Sax; Clarinet/Alto Sax; Tenor Sax; Horn I II; Trumpet I II; Trumpet III; Trombone; Percussion; Piano; Violin I II; Viola I II; Cello; Bass
Comments	HEADS UP! first appeared as ME FOR YOU, with a book by Owen Davis and a score by Rodgers and Hart. ME FOR YOU opened in Detroit on September 15, 1929, and closed two weeks later. In the ensuing weeks, the show was overhauled with a new book, new songs, new cast members, and a new title before premiering in Philadelphia on October 25 as HEADS UP! The original production included Victor Moore as Skippy, two pairs of specialty dancers, and Phil Ohman at the piano. HEADS UP! had a brief London run in 1930.
Location of Original Materials	Script: Rodgers and Hammerstein Theatre Library (most lyrics), Library of Congress (most lyrics) Piano-vocal score: See individual listings Partiturs: Missing Parts: Shubert Archive
	Although most of the HEADS UP! lyrics survive, much of the music is missing; conversely, most of the ME FOR YOU music has been located, but many of the lyrics appear lost. Parts survive for five numbers in the New York production and for six that were dropped on the road. The Rodgers and Hammerstein Theatre Library also has two early drafts of the ME FOR YOU script; their HEADS UP! libretto is missing page 1-3-1.
Rental Status	Currently unavailable for rental
Music Publisher	Marlin Enterprises and Lorenz Hart Publishing Co., c/o Warner Brothers Music
Information	Rodgers and Hammerstein Theatre Library

Overture

Rodgers/Hart
Orchestrator: Unknown

Location of   - Composer's manuscript: -0-
      - Sheet music: Unpublished
      - Most complete music: -0-
      - Most complete lyric: INST
      - Original partitur: -0-
      - Original parts: -0-

You've Got to Surrender

Rodgers/Hart
Orchestrator: Unknown

Location of   - Composer's manuscript: -0-
      - Sheet music: Unpublished
      - Most complete music: -0-
      - Most complete lyric: R&H (scr);
          LoC (scr); CLLH
      - Original partitur: -0-
      - Original parts: -0-

Playboy

Rodgers/Hart
Orchestrator: Unknown

Location of   - Composer's manuscript: -0-
      - Sheet music: Unpublished
      - Most complete music: See note
      - Most complete lyric: R&H (scr);
          LoC (scr); CLLH
      - Original partitur: -0-
      - Original parts: SA (inc)

Only the Horn parts survive.

Mother Grows Younger

Rodgers/Hart
Orchestrator: Unknown

Location of   - Composer's manuscript: -0-
      - Sheet music: Unpublished
      - Most complete music: See note
      - Most complete lyric: R&H (scr);
          LoC (scr); CLLH
      - Original partitur: -0-
      - Original parts: -0-

In the London production (1930), the song was entitled "Daughter Grows Older." The refrain was published in the British piano selection (issued at the time of the London production).

Why Do You Suppose?

Rodgers/Hart
Orchestrator: Unknown

Location of   - Composer's manuscript: -0-
      - Sheet music: NYPL
      - Most complete music: NYPL (sm)
      - Most complete lyric: R&H (scr);
          LoC (scr)
      - Original partitur: -0-
      - Original parts: -0-

The music was used earlier in "How Was I to Know?", which was dropped from SHE'S MY BABY (1928) before its New York opening. The New York Public Library has two partiturs for "How Was I to Know?" (by Stephen O. Jones and F. Henri Klickmann) in its SHE'S MY BABY collection.

Me for You

Rodgers/Hart
Orchestrator: Unknown

Location of   - Composer's manuscript: -0-
      - Sheet music: LoC, NYPL
      - Most complete music: LoC (sm);
          NYPL (sm); R&H (pv-l)
      - Most complete lyric: LoC (sm);
          NYPL (sm); R&H (pv-l); CLLH
      - Original partitur: -0-
      - Original parts: SA (inc)

The orchestra piano part and Horn parts are missing.

Heads Up! (1929)

Ongsay and Anceday
Rodgers/Hart
Orchestrator: Unknown

Location of   - Composer's manuscript: -0-
      - Sheet music: Unpublished
      - Most complete music: -0-
      - Most complete lyric: CLLH
      - Original partitur: -0-
      - Original parts: -0-

Entr'acte
Rodgers/Hart
Orchestrator: Unknown

Location of   - Composer's manuscript: -0-
      - Sheet music: Unpublished
      - Most complete music: -0-
      - Most complete lyric: INST
      - Original partitur: -0-
      - Original parts: -0-

It Must Be Heaven
Rodgers/Hart
Orchestrator: Unknown

Location of   - Composer's manuscript: -0-
      - Sheet music: NYPL
      - Most complete music: NYPL (sm);
          R&H (pv-l)
      - Most complete lyric: NYPL (sm);
          R&H (scr); LoC (scr); CLLH
      - Original partitur: -0-
      - Original parts: SA (inc)

Lass Who Loved a Sailor, The
Rodgers/Hart
Orchestrator: Miller

Location of   - Composer's manuscript: -0-
      - Sheet music: Unpublished
      - Most complete music: SA (parts)
      - Most complete lyric: -0-
      - Original partitur: -0-
      - Original parts: SA (inc)

This number may have been dropped after the New York opening; it is not included in the script. The Horn parts are missing.

My Man Is on the Make
Rodgers/Hart
Orchestrator: Unknown

Location of   - Composer's manuscript: -0-
      - Sheet music: LoC, NYPL
      - Most complete music: LoC (sm);
          NYPL (sm); R&H (pv-l)
      - Most complete lyric: LoC (sm);
          NYPL (sm); R&H (pv-l, ls); CLLH
      - Original partitur: -0-
      - Original parts: -0-

The Shubert Archive has parts for two "My Man Is on the Make" encores.

Ship Without a Sail, A
Rodgers/Hart
Orchestrator: Unknown

Location of   - Composer's manuscript: -0-
      - Sheet music: LoC, NYPL
      - Most complete music: LoC (sm);
          NYPL (sm); R&H (pv-l)
      - Most complete lyric: LoC (sm);
          NYPL (sm); R&H (pv-l); CLLH
      - Original partitur: -0-
      - Original parts: SA (inc)

The parts are marked "Old Parts in D." The orchestra piano part is missing.

Knees

Rodgers/Hart

Orchestrator: Unknown

Location of   - Composer's manuscript: -0-
- Sheet music: Unpublished
- Most complete music: See note
- Most complete lyric: R&H (scr);
        LoC (scr); CLLH
- Original partitur: -0-
- Original parts: -0-

The refrain was published in the British piano selection (issued at the time of the London production).

Specialty

Author(s): Unknown

Orchestrator: Unknown

Location of   - Composer's manuscript: -0-
- Sheet music: -0-
- Most complete music: -0-
- Most complete lyric: -0-
- Original partitur: -0-
- Original parts: -0-

A specialty dance performed by the Reynolds Sisters and Atlas and LaMarr.

Mind Your P's and Q's

Rodgers/Hart

Orchestrator: Unknown

Location of   - Composer's manuscript: -0-
- Sheet music: Unpublished
- Most complete music: R&H (pv)
- Most complete lyric: -0-
- Original partitur: -0-
- Original parts: SA (inc)

Performed in ME FOR YOU, but dropped before the New York premiere of HEADS UP! The orchestra piano part and Horn parts are missing.

It's a Man's World

Rodgers/Hart

Orchestrator: Unknown

Location of   - Composer's manuscript: -0-
- Sheet music: Unpublished
- Most complete music: R&H (pv)
- Most complete lyric: -0-
- Original partitur: -0-
- Original parts: SA (inc)

Performed in ME FOR YOU, but dropped before the New York premiere of HEADS UP! The orchestra piano part and Horn parts are missing.

Bootlegger's Chantey, The

Rodgers/Hart

Orchestrator: Unknown

Location of   - Composer's manuscript: -0-
- Sheet music: Unpublished
- Most complete music: R&H (pv)
- Most complete lyric: -0-
- Original partitur: -0-
- Original parts: -0-

Performed in ME FOR YOU, but dropped before the New York premiere of HEADS UP! Alternate title: "We're an English Ship."

Finale Act I

Rodgers/Hart

Orchestrator: Unknown

Location of   - Composer's manuscript: -0-
- Sheet music: Unpublished
- Most complete music: -0-
- Most complete lyric: -0-
- Original partitur: -0-
- Original parts: -0-

Performed in ME FOR YOU, but dropped before the New York premiere of HEADS UP! Alternate title: "Now Go to Your Cabin."

Heads Up! (1929)

Harlem on the Sand

Rodgers/Hart
Orchestrator: Unknown

Location of
- Composer's manuscript: -0-
- Sheet music: Unpublished
- Most complete music: R&H (pv)
- Most complete lyric: -0-
- Original partitur: -0-
- Original parts: -0-

Performed in ME FOR YOU, but dropped before the New York premiere of HEADS UP!

Sweetheart, You Make Me Laugh

Rodgers/Hart
Orchestrator: Unknown

Location of
- Composer's manuscript: -0-
- Sheet music: Unpublished
- Most complete music: R&H (pv)
- Most complete lyric: CLLH
- Original partitur: -0-
- Original parts: SA (inc)

Performed in ME FOR YOU, but dropped before the New York premiere of HEADS UP! The Horns parts are missing.

Jazz Reception

Rodgers/Hart
Orchestrator: Unknown

Location of
- Composer's manuscript: LoC
- Sheet music: Unpublished
- Most complete music: R&H (pv); SA (pv)
- Most complete lyric: R&H (ls); CLLH
- Original partitur: -0-
- Original parts: -0-

This ME FOR YOU Act I Opening was dropped before the New York premiere of HEADS UP! Alternate title: "Kindly Nullify Your Fears."

Sky City

Rodgers/Hart
Orchestrator: Unknown

Location of
- Composer's manuscript: -0-
- Sheet music: LoC, NYPL
- Most complete music: LoC (sm); NYPL (sm); R&H (pv-l)
- Most complete lyric: LoC (sm); NYPL (sm); R&H (pv-l, ls); CLLH
- Original partitur: -0-
- Original parts: SA (inc)

Performed in ME FOR YOU, but dropped before the New York premiere of HEADS UP! The orchestra piano part and Horn parts are missing.

I Can Do Wonders With You
Rodgers/Hart
Orchestrator: Unknown

Location of - Composer's manuscript: -0-
 - Sheet music: LoC, NYPL
 - Most complete music: LoC (sm);
     NYPL (sm); R&H (pv-l)
 - Most complete lyric: LoC (sm);
     NYPL (sm); R&H (pv-l, ls); CLLH
 - Original partitur: -0-
 - Original parts: SA (inc)

Performed in ME FOR YOU, but dropped before the New York premiere of HEADS UP! Later used in SIMPLE SIMON (1930). The orchestra piano part and Horn parts are missing.

As Though You Were There
Rodgers/Hart
Orchestrator: Unknown

Location of - Composer's manuscript: -0-
 - Sheet music: See note
 - Most complete music: R&H (pv-l);
     LoC (pv-l)
 - Most complete lyric: R&H (ls);
     LoC (ls); CLLH
 - Original partitur: -0-
 - Original parts: SA (inc)

Performed in ME FOR YOU, but dropped before the New York opening of HEADS UP! Initial publication in 1940 following a recording by Lee Wiley on an album of Rodgers and Hart songs. The orchestra piano part and Horn parts are missing.

Finaletto Scene 1
Rodgers/Hart
Orchestrator: Unknown

Location of - Composer's manuscript: -0-
 - Sheet music: Unpublished
 - Most complete music: -0-
 - Most complete lyric: -0-
 - Original partitur: -0-
 - Original parts: -0-

Performed in ME FOR YOU, but dropped before the New York premiere of HEADS UP!

Color of Her Eyes, The
Rodgers/Hart
Orchestrator: Unknown

Location of - Composer's manuscript: LoC
 - Sheet music: LoC
 - Most complete music: LoC (sm); R&H (pv)
 - Most complete lyric: CLLH
 - Original partitur: -0-
 - Original parts: -0-

Performed in ME FOR YOU, but dropped before the New York premiere of HEADS UP! Also dropped during the pre-Broadway tryout of SPRING IS HERE (1929). Finally used in EVER GREEN (1930), at which time it was published as "The Colour of Her Eyes."

They Sing! They Dance! They Speak!
Rodgers/Hart
Orchestrator: Unknown

Location of - Composer's manuscript: -0-
 - Sheet music: Unpublished
 - Most complete music: See note
 - Most complete lyric: R&H (ls); CLLH
 - Original partitur: -0-
 - Original parts: -0-

Dropped before the ME FOR YOU tryout. Revised and expanded, this number became the Act II Opening of AMERICA'S SWEETHEART (1931). Tams-Witmark Music Library and the Rodgers and Hammerstein Theatre Library have piano-vocals from the later version.

SIMPLE SIMON

Music   **RICHARD RODGERS**
Lyrics   **LORENZ HART**

Musical comedy in two acts. Opened February 18, 1930 in New York and ran 135 performances (World premiere: January 27, 1930 in Boston). Libretto by Ed Wynn and Guy Bolton. Additional songs by Walter Donaldson and Gus Kahn, Fred Fisher and Billy Rose. Produced by Florenz Ziegfeld. Directed by Zeke Colvan. Choreographed by Seymour Felix. Musical direction by Oscar Bradley.

Synopsis and Production Information

Simple Simon, the lovable proprietor of a newspaper shop on Coney Island, befriends two young lovers, Tony and Ella, whose feuding fathers are determined to keep them apart. Later, Simon falls asleep and dreams that Cinderella (Ella) and her father, King Cole, are driven from their throne by the wicked Bluebeard and forced to wander through an enchanted forest on Christmas Eve. After adventures in the Kingdom Drugstore, the Walled City, and the Kissing Forest, they are rescued by Prince Charming (Tony). Simon then awakes and relates his dream to the two families; miraculously, they make sense out of all this, and the fathers resolve their differences.

Other characters include Sal, a dance hall hostess, and Jack and Jill, a Coney Island couple who perform several numbers in and out of the dream. There is also a full singing and dancing ensemble, several live animals, and a contortionist who plays the part of a giant green frog.

Orchestration

Flute; Oboe; Clarinet I II; Bassoon; Horn I II; Trumpet I II; Trumpet III; Trombone; Drums; Harp; Piano; Violin I II; Viola; Cello; Bass

Comments

A Ziegfeld extravaganza, SIMPLE SIMON served primarily as a showcase for a sumptuous physical production and for the antics of Ed Wynn as Simon. The original cast also included Ruth Etting as Sal.

Location of Original Materials

Script: New York Public Libary (few lyrics)
Piano-vocal score: See individual listings
Partiturs: Rodgers and Hammerstein Theatre Library
Parts: Rodgers and Hammerstein Theatre Library

Much of the piano-vocal score is still missing. In addition, partiturs and parts for only one number have been located.

Rental Status

Currently unavailable for rental

Music Publisher

Marlin Enterprises and Lorenz Hart Publishing Co., c/o Warner Brothers Music

Information

Rodgers and Hammerstein Theatre Library

Overture

Rodgers/Hart
Orchestrator: Unknown

Location of   - Composer's manuscript: -0-
- Sheet music: Unpublished
- Most complete music: -0-
- Most complete lyric: INST
- Original partitur: -0-
- Original parts: -0-

Magic Music

Rodgers/Hart
Orchestrator: Unknown

Location of   - Composer's manuscript: -0-
- Sheet music: Unpublished
- Most complete music: -0-
- Most complete lyric: R&H (ls);
      NYPL (scr); CLLH
- Original partitur: -0-
- Original parts: -0-

Coney Island

Rodgers/Hart
Orchestrator: Unknown

Location of   - Composer's manuscript: -0-
- Sheet music: Unpublished
- Most complete music: -0-
- Most complete lyric: R&H (ls);
      NYPL (scr); CLLH
- Original partitur: -0-
- Original parts: -0-

Alternate title: "Opening Act I."

I Still Believe in You

Rodgers/Hart
Orchestrator: Unknown

Location of   - Composer's manuscript: LoC
- Sheet music: LoC, NYPL
- Most complete music: LoC (sm);
      NYPL (sm)
- Most complete lyric: LoC (sm);
      NYPL (sm); CLLH
- Original partitur: R&H
- Original parts: R&H (inc)

Dropped during the New York run. The same music, except for part of the verse, had been used for "Singing a Love Song" in CHEE-CHEE (1928).

Don't Tell Your Folks

Rodgers/Hart
Orchestrator: Unknown

Location of   - Composer's manuscript: LoC
- Sheet music: LoC, NYPL
- Most complete music: LoC (sm);
      NYPL (sm); R&H (pv-l)
- Most complete lyric: LoC (sm);
      NYPL (sm); R&H (pv-l, ls); CLLH
- Original partitur: -0-
- Original parts: -0-

Send for Me

Rodgers/Hart
Orchestrator: Unknown

Location of   - Composer's manuscript: LoC
- Sheet music: LoC, NYPL
- Most complete music: LoC (sm);
      NYPL (sm)
- Most complete lyric: LoC (sm);
      NYPL (sm); CLLH
- Original partitur: -0-
- Original parts: -0-

The music to the refrain had been used for the refrain of "I Must Love You" in CHEE-CHEE (1928).

Dull and Gay
Rodgers/Hart
Orchestrator: Unknown

Location of - Composer's manuscript: -0-
- Sheet music: Unpublished
- Most complete music: -0-
- Most complete lyric: -0-
- Original partitur: -0-
- Original parts: -0-

Mocking Bird
Author(s): Unknown
Orchestrator: Unknown

Location of - Composer's manuscript: -0-
- Sheet music: Unpublished
- Most complete music: -0-
- Most complete lyric: -0-
- Original partitur: -0-
- Original parts: -0-

Probably a sketch or production number with no lyric.

Sweetenheart
Rodgers/Hart
Orchestrator: Unknown

Location of - Composer's manuscript: LoC
- Sheet music: LoC, NYPL
- Most complete music: LoC (sm);
     NYPL (sm); R&H (pv-l)
- Most complete lyric: LoC (sm);
     NYPL (sm); R&H (pv-l, ls); CLLH
- Original partitur: -0-
- Original parts: -0-

Finaletto Act I, Scene 5 ["Come on, men, seize them!"]
Rodgers/Hart
Orchestrator: Unknown

Location of - Composer's manuscript: LoC
- Sheet music: Unpublished
- Most complete music: R&H (pv-l);
     LoC (pv)
- Most complete lyric: R&H (ls); CLLH
- Original partitur: -0-
- Original parts: -0-

Hunting the Fox
Rodgers/Hart
Orchestrator: Unknown

Location of - Composer's manuscript: -0-
- Sheet music: Unpublished
- Most complete music: -0-
- Most complete lyric: CLLH
- Original partitur: -0-
- Original parts: -0-

I Love the Woods
Authors: Unknown
Orchestrator: Unknown

Location of - Composer's manuscript: -0-
- Sheet music: Unpublished
- Most complete music: -0-
- Most complete lyric: See note
- Original partitur: -0-
- Original parts: -0-

Ed Wynn's comic specialty. It has no lyric, but the routine is included in the script.

Entr'acte
Rodgers/Hart
Orchestrator: Unknown

Location of - Composer's manuscript: -0-
            - Sheet music: Unpublished
            - Most complete music: -0-
            - Most complete lyric: INST
            - Original partitur: -0-
            - Original parts: -0-

Ten Cents a Dance
Rodgers/Hart
Orchestrator: Unknown

Location of - Composer's manuscript: LoC (x)
            - Sheet music: NYPL
            - Most complete music: NYPL (sm);
                 R&H (pv-l); LoC (pv-l)
            - Most complete lyric: NYPL (sm);
                 R&H (pv-l); LoC (pv-l); CLLH
            - Original partitur: -0-
            - Original parts: -0-

On With the Dance
Author(s): Unknown
Orchestrator: Unknown

Location of - Composer's manuscript: -0-
            - Sheet music: Unpublished
            - Most complete music: -0-
            - Most complete lyric: -0-
            - Original partitur: -0-
            - Original parts: -0-

This may have been a dance number with no lyric.

In Your Chapeau
Author(s): Unknown
Orchestrator: Unknown

Location of - Composer's manuscript: -0-
            - Sheet music: Unpublished
            - Most complete music: -0-
            - Most complete lyric: -0-
            - Original partitur: -0-
            - Original parts: -0-

Probably a comedy sketch with no lyric. Dropped during the New York run.

I Can Do Wonders With You
Rodgers/Hart
Orchestrator: Unknown

Location of - Composer's manuscript: -0-
            - Sheet music: LoC, NYPL
            - Most complete music: LoC (sm);
                 NYPL (sm); R&H (pv-l)
            - Most complete lyric: LoC (sm);
                 NYPL (sm); R&H (pv-l, ls); CLLH
            - Original partitur: -0-
            - Original parts: SA (inc)

Initially performed in ME FOR YOU (1929). Dropped during the New York run of SIMPLE SIMON. The parts at the Shubert Archive are with the HEADS UP! material; the orchestra piano part and Horn parts are missing.

Roping
Author(s): Unknown
Orchestrator: Unknown

Location of - Composer's manuscript: -0-
            - Sheet music: Unpublished
            - Most complete music: -0-
            - Most complete lyric: -0-
            - Original partitur: -0-
            - Original parts: -0-

Probably a comedy sketch with no lyric.

Simple Simon (1930)

Kissing Forest Ballet, The
    Author(s): Unknown
    Orchestrator: Unknown

    Location of   - Composer's manuscript: -0-
                 - Sheet music: Unpublished
                 - Most complete music: -0-
                 - Most complete lyric: INST
                 - Original partitur: -0-
                 - Original parts: -0-

I Want That Man
    Rodgers/Hart
    Orchestrator: Unknown

    Location of   - Composer's manuscript: -0-
                 - Sheet music: Unpublished
                 - Most complete music: -0-
                 - Most complete lyric: -0-
                 - Original partitur: -0-
                 - Original parts: -0-

Added and dropped during the New York run.

Trojan Horse, The
    Author(s): Unknown
    Orchestrator: Unknown

    Location of   - Composer's manuscript: -0-
                 - Sheet music: -0-
                 - Most complete music: -0-
                 - Most complete lyric: -0-
                 - Original partitur: -0-
                 - Original parts: -0-

Appears to have been a production number with no lyric.
Dropped during the New York run.

Happy Days and Lonely Nights
    Fisher/Rose
    Orchestrator: Unknown

    Location of   - Composer's manuscript: -0-
                 - Sheet music: NYPL
                 - Most complete music: NYPL (sm)
                 - Most complete lyric: NYPL (sm)
                 - Original partitur: -0-
                 - Original parts: -0-

Added during the New York run.

Rags and Tatters
    Rodgers/Hart
    Orchestrator: Unknown

    Location of   - Composer's manuscript: -0-
                 - Sheet music: Unpublished
                 - Most complete music: -0-
                 - Most complete lyric: CLLH
                 - Original partitur: -0-
                 - Original parts: -0-

Love Me or Leave Me
    Donaldson/Kahn
    Orchestrator: Unknown

    Location of   - Composer's manuscript: -0-
                 - Sheet music: NYPL
                 - Most complete music: NYPL (sm)
                 - Most complete lyric: NYPL (sm)
                 - Original partitur: -0-
                 - Original parts: -0-

Added during the New York run. Originally in WHOOPEE (1928).

Cottage in the Country

Donaldson/Donaldson
Orchestrator: Unknown

Location of
- Composer's manuscript: -0-
- Sheet music: LoC, NYPL
- Most complete music: LoC (sm); NYPL (sm); R&H (pv-l)
- Most complete lyric: LoC (sm); NYPL (sm); R&H (pv-l)
- Original partitur: -0-
- Original parts: -0-

Added during the New York run as part of the Act II Finale.

He Was Too Good to Me

Rodgers/Hart
Orchestrator: Unknown

Location of
- Composer's manuscript: LoC (x)
- Sheet music: LoC, NYPL
- Most complete music: LoC (sm); NYPL (sm); R&H (pv-l)
- Most complete lyric: LoC (sm); NYPL (sm); R&H (pv-l); CLLH
- Original partitur: -0-
- Original parts: -0-

Dropped during the pre-Broadway tryout.

Bluebeard's Beard

Author(s): Unknown
Orchestrator: Unknown

Location of
- Composer's manuscript: -0-
- Sheet music: -0-
- Most complete music: -0-
- Most complete lyric: -0-
- Original partitur: -0-
- Original parts: -0-

Added for the post-Broadway tour, this appears to have been a production number without a lyric.

Say When – Stand Up – Drink Down

Rodgers/Hart
Orchestrator: Unknown

Location of
- Composer's manuscript: -0-
- Sheet music: Unpublished
- Most complete music: -0-
- Most complete lyric: -0-
- Original partitur: -0-
- Original parts: -0-

Dropped during the pre-Broadway tryout.

Peter Pan

Rodgers/Hart
Orchestrator: Unknown

Location of
- Composer's manuscript: -0-
- Sheet music: Unpublished
- Most complete music: -0-
- Most complete lyric: CLLH
- Original partitur: -0-
- Original parts: -0-

Added for the post-Broadway tour.

Drugstore Opening

Rodgers/Hart
Orchestrator: Unknown

Location of
- Composer's manuscript: -0-
- Sheet music: Unpublished
- Most complete music: -0-
- Most complete lyric: R&H (ls); CLLH
- Original partitur: -0-
- Original parts: -0-

Probably unused.

Oh, So Lovely
    Rodgers/Hart
    Orchestrator: Unknown

    Location of   - Composer's manuscript: LoC
                - Sheet music: Unpublished
                - Most complete music: R&H (pv-l); LoC (pv)
                - Most complete lyric: R&H (pv-l, ls); CLLH
                - Original partitur: -0-
                - Original parts: -0-

Unused, although prepared for publication.

Hunting Song
    Rodgers/Hart
    Orchestrator: Unknown

    Location of   - Composer's manuscript: LoC
                - Sheet music: Unpublished
                - Most complete music: R&H (pv)
                - Most complete lyric: R&H (ls); CLLH
                - Original partitur: -0-
                - Original parts: -0-

Probably unused.

Simple Simon Instep, The
    Rodgers/Hart
    Orchestrator: Unknown

    Location of   - Composer's manuscript: -0-
                - Sheet music: Unpublished
                - Most complete music: -0-
                - Most complete lyric: R&H (ls); CLLH
                - Original partitur: -0-
                - Original parts: -0-

Unused.

Come Out of the Nursery
    Rodgers/Hart
    Orchestrator: Unknown

    Location of   - Composer's manuscript: -0-
                - Sheet music: Unpublished
                - Most complete music: -0-
                - Most complete lyric: CLLH
                - Original partitur: -0-
                - Original parts: -0-

Dropped during the pre-Broadway tryout.

Prayers of Tears and Laughter
    Rodgers/Hart
    Orchestrator: Unknown

    Location of   - Composer's manuscript: -0-
                - Sheet music: Unpublished
                - Most complete music: -0-
                - Most complete lyric: R&H (ls); CLLH
                - Original partitur: -0-
                - Original parts: -0-

Apparently dropped before the New York opening.

Sing Glory Hallelujah
    Rodgers/Hart
    Orchestrator: Unknown

    Location of   - Composer's manuscript: -0-
                - Sheet music: Unpublished
                - Most complete music: -0-
                - Most complete lyric: CLLH
                - Original partitur: -0-
                - Original parts: -0-

Probably dropped before the pre-Broadway tryout.

He Dances on My Ceiling

Rodgers/Hart

Orchestrator: Unknown

Location of   - Composer's manuscript: LoC (x)

                - Sheet music: LoC, NYPL

                - Most complete music: LoC (sm);

                      NYPL (sm); R&H (pv-l)

                - Most complete lyric: LoC (sm);

                      NYPL (sm); R&H (pv-l, ls); CLLH

                - Original partitur: -0-

                - Original parts: -0-

Dropped before the New York opening. Later included in
EVER GREEN (1930) as "Dancing on the Ceiling."

EVER GREEN

Music   **RICHARD RODGERS**
Lyrics   **LORENZ HART**

Musical comedy in two acts. Opened December 3, 1930 in London and ran 254 performances (World premiere: October 13, 1930 in Glasgow). Libretto by Benn W. Levy, based on an idea by Richard Rodgers and Lorenz Hart. French lyrics by J. Lenoir. Produced by Charles B. Cochran. Directed by Frank Collins. Choreographed by Buddy Bradley and Billy Pierce. Musical direction by Richard Crean. Orchestrations by Robert Russell Bennett.

Synopsis and Production Information

Harriet Green is a young English actress who becomes a star in Paris by posing as a sixty-year-old woman who looks twenty. Complications arise when she falls in love with Tommy Thompson, since she's afraid if she tells him the truth, she'll lose her fame. In the end, she eats her cake and has it, too.

Other characters include Mary Tucket, Harriet's fellow actress and accomplice; Mrs. Platter, Harriet's mother (who is passed off as Harriet's daughter); Eric Merivale, Tommy's buddy, also an aspiring young actor; Saint-Didier, the grand director of the Casino des Folies in Paris; and Miss Cheltenham, a beauty contestant who sings a song at the top of the show and then disappears for the rest of the evening. There is a full singing and dancing ensemble (including a pair of specialty dancers) and elaborate sets and costumes.

Orchestration   Unknown

Comments   Two numbers and portions of the dialogue are performed in French.

Location of Original Materials

Script: Rodgers and Hammerstein Theatre Library (most lyrics)
Piano-vocal score: See individual listings
Partiturs: Missing
Parts: Missing

Rental Status   Currently unavailable for rental

Music Publisher   Marlin Enterprises and Lorenz Hart Publishing Co., c/o Warner Brothers Music

Information   Rodgers and Hammerstein Theatre Library

Overture

Rodgers/Hart
Orchestrator: Unknown

Location of - Composer's manuscript: -0-
        - Sheet music: Unpublished
        - Most complete music: -0-
        - Most complete lyric: INST
        - Original partitur: -0-
        - Original parts: -0-

Doing a Little Clog Dance

Rodgers/Hart
Orchestrator: Unknown

Location of - Composer's manuscript: LoC
        - Sheet music: Unpublished
        - Most complete music: LoC (pv)
        - Most complete lyric: R&H (scr); CLLH
        - Original partitur: -0-
        - Original parts: -0-

Alternate title: "Doing a Little Waltz Clog."

Opening Act I

Rodgers/Hart
Orchestrator: Unknown

Location of - Composer's manuscript: LoC
        - Sheet music: Unpublished
        - Most complete music: R&H (pv); LoC (pv)
        - Most complete lyric: R&H (scr); CLLH
        - Original partitur: -0-
        - Original parts: -0-

Alternate title: "The Beauty Contest."

Dear! Dear!

Rodgers/Hart
Orchestrator: Unknown

Location of - Composer's manuscript: -0-
        - Sheet music: NYPL
        - Most complete music: NYPL (sm);
            R&H (pv)
        - Most complete lyric: R&H (scr, ls); CLLH
        - Original partitur: -0-
        - Original parts: -0-

The script also contains a few alternate lyrics.

Harlemania

Rodgers/Hart
Orchestrator: Unknown

Location of - Composer's manuscript: LoC
        - Sheet music: LoC
        - Most complete music: LoC (sm); R&H (pv)
        - Most complete lyric: LoC (sm);
            R&H (scr, ls); CLLH
        - Original partitur: -0-
        - Original parts: -0-

Nobody Looks at the Man

Rodgers/Hart
Orchestrator: Unknown

Location of - Composer's manuscript: LoC
        - Sheet music: Unpublished
        - Most complete music: R&H (pv); LoC (pv)
        - Most complete lyric: R&H (scr); CLLH
        - Original partitur: -0-
        - Original parts: -0-

Waiting for the Leaves to Fall
Rodgers/Hart
Orchestrator: Unknown

Location of   - Composer's manuscript: LoC
              - Sheet music: Unpublished
              - Most complete music: R&H (pv); LoC (pv)
              - Most complete lyric: R&H (scr); CLLH
              - Original partitur: -0-
              - Original parts: -0-

The piano-vocals are entitled "She Was Poor."

No Place But Home
Rodgers/Hart
Orchestrator: Unknown

Location of   - Composer's manuscript: LoC
              - Sheet music: LoC, NYPL
              - Most complete music: LoC (sm);
                      NYPL (sm); R&H (pv)
              - Most complete lyric: LoC (sm);
                      NYPL (sm); R&H (scr); CLLH
              - Original partitur: -0-
              - Original parts: -0-

The script also contains a few alternate lyrics. The manuscript is entitled "If We're in China."

Lion King, The
Rodgers/Hart
Orchestrator: Unknown

Location of   - Composer's manuscript: -0-
              - Sheet music: Unpublished
              - Most complete music: -0-
              - Most complete lyric: R&H (ls); CLLH
              - Original partitur: -0-
              - Original parts: -0-

Alternate title: "The Lion Song." The lyric is not in the script.

Quand Notre Vieux Monde Etait Tout Neuf [When the Old World Was New]
Rodgers/Hart & Lenoir
Orchestrator: Unknown

Location of   - Composer's manuscript: LoC
              - Sheet music: Not published separately
              - Most complete music: R&H (pv); LoC (pv)
              - Most complete lyric: R&H (scr) & CLLH
              - Original partitur: -0-
              - Original parts: -0-

The script contains Lenoir's French lyric (which was sung in the show); The Complete Lyrics of Lorenz Hart contains Hart's English lyric. The refrain was published in the piano selection, which can be found at the Rodgers and Hammerstein Theatre Library and the New York Public Library.

La Femme A Toujours Vingt Ans! [Lovely Woman's Ever Young]
Rodgers/Hart & Lenoir
Orchestrator: Unknown

Location of   - Composer's manuscript: LoC
              - Sheet music: Unpublished
              - Most complete music: LoC (pv)
              - Most complete lyric: R&H (scr) & CLLH
              - Original partitur: -0-
              - Original parts: -0-

The script contains Lenoir's French lyric (which was sung in the show); The Complete Lyrics of Lorenz Hart contains Hart's English lyric.

Entr'acte
Rodgers/Hart
Orchestrator: Unknown

Location of   - Composer's manuscript: -0-
              - Sheet music: Unpublished
              - Most complete music: -0-
              - Most complete lyric: INST
              - Original partitur: -0-
              - Original parts: -0-

Colour of Her Eyes, The
Rodgers/Hart
Orchestrator: Unknown

Location of - Composer's manuscript: LoC
- Sheet music: LoC
- Most complete music: LoC (sm); R&H (pv)
- Most complete lyric: LoC (sm);
    R&H (scr); CLLH
- Original partitur: -0-
- Original parts: -0-

The Complete Lyrics of Lorenz Hart also contains earlier lyrics written for SPRING IS HERE (1929) and HEADS UP! (1929).

In the Cool of the Evening
Rodgers/Hart
Orchestrator: Unknown

Location of - Composer's manuscript: LoC
- Sheet music: LoC, NYPL
- Most complete music: LoC (sm);
    NYPL (sm); R&H (pv)
- Most complete lyric: LoC (sm);
    NYPL (sm); R&H (ls, scr); CLLH
- Original partitur: -0-
- Original parts: -0-

Dancing on the Ceiling
Rodgers/Hart
Orchestrator: Unknown

Location of - Composer's manuscript: LoC
- Sheet music: R&H (x)
- Most complete music: R&H (sm-x)
- Most complete lyric: R&H (sm-x); CLLH
- Original partitur: -0-
- Original parts: -0-

Intended for SIMPLE SIMON (1930). Initially published (with the SIMPLE SIMON sheet music) as "He Dances on My Ceiling". The Library of Congress manuscript is with the SIMPLE SIMON material.

Je M'en Fiche du Sex-Appeal
Rodgers/Hart
Orchestrator: Unknown

Location of - Composer's manuscript: LoC
- Sheet music: Unpublished
- Most complete music: R&H (pv); LoC (pv)
- Most complete lyric: R&H (scr); LoC (ls);
    CLLH
- Original partitur: -0-
- Original parts: -0-

Impromptu Song
Rodgers/Hart
Orchestrator: Unknown

Location of - Composer's manuscript: LoC
- Sheet music: Unpublished
- Most complete music: R&H (pv); LoC (pv)
- Most complete lyric: R&H (scr); CLLH
- Original partitur: -0-
- Original parts: -0-

The piano-vocals are entitled "Talking Song."

If I Give in to You
Rodgers/Hart
Orchestrator: Unknown

Location of - Composer's manuscript: LoC
- Sheet music: LoC, NYPL
- Most complete music: LoC (sm);
    NYPL (sm); R&H (pv)
- Most complete lyric: LoC (sm);
    NYPL (sm); R&H (ls, scr); CLLH
- Original partitur: -0-
- Original parts: -0-

AMERICA'S SWEETHEART

Music   **RICHARD RODGERS**
Lyrics   **LORENZ HART**

Musical comedy in two acts. Opened February 10, 1931 in New York and ran 135 performances (World premiere: January 19, 1931 in Pittsburgh). Libretto by Herbert Fields. Produced by Lawrence Schwab and Frank Mandel. Directed by Monty Woolley. Choreographed by Bobby Connolly. Musical direction by Al Goodman. Orchestrations by Robert Russell Bennett.

Synopsis and Production Information

Michael Perry and Geraldine March, two hicks from the Midwest, travel to Hollywood to become rich and famous so that they can marry. When S.A. Dolan, general manager of Premier Pictures, makes Gerry a star of the silent screen, she forgets her humble beginnings and snubs Michael. Soon talkies replace silent films, however, and Michael becomes the new sensation. He forgives Gerry and publicly proposes to her.

Musical support is provided by Larry Pitkin and Madge Farrell (an aspiring comedy team) and by French star Denise Torel. There is a full singing and dancing ensemble, and a female vocal trio.

Orchestration

Reed I (Alto Sax, Clarinet, Flute); Reed II (Alto Sax, Clarinet); Reed III (Tenor Sax, Clarinet, Oboe); Trumpet I II; Trumpet III; Trombone; Banjo; Percussion; Piano; Violin I; Violin II; Violin III; Cello; Bass

Location of Original Materials

Script: Tams-Witmark Music Library (no lyrics)
Piano-vocal score: See individual listings
Partiturs: Tams-Witmark Music Library
Parts: Tams-Witmark Music Library

The complete piano-vocal score from the New York production has surfaced with the exception of one number; most of the partiturs and parts survive as well. Early drafts of the script can be found at Tams-Witmark Music Library, the Library of Congress, and the Rodgers and Hammerstein Theatre Library.

Rental Status

Currently unavailable for rental

Music Publisher

Warner Brothers Music

Information

Rodgers and Hammerstein Theatre Library

Overture

Rodgers/Hart

Orchestrator: Bennett

Location of
- Composer's manuscript: -0-
- Sheet music: Unpublished
- Most complete music: TW (parts)
- Most complete lyric: INST
- Original partitur: TW (inc)
- Original parts: TW

My Sweet

Rodgers/Hart

Orchestrator: Bennett

Location of
- Composer's manuscript: LoC (sk)
- Sheet music: Unpublished
- Most complete music: TW (p)
- Most complete lyric: TW (ls)
- Original partitur: TW
- Original parts: TW (inc)

Pages 23-28 and 33-34 of the partitur are with the Overture material. The orchestra piano part is missing.

Mr. Dolan Is Passing Through

Rodgers/Hart

Orchestrator: Bennett

Location of
- Composer's manuscript: LoC (sk)
- Sheet music: Unpublished
- Most complete music: R&H (pv); TW (pv)
- Most complete lyric: TW (ls)
- Original partitur: TW
- Original parts: TW (inc)

The orchestra piano part is missing.

I've Got Five Dollars

Rodgers/Hart

Orchestrator: Bennett

Location of
- Composer's manuscript: LoC (sk)
- Sheet music: LoC, NYPL
- Most complete music: LoC (sm);
  NYPL (sm); R&H (pv); TW (pv)
- Most complete lyric: LoC (sm);
  NYPL (sm); CLLH
- Original partitur: TW
- Original parts: TW (inc)

The orchestra piano part is missing. The Tams-Witmark piano-vocal also includes a description of the number's original routine.

In Californ-i-a

Rodgers/Hart

Orchestrator: Bennett

Location of
- Composer's manuscript: LoC (sk)
- Sheet music: Unpublished
- Most complete music: R&H (pv); TW (pv)
- Most complete lyric: TW (ls)
- Original partitur: TW
- Original parts: TW (inc)

The orchestra piano part is missing. The Tams-Witmark piano-vocal also includes a description of the number's original routine.

Sweet Geraldine

Rodgers/Hart

Orchestrator: Unknown

Location of
- Composer's manuscript: TW
- Sheet music: Unpublished
- Most complete music: TW (pv)
- Most complete lyric: TW (ls)
- Original partitur: -0-
- Original parts: -0-

The first of two numbers performed by Hilda, Louise, and Maxine Forman (playing characters named Georgia, Georgiana, and Georgette), who were apparently not accompanied by the pit orchestra.

America's Sweetheart (1931)

There's So Much More

Rodgers/Hart

Orchestrator: Bennett

Location of - Composer's manuscript: -0-
- Sheet music: LoC, NYPL
- Most complete music: LoC (sm);
    NYPL (sm); R&H (pv); TW (pv)
- Most complete lyric: LoC (sm);
    NYPL (sm); CLLH
- Original partitur: TW
- Original parts: TW (inc)

The music was previously used for "Someone Should Tell Them" in A CONNECTICUT YANKEE (1927). The piano-vocal also includes a description of the number's original routine.

We'll Be the Same

Rodgers/Hart

Orchestrator: Unknown

Location of - Composer's manuscript: -0-
- Sheet music: LoC, NYPL
- Most complete music: LoC (sm);
    NYPL (sm); TW (pv)
- Most complete lyric: LoC (sm);
    NYPL (sm); CLLH
- Original partitur: -0-
- Original parts: TW (inc)

The orchestra piano part is missing. The piano-vocal also includes a description of the number's original routine.

How About It?

Rodgers/Hart

Orchestrator: Unknown

Location of - Composer's manuscript: -0-
- Sheet music: NYPL
- Most complete music: NYPL (sm);
    R&H (pv-l); TW (pv)
- Most complete lyric: NYPL (sm);
    R&H (pv-l); CLLH
- Original partitur: -0-
- Original parts: TW (inc)

The orchestra piano part is missing.

Innocent Chorus Girls of Yesterday

Rodgers/Hart

Orchestrator: Unknown

Location of - Composer's manuscript: LoC (sk)
- Sheet music: Unpublished
- Most complete music: TW (pv)
- Most complete lyric: TW (ls); CLLH
- Original partitur: TW
- Original parts: TW (inc)

The orchestra piano part is missing.

Lady Must Live, A

Rodgers/Hart

Orchestrator: Bennett

Location of - Composer's manuscript: LoC (sk)
- Sheet music: LoC, NYPL
- Most complete music: LoC (sm);
    NYPL (sm); R&H (pv-l); TW (pv)
- Most complete lyric: LoC (sm);
    NYPL (sm); R&H (pv-l); CLLH
- Original partitur: TW
- Original parts: TW (inc)

The orchestra piano part is missing.

Entr'acte

Rodgers/Hart

Orchestrator: Unknown

Location of - Composer's manuscript: -0-
- Sheet music: Unpublished
- Most complete music: TW (parts)
- Most complete lyric: INST
- Original partitur: -0-
- Original parts: TW (inc)

The orchestra piano part is missing. Tams-Witmark also has the original conductor's score.

Opening Act II ["Hello! Hello! Yes, Mr. Dolan's busy now!"]
Rodgers/Hart
Orchestrator: Bennett

Location of - Composer's manuscript: -0-
- Sheet music: Unpublished
- Most complete music: TW (pv); R&H (pv)
- Most complete lyric: TW (ls)
- Original partitur: TW
- Original parts: TW (inc)

A revised and expanded version of "They Sing! They Dance! They Speak!", originally intended for ME FOR YOU (1929). The orchestra piano part is missing.

You Ain't Got No Savoir-Faire
Rodgers/Hart
Orchestrator: Bennett

Location of - Composer's manuscript: -0-
- Sheet music: Unpublished
- Most complete music: TW (pv); R&H (pv)
- Most complete lyric: TW (ls)
- Original partitur: TW
- Original parts: TW (inc)

The orchestra piano part is missing.

Two Unfortunate Orphans
Rodgers/Hart
Orchestrator: Bennett

Location of - Composer's manuscript: -0-
- Sheet music: Unpublished
- Most complete music: TW (pv); R&H (pv)
- Most complete lyric: TW (ls)
- Original partitur: TW
- Original parts: TW

The parts were removed from the orchestra books, suggesting that the number may have been dropped during the New York run.

I Want a Man
Rodgers/Hart
Orchestrator: Bennett

Location of - Composer's manuscript: TW (sk)
- Sheet music: LoC, NYPL
- Most complete music: LoC (sm);
      NYPL (sm); R&H (pv-l)
- Most complete lyric: LoC (sm);
      NYPL (sm); R&H (pv-l); CLLH
- Original partitur: TW
- Original parts: TW (inc)

The third and final version of a song previously intended for WINKLE TOWN (1922) and LIDO LADY (1926). One dance chorus of the partitur is with the Overture material. The orchestra piano part is missing.

Tennessee Dan
Author(s): Unknown
Orchestrator: Unknown

Location of - Composer's manuscript: -0-
- Sheet music: -0-
- Most complete music: -0-
- Most complete lyric: -0-
- Original partitur: -0-
- Original parts: -0-

The second of two numbers performed by Hilda, Louise, and Maxine Forman, apparently unaccompanied by the pit orchestra.

God Gave Me Eyes
Rodgers/Hart
Orchestrator: Bennett

Location of - Composer's manuscript: -0-
- Sheet music: Unpublished
- Most complete music: TW (pv); R&H (pv)
- Most complete lyric: -0-
- Original partitur: TW
- Original parts: TW

Replaced by "My Sweet" during the pre-Broadway tryout.

America's Sweetheart (1931)

Cat Can Look at a Queen, A
    Rodgers/Hart
    Orchestrator: Bennett

    Location of   - Composer's manuscript: -0-
                 - Sheet music: Unpublished
                 - Most complete music: TW (pv); R&H (pv)
                 - Most complete lyric: -0-
                 - Original partitur: TW
                 - Original parts: TW

Dropped before the New York opening. The Tams-Witmark piano-vocal also includes a description of the number's original routine.

Tonight or Never
    Rodgers/Hart
    Orchestrator: Unknown

    Location of   - Composer's manuscript: -0-
                 - Sheet music: Unpublished
                 - Most complete music: -0-
                 - Most complete lyric: -0-
                 - Original partitur: -0-
                 - Original parts: -0-

Dropped before the pre-Broadway tryout.

I'll Be a Star
    Rodgers/Hart
    Orchestrator: -0-

    Location of   - Composer's manuscript: -0-
                 - Sheet music: Unpublished
                 - Most complete music: TW (pv); R&H (pv)
                 - Most complete lyric: -0-
                 - Original partitur: TW
                 - Original parts: TW

Dropped before the pre-Broadway tryout.

JUMBO

Music   RICHARD RODGERS
Lyrics   LORENZ HART

Musical comedy/extravaganza in two acts. Opened November 16, 1935 in New York and ran 233 performances. Libretto by Ben Hecht and Charles MacArthur. Additional lyrics by Jimmy Durante. Produced by Billy Rose. Directed by John Murray Anderson, George Abbott. Choreographed by Allen K. Foster. Musical direction by Adolph Deutsch. Orchestrations by Adolph Deutsch, Murray Cutter, Joseph Nussbaum, Hans Spialek, Robert Russell Bennett, Conrad Salinger, Roy Bargy.

Synopsis and Production Information	Circus owners John Considine and Matthew Mulligan are arch rivals, which causes great distress to their respective children, Mickey and Matt, who are in love. When Considine's circus fall into debt, he is forced to sell his prize elephant, Jumbo, to Mulligan. All looks lost for Considine (as well as for the two young lovers) until he saves the day by rescuing the town from a rampaging Jumbo. His circus is restored, he and Mulligan reconcile their differences, Mickey and Matt marry, and the clowning around continues.
	Other characters include Mr. Jellico, faithful manager of Considine's circus; Claudius B. Bowers, Considine's devoted right-hand man; and the United States Marshall. The show requires a full singing and dancing ensemble, numerous circus specialty acts, and a well-trained elephant.
Orchestration	Reed I (Flute, Piccolo, Clarinet); Reed II (Clarinet, Alto Sax); Reed III (Clarinet, Alto Sax); Reed IV (Clarinet, Alto Sax); Reed V (Clarinet, Tenor Sax); Reed VI (Alto Sax, Baritone Sax); Trumpet I; Trumpet II; Trombone I; Trombone II; Tuba I II; Drums; Organ, Piano; Accordion/Celeste; Guitar; Violin A B C; Viola; Cello; Bass
Comments	The original production included Jimmy Durante (as Claudius B. Bowers) and Paul Whiteman and his Orchestra.
Location of Original Materials	Script: Rodgers and Hammerstein Theatre Library (few lyrics) Piano-vocal score: See individual listings Partiturs: New York Public Library, Rodgers and Hammerstein Theatre Library Parts: Rodgers and Hammerstein Theatre Library
	Most of the songs survive. Of the orchestra parts, only the 1st Violin, Organ, and Conductor parts have been found for the major numbers. The orchestral material at the New York Public Library and the Rodgers and Hammerstein Theatre Library contains a great deal of incidental music appropriate to a circus show, including fanfares, codas, entrances, and playoffs. There are also arrangements for a wind and brass orchestra.
Rental Status	Currently unavailable for rental
Music Publisher	Chappell Music
Information	Rodgers and Hammerstein Theatre Library

Jumbo (1935)

Overture

Rodgers/Hart

Orchestrator: Unknown

Location of - Composer's manuscript: -0-
- Sheet music: Unpublished
- Most complete music: -0-
- Most complete lyric: INST
- Original partitur: -0-
- Original parts: -0-

Most Beautiful Girl in the World, The

Rodgers/Hart

Orchestrator: Cutter, Nussbaum

Location of - Composer's manuscript: LoC
- Sheet music: LoC, NYPL
- Most complete music: R&H (pv-I)
- Most complete lyric: R&H (pv-I);
    LoC (pv-I); CLLH
- Original partitur: NYPL
- Original parts: R&H (inc)

The trio patter was not published.

Over and Over Again

Rodgers/Hart

Orchestrator: Deutsch, Cutter, Nussbaum

Location of - Composer's manuscript: -0-
- Sheet music: LoC, NYPL
- Most complete music: R&H (pv-I)
- Most complete lyric: R&H (pv-I); CLLH
- Original partitur: NYPL
- Original parts: R&H (inc)

The music, original entitled "The Party Waltz," was
written for the film HOLLYWOOD PARTY (1934).

March of the Clowns

Rodgers

Orchestrator: Cutter, Spialek, Bargy, Nussbaum

Location of - Composer's manuscript: LoC
- Sheet music: Unpublished
- Most complete music: R&H (pv)
- Most complete lyric: INST
- Original partitur: NYPL
- Original parts: R&H (inc)

Circus Is On Parade, The

Rodgers/Hart

Orchestrator: Nussbaum, Cutter

Location of - Composer's manuscript: LoC
- Sheet music: LoC, NYPL
- Most complete music: LoC (sm); NYPL (sm)
- Most complete lyric: LoC (sm); NYPL (sm);
    CLLH
- Original partitur: NYPL
- Original parts: R&H (inc)

Laugh

Rodgers/Hart & Durante

Orchestrator: Cutter, Nussbaum

Location of - Composer's manuscript: LoC (sk)
- Sheet music: Unpublished
- Most complete music: NYPL (ptr)
- Most complete lyric: R&H (scr); CLLH
- Original partitur: NYPL
- Original parts: R&H (inc)

Alternate title: "Ya Gotta Laugh."

My Romance

Rodgers/Hart
Orchestrator: Cutter, Spialek, Deutsch, Bennett

Location of   - Composer's manuscript: LoC
              - Sheet music: LoC, NYPL
              - Most complete music: LoC (sm);
                NYPL (sm); R&H (pv-l)
              - Most complete lyric: LoC (sm);
                NYPL (sm); R&H (pv-l); CLLH
              - Original partitur: NYPL
              - Original parts: R&H (inc)

Song of the Roustabouts

Rodgers/Hart
Orchestrator: Bennett, Nussbaum, Cutter

Location of   - Composer's manuscript: LoC (sk)
              - Sheet music: Unpublished
              - Most complete music: See note
              - Most complete lyric: CLLH (frag)
              - Original partitur: NYPL
              - Original parts: R&H (inc)

Alternate titles: "Song of the Razorbacks" and "No Job in Omaha." The most complete music manuscript is the Conductor part, one of the three surviving orchestra parts.

Little Girl Blue

Rodgers/Hart
Orchestrator: Unknown

Location of   - Composer's manuscript: LoC
              - Sheet music: LoC, NYPL
              - Most complete music: LoC (sm);
                NYPL (sm); R&H (pv-l)
              - Most complete lyric: LoC (sm);
                NYPL (sm); R&H (pv-l); CLLH
              - Original partitur: -0-
              - Original parts: R&H (inc)

Women

Rodgers/Hart & Durante
Orchestrator: Cutter, Deutsch, Bennett

Location of   - Composer's manuscript: LoC
              - Sheet music: Unpublished
              - Most complete music: R&H (pv-l)
              - Most complete lyric: LoC (pv-l)
                & R&H (scr); CLLH
              - Original partitur: NYPL
              - Original parts: R&H (inc)

There are two versions of the lyric.

Entr'acte

Rodgers/Hart
Orchestrator: Nussbaum, Cutter

Location of   - Composer's manuscript: -0-
              - Sheet music: Unpublished
              - Most complete music: NYPL (ptr)
              - Most complete lyric: INST
              - Original partitur: NYPL
              - Original parts: R&H (inc)

Memories of Madison Square Garden

Rodgers/Hart
Orchestrator: Nussbaum, Cutter, Deutsch

Location of   - Composer's manuscript: -0-
              - Sheet music: Unpublished
              - Most complete music: R&H (pv-l)
              - Most complete lyric: R&H (pv-l); CLLH
              - Original partitur: NYPL
              - Original parts: R&H (inc)

Diavolo

Rodgers/Hart

Orchestrator: Nussbaum, Cutter

Location of - Composer's manuscript: LoC
          - Sheet music: LoC, NYPL
          - Most complete music: LoC (sm);
             NYPL (sm)
          - Most complete lyric: LoC (sm);
             NYPL (sm); CLLH
          - Original partitur: NYPL
          - Original parts: R&H (inc)

More I See of Other Girls, The

Rodgers/Hart

Orchestrator: Cutter

Location of - Composer's manuscript: -0-
          - Sheet music: Unpublished
          - Most complete music: R&H (pv-l)
          - Most complete lyric: R&H (pv-l); CLLH
          - Original partitur: NYPL
          - Original parts: -0-

Dropped before the New York opening. Alternate title: "Elephant Song."

ON YOUR TOES

| Music | RICHARD RODGERS |
| Lyrics | LORENZ HART |

Musical comedy in two acts. Opened April 11, 1936 in New York and ran 315 performances (World premiere: March 21, 1936 in Boston). Libretto by Richard Rodgers, Lorenz Hart and George Abbott. Produced by Dwight Deere Wiman. Directed by Worthington Miner and George Abbott (uncredited). Choreographed by George Balanchine. Musical direction by Gene Salzer. Orchestrations by Hans Spialek; additional orchestrations by David Raksin.

Synopsis and Production Information	Junior Dolan, music professor and former child vaudeville star, presents his student's jazz composition, SLAUGHTER ON TENTH AVENUE, to the Russian Ballet. Prima Ballerina Vera Barnova takes a fancy to Junior and sees to it that the ballet is produced with Junior dancing the male lead. Vera's former partner and lover, Konstantine Morrosine, becomes extremely jealous, and during a performance, tries to turn a stage killing into a real one. At the last minute, Junior is warned by his devoted student, Frankie.
	Other characters include Junior's vaudevillian parents, Phil and Lil; Peggy Porterfield, the wealthy American backer of the Russian Ballet; and Sergei Alexandrovitch, the Ballet's director. There is a full singing and dancing ensemble.
Orchestration	Reed I (Flute, Piccolo); Reed II (Oboe, English Horn, Celeste); Reed III (Alto Sax, Flute, Bass Clarinet); Reed IV (Alto Sax, Clarinet); Reed V (Tenor Sax, Clarinet); Horn; Trumpet I II; Trumpet III; Trombone; Piano I; Piano II (Celeste); Percussion; Violin A B C; Viola I II; Cello; Bass
Comments	In the original production, Junior was played by Ray Bolger.
Location of Original Materials	Script: Rodgers and Hammerstein Theatre Library (all lyrics), New York Public Library (all lyrics) Piano-vocal score: Rodgers and Hammerstein Theatre Library (Published: Chappell & Co., 1985) Partiturs: Rodgers and Hammerstein Theatre Library Parts: Rodgers and Hammerstein Theatre Library All of the original parts survive, as do most of the partiturs.
Rental Status	The Rodgers and Hammerstein Theatre Library rents a version based on the 1983 Broadway revival. The piano-vocal score and orchestration are similar to those of the original show; the book is heavily revised.
Music Publisher	Chappell Music
Information	Rodgers and Hammerstein Theatre Library

On Your Toes (1936)

Overture

  Rodgers/Hart

  Orchestrator: Spialek

  Location of - Composer's manuscript: -0-
  - Sheet music: Not published separately
  - Most complete music: R&H (pv score)
  - Most complete lyric: INST
  - Original partitur: R&H (inc)
  - Original parts: R&H

It's Got to Be Love

  Rodgers/Hart

  Orchestrator: Spialek, Raksin

  Location of - Composer's manuscript: -0-
  - Sheet music: LoC, NYPL
  - Most complete music: LoC (sm);
      NYPL (sm); R&H (pv score)
  - Most complete lyric: R&H (pv score,
      scr); CLLH
  - Original partitur: R&H
  - Original parts: R&H

Two a Day for Keith

  Rodgers/Hart

  Orchestrator: Unknown

  Location of - Composer's manuscript: LoC
  - Sheet music: Not published separately
  - Most complete music: R&H (pv score);
      LoC (pv-l)
  - Most complete lyric: R&H (pv score, scr);
      LoC (ls); CLLH
  - Original partitur: R&H
  - Original parts: R&H

Too Good for the Average Man

  Rodgers/Hart

  Orchestrator: Spialek

  Location of - Composer's manuscript: -0-
  - Sheet music: LoC, NYPL
  - Most complete music: LoC (sm);
      NYPL (sm); R&H (pv score)
  - Most complete lyric: CLLH
  - Original partitur: R&H
  - Original parts: R&H

Three B's, The

  Rodgers/Hart

  Orchestrator: Spialek

  Location of - Composer's manuscript: LoC
  - Sheet music: Not published separately
  - Most complete music: R&H (pv score);
      LoC (pv-l)
  - Most complete lyric: R&H (pv score, scr);
      LoC (pv-l); CLLH
  - Original partitur: R&H
  - Original parts: R&H

There's a Small Hotel

  Rodgers/Hart

  Orchestrator: Spialek

  Location of - Composer's manuscript: LoC (sk)
  - Sheet music: LoC, NYPL
  - Most complete music: LoC (sm);
      NYPL (sm); R&H (pv score)
  - Most complete lyric: CLLH
  - Original partitur: R&H
  - Original parts: R&H

The manuscript sketch is only for the verse and patter.
The Complete Lyrics of Lorenz Hart also contains an
alternate couplet.

Heart Is Quicker Than the Eye, The
Rodgers/Hart
Orchestrator: Spialek, Raksin

Location of - Composer's manuscript: LoC (sk)
              - Sheet music: LoC, NYPL
              - Most complete music: R&H (pv score
                     & ptr)
              - Most complete lyric: CLLH
              - Original partitur: R&H
              - Original parts: R&H

Quiet Night
Rodgers/Hart
Orchestrator: Spialek, Raksin

Location of - Composer's manuscript: -0-
              - Sheet music: LoC, NYPL
              - Most complete music: LoC (sm);
                     NYPL (sm); R&H (pv score)
              - Most complete lyric: LoC (sm);
                     NYPL (sm); R&H (pv score, scr);
                     CLLH
              - Original partitur: R&H
              - Original parts: R&H

La Princesse Zenobia Ballet
Rodgers
Orchestrator: Spialek, Raksin

Location of - Composer's manuscript: -0-
              - Sheet music: Not published separately
              - Most complete music: R&H (pv score)
              - Most complete lyric: INST
              - Original partitur: R&H (inc)
              - Original parts: R&H

Glad to Be Unhappy
Rodgers/Hart
Orchestrator: Spialek

Location of - Composer's manuscript: -0-
              - Sheet music: LoC, NYPL
              - Most complete music: LoC (sm);
                     NYPL (sm); R&H (pv score)
              - Most complete lyric: LoC (sm);
                     NYPL (sm); R&H (pv score, scr);
                     CLLH
              - Original partitur: R&H
              - Original parts: R&H

Entr'acte
Rodgers/Hart
Orchestrator: Unknown

Location of - Composer's manuscript: -0-
              - Sheet music: Not published separately
              - Most complete music: R&H (pv score)
              - Most complete lyric: INST
              - Original partitur: -0-
              - Original parts: R&H

On Your Toes
Rodgers/Hart
Orchestrator: Spialek, Raksin

Location of - Composer's manuscript: -0-
              - Sheet music: LoC, NYPL
              - Most complete music: LoC (sm);
                     NYPL (sm); R&H (pv score)
              - Most complete lyric: LoC (sm);
                     NYPL (sm); R&H (pv score, scr);
                     CLLH
              - Original partitur: R&H
              - Original parts: R&H

Slaughter on Tenth Avenue Ballet

    Rodgers

    Orchestrator: Spialek

Location of   - Composer's manuscript: LoC (sk)

               - Sheet music: NYPL

               - Most complete music: R&H (pv score)

               - Most complete lyric: INST

               - Original partitur: R&H

               - Original parts: R&H

BABES IN ARMS

Music   RICHARD RODGERS
Lyrics   LORENZ HART

Musical comedy in two acts. Opened April 14, 1937 in New York and ran 289 performances (World premiere: March 31, 1937 in Boston). Libretto by Richard Rodgers and Lorenz Hart. Produced by Dwight Deere Wiman. Directed by Robert Sinclair. Choreographed by George Balanchine. Musical direction by Gene Salzer. Orchestrations by Hans Spialek.

Synopsis and Production Information	The Babes in Arms, children of a troupe of past-prime vaudevillians, are doomed to a work camp unless they can raise some money. They put on a big musical show, but still lack the necessary funds. Just when all seems hopeless, Rene Flambeau, the famous French aviator who is flying non-stop from Paris to Newark, makes an emergency landing on their property. The Babes convince the community that the land could be a valuable airstrip, thus solving their financial problems.
	The romantic Babes (and the leads) are Billie Smith, a 17-year-old free spirit and hitchhiker, and Val La Mar, a clever lad who saves the day by masquerading as Flambeau (who has been knocked unconscious by the crash) and delivering a radio speech in broken English.[7] The brassiest Babe is Baby Rose, a former child star with a breezy personality and a whale of a voice; the dancing Babes are Ivor and Irving, black brothers who are light on their feet; and the comic Babes are Dolores and Gus, who wish they were in love again. There is a singing and dancing ensemble known affectionately as "the gang," and a second-act ballet entitled "Peter's Journey."
Orchestration	Reed I (Flute); Reed II (Oboe, English Horn); Reed III (Alto Sax I, Flute, Clarinet); Reed IV (Alto Sax II, Clarinet); Reed V (Tenor Sax, Clarinet), Reed VI (Bass Clarinet, Clarinet, Basset Horn); Trumpet I II; Trumpet III; Trombone; Piano I; Piano II; Percussion; Violin A; Violin B; Violin C; Violin D; Cello; Bass
Location of Original Materials	Script: Rodgers and Hammerstein Theatre Library (all lyrics) Piano-vocal score: See individual listings Partiturs: Missing Parts: Rodgers and Hammerstein Theatre Library
	All of the original piano-vocal score and parts survive. In addition, partiturs were reconstructed from most of the parts in 1987; these are now at the Rodgers and Hammerstein Theatre Library.
Rental Status	The Rodgers and Hammerstein Theatre Library rents an updated version from 1959, with a new book (by George Oppenheimer), most of the original songs, and an orchestration for 21-23 players. The piano-vocal score to this revision was published by Chappell in 1960.
Music Publisher	Chappell Music
Information	Rodgers and Hammerstein Theatre Library

---

[7]   "My friends, I am so happee I can hardly -- what you say? -- to breathe."

Babes in Arms (1937)

Overture
Rodgers/Hart
Orchestrator: Unknown

Location of - Composer's manuscript: -0-
    - Sheet music: Unpublished
    - Most complete music: R&H (parts)
    - Most complete lyric: INST
    - Original partitur: R&H (1988)
    - Original parts: R&H

I Wish I Were in Love Again
Rodgers/Hart
Orchestrator: Unknown

Location of - Composer's manuscript: LoC
    - Sheet music: LoC, NYPL
    - Most complete music: LoC (sm);
        NYPL (sm); R&H (1960 pv score)
    - Most complete lyric: LoC (sm);
        NYPL (sm); R&H (1960 pv score, scr);
        CLLH
    - Original partitur: R&H (1987)
    - Original parts: R&H

The piano-vocal score also contains additional (uncredited) lyrics written for the 1959 revision.

Where or When
Rodgers/Hart
Orchestrator: Unknown

Location of - Composer's manuscript: LoC
    - Sheet music: LoC, NYPL
    - Most complete music: LoC (sm);
        NYPL (sm); R&H (1960 pv score)
    - Most complete lyric: LoC (sm);
        NYPL (sm); R&H (1960 pv score, scr);
        CLLH
    - Original partitur: R&H (1987)
    - Original parts: R&H (inc)

The Tenor Sax part is missing.

All Dark People
Rodgers/Hart
Orchestrator: Unknown

Location of - Composer's manuscript: -0-
    - Sheet music: LoC, NYPL
    - Most complete music: LoC (sm);
        NYPL (sm); R&H (pv-I)
    - Most complete lyric: LoC (sm);
        NYPL (sm); R&H (pv-I, scr); CLLH
    - Original partitur: R&H (1987)
    - Original parts: R&H

This song is not included in the current rental edition.

Babes in Arms
Rodgers/Hart
Orchestrator: Unknown

Location of - Composer's manuscript: -0-
    - Sheet music: LoC, NYPL
    - Most complete music: LoC (sm);
        NYPL (sm); R&H (1960 pv score)
    - Most complete lyric: LoC (sm);
        NYPL (sm); R&H (1960 pv score, scr);
        CLLH)
    - Original partitur: R&H (1987)
    - Original parts: R&H

Way Out West
Rodgers/Hart
Orchestrator: Unknown

Location of - Composer's manuscript: -0-
    - Sheet music: LoC, NYPL
    - Most complete music: LoC (sm);
        NYPL (sm); R&H (1960 pv score)
    - Most complete lyric: R&H (1960 pv score,
        scr); CLLH
    - Original partitur: -0-
    - Original parts: R&H

My Funny Valentine

Rodgers/Hart

Orchestrator: Unknown

Location of   - Composer's manuscript: LoC
           - Sheet music: NYPL
           - Most complete music: NYPL (sm);
               R&H (1960 pv score)
           - Most complete lyric: NYPL (sm);
               R&H (1960 pv score); CLLH
           - Original partitur: R&H (1987)
           - Original parts: R&H

Imagine

Rodgers/Hart

Orchestrator: Unknown

Location of   - Composer's manuscript: LoC
           - Sheet music: Not published separately
           - Most complete music: LoC (pv-l);
               R&H (1960 pv score)
           - Most complete lyric: R&H (scr); CLLH
           - Original partitur: R&H (1987)
           - Original parts: R&H

The piano-vocal score contains additional (uncredited) lyrics written for the 1959 revision.

Johnny One-Note

Rodgers/Hart

Orchestrator: Unknown

Location of   - Composer's manuscript: LoC
           - Sheet music: LoC, NYPL
           - Most complete music: LoC (sm);
               NYPL (sm); R&H (1960 pv score)
           - Most complete lyric: LoC (sm);
               NYPL (sm); R&H (1960 pv score, scr);
               CLLH
           - Original partitur: R&H (1987)
           - Original parts: R&H

This number is followed by a 675-measure "Johnny One-Note" Ballet, for which a conductor's score and parts survive at the Rodgers and Hammerstein Theatre Library.

All at Once

Rodgers/Hart

Orchestrator: Unknown

Location of   - Composer's manuscript: LoC
           - Sheet music: LoC, NYPL
           - Most complete music: LoC (pv-l);
               R&H (ptr)
           - Most complete lyric: LoC (ls);
               R&H (scr); CLLH
           - Original partitur: R&H (1987)
           - Original parts: R&H (inc)

The patter was not published. The Piano I part is missing. The piano-vocal score contains additional (uncredited) lyrics written for the 1959 revision.

Entr'acte

Rodgers/Hart

Orchestrator: Unknown

Location of   - Composer's manuscript: -0-
           - Sheet music: Unpublished
           - Most complete music: R&H (parts)
           - Most complete lyric: INST
           - Original partitur: -0-
           - Original parts: R&H

Peter's Journey

Rodgers/Hart

Orchestrator: Unknown

Location of   - Composer's manuscript: LoC
           - Sheet music: Unpublished
           - Most complete music: R&H (parts)
           - Most complete lyric: INST
           - Original partitur: -0-
           - Original parts: R&H

Babes in Arms (1937)

Lady Is a Tramp, The

Rodgers/Hart
Orchestrator: Unknown

Location of   - Composer's manuscript: LoC
                 - Sheet music: LoC, NYPL
                 - Most complete music: LoC (sm);
                         NYPL (sm); R&H (1960 pv score)
                 - Most complete lyric: CLLH
                 - Original partitur: R&H (1987)
                 - Original parts: R&H

The piano-vocal score contains additional (uncredited) lyrics written for the 1959 revision.

You Are So Fair

Rodgers/Hart
Orchestrator: Unknown

Location of   - Composer's manuscript: LoC
                 - Sheet music: Unpublished
                 - Most complete music: LoC (pv-l);
                         R&H (pv)
                 - Most complete lyric: R&H (scr); CLLH
                 - Original partitur: R&H (1987)
                 - Original parts: R&H

This song is not included in the current rental edition.

I'D RATHER BE RIGHT

Music	RICHARD RODGERS
Lyrics	LORENZ HART

Musical satire in two acts. Opened November 2, 1937 in New York and ran 290 performances (World premiere: October 11, 1937 in Boston). Libretto by George S. Kaufman and Moss Hart. Produced by Sam H. Harris. Directed by George S. Kaufman. Choreographed by Charles Weidman and Ned McGurn. Musical direction by Harry Levant. Orchestrations by Hans Spialek, Maurice B. DePackh, Don Walker.

Synopsis and Production Information

Peggy and Phil can't marry until Phil gets a raise, which in turn will only happen when the national budget is balanced. One evening in Central Park, they dream that they meet President Roosevelt, who tirelessly tries to help them despite obstacles created by his Cabinet, Supreme Court, and fellow Democrats. When the President is unable to find a solution, he simply advises Peggy and Phil to have faith and marry. When they awaken, they decide to do so.

The cast includes numerous Secretaries from Roosevelt's cabinet, Roosevelt's mother, and his two grandchildren. The full singing and dancing ensemble includes the Supreme Court Justices, their girlfriends, ten cabinet members, and players in the Federal Theatre Company.

Orchestration

Reed I (Flute, Clarinet, Alto Sax); Reed II (Oboe, English Horn); Reed III (Clarinet, Alto Sax, Bass Clarinet); Reed IV (Tenor Sax, Flute); Reed V (Clarinet, Tenor Sax, Bassoon); Horn; Trumpet I II; Trumpet III; Trombone; Piano; Harp; Percussion; Violin A B C; Viola I II; Cello; Bass

Comments

In the original production, President Roosevelt was played by George M. Cohan.

Location of Original Materials

Script: Rodgers and Hammerstein Theatre Library (some lyrics)
      (Published: Random House, Inc., 1937)
Piano-vocal score: Rodgers and Hammerstein Theatre Library
Partiturs: Rodgers and Hammestein Music Library
Parts: Rodgers and Hammerstein Theatre Library

All of the piano-vocal material and parts survive, as do most of the partiturs.

Rental Status

As of this writing, the Rodgers and Hammerstein Theatre Library is preparing a rental edition based on the original show.

Music Publisher

Chappell Music

Information

Rodgers and Hammerstein Theatre Library

I'd Rather Be Right (1937)

Overture
Rodgers/Hart
Orchestrator: Spialek, unknown

Location of   - Composer's manuscript: -0-
- Sheet music: Unpublished
- Most complete music: R&H (pv score)
- Most complete lyric: INST
- Original partitur: R&H (inc)
- Original parts: R&H

Homogeneous Cabinet, A
Rodgers/Hart
Orchestrator: DePackh, Spialek

Location of   - Composer's manuscript: R&H
- Sheet music: Unpublished
- Most complete music: R&H (pv score
    & pv-l)
- Most complete lyric: R&H (pv score
    & pv-l)
- Original partitur: R&H
- Original parts: R&H

Have You Met Miss Jones?
Rodgers/Hart
Orchestrator: Spialek

Location of   - Composer's manuscript: LoC
- Sheet music: NYPL
- Most complete music: NYPL (sm);
    R&H (pv score); LoC (pv-l)
- Most complete lyric: CLLH
- Original partitur: R&H
- Original parts: R&H

Beauty Sequence ["Here he is!"]
Rodgers/Hart
Orchestrator: Spialek

Location of   - Composer's manuscript: LoC
- Sheet music: Unpublished
- Most complete music: R&H (pv score);
    LoC (pv-l)
- Most complete lyric: R&H (pv score, ls);
    CLLH
- Original partitur: R&H
- Original parts: R&H

Take and Take and Take
Rodgers/Hart
Orchestrator: Spialek

Location of   - Composer's manuscript: LoC
- Sheet music: NYPL
- Most complete music: NYPL (sm);
    R&H (pv score); LoC (pv-l)
- Most complete lyric: NYPL (sm);
    R&H (pv score); LoC (pv-l); CLLH
- Original partitur: R&H
- Original parts: R&H

Spring in Vienna
Rodgers/Hart
Orchestrator: Spialek

Location of   - Composer's manuscript: -0-
- Sheet music: Unpublished
- Most complete music: R&H (pv score)
- Most complete lyric: R&H (pv score);
    CLLH
- Original partitur: R&H
- Original parts: R&H

The title was changed to "Spring in Milwaukee" in May, 1938, possibly because of the German annexation of Austria the previous March; the "Spring in Milwaukee" lyric is probably the same as "Spring in Vienna" lyric, with the name of the city changed throughout. The partitur at the Rodgers and Hammerstein Theatre Library is titled "The World Is My Oyster," an unused number with the same music as "Spring in Vienna."

387

Little Bit of Constitutional Fun, A
Rodgers/Hart
Orchestrator: Spialek, unknown

Location of   - Composer's manuscript: See note
        - Sheet music: Unpublished
        - Most complete music: R&H (pv score)
        - Most complete lyric: CLLH
        - Original partitur: R&H
        - Original parts: R&H

The partitur and parts are titled "Not So Innocent Fun," an earlier number with the same music as "A Little Bit of Constitutional Fun." The Library of Congress has a Rodgers manuscript for "Not So Innocent Fun"; it contains a verse that was not used in the later number.

Sweet Sixty-Five
Rodgers/Hart
Orchestrator: Spialek, Walker

Location of   - Composer's manuscript: R&H
        - Sheet music: NYPL
        - Most complete music: NYPL (sm);
            R&H (pv score)
        - Most complete lyric: NYPL (sm);
            R&H (pv score); CLLH
        - Original partitur: R&H
        - Original parts: R&H

We're Going to Balance the Budget
Rodgers/Hart
Orchestrator: Unknown

Location of   - Composer's manuscript: LoC
        - Sheet music: Unpublished
        - Most complete music: R&H (pv-l)
        - Most complete lyric: R&H (pv-l); CLLH
        - Original partitur: R&H
        - Original parts: R&H

Listed in the Boston programs as "Tune Up, Bluebird."

Entr'acte
Rodgers/Hart
Orchestrator: Unknown

Location of   - Composer's manuscript: -0-
        - Sheet music: Unpublished
        - Most complete music: R&H (pv score)
        - Most complete lyric: INST
        - Original partitur: -0-
        - Original parts: R&H

What It's All About
Rodgers/Hart
Orchestrator: Unknown

Location of   - Composer's manuscript: -0-
        - Sheet music: Unpublished
        - Most complete music: R&H (pv-l)
        - Most complete lyric: R&H (pv-l, ls);
            CLLH
        - Original partitur: See note
        - Original parts: R&H

Alternate title: "We Just Dance and Sing." Replaced before the New York opening by "An American Couple," then reinstated early in the Broadway run to replace "An American Couple." Although the partitur to the vocal is missing, the Rodgers and Hammerstein Theatre Library has a partitur titled "New Tapps Routine" that was used as part of this number.

Labor Is the Thing
Rodgers/Hart
Orchestrator: Spialek

Location of   - Composer's manuscript: LoC
        - Sheet music: Unpublished
        - Most complete music: R&H (pv score)
        - Most complete lyric: R&H (pv score);
            CLLH
        - Original partitur: R&H
        - Original parts: R&H

I'd Rather Be Right (1937)

I'd Rather Be Right [second version]
Rodgers/Hart
Orchestrator: Spialek

Location of   - Composer's manuscript: -0-
       - Sheet music: NYPL
       - Most complete music: NYPL (sm);
          R&H (pv score)
       - Most complete lyric: NYPL (sm);
          R&H (pv score); CLLH
       - Original partitur: R&H
       - Original parts: R&H

American Couple
Rodgers/Hart
Orchestrator: Unknown

Location of   - Composer's manuscript: -0-
       - Sheet music: Unpublished
       - Most complete music: -0-
       - Most complete lyric: INST
       - Original partitur: -0-
       - Original parts: -0-

Replaced early in the New York run by "What It's All About."

Off The Record
Rodgers/Hart
Orchestrator: Unknown

Location of   - Composer's manuscript: -0-
       - Sheet music: Unpublished
       - Most complete music: R&H (pv score);
          LoC (pv-I)
       - Most complete lyric:R&H (pv score);
          CLLH
       - Original partitur: R&H
       - Original parts: R&H

The Complete Lyrics of Lorenz Hart also has additional lyrics used in the 1942 film, YANKEE DOODLE DANDY.

Ev'rybody Loves You
Rodgers/Hart
Orchestrator: Spialek

Location of   - Composer's manuscript: LoC
       - Sheet music: See note
       - Most complete music: R&H (pv-I)
       - Most complete lyric: R&H (pv-I, ls); CLLH
       - Original partitur: R&H
       - Original parts: -0-

Dropped before the New York opening. Issued as a professional copy in 1937; later published in Rodgers and Hart: A Musical Anthology (Hal Leonard Publishing Corp.: 1984).

Baby Bond for Baby, A
Rodgers/Hart
Orchestrator: Walker

Location of   - Composer's manuscript: R&H
       - Sheet music: Unpublished
       - Most complete music: R&H (pv score)
       - Most complete lyric: R&H (pv score);
          CLLH
       - Original partitur: R&H
       - Original parts: R&H

Treaty, My Sweetie, With You, A
Rodgers/Hart
Orchestrator: Unknown

Location of   - Composer's manuscript: LoC (sk)
       - Sheet music: See note
       - Most complete music: R&H (pv-I)
       - Most complete lyric: R&H (pv-I, ls);
          CLLH
       - Original partitur: -0-
       - Original parts: -0-

Dropped before the New York opening. Prepared for publication, but never issued.

I'd Rather Be Right [first version]

    Rodgers/Hart

    Orchestrator: DePackh, unknown

    Location of   - Composer's manuscript: -0-

               - Sheet music: Y

               - Most complete music: Y (sm); R&H (pv-I)

               - Most complete lyric: Y (sm); R&H (pv-I);

                    CLLH

               - Original partitur: R&H

               - Original parts: -0-

Replaced before the New York opening by the second
version of "I'd Rather Be Right." The music was later
used with a new lyric for "Now That I Know You" in the
1940 summer revue TWO WEEKS WITH PAY.

Finaletto ["His chances are not worth a penny..."]

    Rodgers/Hart

    Orchestrator: Unknown

    Location of   - Composer's manuscript: LoC (sk)

               - Sheet music: Unpublished

               - Most complete music: R&H (pv-I)

               - Most complete lyric: R&H (pv-I, ls);

                    CLLH

               - Original partitur: -0-

               - Original parts: -0-

Dropped before the New York opening.

World Is My Oyster, The

    Rodgers/Hart

    Orchestrator: Spialek

    Location of   - Composer's manuscript: -0-

               - Sheet music: Unpublished

               - Most complete music: R&H (pv-I)

               - Most complete lyric: R&H (pv-I, ls);

                    CLLH

               - Original partitur: R&H

               - Original parts: R&H

The lyric was changed before the New York opening to
"Spring in Milwaukee," and the same orchestration was
used.

I MARRIED AN ANGEL

Music RICHARD RODGERS
Lyrics LORENZ HART

Musical comedy in two acts. Opened May 11, 1938 in New York and ran 338 performances (World premiere: April 14, 1938 in New Haven). Libretto by Richard Rodgers and Lorenz Hart, adapted from the play by John Vaszary. Produced by Dwight Deere Wiman. Directed by Joshua Logan. Choreographed by George Balanchine. Musical direction by Gene Salzer. Orchestrations by Hans Spialek.

Synopsis and Production Information

World weary Count Willy Palaffi, fed up with jaded continental women, wishes for an angel to marry. Miraculously, one appears from heaven, and they immediately elope. In her innocence, the angel makes several faux pas that get Willy into financial and social trouble. Willy's sister, Countess Peggy Palaffi, then shows her the sly ways of women of the world, and the marriage is a success.

Other characters include Peter, Willy's right-hand man; Anna, a wild young American schoolgirl; and Harry Szigetti, Willy's wealthy businessman friend. The show requires a full singing and dancing ensemble. There are two ballet sequences.

Orchestration

Reed I (Flute, Piccolo, Clarinet, Alto Sax); Reed II (Oboe, English Horn, Celeste); Reed III (Clarinet, Alto Sax, Bass Clarinet); Reed IV (Tenor Sax, Flute, Clarinet, Bass Clarinet); Horn; Trumpet I II; Trumpet III; Trombone; Piano; Harp; Percussion; Violin A B C D; Viola I II; Cello; Bass

Comments

In 1933, Rodgers and Hart teamed with Moss Hart on a musical film (based on a Hungarian play) entitled I MARRIED AN ANGEL; it was intended as a vehicle for Jeanette MacDonald. Although the film never materialized, I MARRIED AN ANGEL became a Broadway musical in 1938, utilizing some of the songs written in 1933. Four years later, the stage version was made into a movie starring Jeanette MacDonald and Nelson Eddy.

The original New York production included Dennis King as Willy, Vivienne Segal as Peggy, and Vera Zorina as the angel.

Location of Original Materials

Script: Rodgers and Hammerstein Theatre Library (most lyrics)
Piano-vocal score: See individual listings
Partiturs: Missing
Parts: Rodgers and Hammerstein Theatre Library

All of the songs and orchestra parts from the original New York production survive.

Rental Status

Currently unavailable for rental

Music Publisher

Robbins Music Corporation

Information

Rodgers and Hammerstein Theatre Library

Overture

Rodgers/Hart
Orchestrator: Unknown

Location of   - Composer's manuscript: -0-
      - Sheet music: Unpublished
      - Most complete music: R&H (p)
      - Most complete lyric: INST
      - Original partitur: -0-
      - Original parts: R&H

Did You Ever Get Stung?

Rodgers/Hart
Orchestrator: Unknown

Location of   - Composer's manuscript: -0-
      - Sheet music: NYPL
      - Most complete music: NYPL (sm);
         R&H (pv-l)
      - Most complete lyric: NYPL (sm);
         R&H (pv-l, scr); CLLH
      - Original partitur: -0-
      - Original parts: R&H

The script also contains the original vocal arrangement, which includes additional lyrics in the second refrain.

I Married an Angel

Rodgers/Hart
Orchestrator: Unknown

Location of   - Composer's manuscript: -0-
      - Sheet music: NYPL
      - Most complete music: NYPL (sm);
         R&H (pv-l)
      - Most complete lyric: NYPL (sm);
         R&H (pv-l, scr); CLLH
      - Original partitur: -0-
      - Original parts: R&H

The refrain was written in 1933 for the unproduced film version.

Modiste, The

Rodgers/Hart
Orchestrator: Unknown

Location of   - Composer's manuscript: -0-
      - Sheet music: Unpublished
      - Most complete music: R&H (pv-l)
      - Most complete lyric: R&H (pv-l, scr);
         CLLH
      - Original partitur: -0-
      - Original parts: R&H

A revision of "Bath and Dressmaking Sequence," written in 1933 for the unproduced film version.

Honeymoon Ballet

Rodgers/Hart
Orchestrator: Unknown

Location of   - Composer's manuscript: -0-
      - Sheet music: Unpublished
      - Most complete music: R&H (p)
      - Most complete lyric: INST
      - Original partitur: -0-
      - Original parts: R&H

I'll Tell the Man in the Street

Rodgers/Hart
Orchestrator: Unknown

Location of   - Composer's manuscript: -0-
      - Sheet music: NYPL
      - Most complete music: NYPL (sm);
         R&H (pv-l)
      - Most complete lyric: CLLH
      - Original partitur: -0-
      - Original parts: R&H

How to Win Friends and Influence People
Rodgers/Hart
Orchestrator: Unknown

Location of   - Composer's manuscript: LoC (sk)
      - Sheet music: NYPL
      - Most complete music: NYPL (sm);
        R&H (pv-l)
      - Most complete lyric: NYPL (sm);
        R&H (pv-l, scr); CLLH
      - Original partitur: -0-
      - Original parts: R&H

Angel Without Wings
Rodgers/Hart
Orchestrator: Unknown

Location of   - Composer's manuscript: LoC (sk)
      - Sheet music: Unpublished
      - Most complete music: R&H (pv-l)
      - Most complete lyric: R&H (pv-l, scr);
        CLLH
      - Original partitur: -0-
      - Original parts: R&H

Entr'acte
Rodgers/Hart
Orchestrator: Unknown

Location of   - Composer's manuscript: -0-
      - Sheet music: Unpublished
      - Most complete music: R&H (parts)
      - Most complete lyric: INST
      - Original partitur: -0-
      - Original parts: R&H

Twinkle in Your Eye, A
Rodgers/Hart
Orchestrator: Unknown

Location of   - Composer's manuscript: LoC (sk)
      - Sheet music: NYPL
      - Most complete music: NYPL (sm);
        R&H (pv-l)
      - Most complete lyric: R&H (scr); CLLH
      - Original partitur: -0-
      - Original parts: R&H

The manuscript sketch is for the verse only.

Spring Is Here
Rodgers/Hart
Orchestrator: Unknown

Location of   - Composer's manuscript: -0-
      - Sheet music: NYPL
      - Most complete music: NYPL (sm);
        R&H (pv-l)
      - Most complete lyric: NYPL (sm);
        R&H (pv-l, scr); CLLH
      - Original partitur: -0-
      - Original parts: R&H

I'm Ruined
Rodgers/Hart
Orchestrator: Unknown

Location of   - Composer's manuscript: -0-
      - Sheet music: Unpublished
      - Most complete music: R&H (pv-l)
      - Most complete lyric: R&H (pv-l, scr);
        CLLH
      - Original partitur: -0-
      - Original parts: R&H

This number leads directly into the verse of "At the Roxy Music Hall."

At the Roxy Music Hall

Rodgers/Hart
Orchestrator: Unknown

Location of - Composer's manuscript: -0-
            - Sheet music: See note
            - Most complete music: R&H (pv-l)
            - Most complete lyric: R&H (scr); CLLH
            - Original partitur: -0-
            - Original parts: R&H

Issued in 1938 as a professional copy; later published in Rodgers & Hart: A Musical Anthology (Hal Leonard Publishing Corp.: 1984). This number segues into a Roxy Music Hall parody, commencing with 1) an Overture, 2) a take-off on Charlie McCarthy and Edgar Bergen performed by Peter, and 3) an entire Rockette kick-line simulated by Peggy and Anna. All parts survive.

Men From Milwaukee

Rodgers/Hart
Orchestrator: Unknown

Location of - Composer's manuscript: -0-
            - Sheet music: Unpublished
            - Most complete music: R&H (pv-l)
            - Most complete lyric: R&H (pv-l); CLLH
            - Original partitur: -0-
            - Original parts: R&H

Although the lyrics to Willy's operatic parody (part 4 of the Roxy Music Hall sequence) are not in the script, they were probably sung in the original production: A "Roxy Music Hall" reprise later asks, "Did you hear what they sang about Milwaukee beer?"

Othello

Rodgers
Orchestrator: Unknown

Location of - Composer's manuscript: -0-
            - Sheet music: Unpublished
            - Most complete music: R&H (p)
            - Most complete lyric: INST
            - Original partitur: -0-
            - Original parts: R&H

Following an untitled dance by Harry (for which parts survive), this "surrealist ballet" featuring the Angel concludes the Roxy Music Hall sequence.

Women Are Women

Rodgers/Hart
Orchestrator: Unknown

Location of - Composer's manuscript: LoC
            - Sheet music: Unpublished
            - Most complete music: LoC (pv)
                & R&H (parts)
            - Most complete lyric: -0-
            - Original partitur: -0-
            - Original parts: R&H

Dropped before the New York opening. The lyric may be based on a section of "Love Is Queen, Love Is King," written for the unproduced film version.

Yodel if You Can

Rodgers/Hart
Orchestrator: Unknown

Location of - Composer's manuscript: LoC
            - Sheet music: Unpublished
            - Most complete music: R&H (pv & parts)
            - Most complete lyric: -0-
            - Original partitur: -0-
            - Original parts: R&H

Dropped before the New York opening.

THE BOYS FROM SYRACUSE

Music	RICHARD RODGERS
Lyrics	LORENZ HART

Musical comedy in two acts. Opened November 23, 1938 in New York and ran 235 performances (World premiere: November 3, 1938 in New Haven). Libretto by George Abbott, based on the play THE COMEDY OF ERRORS by William Shakespeare. Produced and directed by George Abbott. Choreographed by George Balanchine. Musical direction by Harry Levant. Orchestrations by Hans Spialek, Maurice B. DePackh, Menotti Salta.

Synopsis and Production Information

Antipholus of Syracuse travels to Ephesus in search of his long-lost twin. He takes along his slave, Dromio, whose own long-lost twin happens to be the slave of Antipholus of Ephesus. Mistaken for their siblings, the pair get into marital and legal troubles, until at last the brothers are reunited.

The distaff principals are Adriana and Luce, wives to Antipholus of Ephesus and his servant, and Adriana's sister, Luciana. A courtesan, her secretary, and a dancing policeman handle several dance specialties. There is also a full singing and dancing ensemble.

Orchestration

Reed I (Flute, Tenor Sax); Reed II (Oboe, English Horn); Reed III (Clarinet, Alto Sax, Bass Clarinet); Reed IV (Clarinet, Baritone Sax, Alto Sax, Eb Clarinet, Flute, Piccolo); Horn; Trumpet I; Trumpet II; Trombone; Piano; Harp; Percussion; Violin A B C D; Viola I II; Cello; Bass

Location of Original Materials

Script: Rodgers and Hammerstein Theatre Library (most lyrics)
Piano-vocal score: Rodgers and Hammerstein Theatre Library
    (Published: Chappell & Co., 1965)
Partiturs: Rodgers and Hammerstein Theatre Library
Parts: Rodgers and Hammerstein Theatre Library

Nearly all the partiturs and parts survive.

Rental Status

The Rodgers and Hammerstein Theatre Library rents a version based on a 1960's revival; it includes the original piano-vocal score and a new orchestration for 17 players.

Music Publisher

Chappell Music

Information

Rodgers and Hammerstein Theatre Library

Overture

Rodgers/Hart
Orchestrator: Spialek

Location of
- Composer's manuscript: -0-
- Sheet music: Unpublished
- Most complete music: R&H (parts)
- Most complete lyric: INST
- Original partitur: R&H (inc)
- Original parts: R&H

The Overture in the published piano-vocal score is not the one used in the original production.

I Had Twins

Rodgers/Hart
Orchestrator: Spialek

Location of
- Composer's manuscript: LoC
- Sheet music: Not published separately
- Most complete music: R&H (pv score); LoC (pv-l)
- Most complete lyric: R&H (pv score); LoC (pv-l); CLLH
- Original partitur: R&H
- Original parts: R&H

The Rodgers manuscript also contains a few lyrics that were eventually cut.

Dear Old Syracuse

Rodgers/Hart
Orchestrator: Spialek, unknown

Location of
- Composer's manuscript: LoC
- Sheet music: Not published separately
- Most complete music: R&H (pv score); LoC (pv-l)
- Most complete lyric: R&H (pv score, scr); CLLH
- Original partitur: R&H
- Original parts: R&H

The Complete Lyrics of Lorenz Hart also contains an alternate lyric for the second refrain.

What Can You Do With a Man?

Rodgers/Hart
Orchestrator: Spialek

Location of
- Composer's manuscript: LoC
- Sheet music: Not published separately
- Most complete music: R&H (pv score, pv-l); LoC (pv-l)
- Most complete lyric: R&H (pv score, scr); CLLH
- Original partitur: R&H
- Original parts: R&H

Falling in Love With Love

Rodgers/Hart
Orchestrator: Spialek

Location of
- Composer's manuscript: LoC
- Sheet music: LoC, NYPL
- Most complete music: LoC (sm); NYPL (sm); R&H (pv score)
- Most complete lyric: LoC (sm); NYPL (sm); R&H (pv score, scr): CLLH
- Original partitur: R&H
- Original parts: R&H

Shortest Day of the Year, The

Rodgers/Hart
Orchestrator: Spialek, unknown

Location of
- Composer's manuscript: LoC
- Sheet music: LoC, NYPL
- Most complete music: LoC (sm); NYPL (sm); R&H (pv score)
- Most complete lyric: LoC (sm); NYPL (sm); R&H (pv score, scr); CLLH
- Original partitur: R&H
- Original parts: R&H (inc)

The orchestra piano part is missing.

The Boys From Syracuse (1938)

This Can't Be Love
Rodgers/Hart
Orchestrator: Spialek, unknown

Location of
- Composer's manuscript: -0-
- Sheet music: LoC, NYPL
- Most complete music: LoC (sm); NYPL (sm); R&H (pv score, pv-l)
- Most complete lyric: R&H (pv score); CLLH
- Original partitur: R&H
- Original parts: R&H

The comic reprise is not included in the script.

Ladies of the Evening
Rodgers/Hart
Orchestrator: Spialek

Location of
- Composer's manuscript: LoC
- Sheet music: Not published separately
- Most complete music: R&H (pv score); LoC (pv-l)
- Most complete lyric: R&H (pv score, scr); LoC (pv-l); CLLH
- Original partitur: R&H
- Original parts: R&H

Let Antipholus In
Rodgers/Hart
Orchestrator: Unknown

Location of
- Composer's manuscript: LoC
- Sheet music: Not published separately
- Most complete music: R&H (pv score), LoC (pv-l)
- Most complete lyric: LoC (pv), CLLH
- Original partitur: -0-
- Original parts: R&H

Alternate title: "Finale Act I."

He and She
Rodgers/Hart
Orchestrator: Spialek

Location of
- Composer's manuscript: LoC
- Sheet music: Not published separately
- Most complete music: R&H (pv score, pv-l); LoC (pv-l)
- Most complete lyric: R&H (pv score, scr); CLLH
- Original partitur: R&H
- Original parts: R&H

Entr'acte
Rodgers/Hart
Orchestrator: Spialek

Location of
- Composer's manuscript: -0-
- Sheet music: Unpublished
- Most complete music: R&H (parts)
- Most complete lyric: INST
- Original partitur: R&H (inc)
- Original parts: R&H

The Entr'acte in the published piano-vocal score is not the one used in the original production.

You Have Cast Your Shadow on the Sea
Rodgers/Hart
Orchestrator: Spialek

Location of
- Composer's manuscript: LoC
- Sheet music: LoC, NYPL
- Most complete music: LoC (sm); NYPL (sm); R&H (pv score)
- Most complete lyric: R&H (pv score); CLLH
- Original partitur: R&H
- Original parts: R&H

Come With Me
Rodgers/Hart
Orchestrator: Unknown

Location of - Composer's manuscript: LoC
  - Sheet music: Not published separately
  - Most complete music: R&H (pv score);
    LoC (pv-l)
  - Most complete lyric: R&H (pv score, scr);
    LoC (pv-l); CLLH
  - Original partitur: R&H
  - Original parts: R&H

Sing For Your Supper
Rodgers/Hart
Orchestrator: Spialek, DePackh, Salta

Location of - Composer's manuscript: LoC
  - Sheet music: LoC, NYPL
  - Most complete music: LoC (sm);
    NYPL (sm); R&H (pv score)
  - Most complete lyric: LoC (sm);
    NYPL (sm); R&H (pv score, scr);
    CLLH
  - Original partitur: R&H
  - Original parts: R&H

The Rodgers and Hammerstein Theatre Library also has the original vocal arrangement, most of which was published in the piano-vocal score.

Big Brother
Rodgers/Hart
Orchestrator: Unknown

Location of - Composer's manuscript: LoC
  - Sheet music: Not published separately
  - Most complete music: R&H (pv score);
    LoC (pv-l)
  - Most complete lyric: R&H (pv score, scr);
    LoC (pv-l); CLLH
  - Original partitur: R&H
  - Original parts: R&H

Oh, Diogenes
Rodgers/Hart
Orchestrator: DePackh, unknown

Location of - Composer's manuscript: LoC
  - Sheet music: LoC, NYPL
  - Most complete music: LoC (sm);
    NYPL (sm); R&H (pv score)
  - Most complete lyric: LoC (sm);
    NYPL (sm); R&H (pv score, scr);
    CLLH
  - Original partitur: R&H
  - Original parts: R&H

Ballet
Rodgers
Orchestrator: Unknown

Location of - Composer's manuscript: -0-
  - Sheet music: Not published separately
  - Most complete music: R&H (parts)
  - Most complete lyric: INST
  - Original partitur: -0-
  - Original parts: R&H

Greeks Have No Word For It, The
Rodgers/Hart
Orchestrator: Unknown

Location of - Composer's manuscript: -0-
  - Sheet music: Unpublished
  - Most complete music: See note
  - Most complete lyric: CLLH
  - Original partitur: -0-
  - Original parts: -0-

Added for the film version (1940). No musical manuscript was found.

Who Are You?

Rodgers/Hart

Orchestrator: Unknown

Location of   - Composer's manuscript: LoC (sk)

                - Sheet music: LoC

                - Most complete music: LoC (sm)

                - Most complete lyric: LoC (sm); CLLH

                - Original partitur: -0-

                - Original parts: -0-

Added for the film version (1940).

TOO MANY GIRLS

Music   RICHARD RODGERS
Lyrics   LORENZ HART

Musical comedy in two acts. Opened October 18, 1939 in New York and ran 249 performances (World premiere: October 2, 1939 in Boston). Libretto by George Marion, Jr. Produced and directed by George Abbott. Choreographed by Robert Alton. Musical direction by Harry Levant. Orchestrations by Hans Spialek, F. Marks. Vocal arrangements by Hugh Martin.

Synopsis and Production Information	In order to be near a playwright she fancies, Connie Casey abandons her madcap European travels and enrolls in her dad's old Alma Mater, Pottawatomie University (in Stop Gap, New Mexico). Her father decides to hire four bodyguards to keep an eye on her, and ends up choosing the top football players from Harvard, Yale, Princeton, and South America. Naturally, the Pottawatomie football team, now boasting the four best players in the Western Hemisphere, wins the national championship. One of the players, Clint, wins Connie's hand as well.
	The cast also includes an assortment of co-eds, including Student Body President Eileen ("long-limbed, lovely, and loud") and a Spanish spitfire, Peppy. There is a full singing and dancing ensemble.
Orchestration	Reed I (Flute, Piccolo, Tenor Sax); Reed II (Oboe, English Horn, Celeste); Reed III (Clarinet, Bass Clarinet, Bassett Horn, Tenor Sax); Reed IV (Clarinet, Alto Sax, Flute); Reed V (Bassoon, Tenor Sax, Clarinet); Horn; Trumpet I II; Trumpet III; Trombone; Piano; Percussion; Violin A B C D (dbl. Guitar); Cello; Bass
Location of Original Materials	Script: Rodgers and Hammerstein Theatre Library (all lyrics), Library of Congress (all lyrics) (Published: Dramatists Play Service, 1940) Piano-vocal score: See individual listings Partiturs: Rodgers and Hammerstein Theatre Library Parts: Rodgers and Hammerstein Theatre Library
	All the piano-vocal material and parts survive, as do most of the partiturs.
Rental Status	Currently unavailable for rental
Music Publisher	Chappell Music
Information	Rodgers and Hammerstein Theatre Library

Too Many Girls (1939)

Overture

Rodgers/Hart

Orchestrator: Spialek

Location of   - Composer's manuscript: -0-
- Sheet music: Unpublished
- Most complete music: R&H (parts)
- Most complete lyric: INST
- Original partitur: R&H (inc)
- Original parts: R&H

The partitur contains only the introduction and the links between numbers.

My Prince

Rodgers/Hart

Orchestrator: Spialek

Location of   - Composer's manuscript: R&H (x)
- Sheet music: Unpublished
- Most complete music: R&H (pv-l)
- Most complete lyric: R&H (pv-l, scr); LoC (scr); CLLH
- Original partitur: R&H
- Original parts: R&H

Heroes in the Fall

Rodgers/Rodgers & Hart

Orchestrator: Spialek

Location of   - Composer's manuscript: -0-
- Sheet music: Unpublished
- Most complete music: R&H (pv)
- Most complete lyric: R&H (scr); LoC (scr); CLLH
- Original partitur: R&H
- Original parts: R&H

Pottawatomie

Rodgers/Hart

Orchestrator: Unknown

Location of   - Composer's manuscript: LoC
- Sheet music: Unpublished
- Most complete music: R&H (pv-l)
- Most complete lyric: R&H (pv-l, scr); LoC (scr); CLLH
- Original partitur: R&H
- Original parts: R&H

Tempt Me Not

Rodgers/Hart

Orchestrator: Unknown

Location of   - Composer's manuscript: LoC
- Sheet music: Unpublished
- Most complete music: R&H (pv-l)
- Most complete lyric: CLLH
- Original partitur: -0-
- Original parts: R&H

The lyric in the published script contains slight inaccuracies.

'Cause We Got Cake

Rodgers/Hart

Orchestrator: Spialek, Marks

Location of   - Composer's manuscript: LoC
- Sheet music: Not published separately
- Most complete music: R&H (pv-l)
- Most complete lyric: R&H (pv-l, scr); LoC (scr); CLLH
- Original partitur: R&H
- Original parts: R&H

Initial publication in Rodgers & Hart: A Musical Anthology (Hal Leonard Publishing Corp.: 1984).

Love Never Went to College

Rodgers/Hart
Orchestrator: Spialek

Location of - Composer's manuscript: LoC
 - Sheet music: LoC, NYPL
 - Most complete music: LoC (sm);
   NYPL (sm); R&H (pv-l)
 - Most complete lyric: LoC (sm, scr);
   NYPL (sm); R&H (pv-l, scr); CLLH
 - Original partitur: R&H
 - Original parts: R&H

Look Out

Rodgers/Hart
Orchestrator: Spialek

Location of - Composer's manuscript: LoC
 - Sheet music: Unpublished
 - Most complete music: R&H (pv-l)
 - Most complete lyric: R&H (pv-l, scr);
   LoC (scr); CLLH
 - Original partitur: R&H
 - Original parts: R&H

Spic and Spanish

Rodgers/Hart
Orchestrator: Spialek

Location of - Composer's manuscript: LoC
 - Sheet music: LoC, NYPL
 - Most complete music: LoC (sm);
   NYPL (sm); R&H (pv-l)
 - Most complete lyric: LoC (scr & sm);
   CLLH
 - Original partitur: R&H
 - Original parts: R&H

The script has the version performed in the show; the
sheet music has different lyrics to the verse.

Entr'acte

Rodgers/Hart
Orchestrator: Spialek

Location of - Composer's manuscript: -0-
 - Sheet music: Unpublished
 - Most complete music: R&H (parts)
 - Most complete lyric: INST
 - Original partitur: R&H (inc)
 - Original parts: R&H

I Like to Recognize the Tune

Rodgers/Hart
Orchestrator: Spialek

Location of - Composer's manuscript: LoC
 - Sheet music: LoC, NYPL
 - Most complete music: LoC (sm);
   NYPL (sm); R&H (pv-l)
 - Most complete lyric: R&H (scr);
   LoC (scr); CLLH
 - Original partitur: R&H
 - Original parts: R&H

The Rodgers and Hammerstein Theatre Library also has a
conductor's score with Hugh Martin's original vocal
arrangement. The lyrics for this arrangement are in the
published script.

Sweethearts of the Team, The

Rodgers/Hart
Orchestrator: Spialek

Location of - Composer's manuscript: LoC
 - Sheet music: Unpublished
 - Most complete music: R&H (pv-l)
 - Most complete lyric: R&H (scr);
   LoC (scr); CLLH
 - Original partitur: R&H
 - Original parts: R&H

Too Many Girls (1939)

She Could Shake the Maracas
Rodgers/Hart
Orchestrator: Spialek

Location of
- Composer's manuscript: LoC
- Sheet music: LoC, NYPL
- Most complete music: LoC (sm);
  NYPL (sm); R&H (pv-l)
- Most complete lyric: LoC (sm);
  NYPL (sm); R&H (pv-l); CLLH
- Original partitur: R&H
- Original parts: R&H

I Didn't Know What Time It Was
Rodgers/Hart
Orchestrator: Spialek

Location of
- Composer's manuscript: LoC
- Sheet music: LoC, NYPL
- Most complete music: LoC (sm);
  NYPL (sm); R&H (pv-l)
- Most complete lyric: R&H (ls, scr);
  LoC (scr); CLLH
- Original partitur: R&H
- Original parts: R&H

The Rodgers and Hammerstein Theatre Library also has a partitur by Ted Royal for an instrumental version.

Too Many Girls
Rodgers/Hart
Orchestrator: Marks

Location of
- Composer's manuscript: LoC
- Sheet music: Unpublished
- Most complete music: R&H (pv-l)
- Most complete lyric: R&H (pv-l, scr);
  LoC (scr); CLLH
- Original partitur: R&H
- Original parts: R&H

Give It Back to the Indians
Rodgers/Hart
Orchestrator: Spialek

Location of
- Composer's manuscript: LoC
- Sheet music: LoC, NYPL
- Most complete music: LoC (sm);
  NYPL (sm); R&H (pv-l)
- Most complete lyric: R&H (scr);
  LoC (scr); CLLH
- Original partitur: R&H
- Original parts: R&H

Hunted Stag
Rodgers/Hart
Orchestrator: Unknown

Location of
- Composer's manuscript: LoC
- Sheet music: Unpublished
- Most complete music: R&H (pv-l)
- Most complete lyric: R&H (ls); CLLH
- Original partitur: -0-
- Original parts: -0-

Dropped before the New York opening.

You're Nearer
Rodgers/Hart
Orchestrator: Unknown

Location of
- Composer's manuscript: LoC
- Sheet music: LoC, NYPL
- Most complete music: LoC (sm);
  NYPL (sm)
- Most complete lyric: LoC (sm);
  NYPL (sm); CLLH
- Original partitur: -0-
- Original parts: -0-

Written for the film version (1940). By October of 1940, it had replaced "My Prince" in the stage production's post-Broadway tour. The Rodgers and Hammerstein Theatre Library has a Spialek partitur for a reduced orchestration.

HIGHER AND HIGHER

Music   RICHARD RODGERS
Lyrics   LORENZ HART

Musical comedy in two acts. Opened April 4, 1940 in New York and ran 108 performances (World premiere: March 7, 1940 in New Haven). Libretto by Gladys Hurlbut and Joshua Logan, based on an idea by Irving Pincus. Produced by Dwight Deere Wiman. Directed by Joshua Logan. Choreographed by Robert Alton. Musical direction by Al Goodman. Orchestrations by Hans Spialek, Ted Royal, Don Walker.

Synopsis and Production Information	The servants of the Drake household try to save the estate from bankruptcy by presenting the scullery maid Minnie Sorenson as Mrs. Drake's daughter Deborah at the debutante ball. Her cover is almost ruined by a pet seal owned by the real Deborah Drake, who lives in Iceland, but in the end, the plan works to the servants' favor.
	Principal characters include Zachary, who works in the Drake household; Zachary's old friend Sandy; Patrick, the private guard from across the street who falls in love with Minnie; and Byng, the head of the Drake household. There is a full singing and dancing ensemble.
Orchestration	Reed I (Oboe, English Horn); Reed II (Alto Sax, Flute, Clarinet); Reed III (Alto Sax, Flute, Piccolo, Clarinet); Reed IV (Tenor Sax, Flute, Clarinet); Reed V (Tenor Sax, Bass Clarinet, Oboe, English Horn, Clarinet); Trumpet I II; Trombone; Piano; Harp; Percussion; Violin A B C D; Viola I II; Cello; Bass
Location of Original Materials	Script: Rodgers and Hammerstein Theatre Library (all lyrics), New York Public Library (all lyrics) Piano-vocal score: See individual listings Partiturs: Rodgers and Hammerstein Theatre Library Parts: Rodgers and Hammerstein Theatre Library
	Most of the songs survive in piano-vocal form; the rest can be reconstructed from the partiturs and parts, which are virtually complete.
Rental Status	Currently unavailable for rental
Music Publisher	Chappell Music
Information	Rodgers and Hammerstein Theatre Library

Higher and Higher (1940)

Overture
Rodgers/Hart
Orchestrator: Spialek, unknown

Location of   - Composer's manuscript: -0-
            - Sheet music: Unpublished
            - Most complete music: R&H (parts)
            - Most complete lyric: INST
            - Original partitur: R&H (inc)
            - Original parts: R&H

Barking Baby Never Bites, A
Rodgers/Hart
Orchestrator: Walker

Location of   - Composer's manuscript: LoC
            - Sheet music: Unpublished
            - Most complete music: R&H (pv-l);
                LoC (pv-l)
            - Most complete lyric: R&H (ls, scr);
                NYPL (scr); CLLH
            - Original partitur: R&H
            - Original parts: R&H

The Rodgers and Hammerstein Theatre Library also has an unused Spialek partitur, as well as a Royal partitur (and parts) for "Barking Baby Dance."

From Another World
Rodgers/Hart
Orchestrator: Spialek, unknown

Location of   - Composer's manuscript: LoC
            - Sheet music: LoC, NYPL
            - Most complete music: R&H (ptr)
            - Most complete lyric: R&H (scr);
                NYPL (scr); CLLH
            - Original partitur: R&H
            - Original parts: R&H

The orchestrator of the song proper is unknown, but the development section that follows (for which no piano-vocal has been located) was scored by Spialek.

Morning's at Seven
Rodgers/Hart
Orchestrator: Walker

Location of   - Composer's manuscript: LoC
            - Sheet music: Unpublished
            - Most complete music: R&H (pv-l);
                LoC (pv-l)
            - Most complete lyric: R&H (pv-l, ls, scr);
                LoC (pv-l); NYPL (scr); CLLH
            - Original partitur: R&H
            - Original parts: R&H

The Rodgers and Hammerstein Theatre Library also has an unused Spialek partitur with parts.

Nothing But You
Rodgers/Hart
Orchestrator: Spialek, unknown

Location of   - Composer's manuscript: LoC
            - Sheet music: LoC, NYPL
            - Most complete music: R&H (pv & ptr)
            - Most complete lyric: CLLH
            - Original partitur: R&H
            - Original parts: R&H

The partitur has the version performed in the show; the sheet music has a different verse.

Disgustingly Rich
Rodgers/Hart
Orchestrator: Spialek, Royal

Location of   - Composer's manuscript: LoC (sk);
                R&H (neg)
            - Sheet music: Not published separately
            - Most complete music: R&H (pv-l)
            - Most complete lyric: R&H (scr);
                NYPL (scr); CLLH
            - Original partitur: R&H
            - Original parts: R&H

Initial publication in Rodgers & Hart: A Musical Anthology (Hal Leonard Publishing Corp.: 1984).

Entr'acte

Rodgers/Hart

Orchestrator: Spialek, unknown

Location of
- Composer's manuscript: -0-
- Sheet music: Unpublished
- Most complete music: R&H (parts)
- Most complete lyric: INST
- Original partitur: R&H (inc)
- Original parts: R&H

Lovely Day for a Murder, A

Rodgers/Hart

Orchestrator: Spialek, Royal

Location of
- Composer's manuscript: LoC
- Sheet music: Not published separately
- Most complete music: R&H (pv-l);
  LoC (pv-l)
- Most complete lyric: R&H (pv-l, scr);
  LoC (pv-l); NYPL (scr); CLLH
- Original partitur: R&H
- Original parts: R&H

Initial publication in Rodgers & Hart: A Musical Anthology
(Hal Leonard Publishing Corp.: 1984).

Blue Monday

Rodgers/Hart

Orchestrator: Spialek

Location of
- Composer's manuscript: LoC (sk)
- Sheet music: Unpublished
- Most complete music: R&H (pv-l)
- Most complete lyric: R&H (scr);
  NYPL (scr); CLLH
- Original partitur: R&H
- Original parts: R&H

How's Your Health?

Rodgers/Rodgers & Hart

Orchestrator: Unknown

Location of
- Composer's manuscript: LoC
- Sheet music: Unpublished
- Most complete music: R&H (pv-l);
  LoC (pv-l)
- Most complete lyric: R&H (pv-l, ls, scr);
  LoC (pv-l); NYPL (scr); CLLH
- Original partitur: R&H
- Original parts: R&H

Ev'ry Sunday Afternoon

Rodgers/Hart

Orchestrator: Spialek

Location of
- Composer's manuscript: LoC
- Sheet music: LoC, NYPL
- Most complete music: LoC (sm);
  NYPL (sm); R&H (pv-l)
- Most complete lyric: LoC (sm);
  NYPL (sm); R&H (pv-l, ls); CLLH
- Original partitur: R&H
- Original parts: R&H

It Never Entered My Mind

Rodgers/Hart

Orchestrator: Spialek

Location of
- Composer's manuscript: LoC (sk)
- Sheet music: LoC, NYPL
- Most complete music: LoC (sm);
  NYPL (sm)
- Most complete lyric: R&H (scr);
  NYPL (scr); CLLH
- Original partitur: R&H
- Original parts: R&H

Higher and Higher (1940)

I'm Afraid

Rodgers/Hart
Orchestrator: Spialek

Location of   - Composer's manuscript: -0-
        - Sheet music: Unpublished
        - Most complete music: R&H (ptr)
        - Most complete lyric: R&H (scr);
            NYPL (scr); CLLH
        - Original partitur: R&H
        - Original parts: R&H

Life! Liberty!

Rodgers/Hart
Orchestrator: Unknown

Location of   - Composer's manuscript: LoC
        - Sheet music: Unpublished
        - Most complete music: R&H (pv-l);
            LoC (pv-l)
        - Most complete lyric: R&H (pv-l, ls);
            LoC (pv-l, ls); CLLH
        - Original partitur: R&H
        - Original parts: R&H

Replaced during the pre-Broadway tryout by "I'm Afraid."

It's Pretty in the City

Rodgers/Hart
Orchestrator: Spialek

Location of   - Composer's manuscript: LoC
        - Sheet music: Unpublished
        - Most complete music: R&H (pv-l);
            LoC (pv-l)
        - Most complete lyric: R&H (pv-l, ls);
            LoC (pv-l, ls); CLLH
        - Original partitur: R&H
        - Original parts: R&H

Dropped during the pre-Broadway tryout.

PAL JOEY

Music	**RICHARD RODGERS**
Lyrics	**LORENZ HART**

Musical play in two acts. Opened December 25, 1940 in New York and ran 374 performances (World premiere: December 16, 1940 in Philadelphia). Libretto by John O'Hara, based on a series of short stories in The New Yorker by Mr. O'Hara. Produced and directed by George Abbott. Choreographed by Robert Alton. Musical direction by Harry Levant. Orchestrations by Hans Spialek.

Synopsis and Production Information

Joey Evans, an ambitious two-bit nightclub entertainer, attracts the attentions of Vera Simpson, a wealthy society lady. An intrigued Vera uses her husband's money to tailor Joey, keep Joey, and even build Joey a nightclub. Eventually, however, Joey becomes more a nuisance than a diversion (particularly when a charming blackmailer threatens to expose their arrangement), and Vera disposes of him.

Other characters include sweet Linda English, a trusting young thing taken in by Joey's lies till the very end, and sassy Gladys Bumps, a nightclub performer who's taken in by no man. A hard-nosed female reporter has one scene, which climaxes with an intellectual tribute to Gypsy Rose Lee. There is a full singing and dancing ensemble, and a ballet entitled "Joey Looks Into the Future" that closes Act I.

Comments

The original production starred Gene Kelly as Joey and Vivienne Segal as Vera. PAL JOEY enjoyed even greater success in its 1952 Broadway revival, in which Vivienne Segal again portrayed Vera; that production ran 542 performances and won the N.Y. Drama Critics Circle Award for Best Musical, 1951-52.

Orchestration

Reed I (Alto Sax, Clarinet, Flute); Reed II (Alto Sax, Oboe, English Horn); Reed III (Alto Sax, Clarinet, Bass Clarinet); Reed IV (Alto Sax, Clarinet, Bass Clarinet, Tenor Sax); Reed V (Clarinet, Bass Clarinet, Bassoon, Tenor Sax); Horn; Trumpet I II; Trumpet III; Trombone; Percussion; Piano; Violin A B C; Viola; Cello; Bass

Location of Original Materials

Script: Rodgers and Hammerstein Theatre Library
    (Published: Duel, Sloane and Pearce, New York, 1941)
Piano-vocal score: Rodgers and Hammerstein Theatre Library, Library of Congress,
    New York Public Library (Published: Chappell & Co., 1962)
Partiturs: Missing
Parts: Rodgers and Hammerstein Theatre Library

Rental Status

The Rodgers and Hammerstein Theatre Library rents the original piano-vocal score, along with orchestra parts adapted from the originals and the book from the 1952 revival. This book, which was published by Random House in 1952, contains minor dialogue and lyric revisions.

Music Publisher

Chappell Music

Information

Rodgers and Hammerstein Theatre Library

Pal Joey (1940)

Overture
Rodgers/Hart
Orchestrator: Unknown

Location of
- Composer's manuscript: -0-
- Sheet music: Not published separately
- Most complete music: LoC (pv score);
  NYPL (pv score); R&H (pv score)
- Most complete lyric: INST
- Original partitur: -0-
- Original parts: R&H

Great Big Town, A
Rodgers/Hart
Orchestrator: Unknown

Location of
- Composer's manuscript: LoC
- Sheet music: Not published separately
- Most complete music: LoC (pv score);
  NYPL (pv score); R&H (pv score)
- Most complete lyric: LoC (pv score);
  NYPL (pv score); R&H (pv score);
  CLLH
- Original partitur: -0-
- Original parts: R&H

Alternate title: "Chicago." In the 1952 revival, this song was reprised in the second act as "Morocco."

You Musn't Kick It Around
Rodgers/Hart
Orchestrator: Unknown

Location of
- Composer's manuscript: LoC
- Sheet music: LoC, NYPL
- Most complete music: LoC (sm, pv score);
  NYPL (sm, pv score); R&H (pv score)
- Most complete lyric: LoC (sm, pv score);
  NYPL (sm, pv score); R&H (pv score);
  CLLH
- Original partitur: -0-
- Original parts: R&H

I Could Write a Book
Rodgers/Hart
Orchestrator: Unknown

Location of
- Composer's manuscript: LoC
- Sheet music: LoC, NYPL
- Most complete music: LoC (sm, pv score);
  NYPL (sm, pv score); R&H (pv score)
- Most complete lyric: LoC (pv score);
  NYPL (pv score); R&H (pv score);
  CLLH
- Original partitur: -0-
- Original parts: R&H

That Terrific Rainbow
Rodgers/Hart
Orchestrator: Unknown

Location of
- Composer's manuscript: R&H
- Sheet music: Not published separately
- Most complete music: LoC (pv score);
  NYPL (pv score); R&H (pv score)
- Most complete lyric: LoC (pv score);
  NYPL (pv score); R&H (pv score);
  CLLH
- Original partitur: -0-
- Original parts: R&H

What Is a Man?
Rodgers/Hart
Orchestrator: Unknown

Location of
- Composer's manuscript: -0-
- Sheet music: LoC
- Most complete music: LoC (pv score);
  NYPL (pv score)
- Most complete lyric: CLLH
- Original partitur: -0-
- Original parts: R&H

Originally entitled "Love Is My Friend"; the lyric was changed after the New York opening. The lyric to "Love Is My Friend" is missing. The patter section was not published in the sheet music.

Happy Hunting Horn
    Rodgers/Hart
    Orchestrator: Unknown

    Location of   - Composer's manuscript: LoC (sk)
              - Sheet music: LoC
              - Most complete music: LoC (sm, pv score);
                  NYPL (pv score); R&H (pv score)
              - Most complete lyric: LoC (sm, pv score);
                  NYPL (pv score); R&H (pv score);
                  CLLH
              - Original partitur: -0-
              - Original parts: R&H

Entr'acte
    Rodgers/Hart
    Orchestrator: Unknown

    Location of   - Composer's manuscript: -0-
              - Sheet music: Not published separately
              - Most complete music: LoC (pv score);
                  NYPL (pv score); R&H (pv score)
               - Most complete lyric: INST
              - Original partitur: -0-
              - Original parts: R&H

Bewitched
    Rodgers/Hart
    Orchestrator: Unknown

    Location of   - Composer's manuscript: LoC
              - Sheet music: LoC, NYPL
              - Most complete music: LoC (sm, pv score);
                  NYPL (sm, pv score); R&H (pv score)
              - Most complete lyric: CLLH
              - Original partitur: -0-
              - Original parts: R&H

Alternate title: "Bewitched, Bothered and Bewildered."
The sheet music also contains a few alternate lyrics.

Flower Garden of My Heart, The
    Rodgers/Hart
    Orchestrator: Unknown

    Location of   - Composer's manuscript: LoC
              - Sheet music: Not published separately
              - Most complete music: LoC (pv score);
                  NYPL (pv score); R&H (pv score)
              - Most complete lyric: CLLH
              - Original partitur: -0-
              - Original parts: R&H

Pal Joey
    Rodgers/Hart
    Orchestrator: Unknown

    Location of   - Composer's manuscript: -0-
              - Sheet music: Not published separately
              - Most complete music: LoC (pv score);
                  NYPL (pv score); R&H (pv score)
              - Most complete lyric: LoC (pv score);
                  NYPL (pv score); R&H (pv score);
                  CLLH
              - Original partitur: -0-
              - Original parts: R&H

Alternate title: "What Do I Care for a Dame?"

Zip
    Rodgers/Hart
    Orchestrator: Unknown

    Location of   - Composer's manuscript: LoC
              - Sheet music: LoC
              - Most complete music: LoC (sm, pv score);
                  NYPL (pv score); R&H (pv score)
              - Most complete lyric: CLLH
              - Original partitur: -0-
              - Original parts: R&H

Pal Joey (1940)

Plant You Now, Dig You Later
Rodgers/Hart
Orchestrator: Unknown

Location of - Composer's manuscript: LoC
        - Sheet music: LoC, NYPL
        - Most complete music: LoC (sm, pv score);
           NYPL (sm, pv score); R&H (pv score)
        - Most complete lyric: CLLH
        - Original partitur: -0-
        - Original parts: R&H

Take Him
Rodgers/Hart
Orchestrator: Unknown

Location of - Composer's manuscript: LoC
        - Sheet music: LoC
        - Most complete music: LoC (sm, pv score);
           NYPL (pv score); R&H (pv score)
        - Most complete lyric: CLLH
        - Original partitur: -0-
        - Original parts: R&H

Den of Iniquity
Rodgers/Hart
Orchestrator: Unknown

Location of - Composer's manuscript: LoC
        - Sheet music: LoC
        - Most complete music: LoC (sm, pv score);
           NYPL (pv score); R&H (pv score)
        - Most complete lyric: LoC (pv score);
           NYPL (pv score); R&H (pv score);
           CLLH
        - Original partitur: -0-
        - Original parts: R&H

The Complete Lyrics of Lorenz Hart also contains an
alternate line.

I'm Talking to My Pal
Rodgers/Hart
Orchestrator: Unknown

Location of - Composer's manuscript: LoC
        - Sheet music: Unpublished
        - Most complete music: LoC (pv-l)
        - Most complete lyric: LoC (pv-l, ls); CLLH
        - Original partitur: -0-
        - Original parts: -0-

Dropped before the New York opening.

Do It the Hard Way
Rodgers/Hart
Orchestrator: Unknown

Location of - Composer's manuscript: LoC
        - Sheet music: LoC, NYPL
        - Most complete music: LoC (sm, pv score);
           NYPL (sm, pv score); R&H (pv score)
        - Most complete lyric: LoC (sm, pv score);
           NYPL (sm, pv score); R&H (pv score);
           CLLH
        - Original partitur: -0-
        - Original parts: R&H

BY JUPITER

Music	RICHARD RODGERS
Lyrics	LORENZ HART

Musical comedy in two acts. Opened June 3, 1942 in New York and ran 427 performances (World premiere: May 11, 1942 in Boston). Libretto by Richard Rodgers and Lorenz Hart, based on the play THE WARRIOR'S HUSBAND by Julian F. Thompson. Produced by Dwight Seere Wiman and Richard Rodgers in association with Richard Kollmar. Directed by Joshua Logan. Choreographed by Robert Alton. Musical direction by Johnny Green. Orchestrations by Don Walker. Vocal arrangements by Johnny Green and Clay Warnick.

Synopsis and Production Information	The Amazon women warriors, symbols of female supremacy, fight men for the first time in a battle against the Greeks. They are defeated and from then on are subordinate to men.
	Principals include Hippolyta (Queen of the Amazons) and Sapiens, son of the Queen's concellor, "a delicate example of masculine grace." Most of the romantic musical material is handled by the Queen's sister Antiope and Theseus, a Greek warrior. There is a full singing and dancing ensemble.
Orchestration	Reed I (Alto Sax); Reed II (Clarinet, Bass Clarinet, Alto Sax); Reed III (Oboe, English Horn, Clarinet, Tenor Sax); Reed IV (Clarinet, Tenor Sax, Flute, Bassoon, English Horn); Reed V (Alto Sax, Baritone Sax, Clarinet); Trumpet I II; Trumpet III; Trombone I; Trombone II; Trombone III; Piano; Guitar; Percussion; Violin A B C; Viola; Cello; Bass
Comments	In the original production, Sapiens was played by Ray Bolger.
Location of Original Materials	Script: Rodgers and Hammerstein Theatre Library (all lyrics), New York Public Library (all lyrics) Piano-vocal score: Rodgers and Hammerstein Theatre Library Partiturs: Missing Parts: Rodgers and Hammerstein Theatre Library
	The piano-vocal score is based on the 1967 revival, but it is nonetheless quite close to the original score. Roughly half the parts are missing; only the Reed II book is complete. The Rodgers and Hammerstein Theatre Library also has an early draft of the script.
Rental Status	The Rodgers and Hammerstein Theatre Library rents a version based on the 1967 revival, with the original score, additional book material by Fred Ebb, and an orchestration for ten players.
Music Publisher	Chappell Music
Information	Rodgers and Hammerstein Theatre Library

By Jupiter (1942)

Overture
Rodgers/Hart
Orchestrator: Unknown

Location of   - Composer's manuscript: -0-
- Sheet music: Unpublished
- Most complete music: R&H (parts)
- Most complete lyric: INST
- Original partitur: -0-
- Original parts: R&H (inc)

For Jupiter and Greece
Rodgers/Hart
Orchestrator: Unknown

Location of   - Composer's manuscript: -0-
- Sheet music: Unpublished
- Most complete music: R&H (pv score)
- Most complete lyric: R&H (scr);
    NYPL (scr); CLLH
- Original partitur: -0-
- Original parts: R&H (inc)

Jupiter Forbid
Rodgers/Hart
Orchestrator: Unknown

Location of   - Composer's manuscript: LoC
- Sheet music: R&H, NYPL
- Most complete music: R&H (sm, pv score);
    NYPL (sm), LoC (pv-l)
- Most complete lyric: R&H (sm, pv score,
    scr); NYPL (sm, scr); LoC (pv-l, ls);
    CLLH
- Original partitur: -0-
- Original parts: R&H (inc)

The scripts also contain the lyric for the original vocal
arrangement.

Life With Father
Rodgers/Hart
Orchestrator: Unknown

Location of   - Composer's manuscript: LoC
- Sheet music: Unpublished
- Most complete music: R&H (pv score);
    LoC (pv-l)
- Most complete lyric: R&H (pv score, scr);
    NYPL (scr); CLLH
- Original partitur: -0-
- Original parts: R&H (inc)

Nobody's Heart
Rodgers/Hart
Orchestrator: Unknown

Location of   - Composer's manuscript: LoC
- Sheet music: NYPL
- Most complete music: NYPL (sm);
    R&H (pv score); LoC (pv-l)
- Most complete lyric: NYPL (scr);
    R&H (pv score, scr); CLLH
- Original partitur: -0-
- Original parts: R&H (inc)

Gateway of the Temple of Minerva, The
Rodgers/Hart
Orchestrator: Unknown

Location of   - Composer's manuscript: LoC
- Sheet music: Unpublished
- Most complete music: R&H (pv score)
- Most complete lyric: R&H (scr);
    NYPL (scr); CLLH
- Original partitur: -0-
- Original parts: R&H (inc)

Here's a Hand
Rodgers/Hart
Orchestrator: Unknown

Location of   - Composer's manuscript: LoC
- Sheet music: NYPL
- Most complete music: NYPL (sm);
     R&H (pv score); LoC (pv-l)
- Most complete lyric: NYPL (sm, scr);
     R&H (pv score, scr); LoC (pv-l, ls);
     CLLH
- Original partitur: -0-
- Original parts: R&H (inc)

Boy I Left Behind Me, The
Rodgers/Hart
Orchestrator: Unknown

Location of   - Composer's manuscript: LoC
- Sheet music: Unpublished
- Most complete music: R&H (pv score);
     LoC (pv-l)
- Most complete lyric: R&H (pv score, scr);
     NYPL (scr); CLLH
- Original partitur: -0-
- Original parts: R&H (inc)

No, Mother, No
Rodgers/Hart
Orchestrator: Unknown

Location of   - Composer's manuscript: LoC
- Sheet music: Unpublished
- Most complete music: R&H (pv score)
- Most complete lyric: R&H (scr);
     NYPL (scr); CLLH
- Original partitur: -0-
- Original parts: R&H (inc)

The Act I Finale. The manuscript is from an early
version; it contains an early set of lyrics that are also
found in The Complete Lyrics of Lorenz Hart.

Ev'rything I've Got
Rodgers/Hart
Orchestrator: Unknown

Location of   - Composer's manuscript: LoC
- Sheet music: NYPL
- Most complete music: NYPL (sm);
     R&H (pv score); LoC (pv-l)
- Most complete lyric: NYPL (scr);
     R&H (scr); CLLH
- Original partitur: -0-
- Original parts: R&H (inc)

The piano-vocal score contains some alternate lyrics that
are probably not by Lorenz Hart.

Entr'acte
Rodgers/Hart
Orchestrator: Unknown

Location of   - Composer's manuscript: -0-
- Sheet music: Unpublished
- Most complete music: R&H (parts)
- Most complete lyric: INST
- Original partitur: -0-
- Original parts: R&H (inc)

Bottoms Up
Rodgers/Hart
Orchestrator: Unknown

Location of   - Composer's manuscript: -0-
- Sheet music: Unpublished
- Most complete music: R&H (pv score)
- Most complete lyric: R&H (scr);
     NYPL (scr); CLLH
- Original partitur: -0-
- Original parts: R&H (inc)

The scripts also have the original vocal arrangement,
which contains additional lyrics.

By Jupiter (1942)

Careless Rhapsody
Rodgers/Hart
Orchestrator: Unknown

Location of   - Composer's manuscript: LoC
              - Sheet music: NYPL
              - Most complete music: NYPL (sm);
                  R&H (pv score); LoC (pv-l)
              - Most complete lyric: NYPL (sm);
                  R&H (pv score); CLLH
              - Original partitur: -0-
              - Original parts: R&H (inc)

Finaletto Act II, Scene 1 ["The Greeks have got the girdle."]
Rodgers/Hart
Orchestrator: Unknown

Location of   - Composer's manuscript: LoC
              - Sheet music: Unpublished
              - Most complete music: R&H (pv score)
              - Most complete lyric: R&H (pv score, scr);
                  NYPL (scr); LoC (ls); CLLH
              - Original partitur: -0-
              - Original parts: R&H

Wait Till You See Her
Rodgers/Hart
Orchestrator: Unknown

Location of   - Composer's manuscript: LoC
              - Sheet music: NYPL
              - Most complete music: NYPL (sm);
                  R&H (pv score); LoC (pv-l)
              - Most complete lyric: NYPL (sm);
                  R&H (pv score); LoC (pv-l, ls); CLLH
              - Original partitur: -0-
              - Original parts: -0-

Dropped during the New York run; the lyric is not in
either script.

Now That I've Got My Strength
Rodgers/Hart
Orchestrator: Unknown

Location of   - Composer's manuscript: -0-
              - Sheet music: Unpublished
              - Most complete music: R&H (pv score)
              - Most complete lyric: R&H (scr);
                  NYPL (scr); CLLH
              - Original partitur: -0-
              - Original parts: R&H (inc)

Added during the pre-Broadway tryout, replacing "Life Was
Monotonous." The piano-vocal score contains additional
lyrics that may not have been written by Hart.

Life Was Monotonous
Rodgers/Hart
Orchestrator: Unknown

Location of   - Composer's manuscript: LoC
              - Sheet music: Unpublished
              - Most complete music: LoC (pv-l)
              - Most complete lyric: LoC (pv-l, ls);
                  CLLH
              - Original partitur: -0-
              - Original parts: -0-

Replaced by "Now That I've Got My Strength" during the
pre-Broadway tryout.

Fool Meets Fool
Rodgers/Hart
Orchestrator: Unknown

Location of   - Composer's manuscript: LoC
              - Sheet music: Unpublished
              - Most complete music: LoC (pv-l)
              - Most complete lyric: LoC (pv-l, ls);
                  CLLH
              - Original partitur: -0-
              - Original parts: -0-

Dropped during the pre-Broadway tryout.

Nothing to Do But Relax

Rodgers/Hart

Orchestrator: Unknown

Location of   - Composer's manuscript: LoC
            - Sheet music: Unpublished
            - Most complete music: LoC (pv-I)
            - Most complete lyric: LoC (pv-I, ls);
                CLLH
            - Original partitur: -0-
            - Original parts: -0-

Dropped during the pre-Broadway tryout.

A CONNECTICUT YANKEE (1943)

Music   **RICHARD RODGERS**
Lyrics   **LORENZ HART**

Musical comedy in two acts. Opened November 17, 1943 in New York and ran 135 performances (World premiere: October 28, 1943 in Philadelphia). Libretto by Herbert Fields, adapted from A CONNECTICUT YANKEE IN KING ARTHUR'S COURT by Mark Twain. Produced by Richard Rodgers. Directed by John C. Wilson. Choreographed by William Holbrook and Al White, Jr. Musical direction by George Hirst. Orchestrations by Don Walker.

Synopsis and Production Information	Lt. Martin Barrett's old girlfriend Alice turns up the night before his marriage to Fay Morgan. Fay appears and, upon seeing the two together, knocks Martin out with a bottle. An unconscious Martin then dreams that he is back in the court of King Arthur, in love with a mere maiden, Alisande, but forced to marry the King's sister, Morgan Le Fay. When Martin awakes, he realizes that he truly wants to marry Alice.

Other characters include Sir Galahad and lady-in-waiting Evelyn, who team up for a couple of numbers. There is a full singing and dancing ensemble. |
| **Orchestration** | Reed 1 (Flute, Clarinet); Reed 2 (Oboe, English Horn); Reed 3 (Clarinet); Reed 4 (Clarinet, Bass Clarinet, Tenor Sax); Reed 5 (Clarinet, Bass Clarinet, Bassoon, Tenor Sax); Horn; Trumpet I II; Trumpet III; Trombone; Percussion; Piano; Violin A B C; Viola; Cello; Bass |
| **Comments** | This production of A CONNECTICUT YANKEE was an updated revision of the 1927 show, which is also included in this catalog; it featured Vivienne Segal in the enlarged role of Morgan Le Fay. |
| **Location of Original Materials** | Script: Tams-Witmark Music Library (some lyrics)
Piano-vocal score: Tams-Witmark Music Library
Partiturs: Missing
Parts: Tams-Witmark Music Library

The Rodgers and Hammerstein Theatre Library has an early draft of the 1943 script. |
Rental Status	Tams-Witmark rents the 1943 show.
Music Publisher	Marlin Enterprises and Lorenz Hart Publishing Co., c/o Warner Brothers Music
Information	Tams-Witmark Music Library

Overture
Rodgers/Hart
Orchestrator: Unknown

Location of   - Composer's manuscript: -0-
      - Sheet music: Unpublished
      - Most complete music: TW (pv score)
      - Most complete lyric: INST
      - Original partitur: -0-
      - Original parts: TW

Here's Martin the Groom
Rodgers/Hart
Orchestrator: Unknown

Location of   - Composer's manuscript: -0-
      - Sheet music: Unpublished
      - Most complete music: TW (pv score)
      - Most complete lyric: TW (pv score, scr)
      - Original partitur: -0-
      - Original parts: TW

Written for the 1943 version. This Act I opening, not listed in the New York programs, segues into "This Is My Night to Howl."

This Is My Night to Howl
Rodgers/Hart
Orchestrator: Unknown

Location of   - Composer's manuscript: LoC
      - Sheet music: Unpublished
      - Most complete music: TW (pv score)
      - Most complete lyric: TW (pv score); CLLH
      - Original partitur: -0-
      - Original parts: TW

Written for the 1943 version. The piano-vocal score also contains the 1943 vocal arrangement, which includes additional lyrics.

My Heart Stood Still
Rodgers/Hart
Orchestrator: Unknown

Location of   - Composer's manuscript: -0-
      - Sheet music: LoC, NYPL
      - Most complete music: LoC (sm);
         NYPL (sm); R&H (pv-l);
         TW (pv score)
      - Most complete lyric: TW (pv score, scr)
      - Original partitur: -0-
      - Original parts: TW

The original lyric was updated for the 1943 version. For the most complete version of the 1927 lyric, see the listing under A CONNECTICUT YANKEE (1927).

Thou Swell
Rodgers/Hart
Orchestrator: Unknown

Location of   - Composer's manuscript: -0-
      - Sheet music: LoC, NYPL
      - Most complete music: LoC (sm);
         NYPL (sm); R&H (pv-l);
         TW (pv score)
      - Most complete lyric: LoC (sm);
         NYPL (sm, 1927 scr); R&H (pv-l,
         1927 scr); TW (pv score); CLLH
      - Original partitur: -0-
      - Original parts: TW

The piano-vocal score also contains the 1943 vocal arrangement, which includes additional lyrics.

At the Round Table
Rodgers/Hart
Orchestrator: Unknown

Location of   - Composer's manuscript: -0-
      - Sheet music: Not published separately
      - Most complete music: TW (pv score)
      - Most complete lyric: CLLH
      - Original partitur: -0-
      - Original parts: TW

Alternate title: "Knights' Opening." The refrain was published in the piano selection.

A Connecticut Yankee (1943)

On a Desert Island With Thee
Rodgers/Hart
Orchestrator: Unknown

Location of   - Composer's manuscript: -0-
         - Sheet music: LoC, NYPL
         - Most complete music: LoC (sm);
             NYPL (sm); R&H (pv); TW (pv score)
         - Most complete lyric: LoC (sm);
             NYPL (sm, 1927 scr); R&H (1927 scr);
             TW (pv score, scr); CLLH
         - Original partitur: -0-
         - Original parts: TW

Entr'acte
Rodgers/Hart
Orchestrator: Unknown

Location of   - Composer's manuscript: -0-
         - Sheet music: Unpublished
         - Most complete music: TW (pv score)
         - Most complete lyric: INST
         - Original partitur: -0-
         - Original parts: TW

To Keep My Love Alive
Rodgers/Hart
Orchestrator: Unknown

Location of   - Composer's manuscript: -0-
         - Sheet music: LoC, NYPL
         - Most complete music: LoC (sm);
             NYPL (sm); TW (pv score)
         - Most complete lyric: TW (pv score); CLLH
         - Original partitur: -0-
         - Original parts: TW

Written for the 1943 version.

Ye Lunchtime Follies
Rodgers/Hart
Orchestrator: Unknown

Location of   - Composer's manuscript: -0-
         - Sheet music: Unpublished
         - Most complete music: TW (pv score)
         - Most complete lyric: TW (pv score, scr)
         - Original partitur: -0-
         - Original parts: TW

Written for the 1943 version.

Finale Act I ["Ibbidi bibbidi sibbidi sab..."]
Rodgers/Hart
Orchestrator: Unknown

Location of   - Composer's manuscript: -0-
         - Sheet music: Unpublished
         - Most complete music: TW (pv score)
         - Most complete lyric: TW (pv score); CLLH
         - Original partitur: -0-
         - Original parts: TW

The original lyric was updated for this production.

Can't You Do a Friend a Favor?
Rodgers/Hart
Orchestrator: Unknown

Location of   - Composer's manuscript: LoC
         - Sheet music: LoC, NYPL
         - Most complete music: TW (pv score)
         - Most complete lyric: TW (pv score)
         - Original partitur: -0-
         - Original parts: TW

Written for the 1943 version.

I Feel at Home With You
    Rodgers/Hart
    Orchestrator: Unknown

    Location of   - Composer's manuscript: -0-
                  - Sheet music: LoC, NYPL
                  - Most complete music: LoC (sm);
                        NYPL (sm); R&H (pv-l);
                        TW (pv score)
                  - Most complete lyric: TW (pv score)
                        & CLLH
                  - Original partitur: -0-
                  - Original parts: TW

Camelot Samba, The
    Rodgers/Hart
    Orchestrator: Unknown

    Location of   - Composer's manuscript: -0-
                  - Sheet music: Unpublished
                  - Most complete music: TW (pv score)
                  - Most complete lyric: TW (pv score)
                  - Original partitur: -0-
                  - Original parts: TW

Written for the 1943 version.

You Always Love the Same Girl
    Rodgers/Hart
    Orchestrator: Unknown

    Location of   - Composer's manuscript: LoC
                  - Sheet music: LoC, NYPL
                  - Most complete music: TW (pv score)
                  - Most complete lyric: TW (pv score, sm);
                        CLLH
                  - Original partitur: -0-
                  - Original parts: TW

Written for the 1943 version.

APPENDIX

List of Abbreviations and Addresses

The following abbreviations are used throughout the <u>Catalog of the American Musical</u>:

AC	Amherst College Library
CLCP	<u>The Complete Lyrics of Cole Porter</u>, edited by Robert Kimball (Alfred A. Knopf, Inc.: 1983)
CLLH	<u>The Complete Lyrics of Lorenz Hart</u>, edited by Dorothy Hart and Robert Kimball (Alfred A. Knopf, Inc.: 1986)
CPT	Cole Porter Musical and Literary Property Trusts
frag	fragment
IB	Irving Berlin Music Corporation
IG	Ira Gershwin Estate
JF	James J. Fuld
INST	instrumental
inc	incomplete
l	lyrics
lead	lead sheet (a melody line with chords)
LoC	Library of Congress
LOSO	<u>Lyrics on Several Occasions</u>, by Ira Gershwin (Alfred A. Knopf, Inc.: 1959)
ls	lyric sheet(s)
m	melody line
MTI	Music Theatre International
nb	notebook
neg	negative photocopy (white on black)
NYPL	New York Public Library
p	piano arrangement[8]
p sel	piano selection (a medley of songs from a show, printed without lyrics)
prof	professional copy (a song printed for noncommercial use)
ptr	partitur (orchestra score)
pv	piano-vocal arrangement (arranged for piano with a separate vocal line)
pv score	piano-vocal score (all the songs from a show, arranged for piano-and-voice)
r	refrain
R&H	Rodgers and Hammerstein Theatre Library
scr	script
SA	Shubert Archive
SF	Samuel French, Inc.
sk	sketch
sm	sheet music
TW	Tams-Witmark Music Library
v	verse
v sel	vocal selections (a collection of songs, usually the sheet music arrangements)
WB	Warner Brothers Music Publication
x	photocopy
Y	Yale University Library

---

[8]　In the case of vocal numbers, a melody line is contained within the piano arrangement unless otherwise noted.

The following rental agents, authors' estates, and repositories of scripts and musical manuscripts are listed in the Catalog of the American Musical:

Amherst College Library
Special Collections
Amherst College
Amherst, MA 01002

Irving Berlin Music Corporation
1290 Avenue of the Americas
New York, NY 10104

Chappell & Co.
810 Seventh Avenue
New York, NY 10019

Ira Gershwin Estate
c/o Ronald L. Blanc, Esq.
Blanc, Gilburne, Williams & Johnston
1900 Avenue of the Stars Suite 1200
Los Angeles, CA 90067

George Gershwin Family Trust
c/o Marc Gershwin
101 Central Park West
New York, NY 10023

James J. Fuld
New York City

Alfred A. Knopf, Inc.[9]
201 East 50th St.
New York, NY 10022

Library of Congress
Music Division
Washington, DC 20540

Music Theatre International
545 Eighth Avenue
New York, NY 10018

New York Public Library
c/o Lincoln Center Library of
      the Performing Arts
Third Floor Research Divisions
111 Amsterdam Avenue
New York, NY 10023

Cole Porter Musical and Literary Property
      Trusts
c/o Robert H. Montgomery, Jr., Trustee
Paul, Weiss, Rifkind, Wharton & Garrison
1285 Avenue of the Americas
New York, NY 10019

Robbins Music Corporation
c/o SBK Entertainment World Inc.
810 Seventh Avenue
New York, NY 10019

The Rodgers and Hammerstein Theatre Library
598 Madison Avenue
New York, NY 10022

---

[8]   Lyrics on Several Occasions is currently out of print; inquiries about its contents are best directed at this time to the Ira Gershwin Estate. Similarly, the Cole Porter Musical and Literary Property Trusts and the Rodgers and Hammerstein Theatre Library can provide information from The Complete Lyrics of Cole Porter and The Complete Lyrics of Lorenz Hart, respectively.

Appendix

Samuel French, Inc.
45 West 25th St.
New York, NY 10010

G. Schirmer, Inc.
24 E. 22nd St.
New York, NY 10010

Shubert Archive
Lyceum Theatre
149 W. 45th St.
New York, NY 10036

Tams-Witmark Music Library, Inc.
560 Lexington Avenue
New York, NY 10022

Warner Brothers Music Publication
265 Secaucus Rd.
Secaucus, NJ 07094

Yale University Library
Historical Sound Recordings
Box 1603A Yale Station
New Haven, CT 06520

The Catalog of the American Musical covers the book musicals of Irving Berlin, George and Ira Gershwin, Cole Porter, and Richard Rodgers and Lorenz Hart. Inquiries about other works by these songwriters should be directed as follows:

For the works of IRVING BERLIN:
Irving Berlin Music Corporation
1290 Avenue of the Americas
New York, NY 10104

For the works of COLE PORTER:
Cole Porter Musical and Literary Property
    Trusts
c/o Robert H. Montgomery, Jr., Trustee
Paul, Weiss, Rifkind, Wharton & Garrison
1285 Avenue of the Americas
New York, NY 10019

For the works of GEORGE & IRA GERSHWIN:
Ira Gershwin Estate
c/o Ronald L. Blanc
Blanc, Gilburne, Williams & Johnston
1900 Avenue of the Stars Suite 1200
Los Angeles, CA 90067

For the works of RICHARD RODGERS &
LORENZ HART:
The Rodgers and Hammerstein Theatre Library
598 Madison Avenue
New York, NY 10022

INDEX OF SONGS

All songs listed in the Catalog of the American Musical are included in this index, with the exception of Overtures, Entr'actes, and generic titles (e.g., "Dance," "Duet").

Index of Songs